JASON PINTER
THE STOLEN

ISBN-13: 978-0-7783-2572-7
ISBN-10:   0-7783-2572-5

THE STOLEN

www.MIRABooks.com

Printed in U.S.A.

To my sister, who taught me the meaning of friendship.
To my father, who taught me the meaning of generosity.
To my mother, who taught me the meaning of strength.

ACKNOWLEDGMENTS

The first thanks go to my beautiful wife, Susan, who more so than on any of my previous books humbled me with her patience and understanding. After many coffee-fueled late nighters and supportive pep talks, this book is as much yours as it is mine.

Joe Veltre, who has proved time and time again that the best business relationships are also great friendships. Thank you for both. Thanks also to Diane Bartoli and Sara Wolski, who are always gracious with their time.

Adam Wilson. Thanks for always being there in a pinch, and answering even the silliest questions faster than humanly possible. I'll stump you soon, I promise....

Donna Hayes, Dianne Moggy, Margaret O'Neill Marbury, Heather Foy, Maureen Stead, Ana Luxton, Jayne Hoogenberk, Ken Foy, Michelle Renaud, Don Lucey, Andi Richman, Katherine Orr, Craig Swinwood, Loriana Sacilotto and Stacy Widdrington. The best is yet to come. Thank you, thank you, thank you all.

I also owe a debt to George Witte, Sally Richardson, Andy Martin, Kylah McNeill, Keith Kahla and Kelley Ragland. I'm sorry our time together was cut short, but every day was a real treat. I'm lucky to have spent so much time working with people who know how to publish the right way.

Susan Schwartzman. After knowing you for just two weeks, I was in awe. By the time this book comes out, I can only imagine what you'll have accomplished.

Bonnie and Joe, Maggie Griffin and Terry Lucas. I still have a lot to learn about this crazy thing called writing, but when you've had friends like these, everything seems possible.

Linda McFall. Three down, and hopefully many, many more to go. If I feel spoiled, it's your fault for being such a terrific editor. Thanks also for your help on understanding the (often frightening) mind of the American toddler. Thank you again, ad infinitum.

To the booksellers and librarians who have made it possible for people to read my stuff.

To everyone who's read one of my books, thanks for giving me the greatest job in the world. You keeping reading 'em, I'll keep writing 'em.

And to reporters around the world who risk so much to write about good, evil and everything in between, Henry Parker offers a sincere thank-you. He wouldn't be here without your inspiration.

Dear Reader,

It is said that the most painful experience a parent can endure is losing a child. The pain and anguish must be simply incalculable. But what happens when a child presumed gone forever returns suddenly with no explanation, no injuries and no recollection of where they've been?

In *The Stolen*, Henry Parker must face perhaps the most difficult, and most personal, story of his young career. Because when he investigates the sudden reappearance of ten-year-old Daniel Linwood, Henry soon realizes that despite the jubilation of Daniel's parents, something far more sinister is beginning to take shape. And as Henry fights to uncover the truth, caught in the balance are a family, a community and several people who will stop at nothing to make sure those questions stay unanswered, and that Henry is silenced—permanently.

I hope as you read *The Stolen*, you might ask yourself the same question that drives Henry to find the truth: How far would you go to protect your loved ones?

Enjoy *The Stolen*...

Jason Pinter
January 2008

Prologue

"Finished."

I saved the document and eased back in my chair. My body had grown accustomed to long days and nights spent in its discomfort. The last few months, I had arrived home nearly every night with a sore tailbone or stiff back, wondering if the supplies department would turn a blind eye and let me expense a newer model. Eventually I forgot about it. Then one day, I noticed I hadn't thought about the aches and pains in a long time. They were a part of me now.

The past three days and nights had sped by in a blur of keystrokes, Chinese food containers and discarded coffee cups. I was on the kind of crash deadline that a year ago would have had me sweating rivulets, but now barely raised my pulse. The fact was, without those deadlines to keep me focused, the pains might not have ebbed away.

Saving the file, I looked outside my window over Rockefeller Plaza. The view had changed—bright morning into gauzy summer afternoon, fading into the kind of New York night where the constant bright lights disguised any sense of time.

Until recently, the night always heralded the end of my

workday. I would file my story with Evelyn Waterstone, the *Gazette*'s Metro editor, pack up my things, throw some goodbyes to my night-shift colleagues and one or two guys at the sports desk who were putting together the box scores, and head home to meet Amanda. Good conversation, a hot shower, maybe a movie or a show we'd recorded, they'd all be waiting. Then I'd fall asleep with a whisper of her hair across my face.

Amanda.

We met two years ago. Our introduction wasn't exactly the setup for your average romantic comedy. Our paths crossed while I was on the run after being falsely accused of murder. I had nobody to turn to. Nowhere to go. And just when the situation was at its bleakest, Amanda offered a hand to me, a total stranger. She saved my life. She was running from her own demons, having come from a broken home, spending her childhood recapping her life in small notebooks because she assumed everyone she met would eventually abandon her. It was this that brought us together. We were both damaged, broken, but together we were whole. She was everything I wanted in a partner. Strong, brilliant, beautiful. And she laughed at my jokes that made everyone else cringe. I repaid her by offering all the love I had to give. Had I offered merely love, it would have been more than enough. It's the other baggage I brought along that was too heavy for our relationship to bear.

Six months ago, a killer began terrorizing the city by publicly executing those he felt deserved his wrath. I was able to weave together the strands of his mysterious past and learned the horrific truth about his ancestry. During my search, the killer turned his sights not just toward me, but to those I loved.

He brutally attacked my ex, Mya Loverne, and left her fighting for her life. He broke into Amanda's office at the New York Legal Aid Society and nearly killed her. It was then, in the aftermath of those acts of violence, that I realized what I had to do. To protect those I loved, I had to turn away. I had to shield them from myself.

There was nothing more I would have wanted than to spend the rest of my life with her, playing shuffleboard and eating dinner at noon, doing whatever old couples did. It should have been easy. I mean, everyone complains about how hard it is to find someone in New York City. Once you find the right person, you hold on to them for dear life. Unfortunately I had to do the opposite.

Amanda nearly lost her life because of me, because of my work. And because being a reporter was in my blood, I shuddered to think that it was only a matter of time before those odds caught up. So I left her. In the middle of the street. And every day since I've had ample time to think about my decision.

We have not spoken in six months. My apartment, once warm with her presence, was now cold and uninviting. The stove, where we used to burn our attempts at lasagna, hadn't seen a pan in weeks. The place reeked of carelessness, abandoned by a man who felt like a stranger in his own home.

Work had always been my passion. Now it was my whole life.

Underneath my desk was a small duffel bag in which I kept a clean shirt, slacks and a pair of loafers. Every other day I would venture back to that unfamiliar home, unload the dirty laundry and pack up a clean change of clothes. Every other week the accumulation of soiled attire would be sent to the cleaners, and the cycle would start again. I would change in the men's room, always drawing a few *weren't you just wearing that?* looks from my colleagues.

I heard a noise behind me, turned to see Evelyn Waterstone striding up to my desk. Evelyn had barely given me the time of day when I first started working at the *Gazette,* but she'd warmed considerably over the past few months. Evelyn was in her late fifties, a solid tree stump of a woman who commanded attention, respect, and made everyone leap to the side when she walked by. Like many of the newspaper's top talent, Evelyn was unmarried and childless. She was also one of the best editors in the business. Somehow I'd grudgingly gained her respect. I figured as long as I kept my head down and did what I did best, it would stay that way.

"Got your story, Parker," she said, barely slowing down as she approached, then stopping abruptly before she knocked my desk over. "I swear you must have replaced your brain this year or taken basic grammar and spelling lessons. I haven't had to smack my head in frustration at your copy in almost a month. You keep it up like this, I might actually be able to cut back on the migraine medication."

"They say reading is the cure for all ills," I said.

Evelyn eyed me skeptically. "Who said that?"

"You know…they."

"Tell 'they' that they can shove their quotations up my keester. Anyway, keep up the not-so-terrible work. You're giving me more time to spend with crustaceans whose brains haven't fully grasped the '*i* before *e*' concept." Evelyn shot a glance toward Frank Rourke, the city's top sports columnist, to whom *grammar* was a term of endearment for his mother's mother.

Then Evelyn leaned forward. Sniffed. Scrunched up her nose.

"My God, Parker, you stink worse than O'Donnell the morning after St. Patrick's Day. Your pieces might be clean, but you reek like my nephew's diaper. Go home and shower, seriously, otherwise I'll tell Wallace he has a rodent infestation in the vicinity of your desk."

"I'm not that bad, am I?" I raised an arm, took a whiff, and immediately nodded in agreement. "I'm on my way."

When Evelyn left, I took the duffel out from beneath my desk, opened it. Sniffed. Closed it right up. Maybe it was best to just burn this load.

I grabbed the bag, left the office, took a cab to my apartment. I blew in the door, took a three-minute shower, and seven minutes after that I was wearing a fresh outfit with a spare packed away. Another cab brought me back to Rockefeller, where I strode into the office with a sense of pride that I knew was well undeserved. I waved to the night security team. They were too busy watching a ball game to wave back.

The newsroom was nearly empty. A quiet newsroom felt like an unnatural beast, but I'd grown used to it.

I opened my drawer, pulled out a down pillow I'd bought myself as a present. I took a fresh pillow cover from the bag, pulled it on. Buried somewhere in those drawers, beneath a mountain of papers, was a photo of Amanda. I'd taken it at a concert at Jones Beach last summer. It was raining. I was concerned the camera would be ruined. Amanda told me not to worry, that if special moments weren't worth some sort of risk, how special could they be?

Without saying another word I snapped the photo. She was right. The moment was worth far more than the risk.

Her brown hair was plastered to her cheeks, her neck. Her tank top clinging to her rain-slick body like silk. Her eyes were closed, the music pouring through her. That was my favorite photo of Amanda. It used to sit on my desk. Now I couldn't even look at it, because it only made me think of the night I ended the best thing in my life.

Then I did what I'd been doing every night for the past four months. I placed the pillow on my desk, put my head down, and slept.

1

"James, get your behind down here and finish your greens!"

Shelly's voice boomed through the house, and even though it took eight-year-old James Linwood only thirty seconds to turn off his Xbox 360 and race down the stairs, his younger sister, Tasha, was already sitting at the table, eyeing him while munching loudly on a celery stalk. When James sat down, Tasha, six years old but already a grandmaster at winning the game of sibling rivalry, stuck a green, mush-filled tongue out at her brother, who was more than happy to return the favor.

"That's enough, both of you. James, baby, I never excused you from the table. You have to *ask* to be excused." James looked at his mother and gave an exaggerated sigh, then picked up a single piece of lettuce. He took a bite, grimacing as if it had been marinating in oyster juice. "I don't know what you're looking at me for," Shelly said. "Some people actually think vegetables taste good."

Tasha nodded along with her mother, opened wide and shoved a whole stalk of celery in her mouth.

"Those people are stupid," James said, nibbling at the lettuce.

"No, if you knew what kind of vitamins and minerals veggies had, you'd know those people are quite smart," Shelly said. "Did you know LeBron James eats a double helping of carrots before every game?"

"Does not," James replied.

"Does too," said Shelly.

"Does too," said Tasha.

James gave his sister a cold glare. He tore off a piece of lettuce and chewed it with vigor, letting several shreds of green gristle fall onto the table.

Shelly watched her children eat, their eyes more concerned with her approval than their nutrition. The soft jingle of a wind chime could be heard from the back porch, as well as the noise of a television set blaring from the house next door. Mrs. Niederman's hearing had begun to go last year, and now she watched Alex Trebek at a volume that could be heard from space.

Shelly took a moment to gaze around her house. Just a few years ago, the back porch was riddled with termites, the wood rotted, the whole structure ready to collapse. She never would have let Tasha and James play on it. Randy was never very good with tools, and they simply didn't have the money to rebuild it. Not yet.

After their terrible ordeal, when their family had been fractured, the Good Samaritans of Hobbs County had reached out to help the Linwoods. Now barely a day passed where James and Tasha weren't outside shooting off water guns, dangling from the railing like a pair of spider monkeys. At least the porch had been rebuilt.

While the kids were at school, while Randy was away at work, Shelly would often find herself looking at the old photos of their house, taken when they'd first moved in years ago. She barely recognized what it had become.

The white paint was fresh, blue trim even, the mailbox upright. Nobody egged their house on Halloween, and she never had to call the police to report the teenagers who used to drive by once a week and knock the mailbox sideways with wielded baseball bats. Those kinds of things never happened anymore. There were more cops; she could feel their presence. They stopped by every so often, just to see how she and Randy were holding up. *I'm fine,* Shelly would say. *We're fine.*

The cops always turned down a cup of coffee. As though being any closer to the sorrow might somehow infect them.

James was grimacing through his last scraps of food when Shelly heard the doorbell.

"That's got to be Daddy," Shelly said. "He probably forgot his keys again this morning. James, would you let your father in?" James didn't move. "Did you hear me?"

"I'm cleaning my plate like you told me. I can't answer the door and eat at the same time." He smiled at this catch-22. Shelly sighed, though silently proud of her son's intelligence.

"Fine, you can stop eating if you let your father in. But if I hear that video game start up before you finish your social studies homework, you won't watch television until you graduate college."

James sprung up like he'd been shot from a cannon, then bolted from his chair.

Shelly smiled at her daughter. Tasha. Her beautiful, young daughter, who would grow up to be strong and vivacious like her mother had never been. Shelly felt an ache in her stomach and placed her palm on Tasha's cheek. Tasha smiled at her, that big goofy grin full of baby teeth.

"Mom?" James's voice bellowed from the hallway. "There's a kid here. Do you know anyone named Daniel?"

A napkin fell from Shelly's hand and fluttered to the floor.

"Wha…what did you say, baby?"

"Daniel. There's some kid at the door says he knows you. Wait, huh? Uh, Mom? He says…he says you're his mom."

Shelly leapt from her seat. She dashed through the house, nearly knocking over the coffee table, and sprinted into the front hallway.

The wooden frame was open to reveal the screen door. A boy was standing behind the screen, looking confused as to why he hadn't been allowed in yet. Shelly covered her mouth to prevent a scream from escaping her lips.

On the other side of the door stood a boy Shelly both knew and didn't know. He was about five foot three with a lock of dark hair that fell over his hazel eyes. His father's eyes. His limbs were gangly, full of sharp angles, as if he'd grown a great deal in a short amount of time and the flesh hadn't caught up to his bones. Everything and nothing was just like she remembered.

"Baby, oh my God…"

She gently pushed James away from the door and tore open the screen. The boy stood on the front porch with a look of slight bewilderment, a twinkle of recognition, a blurry memory slowly coming into focus. He didn't move. Instead, the boy's eyes met Shelly's as though waiting for something, and before another second passed Shelly Linwood gathered the boy up into her arms and squeezed him like there was no tomorrow, until his arms tentatively wrapped themselves around her body and held on. She remembered how he'd felt in her arms, and though heavier, he was the same child she'd held in her arms for the first six years of his life. She showered the boy's head with kisses until he pulled away slightly, an embarrassed grin on his young face.

"Oh my God," she whispered. "Oh my God, oh my God, oh my God. Baby, is it really you?" The boy shrugged, then was muffled as Shelly attempted to squeeze the life out of him again.

Shelly heard a car pull up. When the engine cut off, she looked up to see Randy's silver V70 Volvo in the driveway. The door opened, and her husband climbed out with a groan. Randy was forty-one, just ten pounds heavier than when they'd met in high school. His jawline was still visible above a slight jowl, his arms still maintaining some of the tone from his linebacker days at Hobbs High. Shelly loved to run her hands down his arms when he lay on top of her, the definition of his triceps making her shiver. It had been a year since she last felt that, but now she needed to feel him closer more than ever.

Her family.

Randy stretched his back, ran his fingers through his thinning hair, then reached back inside to grab his briefcase.

"Honey," he said, noticing the commotion on the front porch. "Please tell me there's a Michelob left in the fridge, I—"

"It's Daniel," Shelly blurted. "He's back."

Randy looked up, confused. Then when everything came into focus, his briefcase fell to the ground. He stared for a moment, shaking his head, then ran up the steps to join his wife. He placed his palm over the boy's forehead, pulled his hair back, gazing into the young, confused eyes. Then he joined his wife in the embrace.

"You people are weird," James muttered. "I don't get it. Who is he?"

"This," Randy said, turning the boy to face him, tears streaming down his face, "is your brother. His name is Daniel. Do you remember him?"

James had been just three when it all happened. Shelly didn't take it personally when Daniel looked at his sibling, bewilderment reigning over his face, a slight twinkle of memory.

"My brother?" James said. "I thought he was, like, stolen or something."

"He was," Shelly said, stroking Daniel's hair. "But thank you, *God,* somehow our boy has found his way home."

James looked at Daniel. There were no bruises on his body; no cuts or scrapes. His clothes looked new enough to still have the tags on them. Though he was so young, Shelly wondered if James remembered all those people rushing in and out of their house. Men and women with badges, other loud people with cameras and microphones. Once on an Easter egg hunt, Shelly had entered the bedroom to find James and Tasha rifling through a trunk stuffed full of newspaper clippings about Daniel's disappearance. James had asked Shelly about Daniel once, and she answered with a single tear, a trembling lip. He never asked again.

To Shelly, this was God's will. It was fate that her family be reunited.

To James Linwood, though, he couldn't understand how his brother, who'd disappeared nearly five years ago without a trace, could simply reappear like magic without a scratch on him.

2

The bar was sweltering hot, but the swirling fans made it more palatable than the thick sweater choking the New York streets. It didn't take long to learn that Augusts in New York could be brutal. My first summer in the city, I made the mistake one day of wearing a T-shirt and sweater to the office. Jack told me between my clothes and the *Gazette*'s sporadic air-conditioning, I'd lose ten pounds before the day was up. While I doubted the New York summer could get any hotter than my childhood years in Bend, Oregon, when later that night I peeled off my sweater and squeezed out the moisture, I realized East Coast summers were just as brutal as their West Coast counterparts.

I took another sip of my beer—my third of the night, and third in slightly under an hour—and casually glanced up at the baseball game. Out of the dozen or so patrons, only two or three seemed to care about the outcome. The others were nursing a drink, chatting up the bartender or, like the six people my age playing darts, far too busy reveling in their own bliss.

I'd gotten to know the bartender, Seamus. Things like that happen when you become a regular. Some nights I had trouble sleeping. This necessitated finding somewhere to go to kill time. Somewhere I could be lost in my own thoughts. That's how I stumbled upon Finnerty's. Quiet enough to lose yourself. Loud enough to drown everything out.

Most nights I was happy to imbibe among young Irish gents and apple-cheeked female bartenders. U2 and Morrissey seemed to emanate from the jukebox on an endless loop. Though I enjoyed the Irish pub, sitting in Finnerty's made me feel that much closer to the elder drinkers, sitting with bottomless glasses of whiskey, talking to the bartender because he was cheaper than a psychiatrist. All of this, by proxy, made me feel more and more like I was becoming Jack O'Donnell. In many ways being compared to Jack would be a compliment. Just not this one.

Jack O'Donnell, to put it bluntly, was my idol. He'd worked the city beat for going on forty years, and any conversation about New York journalism was incomplete without mention of the old man. Growing up, I'd gone out of my way to read every story O'Donnell wrote, not an easy task for a kid who lived three thousand miles away from New York. I had our library special-order the *Gazette* on microfiche. I would take on an extra newspaper route just so I could afford the next O'Donnell book in hardcover when it hit stores. I couldn't, or wouldn't, wait for the paperback.

A few years ago I'd arrived at the *New York Gazette* a fresh-faced newbie reporter who deigned only to shine O'Donnell's shoes. He was a journalistic institution, writing some of the most important stories of the past half century. Despite his age, Jack seemed to grow younger with every word he typed. Even though Jack's first assignment for me led to disaster—namely me being accused of murder—he was the first person at the newspaper to give me an honest shot at showing what I was worth. Both Jack and Wallace Langston, the *Gazette*'s editor-in-chief, had taken me under their wings, given me stories that I grabbed on to tenaciously and reported the hell out of. Without Jack I probably wouldn't have come to New York. Because of him I found my calling.

Like any idol, though, once you got closer you could see that some of the gold paint covered a chipped bronze interior. For all his brilliance with a pen, Jack's personal life was a disaster. Several times married and divorced. On the highway to alcoholism while seeming to hit every speed bump at sixty miles an hour. Yet, despite Jack's faults, he was the tent pole to which I aspired to in this business. As long as I could stop there.

Nights like tonight, I was content to sit on the aged bar stool and ignore everything. It was easier that way.

Then I felt a cold splash on my back, whipped around to see a tall, lithe redhead standing over my shoulder, her hand over her mouth as if she'd just seen a bad car accident.

"Oh, my gosh!" she said, grabbing a pile of napkins off the bar and mopping at my shirt where she'd spilled her drink. From the look and smell, I could tell she'd spilled a cosmopolitan. I'd say I was thankful it wasn't one of my good shirts, but the truth was I didn't own any good shirts. Just one more article of clothing with an unidentifiable stain.

"No big deal," I said, wringing as much liquid from the cloth as I could. "It's a bar. You kind of expect to be hit with a drink or two."

She smiled at me. I wondered if she thought I was funny, or if she was just relieved I wasn't the kind of asshole who would bark and shout at a girl who'd accidentally spilled a drink on him.

She was pretty. Tall, in good shape, but I could tell a lot of effort went into her appearance. Probably too much. Her jeans were tight, light blue tank top with a neckline that plunged far down enough to catch the eyes. Her cheeks and eyelids glistened with sweat on top of sweat-proof makeup. She was probably a natural beauty but simply didn't trust herself. I thought I noticed a small dark spot, a mole perhaps, by her right collarbone, but quickly realized it was a passing shadow. She was the prettiest girl I'd noticed in Finnerty's in a long while. Either that, or I just never bothered to notice.

"Here," she said, putting down the soiled napkins and reaching into her purse, "let me buy you a drink. Least I can do, right, since you're being such a gentleman? What kind of beer is that?"

I shook my head. "No need. It happens." I caught the ball game from the corner of my eye. The fans were on their feet. Looked like someone had hit a home run.

"Well, can I just buy you a drink to buy you a drink?"

I looked at her, a cautious smile. My beer was almost empty. And my wallet was running light.

"It's okay," I said after a moment. "Really, it's not necessary." She put her purse away, eyed me with a combination of skepticism and curiosity.

"Are you here with friends?" she asked.

"Nope. Just watching the game."

She glanced around the bar, watched the guys with gelled hair and long button-down shirts hanging over expensive jeans, high-fiving one another while a gaggle of girls cheered every dart throw.

"So you're just here to, what…hang out by yourself?"

"That's the idea," I said. Her smile turned demure. I felt her move closer. Her arm brushed mine, and for a moment

I felt that tingle of electricity. It had been so long. I didn't move my arm.

"That's kind of cool," she said. "Lot of guys try too hard to be all macho and stuff. It takes confidence to stay quiet."

I had to stop myself from laughing, considering I was afraid of my own apartment and came here precisely so I could avoid the braying of testosterone-drenched i-bankers.

"Trust me, it's not confidence," I said. "Just comfort."

"See, that's confident right there!" Then she extended her hand. "I'm Emily."

"Henry," I said. For a moment I waited, then shook her hand. Didn't want to be rude.

"I'm here with some old college friends who are in town for the weekend," Emily said, "but we're probably going to ditch this place soon and go somewhere else more, like, alive. I know you're happy to be by yourself—" she used finger quotation marks to accent this statement "—but it might be cool if you came with us."

Right then I could see the night laid out before me. Two paths. I could accept Emily's invitation, and presuming I played my cards right, that electric sensation of skin on skin would later become a wildfire.

Or I could sit here, sip my beer, stare at my reflection in the mirror and think about all the other paths I'd simply passed right by.

"I appreciate the offer, Emily," I said. "But I think I'll stay here for the night."

"You sure?" she said.

"Sure."

"Suit yourself." She grabbed a clean napkin from the bar, removed a tube of eyeliner from her purse and painstakingly drew something on the paper. When she was done, she smiled, handed me the napkin and walked away.

Her phone number was written in black, smudgy ink. Emily offered one last wave as she went through the door, pausing for a moment to give me one last chance to reconsider. I raised the rest of my beer to her. She shrugged and left. Then I let the napkin fall to the floor.

I downed the last of my beer. Seamus took a pair of empty pitchers down off the bar and came over to me.

"Another?" he said.

I looked at my glass, felt the buzz swirling in my head and decided against it.

"That's it for me tonight." He took my glass and went to serve a man shaking his glass for a refill. I stood up, steadying myself as the blood swam to my head. When my equilibrium settled, I left the bar.

I checked my phone. Four missed calls, beginning at 11:00 p.m. They were all from the same prefix, which I recognized as the *Gazette*. I checked my watch. Late job-related calls were no longer a nuisance; they were a part of my life. Perhaps that's why I turned down another beer. Somehow I had a feeling I'd have to return someone's call while relatively sober.

I walked down to the corner and bought a pack of Certs, slipping one in my mouth to try to remove the beer after-taste. Then I dialed the *Gazette*. Wallace Langston, editor-in-chief, picked up his private line on the first ring.

"Henry, Christ, where the hell've you been?"

"It's a Friday night. You don't pay me enough to have a 24/7 retainer."

"Okay, you don't want to answer your phone, I have half a newsroom of reporters who'd drop their off days faster than a hot iron for what I'm about to tell you, so let me know if this is an inconvenient time."

"What if I said it was?"

"I'd say two things," Wallace said. "First, you're a liar. It sounds like you're standing on the street, which means you can't be that busy. Second, I'd say I don't give a crap because if you turn down this assignment, I can find another reporter who'll grab it faster than you can hang up."

"Sounds like a hot one," I said. "So maybe I'm interested."

"*Hot* isn't the word," Wallace said. "Scorching. Actually no, forget that. The only appropriate word is *exclusive.*"

"Oh, yeah? What kind of exclusive?"

"You hear about this Daniel Linwood case up in Hobbs County?"

Immediately my buzz wore off. "Kid who was kidnapped five years ago and suddenly reappeared on his parents' doorstep, right?"

"So you follow the news. Glad to know we pay you for something. Daniel Linwood was five years old when he disappeared from his parents' home in Hobbs County, New York. That was five years ago. One moment he's playing outside, then all of a sudden he's just gone. No witnesses, nobody saw or heard anything. His disappearance shakes the Hobbs County community to its roots. There's a media frenzy, politicians come out of the woodwork to show their support, but the cops come up empty. Then last night, Daniel shows up at his parents' house like he's been at the movies. Not a scratch on him. And get this—the kid has as much memory of the past five years as I have of my first marriage. He doesn't remember where he's been, who took him or how he even got home. Half the known world is waging war to talk to Daniel and his parents and get the story, but up until now it's been radio silence."

"Until now?" I said.

"Until you," Wallace said. "I've been calling the Linwoods for twenty-four hours nonstop."

"I bet they appreciate that," I said snidely.

"Shut up, Parker, or I'll smack that booze right off your breath."

"You don't know I've been drinking," I said, regretfully slurring the last word.

"I've worked with Jack O'Donnell for more than twenty years. You can't fool a professional bullshit detector. Anyway, tonight I get a call from Shelly Linwood out of nowhere. She says she's ready to talk. And before I can say another word, she says she and Daniel will talk to you, and only you."

"Me?" I said. "Why?"

Wallace said, "Shelly knows she can't keep silent forever, that at some point she and Daniel will need to speak to the press. So she said when he does speak to someone, she wants it to be to a reporter he won't be intimidated by. Someone who doesn't remind him of his parents. She wants Daniel to talk to someone he can trust, whom she can look in the eye and know he won't exploit her son. Between all of that, I offered you. And she accepted."

"Holy crap, are you serious?" I said. "This is a major story, Wallace. We're going to make a lot of reporters pretty jealous."

"And I'm going to revel in it," Wallace said. "This is your story now, Parker. Daniel Linwood has probably been through a kind of hell you and I can't even imagine, and his parents have spent almost five years assuming their oldest son was dead. Be gentle. Daniel is ten years old, and we still don't know the full psychological damage he's suffered. If you press the wrong button, touch the wrong nerve, he and Shelly will clam up fast. And the *Dispatch* will be on top of this as fast as Paulina Cole can get up to Hobbs County."

"I'd die before Paulina scoops us," I said.

"Don't make it come to that, Henry. The Linwoods are expecting you tomorrow at two. Get there at noon, spend a few hours checking out the neighborhood for local color. But if Daniel wants to talk to you at one-forty-five, two-fifteen or three o'clock in the morning, you'll have your tape recorder ready to go."

"You got it."

"That means going home right now and sobering up."

"I'm on my way." This included a hot shower, a fresh set of clothes, suit and tie. I prayed these were all at the ready, otherwise an all-night Laundromat would soon be graced by my clothes' aromatic presence.

"Call me before you leave tomorrow," Wallace said. "And I mean that. *Call me.* I don't want to come into the office tomorrow and see you asleep and drooling on your keyboard. You have a home. Go there."

I said nothing. Telling Wallace that my apartment didn't feel like a home was neither his business nor concern. All he cared about, and rightfully so, was this story. I'd been granted leeway the past few years most young reporters never got. Many in my position would have been shown the door, either landing in the safety net of a small-town paper or spewing angry blogs about the dumbing-down of American media. I had no desire to do either, and preferred to help from the inside. Big-time news was in my blood. A while ago Jack O'Donnell had told me that to truly become a legend in your field, you had to lead a life with one purpose. You had to devote yourself to your calling.

Splitting your passions between that and other pursuits—hobbies, family—would only make each endeavor suffer. The past few months I'd whittled down my extracurriculars to nothing. All for stories like this.

"You'll hear from me first thing tomorrow morning," I said. "And, Wallace?"

"Yeah, kid?"

"Thanks for the opportunity."

"Don't thank me, thank Shelly Linwood. I'm not the only one counting on you to do the right thing."

The call ended. I stood there in the warm night, the sounds of the bar and the street fading away. This night held nothing else for me, but tomorrow presented a golden opportunity. So many circumstances surrounding Daniel Linwood's disappearance were a mystery, and because the boy himself couldn't remember, I wondered how much, if any of it, would ever come to light. I wondered if never getting that closure would bother the Linwood family. Or if they were just thankful to have their son back.

I put the phone in my pocket, went to the corner and hailed a cab back to my apartment. For a moment I wondered if, like Daniel Linwood, I was returning to a place both strangely familiar, yet terribly foreign at the same time.

3

The Lincoln Town Car pulled up at 10:00 a.m. on the dot, shiny and black and idling in front of my apartment as inconspicuous as a black rhinoceros. I'd heeded Wallace's advice and gone home, sleeping in my own bed for the first time in weeks. I stripped the sheets, used a few clean towels in their place, and got my winks under an old sleeping bag.

I woke up at eight-thirty, figured it'd be plenty of time, but it took forty-five minutes to clean the crud out of my coffee machine and brew a new pot, so by the time the driver buzzed my cell phone I was tucking my shirt in, making sure my suit jacket was devoid of any lint. Unfortunately I missed the open fly until we'd merged off the West Side Highway onto I-87 North. My driver was a Greek fellow named Stavros. Stavros was big, bald and had a pair of snake-eyed dice tattooed on the back of his neck that just peeked out over the headrest.

I sipped my Thermos of coffee, grimaced and double-checked my briefcase. Pens, paper, tape recorder, business cards, digital camera in case I had a chance to take some shots of the neighborhood surrounding the Linwood residence in Hobbs County. Perhaps we'd use them in the article, give the reader a sense of local color recorded words could not.

Hobbs County was located about thirty miles north of New York City, nestled in between Tarrytown and the snuggly, wealthy confines of Chappaqua. Just a few years ago Hobbs County was an ingrown toenail between the two other towns, but recently a tremendous influx of state funds and pricey renovations had things moving in the right direction. Good thing, too, because statistically, Hobbs County had crime rates that would have made Detroit and Baltimore shake their heads.

According to the FBI Report of Offenses Known to Law Enforcement, the year before Daniel Linwood disappeared, Tarrytown, with 11,466 residents, had zero reported murders, zero rapes, one case of arson (a seventeen-year-old girl setting fire to her ex-boyfriend's baseball card collection), zero kidnappings and ten car thefts. Each of these numbers were microscopic compared to the national average.

That same year, Hobbs County, with 10,372 residents, had sixteen reported murders, five rapes, nine cases of arson, twenty-two car thefts and two kidnappings. If Hobbs County had the population of New York City, it would be on pace for more than twelve thousand murders a year.

Hobbs County was literally killing itself.

One of those two reported kidnappings was Daniel Linwood. The other was a nine-year-old girl whose body was later found in a drainage ditch. Since then, those crime rates had dropped like a rock. This past year, Hobbs had four murders. One rape. Eleven car thefts. And no kidnappings. There was still a lot of work to be done, but something had lit a fire under Hobbs County. It was righting itself.

And then Daniel Linwood reappeared, hopefully speeding the cleansing process even more.

The rebuilding had naturally raised property values, and between the drop in crime and influx of new money, Hobbs County found itself awash with wealthy carpetbaggers interested in the refurbished schools, reseeded parks and investment opportunities. Five years ago you could have bought a three-bedroom house for less than two hundred and fifty thousand dollars. Today, if you scoured the real estate pages and found one for less than three quarters of a million, you'd be an idiot not to snap it up.

While there was no getting back Daniel Linwood's lost years, his family could at least be thankful he had come back to a town far safer than the one he'd left.

"Only been to Hobbs once," Stavros piped in from the front seat. "Few years ago. Pro football player going to visit his aunt just diagnosed with Hodgkins. She lived in the same house for thirty years, give or take. Guy told me he'd tried to buy her a new place, get her out of the life, but you know how old folks are. Rather die at the roots than reach for a vine. You know, even if the client's only booked for a one-way trip, I'll usually offer to hang around in case they decide they need a ride back to wherever. Hobbs, though, man, you could offer me double the rate and I would have jetted faster than one of them Kenyan marathon runners. Not the kind of place you want to be sitting in a car alone at night. Or anytime, really."

I eyed those dice tattoos. Wondered what it took to scare a man who wasn't afraid to get ink shot into his neck with a needle.

"I hear the town is different now," I said. "A lot's changed in five years."

"New coat of paint, same cracked wood underneath," Stavros said. "You don't start from the ground up, poison's still gonna be there. Anyway, you're booked for a return trip, right? I'm sure you'll be fine, long as you're finished before the sun goes down. The dealers and hoods come out thinking you're the po-lice."

"I really think you're wrong," I said, my voice trying to convince me more than Stavros. "Anyway, when we get there, I don't think you'll have to worry too much about being alone. If I know the press, they'll be camped out at this house like ants at a picnic."

"That so? Where exactly you headed?"

"Interview," I said. "A kid."

"Not that kid who got kidnapped. Daniel something, right?"

"Daniel Linwood, yeah."

"Hot damn, I've been reading about that! Awful stuff. I mean great he came back, but I got a six-year-old and I'd just about tear the earth apart if she ever went missing. Those poor parents. Can't even imagine."

"Better you don't."

We merged onto 287, then headed north on Route 9, driving past a wide white billboard announcing our entry into the town limits.

Hobbs County was covered in lush green foliage, the summer sun shining golden through the thick leaves. Trees bracketed sleepy homes, supported by elegant marble columns. I lowered the window and could hear running water from a nearby stream. This was New York, but not the big city you read about in newspapers. It was the kind of place where you bought homemade preserves and knew everybody's name. Over the past few years, though, the names got wealthier, the jams more expensive. Shelly

Linwood didn't work. I wondered how the Linwoods were able to afford the newfound royalty of Hobbs County. And whether Daniel had come back to any sort of recognizable life.

We wound our way to Eaglemont Terrace, threading down Main Street. All the stores were open, Hobbs residents walking small, freshly groomed dogs while carrying bags from the town's boutique shops. Lots of cell phones and BlackBerries. Pretty much the same ratio of technology to people as NYC.

It was just before noon. I had two hours before the interview was scheduled to begin. As we turned onto Woodthrush Court, I made out a row of cars and vans clogging the street, metal lodged in an artery. The main cluster looked to be centered around one house, no doubt the Linwood residence. I didn't want to make any sort of grand entrance, and once the other reporters saw me, they wouldn't leave me alone. They knew I had the exclusive, and they wouldn't make my job any easier.

"Do me a favor, stop here," I said to Stavros. The Greek man obliged, eased on the brakes until we were stopped a few blocks down from the mess.

"You want to hang out here? I can put the radio on, even got a few CDs in the glove. You like The Police?"

"Eh. Sting never really did it for me. Just want to walk around the neighborhood for a few minutes. Get a sense of the place."

"Your time," Stavros said. "Tell you something, it might have been a few years ago and my memory's as soft as my dick, but this sure ain't the same town I drove through a while back."

"Hold that thought," I said to Stavros, unbuckling my seat belt. "The last one, not the one about your...never mind. I have your cell number, so I'll just call when I'm ready to leave, right? You'll be here?"

"Faster 'n instant coffee."

"Glad to hear that, thanks."

I grabbed my briefcase, stepped out of the car. It was a sunny day, high seventies, a light breeze rattling leaves and lowering the humidity. I breathed in the fresh air, wished I could find it in the city outside of Central Park. It was strange to be in a town where you could see the horizon miles away. Unobstructed views over houses just a story or two tall.

While what I said to Stavros was partly true, about wanting to stay incognito to the press as long as possible, I also didn't want to give the wrong impression to the Linwoods themselves. I didn't want to roll up in a Lincoln with a driver, step out of the backseat like some dignitary. If I was going to talk to Daniel Linwood, it was going to be on his level. With all the attention he'd be facing over the coming weeks, his family didn't need to feel like they were being talked down to.

I walked to the opposite side of the street, slow enough to avoid arousing suspicion, fast enough that residents wouldn't think a solicitor was creeping around in their front yards.

When I was just a block away, still unnoticed, I stepped into the pathway between two clapboard houses and sat down on a stone bench. I gathered my notes, made sure the tape recorder had fresh batteries. And then I sat and watched the beehive.

The reporters camped outside the Linwood home were standing on the grass, their vans having left tire tracks in yards all across the street. No doubt the locals would complain to the city council about this, but with a story this big there was no stopping the boulder from rolling downhill.

Since the night Daniel came back, the only comment from the Linwood home had been "no comment." Today that would change.

I sketched brief descriptions of the homes, the climate, the scene in front of me. Enough to give Hobbs County some color. I snapped a few pictures of the houses, even took a few of the press corps just for kicks. Then I waited.

At one-forty I stood up, stretched and started to walk over. My heart was beating fast, and I wiped my palms on the inside of my jacket. One of the tricks of the trade Jack taught me. Most people wipe their hands on their pants, and that does nothing but make your source think they're being interviewed by a guy who can't jiggle out the last few drops of piss. Inside the jacket, nobody could see you were hiding the Hoover Dam in your armpits. Good thing Jack was a classy guy.

I was hoping to enter the Linwood residence as quickly as possible. I didn't want to answer any questions, or see my face on any newscasts. I'd had enough of that.

Silently I crept toward the house, when all of a sudden a gravelly voice said, "Look who crawled out of the sewer," and I knew I had a better chance of finding a winning lottery ticket in my hamper than staying incognito.

One by one the heads turned. Clean-shaven newsmen with three-hundred-dollar haircuts, women wearing makeup so thick it could have been a layer of skin. They all looked at me with sneers reserved for subjects they were used to interviewing in solitary confinement. A piece of gum snapped, then landed on my shoe. I flicked it off, kept walking without looking to see who was guilty. Never let them see you angry.

I nudged my way through the crowd without making eye contact with anyone. I recognized a male reporter from the *New York Dispatch,* somewhat surprised to see that Paulina Cole hadn't taken on the story herself. Paulina Cole was the *Dispatch*'s top columnist, a post she took after leaving the *Gazette.* We'd actually worked next to each other for several months, but now there was as much love between us as Hillary and Monica.

You'd never picture the devil as a five-foot-six woman with platinum-blond hair, impeccable skin tone and a take-no-prisoners, ball-busting attitude that could have made the toughest Viet Cong piss his pants. At first I admired Paulina. The newsroom had very much been an old boys' club during her climb, and she'd had to endure a lot and work fantastically hard to get where she was. But then she showed her true colors. She showed that one thing's for certain in the media: throwing someone under the bus can make quite a lucrative career.

After publicly criticizing me in print, Paulina later ran a story focusing on the sordid family affairs of my ex-girlfriend. It was this story that led to Mya being brutally attacked and nearly killed. I'd spent many hours at Mya's hospital bed, beside her at physical therapy, comforting her mother, who was widowed at the hands of the same killer who nearly took her daughter's life. Though Paulina had fewer friends than O. J. Simpson, her notoriety was entirely part of the game. Brazen, provocative, pushing every hot button as though her life depended on it. Rumor had it Ted Allen, the *Dispatch*'s editor-in-chief, gave her a five-figure expense account to dress the part, as well. If perception was reality, Paulina Cole was the grand bitch goddess of the news.

I heard audible whispers as I walked up to the Linwood

porch. *Punk. Asshole. Little shit.* I'd taken a beating both in the press and from other reporters since my first few months at the *Gazette,* and as much as the words stung, sadly, I'd grown used to them.

Screw them.

The Linwood house was a small, Victorian-style dwelling, with jigsaw trim and spindles. It was three stories high, the top floor with a small square window, most likely an attic rarely used. Two unadorned columns were mounted on the front porch, the marble clean. The paint job was an off-white, and looked recently refreshed. I could see a small swing set around the back, a shovel and pail sitting abandoned. Surprised a reporter hadn't snagged it yet. I stepped up to the porch and took a breath, preparing to ring the doorbell.

Just then the front door swung open, nearly knocking me on my ass, and a caravan of steely-postured suited men and women came pouring out. The first few were all hefty men wearing identical pants and blazers. They wore single wire earpieces, transparent tubing with Star ear-mold devices. They didn't wear sunglasses, but the bulges in their jacket pockets said they would be in a matter of seconds.

I stepped aside. The men paid me no attention, stopping at the bottom of the porch, hands clasped behind them. When I turned back to knock, I found myself in front of a tall, lean man in his early fifties. He had wavy gray hair, a sharp, equine nose and the slightest onset of crow's-feet. He wore a smart navy suit and a brilliant smile. I recognized him instantly but tried to hide my surprise. He was talking to somebody inside I couldn't see, but when he turned around, the look on his face confirmed that he recognized me, as well. I swallowed hard.

The man cocked his head, flashed that smile again and put his hand out.

"Henry Parker, right? *New York Gazette?*"

"Yes, yes, sir." I was flattered that he'd heard of me. Either that, or he knew why I was here.

"Pleasure to meet you, Henry. Gray Talbot."

"Pleasure to meet you, too, Senator."

Talbot smiled again. "Walk with me for a moment, won't you, Henry?" It was phrased like the kind of question you couldn't refuse.

I half nodded, then suddenly Talbot's arm was around me, leading me down the steps. His grip was just strong enough to let me know I didn't have a choice, light enough to let onlookers know this would be a friendly chat. Everything about the man spoke volumes of an effortless confidence, a confidence that had captured the hearts and minds of New Yorkers desperate for a politician who deep down wasn't *quite* a politician.

Gray Talbot was currently in his fourth term as a Democratic New York State senator. In his four elections, he'd averaged sixty-two percent of the vote, and it was assumed Talbot would hold that seat until he either retired, died or decided he preferred a larger, whiter house. Talbot was currently the third-highest-ranking Democrat in the senate, behind the senate majority leader and senate majority whip. As the current majority chairman on the United States Committee on Banking, Housing, and Urban Affairs, Talbot was one of the most outspoken proponents of lowering the federal interest rate. "A home for every American who wants one" was his slogan. He was often photographed with his trademark plaything, a Rubik's Cube, constantly fiddling and working out solutions. He was quoted as saying the game kept his mind limber. Every cube he'd ever completed was kept in his home. Rumor was he needed a bookcase to house them all.

In the previous election, three years after Daniel Linwood's disappearance, Gray Talbot had outdone himself, garnering an unheard of seventy-three percent of the popular vote. And now that man had his arm around me. Talbot wasn't visiting Daniel Linwood for a simple photo-op. The stakes were much higher. Daniel's reappearance wasn't merely a human-interest story, it was important enough that one of the most powerful men in the country made it his business. Yet as we walked, there were no staged photo-ops. No handshakes. No teary hugs with Shelly Linwood. Gray Talbot, as far as I could tell, was here because he *wanted* to be.

And he was the kind of man who, if he felt like it, could squash reporters with his pinkie finger.

As Talbot led me across the lawn, I could hear groans of protest as his bodyguards held the throng of reporters back. When we were out of earshot, Talbot took his arm from my shoulder and said, "I'm glad Wallace chose you to report on Daniel. Shelly and Randy think they can trust you. I'm inclined to believe them."

"Then can trust me, sir, I promise that."

"Good." Talbot turned slightly as the angry catcalls grew louder. "Ignore the parasites," he said. "They're jealous, that's all. Any one of them would trade their press badge to be where you are and do what you've done in such a short amount of time."

I felt a tingle down my side where a bullet had shattered my rib and punctured my lung just a few years ago, and wondered if that was really true.

"You know I used to live in a place just like this," Talbot said, his eyes searching the tree line as though looking for a familiar sign. "Not like it is now, the way it was back when Daniel disappeared. The kind of town where you woke up every day assuming a crash position, trying just to hold on to a sliver of hope. My biggest dream growing up was to just get the hell out and make something of myself before the evil swallowed me whole. The strongest men and women aren't the ones born with everything, Henry, they're the ones who are born with nothing but fight like hell to get it. I know how hard you've fought. And I know you'll understand what this family has gone through. To lose a child? To assume your child is dead, that you've outlived your firstborn? I can't even imagine it. So be respectful. Daniel will never get back those years, and his parents will never fully repair that hole in their hearts. If their boy's story is given the respect and honesty it deserves, well, that might go a little way toward helping. I know you have a responsibility to your job. But your job is also to mend fences when you can. This is not a tabloid story. This is not a family to be exploited. So don't you dare treat them like one."

"I wouldn't dare," I said.

"I know that, Henry." Talbot stopped, turned around, made a brief gesture, and the bodyguards began walking over. A limousine pulled up, a chauffeur getting out to open the door for the senator. He shook my hand one last time, then said, "You're a fine young man and a terrific reporter. Hopefully Daniel Linwood will have the chance to grow up and find his calling just the same."

Then he got in and was gone.

I turned back to the house, tried to figure out what to make of the encounter. Gray Talbot was known to be a humanitarian, and his troubled background only solidified his resolve to help those in need. The Linwoods obviously fit that bill, and he was more than happy to put more weight on my story. To make sure I didn't color outside the lines. Not that I planned to, but there's a difference between moral obligation and having a politician flat-out tell you.

I walked back to the Linwoods' house. This time the other reporters were silent. I rang the doorbell, and barely a moment passed before it opened to reveal a woman wearing an apron. She had curly brown hair pulled back in a ponytail, a look of both joy and exhaustion in her face. The apron was covered with stains of various colors. She smiled. Her eyes were bloodshot and weary, but happy.

"Henry, right?"

"That's right. Mrs. Linwood?"

"Please, call me Shelly. Come in. Daniel will be so happy to meet you. From what Senator Talbot told me, you two actually have a lot in common."

4

Shelly led me through the foyer and into what looked like their family room. A thirty-eight-inch television sat on a wooden stand; toys and video-game cartridges were spread about haphazardly. The couches and chairs were all dark fabric and wood, the kind you buy when you expect stains to make regular appearances.

"I was going to clean up for the senator, but…you know…" Shelly said, slightly embarrassed at the mess.

"You want Daniel to get used to living in a normal home," I said.

"Best for him to get used to a real home again," Shelly said, nodding.

A man entered the room. He looked weary but happy. He was a slightly paunchy man with a receding hairline and deep bags under his eyes.

"You must be Henry," he said, offering his hand. "Randall Linwood."

"Mr. Linwood," I said. "Thanks so much for having me. I'm grateful for you letting me into your home."

"Thank you, Mr. Parker. With so many vultures circling us since Daniel's return, it's good to have someone we feel we can trust handling the story. Shelly and I have done our homework on you and your newspaper. I think we're all in good hands."

"You are, sir. I ask for nothing but the truth, and I give nothing but my word." Shelly smiled at this, flicked at her eye as though wiping away a nonexistent tear.

"Anyway, I have to get back to the office. I wanted to be here to meet the senator, but if I miss any more time, Daniel'll have to eat Spaghetti O's for the next few weeks. Pleasure to meet you, Henry."

"Likewise, sir."

When Randy Linwood left, I heard a brief scuffle come from another room. Looking through the doorway, I saw two pairs of eyes peering at me from between the slats on a staircase. Just as quickly as they appeared, the legs they were attached to ran back up the stairs, whispers following.

"James and Tasha," Shelly said, brushing a strand of hair from her face, the red still there. "They're not really sure how to deal with all of this. We're so happy, but all this…attention, it's not what they're used to. They deal with it in their own way."

"I can't imagine going through what you've been through. But I have to say, Mrs. Linwood, you're handling it well."

"I'd say thank you, but it's not on purpose."

"Have the police been helpful?"

"Oh, my, incredibly so. I actually thought it'd be much worse, but they've barely spent more than half an hour here since Danny came back. In fact, when the senator came, that's the first time I saw more than two of them at the same time." I found that strange, but allowed Shelly to continue. She paused for a moment, said softly, "We're just so glad to have Daniel back. It's like, a wave crashing over you when you're ready to burst into flame. I can't explain it. All I know is I love him now more than I ever did."

Without thinking, my hand went to my briefcase and I started to unlatch it. My eyes snapped back to Shelly, a sheepish grin on my face.

"I'm sorry," I said. "I'd kind of like to keep the tape recorder running, if you don't mind. Things like that, what you just said, they'd add a lot to the story. I don't want the piece to be just about Daniel and how his return has affected him, but what it's meant to your family. How it affects you, your husband, your other children." Shelly smiled, nodded once. I took out the recorder, raised my eyebrows, clicked it on.

"Are you recording now?" she asked.

"I am."

"So this will go in your interview?"

I laughed. "Not everything. Not what you just said, only if it relates to Daniel and your family."

"Can you print swear words?" she asked.

"Uh…no."

"Okay, I curse sometimes and I don't want Daniel to get embarrassed by his potty-mouthed mother."

I smiled at her.

Behind Shelly, I noticed a row of photographs lining a gray shelf. Inside the frames were pictures of the Linwood family. Most of the photos had just four people in them. Shelly, Randy, James and Tasha. Two pictures had been placed in front of the others. One was of all five Linwoods: Randy, Shelly, Tasha, James and Daniel. It looked like a photo from a Christmas card, all five bundled in warm sweaters, posed on a couch with smiles as big as they could muster.

"The last photo we took as a family," Shelly said. "Tasha was only a year old."

"It's beautiful," I said. Then I looked at the photo next to it.

The picture was of their daughter, Tasha, when she was just a child, maybe one or two years old. Tasha wasn't facing the camera. Her head and body were turned away, short blond hair caught in the wind. There was nothing particularly photogenic about the pic, nothing that seemed extraordinary.

"Tasha's birthday," Shelly was quick to point out. "There was a leak in the basement. We lost so many photo albums. This is the only one we could save. Not the best shot, but it's what's in it that matters. She's just so carefree."

I smiled back at her. "Should we get Daniel?"

Shelly bit her lip, then relaxed. "Have a seat. I'll be right back."

I sat down on the couch. An oak coffee table separated me from a chair where I assumed Daniel would sit. The couch was dark brown, microfiber, half a dozen stains of varying color and size spattered about. A silver robot peeked out from beside the television set, and a few stray doll hairs were tucked between the cushions. The Linwoods' living room was well worn, well used. The photos on the mantel didn't look like they were placed there for Senator Talbot. I could tell from the dust patterns and slightly faded wood surrounding them that they were barely ever moved. That photo of Tasha, though, captivated my interest. It just seemed so out of place.

I placed the tape recorder on the coffee table; better to keep it in plain sight than unnerve Daniel by taking it out after he'd settled down. I breathed easy. Waited.

I heard Shelly say, "Come on, sweetheart," and into the room stepped a young boy. He was a little over five feet tall, with dark, tousled hair and hazel eyes. Those eyes appeared less curious than slightly fearful, as though he was being led through a curtain into somewhere unknown. His cheeks bore a few freckles that surely got him teased as a kid, but in ten years would make him look cute, even handsome. His limbs were gangly, face thin. I remembered my growth spurt at about the same age, thinking I'd end up being eight feet tall and starting at center for the Lakers. Of course neither happened. For a moment I believed Daniel's tentativeness was directed toward me, but then I realized that there was a gap of nearly five years in this boy's memory. He wasn't just feeling me out, but his whole life.

Shelly kept her hands on his shoulders, gentle but muscles tensed, as though he could topple over at any moment and shatter. Daniel's only hesitation was in his gait, otherwise he looked like a regular boy, ready to lose himself in too much homework, too many video games, and the dreams of years he had yet to know.

"Hey, Daniel," I said, standing up slightly, trying to make him relax. "I'm Henry. It's nice to meet you."

"Danny," he said. "Just Danny." No hesitation there. I saw a frown glimmer across Shelly's face, but she said nothing.

"Danny," I said. "Well, Danny, thanks for letting me talk to you." His nod said he wasn't quite as happy as me.

He smiled tentatively, sat down in a wicker-backed chair across the table from me. "Could I have a soda?" he said to Shelly. She was up and heading to the kitchen before the question was finished. When she'd disappeared, he looked at the tape recorder. "Is that thing on?"

"Yeah, it is. See that red light?" He nodded. "That means it's on."

"So it's recording what I'm saying right now?"

"That's right."

"Okay. Shit." I looked up at him. Danny had a mischievous grin on his face, slightly red with embarrassment. "Sorry, just wanted to, you know..."

"Yeah, I know."

"That won't be in your story, will it?"

"Nah. I'll keep the uncensored version for my personal files."

Shelly came back in carrying a tray with a glass of soda, another glass of water and a plate of assorted vegetables. Danny and I shared a smirk. Then I noticed what else was on the tray: a gauze pad, a bottle of what appeared to be rubbing alcohol, a cylindrical tube the size of a pen and a vial.

Shelly noticed me looking at this and said, "Daniel, sorry, *Danny* has diabetes. I thought it'd be good to give him his insulin before you got started."

"Fine with me," I said. "Danny?"

He nodded. Shelly said, "We did your arm this morning, right? Let's go with your leg."

Danny rolled up his right pant leg, exposing his calf. Shelly inserted the vial into the pen until it clicked. Then she unscrewed the cap from the rubbing alcohol, tipping just enough onto the gauze pad to wet it. She rubbed the pad on Danny's calf until it shone. Then she took the pen, pressed it against his skin and depressed the plunge. Danny winced slightly.

Shelly removed the pen, wiped down Danny's leg with a towel, then took the materials back into the kitchen. Danny rolled down his pant leg as Shelly returned.

"Sucks," he said. "Dr. Petrovsky says I have to take it three times a day."

"Petrovsky?" I said.

"Dmitri Petrovsky. He's Daniel's pediatrician," Shelly answered.

I nodded. "You should listen to your doctor. This medicine helps to keep you healthy," I told Danny.

"Still sucks."

"Do you mind if I stay during the, the interview?" she asked.

"Not at all. If it makes Danny more comfortable, I'd prefer it."

"Honey," she said, "do you mind if Mommy stays?"

"No, I don't mind if *Mommy* stays." "Mommy" came out with a slightly sarcastic bent. I smiled. I kind of liked Danny Linwood.

Shelly, satisfied, nestled into a love seat, holding a lace throw pillow on her lap.

"So, Danny," I said, "how are things going here? Are you having a hard time adjusting?" He shrugged. "I need a little more than that, buddy."

"It's okay, I guess. I'm supposed to start school in two weeks, but I don't really want to."

"Why not?"

"I don't know anybody. They're all going to think I'm some sort of freak."

"They do know you, Daniel," Shelly interrupted. "You started out in grade school with most of them. Like Cliffy Willis, remember Cliffy? Or Ashley Whitney?"

I listened.

"No, *Mommy,* I don't remember Cliffy. Or Ashley. I don't remember anyone."

"Mrs. Linwood?" I said. She looked at me. Nodded. Got it. She held the pillow tighter.

"Danny, tell me about the day you came home. You came to this house, knocked on the door." Danny nodded. "Can you tell me what happened right before that?"

Danny shifted in his chair. "I remember lying down,

then suddenly waking up. I was on the ground, like I'd fallen asleep or something. I recognized where I was."

"And where was that?"

"Doubleday Field," Danny said. "I played peewee baseball there."

"What position?"

"Third base."

"Like A-Rod," I said.

"No, he's a shortstop for the Rangers."

I was about to disagree, when I remembered that in Danny's mind, he was correct. The year Danny disappeared, Rodriguez hadn't yet become a Yankee, hadn't yet changed positions. I wondered how much else of Danny Linwood's world had changed unbeknownst to him.

"What happened then?"

"I remember hearing a siren. Like a police car or an ambulance. And then I just started walking home."

"You knew how to get home?"

"Yeah, I used to walk home every day with…" Danny searched for the rest of his sentence.

"Cliffy Willis and his mother," Shelly offered quietly. Danny looked at her angrily, then the reaction slipped away.

"Where did you walk?" I asked.

"Home," he said. "Past the corner store and that brick wall with the graffiti of the boy that got shot a long time ago. I got scared for a second when I saw the police car pull up at the field I just left, but I didn't think I did anything wrong so I just went home."

"Were you hurt?"

"No. Maybe a little tired, s'all. The doctors said they found something in my system, dia-something."

"Diazepam," I said. "It's a drug used to sedate. The police report said it was administered a few hours before you woke up. When you woke up, that's when it wore off." I said this as much to Shelly as Daniel. "I'm sorry, keep going."

"So, anyway, I walked home, knocked on the door. James opened it. I knew it was James, but he was, like, three feet taller than I remembered. And all of a sudden everyone is squishing the life out of me. Mom, Dad, Tasha, my brothers." I saw Shelly smile, the pillow gripped tight in her arms.

"Brothers?" I said.

"James," he said, "my brother."

"Right," I continued. "Do you know how long you were gone?"

"Mom says almost five years."

"Does it feel like you've been gone a long time?"

"Not really," Danny said. "I mean, it's hard when I, like, go to do something and can't do it. Like there used to be a radiator in my room where I could turn up the heat, but now we have these electronic-control things. And I don't recognize anything on TV, which sucks. All of a sudden my brothers and sister are, like, old." I felt a strange mental tugging sensation. Something Danny had said triggered it, but I couldn't quite put my finger on it.

"Danny, I know the police have probably asked you these questions already, but did you have any enemies at school? On the team? Someone you were scared of?" He shook his head vehemently.

"I remember breaking up with my girlfriend once and she got mad and cried, that's it."

"You had a girlfriend?" Shelly said. "When was this?"

"Mom, come on," he said.

"What, you can tell the whole world but you can't tell me?"

Danny looked at me, his eyes pleading. I smiled at him. Six-year-old Danny Linwood with a girlfriend. I wondered if she'd missed him, or even understood what had happened.

"Mrs. Linwood. Shelly," I said, looking at Danny from the corner of my eye. "I need to be able to talk to your son with his full concentration. I know this is hard and you have a lot to catch up on with Danny, but I need this to do my job."

"Your job." She sneered. "My job is my son."

"I know that. All I want to do is tell the truth about your boy. Trust me, I don't want to upset your family at all."

"Mom…" Danny said softly. This was likely the first chance Danny had had to talk about what happened, and it seemed to even be a bit cathartic for him.

"You're right. I'm sorry. Henry, please."

"Thank you," I said politely. "Danny, what was the last thing you remember before you woke up on that field?"

"I remember being at baseball practice," he said. "I don't know if that's the last thing that happened. But I remember Mike Bursaw got hit in the knee by a line drive and was crying, and Coach was going to send him to the nurse but Mike wouldn't let him. And I remember watching the Yankees on TV and my dad saying Jason Giambi couldn't get a hit to save his life, which is weird because he used to be so good. I mean, I had his poster on my wall, and every night I'd tell it to go three-for-four with a home run. I noticed the poster wasn't on my wall anymore. My dad said he took it down but didn't tell me why."

I didn't have the heart to bring up the fact that Jason Giambi had admitted using steroids, and his deteriorating performance was likely the result of his body breaking down. Danny Linwood was going to have enough problems reentering society; tearing down his boyhood heroes would happen eventually. Yet I understood his father's hesitance to wield the sledgehammer.

"Do you remember feeling pain?" I asked.

"No."

"Do you remember a face, someone unfamiliar, something frightening you?"

"Not really."

"Do you remember anything about the past few years? Sights? Sounds? Memories?"

Daniel sat there for a few moments. He seemed almost to be in pain, searching his thoughts as hard as he could for something, straining to find what wasn't there.

"A room," he said. "Like mine, but…I don't know."

"How like yours?"

"I think there were toys, but I don't know."

"Okay…what was the first thing you thought when your mom came out the door that day? The day you came back?"

"I remember being kind of confused. She didn't hug me like that when I came back from school or practice usually, so I kind of knew something was different. I was a little scared, like something might have happened to James or Tasha or my brothers. When my dad got home and started crying, that's when I started crying, too. Like maybe I was sick and didn't know it or something. All those TV shows where someone gets sick and then everyone is really nice to them, it's usually because they're going to die." Again I got that feeling. There was more to what Danny Linwood was saying than even he knew.

I noticed Shelly Linwood's lip trembling. She was aching to say something, gather her son up and hold him. My heart hurt for her.

"How did you find out what actually happened?"

"I still don't know what happened," Danny said, anger rising.

"I didn't mean…Who told you that you'd been gone?"

"My mom," he said, looking at Shelly. "She took me in here, sat me down where you're sitting. James and Tasha and my dad were with her. Then Mom told me."

"What did you think when she told you?"

"I didn't believe her," he said. "I thought it was, like, April Fools' or something."

"How did you realize she was telling the truth?"

"My dad showed me the Derek Jeter baseball rookie card he bought me for my birthday a while ago. He told me to look at the back. He said he'd bought the card the year I was born, 1996, Derek Jeter's rookie year. Jeter was twenty-two. Then he showed me a brand-new Jeter card. From this year. And on the back of that card, Jeter was thirty-three."

"How did you feel?"

"Scared. Upset. I mean, he'd been my favorite player and I didn't get to watch him grow up."

"What did you think about what your parents told you?" I clarified.

"Really scared," Danny said. "I cried, I think, because I didn't know what else to do. But I didn't really know why. I mean, I didn't feel sick, I wasn't hurt, it's not like I missed anyone, it was just…like, weird. Like you know when you wake up from a nap and you're not really sure what time it is?"

I nodded. The past few months of my life could have been accurately described that way.

"Do you think it'll be hard going back to school? Starting your life again? Just being a kid?"

Danny chewed his lip, looked at his mother. I could tell it was killing her to stay quiet, but she also knew her son needed to heal. And talking would help that process.

"I don't feel different. And I probably won't until I go back and, like, see people. Or like today when I want to watch a show but don't recognize anything that's on. I don't even really recognize myself, if that makes sense."

"In what way don't you recognize yourself?"

"Just, ways."

"Like what?"

He eyed his mother, a look of worry on his face. "I don't know if I can say with my mom here."

"Say whatever you need to, baby," Shelly added, for once chiming in at the right time.

"Well…I don't think I remember having hair down there."

I snorted a laugh without thinking. Shelly's face turned beet-red.

I said, "Moms don't usually like hearing things like that."

Danny shrugged. "She told me to say whatever I needed to."

"She sure did."

"How's your mom taking it?" I said. I looked at Shelly. She knew I needed this from him, as well.

"I don't know. Fine, I guess. I mean, she's always hugging me and kissing me. I mean, like the kids don't have enough to make fun of already, I don't want to show up at school covered in lipstick."

"She missed you is all," I said.

"Yeah, I know, but she could back off a little bit."

"I was your age once," I said. "I kind of wish my mom was more like yours."

Danny laughed. "Yeah, right," he said. "I guess she's just glad to have me back." Shelly was nodding, her face in the pillow. Danny looked somewhat at ease. I knew that likely wouldn't last long.

"My mom told me you got in trouble a while ago," Danny said. "She looked you up in the newspapers when she found out you were coming. Was she telling the truth? Were you in trouble?"

I felt the air rush from my lungs. I nodded. "Yeah, she's telling the truth."

"What did you do?"

I took a breath. "Some people thought I hurt someone," I said.

Danny looked at me, riveted.

"Did you?"

"Not on purpose," I said.

"What did it feel like?"

I thought for a moment, then said, "Probably a little like what you're going through. I felt like a stranger everywhere I went. Like nobody knew who I really was, they just saw what they read about or watched on TV."

"That's what'll happen to me, right? People will think I'm some freak weirdo when they don't even know who I am."

"They'll think that for a little while. Then it's up to you to prove them wrong."

"I don't see why they need me to prove anything," he said quietly. "It's not like I'm a different person or something."

I couldn't say this to Danny, but no matter what he or Shelly wanted to believe, he was a different person. Scandals resonated for a long time. Perceptions died hard.

Danny took a celery stalk, munched on it, leafy threads stuck between misaligned teeth. Shelly watched approvingly. Danny would need braces, that was for sure. No escaping that part of adolescence.

"I don't remember the house being so clean," Danny said. "And the color on the walls outside used to be gross."

"I had it repainted a few years ago," Shelly said. She turned to me. "I wanted things to be clean in case...in case my boy ever came back. I wanted him to know things would be different."

"You never lost hope, did you?" I asked.

"Never."

"Do you think things will be different?" I asked Shelly. "For Danny and your family?"

She gave me a smile, weaker than she likely thought it came off.

"Yes, they will. For the first time I truly know my babies will be safe."

Danny and I both looked at her, wondering just how she could be so certain.

5

I listened to the recording of my interview with Daniel on the ride back to the city. I tried to focus as much on Danny Linwood's cadences, his voice inflections, as what he actually said. I'd spoken to abducted children before, as well as men and women responsible for kidnapping children. The children were always withdrawn, as if a piece of their soul had been sucked out. Only they never knew why. The luckier ones, the ones that were found quicker, had withdrawn into a shallower hole. Eventually they could rejoin society, restart their lives. The ones like Daniel, who were removed for years, they weren't so lucky. It was fortunate enough they beat the tremendous odds to survive, but more than likely they'd be stuck in that hole their entire lives. They would spend as much time scrabbling for footing as they did living. With Daniel Linwood, it was as though four-plus years had simply been lopped off clean. No ragged edges to be caught on. Just a gaping hole that left barely a trace.

When Stavros dropped me at Rockefeller Plaza, I entered the *Gazette* and headed to my desk. First I would have the tape duplicated, then transcribed. I couldn't promise Daniel and Shelly that they would see my story before it ran, but I had given them my word that Daniel would be treated with respect. Right before I left, Shelly Linwood told me that Paulina Cole had been calling every fifteen minutes, begging her to reconsider giving me the exclusive. Apparently Paulina promised to set Shelly up with the *Dispatch*'s parent company, which had subsidiaries in television, film and publishing. News would be the beginning. Film deals and book deals would follow. The money would come rolling in.

According to Paulina, "The Linwoods will no longer be victims. They'll be a brand name for survival."

Shelly said their family wanted no part of it. Once my story ran, what she wanted more than anything was for her children to lead normal lives. Shockingly, Haley Joel Osment cast as Danny didn't fit in.

I sat down at my desk, checked my messages. There was one from Wallace asking me to stop by as soon as I got back. There was another from Jack O'Donnell asking if I wanted to grab a beer and a shot after work. Both sounded like great ideas.

I walked into Wallace's office, found the editor-in-chief balancing the phone in the crook of his neck while simultaneously typing on his keyboard. The receiver fell twice, and finally Wallace gave up, slamming it back in the cradle and offering a string of colorful profanities.

"You know they make earpieces for people just like you," I said.

"No way. Next thing you know I'll have a chip implanted in my cerebellum instead of a laptop. I know I can't stop technology, but I can keep it from plowing me over like a Thoroughbred. I swear, this industry was more efficient before stupid Al Gore invented the Internet."

"Hey, once the Atlantic swallows the city up, the Internet will be the least of your concerns. So what's up?"

"You talked to the Linwoods?"

"I did," I said, holding the tape recorder out for him.

"Fantastic." He looked at his watch. "How'd it go?"

"I got as much as you can expect from a ten-year-old who fell into a black hole and can't remember the last five years of his life. You get as much from looking at Shelly Linwood's face as you do hearing the story. Just heartbreaking. Strange, though. The kid disappears for almost five years, yet talks and acts like your typical ten-year-old. Nobody has any idea where Danny Linwood went, but somehow his body and mind developed like a normal adolescent boy's."

Wallace looked a minimum of disturbed by this, more distracted if anything. I had to remember that Wallace had been in this industry for longer than I'd been alive. He'd seen atrocities like this day after day, year after year. My conscience hadn't calloused over the years. Stories like this still angered me.

"That's good work, Henry. I need thirty inches for tomorrow's page one. I swear, Ted Allen over at the *Dispatch* is probably trying to bug this building as we speak to get what's on that tape."

"Shelly Linwood told me Paulina Cole all but offered her body and soul in exchange for this interview."

"Just what the world needs, another forty-year-old woman sleeping with a toddler. For the sake of Daniel's future and his sanity, he's lucky his mother picked us."

"For Danny's sake, sir."

"Danny?"

"That's what Daniel Linwood prefers to be called now. Danny."

"I'm taking it this is a new development."

"Shelly doesn't seem too keen on it."

"Makes you wonder just what happened to Daniel—Danny—during the past few years," Wallace said. "Speaking of memory lapses, have you spoken to Jack today?"

"Not in person, but he left me a message about grabbing a drink after work."

Wallace's faced showed a mixture of anger and concern. "You're going to politely decline that offer," he said.

I was about to ask why, but didn't need to. Over the past year I'd noticed a change in Jack's drinking habits. One-martini lunches had turned into three shots of Jim Beam. Drinks after work turned into drinks during work. Veins began popping up where I hadn't seen them before, the old newsman's equilibrium always seeming a little off. It was clear Jack was developing a problem. Either that, or the problem was already here and we'd just been enabling him, turning a blind eye for months.

"Anytime Jack requests your company for a drink," Wallace continued, "make it clear you don't approve and you're more than aware. A little humiliation goes a long way for a proud man. That's all we can do short of sending him to rehab."

"Would that be such a terrible thing?" I asked.

"Actually, yes. Our circulation has been flat since your reporting on William Henry Roberts last year. Paulina Cole has the *Dispatch* breathing down our necks, and Ted Allen is using every dirty trick in the book to up their numbers. Giving out more free newspapers than high schools give out condoms, dropping thousands of copies in Dumpsters and recording them as part of their circulation."

"But if the numbers are inflated," I said, "who cares?"

"Advertisers," Wallace said. "Not to mention subjects who, unlike Shelly Linwood, truly care about maximizing their publicity. If our top writer goes into the detox, it's one less leg for us to stand on, one more piece of ammo for Paulina's slime cannon."

"I'll ease off with Jack," I said. "I need to cut back on my own extracurriculars as it is."

"Glad to hear you say that, Henry. Don't think I'm unaware that you seemed to have mistakenly thought your desk came from 1-800-MATTRESS. Speaking of social lives, how's that girlfriend of yours? Amanda, right?"

I toed the floor. Looked away.

"We aren't seeing each other anymore," I said. "Haven't talked in a while, actually."

"That's a shame. Remember you talking about her from time to time. In a good way."

She was worth talking about, I wanted to say. Instead, I let my silence speak for me. It was an issue I couldn't talk about with Wallace. Or Jack. Or anyone. I wasn't fully ready to face it myself. Knowing the woman I loved was out there in the same city walking the same streets, it was enough to tear me apart if I thought about it too much. Knowing what I'd let—what I'd *forced* away.

"Not to get too parental, but you'll meet someone nice," Wallace said. "All these bylines, your name in the paper, lots of girls would probably kill to go out with a hotshot journalist."

"Yeah, nothing sexier than a guy with half a dozen cartons of half-eaten Chinese food, who makes less money than a public school teacher and doesn't own a mattress cover."

I could tell Wallace didn't find that funny. I decided to change the subject.

"Hey, know who showed up at the Linwoods' place today? Gray Talbot."

"No kidding?"

"In the flesh. Or suit."

"The savior of suburbia checking on his constituents."

"What do you mean, savior?"

"After Daniel Linwood disappeared, Gray Talbot came in and rattled the cage until someone changed the lining. Made a big stink about how the town was becoming a cesspool, how the crime rate was simply unacceptable. He got state and federal funding to rebuild Hobbs County pretty much from the ground up. Nearly doubled the police force, turned a hellhole of a town into a damn fine place to raise a family. There's still work to be done, but that place is pretty unrecognizable compared to what it was."

I thought about what Wallace said, and agreed with him. Even Stavros, the driver, had said the same thing.

"Daniel Linwood's kidnapping was a terrible thing, but the silver lining is he forced change," he continued. "That boy basically returned to a brand-new, safer home and community. That's all Gray Talbot. Rumor has it he contributed close to a million from his own coffers to aid the effort."

"I thought his suits looked nice. Guess he's got enough money for them."

"I have Gray's home phone number. It'd be great to get him on record for this story as well. He's got a lot invested in Hobbs County, both in time and money, and I'm sure he's expecting a heck of a story from you as well. You don't construct a house and then not care how it's decorated. Get to it," Wallace said. "All story, all the time. I want to see ink on your eyeballs. If I hear you had a single drink with Jack, you'll be reporting on the passing of venereal diseases in the champagne room. Show me the copy before you send it to Evelyn."

"No problem," I said.

"Then tomorrow morning, I'll send over a copy of the paper with a fruit basket to Ted Allen and Paulina Cole."

"Do me a favor, leave my name off the card,' I said. "Enough people in this town hate me."

"If they hate you it's because you're doing a good job. You're getting the scoops they want. So go make some enemies. Just make sure they're the *right* enemies."

"Operation Piss People Off to commence immediately, sir."

I gave Wallace a halfhearted salute and returned to my desk. I sent Jack a quick e-mail declining drinks.

I pushed all that aside and got to work. Punching keys. Making enemies of the right people. Something still didn't sit right with me about the interview. I needed to pinpoint it. To do justice to the story. To give justice to Danny Linwood.

6

"It's called 'declared dead in absentia,'" Amanda said. "It's when a person is presumed dead, yet there is insufficient evidence to prove such a death occurred."

Darcy Lapore chewed her gum thoughtfully. At least Amanda assumed it was thoughtful, because her brows were furrowed as if creating space for a gopher to hibernate. Regardless, she continued. Amanda Davies had been working at the New York Legal Aid Society for several years. In that time, she'd witnessed some of the most horrific cases of neglect and abuse. And she'd seen children taken from the depths of hell and given hope. Yet, as she sat there with Darcy Lapore, Amanda couldn't recall ever working on a case as bizarre as that of Daniel Linwood.

"However, if a person has either been missing for a significant amount of time—for adults it's usually seven years—or has disappeared under unusual circumstances, the death certificate can be sped up. It's a way to both give the family some closure, and to make sure they get any benefits they're entitled to, like life insurance."

"So…the Linwoods have been collecting their son's life insurance?" Darcy asked. Amanda mentally slapped her head, then for fun mentally slapped Darcy's head. Then she reminded herself that no matter how often she wanted to strangle the stupid out of the girl, she couldn't get mad at Darcy. Kind of the same way you couldn't really be upset with a puppy who peed on the rug. Though most puppies did eventually learn to hold their bladders, Amanda did wonder whether Darcy would ever really commit to the job. The girl meant well, but for some reason her ability to recall thousands of shades of lip gloss and memorize every designer from Betsey Johnson to Umbro outweighed her ability to retain legal aid information by a multiple of, oh, about a trillion. The children they worked with needed passionate advocates.

"Daniel didn't have life insurance," Amanda continued, not letting an ounce of condescension drip into her voice. While Darcy would never win employee-of-the-month—or day, or even minute—in addition to being a colleague, she'd been a better friend than most people Amanda had ever known.

Last year, when Henry ended their relationship, when Amanda had no place to sleep, Darcy opened up her home and her sofa bed without thinking twice. Darcy's husband, Nick, moaned for a millisecond, but apparently Darcy gave him a look that first night and Nick never peeped again. Amanda knew Nick brought home a salary closer to seven figures than six, so Darcy didn't need nonprofit work, or any kind of work for that matter. Nick didn't get home most nights until midnight, if not later, so if her generosity was for companionship Amanda didn't know, but she was thankful for it, nonetheless. Which meant forgiving occasional, scratch that, regular lapses in judgment.

"You know, you should have come out last night,"

Darcy said. "They gave out gift bags at the end. Each one had a tube of La Mer. I swear it's like rubbing liquid silk on your skin. And Nick's friend Spencer, remember the one I told you about? He was there, and honey, that boy can wear a Brooks Brothers."

"I'm sorry, Darce, I was tired. I'll be there next time."

"Wow," Darcy said sardonically. "If there ever is a next time, you'll have to clone yourself, like, fifty times to make up for all your excuses."

Amanda turned to her, said, "I'm sorry, it's just…it's not me. I don't get all giggly for that kind of stuff. If I'm going to meet someone, it'll happen the way it's meant to happen. Like…"

"Like a fugitive asking for a ride out of the state."

She smiled. "Yeah. Something like that."

"Well, fine. I'll tell Nick to tell Spencer to find another playmate. But, Amanda?"

"Yeah?"

"Next time you might want to come just for the moisturizer. Your dry-as-dust forehead will thank you."

Amanda shut her gaping mouth, then play-slapped Darcy. She never wanted to be rude, and surely appreciated the effort, but she wasn't a socialite, the kind of woman who spent more time getting dressed than she did sleeping. And that's what she missed most about Henry. Those nights where it was just the two of them, cuddled in sweats and T-shirts, relaxing on his couch, watching a funny movie, talking, making love, then falling asleep. Bodies intertwined as though there was no world other than theirs. And for a while, there wasn't. Then the world decided to have some fun at their expense, and dispatched a killer into their midst. And while they survived, their relationship died horribly. And now Amanda's nights were spent full of sorrow for her loss, guilt for imposing on Darcy, and desire to just move on and forget everything.

"Hey, Amanda, you see this?" Levi Gold, one of the NYLAS's partners, came into their office waving a copy of that morning's *New York Gazette*. He laid it on the table in front of Amanda and Darcy, then underlined the headline with his finger.

"I Just Want To Be a Kid"
Long thought dead, Daniel Linwood grasps for the life nearly taken from him
by Henry Parker

"That's our guy, Daniel Linwood," Levi said. Levi was a short man, yet always walked with his shoulders rolled back as though it might add an extra few inches. His balding pate was neatly combed over, his gold wedding ring always buffed to a polish. As he leaned in close, Amanda could smell a whiff of Hugo Boss. And though she'd never tell him, she'd once spied him inserting lifts into his loafers.

"Whaddaya think, we're handling this city's top legal aid case. Pretty sweet, huh? If my bonus doesn't hit four figures this year, I'll be seriously pissed."

Darcy was out of her seat ready to give Levi a hug, but Amanda couldn't stop staring at the byline. She hadn't spoken to him in months. Hadn't read the *Gazette* since they broke up. Suddenly Amanda grabbed the paper, opened it to Henry's article and began reading.

When Darcy saw the story's continuation, saw the *Gazette*'s emblem atop the margin, noticed the byline, it dawned on her.

"Oh, babe," she said. "You don't need to read this."

"I want to."

"Really, Manda…" She moved to take the paper.

"If you touch it you'll be wearing your wedding band on a stump."

Darcy withdrew, protectively holding her hand.

Amanda read the whole story in silence. When she was finished, she closed the paper and handed it back to Levi.

"Sorry for hoarding your paper."

"Don't worry about it. Least some of the newsprint rubbed off on you instead of me." Levi smiled and walked out.

"Does it still hurt?" Darcy asked. Amanda could tell along with the sympathy there was a note of curiosity in Darcy's voice. She'd never been hurt like that, never had to see an ex-lover's name in front of her. She was the kind of girl men fawned over, men who would never hurt her, because her beauty was what they craved, and they knew she could walk away in an instant. If she left, another man just like them would be waiting around the corner to scoop her up. Amanda never had that luxury. She'd always told herself once she found the right man, she would never let him go. She never wondered what it would be like if *he* left *her.* Never wondered if he was simply carrying on his life while she cried herself to sleep.

"It hurts," Amanda said. Then she turned to Darcy. "Hurts more today than usual."

"Come on," she said, standing up. "Lychee martinis at lunch today. On me. And afterward we'll work on bringing young Mr. Linwood back to life."

For once, Amanda was more than happy to indulge Darcy.

7

I arrived at my desk to find Jack O'Donnell waiting for me. Sitting in my chair, in fact. He was wearing a brown suitcoat and gray slacks with several patches sewn in. In fact, during the few years I'd gotten to know him, Jack had shown as much taste for fashion as your average wino. *Pants are pants,* he told me one night over a beer. *Just because they rip doesn't mean they stop being comfortable. You have any idea how much money I've saved over the years by giving my money to tailors instead of garment salesmen?*

The look on his face read "mildly perturbed." His posture said, "I'm sitting in your chair. So what?"

Big red veins tubed down the sides of his nose. His eyes were mildly bloodshot, and it was clear though I'd declined his drinking invitation last night, he'd hit the town with his more reliable friend Jack Daniel's, maybe met up with their buddy Jim Beam and set sail on a voyage with Captain Morgan as well.

Jack was holding a copy of that morning's edition of the *Gazette,* the front page held up and turned my way so I could see it. He slapped it with his hand and said, "Knocked it out of the park, Henry. Of course you know I plan to take full credit for this. I've already told the whole newsroom you couldn't find an acorn in a squirrel's paw without my help."

"And just when people were starting to respect me," I said. "You think this will convince Rourke to hold off making another shit bag?"

Last year, the *Gazette*'s sports editor, a rough-and-tumble jackass named Frank Rourke, decided it would be funny to leave a paper bag full of shit on my desk. Apparently this was the highlight of the week for a lot of journos. And a month later Jack forwarded me the Photoshop image of my face superimposed onto that of a dog taking a big, steaming poop. That's when I became convinced that the more literate some people are, the more puerile their sense of humor was.

"You should be proud, Henry. Big interview like that, not to mention the sensitive subject matter, you could have had all the media watchdogs all over you if you'd messed up. You want people talking about the story itself before the quality of the coverage. Best kind of press for a reporter is no press."

"That's a trick I haven't quite mastered yet," I said.

"It'll come," Jack offered. "You have the brains and the talent. Just keep doing what you were born to do and the rest will come."

"It felt good to be in there," I said.

"I bet," Jack said, and I knew he must have written a million stories like it. "Good mixture of fastballs and soft-balls. Nobody wanted you to give the Linwood kid the third degree, but there are a lot of unanswered questions."

"That's one thing that's strange. All those questions, and yet I'm the only one asking them."

"What do you mean?"

"This Linwood story, it's really just incredible. I mean,

this family, the Linwoods, it's like the sun has finally come out after a thousand years of darkness. Now they just want to move on with their lives, let Danny be a kid again. But nobody knows where he went, who took him, and why he can't remember a thing before the day he came back."

"So you think he'll, what, just be left alone now?" Jack said. "Uh-uh. Now's when the vultures start circling. Long-lost relatives come out of the woodwork. An uncle somewhere who claims to be Daniel's best friend even though he hasn't seen the kid in years, wants some of the money folks donated. Some cousin will write a book about how Danny wasn't such a good kid, maybe he picked his nose when he was a toddler and put gum in a girl's hair. It's sad how much money there is in the misery of others."

I had to shake my head. I knew Jack was right, but after my interview I hoped the cops would pick up the slack, ask the really tough questions. Though Danny was technically a ten-year-old boy, he'd forever be known as the one who came back. Even strangers would hesitate a second, wondering where they knew his name from. And without that closure, the questions would never cease.

"You know, it's funny," I said. "All this commotion over Daniel returning, yet the cops have no leads and nobody really seems to be digging that hard. Even Shelly Linwood herself seemed unconcerned as to why the cops weren't doing more."

"When your dog runs away, then shows up an hour later, do you really care where it went? You're just happy the thing's back."

"This isn't a dog, Jack. It's a child. Somebody took him and kept him for almost five years."

"Yeah, somebody took him. And then either they got

bored of him or he managed to get away. And the world keeps on spinning."

"That's your answer?"

"I don't need to answer," Jack said. "It's not my kid, and it's not my story."

"You don't think it's weird that Danny doesn't remember a minute of what happened? Or where he went?"

"Strange things occur every day in this world, sport. Just last Thursday I went to get a glass of iced tea, turned out the pitcher was empty. Now, I *know* I didn't finish that sucker, but did I go questioning the neighbors? Nope. I went to the store, bought another jug."

"I have no idea how this relates to an actual human being."

"It's hoopla, is what it is now," Jack said. "You wrote a great piece, Henry. Move on."

"Hoopla? They didn't outlaw that word in, like, 1800?"

"Laugh it up, tiger. A family is back together. You want to give them closure? Right now, *today,* this is the most closure they're probably ever going to get. You think people like Paulina Cole are going to stop calling? You don't think there are people out there who know the juice that can be squeezed from this family is worth money? Just because you think you have scruples, son, doesn't mean everyone else thinks that way."

"Cop cars," I said.

Jack looked puzzled. "Cop cars?"

"Danny Linwood told me that when he woke up, he heard police sirens, and that he saw a cop car pull up right where he'd been lying. I checked the newspapers and police reports from that day, and couldn't find anything about any crimes reported in the vicinity of Doubleday Field."

"Could have been a prank. Could have been a drunk wandered off before they got there. The cops could have come for any number of reasons."

"Could be, sure. But don't you think it's a heck of a coincidence that the cops are called to a scene where just a few minutes ago, a kid who went missing for five years appears out of thin air?"

Jack chewed on his lip, trying to figure out if there was a way to play it like this was no big deal. I felt a lump in my throat. This wasn't the Jack O'Donnell I'd grown up idolizing, the kind who asked questions until there were no more to ask. Who dug until he hit a vein or a nerve. This Jack seemed tired, content to be apathetic, unwilling or unable to go that extra step.

"I'm going to look into this," I said. "Somebody knows who took Danny Linwood and why." Jack didn't say a word, just shrugged his shoulders, stood up and walked away. I debated following him, then decided it wasn't worth it.

I picked up the phone and dialed the Hobbs County Police Department switchboard. I asked to be connected to whoever was investigating the Linwood abduction. Then, surprisingly, the operator hesitated.

"Hold on one moment, sir, I'm going to have to check on that." It seemed odd that despite the fact that Daniel Linwood was likely Hobbs's biggest story since, well, Danny's original disappearance, they couldn't connect me to the investigating officer right away. The operator hadn't been asked many questions.

"Sorry, sir, for the delay. Hold for Detective Lensicki."

A synthesized version of "Copacabana" came over the earpiece. It was all I could do not to slice my ears off. Finally a man answered with a curt "Yeah?"

"Detective Lensicki, Henry Parker with the *New York Gazette*. I was wondering if I could have a minute of your time."

"I know who you are, Parker. I saw you yesterday at the Linwood house. Haven't read your article in today's paper. I'll get right to it when my shift is up." He didn't sound very sincere.

"Yeah, anyway, Detective, I had a question about something Daniel Linwood told me yesterday. He said when he woke up, he heard police sirens. Now, it might have been police, it might have been an ambulance, but I couldn't find any record or report of an investigation at Doubleday Field. Could you comment on that?"

"No problem, Sherlock. There was no investigation because there was no crime. There was no report because nothing happened."

"So who called 911?"

"Excuse me?"

"I assume the police had a reason to show up at Doubleday Field with their sirens on."

"We do have routine patrols, *Mr.* Parker."

"Do you usually keep your sirens on during those routine patrols?" Lensicki stayed silent. "Listen, Officer, I'm not trying to break your balls. I just want to know why it seems like everything's back to normal now that Daniel Linwood has turned up, yet nobody's really turning over any rocks to find out where he went."

"Listen here, you little punk," Lensicki said. "You go back to your typewriter and your fancy paper. The day you tell us how to do our jobs is the day you see us coming down to your office and sticking a Bic up your ass. You want a comment about Daniel Linwood? Here you go. The investigation is ongoing. If and when we have any news to report, don't worry, we'll make sure you and the rest of the *respected* media get all the info."

"So…can I quote you on that pen-in-ass comment?"

"I got nothing else to say to you," Lensicki said. "You have any more questions you direct them to our press secretary. She's eighty-three years old and can't see out of one eye and I'm sure she'll be happy to help."

"Wow. You know, I watched *Columbo,* and always thought cops were helpful and jolly."

"Blow it out your ass, Parker."

"'Detective has strange ass fetish.' That's my headline for tomorrow. What do you think?"

Unsurprisingly, the line went dead. I felt good about myself, not just for pissing off a cop but because Lensicki's standoffishness made it clear the Hobbs County PD wasn't serving and protecting quite as strenuously as their job description called for. Somebody called 911 to alert the cops to Danny's whereabouts when he woke up, and if Lensicki wasn't interested in digging, I'd be happy to pick up his slack.

I debated calling Curt Sheffield to get his take on it. Curt was a young African-American officer with the NYPD. We'd grown close over the past few years, mainly due to our unwanted celebrity, our respect for our jobs and our admiration for a good pint. He'd been a source on numerous stories, and I was happy to repay him with a few good shout-outs for his squad. That's what was most important to Sheffield. That the job was given as much respect as possible. I was happy to help, because they needed all the help they could get.

In the aftermath of 9/11, NYPD recruit applications had dropped more than twenty-five percent. And while the police force still had approximately fourteen applications for every spot they needed to fill, a drop in overall applications meant a drop in quality of applications. That's why a cop like Curt—young, good-looking and ambitious—found himself on every recruiting poster between here and Hoboken.

Many blamed lack of recruits on the NYPD's staggeringly low starting salaries—just $25,100 during the first six months on the job, a salary that would make most janitors shake their heads. Having young men like Curt on the force showed those quality applicants that the best, the brightest and the most appealing citizens made up the NYPD. What pissed Curt off was that he was a damn good cop, yet on the street he was treated like Mickey Mouse. Kids and their parents recognized him from posters. He spent more time signing autographs than patrolling his route. I tried to get him to keep things in perspective, but unlike many cops, Curt's celebrity didn't go to his head. He wanted to stay behind the scenes. Just like a certain reporter who desired celebrity as much as he desired rickets.

I called Curt's desk, got a message saying that today was his day off. Which meant he was probably sitting on his couch watching SportsCenter and eating one of those meat-lovers pizzas that contained a little over eighteen thousand calories per slice. If I had Curt's dietary habits I'd look like Norm from *Cheers,* but the guy had the metabolism of a Thoroughbred. He could eat a cow smothered in steak sauce and not gain an ounce. Sometimes life wasn't fair.

I tried his cell phone. Curt picked up on the third ring. There was a pause between "Curt" and "Sheffield." I must have caught him in the middle of a burp.

"Hey, man, it's Henry."

"S'up, Parker?"

"Let me guess. You're on your fifth slice and third SportsCenter rerun of the day."

"Nope. Gloria's got me on a health kick. She made me some spelt toast with peanut butter, mint jelly and honey. For lunch I got a bowl of plain oatmeal with some raisins and soy milk in the fridge."

"Sounds like a delicious colon-cleansing meal."

"Yeah, it's, uh…it's really tasty." I tried to stifle a laugh. "Dude, if I don't get, like, something that used to moo in my system soon, I'm gonna start pissing soy beans."

"I do owe you a meal or two, but I'll own up later. I got a question for you. When you're investigating a disturbance, what happens if it's a false alarm? Like a burglary or break-in is reported, but when the boys in blue show up there's no evidence of anything illegal?"

"It's investigated, man. Every one. Can't say they spend a ton of time on it, but you gotta make sure it was a false alarm. God forbid it turns out you just missed a clue or someone really needed help and you left instead of lifting a finger."

"That's what I thought."

"What's this about, bro?"

"Not sure yet. I have a few questions about the Daniel Linwood disappearance that nobody's in a rush to answer."

"Kid who got kidnapped then dropped out of the sky, right?"

"That's the one."

"I feel for that family, man. Nobody deserves to go through that. My mom used to hyperventilate if I came home half an hour late from school, let alone five years. Good luck, Henry. If anyone's gonna get those answers it's you, you tunnel-visioned asshole. And hey, don't forget about your tab. Steak and a beer within the week."

"You can count on it."

I hung up and ordered a pizza to be delivered to Curt's house. I just hoped he'd finish it before Gloria got home, otherwise he wouldn't be around long enough for me to repay the rest of the tab.

There had to be more to the Linwood story. Something I'd missed, perhaps. Something in Daniel's voice, his word, his cadences.

I took the tape recorder from my desk, rewound the tape and pushed Play. I listened to the whole tape again. And when it was finished, I was pretty sure I'd discovered one pretty big question. Not to mention an explanation as to why I was confused by certain aspects of Danny's statements. One huge question had been asked by Danny Linwood himself. Only the boy didn't even know he was asking it.

8

Paulina Cole forwarded three e-mails to her assistant, James Keach, then turned off her computer and put on her Burberry trenchcoat. James had asked several times if he could leave for the day, but each time Paulina answered him by not answering him—ignoring him was her favorite form of communication—and he soon slunk back to the cubicle zoo where the other peons sat and stewed. It had become somewhat of an amusing ritual. At the end of each day Paulina would send whatever hate mail she received to James, who would make copies for three departments: Human Resources, Public Relations and the *Dispatch*'s editor-in-chief, Ted Allen. Paulina had requested the *Dispatch* print her e-mail address at the end of every column. She invited readers to write in, and in fact went home depressed on the days where she got no hate mail. Pissed-off folks tended to be more vocal than satisfied ones, so the next day she would try even harder to kneel on the public's pressure points.

She sent the e-mails to HR because it was mandated by corporate. PR wanted it in case any public figures wrote in. Ted Allen demanded it because he liked nothing more than employing a reporter who so riled up readers that they took time out of their busy (or tragically not busy) day to pen her a missive so vile that they would tell all their friends to buy the paper to *see what that bitch wrote.*

When the media reporter for the *New York Gazette* had questioned Paulina's ethics in reporting on a congressman she'd allegedly had a romantic liaison with years back, Cole responded in her column questioning the reporter's manhood. More specifically, she stated her doubt that his manhood was longer than his pencil's eraser. Both she and Ted had gotten a kick out of it, and HR needed a new folder to house all the letters she received. Naturally, the paper sold 50,000 more copies that day than the previous one, and her story was linked to by dozens of influential media Web sites. Nobody was better at riling up the bourgeoisie than Paulina Cole, and in today's America people paid good money to be pissed off.

Paulina began her career in journalism nearly two decades ago working in the Style section at a New York alternative weekly paper. Boring easily of reporting on asinine trends and mindless models, Paulina took a job on the news desk at the *New York Gazette*. Widely considered one of the city's most prestigious dailies, it was at the *Gazette* where Paulina first made a name for herself. And while her progress at the *Gazette* matched her drive, she quickly tired of the politics and backroom handshakes that were staples of the old boys' club. Wallace Langston and Jack O'Donnell were dinosaurs, analogs in a digital world. The newsroom needed a swift stiletto in the ass, but they were too busy sniffing brandy to realize the world was passing them by. And when Wallace brought in Henry Parker, then stood by him when the weasel was accused of murder, it sickened Paulina more than anything in her career had before. And she was not a woman who sickened easily.

Leaving the *Gazette* was the easiest decision she'd ever made. To her, that newspaper represented everything wrong with the current system. Old. Stale. Clueless about technology, and out of touch with the average reader. People wanted pizzazz, something to shock them, something to ignite their senses. They didn't care about politics unless there was sleaze behind the suit. Didn't care about crime unless it was a celebrity drunk behind the wheel. So Paulina was happy to dig and dish the dirt. She was happy to be hated by the highbrow, embraced by the lowbrow. But everyone had an opinion.

Once safely nestled in the bosom of the *New York Dispatch,* Paulina had made it her goal to not only boost the paper's circulation rates, but to do it at the expense of the *Gazette.* She would topple their leaders, set fire to the old guard and burn the paper to the ground. She'd laid the groundwork with her articles focusing on Henry, to the point where nearly half the city would answer "Henry Parker" when asked what was wrong with the current state of journalism.

But Henry was young. Not yet thirty, his proverbial balls had not yet dropped. Going after him was like shooting a fish in a barrel, and its ripples wouldn't travel far. To truly bring down the *Gazette,* she had to stop worrying about the epidermis, and instead dig down to its skeleton. The old guard. The reporter the paper staked its very reputation on.

Jack O'Donnell.

For years Jack O'Donnell had been the public face of the *Gazette.* He'd won countless awards, brought respectability, integrity and readership to Wallace Langston's newspaper. Yet during her tenure there, Paulina had noticed the old man begin to slip. His reporting had been shoddy, numerous quotes and sources had to be spiked by the managing editor. Not to mention the unmistakable odor that wafted from his desk, strong enough to make you fail a sobriety test just by inhaling.

It was only a matter of time before somebody took a sledgehammer to the pillar of the *Gazette,* and it was only fitting for it to be wielded by someone who'd seen the cracks up close.

Paulina turned off her office light, took the umbrella from under her desk. Her office had a beautiful view of the Manhattan skyline, twinkling lights amid the dark hues of night. The skies had opened, drenching the pavement, and the N train was several blocks away. As she strolled through the corridors of the *Dispatch,* Paulina stopped by the one office she'd asked Ted Allen to clear out for her a few months ago. A junior media reporter had been given the office, a reward for a promotion, but when Paulina informed Ted Allen what she had in mind, the young man was given a nice little cubicle by the Flavia coffeemaker.

The office was enclosed, sealed off. Exactly what she needed.

On Paulina's orders, the office had been cleared out; not even a dustball remained. Instead three rows of shelves had been installed, forming a U around the walls. What was inside the office had to be kept a secret until her story was ready. And then the bombshell would drop.

Only two people had a key: Paulina and Ted Allen himself. The key was removed from the rings of the entire janitorial staff, and Paulina only entered when she was positive there were no looming eyes peeking over her shoulder.

Tonight, she had a tremendous urge to look inside. She needed to be reminded of what all her hard work was preparing for.

Checking once more to make sure she was alone, Paulina twisted the key in the lock, opened the door and flicked on the overhead light.

What she saw inside made her glow with delight. The way the room glittered, the light reflecting on everything she'd painstakingly gathered over the past few months. And her treasure trove was growing by the day. It was only a matter of time before the contents of this room, these seemingly innocuous items, changed the face of New York journalism.

Satisfied, Paulina turned off the light, closed the door and got out her umbrella, preparing for her journey into the rain.

9

"Right here," I said to Wallace. He was holding a copy of the transcript of my interview with Daniel Linwood. I'd asked him to read it in its entirety before we spoke. So far he'd only read what was printed in the *Gazette*. There were many quotes that were cut for space, details that didn't make it into the final piece. I wanted to see if Wallace noticed what I had just minutes ago.

I hadn't noticed it upon my first few listenings. It was so subtle, yet because I was already skeptical of the whole situation, it stood out in neon lights.

"I'm not following, Henry," Wallace said. He turned off the tape recorder. "Please, placate an old man whose hearing is going. Enlighten me as to what the hell you're talking about."

"First off," I said, "Daniel mentions he heard sirens when he woke up. Yet there's no record of any complaints or investigations by the Hobbs County PD in that vicinity. And when I spoke to the detective assigned to the case, he was only slightly more helpful than your average retail clerk. And then I heard this."

I rewound to the spot in question. Then I pressed Play. When Daniel spoke that word, I stopped the tape.

"Brothers," I said. "Daniel Linwood talks about seeing his family for the first time when he got back home that day. He refers to his sister, Tasha, but then he uses the word *brothers.* As in plural. Daniel Linwood has one brother, James. There's no record of Shelly and Randall having any other sons. And then he uses the word several more times. As though he can't help it. Once is a slip of the tongue. Twice is a heck of a coincidence. Three times, like Danny says on the tape, that means something's wrong."

Wallace looked at the transcript, found what I was referring to, stared at it so intently I expected a hole to be seared through it.

"I think Daniel was referring to brothers because there was another brother in his life."

"But you just said he only has one brother, this James. I don't follow."

"I think the other brother, the plural brother, was with Danny during the years he was missing. I think whoever kidnapped Daniel Linwood had another young boy. I think even though he can't force himself to remember details of the past five years, Danny subconsciously *is* referring to it. I think whoever took him had another child, and Daniel was made to believe they were brothers. And even though James is his only biological brother, his memory still retains a stamp of some sort. A footprint of the lost years."

"Is that even medically possible?" Wallace asked skeptically.

"In 1993," I said, "medical records showed that Sang Min Lee, a thirteen-year-old Korean boy who'd been in a coma for three years, suddenly woke up and claimed to smell flowers. Sang's mother had brought fresh roses to Sang's hospital room every day for the first year of his hospitalization, then stopped when it became too expensive.

Somehow Sang's brain retained the memory of those smells, despite the fact that the boy himself wasn't even awake."

Wallace scratched his beard, put the papers down. I could tell he was thinking about this, debating whether my discovery warranted looking into, or was just a dead end that would eat up time and resources.

"Let me dig a bit," I said. "I know there's no way to tell right now, but if there is, and we can report exclusively…"

Wallace's head snapped up. I stopped speaking. He knew my engine was running, that if he unleashed the harness I'd be on this like a dog on fresh meat. I was aching to run with this story. It burned to think that nobody else seemed to care where Daniel Linwood had been for five years, why he couldn't remember anything about his disappearance or why the HCPD seemed content to vacuum it all up. I hated that if nobody stepped up, Daniel Linwood would just be another headline. A child with no past, whose future would always be clouded.

"This is awful thin," Wallace said. "You realize it might have been a slip of the tongue. A fault in the recording. My mother used to call me Beth—that was my sister's name, but she was just absentminded. There are a dozen ways to explain what Daniel said, not all of them having anything to do with some Korean boy."

"But you and I both want to know whether there's more."

I looked at Wallace, trying to will him to say it. Then he looked up at me, hands folded in front of him.

"Check it out. Report back if you find anything. And if it turns out there's another way to explain it, you stop digging *immediately*. We promised to treat the Linwood family with respect—the last thing we need is to accidentally hit a nerve that doesn't need to feel pain. There's a family at stake here, not to mention a town trying to rebuild. So use a pipe cleaner to dig instead of a pickax."

"Gentle is my middle name."

"That's a goddamned lie," Wallace said, "but I'll give you the benefit here. Good luck, Parker."

With Wallace's blessing, I went back to my desk and took out the Linwoods' phone number. I held the Post-it between my fingers and thought about the promise I'd made to Shelly. Her family had been torn apart, and it would take years before they could even hope to begin the reparations. By giving me access to their home and to their son, the Linwoods trusted me to do what was right. And I had every intent of doing just that.

First I had to make sure there wasn't a simpler explanation.

I called the Linwood house. It went right to voice mail. An automated system saying, "The person you wish to call is not available at this time. Please leave a message at the tone." I figured they'd disconnected their phone, changed their number to confuse the vultures. Only now I'd become one, too.

At the tone, I said, "Hi, Shelly, Randall, this is Henry Parker. I wanted to thank you for the other day. I did have one follow-up question, and I was wondering if one of you could give me a call back at the office. Again, this is Henry Parker at the *New York Gazette.*"

Then I hung up. And sat there. Twiddling my thumbs, chewing a number two pencil, praying the wait wouldn't be long.

Perhaps the most difficult thing about being a reporter was waiting for a callback. If I was on deadline, and knew that one transforming piece of information was available yet just beyond reach, the minutes crawled by like hours. Waiting for that callback could drive you insane. I propped my feet up on the desk, stuck a pencil between my teeth and waited.

Thankfully I didn't have to worry about my sanity, because my phone rang barely a minute after I'd hung up.

"This is Parker."

"Henry, it's Shelly Linwood." She sounded apprehensive, a little concerned. She had probably assumed once my story ran I'd be out of her life.

"Shelly, thanks so much for getting back to me."

"It's no problem. We have to screen our calls, otherwise we'd never get off the line. We're probably going to have to change our number." She said this with an air of apology. She still saw me as a friend. Unlike the other vultures who wanted to pick the bones.

"I understand that. Again, I appreciate you and Daniel talking to me the other day."

"It's Danny," she said, her voice less than enthusiastic. "That's what he wants to be called now."

"Right. I remember. Anyway, Mrs. Linwood, Shelly, I was going back over the tape of the interview, and something seemed a little strange to me."

"Strange? How so?"

"When Danny is talking about reuniting with his family, he says the word *brothers*. As in more than one. And he says it several times. I know this is a silly question, but Daniel doesn't have any other siblings besides Tasha and James, right?"

"That's right." The acceptance was gone. At that moment I knew I was an outsider again.

"Any close friends he might consider a part of the family? A cousin so close he might call him a brother?"

"No."

"Has he mentioned anything to you about his abduction? Any memories that might offer a clue as to why he said that?"

"I said no, Mr. Parker." Not Henry. *Mr. Parker.* "It's just the five of us. Thank God. Now, if you'll excuse me, I have a pot roast in the oven." I checked my watch. It was eleven in the morning. Kind of early for a pot roast.

She didn't wait for me to respond, and I knew when the line went dead Shelly Linwood would no longer be returning any more of my calls. I sent off a quick e-mail to Wallace.

Shelly Linwood doesn't know where "brothers" came from. Got very defensive. Will update you on progress. H

I tapped my pencil against the desk. Wherever Danny Linwood was during those years, there was another person he'd called "brother." I was sure of it. Of course, there was a chance his mind had simply been damaged from the absence, but something in Shelly's voice and the lack of cooperation from the HCPD told me if I asked more questions, I'd find very unhappy answers. Which meant they had to be asked.

I decided to take a stab at something, then work from there.

I performed a LexisNexis search for child abductions within the past ten years, then narrowed the search to cases where the child returned alive. Sadly, there were over one thousand reported cases of child abductions in the United States during that span, and less than fifty of those thousand children had been found alive. The others had either been found dead, or never found at all.

I searched through the results looking for any similarities, specifically cases, like Danny Linwood's, where the abducted was returned to his or her home with no memory of their time gone.

I was surprised when one hit came back. Seven years ago, an eight-year-old girl named Michelle Oliveira disappeared outside of Meriden, Connecticut, following a playdate at a neighbor's house. The Oliveiras lived just four houses down the block from their friends, a family of four named the Lowes, which explained why she was unsupervised upon her return home. The investigation turned up nothing but a tassel from Michelle's hair that had been caught on a nearby branch. After a month the search was called off. Two years later Michelle Oliveira was declared deceased.

And three years after that, Michelle Oliveira appeared in her parents' front yard in Meriden, in perfect health with the exception of some vitamin deficiencies. According to a newspaper report, Michelle had no recollection of the intervening years.

The police had conducted numerous interviews with Michelle, her parents and younger brother, as well as with the Lowe family. The records had been sealed off due to the victim's young age. The abductor or abductors were never found. And Michelle went on with her life.

While Michelle clearly wasn't a "brother," it did make me wonder. Meriden was just a few hours from Hobbs County, and more important, it set a precedent for this kind of unexplained absence and subsequent reappearance.

I needed to see those records. Fortunately I knew someone who could help. Time to add another lunch to my growing tab.

Curt Sheffield picked up, but it took major convincing to get him to not hang up on me.

"Ain't no way I'm going to even touch a child abduction case, bro. Not to mention that it's in a different state, and I'd have to explain why I'm asking those kind of questions. If I tell them it's to sate some reporter's curiosity, I might as well tell them I deal crack while downloading underage porn. I'll get booted faster than you can say 'Starsky minus Hutch.'"

"So how could I get hold of those records if not through the police?" I asked, praying Curt's reach extended beyond that of his precinct.

"Only other firms who have access to those kinds of documents are the legal aid societies. They keep a database of all child-related abuse cases. I'm guessing this falls under their jurisdiction."

"Even if there was no evidence of actual abuse?"

"Just 'cause there ain't no scars on the outside don't mean they're not on the inside."

"That's deep, Curt. You write poetry, too?"

"Yeah, I'll Robert Frost your ass if you try to squeeze anything else out of me. Good luck, sorry I couldn't help more."

"Yeah, thanks for nothing."

"When can I collect on that tab?"

"I'll have my people call your people."

"Yeah, whatever. Later, Parker."

I had to get more information on Michelle Oliveira's abduction, but I wasn't going to be able to go through the police department. I sat there in silence, thinking about what Curt had said. The legal aid society.

I knew one person who worked at the legal aid society. But calling her would touch nerves much closer to my heart than Daniel Linwood.

I opened my desk drawer. I could almost sense it down there. It had been months since I'd spoken to her. But

rarely a day passed when I didn't feel that ache, that
gnawing in my gut that seemed to only get worse over
time.

Six months ago I'd made a choice. I decided I had to
give her up. I told myself at the time it was the right thing
to do. A man had to put his love before himself. And since
Amanda had nearly been killed twice because of me, in
my mind there was no other option.

So I said goodbye to Amanda. I hadn't been truly happy
in months. It didn't take a great reporter to figure out the
two were directly correlated. But I still couldn't be with her.

There had been times over the past few months where
I had wanted to call, where I'd gone so far as to pick up
the phone and dial everything but the last number on her
cell phone, nearly crying when I hung up before pushing
the final key. Nights where the booze loosened up my inhibitions, and only that last vestige of clarity prevented me
from calling. Like that terrible night six months ago, today
there was only one choice to make.

Amanda worked for the New York Legal Aid Society.
She would have access to Michelle Oliveira's records. She
could help the investigation. She could provide answers.

She could also throw it back in my face.

And I would deserve it.

Maybe this was the opening I needed, I wanted. A way
to tell myself it wasn't about her, even though deep down
I couldn't even fool myself. Maybe it was fate. Or maybe
fate was a cruel son of a bitch.

Before I had a chance to think again, I picked up the
phone and dialed.

Amanda picked up on the first ring.

"Hey," I said. "It's me."

10

The girl woke up with a slight headache. Her first thought was that she'd fallen, maybe hit her head on the sidewalk or bumped into the same tree she'd rammed her bike into the other day. But she didn't remember putting on a helmet, didn't remember actually falling. And she only rode her bike when her mommy was watching. And right away she felt the terror that she was alone.

She stood up warily. Her breathing was harsh, and she felt hot tears rush to her eyes. She reached out for her bed, the couch, some familiar sign. But she found nothing. She grew desperate and called out. There was no answer.

The room was pitch-black. Had her mommy just put her to bed, accidentally left the Bratz night-light unplugged? No, there was a smell in the room, something different, something rotted. She didn't belong there. Yet when she cried, nobody came.

The girl smelled something that reminded her of her dad's breath after he came home on Sunday evenings. Mommy said he was watching the football games at the bar with his friends. His breath had that sweet smell, and her mom never let her get too close to him when he was like that. There was a smell in the air that reminded her of that. Reminded her to be afraid of getting too close.

After a few minutes her eyes adjusted. The room was small, about the size of her baby brother's bedroom. There was a small bench by the wall, and the floor was made of wood. A slit of light shone from a crack under the door, but other than that she couldn't see a thing.

Her throat began to choke up. She didn't know this place. She wanted to feel her mommy's arms. Wanted to smell her daddy's sweet breath.

Suddenly she remembered walking home from the park, remembered feeling a hand clamp over her mouth. She couldn't remember anything past that.

The girl let out a cry of help, then ran toward the door. She gripped the knob and twisted as hard as she could, but it didn't budge. She pushed and pulled and cried, but the door stayed shut.

Finally she collapsed onto the floor and began to cry.

She wiped the snot away from her nose. She needed a tissue. She could wipe it on her clothes, but she loved the sundress she was wearing. Bright pink with pretty sunflowers. Her mom had picked it out for her at the mall, the same day she'd bought that nice barrette in the shape of a butterfly that mommy wore to the park.

She began to cry again. She screamed for her mother. For her father. And nobody came.

Then she lay back down, curled into a ball, and hoped maybe somebody could hear her through the floor.

And that's when she heard footsteps.

She sat back up. Looked at the door. Saw a shadow briefly block out that sliver of light. She wiped her eyes and nose. She held her breath as the doorknob turned.

Then nearly screamed when it opened. She would have screamed. If she wasn't too scared.

There was a man in the doorway. He was bald, with thinning hair and glasses that were too small for his head. He was wearing light jeans with a hole by one knee. On his hands were leather gloves. When she saw the gloves, she finally managed to scream.

The man flicked a switch on the outside of the door, and a lightbulb came on, bathing the room in harsh white. She closed her eyes, blinked through the glare, then opened them. The man was now barely a foot in front of her. He was staring at her. Not in a scary way, not like bad men on television did. In the way her daddy did when he tucked her in at night. He'd taken the gloves off. He held them out to her, then made a show of putting them in his pocket.

"Don't be scared," he said. "I would never hurt you."

The man reached out, took her chin in his hands. They were calloused, rough. She was too scared to move, felt her head pounding, mucus running down her nose and onto his hand.

When he noticed the snot on his fingers, the man reached into his pocket. She closed her eyes. When she opened them, he'd taken out a handkerchief and was wiping her nose, her face.

"That's better," he said. He had a glass of water with him. He handed it to her. "Go on. Drink some."

She took it, her hand trembling. She didn't know what was in it, whether he'd poisoned it, whether he'd spit in it, but she was so thirsty she downed almost all of it in one gulp. When she was finished, he took the clean side of the handkerchief and wiped her mouth.

Then he handed her two small pills. She looked at him, looked at the pills.

"You must have a bad headache," he said. "This will make you feel better."

Then he smiled at her.

She didn't know how he knew about her headache, but if the pills would help...

"How do you feel?" he asked.

"Hurts," she moaned.

"It won't for long."

She looked at him. He was wearing a wedding ring. It was polished and it gleamed something pretty.

He stood up. Motioned for her to do the same. The girl stood up reluctantly, then smelled the aroma of pancakes coming from somewhere. Her favorite.

"Strawberry and chocolate chip. Fresh off the griddle," he said, smiling. "Let's get you fed, you can meet your new mommy and new brother, and then I'll show you to your room."

She took the man's hand, his grip gentle, and followed him out of the darkness.

11

It would have been easy to say no. For years she'd grown accustomed to disappointments, to a life that never quite went the way she planned.

The wound still hurt terribly. Doing this could rub salt in deep. And who knows? Another few weeks, few months, and the pain might have begun to die down. And given a few years, she might have never thought about him again. Things would have gone back to the way they were before the day they met.

None of that mattered, though, because when Henry called, for the first time in months his voice coming over the phone, she agreed to meet him almost immediately.

Just a few years ago, Amanda had nothing, no friends, nobody to trust but herself. Her life had been a series of half-hearted relationships, embarked upon mainly because that's what she assumed was normal. That's what she was used to. Men who were more interested in their own success than how it could be used to make others happy. She'd grown weary of that scene, and at some point, like many other girls her age, Amanda Davies had simply given up.

The irony was when she'd met Henry, the very first thing he did was lie right to her face. Looking back, she knew he'd done it to save his own life without implicating her. And while back then she contemplated literally ditching him on the side of the road, she could look back at his brazen behavior fondly.

He'd tricked her into giving him a ride out of town when he was mistakenly wanted for murder. In the end Henry was able to clear his name, yet there was a moment, that moment when he'd come clean, admitting his lie, when she could have left him on the side of the road to die. But in that moment Amanda was able to look into Henry Parker's eyes and tell one thing. This was more real than anyone she'd ever known.

Henry's eyes gave away everything. The year they knew each other, he could never hide anything. She could read his language—words and body—like nobody else. And he offered himself in a way that was both selfless and confident, and utterly consuming.

That's why when he ended their relationship, it wasn't simply another thing to forget. Being with him was the first time Amanda felt a future. She couldn't be the only one who thought that way, though, so when he decided to end it, for her own sake in his words, she didn't fight. She didn't want to be another one of those sad girls, trying to convince a guy to stay.

If she was meant to be happy, she would be. If not, that was life.

So when Henry called her out of the blue, after radio silence for nearly six months, the easy thing to do would have been to hang up. To tell him to go screw himself.

Instead she found herself sitting on a bench in Madison Square Park, waiting for him to arrive, looking at every boy that walked by, waiting to see if the months had been as cruel to him as they had to her.

The park was neutral ground. That was one condition she made him agree to. They had to meet far enough away from both their offices that they could sit, and talk, and see what was what, without any distractions.

Amanda folded her arms across her chest. The sun was bright over the trees. She sat and watched couples lounging on the green grass. The line snaking outside the Shake Shack, home of the best burgers in NYC. Her purse was splayed open slightly, and Amanda noticed the glint of her keychain. Attached to the silver loop that held her keys was a small red heart made of leather. Henry had brought it home one day. He'd attached it to the chain when she was in the shower. When she asked what it was for, he said it was because she had the keys to his heart. At first she laughed. It was a pretty cheesy gesture, something out of a bad romantic comedy, but that night they made love, and as Henry lay there, naked, staring at her, she knew that he'd meant it.

It would have been easy to throw the heart away. Looking at it now, she was glad she'd kept it.

She buttoned the purse and looked up to see Henry walking down the gated path. He stopped briefly beside the dog run to make faces at a small shih tzu that was trying to leap at him with its tiny legs. Henry was making bug-eyed faces at the dog, and Amanda couldn't help but smile. He looked up, looking for her, saw her, and Amanda saw his cheeks flush red. He quickened his pace and walked over to her bench, sat down next to her. A foot separated them. It felt like a mile and a millimeter at the same time.

"Hey," she said, offering a purposefully bland greeting.

"Hey, Amanda." He half leaned in, unsure of whether to offer a hug, a kiss or nothing. She felt a brief flash of electricity when he did it, felt slightly disappointed when he pulled back, but glad at the same time. "What's up?"

He looked good. Better that she'd hoped in some ways. Perhaps if he'd showed up thirty pounds heavier, with an unflattering beard and gut paunch, it'd be easier to move on. Yes, his eyes were bleary and red, probably from late-night deadlines, but it was still Henry. She'd gotten used to those eyes, his near-constant state of exhaustion. And despite that, every night she missed falling asleep next to him, Amanda remembered how proud it used to make her to see his name headline a terrific story. She looked at his shock of brown hair, an inch or so too long, and couldn't help but smile.

"You need a haircut," she said.

"Really?" He ran his hand through his hair. Amanda remembered doing that for him. "You think?"

"Yeah, you could use a trip to Supercuts."

"So," he said tentatively, "what's up?"

"I don't know. Work. Life. What's usually up," she replied. He nodded. She wanted to say *you called me,* but that was combative. "You know you called me." Screw it, she had to say it. Henry nodded, chewed on his thumbnail for a moment.

"Just want to start by saying I'm sorry about what happened. You know, between us. I didn't…"

"Stop," she said, her face growing warm, slight anger bubbling up. "You said your apologies a long time ago. If I wanted to hear them again, I've got a good memory and a lot of sad songs on my iPod."

"That's not why I called you," Henry said. "I just… You know, I don't really know how to start it."

"Why do you need to in the first place?" she asked. Her heart was beating fast, frustration building. She'd begun to wish she'd stayed at the office, hung up the phone, let everything heal the way maybe it was meant to. Seeing him was maddening and invigorating at the same time. And she wasn't ready to open back up.

"I need your help," Henry said. "It's not for me. It's for a kid."

"A kid?" she asked, surprised.

"Daniel Linwood, have you heard about him?"

"Of course. My office is handling the paperwork. You know, I never realized bringing someone back from the dead was as easy as filling out a bunch of paperwork. Scary to think there's enough precedent that we have the forms on file. I'm actually thinking I might do the same thing with my aunt Rose, freak the hell out of Lawrence and Harriet. That'd make a pretty neat headline. 'Girl brings dead, smelly aunt back to life, scares the hell out of her adoptive parents.'"

"It's been a while since I wrote obituaries," Henry said. "But I bet it's like riding a bike."

"Think of it as an anti-obituary."

"Now, those I don't have a lot of experience with."

"So Daniel Linwood. The boy who came back after five years. I saw your story in the paper. What do you need to know about him?"

"Well, long story short, there's a lot about his disappearance and reappearance that doesn't sit well with me. For one thing, there haven't been any suspects arrested in his kidnapping or disappearance, and from my talks with the detectives in Hobbs County they're looking as hard for him as O.J. is for the real killer."

"I'm waiting to hear what this has to do with me."

"I'm getting to that. So I interviewed Danny for that story…"

"Danny?"

"Yeah, that's what he likes to be called now. Anyway,

during the interview, he said something kind of strange. He used the word *brothers*. As in more than one. And he used it several times, even when I corrected him, like his brain was hardwired to do it. But Danny's only got one brother. It might have been a slip of the tongue, but there's also a chance he retained something from his disappearance, something about his kidnappers or where he was. Maybe he remembers somebody else, somebody his own age, being wherever he's been the past five years."

Amanda sat, listened intently. She felt the familiar rush Henry got when he was excited about a story, the same sense of pride she felt *(used to feel)* when she was proud of her man.

"I did some digging," he continued, "and it turns out a girl named Michelle Oliveira went missing several years before Danny. Similar circumstances, both children disappearing without a trace, then suddenly reappearing out of nowhere, remembering nothing about their disappearance. No suspects ever arrested. Nobody ever found out how or why she went missing."

"I think I get where this is going."

Henry nodded. "Michelle Oliveira's records are sealed," he said. Henry waited, knowing she would respond.

"But you know I have access to them at the legal aid society."

"That's right."

"That's why you called me."

Henry stayed silent, looked at Amanda, his eyes full of remorse. It was genuine. "I've been an asshole. I'm not apologizing again, we both know that's over and done with. But this is important. It's a boy's life, Amanda, and I didn't know who else I could turn to or trust. I still trust you."

"I don't know if I trust you."

"I'm not asking you to trust me. I'm asking you to help me for the sake of someone else."

Amanda was struck by the tone of his voice, the sense of coldness. But she knew it wasn't meant to hurt her. In a way it was meant to protect her.

"I'm not asking you to take me back, or anything like that. I know you don't want to. I'm asking you to help because you're the only person I know who can do this, who has access to those records. The only person who *would* do this. Something is wrong with this story, and I need to know what." He added, "For Danny Linwood's sake."

Amanda sat for a moment. A cool breeze whipped through the park. She watched a smiling couple holding hands, eating sandwiches just a few feet from them, as though their whole lives existed in this small world where problems were as light as the leaves. She thought about her life, what it was like before and after Henry. How there didn't seem to be enough of it lived.

"I can get you those records," she said. "But that's all I'll do. I'll help you with whatever information you need in regard to this Oliveira girl, but I'm not going to ask for anything in return. And I don't even want you to offer."

"I won't," he said, though the words seemed hard for him to say.

Amanda stood up. Smoothed out her skirt. Henry stood as well.

"Michelle Oliveira?" Henry nodded. Amanda clutched her purse, felt the sharp edges of her keys. "I'll call you later when I get the files. One thing, I'll only give them to you in person. I could get in deep doo-doo if my supervisor knows I'm doing this, so I'll contact you discreetly. Don't send me any e-mails, don't call or text message. I don't even want to see a carrier pigeon. You might trust me, but I sure as hell don't trust Verizon."

"That's a deal."

"Then I'll call you," she said. Amanda turned around to leave.

"Hey, Amanda," Henry said.

"Yeah?"

"It was good to see you."

"I'll call you," she said, glad the smile on her face couldn't be seen as she walked away.

12

Sometimes all you can do is wait. That's what I did back at the office while waiting to hear from Amanda. I went over the Daniel Linwood transcript half a dozen times, word by word, line by line, to make sure I hadn't missed anything else. I listened to the tape, tried to hear the cadences in his voice, catch a sense of apprehension, a feeling that he was holding back. And though I strained hard to hear it to the point where I tried to convince myself, it simply wasn't there. Daniel Linwood had laid it all out. At least the way he remembered it. Or didn't remember.

Those words stuck in my head. *Brothers*. Such a small thing, Danny himself hadn't even noticed it. When a person misspeaks, they often correct themselves. If not, they won't make the mistake again. Not Danny Linwood.

At about five o'clock, when I was beginning to think it wasn't coming, that tomorrow would be a repeat of today, I got an e-mail. The subject heading read "Marion Crane." Right away I knew who it was. It was tough to hold back a smile.

When I'd been on the run for my life a few years ago, Amanda and I had stopped at a hole-in-the-wall hotel to plan our next move. She signed the ledger using the same name, Marion Crane. The Janet Leigh role from Hitchcock's *Psycho*. Marion Crane, the girl who would have done anything, including stealing thousands of dollars, just for a better life.

The e-mail was brief.

Battery Park City. Starbucks. Bring money to buy me a double latte and maybe a scone if I'm feeling adventurous.

I wondered why the hell she had to pick Battery Park City of all places. Battery Park was at the southernmost tip of New York City, but was barely in New York City. I'd been there a few times, reporting on a new housing development that was alleged to be one of the city's first "green" buildings, but a little digging turned up that the solar panels alleged to power thirty percent of the building's generator were nothing more than fancy aluminum, and the developer had pocketed a few hundred grand from snookered tenants.

Since I wasn't calling the shots, I hopped on the 4 train and rode it to the Bowling Green stop. When I got off, I immediately saw two Starbucks (or was it Starbuckses? Starbucksi?) across the street from each other. I walked into the first one, didn't see Amanda, and sheepishly left.

Battery Park had a stunning view of the Hudson River, the grand Statue of Liberty easily visible from the shore. Because of its proximity to the ocean, the temperature in Battery Park was ten to fifteen degrees cooler than the rest of Manhattan, so in August it was still a brisk sixty-five. I was glad I'd decided to wear a sport jacket.

The second Starbucks thankfully was the right one, though if I came up empty I didn't doubt there was another one right around the corner, or even inside the restroom.

Amanda was sitting by a back table reading a discarded copy of the *Dispatch*. Next to her purse was a small tote bag. Inside it I could see a thick folder with stark white printouts spilling out. She saw me coming and put down the paper. I pulled out the chair to sit down, but Amanda shook her head.

"Uh-uh." I stood there, confused. "Double latte. One sugar."

"Scone?"

"Nope. Gotta watch my girlish figure."

I wanted to tell her she needed to watch her figure like Britney needed another mouth to feed, but decided against it.

I nodded, bought the drink, fixed it to her specifications, set it down on the table and sat down.

"The *Dispatch*?" I said, gesturing to the discarded paper. "Really?"

"It's for show, stupid. I'm here incognito."

"Right. So that's it? The Oliveira file?" I said, gesturing to the tote bag. She sipped her drink, nodded.

"I feel like we're investigating Watergate or something," she replied. "Passing folders under the table."

"If that were the case, I could think of a few places a little less conspicuous than Starbucks."

"That why we're in Battery Park. You think either of us knows a soul down here? Besides, I thought you loved the Woodward and Bernstein stuff."

"I do, but Robert Redford is a little too old and leathery to play me. And Dustin Hoffman's too short for you."

Amanda looked around exaggeratedly. She eyed the barista, squinted her eyes. I had no idea what in the hell she was doing. It was as if she was expecting a rogue team of FBI agents to come out of nowhere and load her in the back of a van. Sadly, it wasn't even two years ago when two FBI agents *did* break into her house and shoot someone in her bedroom.

Maybe that's what made it funnier.

She pressed her foot up against the tote bag underneath the table. Then she kicked it toward me. Then she gestured at the bag before taking a long, slow sip of her latte.

"Oh, is that for me?"

She eyed me contemptuously. "Oh, for Christ's sake, open the damn thing."

I picked up the tote and pulled out the folder. The top sheet was Michelle Oliveira's birth certificate. She was born on November 15, 1991. That would make her sixteen today. Michelle Oliveira's parents were Carlos and Jennifer Oliveira. At the time of the abduction, the family resided in Meriden, Connecticut. According to tax records, Carlos worked as a housepainter, and Jennifer had worked in a variety of temp jobs over the years. Secretary to an orthodontist. Court stenographer. Doctor's office receptionist. Telemarketer.

Together, the Oliveiras' income never exceeded thirty-four-thousand dollars a year. They had two other children, a boy, Juan, now fourteen, and a girl, Josephine, twelve. Juan was a high school freshman, Josephine was just about to begin the seventh grade. Their sister Michelle was kidnapped on March 23, 1997, not yet six years old. She returned on February 16, 2001, nearly four years later.

According to the report, Michelle had spent that afternoon at the home of Patrick and Lynette Lowe. Michelle was in grade school with their daughter Iris, and according to interviews with the Lowes, and confirmed by the Oliveiras, Michelle often went to the Lowes' home after school to play. She would often stay at the Lowes' from approximately three-thirty to six, at which time she would come home to get ready for dinner. As the Lowes lived just four houses down on the same block as the Oliveiras, the families admitted she walked home on most occasions unsupervised. On March 23 she left the Lowes' home at approximately a quarter to six. At six-fifteen Jennifer Oliveira called Lynette Lowe to ask when Michelle would be home. When Lynette Lowe informed Jennifer that Michelle had left half an hour earlier, and Josephine could not find Michelle on their block, she called the police.

The Meriden PD found no trace of Michelle Oliveira. They compared tire tracks found on Warren Street to all vehicles registered to inhabitants of the block. All vehicles checked out. Nobody had seen Michelle after she left the Lowes. No neighbor glimpsed the girl. Nobody came forward. Michelle Oliveira had simply vanished.

The next page contained her social security number, employment records, known addresses. And her parents'.

I looked at Amanda. She was absently sipping her coffee while eyeing me.

"Did you read this already?" I asked. She nodded.

I continued reading. In 2003, two years after Michelle's reappearance, the Oliveiras moved from Meriden to Westport. Westport, I knew, was a much more affluent part of Connecticut. Records indicated that the Oliveiras were able to sell their home in Meriden for nearly $800,000, nearly triple what they'd paid for it ten years earlier. That was quite a profit for a family who couldn't afford to do much refurbishing.

"What are you thinking?" Amanda asked.

"I'm thinking I'm throwing away money by renting my apartment."

"Seriously," she said. "As soon as I can afford it, I'm leaving Darcy and buying a studio."

"Good luck coming up with half a million dollars," I replied.

"No way."

"You want three hundred and fifty square feet in Manhattan? Damn right you'll need half a mil." Amanda shook her head, obviously realizing that living for free with Darcy wasn't so bad.

"One thing's for sure," I said. "The Oliveiras couldn't wait to get the heck out of Meriden after Michelle turned up."

"Can you really blame them? I mean, their daughter disappears, do you really want to hang around and subject her to those memories? Subject your other children to that? I'd want to start my life over, that's for sure."

"I guess you're right," I said "God, that has to be every parent's worst nightmare come true."

I thumbed through the papers and the rest of the police reports, paying particular attention to the reports from the day Michelle disappeared and the day she returned. The police work had been thorough. More than thirty neighbors and friends had been interviewed, as well as all of Michelle's classmates, teachers and her private music instructor, which the Oliveiras admitted cost nearly a hundred dollars a session. In the report, Carlos and Jennifer acknowledged the expense, stating their daughter was a gifted violinist and they simply wanted to give her the best chance to "make it."

"Michelle's currently enrolled at Juilliard," Amanda said. "Full scholarship."

"You don't say. I guess Michelle did make it. That's called beating the odds."

I found an interview the police had conducted with Michelle's violin teacher, a Ms. Delilah Lancaster. Ms.

Lancaster was scheduled for her weekly lesson with Michelle the evening she disappeared. At eight o'clock she showed up, unaware of the situation. According to the report, Ms. Lancaster had seen the police, got spooked, tried to run away, which led to her questioning and being a part of the police report. Delilah had confirmed their relationship, mentioning that Michelle had recently begun working through a book called *Solo Pieces for the Intermediate Violinist*. They had just begun lessons on George Frideric Handel's "Air," from the *Water Music*. She had just completed works by Vivaldi and Mendelssohn.

Four years later, when Michelle returned, the first person she asked to speak to was Delilah Lancaster. According to the Oliveiras, nobody was closer to Michelle than Delilah Lancaster. The police ran a cursory investigation into the woman on the chance they'd find some sort of impropriety. They uncovered dozens of e-mail correspondences between the two and many phone calls to and from each other's homes, but they seemed to be more of the gifted student/dedicated teacher variety. Lancaster taught Michelle Bach and Mozart and Vivaldi, fingerboards and upper bouts. She was clearly a gifted student, but nothing seemed out of the ordinary.

Carlos Oliveira remarked to the Meriden *Record-Journal* after Michelle's reappearance that socially, his daughter seemed to have withdrawn. She was unsure of herself, timid.

"She spends hours, I mean, hours a day locked in that room of hers, fiddling with the violin as if it's all she's got in the world. We try to push her to go outside, play like a normal girl, but all she cares about are those strings. She used to have so many friends. She was such a popular girl. At least she's safe now, that's what matters most."

"The music teacher," I said. "I think I'll give Ms. Delilah a ring. It seems like she was the closest person to Michelle Oliveira, and spoke to her the most after she came back. All Michelle had left was her violin. If anybody knows anything it might be the music teacher." I held up the folder. "Can I keep these?"

"Sure," Amanda said. "But I swear, Henry, my career is on the line."

"No worries. I'll take good care of this."

She looked at me, as if debating whether I could be trusted. Finally Amanda stood up. She downed the rest of her coffee, flung it at the garbage. It rattled around and fell in.

"Keep me in the loop, will you? It sickens me to think this has happened to more than one child. That it even happened to one is just…God, horrible."

"You know I will. I know what this means to you. I hope you know what it means to me. And not just from a professional perspective."

"I know." Amanda gathered her purse and began to walk out of the store.

"That's it?"

She looked at me, her eyes a mixture of hurt and confusion.

"That's it," she said. "For now, that's all I can take." Then Amanda left.

I watched her until the door had closed and Amanda had rounded the corner. It took a moment to regain focus.

I decided the next step was to call Delilah Lancaster. It was clear she and Michelle were very close, to the point where Delilah was contacted before any of Michelle's school friends. I figured there was a reason for that. If the violin was all Michelle had left, I needed to speak to the person who probably influenced her more than any.

I sat in the store for another few minutes, then gathered up the folder and left. I hoped that somewhere, Daniel Linwood and Michelle Oliveira knew two people were going to fight for them.

13

The next morning I went to Penn Station first thing and bought a ticket on the 148 regional Amtrak en route to Meriden, Connecticut. Delilah Lancaster was scheduled to meet me. I'd spent the previous night going over her comments, trying to gain a better understanding of her relationship with Michelle Oliveira.

I took a copy of the file on Michelle Oliveira, a copy of that morning's *Gazette* and a large iced coffee that promptly spilled all over my linen jacket when a kind man with a Prada briefcase elbowed me in the head. I went to the bathroom compartment on the train to clean it, and though I was able to avoid stepping in the unidentified brown goop on the floor, I left with a softball-size blotch on my chest. I debated finding Prada man and throwing him onto the tracks, but I needed my composure. Not to mention I needed to stay out of jail.

When the train pulled out of the station, I cracked open the *Gazette* and read the story Jack had written for this edition. The piece focused on the looming gentrification of Harlem, how real estate prices were soaring, speculative investors, many of them foreign, were snapping up town houses and condos like they were Junior Mints. The

average two-bedroom had nearly doubled in price over
past decade. Foreign investors, emboldened by the weak
dollar, were monopolizing the market. The prices Jack
quoted quickly confirmed that if I ever desired to buy in
New York rather than rent, I'd either have to win the lottery
or find a sugar mama.

The reporting was solid, one of Jack's better recent
efforts. Too many of his recent articles felt slapped
together, rushed, pieces he forced past Evelyn and the copy
editors simply because he was the man. Had the stories
been written by a younger reporter who hadn't yet cut his
teeth, won major awards and written a shelfful of bestsell-
ers, many of them would have been spiked. The old man
needed an intervention. The ink of the newsroom was still
the blood that pumped through his veins, but he was a
train slowly careening off the tracks. Without some
straightening out, the impending crash would permanently
derail his career.

The train took about an hour and forty-five minutes to
reach Meriden. I finished the *Gazette* and spent a good twenty
minutes staring at an advertisement featuring a man quizzically holding an empty bottle of water before realizing it was
hawking Viagra. When the train came to a stop, I noticed a
man with a friar's patch of baldness jotting down the ad's
Web site before hustling off the train. One new customer.

I disembarked the train and took in the city of Meriden.
I hadn't spent much time in Connecticut, only having
traveled here once to interview a fast-food worker who'd
witnessed a murder while on vacation in NYC. A lot of
New Yorkers commuted into the city from parts of Connecticut—Greenwich being a popular hub—in large part
due to the ever-booming Manhattan real estate market. For
just a thirty-minute train commute, a million bucks could

buy you a home or large condo as opposed to a one-bedroom with the view of fire escape.

Meriden, though, was no Greenwich.

What struck me first was that the Meriden train station resembled less of an actual station and more like a glorified bus stop. A small hut was the only building on the gravelly lot. It had boarded-up windows, graffiti sprayed layer upon layer. A ticket vending machine sat lonely outside the hut, like a relic from the 1970s. I wasn't even sure if it accepted credit cards. A dirty, bearded man sat on a bench fully asleep, his yellow windbreaker also looking as if it hadn't been removed since long before the man's last shave. He looked comfortable, and clearly wasn't waiting for the train.

The air was cool, but I had no doubt the day would grow hotter throughout the morning. I buttoned up my jacket, stuck my hands in my pockets, and waited. The surrounding buildings were low, squat, though they seemed to have an air of vigor. Fresh coats of paint. Newly cemented sidewalks, clear of footprints and cracks. It looked like a city wrenching itself toward respectability, while experiencing a few hiccups along the way.

As well as brushing up on the Oliveira case file, I also read about the demographics and income of the city of Meriden, specifically how both had changed over the years during Michelle Oliveira's disappearance. In 1997, when Michelle was abducted, more than forty percent of Meriden residents lived below the poverty line. The median income was a shade over $28,000. And more than sixty percent of residents had one or more children.

Today, the median income was more than $45,000, and was growing at a rate far larger than the national average. Plus, only nineteen percent of residents currently lived below the poverty line. Yet less than half of residents now lived with children. I wondered if Michelle's abduction had anything to do with this. Whether the horrific nature of Michelle's disappearance convinced families it simply wasn't safe to raise a family here.

From what I could tell, this was a city that seemed to want to right the wrongs of its past. A city that desperately wanted to prove it was safe for girls like Michelle. And whatever part of the city didn't want to improve, it would remain contentedly criminal. A place where a girl could be abducted, and her abductors could remain free. That part of the city would be what it always was, and whatever happened was simply God's—or the criminal's—will.

I stood outside for a moment, unsure of what to look for, until a honking car horn brought my attention to the Chrysler sitting alone in the lot. A woman was in the driver's seat. I could see her through the windshield, an uncomfortable look on her face. She didn't want to be here. I walked over, peered in through the passenger-side window.

"Delilah Lancaster?" I said.

She nodded, said, "Get in."

I obeyed. She started the engine as I buckled my seat belt. We peeled away from the station, leaving the tracks in our wake.

Her car was if not new then new*er*. A black 300 model, it had less than ten thousand miles on it, and there were no telltale signs of wear and tear on the interior. A classical station played on the radio, and I noticed Delilah's hand moving in nearly perfect rhythm, sliding gently up and down the steering-wheel cover as though she was conducting the symphony herself.

Delilah Lancaster was in her early forties. Her black hair was pulled back in a tight bun, a few errant streaks of gray shining through like silver threads. Her face had aged gracefully, the lines and striations of a woman who was comfortable in growing older. She moved delicately but with purpose, her eyes fixed on the road.

We sat in the car for several minutes, neither of us speaking. She drove past several streets of well-maintained homes. We passed by those into a less-friendly part of town that resembled the train station in its sense of abandonment. When we stopped in front of an empty building, I turned toward her to ask where we were.

"I agreed to talk to you," she said, her hands still on the wheel despite the engine being off. "But I don't want it in my house or in any place of business or pleasure. That's the agreement."

I nodded, reached into my bag for a tape recorder. She eyed it, curled her lip.

"This is also part of the agreement," I said. "You have to go on the record." She nodded. I turned the recorder on.

"You know I went through all this seven years ago," she said. "The police questioned me many times. I know I got scared that night, but all those police, I thought somebody had been killed. For a moment I thought it might have been Michelle. All I know is, one day I was Michelle Oliveira's tutor, the next day she was gone from this world, and then several years later she rose like the phoenix."

"Why did you think she might have been killed? That seems like you were jumping to a pretty terrible conclusion."

"When you've lived in this city as long as I have, you've seen young boys killed because they were targeted by rival dealers. When you've seen young girls caught in the cross fire, then you can say that I'm jumping to conclusions. I did think Michelle might have been another victim. That she'd been taken away forever."

"Well, now she's at Juilliard," I said. A slight smile crossed Delilah Lancaster's lips.

"She's the most talented individual I've ever had the pleasure of working with," Delilah said. "The moment I walked into the Oliveira home for the first time and listened to that girl play, the French bow moving in her hand like the wind, I knew it. French bows are mainly used by soloists, and most young students don't even know the difference. But Michelle, she made her father buy a French bow. Nothing else would suffice. Most young girls have posters on their walls of their favorite bands, their favorite athletes, boys they have crushes on. Do you know what Michelle Oliveira had posted on her wall?"

I said I didn't.

"You're aware that most girls that age don't have posters, or much of anything on their walls. They haven't yet begun to have crushes, and wouldn't know who Orlando Bloom was compared to Barack Obama. But Michelle, she had a poster on her wall. I don't even know where she got it, or how. But right on her wall, above her bed, was a picture of Charles IX."

I waited for an explanation. "Is that a King of England or something?"

Delilah shook her head. "Charles IX is the oldest violin in existence. It was made in 1716 by Antonio Stradivari. It is kept in pristine condition at the Ashmolean museum in Oxford. You can imagine this is not exactly a common item for a five-year-old to worship."

"Stradivari—is he related to the Stradivarius?"

"The same," she said.

"For a young child to hold such an instrument in this regard, it simply made my heart float. When she disappeared—" Delilah lowered her head, clasped her hands together "—I felt like I'd lost a kindred spirit. Someone who understood the beauty and passion of music like so few do in their lives. And to lose her at such a young age—I thought a great student had been taken. A shame in so many ways. And when Michelle came back, I thanked God for keeping one of his finest creatures on this earth."

"You really cared for Michelle, didn't you?" I asked.

Delilah looked at me. "*Still* care. I do care for her the way a teacher looks at a prized pupil, yes. But our bond went deeper than that. I cared more for Michelle than I did most of my friends and—" she sighed "—perhaps most of my family."

I looked at Delilah's hand, barren of any rings. She noticed this.

"My husband died three years ago. Pulmonary embolism. Life hits you when you never expect it. But I still have my music. That, at least, is everlasting. And one day Michelle will create a composition that will stand the test of time. That students, like she once was, will study."

Delilah looked out over her town, the barren building in front of her.

"This city has changed so much. So many people left after what happened to Michelle. I didn't blame them. I have no children, but if I did I couldn't justify raising them here. Now young families, dare I say *yuppies,* have moved into those houses. Rats joining a ship. I never thought I would see that in Meriden."

"You're against gentrification?" I asked.

"It pays my bills," she said. "And allows me more leisure time than I previously had. But Lord, if I could find one truly talented student in the bunch, it would make my year."

"Not many children like Michelle come along," I said.

"No," she agreed. "No, they don't."

"Aside from the obvious, was there anything about Michelle that was different when she came back? Did she ever mention a family member, a friend, somebody you didn't recognize?"

Delilah shook her head. "Michelle didn't have many friends. The gifted ones never do."

"Did she strike you as different in any way? After she returned?"

Delilah thought for a moment. "She became more withdrawn. Michelle was once a vibrant, popular girl, but she never fit in again. You can't explain to a young girl why people are staring at her, knowing she can't possibly understand exactly what happened. One night, a few days after she came back, I thought I saw scarring on her arm, but I decided it was just a pimple, some kind of adolescent puberty thing. It saddened me to see such a lovely girl just have her soul sucked away. But what person wouldn't after going through something like that?"

"Did she ever say anything to you that gave any clue as to where she might have been all those years?"

Delilah shook her head. Stared ahead of her. I looked at the tape recorder. Afraid this was all I was going to get from Delilah Lancaster.

Another song came on the radio, the violin strings prominent. Delilah's fingers flowed with the sound. Then they abruptly stopped.

"What?" I asked. "What is it?"

She cocked her head, looked deep in thought. "Beethoven's sonata," she said.

"Is that what's playing right now?" I asked.

"No," Delilah answered, her voice soft. There was a

tinge of fright in there that made my pulse begin to race. "Beethoven's Sonata no. 6. It's an incredibly difficult piece. It can take months, if not years, to master. Oh, God, I remember that night."

"What happened?"

"It was only the second or third lesson after she returned," Delilah said. "Michelle was so down. Depressed. I asked her to play something that made her happy. And she picked up her bow and began to play…oh, God…"

"What?" I said. "What happened?"

"The sonata. Michelle played it for me that night. I left the house cold, shivering. I didn't sleep for a week."

"Why?" I said, a shiver running down my back.

Delilah Lancaster turned toward me. "In the dozens of lessons I had with Michelle Oliveira, never once had she even attempted to play Beethoven. She had never tried to play that symphony. That sonata was not even in any of the books I purchased for her. Somehow she'd learned to play that piece in between the time she disappeared…"

"…and when she came back."

I looked at Delilah Lancaster. She was trembling, her hands gripping the wheel so hard they'd become white.

"Somebody else taught her how to play that sonata."

_14_

I marched into Wallace Langston's office and sat down. He was poring over a pile of loose pages. He simply looked up and stared at me.

"I don't recall that chair offering you a seat," he said. I stood back up. Without missing a beat, Wallace said, "Now you can sit down, Henry. What's up?"

I took out the tape recorder, put it on the desk in front of Wallace. "I just spent the day in Meriden talking to Michelle Oliveira's old music teacher, Delilah Lancaster. She—"

"Michelle who?" he said. I forgot for a moment that Wallace had dozens of other stories being run past him, and that even though this was hugely important to me, I needed to show him that I was right about my suspicions.

"Seven years before Daniel Linwood disappeared, a girl named Michelle Oliveira vanished from Meriden, Connecticut. For almost four years there was no trace of her. No suspects, no arrests, nada. Then, just like Danny Linwood, she shows up at her parents' doorstep without the vaguest idea what happened. No scrapes, no bruises, and police can't figure out what the hell happened or where she'd been."

Wallace slowly put down the pages. I had his full attention.

"I thought that whole 'brothers' thing was strange, but it seemed clear to me that after Daniel was kidnapped, he retained some information from his time gone. I wanted to find out if this was a common occurrence for kidnapping victims. Upon running a search, I found this Oliveira girl, who disappeared in the exact same way. Michelle was very close to her music teacher, this Delilah Lancaster, so I figured she might be able to shed some light and maybe help me understand Danny's case better. During the interview today, it turns out that in between Michelle Oliveira's disappearance and return, the girl learned an *entire new* violin sonata. Somehow she'd had access to both instruments and music books. So not only was she kidnapped, but she was kidnapped by somebody who knew her well enough to know she was a violin prodigy."

Wallace looked at me, looked at the recorder. "She played violin, this Michelle Oliveira?"

"A prodigy," I said. "She's at Juilliard now."

"There's no chance she started studying this sonata before she disappeared, and simply finished it later?"

I shook my head. "I asked Delilah that. She said they were using a workbook in which that specific sonata was not a part of the lesson. When they resumed lessons after Michelle returned, suddenly this ten-year-old has turned into Yo-Yo Ma."

"How did Lancaster explain it?"

"She couldn't," I said. "And neither could Michelle. Delilah asked her where she learned it, but Michelle didn't know."

"And Lancaster believed her?"

"Without a doubt. Like Danny Linwood, it's an imprint on her brain, the moves in her muscle memory. Unconscious. I did leave several messages for the Oliveiras but haven't heard back yet, and frankly I'm not expecting to. But something strange is happening to these kids while they're gone. Obviously somebody took them, and they're retaining a piece of memory from their time away. It's not much, but it definitively links Michelle Oliveira and Daniel Linwood. I don't know how or why, but their disappearances are connected."

"This is stunning stuff, Parker. And where did you get all this information on Oliveira?" Wallace asked.

"I... Most of it from newspapers. Lancaster was interviewed by the *Journal-Record*."

"You just happened to come upon this?"

"I dig deep," I said, thinking of Amanda, not wanting to get her into any trouble.

Just then there was a knock at Wallace's door. We both turned. Our jaws simultaneously dropped when we saw the striking figure in the doorway.

"Gray," Wallace said. I recognized the man immediately, but for the life of me couldn't imagine why he was here.

The man entered, striding up to Wallace with casual confidence.

Wallace said, "Henry, you've met..."

"Senator Talbot," I said. "We met just the other day."

Gray Talbot smiled at me. "Hello, Henry," he said. "I hope I'm not interrupting anything."

15

I stood out in the hall, trying to hear what Wallace and Gray Talbot were discussing behind closed doors. Though Wallace had told me to wait by my desk, I wasn't nearly patient enough. I felt better pacing a tread on the carpet outside of his office. I wondered what the hell Senator Talbot was doing in the *Gazette* offices. Wallace seemed surprised, and I was pretty sure Gray had stopped by totally unannounced. Generally not the behavior of most politicians who throw a press conference to announce they've voided their bowels.

I felt slightly dirty, like a journalistic Peeping Tom, straining for quick glimpses. I could only make out corners of the office—Wallace had drawn the shades. I could see Talbot pacing back and forth, his face angry. He was looking in one direction, which inferred that Wallace was sitting at his desk, most likely being defensive.

I got the distinct impression that Wallace was being read the riot act for something, I just wasn't sure what.

Finally after about twenty minutes, the door opened and Gray Talbot exited. His navy suit was unruffled, his hair unmussed, his demeanor unshaken. Whatever he'd come for today, he'd gotten it.

As he walked by he slowed up, turned to me slightly, leaned in. I could smell his light aftershave, saw a small nick by his jawbone.

"Parker," he said. "You're better than this. I haven't forgotten what we spoke about. And I hope you haven't, either."

Before I could ask what the hell he was talking about, Talbot was in the elevator.

Without waiting another second, I burst into Wallace's office. The editor-in-chief was sitting down, hands steepled, chin resting on his thumbs. He looked up at me without moving, his eyes flickering.

"Sit down, Henry." I sat.

"How did you get that information about Michelle Oliveira?" he asked. I opened my mouth to speak. "And if you lie to me you're fired."

I sighed, knew I was cornered, knew there was nothing I could do.

"I have a contact at the legal aid society. This person gave me information about the Oliveira case. The police report, and more." I kept it gender nonspecific, just in case. "The rest I did myself. Frankly I didn't really need it, it was just a shortcut—"

"Shortcuts are the death of our industry, Parker," Wallace said. "Jayson Blair took shortcuts. Stephen Glass took shortcuts. I don't expect you to want or need those. And I hope to God you yourself think you're better than them."

"It wasn't like that," I said. "I knew there was more to this Linwood story than was being reported, and I needed something to tie them together. You know there's a connection. And without those papers I might not have found it. You can call it a shortcut, I call it a story worth investigating. My source is reliable, and the papers are authentic."

"Ethics and honesty are not always independent of each other," Wallace said.

I felt my body go slack. "So what now?" I said. "What did Talbot want?"

"You forget about this story now."

I felt my body go numb. "That's ridiculous. He can't spike a story because he doesn't like my sources."

"Gray Talbot has threatened to prosecute you, and by proxy us, if any of what you've told me about Daniel Linwood or Michelle Oliveira ever runs. He knows that you obtained those files and he knows you did it illegally, without the knowledge of the LAS. Like you said, it was one rogue employee. And like a good politician he's going to hold it over our heads until we bend to his will. I know you've worked hard on this, Henry, but let it go."

I stood up. "This is bullshit," I said. "Do you really think it's the right thing to let it go? Do you honestly believe there's nothing more to find on this story?"

"We're not crusaders," Wallace said. "We're not vigilantes, or judges or heroes. You are a reporter. Nothing more or less. It's not my call to say what's right and what's wrong. But I can tell you what your job is. And as of Monday, I'll have a new assignment for you. Now go. Get rid of any files you have. Take the weekend, recharge your batteries and get ready to kick some ass next week."

"Right. Kick some ass," I said lethargically. I left Wallace's office without saying another word. I didn't know if I was going to be able to "recharge" over the weekend, but one thing was for damn sure. I wasn't getting rid of those files. And I sure as hell wasn't letting this story go.

16

I called Amanda as soon as I left the office. The call went straight to her voice mail at work. For a moment my breath caught in my throat. I prayed she hadn't been fired. Then I tried her cell phone. When she picked up, her voice sounded upbeat, familiar. Not the voice of someone whose life had taken a turn for the worse.

"Oh, thank God, are you OK?" I asked.

"Of course, why wouldn't I be? Is that asteroid finally headed for earth or something?"

"No, even worse. Gray Talbot came by our office today."

"The political dude?"

"Senator, yeah."

"What was he doing at the *Gazette?* Doesn't he get enough press?"

"That's the thing, he wasn't there about a story that had already run, he was there to make sure we didn't print anything else about Danny Linwood or Michelle Oliveira."

"That's ridiculous. Why?"

I took a breath. "He knows about the files."

There was silence. Then she spoke. "I assume you're referring to whatever files I definitely had nothing to do with."

"Those are the ones."

"Goddamn it, Henry, you promised you wouldn't say anything!"

"Amanda, I didn't, I swear. But he knew about it and threatened to either fire me or castrate Wallace if we ran any stories about Michelle Oliveira, using the information you gave me. Is it possible someone in your office knows you took the files?"

"It's possible," she said. "I had to log in to our system to print out a lot of it. But if they know I took them, why haven't I been led out by Security?"

"Same reason he came by our office. He wants this kept quiet. You get fired, the press gets hold of that, and he's got much more than Wallace Langston to worry about."

"But why is he taking such an interest in Michelle and Danny?" Amanda asked.

"I don't know," I said. "But I'll find out."

"I want to find out with you," she said. "I'll meet you at your apartment in an hour."

"Amanda," I said. "I don't think—"

"Right, don't think anything. I want to help figure out what the hell is going on. I work with kids seven days a week. Kids that have been beaten and left for dead because nobody fought for them. And now it turns out two of them are missing pieces of their lives and some stuffed shirt wants to step on it? Not on my watch."

I came this close to saying *I love you.* I didn't. But it sounded great in my head.

"I'll be at my place in an hour," I said. "See you then."

"Have a pot of coffee ready," she said. "And please, Henry. Pick up whatever dirty underwear is starting to grow spores in your hamper."

"I have a hamper?"

She hung up.

I caught a cab back home, threw every article of clothing that appeared salvageable into a garbage bag and shoved it into my closet. I was apprehensive about letting her in. Amanda hadn't set foot in my apartment in six months. Like me, Amanda had the inquisitive gene. And especially now that her ass was on the line, she was going to be a part of this until we figured out what happened to the years Michelle and Danny had lost. I just needed to make sure my nasty socks hadn't grown a life of their own in the meantime.

Once the apartment was clean enough to present, I poured a glass of water and sat on the couch, thinking about Daniel Linwood and Michelle Oliveira. It had made me sick to read about how heartbroken their families were when they disappeared, how two families could be shattered in seconds. I could only imagine the joy when they came back, as though a hole in their parents' hearts had suddenly been repaired.

I hadn't spoken to my father or mother in two years. The last time was while I was on the run. I called my father one night, holed up in a dank room, waiting for two men who would either be my saviors or my executioners. I called him for two reasons. The first was to say goodbye, in the event that I didn't make it out alive. The second was out of the hope that that bastard would give me something to keep going, a reason to live, to spite him if nothing more. He gave me that, and I lived. And we hadn't spoken since. I never desired to. I didn't wish him dead, but merely hoped he took care of my poor, absent mother the best he knew how. But I was glad to be gone from that home. I was happy to be living a life where I was the only arbiter

Jason Pinter

of my triumphs or failures. Like Danny and Michelle, I'd been lost, too.

The buzzer jolted me out of my thoughts. I went to the window, looked down to see Amanda standing at the door. She looked up, saw me, gave me the finger. Classy as always. I jogged to the intercom and released the door lock, then did another once-over of the apartment to make sure no dust bunnies—or actual bunnies—were hiding from view.

In the minute I had before Amanda got to the door, I considered how to answer it. Suave, with a Rhett Butler-esque baritone in my voice? Should I leave the door un-latched, sit on the couch and try to act nonchalant? Maybe greet her with a glass of water, or wine? A plate of cheese? A half-eaten Snickers bar from my nightstand?

Then I remembered it was Amanda. She wasn't im-pressed by overdone gestures. She'd spent years of her life sizing people up in mere seconds, a habit brought on by her adoption after the death of her parents. She was a better judge of character than anyone I'd ever known. She could tell who was real and who wanted you to believe they were real. I'd been nothing but real during our rela-tionship. And even though I doubted we'd ever be together again, I couldn't stop being that. She saw past it. And I didn't want her to look any further.

The doorbell rang. I cleared my throat—the least I could do was talk to her phlegm-free—and answered it. She was dressed in fitted jeans, a gray T-shirt and a thin red cardigan. Her hair spilled gently over her shoulders. It was a few seconds before I realized how much I'd missed seeing her, cataloging her beauty on a daily basis. I threw the thoughts from my head, and said, "Hey."

"Hey, yourself." She was holding two cups of coffee,

and offered me one. "I figured you'd forget to brew a pot. Milk and three hundred Splendas, right?"

I smiled. "Perfect. I was kind of hoping my teeth might jitter all night. Come on in."

She entered the apartment, looked around. "Looks good," she said. "It's been a while. I was kind of expecting a bear to attack me, or some sort of underwear monster to run across the room."

"The underwear monster doesn't come out until the sock monster goes to sleep."

"I'm going to ignore you now."

She walked around to the couch, sat down, placed her coffee on the small marble table, already ringed with many old coffee cup stains, including a few that were most likely from Amanda's cups and had never been cleaned.

"This place missed you," I said, then felt silly for saying it.

"Really? It probably has enough festering life forms hiding that it did tell you that."

"Yeah, the comforter and I, we chat sometimes."

"If cleanliness is next to godliness, I think this makes you the Antichrist."

I laughed, took a sip of the coffee. Then we sat in silence for a moment.

"So Gray Talbot," she said, thankfully breaking the tension. "What does he have to do with Michelle and Daniel?"

"I did a bit of a background check on the senator," I said. "Found a few interesting facts."

"Let me guess. This was after Wallace told you to let it be."

"Naturally. Anyway, in 2001, after Michelle Oliveira disappeared from Meriden, Gray Talbot swooped in like an avenging angel and pretty much scorched the earth. He lambasted the government of Connecticut, the social services offices, the police force, criticized them all for betraying the families that lived within their borders. He said it was a sad day when an out-of-stater had to come in because the job wasn't being done right. And Talbot saved his best blasts for then Governor John Rowland."

"Rowland," Amanda said. "That name rings a bell."

"It should. John Rowland resigned from office as governor of the state of Connecticut in 2004 due to charges of massive corruption. Mail fraud, tax fraud, he even served ten months in a federal prison."

"And this guy was running the state when Michelle disappeared?"

"Kind of like having a crack addict babysit your children. Rowland was skimming money for numerous personal projects that had nothing to do with the state. He took state money and paid for improvements to his weekend cottage, took thousands of dollars in gifts from his subcontractors. Of course, after prison he did the whole rehab-image deal, everything but appear on the cover of *People* magazine. Anyway, Talbot came in after Michelle disappeared and tore Rowland a new one for letting the state go to seed. He said the state was not protecting its youth. At the time, Meriden had the second-highest crime rate in the state, and it had gotten worse over the previous few years. Even though Talbot was a New York senator, he was quoted as saying, 'This is a matter so vital to the future of our country that it would be irresponsible to only permit coloring within state lines.'"

"So Talbot ruins Rowland, then what?"

"Talbot institutes a program called 'Not on Our Watch.' He raises millions of dollars earmarked for improving security within Meriden and other surrounding counties. More money for police recruiting, neighborhood watches, more incentives for gang members and criminals to become informants. He raises thousands of dollars for the Oliveira family, basically seals up trust funds for their other children to go to college. Within two years, the crime rate in Meriden drops like a rock. He spent years working to help the Oliveiras move on with their lives."

Amanda said, "And now this guy is knocking on Wallace's door telling him to let the city move on. It sounds to me like Talbot is a guy who worked his ass off to rebuild a community, then sees some punk reporter, no offense…"

"None taken…"

"…digging around, looking for holes in the masonry."

"Not to mention the most interesting part," I said. "Michelle Oliveira grew up in Meriden, but guess where she was born?"

"I don't know, where?"

"Hobbs County."

"Like Danny Linwood?" she said. "Holy shit, that's a hell of a coincidence."

"Or maybe not," I said. "Guess where our favorite senator also grew up?"

Amanda looked at me. She said, "No way…"

"That's right, Hobbs County for two hundred, Alex."

"So this guy has taken protecting his own to a whole new level. No wonder as a New York senator he decided to stick his nose into another state."

"What's also strange, though, is that both Meriden and Hobbs County were essentially cesspools before Michelle Oliveira and Daniel Linwood were kidnapped. Since Talbot came in, they've seen unprecedented growth and community support."

"Talbot seems to have done his job well," she said. "There are certainly enough shitty neighborhoods in New York, maybe he should take care of his own backyard for a bit."

"That's why he was at Danny Linwood's home the day I interviewed him," I said. "He is looking out for his own backyard. Literally."

"What are you thinking we should do?" she asked.

"I'm not sure," I said. "But it concerns me any time a politician does something for the alleged good of the community. It makes me wonder what the quid pro quo is."

"Well, how has Talbot's career been affected since Michelle Oliveira and Danny Linwood came back?"

"Well, he's won by a landslide every time he's run for reelection," I said. "One would assume at some point he'll want to move from the senate to the governor's mansion. All that good press can't hurt."

"You think we might be a little too cynical?" Amanda said. "I mean, this guy seems to have legitimately changed lives. Maybe even saved a few. For all the politicians that talk a big game, this guy actually gets his feet dirty. Yet he ruffles a few feathers at your office and we're ready to string him up."

"I'm not doing anything like that," I said defensively. "But I need to know why two children disappeared into thin air, reappeared years later with no memory of where they went, and nobody seems to be looking too hard into that fact. I have no idea if Gray Talbot is the greatest Samaritan of all time or Jack the Ripper in a good suit. I just want the truth. And one thing I've learned in this job is that anytime somebody tells you not to look under that rock, there's something there they don't want you to find."

"And now you're going to lift that rock. Even if it means your job."

"Even if it means *your* job," I said, looking her dead in the eye. Amanda seemed taken aback, then she took a breath and calmed down.

"Guess I should have expected that."

"I'm sorry, I—"

"Don't be sorry. I want to respect you. If you pulled punches, I wouldn't."

"Sometimes I hit harder than I need to. Against people who don't deserve it."

"Yeah…" she said, eyeing me warily. "I think it's time for me to head home."

"You're sure?" I said. "You want to grab dinner or something?"

Amanda looked at me, sadness in her eyes. "Henry, this is what it is. I'll help you all you need. I want to know everything about Danny and Michelle, too. But this is what we are, now, you and me. And this is a choice you made."

"What was your choice?" I asked.

She looked at me, her cheeks flushing red, anger in her eyes. "I didn't have one," she said. "You made my choice for me."

"I know. And I'm sorry I did that. I wish I could take it back. More than anything."

Amanda took a step closer, her eyes locked on to mine. For a moment I felt embarrassed, wanted to step back.

"Two years ago," Amanda said, "you came clean about who you were. I had a choice. I could have left you on the side of the road for the assholes who wanted you dead. Or I could help you. I made my choice. And here we are. I didn't leave you then, and I wouldn't have left you ever. You decided to make my choice for me. And since you did that, I'm not going to put myself in another

situation where someone can dictate *my* future without my
say-so. It's my life, Henry, and if you don't like what I do
with it, you should have never gotten into my car in the
first place."

I finally stepped back, felt like I'd been slapped across
the face. Though I had no one to blame but myself. "So
what are we, then?" I asked.

Amanda walked forward until I could smell the light
perfume that she must have put on before work. Because
she sure didn't wear it for me.

"We're friends," she said. "Good friends. I'll help you
however I can with this. But just with this. That's my choice.
So either you can deal with it or you can't, but if you can't,
say something now. Otherwise don't waste my time."

"I have nothing to say. I appreciate it. So will Danny
Linwood."

I sat back down. Took out the papers Amanda had given
me regarding Michelle Oliveira's disappearance. I began
to go through them again. Amanda stood there in the hall
for a moment, then came and sat down next to me. She
looked over my shoulder.

"Do you mind?" she asked. She didn't quite phrase it
as a question. She knew there wasn't a chance in hell of
me minding. I smiled. Told her I didn't.

Then I noticed something on Michelle's medical
reports. She used a pediatrician in Hobbs County for
several years before moving to Meriden. I looked at the
name on the birth certificate, the signature of the man who
delivered Michelle Oliveira.

"What is it?" Amanda asked.

"Michelle Oliveira was born at the Yardley Medical
Center in Hobbs County," I said.

"And?"

"The doctor on this birth certificate is named Dmitri Petrovsky," I said. "The same Dmitri Petrovsky who treats Danny Linwood."

17

The girl sat on the couch, listening to the two grown-ups speak as if she wasn't even there.

"I heard her coughing last night," Elaine Reed said. It was cold inside the house. The girl watched with curiosity as Elaine held a cup of tea to her cheek. She'd heard Elaine's husband, Bob, say something about not being able to work the fireplace. Bob talked loud sometimes, and used words that Elaine got mad at him for.

Elaine was a pretty woman, only a little younger than her own mom. She had bright red hair and always wore pretty blue jewelry. When the other day the girl asked what kind it was, Elaine told her that her own daddy had brought it back from Greece. She said the rocks there were as blue as the sea itself.

Bob was shorter, with thinning dark hair and a beard that circled only his upper lip and chin. He wore glasses and didn't say much and spent most of the day reading books and newspapers. He seemed to like to argue about politicians, people he said were doing this country more harm than good. Elaine always nodded and smiled when he talked like that, but didn't really seem to have any opinions of her own in that regard.

The house was so huge, bigger than her old one, and the girl was scared to walk around alone. Not that she ever had to, since Elaine insisted on holding her hand almost everywhere she went. The girl felt strange, this woman she'd just met acting so friendly, but Elaine was nice and it meant not having to be scared. Even though she was still confused, the girl loved running up and down the lengthy hallways, laughing as Bob helped her slide down the banister. Elaine placed both of her hands around the cup, took a sip and placed it on the wooden table. Bob picked it up, frowned at her, then took a glass coaster emblazoned with a bright yellow sunflower and put the cup back down on it.

"She might just have a cold," Bob said. "Kids get colds. Not everything is a life-threatening disease."

She'd heard Elaine mention that the Reed family had lived in this house for just six months, and still hadn't quite grown used to its nooks and crannies, the way it creaked during high wind, the way the linoleum was cool in the spring and hot in the summer. Yet for all the comfort, Elaine said she still felt isolated. The days were sunny and clear, and when the windows were left open the girl could see the trees, high oaks. And the fence surrounding the property.

Bob Reed had a bit of a temper. Or as her daddy would say, his blood got up something. Bob complained that they had to drive three miles just to see a human being. And he had to fiddle with some sort of remote control to work a "stupid" motor-controlled gate that allowed access to the driveway. Not to mention some brick wall that obscured the surrounding area. Elaine would put her hand on Bob's shoulder and say, "We know why this is happening. We need to make the best of it." Bob would look at her, nod, then go off on his own.

But right now they seemed concerned. A few days ago, the girl had come down with a cold. She felt shivery and warm at the same time, and no matter how many blankets Elaine piled on top of her it never went away. When they first realized she was sick, Bob and Elaine grew pale, and this scared the girl.

"Kids cough," he said now, trying to be strong. "Look at Patrick. Hawked up a ball of phlegm every night until he turned three."

"Well, this one is six," Elaine said. "And that coughing doesn't sound right. Maybe we should take her to see someone."

"Not him," Bob said. "I don't trust that man."

"Neither do I, but we have to. He told us if we ever needed medical help, we had to see…"

"Screw that crazy, scarred-up old man," Bob said. "He doesn't have to live like this. He didn't have to change his life for some strange kid."

"Patrick," Elaine said. "Think of Patrick."

Bob sighed, put his head in his hands. "Her cold will pass," he said, reaching for the newspaper. "Can't even get the newspaper delivered because 'he' said so."

"Speaking of which," Elaine said, "I think it's time for her shot."

Bob nodded. He said, "I'll do it this time."

He stood up. Headed toward the bathroom. A minute later Bob came back carrying a plastic bag.

He opened the bag and took out a gauze pad, a syringe, a small vial and a bottle of clear liquid that smelled funny. The girl watched all this. It all seemed vaguely familiar. And though that needle looked huge, like the size of a knife, for some reason she wasn't scared.

"Did you wash your hands?" Elaine asked.

"Of course," Bob replied. He took the small vial and rolled it gently between his fingers. Next he took a cotton ball, opened the bottle of clear liquid, held the ball against the open top until it was wet, then cleaned the top of the vial with the cotton ball.

"That smells funny," the girl said. Elaine scrunched her nose and smiled.

"It does, doesn't it?"

Bob didn't smile. He just kept doing what he was doing.

Bob took the syringe and pulled the stopper back a little bit. Then he pushed the needle into the top of the vial, pressing the stopper again. A small bubble of air entered the vial. Then he turned the vial upside down, the syringe pointing at the ceiling, and pulled the stopper again until a small amount of the liquid was sucked into the syringe.

He tapped the syringe until the air bubbles had risen to the top of the needle. Then he removed the needle from the vial.

Bob turned to Elaine, still holding the needle. "Where did we give it to her this morning?"

"The abdomen," she said.

"Gotcha. Caroline, would you come here?" The girl stood up warily, then went over to Bob. "Here, sweetie, sit down next to me."

She did. Bob rolled up the sleeve of her right arm, then took the smelly cotton ball and rubbed it all over the underside of her arm. Then he blew on it gently.

"That tickles," the girl said.

"Just needs to dry a bit," Bob said. He waited a minute, then took her arm and gently squeezed her skin until a fold stuck out. Caroline winced a bit but stayed still.

"Good girl," Elaine said.

"Now close your eyes," Bob said. When she did, she felt a sting as the needle entered her skin. She felt Bob's grip tighten, then a few seconds later it eased up. She opened her eyes. The needle was on the table and Bob was swabbing her arm with another cotton ball.

"You're such a brave girl," Elaine said. Caroline smiled.

18

The rental car zipped along like only a Hyundai with a hundred-and-twenty-five thousand miles could. Now that I'd been summarily dismissed from the Daniel Linwood story by Wallace, I couldn't expect to be reimbursed for expenses anytime soon. Which meant watching my budget until I proved that it was worth potentially disrupting the lives of several families, not to mention putting my career on the line, to find out what happened to two missing children. Which meant that, for the time being, the $44.95-a-day rates of the Rent-a-Wreck of Yonkers was the only thing that could fit my ever-extended budget.

As soon as I realized that both Michelle Oliveira and Daniel Linwood not only were born in the same hospital, but were treated by the same doctor, I decided to speak to this man to see what, if anything, he could shed light on. Dr. Dmitri Petrovsky worked in the pediatrics unit at the Yardley Medical Center in Hobbs County. Amanda and I were on our way to speak to the good doctor. Like good guests we were coming uninvited.

As I drove up I-287, Amanda gripped the side door handle as though the car might split in half at any moment. Ironic, considering a few years back Amanda had driven us to St. Louis at an average speed that would make Jeff Gordon cry for mama.

I noticed her clutching the side, smirked and said, "Come on, you really think I'm going to spin out or drive us both into the Hudson? Besides, between the two of us, who do you think has racked up more points on their license?"

She glared at me. "I've never had an accident in all the time I've been driving. And I've been in a car with you, oh, a total of, like, three times. Forgive me if I don't quite trust your instincts. Not to mention my Toyota was sturdier than the Verrazano bridge."

"I have such fond memories of that car."

Though Amanda and I had now been on speaking terms for just a few days, I was surprised at how easily we fell back into old patterns, the give-and-take of conversation. I was actually uncomfortable with it. Specifically, the fact that she seemed so calm. As if she knew our banter was nothing more than that, and would never get past the surface.

Two young children, both vanishing into nothing, reappearing after years, neither with any memory of their time gone. Both having been born in the same town, to low-income families with other siblings. I had no idea exactly what we were looking for, or what I expected to find, but I hoped that Dmitri Petrovsky, having borne witness to the birth of both Michelle and Danny, could yield new information.

We arrived at Yardley Medical Center a little after nine in the morning.

We stepped out of the Hyundai. It was warm outside, the sun hot and vivid. I was wearing a pair of brown khakis and a navy-blue sport coat. Amanda was in a sweater and light blue jeans. She looked a millions times better than I did, which wasn't surprising, since I had to dig through a pile of unmentionables just to find two matching socks.

The Yardley Medical Center was a long building, twelve stories high, shaped like an L, with one taller side made of red brick, the other, shorter part windowed by steel and blue glass. We walked around to the main entrance, passing ambulatory care, and entered. The lobby was not large, but it was impeccably clean. Off to the side was a flower shop, a newsstand and a small cafeteria, and another path leading to a bank of elevators. In the middle was an information desk and security checkpoint. Half a dozen people were in line. When they finished talking to the attendant, she handed them a sticker to show Security, who let them enter the elevator bank.

We walked up to the information booth. The attendant, a heavyset black woman, said, "May I help you?"

"We're here to see Dr. Dmitri Petrovsky in Pediatrics," I said.

"Your names?"

"Henry Parker and Amanda Davies."

"Do you have identification?"

We both handed over our drivers licenses. I didn't want to announce myself as a member of the press just yet. In case Petrovsky knew anything, I didn't want to give him time to prepare.

The woman looked at our IDs, then at us, then handed them back. She scribbled our names on two orange stickers, then signed each one before peeling them off and pressing them against our shirts.

"Petrovsky, Pediatrics. Suite 1103."

We thanked her, showed the stickers to the guard and

rode the elevator to the eleventh floor. The elevator was jam-packed, and the ride took forever. Finally we got off on eleven and followed the signs to the correct suite.

The eleventh-floor hallway was painted light blue. Very soothing. When we found 1103, a door marked Pediatrics, we paused for a moment, then entered.

We found ourselves in a waiting room littered with toys and parenting magazines. Various brochures were available. There were about a dozen chairs, almost all of which were filled with mothers, fathers and their tykes. I counted three pregnant women. Some of the kids were playing, some sleeping, and at least two were bawling their eyes out. Amanda took a seat, picked up a copy of *Parenting* magazine, and nodded toward the secretary.

"Would you mind signing us in, hon?"

"My pleasure, *hon*."

I approached the secretary, a middle-aged woman with frizzy hair and a pair of red glasses perched on her nose. "Help you?" she said.

"I'm here to see Dr. Petrovsky," I said.

"Do you have an appointment?"

"No, I'm sorry, we don't."

She swiveled to a computer, pressed a few keys, then swiveled back. "He can see you today, but not likely until eleven-thirty." She handed me a clipboard with several forms on it. "If you and your wife would please fill these out and return it back to me."

I opened my mouth to explain the whole *not wife* thing, but didn't think it was worth the time or explanation.

I took the papers and a pen, sat down next to Amanda. "If anyone asks, you're my wife."

"'Scuse me?"

"Just go with it."

"Come on, Henry, these kind of matrimonial decisions should be made by both of us for Christ's sake."

A lady holding her infant son glared at us.

"Sorry," I said, turning to Amanda. "Honey, there are children present."

Amanda gave me a look that could have melted steel. I concentrated on filling out the forms, being as vague as possible, while leaving most responses blank.

When they were completed, I went back up to the receptionist. Handing them over, I said, "I left a lot of this blank. Frankly, there are some personal issues I'd rather discuss with Dr. Petrovsky first, if you don't mind."

The woman rolled her eyes at me, said, "Suit yourself," and took the papers. When I returned to Amanda, she was buried in a copy of *Parenting* magazine.

"Wow," Amanda said, eyebrows raised. "Did you know that the World Health Organization recommends breast-feeding your child until they're at least two years old, and sometimes until they're four?"

"Why not?" I said. "Nothing brings a mother and her child closer than reading, writing and breast-feeding."

Amanda snorted a laugh, causing the other mothers to sneer at her in unison. She went back to reading the magazine. I did a cursory search through the reading material available. Since I had no aching desire to sift through a Learning Annex pamphlet or a four-month-old issue of *Cosmopolitan,* I just sat there and waited.

Finally after a two-hour wait, the receptionist called, "Mr. and Mrs. Parker."

I looked at Amanda, her face suddenly nervous. We stood up and followed the receptionist down a wood-paneled hallway into an examination room.

"Dr. Petrovsky will be with you in just a moment."

When she left, I turned to Amanda and said, "Here we go."

"You really think this guy knows anything about Danny and Michelle?"

"That's why we're here," I said. "I just want something to prove to Wallace this story deserves looking into, regardless of what some stuffed shirt says."

We sat there waiting for fifteen minutes. I looked around the room. Nothing out of place, and because we were in a simple examining room rather than Petrovsky's office, it prevented me from snooping around his framed degrees.

Then the door opened, and a fifty-something barrel-chested man walked in. He was about five-ten with a thick gray beard and a white coat that barely concealed his protruding midsection. Beneath the beard his cheeks were slightly red. He walked with a slight limp. I guessed he'd undergone a hip or knee replacement surgery recently.

"Mr. and Mrs. Parker, I am Dr. Dmitri Petrovsky." He spoke with a thick Russian accent. I took his extended hand, as did Amanda.

"Thanks for seeing us on such short notice," I said.

"It is my pleasure. Now, if you will do me one more, please, have a seat." Amanda sat down on a small metal chair. Petrovsky laughed. "No, not there. Here."

Petrovsky approached the examining table. He reached underneath, fiddled around for a few seconds, and then pulled up a pair up stirrups which he latched into place. He then slapped the green cushion and said, "Mrs. Parker, if you please."

He put his palms together and then opened them as if he were reading a book.

Amanda's eyes went wide. "Oh, hell no. Henry, this is where I get off the train. Good luck."

"Mrs. Parker?" Petrovsky said. He turned to me. "I do not understand. This is a routine part of a first examination."

Time to come clean. Or at least cleaner.

"Dr. Petrovsky, my name is Henry Parker, and I'm a reporter with the *New York Gazette.* Now, first off, I want you to know that I'm here in the best interests of two children. All I want to do is ask you a few questions. We don't want to make any trouble, I promise. And I would appreciate your complete candor. It's vital in our investigation."

"Investigation?" Petrovsky's eyes were frightened, but I couldn't tell if it was from the surprise or something else. "Please, I do not understand. You lied to Maggie at reception?"

"Not exactly, Doctor. I just needed to speak with you. If after we talk you think my motives aren't genuine, you can do what you want. But please, just hear me out. I mean well."

Petrovsky folded his arms. I took that to mean he was listening.

"I'm investigating the disappearance of Daniel Linwood," I said. "The records show that Daniel Linwood was born in this hospital, and that you were the attending during the birth. In conjunction with Daniel Linwood, we're investigating a similar disappearance, a girl named Michelle Oliveira. Michelle also was born here, under your supervision.

"Daniel Linwood," Petrovsky said, his eyes yielding a glimmer of recognition. "The name does sound familiar, yes. What has happened that you are investigating?"

This surprised me a little. The Linwood disappearance was major news in Hobbs County. Petrovsky had worked here dating back years. Either his memory had slipped, or he was being obstinate for a reason.

"A week ago, Daniel Linwood returned to his family after being kidnapped nearly five years ago. I'm looking into who kidnapped him and why."

"But you say Daniel was found, yes? He is with his family?"

"Yes, he is."

"Then all should be happy, no?"

"Not if you want a sense of justice. And I think Daniel's disappearance is related in some way to Michelle Oliveira. You know both children were born at Yardley," I said. "And they're both from Hobbs County."

"I did not know this, and I do not know this Michelle person you speak of."

Petrovsky reached into his pocket and took out a handkerchief, mopping a few beads from his brow. He put it back in, laughed slightly, then held his hands to his stomach.

"My wife," he said. "Says I should lose about fifty pounds to stay healthy. Perhaps, she says, this is the reason I have a titanium knee. I think she may be right, but she cannot tell me *how* to lose that weight."

"Doctor," I said, "Daniel Linwood has no recollection of his missing years. I need to know what could happen to a child that could do that to their brain, to their memory. If you know anything about Daniel, or what happened, that could explain it."

"Please, Mr. Parker, I am just here to do my job. I have delivered many hundreds of children in my career, and now you ask me to remember two as if they were delivered this morning? You have lied to me, and now you expect me to answer you like a man at a cocktail party who has medical questions? If you have medical questions, I would be happy to refer you to another physician in this clinic. Or if you prefer to continue down this path, I would be happy to refer you to hospital security, who will refer you to a good lawyer. That is all I have to say. Now I suggest you leave. Right away."

The look Petrovsky gave us confirmed that he was not bluffing. I had no intention of calling his bluff. I merely thanked him for his time, apologized again for the ruse, and we left.

We exited Yardley in silence. When we got to the parking lot, Amanda said, "Goddamn, that guy knows something."

I nodded, picked up the pace and headed toward our Hyundai, hoping a strong wind hadn't caused it to blow away.

"I agree," I said. "He'd heard the name Michelle Oliveira before. And I don't buy that he didn't know about Danny Linwood." I stood in front of our car, thinking about what to do next.

"Think we should head back?" Amanda asked.

"No," I said.

"Why not?"

"I'm going to wait for him. Petrovsky. I'm going to follow him when he gets off work and see where he goes. If necessary, confront him off hospital grounds. Where there's no security, nobody but us."

Amanda sighed.

"The least you could have done was tell me that upstairs. I would have grabbed a magazine from the waiting room."

She smiled at me, and we both piled into the car, waiting for the good doctor to emerge.

_19_

The phone call was not unexpected, but it rattled Raymond Benjamin nonetheless. He'd been sitting in his loft, sipping a glass of pinot noir, from the Argyle wineries, 2005 vintage. There were few things that beat a glass of red and a cigarette at night. Perhaps a little Coltrane. Getting a phone call from this number ruined all of it.

He recognized the area code and extension immediately, and as soon as they appeared in the caller-ID display, Benjamin knew there was a problem. Petrovsky was only supposed to call if there was an emergency. And Benjamin made it very clear about what constituted an emergency.

He answered the phone. "Doctor," Ray said. "There'd better be a fucking good reason for this."

Raymond Benjamin listened as Dmitri Petrovsky filled him in on what had occurred at the hospital that day. He ended the conversation by saying he'd watched the two people—Henry Parker and Amanda Davies—leave the hospital. Only, when they left, they didn't drive away. In fact, they'd been sitting in their car for several hours. Petrovsky and Benjamin came to the same conclusion: they were planning to follow the doctor when he left work.

When Ray Benjamin hung up the phone, he sat there for a moment, thinking. Then he got up, tossing the rest of his glass into the sink, stubbing out his cigarette in the ashtray. He called Vince and told him to be at the garage in fifteen minutes. Ray had a lot of phone calls to make.

First he called the house. The couple took it as well as he expected. He told them they'd prepared for a day like this. And if they kept up their end of the deal, it would all be worth it. And if they didn't, he only needed to remind them of the photograph.

When everything was in motion, and Petrovsky confirmed that Parker was still at Yardley, Ray Benjamin went to the garage. Vince was waiting for him. Vincent Cann was a tall, slender man of thirty-eight. His jet-black hair was slicked back, his face clean-shaven as always. A pair of designer sunglasses sat on his face. He nodded when he saw Benjamin approaching.

"Clusterfuck, ain't it, boss?"

Ray answered by not answering at all.

They piled into the car. Ray opened his window a crack. The younger man was chewing gum, his jaws working overtime. Ray reached into his pocket and pulled out a fresh pack of Chesterfields. He depressed the electric lighter, unwrapped the pack, stuck the cig in his mouth and waited.

Vince said, "Should we get going?"

"Wait a second," the older man said. The lighter wasn't ready yet.

When the metal knob popped out, Ray took the end, pressed it to the tip and inhaled deeply. There was nothing like a good Chesterfield. When the butt was half smoked, a long finger of ash hanging off the end, Ray flicked it out the window.

"Clear your schedule for the next few days," Ray said to Vince as he pulled into traffic. "We're going to be busy cleaning this mess up, and there's not a lot of time."

20

Paulina arched her back, feeling the convulsions ripple through her body. She embraced the aches of pleasure, the slightest hint of pain as Myron Bennett raked his too-long nails down her stomach. She felt the final shudder of orgasm, the sweat dripping down her chest, waiting until everything was calm before finally becoming still. Paulina looked down. She was still wearing her bra, a slight puddle of moisture collecting in between the cups.

Gathering herself, Paulina climbed off Myron, taking one more glimpse at his naked body, his erection like a flag of surrender. The boy had a beautiful body, that's for sure, and though nobody would ever know of their tryst, it secretly thrilled her to know she'd just fucked a man thousands of women would ditch their husbands and 2.4 children for.

She located her underwear, snagged the band on her shoe, kicked it into her hands and headed for the bathroom.

"Hey," Myron called out as Paulina groped her way to the bathroom door. "I didn't come yet!"

"Nobody's watching if you want to finish yourself off," she said, closing the bathroom door. Paulina looked at herself in the mirror. Her mascara was streaked. She ran the faucet and washed it off. She looked at her breasts, felt a twinge of sadness, noticed they were sagging slightly more than she remembered. For years Paulina had taken care of her body, spending countless hours at the gym, countless dollars on every treatment under the sun. But aging happened to everyone, even women who were born to fight everything. Push-up bras did wonders to enhance her natural cleavage, but nobody could fight Father Time, especially since he had gravity on his side. She thought about having them done, wondered if it was an outpatient procedure. The last thing she needed was to be out of work a day or two, then come with them *enhanced.* Boob jobs were only worth it if no one knew you'd had one.

She could hear Myron moving about in the bedroom. She heard the sound of his zipper, laughed to herself that he was too frustrated to finish the job. Myron was a nice treat, and thankfully she'd never have to see him again. At least not in person.

In Sunday's edition of the *Dispatch,* Paulina would be running a lengthy article about Myron's decade-long affair with Mitsy Russell Henshaw, wife of billionaire venture capitalist Richard Henshaw. Richard Henshaw had been a longtime critic of the *Dispatch,* specifically the paper's editor-in-chief, Ted Allen. It was what Allen called a "have your cake and eat it, too" story. It was both a juicy bit of gossip that would sell papers, while accomplishing the goal of humiliating one of Ted's most vocal enemies. Paulina figured it only fair that if she was going to report the piece, she deserved a piece of the cake, too.

Though Myron was in his late thirties and no longer in the kind of shape that had secured him deals as an underwear model in the nineties—the abs a little softer, the arms not quite as sinewy—he was still a striking bachelor, the kind of man that would turn heads and make very wealthy women think very bad thoughts.

She had interviewed him for three hours, at the end of which Paulina offered to buy him a drink. To make things a little more personal, she said, rinse off the professional. And when they were in the comfort of a pair of martinis, she let Myron know that as long as she was putting her keyboard out, he'd be putting out, too. And so here she was, room 1250 at the W Hotel, the beauty of her exorbitant expense account allowing her the beauty of Myron Bennett.

Yet as much as she'd savored the night's pleasures and would enjoy the media circus surrounding Myron's affair, she'd be glad to get back to work on the real story that had kept her juiced the past few months. Underwear models came and went. It was a rare occasion that you could do something that *mattered*. And in just a matter of weeks, she'd be ready to bring Jack O'Donnell down like a house of cards. And with Jack, the veneer that was the *Gazette* would tumble as well. And that kind of satisfaction would last longer than any orgasm.

Cinching up her robe as she left the bathroom, Paulina took her purse from her wallet and flipped a twenty at Myron. The crumpled bill landed sadly on the pillow. Myron stood there staring at it. He was topless in his jeans, searching around for his shirt. He looked at the money, confused, then looked up and down at Paulina as if she were hanging in a freezer.

"You have the most beautiful tits," he said, a sultry grin on his face that made Paulina feel like retching.

"Please," she said. "Save it for the women who give a shit."

"What, one party and you get all cold on me? It wasn't good for you, beautiful?"

"Ugh, don't call me that. I'm sure Muffy or Tiffani or whatever rich bitch you're going to bang tomorrow night will love that ooey-gooey shit. You're a good lay, Myron. I appreciate it. But enough of the honeydoll, baby stuff. I'm a grown woman, you're a grown man, now help me find my shirt."

"It's under the bed, doll." He smiled at Paulina's grimace. She glanced under the bed, came up with a wrinkled blue shirt. She nodded toward the twenty on the bed.

"Take it."

"What's that for?"

"Whatever you want. A taxi. A beer. Doesn't matter."

He looked at the money. "Really, you don't have to."

"Listen, I spent the better part of an entire day talking to you and listening to the most boring shit on earth. I listened to you whine about your mean parents, your crummy job, how nobody will hire you as a model anymore. And I know you have less money in the bank than you have brains up in that head of yours. I don't think you'll say no to cab fare. So just say thank-you and go home."

He watched her for a moment, looked at the money. "Thank you," he said. "But you don't have to be a bitch about it."

Paulina's mouth dropped, a startled laugh escaping her lips. "Bitch? You call me a bitch because, what, I just repeated what you've been blabbing about all night? If you don't like hearing the whole, cold, hard, clean truth, just continue to delude yourself. Facts are facts. Nobody wants to hire a forty-year-old has-been when twenty years old can be bought for less, and without the baggage. And if you didn't fuck Mitsy for a decade, you'd keep that irrelevant streak of yours going. So you don't want to believe the truth? Then, buddy, don't read the newspaper. But if you want a reality check, you little baby, what I say shouldn't hurt you any more than your life hurts you."

"See," Myron said. "That's what I mean. Most women, when you give them an orgasm, they don't treat you like you're a piece of, a, a dust ball or a termite or something. Something they can pick up and throw in the trash like it didn't exist."

"Listen, Myron. You're a sweet guy. But sweet guys get as much out of life as a little teacup puppy that someone carries around in their purse. You get fed when your master wants to feed you, but pretty soon you're a nuisance and not quite as much fun to look at. If you want more out of life than that, you have to take it. If that means being a bitch, well, I'd rather be a bitch than a pussy."

Myron stared at her. "I'm looking forward to reading the article."

Paulina nodded. "It'll be a good one, I promise you that much. I'll make sure a copy of the *Dispatch* is delivered to you first thing Sunday morning." Then she strode across the room until she was nearly mouth to mouth with Myron. "And if you so much as mention this night to anyone, I'll run a correction on Monday about your chronic herpes outbreaks."

"My what?"

"Exactly."

"Even you wouldn't stoop so low," Myron said, though he looked unconvinced.

"Try me," Paulina replied. "I love it when people think they're calling my bluff."

Myron nodded, put his shirt on, found his shoes. He thanked Paulina, grabbed the twenty and left. Paulina stood there in a room full of rumpled sheets, the air stinking of sweat and sex. Then she gathered up her belongings, went outside and caught a cab home.

21

By three o'clock, my legs were growing stiff. We'd watched countless people arrive and leave Yardley since that morning, with no sign of Dmitri Petrovsky. We'd taken turns going in to the cafeteria for cups of coffee and bathroom breaks, doing everything we could to stay alert without going insane, but I was growing impatient. And even worse, worried.

Doctors came and went, but nobody who looked like Petrovsky.

At four o'clock, Amanda asked, "Do you think we might have missed him?"

I shook my head. "I hope not. Let's make sure."

I took out my cell phone, called the Yardley switchboard, asked to be connected to Pediatrics. When a woman's voice picked up, I asked if Dr. Petrovsky would be available for any more appointments today.

"I'm sorry, sir, he's got two more patients scheduled for this afternoon, then he'll be out again until Monday."

"Do you have any idea what time he'll be finished with his patients?"

"No, sir, I'm sorry, but if you want to come in next week I'd be happy to schedule you for an appointment."

"No, thanks, I'll call back later." I hung up. "He's still there, but probably not for much longer."

Amanda nodded. She began to rub her shoulders.

"You okay?" I asked.

"Just a little stiff."

"Can I do anything to help?"

"Nah, thanks, though."

For a moment I had an ache to reach out, put my arm around her and rub her shoulders myself. Not too long ago it wouldn't have been a big deal at all, just something else that happened over the normal day of a relationship. Small gestures like that in the end meant so much, and it was only when they ended that I realized their significance.

"Henry, look," Amanda suddenly said, pointing in the direction of the entrance. "There he is."

Sure enough, Dmitri Petrovsky was leaving Yardley. He was easily identifiable with his bushy beard, ambling gait. He'd changed out of his hospital whites and was wearing a bulky overcoat, carrying a stuffed briefcase. He trudged through the parking lot as our eyes followed him. He stopped for a moment to yell at another motorist whose Saab edged a little too close, and for a moment I worried that the argument would escalate and our whole plan would be shot. Thankfully, after a heated exchange and a middle-finger gesture that left the driver steaming, Petrovsky continued walking, eventually stopping at a dark blue Nissan.

"Do me a favor," I said. "Take my tape recorder out of my bag." She did so. "Now turn it on."

She clicked the record button.

I said, "I want to record the directions. Just in case."

"Smart," Amanda said.

I started the engine, waited until I saw the brake lights

on Petrovsky's car turn red before I edged out of the parking space. I turned the corner of our row just as Petrovsky finished backing out. I allowed another car to move in front of us as all three vehicles headed for the exit.

"What if he sees us?" Amanda said.

"I don't know," I said truthfully. "Let's just hope he doesn't."

Petrovsky pulled up to the exit and put his right-turn signal on. He made the right, and the car in front of us turned left. I put my right blinker on, waited until Petrovsky's Nissan was about thirty yards away, then I pulled onto the exit ramp and began to follow the doctor.

Petrovsky kept an even speed as he circled the exit ramp that led away from Yardley. I stayed far enough behind that it would be tricky for him to see me in his rearview mirror. Neither Amanda nor I spoke. We were both focused on the road, the car and what would happen next.

When the ramp came to an end, Petrovsky kept on straight and merged onto the freeway. He pulled into the left lane; I took the middle, kept pace three cars behind. There was still light in the sky, sundown not yet for another hour, so I was able to make out his car pretty clearly. The hum of our engine seemed as loud as a bullhorn as we kept pace, threatening to give us away.

After a few miles, Petrovsky drifted over to the middle lane, then turned on his right-turn signal and headed toward a sign that read Exit 62. I relayed this to the tape recorder. When he pulled into the right lane, I allowed a silver Mercedes to do the same and I pulled in behind it. I took the exit ramp behind both cars, watching Petrovsky closely. I could make out the man hunched over the steering wheel, felt lead in my stomach as I prayed we were being cautious, keeping out of sight.

I followed his car down a one-lane highway, our speeds decreasing as the road became more residential. The doctor was steadfastly observing the thirty-five-mile-an-hour speed limit. The silver Mercedes was only a buffer for a few minutes, as it peeled into a strip mall soon after, leaving our car as the only one behind Petrovsky.

We followed him down this road for some time. Eventually the sun began to set. The sky grew darker. Soon all I could make out of Petrovsky's car were the taillights. The faint hum of the tape recorder was the only noise in the car. My pulse was quickening. I had no idea how this night would end.

About twenty minutes later, Petrovsky turned on his left blinker and pulled off onto a narrow street. I had to follow, had to hope it was too dark for him to recognize our car or see me behind the wheel. I was still about thirty yards behind him, but when his Nissan made another right and then a left within seconds of each other, I had to speed up before losing him among the turns.

"There's no way he doesn't know we're following him," Amanda said, her voice quiet, fearful. "No way."

I said nothing. Just spoke the directions into the recorder and kept driving.

We passed through streets lined with houses, lamps illuminating rows of homes. Most of them were in disrepair, casting an aura of poverty, carelessness, hopelessness. I tried not to look at them, focused on the car in front of us, felt cold sweat beading down my back. Fear and adrenaline coursed through me, and I wondered how much longer this chase would last.

Then Petrovsky made a right onto another road, this one dimly lit. I couldn't see any houses on either side. There were no lamps. It was just him and us.

I glimpsed the street sign, stated into the recorder, "Turned right onto Huntley Terrace."

Huntley Terrace was a narrow road. Once we'd driven a few miles, we passed by a few houses spaced sporadically apart, driveways hidden behind thick brush and wooden fences. There were no streetlights, no road signs. We were still twenty yards behind Petrovsky, but we were the only cars traveling this road. By this point, the gig was up.

"Henry," Amanda said. "What is that?"

I squinted my eyes, felt my stomach lurch as I saw that we were approaching a pair of metal double gates up ahead. The were bracketed by a brick wall that encircled the property within. The woods were thick on either side. I couldn't see anything beyond them.

"Oh, fuck," I said. Petrovsky had slowed down as he approached.

"What now?" Amanda asked.

"I don't know."

"I'm scared," she said. She turned to me. In her eyes I could tell she knew what I was thinking. We had to keep going.

I slowed the car down, pulled to a stop and put the car in Park. I waited to see what Petrovsky would do next. His car stopped at the gates. It stayed there for close to a minute, then I heard the sound of metal screeching as the gates swung inward. They did not look like they enclosed a residential area. They were protecting a single home. Was this where Petrovsky lived?

When the gates were open, the doctor pulled onto a gravel road and then disappeared out of sight. I waited, unsure of what to do.

And after a minute of waiting, I realized something strange.

The gates hadn't closed.

They were wide open.

Whoever was inside those gates was waiting for us.

"Too late to turn back," I said.

I put the car into Drive and slowly approached the gates. I still couldn't see anything beyond them, but as I got closer I could make out a red hue around the bend. Definitely Petrovsky's brake lights.

I drove through the gates, half expecting a Sonny Corleone sneak attack. But we passed through without anything out of the ordinary. I made the turn, then jumped as I heard the metal sounds again.

The gates were closing behind us.

"We shouldn't be here," Amanda said. "We should go."

"We can't now," I said. "Let's just see what's what."

As I continued down the path, Petrovsky's Nissan came into view. It was parked at the end of a driveway. The driveway was next to a house. It was shrouded in darkness, but there was just enough light from the moon to illuminate the seven-foot-high brick wall surrounding the entire property. It confused me. The wall wasn't high enough that an adult would have a problem climbing over it. I also noticed that every tree on the property was at least ten or twenty feet from the fence. There were no limbs that could reach the fence. It had been clearly built to keep someone smaller from getting out.

Down the driveway, I could see Petrovsky. He was standing next to his car. Hands in his pockets. He was waiting for us.

I pulled up close until I was directly behind the Nissan, then put the car into Park and shut the engine off.

"Stay here," I said to Amanda.

"The hell with that," she said, unbuckling her seat belt.

We both stepped out of the car. Petrovsky was standing in the middle of the driveway. He did not move as we approached. He did not seem surprised to see us.

As we got closer, I could see that the doctor was trembling slightly. His hands were in his pockets, his body too rigid. As I got closer, a wave of fear coursed through me. I saw that Petrovsky was shaking. The man was afraid.

"Dr. Petrovsky," I said. "It's Henry Parker. I know you saw us following you. I'm sorry to approach you under these circumstances, but I have more questions."

"Yes, Mr. Parker," the doctor said, his voice low, remorseful. "I am very sorry, too."

I heard a faint rustle come from behind us, then there was a sharp pain in my leg. Before I could shout, the gravel of the driveway came hurtling up to meet me, and then everything swam away.

22

I woke up groggy, with pain in my head and my leg. It took a moment for my eyes to adjust to the faint crack of light coming from a doorway on the far side of the room that was otherwise pitch-black. I was standing up. I was shirtless, my bare torso cold against a metal pole behind me. My head pounded, and when I tried to move I realized my hands were bound above me, my legs bound below. My arms were bound and tied to what felt like a metal pipe. I groped around, felt that the pipe went straight back into the brick wall behind me. My feet were bound behind the same pipe. I wriggled but it did no good.

Suddenly my eyes flew open. Amanda. Oh, God, where was she?

I struggled against the bonds, but I couldn't see anything, couldn't reach the rope that bound my hands.

Then a voice spoke out from the darkness, and I stopped moving.

"Don't worry, she's fine. I'm sorry my associate had to restrain you, but I promise it's for your own good." The voice was gruff, older, slightly raspy. A smoker's voice.

"Who are you?" I said. "Come over here so I can see you, asshole."

"Listen to you, talking as though you're holding all the cards. When your hand was folded before you even woke up."

I heard a spark, like a match striking flint, and then a small orange flame lit up the darkness. The flame rose until I heard a sucking sound. The flame lit the end of a cigarette, and with a puff was blown out.

I could see the cigarette about ten feet from me, and with each inhalation I caught the outline of a man's face. I couldn't see much detail, but he looked to be in his late fifties. Harsh light to go with the harsh line. He just sat there, sucked his cigarette and said nothing.

"Come on!" I shouted. "What do you want?"

"What do I want," the man said. He flicked away the cigarette and stood up. He must have turned on a light switch, because suddenly an overhead lamp cast a soft glow over the room. I made out what I could. I was in what looked to be some sort of basement. Bare cement walls and a tiled floor. There were no windows I could see. The room wasn't dingy, though, and in fact I was surprised that it appeared to be rather well maintained. A plush leather sofa rested in front of a television set, and a long-forgotten treadmill sat adorned with boxes and discarded clothes. If this was a prison or interrogation room, it wasn't the most intimidating one. The man approached me, took another cigarette from his pocket, lit it and took a deep drag.

Then he approached me, plucked the cigarette from his lips and held it out.

"Want a puff?"

"Yeah, nothing satisfies me more than sucking on a butt that was just in some strange asshole's mouth."

"You sure? It's a Chesterfield."

"Gee, now, that makes a difference. Go screw yourself."

The man shrugged, took another puff.

"I haven't smoked another brand in over thirty years. You know, you can enjoy the pleasures of so many things in life without knowing where it came from. Who made it. Thirty years ago, I would have taken a beating before I smoked. Now I can't get enough of 'em. Ironic, 'swhat it is. That delicious burn inside your lungs, just makes me want to close my eyes, savor the feeling. My ex-wife always asked why I spent so much time reading about crap like that and never listened to her. I'd say, baby, because one's interesting, and one ain't."

I stayed silent. The longer he talked, the longer I stayed alive.

"Chesterfields started to become popular back in the day when Arthur Godfrey ended his radio program by saying, 'This is Arthur buy-'em-by-the-carton Godfrey!' Since the program was sponsored by Chesterfield, pretty soon that's all anyone wanted to smoke. The nonfiltered Chesterfields were popular during Vietnam, allegedly the strongest nonnarcotic stimulant in the country. The government dropped Chesterfields into the jungle by the thousands. And the common man, he figured whatever was good enough for the fighting men and women of this country was good enough for him."

The man stepped into the light, and I finally got a better look at him.

His graying hair was full, skin worn and weatherbeaten. The crow's-feet at his eyes actually made him look handsome, like one of those blue-jeaned cowboys who spent their days on oil rigs, the kind that actually needed a Chevy flatbed. He was lean, about five foot eleven, wearing a dark green T-shirt and jeans. There was a thin scar about an inch long that ran down his right cheek. It was a faint line, slightly jagged, as though it hadn't been stitched up right. He took another pull, let the ash hang on the end for a long while smoldering before tapping it onto the floor.

My heart hammered in my chest. My wrists ached, and the pins and needles in my feet let me know they wouldn't be much help.

"Where is she?" I said.

"You need to be more trusting," the man said. "I told you she's fine. So you should believe that she is fine. I'm not gonna lie to you, Henry. You do me the same courtesy, and things are gonna work out just splendid for Ms. Davies. But let's just focus on the here and now. You and me. Got it?"

"Who are you?" I said.

"Who I am isn't as important as what I have to offer," he said.

"I don't want anything from you," I spat. "People know I'm here. That door's gonna get busted in any second and I'm gonna laugh as they haul your ass away."

"Really...they're coming for you, huh? Who, the CIA? FBI? Batman? Guess you wouldn't mind then if I leave your girl alone for a few weeks. She won't need food or water since, you know, they're *coming* for her."

"You're making a mistake," I said. "She doesn't belong here."

"Well, she's here. No changing that now. Anyway, back to what I was saying. I have something to offer you, Henry, and if you're as smart as I think you are you'll take this offer."

"What is it?" I said.

"It's simple, really," the man said, taking another puff. "I need you to tell me everything the good doctor told you and everything you know about the kids. Spare no detail. It's very important you lay all your cards on the table. And if you do just that, and I believe you, behind door number one will be your girlfriend's life. You spill, she lives. You don't spill, her blood does. Simple as that."

"I'll take the offer," I said, "because we don't know anything. Petrovsky didn't say a word to us. Now, let us go."

"Oh, come on, Henry, you think it's that easy? You think that's it? Nah, we can get some more out of you."

He took the cigarette from his mouth. Looked at the filtered end.

"Chesterfields," he said. "Just about heaven. Can't find the unfiltered bastards anywhere nowadays, but smoke enough of these and they do the trick."

"Hope that lung cancer acts mighty quick," I said.

"If it gets me, it gets me," he said. "But I'll go out with a smile."

A spark fell off the end of the butt. I watched it flutter to the ground. I moved my wrists around, tried to feel the pipe where my hands were tied, sliding my fingers back and forth out of view until my thumb caught on something. A piece of metal. Something jutting out from the pipe.

The man reached into his pocket, brought out his wallet. He pulled out a one-dollar bill. Held it up in front of me. Then he took the lit cigarette between his thumb and forefinger. Slowly he brought the cigarette to the bill. There was a crackling sound as the lit end burned a perfect circle through the paper.

When the cigarette had passed through, he held up the bill, looked at me through the hole, smiled. "Peekaboo, I see you."

He walked toward me, still holding the lit cigarette. As

he got closer, the light illuminated the man more. I began to shiver, my bare torso shaking. Then I noticed something that nearly made me gag. Covering the man's arms were a road map of small, white marks. Scars. Perfectly round. They were cigarette burns. And there were dozens of them.

"So what did Petrovsky tell you?" he said, his voice frighteningly calm.

"I told you, nothing. Leave us alone."

He scratched his chin, looked at me. "Hmm...no."

He took another step forward, leaned down and pressed the lit end of the cigarette against my chest.

I screamed as I heard the sound of burning, waves of pain shooting through me as I bucked and tried to kick to no avail. The pain was horrific. I hoped I would pass out.

Finally the man removed the cigarette from my skin. Then he leaned over and blew gently on the spot where he'd just burned me.

"That's gonna leave a mark," he said.

I was panting. I could felt sweat pouring down my body, getting into my eyes. I felt around where my hands were bound, found that piece of metal I'd felt before. I rubbed it with my thumb. It was a screw attached to a bolt. The end of the screw jutted out from the metal about half an inch. Just maybe...

I slowly moved my wrists until the half-inch screw was fitted snugly inside one of the loops of knot that bound my wrists. I moved it slowly up and down, back and forth, trying to loosen the knot, to create some slack.

The man tossed his cigarette onto the floor, stubbed it out with his shoe. "I hate to waste one, but I don't think you taste quite as good on the end of a butt as tobacco does."

My breath was ragged, but I tried to focus. I gently

tugged down on my wrist bonds, felt the reassuring pull that the screw was fastened inside the knot. I began to work it more, continuously pressing my wrists against the metal to wedge it in even farther. I nearly gasped when I realized the screw was in as far as it would go. I'd created a hole in the knot. Now all I had to do was make it bigger.

"Do you smoke?" the man asked.

"Fuck you," I said.

"That's a brand I'm unfamiliar with. But since you seem to be full of answers now, I'll ask again. What did Petrovsky tell you?"

"He told me your mother's a whore and your father liked to dress up like Raggedy Ann for Christmas."

The man sighed deeply. I didn't care. The longer we played this game the more time I had. I felt the knot begin to loosen, and soon I was able to slip my index finger inside the knot hole. I pulled down on the screw, worked the loop with my finger, felt it began to slip more. I couldn't let him notice, so I did it slowly. Methodically.

My chest hurt like hell, but I blocked it out. Amanda was somewhere in this house, and even if I did talk, there was no way I trusted this guy to let her live. Rule number one, when a sociopath makes a promise, believe the opposite.

"First time I got burned by one of these," the man said, "I was serving time up in Attica. The guards, *hoo,* man, the guards. They sure liked to have their fun with us. One of the prisoners got out of line, talked back, caused a ruckus at the mess hall, they'd take a lit butt to the guy's armpit. Maybe the bottom of his feet. Something sweet like that. Something that wouldn't go away so fast. At least it would smell sweet after they got done with you. I guess you can see they did a little number on my arms here. Fifty-two, if I counted right, and I won't even get into the rest of my body. 'Course, one time they burnt my arches so bad I couldn't walk for a week. So first thing I did when we got a hold of that place? When us boys took over that prison back in '71? I took a cig, lit the mother up, and stuck it in that same man's eye until it started smoking."

I heard the strike of another match, and he lit another cigarette. Another Chesterfield.

"Did you know," he said, taking a long drag, "that the human hand alone has more than nine thousand nerve endings and six hundred pain sensors? And most of that is concentrated in the fingertips?"

"Yeah, I learned that back in health class."

"What do you think it would feel like to experience mind-numbing pain in the most sensitive area of your body? Do you think you'd enjoy that? Better yet, do you think Ms. Davies would enjoy that?"

I couldn't help but think about the scars already on my hand, from when a madman played butcher shop with it a while back. I certainly wasn't aching for more.

I tugged harder, felt my finger slip through one of the rope's cords. Soon I was able to fit two, then three fingers inside, and I slowly unraveled the rope. I grabbed the end gently before it could fall, but my hands were free. My feet, though, were another matter, and there was no way I could get to them without Chesterfield man noticing. Unless…

"See, if you don't answer my question, we're going to find out just how loud you and your friend can scream. And trust me, nobody will be able to hear you."

"It can't be any louder than you scream when your 'associate' sticks his finger up your ass."

The man frowned, again sucked down the cig, leaving a long ash dangling from the tip.

"Come on, dickhead," I said. "Let's see what you got."

The man looked at me, pissed off and confused. "Let's see if you're this much fun in a minute."

He placed the cigarette between his thumb and forefinger, then reached up with his free hand to steady mine before he burned off my fingertips. As he raised the cigarette, I took a deep breath and blew the long piece of ash directly into his face.

It erupted in a cloud of gray smoke, and the man hacked and coughed and clawed at his eyes.

Before he could take a step back, I pulled off the bonds around my wrists, wound up and backhanded him across the face. He went sprawling across the floor. The cigarette skittered away and went out.

Frantically I bent over and began undoing the bonds at my feet. They were tight, but soon I was able to loosen them. Just then the man stood up, blood leaking from a cut across his cheek. He had fire in his eyes as he ran straight toward me. At that moment I pulled the bonds away from my feet, sidestepped the man and shoved his head against the metal pipe. There was a sickening thud as he bounced off it, then crumpled to the floor in a heap.

I was wobbly standing up. I heard a grunt, saw the man begin to push himself up. There was hatred in his eyes. I didn't hesitate.

I ran forward and kicked him in the head as hard as I could. The breath left him as he lay there, motionless.

As I tried to get the blood flowing back to my feet, I noticed the glint of metal coming from a key ring in his pocket. There were three keys on it. I picked it up, ran for the door. Unsurprisingly, it was locked. I took turns inserting each key inside, and on the third one it clicked home. I twisted the knob, opened the door and prayed Amanda was all right. I glanced back, saw the man unmoving but still breathing steadily. Then I braced myself for whatever horrors awaited in the rest of this house.

But when I ran up the stairs to the main floor, I was shocked to see that I wasn't being held in some dungeon. Instead, I was standing in the middle of what looked like the foyer of a typical suburban house.

"What the hell...?" I whispered.

The hardwood floors had been recently sanded and polished, and the carpeting on the stairs was white and clean. Several framed paintings hung from the walls. A crystal chandelier hung above me, and a family room with a large-screen television branched off to the left. There was a doll with braided hair lying on the floor, next to what looked like a scattered set of a child's building blocks. Everything was clean. I didn't know what to make of it.

"Amanda!" I yelled. There was no response.

I sprinted to the other end of the hall, then took the stairs two at a time to the upper floor.

I ran down a narrow hall. There were three doors, both closed. I opened the first one. It was a bathroom. Hand soaps. Clean towels. No window. No Amanda.

I approached the other door. Pushed it. It opened into what looked like a master bedroom. A king-size bed sat in the center, with a floral comforter cleanly tucked in. Oddly there were no photos anywhere, as though the place had been disinfected of humanity.

I looked around. Didn't see anything.

Then I went to the other door. Stopped in front of it. This one was different. It was painted white like the others,

but the paint seemed duller. I touched the surface, immediately recoiled. The other doors were wooden. This one
was metal. And I knew right away that one of the keys on
my chain would open the dead bolt.

I thrust the key inside, got it on the first twist, but then
froze when I heard someone coming up the stairs.

The lock unlatched and I pushed the door open.

And then I was standing in what looked like the dream
room of any young girl. There were toys everywhere.
Coloring books. A large dollhouse filled with tiny furniture. Tapes and CDs and games were stacked high in a
corner. Pink wallpaper, and every book a child could ever
want to read. And there, sitting on a made bed, her face a
mess of fright and relief, was Amanda.

She jumped up and threw her arms around my chest. I
winced as she pressed on the cigarette burn, then took her
arm and said, "We need to go. Right now."

Then I noticed something. On the floor. A small scrap
of paper. I picked it up, unfolded it. It was a receipt. It was
from a store called Toyz 4 Fun. I clenched my jaw. At that
moment I knew where we were. I knew what this house
was.

Panic welled inside me as I shoved the receipt into my
pocket, grabbed Amanda's hand as we went for the door,
still slightly ajar. I heard someone running down the hall,
shouting, "Ray, where the hell are you, buddy?"

I waited until the footsteps were right outside, then I
slammed the heavy metal door closed as hard as I could.
There was an audible *oomph* as whoever was on the other
side was knocked flat off his feet.

I flung open the door and ran past, my heart hammering when I saw that the man I'd just knocked down had a
gun in his right hand.

We sprinted downstairs and toward the front door. Turned the knob. It was locked. One more key left.

I inserted the last key in the lock, let out a breath when it caught, then turned the handle and opened the door to the outside.

As soon as we stepped onto the front porch, Amanda let out a bloodcurdling scream. There was a body in the driveway. It was lying in a pool of blood. The beard gave it away. It was Dmitri Petrovsky, and he was very dead.

"Run!" I shouted.

We ran down the driveway, and I recognized that we were in the exact same place that we'd cornered Petrovsky. The high brick walls and trees obscured the view beyond the house. There was nobody to hear us scream.

We sprinted around the bend, wind whistling past us, and saw the metal gates up ahead.

They were closed. And I had no keys left.

When we reached the brick wall, I knelt down, cupped my hands and said, "Climb on."

Amanda stepped onto my hands.

"One, two, *three*."

I heaved up as she jumped. Her hands caught the rim of the wall. I pushed from below as Amanda pulled herself up, managing to straddle her legs across the wall.

"Come on!" she shouted.

Just as I got ready to jump, I heard a loud bang and a chunk of brick exploded right beside me.

"Come on, Henry, they're shooting at us!"

I jumped up, managed to get hold of the wall. Amanda gripped my wrists and began to pull. I got a small foothold in the chunk of wall that'd been blown out, then pushed off and hoisted myself up. Another shot rang out, and brick flew apart right where my foot had been.

We toppled over the wall, landed on the other side in a tangled mess. I leaped to my feet, helped Amanda up. Then we ran as fast as we could, until the woods swallowed us.

We arrived panting at the road we'd turned off of when we followed Petrovsky. Huntley Terrace. It was dark out. I had no idea where we were or what day it was.

"Come on," I said, taking Amanda's hand again. I thought back to the last time this happened, the last time we were both running for our lives. Back then Amanda was fleeing with a man she didn't know. This time, for better or worse, she knew what she'd gotten into.

We jogged down the dark road, continually looking over our shoulders to see if we were being followed. I heard nothing, saw nothing. My body felt numb. I was still shirtless, and my side ached. Amanda suddenly stopped, put her hand on my chest.

"Is that a burn mark?" she said.

"We don't have time," I panted.

Then out of the darkness a pair of headlights appeared. My eyes widened, and I ran forward waving my hands like a crazy person. I was in the middle of the road, and I only prayed the driver could see well enough not to run me over.

It was a gray Cadillac. It pulled to a stop a yard in front of me. I ran to the driver's-side window, gasping for air. The driver was a woman of about forty, a DVD from Blockbuster on her front dashboard.

"Don't…don't hurt me," she said. Her eyes were frightened. I could only imagine the sight in front of her.

"Please," I said, "my friend and I were attacked. If you could just take us away from here and call the police… Please, they're trying to kill us."

She reached for the shift, prepared to drive away, then saw Amanda huddled next to me, shivering in the lights of her car.

A minute later we were in the backseat of the Cadillac, heading away from one nightmare.

Then I felt the receipt in my pocket, and knew that another nightmare had just begun.

23

The police station was cold. Nobody had gone out of their way to offer Amanda or me a blanket or a drink or anything else to settle our nerves. I was wearing a blue workshirt with the name "Bill" stitched across the front. One of the detectives had given it to me. I didn't want to know where it came from, but didn't get the feeling Bill was looking too hard for it.

Ironically the only hospital within driving distance was Yardley. After the kind Vanessa Milne picked us up on the side of the road in her Cadillac, she took us right to the emergency room. The docs smeared the burn with something called Silvadene, then dressed it, told me to change the dressing every two hours and reapply the cream. It was just a first-degree burn. Would go away in a week, and hopefully wouldn't leave a scar. Amanda didn't have a scratch on her. But she was pissed off beyond belief.

A pair of detectives met us at Yardley, but they made us wait a good two hours before arriving. And even when they did, they didn't seem too keen to help. I found this odd, that two people had escaped from men who wanted to either torture or kill them, and they seemed about as interested as they would be in macroeconomics.

They asked several questions. First, why had we decided to follow Dmitri Petrovsky in the first place, and what we planned to ask him. I told them the truth. That Dmitri Petrovsky was linked to two children born in Hobbs County who'd disappeared, only to reappear several years later. I told them that we had a feeling based on his behavior at the pediatric clinic that he'd been withholding something. They asked for proof of misconduct. I told them we didn't have proof. That was the point of following him.

After we were released, the cops took us back to the Hobbs PD station. We were led through a cubicle farm of desks and eventually seated in a nondescript gray room with a metal table and chairs that were bolted to the floor. A pitcher of water sat in front of us, along with two glasses.

The same two cops joined us and sat down. They poured themselves two cups of water, drank them loudly. I had a strange feeling that we were being treated like the criminals here.

"Can we get some of that?" Amanda asked. The cops just stared at us. They had identical mustaches that rode straight across their upper lips, then down the sides of their mouths at a right angle. I got a gross mental image of them standing over a sink with a razor, shaving those 'staches in neat lines.

"You have any idea what this town is like now?" the fatter one asked. He had a crew cut and a neck full of angry jowls, like he'd recently graduated from the Mike Ditka finishing school. The one next to him was slightly trimmer, yet had the same scornful look in his eye. Between these two and the runaround I'd received from Lensicki earlier, it was tiresome and frustrating to see the lack of support from this department. "What's done is done, and now here you two come, harassing an upstanding member of our community. You should be ashamed of yourselves."

"Damn ashamed," the other cop agreed.

"You've got it all wrong," I said. "I just want to know why there's a doctor working at your hospital who knows two children that were kidnapped, and who ends up dead the same night we're held captive in some house in the middle of Hobbs County. The fact that all of this went down in your neck of the woods should, I don't know, make you just the least bit interested, I'd think."

"About this…captive thing," the fat one said. "I find it hard to believe that you followed this Russian doctor, as you claim, and then *you* end up being taken by some guy with a cigarette fetish? You're a reporter, right?"

"That's right," I said.

"Sure you're not looking to add a little spice to your story?"

"Go to that house and you'll see if I'm adding anything," I said angrily.

The thin one chimed in. "So you followed the doctor to his home, is that right? You waited in the hospital parking lot?"

"I don't know if it was his home," I said. "We just followed his car. In fact, I don't think he lived there at all. I think he knew we were following him, and probably did for a while. Wherever he led us wasn't his home, but he set us up."

The fat one, whom I would guess was playing bad cop, only the lines weren't really that clear, said, "You followed him into, let me go over your statement again, a gated residence off Huntley Terrace?"

"That's right," I said.

"You followed him into a gated community."

"No, it wasn't a gated community, just a home with a gate out front."

"And a brick wall surrounding the property."

"That's right."

"And *you* want us to investigate *him*." He paused, a scowl coming over his face. "Sounds to me like you two are the ones should be reprimanded."

"The gates *were* open," Amanda added. "And Petrovsky spoke to us when we got out of the car."

"That's when," the thin one said, "everything went, ahem, black. Right?"

"Right," I said. "They must have knocked us out or drugged us. I don't remember."

"And why did you follow Petrovsky to begin with?" Fatty said.

"We think he has knowledge about the kidnappings that took place over the past few years. He was the attending physician for the births of both Daniel Linwood and Michelle Oliveira. Both children disappeared and reappeared years later with no memory of their time gone missing."

"And why did you decide to follow the good doctor?" thin man said.

"When we first spoke to him at his office, he claimed to not know anything. It was a blatant lie." I paused, then added, "And I think there's been another kidnapping. In addition to Danny Linwood and Michelle."

"You fucking reporters," Ditka said. "Another kidnapping? You find two pieces of information got no connection, you put 'em together and make up some story 'bout how there's some big conspiracy. All just to sell a few newspapers, make a name for yourself. Do you have any proof of another kidnapping?"

"Proof? Not hard evidence, but…"

"Listen, fuckhead. Hobbs County is a nice town. I've lived here near twenty years. Now, ten years ago I might have said, yeah, we got some problems, not exactly the kind of place I'd want my kids growing up. But all that's different now. Things have changed. It's not right for you to go bringing up the bad times, because we're past that."

"Tell that to Dmitri Petrovsky."

"We will when we find him," the other cop said.

"Let's go right now," I said, standing up. "I'm pretty sure I remember how to get there. Us four, right now."

"Calm your horses, tough guy," Ditka said again. "We're not going anywhere."

We sat there in silence watching the cops drink water for ten minutes. Then right as I was about to grab the thing and douse Amanda and me with it, Wallace Langston entered, followed by Curt Sheffield. I'd never been happier to see anyone in my life.

"I got your message," Wallace said. "And I figured you could use a little backup."

The cops eyed Wallace with skepticism, but when they saw Curt standing there, all six foot three, two hundred sculpted pounds of him, they went right into bully mode once the bullies had been called on their bluff.

Wallace, happy to be good cop to Curt's badass one, passed out his business card to the cops.

"Gentlemen," he said. "My name is Wallace Langston, and Henry Parker is under my employ at the *New York Gazette.* Our legal counsel is on the way, but I do have some familiarity with legal rights, and unless you're holding Mr. Parker or Miss Davies for a crime, I'm going to ask you leave the room so we can speak in private. And then we plan to leave your care posthaste."

The cops conferred in a lame attempt at whispering, but we all heard every word. Since it was primarily lots of cursing under their breath, we didn't learn anything new, but they didn't seem particularly keen to grant Wallace's request. Yet when Curt stepped forward with his hands folded across his chest, they got up right quick and left the room.

As soon as Ditka and his buddy closed the door, I grabbed the pitcher and poured two glasses. We gulped them down in less time than it took Wallace to say, "Thirsty?"

Water dribbling down my chin, I said, "Yeah, thanks. Hope those assholes are better detectives than they are hosts."

"I don't think they're any worse detectives than you'll find in most departments," Curt said. "I get the feeling they're slacking off for a reason that doesn't involve apathy."

Wallace walked around to the other side of the table, pulled a chair out and sat down. He looked tired as he ran his hands through his thinning hair. Curt sat down, as well, much more at ease now that he didn't have to play bodyguard.

"Damn, it's fun to scare assholes," he said. "How you holding up, Henry?"

"My chest hurts like hell and other than getting handcuffed to a pipe and seeing the dead body of the doctor I planned to investigate for his involvement in several kidnappings, I'm doing just peachy."

"Amanda?" he said.

She said, "Hey, Curt. I'm okay." Her words betrayed her. Her eyes gave away the terror we'd just escaped.

"Bullshit, but you're one hell of a trouper, Amanda. You're lucky it's my day off, no way Carruthers would let me come up here to help your ass out on my normal shift. I expect major reciprocation. I mean *major* reciprocation."

"No problem," I said. "I can pull a few strings, get you in the gossip pages at the *Dispatch* for having a thirteen-inch prick or something."

"Friends like these," Curt said.

Amanda was still silent. I could tell she was upset, but there was a lot to choose from. If she was still scared or in shock from what happened last night, or from the fact our leads seemed to have shrunk, I couldn't tell. At some point I'd need time to talk to her.

Wallace said. "Henry, tell me, what the hell were you thinking?"

I was taken aback, said stupidly, "Sir?"

"I can't think of any reason for you to be up here. I spoke to the watch commander. He told me you claimed to be pursuing a Dr. Dmitri Petrovsky about his involvement or knowledge about the disappearances of Daniel Linwood and some girl named Michelle Oliveira. Last I recall, I didn't give you permission to be working this story. In fact, I distinctly remember telling you to stay the hell away from it."

"Sir, I know," I said. "But there is more to this case than we think. Michelle Oliveira disappeared and reappeared in the exact same way as Daniel Linwood. And we were able to confirm that Petrovsky was the attending pediatrician for both children. He's involved. We can be sure about that now. He set us up last night."

"And now, what, you go on stakeouts? You put on a surveillance detail? Who are you, Kojak?"

"No, sir."

"So did you not hear me the other day, Parker? Did you not understand me when I told you to work another story?"

I mumbled under my breath. Loud enough so that everyone at the table could hear me.

"I'm sorry, what was that, Henry?" Wallace said, folding his ear forward mockingly.

"I said nobody else gives a shit. That's why I do."

"I must have missed something," Wallace said. "Where do you get off saying nobody cares?"

"Look at this!" I yelled. "You want me off the story because Gray Talbot sticks his manicured nails into things. He wants the community to heal. And I'm getting the runaround worse in Hobbs County than I did from my dad, and that's saying something. These cops either don't give a shit, or just want to sweep everything under the carpet. And meanwhile, the parents of these poor kids have to deal with the fact that there are five years missing from their children's lives and everyone else is sitting around with their thumbs up their asses like it's a source of protein."

Wallace sat back, stunned for a moment. I caught my breath. Half expected him to fire me on the spot.

"You're wrong, Parker," he said. "We do care. But what's done is done. Those kids are never getting those years back. These kind of wounds need time to heal, and the longer we leave them open, the more gangrene sets in, both for the families and their communities. Hobbs County won't win any 'best place to raise your family' awards, but it's a long way from what it used to be. People in Meriden regrouped after Michelle Oliveira came back. They banded together. Made the town safer. A better place to live. I hate to say this, but that girl disappearing was the best thing that ever happened to that town. I think you can understand why folks aren't keen to reopen old wounds."

"Maybe these wounds are deeper than anyone knows," I said.

"And why do you think that?"

I dug into my pocket. Took out the receipt I found on

the floor in the room Amanda was kept in. Put it on the table, where it sat like a rancid piece of meat.

"What is that?" Wallace asked.

"See for yourself."

He reached across the table, picked it up, unfolded it, smoothed out the crinkles, read it. Then he dropped it back on the table.

"It's a receipt from a toy store for dollhouse accessories. So what?"

"It's from the Toyz 4 Fun store in White Plains," I said. "White Plains is about fifteen minutes from Hobbs County."

"So?"

"Look at the date," I said. Wallace picked the receipt up again, read it. His eyes squinted. I could tell he was starting to follow.

"This receipt was printed less than a week ago. Then it turns up in the house where Amanda and I follow Dr. Petrovsky to, the same house where we're held and nearly killed. This wasn't some ramshackle, broken-down tenement we're talking about. This place was in good condition."

"And there was a large dollhouse in one room," Amanda said. "A girl's room. Every toy you could ever want." Wallace's eyes jerked to her. She locked him dead-on. He turned away. Knew that whatever he thought of me, Amanda wouldn't bullshit him.

"That house was being used as some sort of detainment center," I said. "That brick wall, that gate, they weren't used to keep people from getting in. They were to keep people from getting out."

"Who?" Curt asked.

"Kids," I said. "The family that lived there was holding a child captive. And recently, too. Which is why I think there's been another kidnapping. Just like Daniel Linwood and Michelle Oliveira. Somebody just bought toys for a child that was being held in that very house. And they bought them recently."

"Jesus Christ," Wallace said. "You're sure you found this in that house?"

"Sure as the day is twenty-four hours."

Amanda said, "You could just say yes, you know."

"Yes," I said. "I'm sure."

"And I saw Henry take it," she added. "And I can vouch for what we saw there."

"We need to find out whose name that house is registered under," Wallace said. "We need to get the cops there to search the place. My goodness, if this is all true…"

"Does this mean I'm back on the story?" I asked.

"One step at a time, Parker," he said. I knew this was as good as a yes. "Right now, all we need to do is…"

Just then a loud commotion began outside the conference room. We turned around, could see cops running, grabbing equipment, heading out the door. They looked panicked.

"What the hell…?" Curt said.

We got up simultaneously and headed outside. Half a dozen cops jogged by us.

"What's going on?" Amanda asked nobody in particular. We saw the fat cop from earlier rushing past. Wallace managed to get his attention.

"Officer, what's going on?"

"Four-alarm blaze," he said. "Possible survivors trapped inside the building."

"Oh, God," Amanda said.

"Where?" Wallace asked.

"Not sure exactly," the cop said. "Somewhere off Huntley Terrace."

"Huntley Terrace," Amanda said. "Isn't that…?"

I nodded, a chill running through my blood. "That's the street where we followed Petrovsky."

Wallace stood rigid. "Come on," he said. There was urgency in his voice, but something else as well. Something scared.

We ran outside. Wallace led us to a brown Volvo. We piled in; he and Curt in the front, Amanda and I in the back. He pulled out of the lot and followed the caravan of HCPD police cars as they peeled out, sirens blaring.

The silence in the car was deafening. Nobody wanting to state what was clearly on all our minds. What we were all praying wouldn't be true.

After several miles the caravan made a right onto Huntley Terrace. Amanda nudged me. I nodded back to her.

I felt her hand take mine. And squeeze.

"This is where we were last night," I said.

Wallace just drove.

A few miles along Huntley Terrace, we noticed the flashing lights multiply. I heard the familiar siren of a fire truck. Then the horrible stench of smoke filled the car, and we could see a thick, black cloud rising above the treeline. We parked the car outside the road the cop cars had turned onto. There was a small wooden sign outside the gravel road that read "482." It had been too dark to see any signs the other night. We got out and began to tentatively walk down the road to see what was going on. There was shouting, cursing, and there were more sirens on the way.

My heart was hammering in my chest. We all stayed close together. And then there they were. The same metal gates we'd climbed over last night. Beyond that the very house where we'd barely escaped with our lives.

Only now the house was engulfed in a horrific plumage of red flames. Burning that home right to the very ground.

24

The minivan pulled into the parking lot at a quarter to four in the afternoon. Caroline watched as Bob Reed pushed open the driver's-side door, then paused a moment to let the muscles in his arm and shoulder stretch. He gingerly stepped out one foot at a time, then threw his arms back in an exaggerated stretch, yawning at the top of his lungs.

The were outside of some sort of hotel or motel. Caroline could see other people entering and exiting. She didn't know where they were or why they were here, only that Elaine and Bob had spent nearly the whole car ride in a chilly silence.

When Bob regained his composure, Elaine was out and opening the minivan's door. Caroline watched as Elaine unbuckled Patrick's seat belt, then picked her child up and held him fast in her arms. Caroline felt a longing as she watched this intimate act, and even though both Elaine and Bob smothered her with kisses and presents, they always felt somewhat odd, forced. Last night, when Elaine entered her room with the curt instructions to get ready for a long car trip, Caroline didn't know what to think. She was too confused to be scared, and she hadn't been in that house long enough to really miss it. After placing Patrick on the

ground, Elaine came around to her side. She stroked
Caroline's hair, her fingers gentle, and Caroline smiled at
the warmth of her fingertips. She gently kissed Caroline's
forehead, then turned her attention back outside.

"Mommy?" Patrick said.

"Hey, sweetie," Elaine said. "Did you have a good
nap?"

Patrick nodded, then buried his face back in her
shoulder as she leaned down. Elaine stroked his hair, that
strawberry-blond lock that confused Caroline. Neither
Bob nor Elaine had red hair. She'd asked Elaine how they
could have a boy with different color hair, and she just said,
God makes us all unique.

Elaine turned to Bob, who was digging a pack of gum
from his pocket, and said, "You want to get her?" Caroline
assumed she was the "her" being referred to.

Bob looked at Elaine, then turned toward the van, in no
real rush to say yes. Caroline had noticed that Bob had
become more and more reluctant to spend time with her
over the past few days. In the beginning he came into her
room often, even helped her set up that beautiful new dollhouse. But he'd withdrawn recently, and sometimes even
seemed afraid to touch her.

Thankfully, the coughing fits had passed. Bob and
Elaine seemed relieved at this. Bob had said something
strange that Caroline remembered.

We're supposed to take care of this girl, not kill her.

Elaine had marched out of the room, slammed the door
and didn't speak to him until dinner. And now they were
parked at some strange building, after having left that
house in a matter of minutes.

With a great sigh, Bob went around to the passenger
side, climbed in and unhooked Caroline from her harness.

His fingers weren't nearly as gentle, as if he were unpacking a box rather than handling a human being.

"Ow," Caroline said as one of Bob's fingers accidentally jabbed her ribs.

"Christ, Bob, she's not a piece of meat," Elaine reprimanded. "Be careful."

"Sorry," he muttered.

"Honey, make sure to bring Boo Boo. You don't want to lose him."

Caroline picked the small brown teddy bear off the seat and held it fast to her chest. That bear was the only thing she'd come with. Elaine had thrown together a bag of clothes, but the bear was the only thing she wanted.

It had a goofy smile and button eyes, fur that was soft to the touch. Out of all the presents the Reeds had bought her over the past few weeks, this was by far her favorite.

"Boo Boo," Caroline said. "He's scared. He wants to know where we are."

"Tell Boo Boo he's safe and not to worry," Elaine said. "And make sure he tells you the same thing."

Caroline wanted to believe Elaine, but there was something in her eyes that belied the truth.

Bob reached in and picked up both the girl and Boo Boo, carried them gently out of the van. Caroline blinked sleep from her eyes, looked around.

"Where are we?" she asked.

Bob didn't say a word. Instead he looked at Elaine and shrugged. *You can answer this one.*

Elaine walked over, put her hand against the young girl's cheek.

"We're staying at another house for a little while," she said. "Our home needs a little renovation, so we'll just be staying here until it's ready."

"What about my room?" Caroline asked. Even though she was happy with Boo Boo, she'd be sad if she didn't get to play with her toys again. She couldn't believe all those brand-new toys and dolls Elaine and Bob had bought for her. She'd never had a dollhouse. It would be so sad if she never got to play with it again.

"Hopefully you'll be back in it soon," Elaine said. Then she smiled, gave Boo Boo a peck on the nose and made a funny *grr* noise. Caroline laughed.

"Come on, hon," Bob said. "We should check in."

"I never thought we'd see him again," Elaine said. "At least not until much later down the road. When it was time to, you know."

"I know," Bob said. "But he told us something might come up. Makes me wonder whether we should have ever listened to that scarred-up asshole. Sorry, kids, pardon my French."

"You know why we did," Elaine said. They both looked at Patrick, and for a moment Caroline thought Elaine might cry.

"Who are you talking about?" Caroline asked.

"Nobody," Elaine said. "Just a scary man that hopefully you'll never have to meet. Now, come on, let's get you to your *new* new room."

25

I got to work at six o'clock in the morning. I had to get out of my apartment, where all I could do was think about who burned down that house. And any moments I was able to forget about that, my thoughts turned to Amanda.

I'd spent half an hour the previous evening on the phone with Rent-a-Wreck, trying to explain how their car had disappeared from the scene of a massive fire. Thankfully I'd taken out insurance, but I wasn't looking forward to the paperwork. Still, with that car gone, the company was out, what, a buck ninety-five?

The cops had ushered us from the fire immediately. Before leaving, I saw the two cops who'd been questioning us. They were standing in the driveway, interviewing several people I presumed to be neighbors. There was fear on the cops' faces. They saw us as we left, but this time their attitude was gone. I wondered if this would finally get them to investigate.

Wallace drove us back to New York. He made it very clear that I was to stay on the Linwood investigation. I felt a swell of pride at this. Not only because I'd been right all along, but because now I wanted, *needed* to know what had happened to those children. And why someone seemed willing to kill to keep it quiet.

I spent the first part of the morning reading various newspapers from Hobbs County over the past few years. The archives of the *Hobbs County Register* were available online, and it was easy to see that this was a city on the verge of tremendous change and tremendous gentrification.

At around ten o'clock I stood up to grab a cup of coffee from the pantry, when I looked over at Jack's desk and noticed that the old man wasn't there. It was curious, since most mornings he was in the office before the sun rose, and I knew today wasn't his day off.

Walking over, I noticed that his computer wasn't on and the red message light on his phone was blinking. His caller ID read sixteen missed calls. I checked the log. He hadn't checked a single message since the previous night. That wasn't like Jack, who I knew carried his work home with him, often calling his voice mail to see if a source had gotten back, or if there was a juicy new scoop from one of his many contacts around the city.

Since my nerves were already a bit frayed from the previous few days, I half jogged over to Wallace's office to see what the deal was. He was reading, looked up expectantly.

"Parker. How you holding up?"

"Been better," I said. "Just doing some background work on Hobbs County right now. Hey, have you seen Jack recently?"

Wallace shook his head. "Not since last night. He filed his story, then left. Haven't seen him since."

"Well, it doesn't look like he came in today, and I just wanted to make sure everything's all right."

"Isn't Jack off today?"

I shook my head. "Not till Friday."

Wallace picked up a pen, twirled it as he thought. "I don't know what to tell you. I've known Jack for nearly thirty years, and I've seen him go through some of the toughest times of his life. Three or four wives, a near bankruptcy. Missing a day of work at this point in his career, at this point he's playing with the house's money, so I won't make a stink."

"Sir, if you don't mind, I just want to be sure you're right. He hasn't been himself for a few months now. I'm going to swing by his place, make sure the status quo is, well, safe and sound." *And sober.*

Wallace shrugged. "Do what you must. If he's there, tell him we'll consider it a sick day."

"And if he's not there?"

"He's a grown man. Check the nearest coffee shop or cigar lounge." *Or bar,* I longed to add, but didn't.

"I'll be back soon," I said. "Hopefully he's on the couch watching old Archie Bunker episodes or something."

As I was leaving the office, I heard Wallace say, "Henry?"

I turned around. "Yes?"

"Give me a call if you, well, find anything out of the ordinary." The look in his eyes admitted that as much as he wanted to think Jack was at home watching TV or at a cigar lounge burning through a Macanudo, we both knew that wasn't likely.

"I'll call as soon as I find him."

After grabbing my bag and cell phone, I hopped a cab to Jack's apartment. It was one of those brand-spanking-new NYC cabs with the video monitor in the divider. Some hairsprayed goon was gushing over a musical comedy set to open that week. I put it on Mute, then when I got tired of seeing the primped-and-coiffed anchor I turned the screen off.

I'd never been to Jack's place. He'd invited me over once or twice for a drink, but I always had to decline for one reason or another. He'd stopped by mine a few times, though not in a while. Though I'd considered the man an icon and a mentor, someone without whom I wouldn't have a career, my refusal to spend time with him outside of work seemed like an artificial boundary I'd recently had to create. I couldn't think of spending a night in better company, hearing Jack's thousands of stories about his career, what the news used to be like. I had to deprive myself of that, though, for his own sake.

A few months ago, Jack had told me that to become a legend in any line of work, you had to rid yourself of outside distractions. Focus on the ball, put in your time, and greatness would come. He frowned on taking long vacations, having friends and even giving yourself up to a lover. Jack was thrice divorced and had admitted to me that though he enjoyed the companionship, at least the physical aspect, he'd never allowed himself to become a real husband. He never offered the emotional companionship his lovers needed, and never desired to. To Jack, the perfect relationship was one where he could come home to a delicious meal, talk about his day, make love and fall asleep. He knew he wasn't able to give to someone else the same things he required, and that never bothered him. Most of his wives were aware of it before they met him. Yet they married him either in spite of this or with the misguided belief they could change him.

But Jack would never change. Not for anyone or anything. He was often wrong, but never in doubt. And that's what alarmed me.

Jack lived in a condominium in the Clinton area of New York at Forty-Eighth and Ninth. Floor-to-ceiling windows, he'd told me, and an unobstructed view that looked over the West Side Highway, where you could see past the Hudson River. A killer view. And since he'd bought it as a new construction, he regaled me about his brand-new appliances as though they were grandchildren. As far as I knew, Jack's brand-new Viking stove had been untouched in two years, to the glee of the numerous take-out restaurants in the neighborhood who would have a hard time paying the rent each month if Jack ever decided to take a cooking class.

A colleague once looked up Jack's purchase on streeteasy.com, and learned that he'd bought the apartment for a cool $1.5 million, while also putting down a higher-than-usual twenty percent for the place. It gave me hope that at some point in the future, continuing in this line of work might enable me to afford such luxury. For now, my crummy rental with the friendly rodent staff and unfriendly super would have to do.

We pulled up to his building and I paid the driver. I walked up to the lobby, slightly embarrassed that I was even doing this. Who the hell was I to have any doubts about Jack? The man had built a career any newsperson would die for, and here I was like the parent who thought his kid was playing hooky. That this child was in his sixties with a monthly mortgage payment likely larger than my college tuition was beside the point.

The doorman was an elderly gent with a wisp of gray hair and teeth slightly yellow and askew. He opened the door for me and smiled pleasantly.

"I'm here to see Jack O'Donnell," I said.

"Just a second." He picked up a black phone that looked to be connected to some amazingly fancy and complicated intercom system. He fiddled with the buttons for a minute, then flipped through a Rolodex. "Who may I ask is visiting?"

"Henry Parker."

"Just a moment, Mr. Parker."

He pressed a buzzer, held the phone to his ear and waited. After a minute he put the phone down. "I'm sorry, sir, nobody's answering."

"Hold on one sec," I said. I took out my cell phone, dialed Jack's home phone, then his cell phone. Both went to voice mail before anyone picked up. Odd. "Would you mind trying one more time?"

"Certainly, sir."

He pressed the buzzer again, held the phone to his ear. A few seconds later the man's brow furrowed. "Yes, yes, hello? Mr. O'Donnell?" The doorman seemed either confused or concerned. "Mr. O'Donnell, is everything all right? There's a Mr. Parker here to see you. Hello, Mr. O'Donnell?"

The doorman hung up,

"What happened?" I said, concern seeping into my voice.

"I don't know, it sounded like Mr. O'Donnell, but he sounded, well, I don't mean to judge, but how should I say, out of it?"

"Out of it? Like how?"

"I really don't know." He looked concerned, then said, "How do you know Jack?"

"I work with him at the *Gazette*." He seemed unsure of whether to let me up. "Look, Jack didn't come in to work today and that's not like him. I just want to make sure he's safe."

"Is that right," he said, not as a question. After considering this, he said, "He's on the fifth floor, the second elevator bank on your left."

I thanked the doorman and walked swiftly to the elevator. I rode it to five. Jack occupied the whole floor. Not a bad deal. I approached and rang the doorbell. Immediately I could sense something was wrong. Not from the door itself, but because the entire hallway stank of booze and some sort of rot.

I pressed the bell again, then banged on the door, my heart racing.

"Jack!" I yelled. "Jack, are you in there? Come on, buddy, open up."

I heard a shuffling, and froze. The shuffling came from behind the door, and it was getting closer. I backed up, didn't know what the hell was going on. I heard a sound come from inside the apartment, a soft moan that chilled my blood.

"Jack, goddamn it, open up!"

I heard a lock disengage, then the door opened a crack. It didn't open any farther. I approached the door, pushed it open wider.

"Jack? Where are…?"

My breath caught in my throat when I could see what was behind the door. Jack was lying in a puddle of what looked like vomit. His undershirt was covered in green chunks, and the whole apartment smelled like a rotted distillery. Flecks were stuck to the man's beard.

"Oh, Jesus, Jack."

I shoved the door open and pushed in, gathering the old man in my arms. He was heavy and essentially dead weight, but I managed to drag him over to the couch. The white leather was covered in odd stains. Empty bottles littered the floor, tossed about like they were nothing more than discarded paper clips.

"Jack, come on, talk to me." I patted his cheek, laying him on the couch. Then I rushed into the kitchen, found where he kept his dishes and poured a glass of water. I jogged back, tilted his head up. Raised the glass to his lips. When I poured, the water ran down the sides of his mouth, pooled in the folds of his pants.

"Come *on!*"

I tried again, this time opening his lips with my fingers. When the water entered his mouth, he began to sputter and cough. His eyes flickered open as he wiped the liquid from his lips. He blinked a few times, his eyes red, lids crusty.

"Henry?" he said.

"I'm here, Jack," I replied, cradling his head.

"Forgot to call in sick today," he said, before going slack in my arms.

26

I sat by the side of the bed, thinking about how much time I'd spent in hospitals recently. Jack had been taken to Bellevue, where he was diagnosed with acute alcohol poisoning.

I'd heard sketchy things about Bellevue, some of which were confirmed upon seeing several men clad all in inmate orange walking handcuffed through the halls. I just prayed the doctors here understood how important this patient was, and had passed their medical board exams with flying colors. Unfortunately, I was getting used to white hospital walls. The antiseptic smell. The forced, sad smiles on concerned friends and family members.

My ex-girlfriend, Mya, was finally at home after recovering from several surgeries after her body was shattered by a ruthless sociopath earlier in the year. I'd stayed by Mya's bed for weeks, comforting her mother when we didn't know if Mya would pull through, then comforting Mya when she went through the agony of rehabilitation and coping with the murder of her father by the same man who'd tried to end her life.

When you give yourself to someone, you carry the responsibility of not just being a friend or confidant, or even a lover, but giving yourself to them when they need it most. I knew Mya had desired for us to get back together, and perhaps the most difficult part of those weeks was being a friend while keeping my distance. Physical pain went away, or could be stunted through medication. It broke my heart to deny her my affection when she probably needed it most. But she would have been hurt more later knowing my heart still belonged to another woman.

Seeing Jack lying in bed made me wonder just what I could, or would, give the man. Perhaps I'd been too emotionally reserved. Or perhaps not given enough.

The doctors had measured Jack's blood alcohol level at an astonishing .19, well over double the legal limit in New York.

An IV was hooked into his right arm, tubes in his nose pumping oxygen, his breathing slow and steady. A bag dripped fluids into his veins as they attempted to flush out Jack's poisoned system. The doctors also informed me they would be testing for cirrhosis of the liver. They guessed—correctly—that this kind of drinking binge was not limited to last night.

A doctor entered the room. He was middle-aged, wore thick glasses on his thin nose. His eyes were red, tired. He flipped through the chart at the foot of Jack's bed, then checked out the readings on the monitors by the bedside. He scribbled in the folder, then placed it back.

"How is he?" I asked. "Dr...."

The doctor turned, then said with a faint smile, "Dr. Brenneman. I've seen worse."

"You didn't see him before they cleaned him up."

"There's always a worse, trust me. But he's lucky you found him when you did. The biggest danger with alcohol poisoning is aspiration and asphyxiation. He could have literally choked to death on his own vomit."

"Ordinarily, I'd say he owes me a drink for saving his life, but…"

"I don't think that's the wisest course of action," Brenneman said.

"When will he wake up?" I asked.

"Well, that's all up to him. We're going to keep him for a few days and monitor his fluid levels, make sure his liver functions are all up to par, but he's not unconscious or anything like that. Just sleeping."

"Got it. Thanks, Doc, I appreciate it. And I'm sure Jack does, too."

He waved his hand, dismissing any gratitude. "I'm actually a fan of Mr. O'Donnell's work," he said. "I followed his reportings on the mob wars a few years back. All that violence with Michael DiForio and his murder, it's all so tawdry and terrible, but I just couldn't turn away. They never did find the man who killed DiForio, did they?"

"No, they didn't."

"Scares you to think there's someone out there walking the streets dangerous enough to kill the head of a major organized-crime family, and slippery enough to get away with it."

"I know what you mean," I said. "So did you recognize Jack right away?"

Brenneman laughed. "Are you kidding? The man's a New York legend." Then his brow furrowed, as concern melted into his features. "To be honest, that's what upsets me the most. I've been around enough alcoholics not to judge, but you never expect to see such a, well, *legend* suffer like he has. To do to his body what he has. For some reason, and forgive me for saying this, but I guess I expected more from him."

"Yeah," I replied. "I guess we all did." Brenneman nodded, turned to leave. "Hey, Doc, mind if I ask you one more question?"

"Absolutely," he said, clutching his clipboard to his chest.

"What could cause a person to lose their memory? Not permanently, but, like, a chunk of it. A few years. What could punch a hole in someone's life?"

"Well, a few things. I assume you're referring to a kind of anterograde amnesia. Most of the time amnesia is the result of some traumatic damage to the brain, specifically the hippocampus and the medial temporal lobes. Anterograde, in which there is usually what's called a 'hole' or 'blackout episode,' happens as the result of a chemical imbalance. It's commonly referred to as Korsakoff syndrome."

"What happens when someone is a victim of Korsakoff?"

"Basically, it's a degenerative brain condition that's brought on by a severe lack of thiamine—or vitamin B1—in a person's brain. Thiamine helps metabolize fats and carbohydrates in the body."

"Thiamine—is this a natural substance? Does the body produce it?"

"No, it's like any other vitamin, it has to be absorbed in the system from outside. There's vitamin B1 in dozens of everyday foods, from bread to meat, vegetables, dairy. You'd almost have to go out of your way to deprive yourself of it.

"Is there any way this chemical imbalance—or Korsakoff syndrome—could be induced?"

"Absolutely. Have you heard of GHB or GBL?"

"Date-rape drugs, right?"

"That's the lay term for them, yes. In effect, what

those drugs do is induce a form of retrograde amnesia. Ironically, GHB is sometimes prescribed to help combat alcoholism." Brenneman looked at Jack. He figured I was asking these questions because of him. "GHB and Rohypnol, especially when mixed with alcohol, can be a potent and often lethal mixture."

"But aren't the effects of those drugs pretty short-term?"

"Assuming they're not ingested in lethal amounts, yes, they generally only cause memory lapses of four to ten hours. And though that's not a tremendous amount of time, in the grand scheme of things, people who use them for nefarious purposes can accomplish an awful lot of evil in that time."

"What about long-term anterograde amnesia? Are there any ways to induce Korsakoff syndrome in a way that could affect the brain for months or even years?"

"In severe cases, people either born with dangerously low levels of thiamine, or whose levels are brought down to a certain level, can experience a form of long-term anterograde amnesia. The damage is done to the medial thalamus, and if left untreated, if thiamine levels are left below a certain level, the memory loss can be long-term, or even permanent." Brenneman eyed me. "Ironically again, alcoholism is one of the most common causes of long-term anterograde amnesia."

Again he eyed Jack. And while Jack would face a tremendous struggle in his battle against the bottle, the more pressing fight was to uncover what had happened to Daniel Linwood and Michelle Oliveira. Jack was in good care. I couldn't say the same about Girl X.

Suddenly I heard a buzzing sound, and Brenneman's hand went to his coat. He took out a small pager, clicked it, then said, "I've been summoned. Nice to meet you, Mr...."

"Henry Parker," I said.

"Mr. Parker." He looked at Jack. "Please, take care of him. More important, get him to take care of himself." Then Brenneman left.

I stayed with Jack for another half an hour. I just watched him breathe, waiting for him to wake up. Half wanting to go over there, shake his drunken ass until his eyes opened, letting him have it about how he was throwing his life's reputation away. How he was in danger of throwing his legacy away. Instead I sat there, watching the tubes drip, the machines beep, thinking about how the man who single-handedly brought the *New York Gazette* to prominence had to be carted out of his house like a derelict.

After half an hour I couldn't sit there any longer, so I left and called Wallace from the street.

"How is he?" the man said.

"About what you'd expect, only worse."

"I knew Jack was drinking, more than usual, but I had no idea it was this bad."

"So you knew he was developing a problem." I was this close to screaming at my boss, and I didn't care.

"Yes, but he was still turning his stories in on time and he was still a valuable member of the team here."

"Wallace, we both know his stuff hasn't been top-notch in a while."

"So Jack's lost a little off his fastball. But he's still faster than most reporters, and he's got enough smarts, contacts and writing chops to make up for anything he's lost."

"He doesn't *have* to lose anything, it's being taken from

him, bottle by bottle. He's worked for you for what, thirty years? And you repay him by turning a blind eye?"

"Watch it, Parker," Wallace snapped. "You haven't been here long enough and you haven't known Jack long enough to judge either of us. We'll get O'Donnell the help he needs. Right now your only job is as an employee of this newspaper. Assuming you still want to be."

"Of course I do," I said. "More than ever."

"Good. Then show it."

Wallace hung up. I felt a great anger surge through me. Both at the runaround I was getting on the Linwood/Oliveira kidnappings, and now this. I'd looked up to Jack for so many years, spent so much of my childhood idolizing this pillar of a man, to see him reduced to a lump under a hospital throw rug was like seeing a baseball bat taken to fine crystal. That's one thing I'd learned in my years as a reporter. Every person, no matter the pubic perception, had demons. And the higher regard in which you held them in, the greater the disappointment when you realized their demons were as common as anyone else's. I refused to believe that Jack O'Donnell was a common alcoholic. The kind of guy who scrounged around his cabinets for that one drop of Knob Creek he knew was left. Jack had a gift that defied all of it. And once he got help, he could polish that crystal back to a shine.

I took a cab back to my apartment. Last night I couldn't wait to get to the office. Today I couldn't bear to spend another minute there. I needed a respite, if only brief.

I threw my stuff on the couch, went into the kitchen and found a Corona nestled behind a jar of pickles. The beer tasted flat, but I didn't care. It had alcohol and that's all I wanted right now. I needed a moment to feel oblivious, blissfully ignorant, to have that feeling all alcoholics must have when they pop the first top of the day and know that, pretty soon, the world outside wouldn't bother them for much longer.

Before I could get to the second sip, my phone rang. The caller ID read "Amanda." I picked it up.

"Hello?"

"Henry, everything all right? I've been trying to reach you all day."

"Not really. Jack was admitted to the hospital this morning. Alcohol poisoning. I walked in on him sitting in a pile of his own vileness."

"Oh, God. I remember a while ago you thought he was drinking too much."

"Yeah, I just never thought it would get this bad."

"I'm so sorry to hear that. I called you at the office, and got worried when I couldn't find you. After the past few days my mind's been all out of whack."

"I'm at home now. Having a beer. Feel the same way as you."

There was a pregnant pause, and then Amanda said, "Mind if I come over?"

Without waiting, I said, "No. That'd be nice."

"Be there in half an hour."

After we hung up, I got up and poured the rest of the beer into the sink. Then I sat on the couch and waited.

I wondered: Would Dmitri Petrovsky still be alive if we hadn't followed him? Possibly. But what the hell was he mixed up in?

I still didn't know exactly what his link was to Danny and Michelle. He was their pediatrician, but somehow he was connected to my friend the Chesterfield-chain-smoking sociopath. One more trail to follow. I needed to know who that man was, who lived in that house, and what Dmitri Petrovsky knew that made necessary his permanent silence. One thing was for certain, my digging had opened a can of worms someone very badly wanted kept closed.

I looked around my apartment. Humble even by humble's standards. I knew when I moved to New York that it was one of the most expensive cities in the world, but nothing prepared me for three-dollar cups of coffee or twelve-dollar movie tickets. I was paying about sixty percent of my income to a landlord I never met, who took longer to fix my air-conditioning than it would have taken me to install a hot tub into a Buick Skylark. I had no idea how long it took Jack to make a decent living, but I hoped it wasn't too long in the waiting.

Twenty-five minutes later my buzzer rang. I peeked out the window, saw Amanda standing on the street. She looked up at me, waved. I let her in.

She came upstairs and sat down across the couch from me. Hands folded under her chin. Her hair fell over her shoulders, worry lines at her eyes. Though she was still beautiful, the past few years had aged her slightly. We'd been through so much together, yet strangely I'd known this girl for less than two years. I still saw that brown hair and remembered that on the day we met, despite the circumstances, she had made everything stand still, if only for a moment. Women like Amanda, who were beautiful almost in spite of their lack of effort, beautiful without trying at all, they didn't come along too often.

We sat there in silence. It was the kind of quiet I hadn't experienced with many other women. I longed for that sense of confidence. Of comfort.

After a few minutes had passed, Amanda said, "What do you think the cops will do now?"

"You mean the dedicated men and women of the Hobbs County PD? Probably nothing. I'd bet my life savings that the same guy that mistook me for a barbecue started that fire, but I can't imagine the cops will work very hard to prove it. They want to wipe this whole mess under the bed and be done with it."

"What about Petrovsky?"

"I don't know. They claim they never found a body, either in the driveway or inside the bonfire. All they did was file a missing persons report when his secretary said he didn't show up at work. Petrovsky isn't married, no children, no real family in the States, so until enough time has gone by they won't have anything breathing down their necks. And the press won't be putting pressure on them if there are no weeping widows or no orphaned children to plaster on the front page to stir sympathies."

She looked sad. "It's like a crime was never even committed."

"It wasn't," I said. "Until a body turns up. Or we catch these assholes."

"If someone is willing to kidnap two children, kill a doctor, torture you and set a house on fire, I have a feeling they wouldn't think twice about disposing of a body."

"Tomorrow," I said. "We start from the other end. We've been looking for what happened to Michelle Oliveira and Daniel Linwood, who kidnapped them and why. And we haven't made a lot of headway on that end. So now we follow this." I took a crumpled piece of paper from my pocket. Tossed it at Amanda. She uncrumpled it, read it.

"The receipt," she said. I nodded.

"Toyz 4 Fun," I replied. "Let's see who was buying a young girl some early Christmas presents. And I'll bet whoever it is has another child. Someone who hasn't been reported missing yet. Someone who in a few years is meant to be another Danny Linwood."

27

James Keach walked down the off-white hallway, still shaking after nearly tripping over an old man and his walker, just thankful he didn't rip the old guy's IV from his arm. James's jacket was unzipped, one hand in his pocket while the other one hung loose. Just like Paulina had taught him.

Be cool, she said. *If anyone asks, you're visiting a relative. It's okay to be nervous—nobody likes being in a hospital—but nurses and orderlies are trained to sniff out anyone who doesn't belong. You belong, right, James? Just tell yourself you belong and you'll act like it. Just don't be a pussy, James, and you'll be fine.*

He still couldn't get over that word. His friends used it in casual conversation all the time, usually out at bars or while watching lumberjack competitions on Spike TV. He'd never been called one. And to be called that name by a woman, his boss, on a regular basis, was something James still hadn't come to grips with.

Once this task was complete, he was going home, getting under the covers and sleeping. Tomorrow he'd be joining his father on a golf outing with Ted Allen, and he'd need to be up for that. James knew his father had cashed

in a favor in getting Ted Allen to hire him at the *Dispatch*.
That didn't bother him much. Everybody had connections
and used them. That was the point. Besides, wouldn't you
rather get a recommendation from a close friend than have
to slog through identical résumés from overachieving
losers? That he got stuck working for Paulina Cole was
something totally unexpected. Unlike any boss he'd ever
worked for, Paulina actually scared the piss out of him.

James felt the thin camera in his pocket. Point. Click.
Done.

That's it. This guy from IT, Wilmer or Wilbur or Wilfred
or something, showed him how to use it. *Idiot proof* was
his term. James laughed at that. Wondered who the idiots
were they had to design it for.

He knew the tip was good. Paulina's tips always were.
And while James was used to Paulina's volcanic temperament and mercurial attitude, James had noticed something
different about her the past few weeks. Her moods had
swung heavier, her demeanor more vicious, her attitudes
more severe. Like she was gearing up for something big,
steeling herself. Though he'd been running errands for
her for going on a year now, she was never totally candid
with him. He knew she was working on something big, but
she refused to share the details.

In good time Jamesy, she'd said.

He counted off the doors as he walked down the hall.

703.

704.

705.

706.

He was there.

But the door was closed.

It wasn't supposed to be closed. He hadn't expected it

to be closed. He assumed it would be wide open, people coming and going, nobody noticing a thing. But opening a hospital door, man, someone would definitely notice that. If not a nurse then another patient. He couldn't see inside. A curtain was drawn. If a nurse was in there she'd sure as hell see him, and there was no way he could get it done without drawing suspicion and ruining the whole thing.

James stepped back. Took a breath. Leaned against the wall. He knew this was the very antithesis of what Paulina had advised, but fuck it, he needed a moment to regroup.

What should he do? Open the door, waltz in, pray nobody was in there? Or wait. Maybe someone would open the door and pull the curtain back. Make it easy for him.

A minute passed. Then five more. He was sweating.

He wiped his forehead with the sleeve of his jacket, saw the leather come away wet and shiny.

Time to sack up, Jim. Show the queen bitch what you're made of.

James stepped in front of the door and reached for the handle. He gripped it, closed his eyes and began to pull.

Just then the door swung outward, nearly knocking James off his feet. When he regained his balance, a pretty nurse was standing in the doorway. She was staring at James. His heart was racing. *Ohcrap, ohcrap, ohcrap, ohcrap, ohcrap, ohcrap...*

Then the nurse smiled, whispered to him.

"Are you here to see Mr. O'Donnell?"

James gulped, managed to eke out a "Yes, ma'am. I'm his nephew."

"That's sweet of you to come. He hasn't had many visitors. Mr. O'Donnell is resting right now," she said. "But if you want to sit with him, go right ahead."

"Thanks, I appreciate it."

The nurse held the door for James. Easy as pie.

When the door eased shut, he stepped around the curtain and saw the man in bed.

He was much older than his picture in the paper. Thinner, too, his face with a sickly gray pallor. He was breathing steadily, tubes in each nostril, an IV in his arm.

James quickly took the camera out of his pocket.

He whispered, "Say cheese, Jack."

28

The Toyz 4 Fun store was located at 136 Evergreen Court in White Plains, New York, about eight miles southeast of Hobbs County. Since the Rent-a-Wreck company refused to deal with us after we lost their car, I was forced to make an expensive upgrade at a regular rental company. Thankfully I was now officially working the story, so I was able to expense the ride. Not to mention how much of a relief it was to drive a car that didn't feel like it was in danger of spontaneously combusting at any moment.

The conversation on the ride up was pleasant, if a little awkward. It was hard to put Jack and the Linwood story out of my mind, and I think Amanda could tell I was distracted.

The Toyz 4 Fun store was wedged between a nail salon and a paper goods shop in a strip mall right off Wood-thrush. We parked in the lot next to a beat-up Camry. It was a warm day out. I had on jeans and a white T-shirt, while Amanda had on a yellow sundress. The kind of outfit that made me wish we could forget about work and just sit down on a bench somewhere, sip lemonade or do whatever normal couples did when they weren't investigating kidnappings and disappearing murder victims.

The Toyz logo had the letters spelled out on different-colored building blocks on the awning. A play easel was set up in front of the store. Scribbled on the easel in erasable magic marker was "Deluxe Easel: Special Price $49.99!!!" It was nice to see an easel outside a store that didn't feature the soups of the day.

Each exclamation point was topped with a smiley face. It was the kind of store I loved to see walking down the street when I was a kid. Not the electronics extravaganzas and smutty Bratz dolls that passed for toys these days, but the true-to-heart toy stores, with owners that cared, knew you by name, knew exactly what you wanted. I didn't get many toys when I was a kid, but the once-a-year trip to the Leapin' Lizards toy store in Bend was worth waiting those other three-hundred-and-sixty-four days.

Amanda pushed the door open and a series of wind chimes rang. I couldn't help but smile.

In front of us were rows and rows of toys. Building blocks. Play-Doh. Action figures. Lego sets. Dollhouses. Erector sets. Everything a growing boy or girl needed to have fun and get into loads of trouble.

An elderly man sat behind the counter, thick glasses shielding kind blue eyes. His hair was sparse, combed over, but there was barely enough to do a passable job of it. He was wearing blue overalls with suspenders, like the OshKosh kid in his waning years. He smiled when we entered. His face was lined, but his cheeks were red, veiny, and his enthusiasm was genuine.

"Corolle doll, right?" the man said. "Or if it's a boy, let me see…how about My First Pirate Set?"

"Excuse me?" I said.

"Well, I'm guessing you two to be, what? Twenty-seven, twenty-eight? Thirty tops? Your kid is somewhere between three and six. Those toys are my most popular sellers for that age group. So what'll it be? Corolle or pirates?"

"I'm sorry sir," I said. "You've got us wrong. We don't have any kids."

"Bun in the oven?" he said.

"Nope," Amanda said.

"Gift-hunting then?"

"Sorry," I said. "We're actually here because we're hoping you can answer a few questions for us."

"Oh," the man said, confused. "Okay then, what can I do you for?"

I took the receipt from my pocket.

"Were you working here at around three-thirty on July 27?"

"Assume I was. I'm here every day unless I'm sick, and I haven't been sick in some time. My name's Freddie, by the way. Nobody will be addressed by 'sir' in this store."

"No problem, Freddie," I said. I handed the receipt across the desk. Freddie looked at me, unsure of what to do with it.

"That's a receipt from this store, right?"

He picked it up, glanced at it, said, "Looks like it."

"Is there any way you could look up in your computer and see who this receipt was issued to?"

"I'm sorry," he said. "It says here 'change'" He pointed to a line at the bottom. "Means whoever paid, paid in cash."

I grimaced. "I know it's a long shot, but is there any way you might know who purchased that item?"

Freddie looked at the receipt again, furrowed his brow. "This here is for accessories for a Victorian dollhouse," he said. "I don't do a lot of sales on dollhouse accessories. Sad to say they're a little old-fashioned. But I keep some in stock just in case. Probably to make me happy more than the kids." He thought for another moment, then said, "Elaine Reed."

"Excuse me?"

"Robert and Elaine Reed. Bob and Elaine. They came into my store all the time when their son, Patrick, was born. They bought that boy all sorts of toy soldiers, must have spent more money than they made on those things. I made sure they knew to keep them away from that boy's mouth. All those sharp parts, you know. But I remember Elaine suddenly buying everything under the sun for a girl, including those accessories. Little tables, chairs, even a tiny medicine chest."

"If they have a son, then why were they buying doll-house accessories?" Amanda asked.

Freddie said, "That's what I wondered. It wasn't just the accessories. The first thing they bought was an actual doll-house. I had to special-order it for them. And not a cheap one, mind you. Then they kept coming back over the next few days to buy more doodads for it. I assumed it wasn't for Patrick—don't know if you can tell a boy's, er, sexual orientation at such a young age. So I asked Elaine one day. Said, 'Elaine, what are all these doll parts for?' She told me they'd just had a baby girl."

"Baby girl," I said. "Seems like bad parenting to buy such tiny things for a baby."

"I thought the same thing, remembered what she'd done with Patrick and warned her about that. Elaine told me the girl was actually six years old. I thought, 'That's strange, I didn't remember her being pregnant.'"

"Did you ask her about it?" I said.

"Naw," Freddie said. "It's not my right to pry into my customers' business. But when I asked about it, Elaine kind of looked worried, like I'd pried or something. I figured they might have adopted, or something else was going on, but either way I was happy for the business. And happy for Elaine, because anyone who spends that much money on toys sure must love their child. Not to mention how happy that kid's going to be. But after that day I asked one question, Elaine and Bob never came back to my store. I hate to think I offended them."

"Was Elaine a good parent?" Amanda asked.

"Wonderful," Freddie said. "Some of them, parents, I mean, you can tell they just buy things 'cause they feel obligated to. Like they just want to shut the kid up or think they can buy affection. Elaine, though, she loved it. You could tell she couldn't wait to get home and see the smiles on her kids' faces."

"Did you happen to catch their daughter's name?" I asked.

"No, I didn't."

"I know we're asking a lot, Freddie," I said, "but is there any chance you might have an address for Mr. and Mrs. Reed? It's very important we speak to them."

"I'm sorry, who did you say you were again?"

"My name's Henry Parker," I said, handing Freddie a business card. "We're investigating a story and really need to speak with the Reeds."

"I hope everything's okay," he said. The man was legitimately concerned.

"I hope so, too," I said. "But there's a chance there's something wrong with one of their children and we need to find them."

Freddie nodded. "I'll do whatever I can. I just hope they're safe. I think a while ago Bob bought Patrick one of those Erector sets, only Elaine didn't have enough room in the car and asked for it to be shipped home." Freddie rummaged under the desk, pulled out a large file box. He opened the lid, began to sift through alphabetical orders. "Reed…Reed…Reed…here we go. Elaine and Bob Reed."

"Can you give us the address?"

"No problem. That package was shipped to 482 Huntley Terrace."

My jaw dropped.

Amanda said, "Henry, that's the house…"

"That burned down yesterday."

29

I needed to learn more about the house on Huntley Terrace. If Robert and Elaine Reed had bought it, there would have to be sale records. I could look them up on streeteasy.com. Even if they didn't have contact info for the Reeds, there would surely be a brokerage firm that would. It made sense. There was a dollhouse in the room Amanda was held in, and the place looked like the perfect abode for a family with young children. But what I didn't understand was how the two men who held us that night were connected to the Reeds. Or how the Reeds were connected by proxy to Dmitri Petrovsky.

We drove around the streets looking for an Internet café. I didn't want to have to go all the way back to the city to use the computers at work. We were getting close to something. Many different spools, but I couldn't figure out the common thread that attached them.

"Look, there." Amanda was pointing to a small pizza parlor. A sign posted outside read "Internet Access."

"You up for a slice and a socket?"

"I am a little hungry."

"Cool. Eat first, search later," I said.

We parked, walked in and scarfed down two slices and

a Coke apiece in less than ten minutes. When we finished, we took two seats in front of a lonely computer in the back of the restaurant. The keyboard was dusty, and I imagined it didn't get much use. The counterman eyed us suspiciously, as though we were as likely to rip the computer from the wall as use it properly.

When I clicked the computer off sleep mode, I entered in my credit card number for access. Once we were in, I directed the browser to streeteasy.com.

"What is this?" Amanda asked.

"Streeteasy.com is a pretty useful tool. It's an online database that records any property transactions, along with the buyer, seller, asking price and brokerage firm who handled the deal. I have a log-in."

I plugged in my log-in information and entered the name Robert Reed in the search field. Several listings came up, with records dating back to 1989, and in five different states.

"This can't be right," Amanda said. "How could he live in three different states at the same time?"

"It's probably not all the same Robert Reed. Hold on, I'll narrow the search."

I narrowed the parameters to Hobbs County. The search came up empty. I tried it again, only this time plugging in Elaine Reed instead. Again the search came up empty.

"Maybe someone else bought it for them? Or Elaine bought it under her maiden name?" Amanda asked.

"That's possible," I said. "We might have better luck searching for the exact house." We had enough information to narrow the search range.

According to Freddie at Toyz, the Reeds' son, Patrick, was currently somewhere between three and five years old. Which meant the Reeds had probably moved into the house on Huntley within the past seven years, either when they decided to try to start a family or when Patrick was on the way and space was essential. I entered the date range in the past eight years just to be sure.

The list came back with two thousand, seven hundred and eighty-three hits.

"I think we can narrow it down more," Amanda said. "We know there were at least three bedrooms in that house on Huntley. That should help, right?"

"Definitely, one sec."

I refined the search to only include houses that had a minimum of three bedrooms. The search came back with three hundred and sixty-seven hits. We were making progress.

"Now we just sift through these and look for anything on Huntley. Anything that looks familiar."

We scrolled through page after page of home sales and purchases through the past eight years. It was fascinating to see the range of prices at which houses had been bought, but it also gave an accurate overview of what the most expensive areas in the state were. Unsurprisingly, Hobbs County homes were ridiculously cheap. Until a few years ago at least, when I noticed they began to trend upward by a large margin.

We'd been sitting at the computer for nearly two hours. The computer had charged thirty-six bucks for the access. I hoped Wallace wouldn't spent too much time scrutinizing my expense account.

Finally on the two hundred and twenty-fourth listing, we found it.

"There we go," I said. "Four-eighty-two Huntley Terrace."

"Bingo," Amanda added.

According to the database, the house had been purchased in 2001 for three hundred and forty thousand dollars. There was a picture of the property on the Web site. I clicked to enlarge it.

The house was easily recognizable. As was the driveway and garage we'd seen the other night. We clicked through various photographs of the interior and exterior, looking for anything familiar. The rooms were different; obviously these shots had been taken before any renovations.

What was more surprising was that there was no sign of the metal gates, nor the brick wall surrounding the property. Whoever purchased the house in 2001 had built them custom-made.

"That's odd," I said, clicking onto the "buyer/seller" link. "According to this, the buyer wasn't Bob or Elaine Reed, or anyone named Reed at all."

"Who was it, then?"

"Someone named Raymond Benjamin," I said. "Does that name sound familiar at all?" Amanda shook her head. Then her eyes opened wide.

"Wait a minute," she said, pointing at the name on the screen. "When we were in that house, when you came into the room where I was held, didn't one of the guys call for a Ray?"

I thought hard, vaguely remembered hearing that, but between the cigarette burn and my state of panic I couldn't be sure. "You think this Raymond Benjamin might have been the same guy from the other night?"

"Be a heck of a coincidence, a guy who obviously knows the place well enough to set us up shares the same first name as the man on the property deed."

"Yes, that would be a mighty coincidence. It would also mean that Raymond Benjamin knows Dmitri Petrovsky." I tapped my fingers on the keyboard. "The guy who had me, he'd been in prison before. Attica. He was there during the riot, and that was in '71. If he was telling the truth, he'll have a criminal record."

"I think it's time to leave the pizza place," Amanda said.

"It sure is. Let's see what we can find out about Raymond Benjamin. It's been at least twenty-four hours since I asked Curt Sheffield for a favor. Let's give him a ring."

30

The diner smelled of cooking grease and burned coffee. A plate of eggs sat in front of him, untouched. Raymond Benjamin rubbed his aching jaw, then took another smoke from his pocket, lit it and inhaled deeply. It was all he could do to relax after the events of the past few days. Everything had been going just the way he'd planned, in that there were no disruptions, no mass hysterics. Everything cool, calm and quiet. And then all of a sudden the newshound Parker shows up at Petrovsky's office and everything goes to shit.

He hadn't wanted to torch the house. Benjamin actually had some fond memories of that place. But once Parker decided to follow Petrovsky, it was only a matter of time before somebody came knocking. Burning it down was a necessary evil. There was too much inside for him and Vince to get rid of in the little time they had, not to mention having to dispose of the doctor and that beat-up car Parker drove. Better to torch the whole thing and wipe their hands than risk one little thing turning up and screwing up the whole operation. Ray couldn't afford that. There was too much at stake.

Raymond Benjamin smoked his cigarette, eased back

into the booth and took out his wallet. He looked at the pictures inside. The first one was of a beautiful young couple. Ray barely remembered what life had been like back then. He'd been so impetuous, so violent. He was amazed a woman had actually had the temerity to marry him. The first photo had been a year or so before Ray Jr. was born. The boy had Ray's nose, but got the rest of his features from Ray's wife. Becca. Becca, who'd died while he was holed up in that shithole prison. Ray Jr., born in 1970, the year before the riots changed everything.

Every person was born with a specific skill set. Ray's son was born a technogeek, the kind of guy who could build computer systems out of thin air, could design corporate Web sites and security systems as easily as he buttered a bagel. The last Ray heard, his boy was making nearly a hundred grand a year. He was married with two kids. Ray hadn't seen them in a decade.

Ray himself was born with a different set of skills. And in a cruel irony, it was that skill set that led Ray to spend the majority of his twenties shuffling from prison to prison. He was a born criminal. Burglar, fighter. Age had sapped much of his brawn. No way that Parker kid would have had the upper hand when Ray had his juices flowing, when his fists were like unstoppable pistons. Now, in his late fifties, Ray was holding on to his fighting memories the way a jilted lover holds on to his, afraid of what would become of him when he realized the man he used to be was slipping away. Lives like Ray's didn't have second acts.

He thought about his time in Attica. Somehow the worst and best years of his life. They'd made him what he had become, but he wasn't sure if the pain and sacrifice were worth it. He thought about that day back in '71, when his fellow prisoners had finally risen up against the guards, who'd tortured them for so long. Ray remembered watching *Dog Day Afternoon* as a young man, just a few years after he got loose. He remembered the feeling of pride in his gut when Pacino delivered that electrifying speech. It was simply incredible, like a candle being lit in his stomach, working its way through him until his whole body was warm. He'd *seen* that in person. He'd *been* there. Everyone watched that flick and got that vicarious thrill of what it was like to make a stand. Ray had been there. He'd *made* that stand.

When Vince came back from the bathroom, the red welt above his eye was shining like a Christmas bulb. The younger man slid into the booth across from Ray, went right back to work on his ham, eggs and sausage links. Ray watched Vince eat for a bit, the man shoveling food into his yawning mouth like it was Thanksgiving and he didn't have a care in the world.

"Eat enough of that, it'll kill you before a bullet does."

Vince smiled as he gnawed on a link. "Best to go out having fun," he said.

"You know, as dumb as we were," Ray said, "things could have gone worse the other night. Much worse."

"Sure could have," Vince said, a forkful of dripping egg sliding back onto his plate. "What d'you think would have happened if the cops had come before we'd taken care of the place?"

Vince stopped chewing. Put the fork down. "We would have been in a world of shit. Years wasted," Ray said. Vince nodded as if he'd figured out the right answer on a multiple-choice test.

"Not really wasted. I mean, it's been fun, right? We've made money."

"You know we're not doing this for money, for our health," Ray said. "This isn't some two-bit scam we're pulling. There are lives at stake."

Vince laughed. "You mean like Petrovsky," he said with a goofy smile.

"No," Ray seethed. "Not fucking Petrovsky. Lives that matter. Petrovsky was a degenerate. He was a means to an end. And we have to protect that end, you hear me?"

"I hear you."

Ray lowered his voice. "I'll be talking to our friend later. We need to make sure everything is sealed up on our end. No doubt they'll find out that house was registered in my name. I'll play the 'woe is me' card, but let it end there. There isn't enough evidence in that house of anything. I gave it a once-through before we lit the match. Now I'm not too worried about the Hobbs police. If anything they're doing a good job protecting what we've created. But that Parker reporter, we can't give him anything more to latch onto. The New York media gets hold of this, it goes national. Nobody gives two shits about a poor kid in a poor city."

"I hear you, Ray. Geez, it's not like I don't know this already."

"Fucking Parker," Ray said. "Never been so stupid in my life. Ten years ago, no way that kid gets the jump on me. Never used to underestimate folks. All of a sudden Parker can ID me and probably you. His word against mine, and I've already spoken to our friend who's good with tools who'll claim I was working late that night. So here's what happens. If it even *looks* like this guy might throw a wrench into things, we don't wait for him to fall into our lap. We take him out. And the girl if necessary. No more cigarettes, no more nicey-nice. Quick, simple, and they disappear."

"Like those kids we nabbed," Vince said, satisfied.

"No. Not like those kids. Parker and Davies have to *stay* gone."

31

Manhattan's 19th Precinct was located on Sixty-Seventh Street between Lexington and Third Avenue. I'd only been there once, just a month or so after I'd arrived in New York. It was to report a lost or possibly stolen cell phone. I'd filled out a form with my information, handed it to the cop behind the front desk, and that was the last I ever heard about it. Probably for the best. The NYPD has more important crimes to worry about than who took my Nokia.

Curt had worked at the 19th going on three years. I knew he was well respected within the department, one of those up-and-comers that are a rare breed in that they're both clean-cut enough to stick on a recruiting poster, but hardworking and intuitive enough to gain the respect of the rank and file.

It was this respect that I was counting on as Amanda and I entered the precinct. The majority of cops had no love lost for me, and despite being vindicated many still considered me responsible for the death of one of their own. The irony was that even though the department loved Curt's image, he couldn't have cared less. That's the only reason he agreed to bring me into his precinct. It wouldn't win him any friends, but it would help uncover the truth.

The precinct was up a short flight of stairs. It had a red brick facade and an arched entryway, bracketed by two green lamps, above which hung a yellow banner that read "Thank you for your support." The banner was bookended by two images: the American flag and the badge of the NYPD.

Curt led Amanda and me through the precinct, though not nearly as fast as I would have liked. I could feel eyeballs boring holes through me as we snaked through the corridors, and knew that many of these men had worked with, probably known, John Fredrickson. A few years back, I defended two people Fredrickson was beating to death, and in the struggle the man's gun went off, killing him. I didn't know he was a cop, and his death was the result of choices made long before I came along. Yet perception was reality, and the feeling was if I hadn't stuck my nose in, he'd still be alive.

"Just this way," Curt said. We followed him down the hall into a row of cubicles, each one set up with large, likely obsolete computers. We entered a larger cubicle which was set up in a U-shape, two computers at either end. The walls were covered with crime-scene photos, mug shots, business cards. Curt pulled up a pair of chairs, then sat in a larger one. He shifted around a few times, then leaned forward and scratched his ass.

"That's lovely," Amanda said.

"Hey, if you can convince Chief Carruthers to spend an extra nickel on chairs that don't make your ass feel like it's the wrong side of a Velcro strip, you'd be spared seeing illicit activities such as these."

"Is it really that bad?" I asked.

"Man, come around here during lunchtime when the detectives are all eating at their desks. You'd think a family of porcupines must have made a nest in every seat. Like a messed-up orchestra, all scratching at the time same."

I said, "Think I'll file that under 'visual imagery I hope to file away and never see again.' So what is this here?"

"Here is where we find out about the criminal record for this guy Benjamin, the dude listed on the property deed on Huntley Terrace. You're sure this Ray Benjamin is the same cat who hung you out to dry in that tinderbox out on Huntley?"

"I can't be sure, but that's what we're here to find out."

"Now, you said this guy made a comment about serving time up at Attica, right?"

"That's right."

"Then our boy's damn sure got a record. Which means he's just a mouse click away from being ours."

Curt logged in to a database, then proceeded to enter first name "Raymond," last name "Benjamin," into the fields. He plugged the years 1968 and 1972 into another field marked "date range." He clicked a box marked "Caucasian" and pressed the search key. One of those helpful little hourglass icons appeared on the screen. On my computer, the sand fell through the hourglass at roughly the same speed as cars cruising Fifth Avenue during the Puerto Rican Day parade.

A few minutes and ass scratches later, the hourglass disappeared and a file appeared on the screen. A mug shot appeared in the top-right corner of the page. I recognized the man in the image at once.

"That's him," I said, pointing to the screen like I was picking him out of a lineup. "Holy shit, that's the guy."

"From the other night?" Curt said. "This is Raymond Benjamin."

I nodded. "No doubt."

Despite the picture being at least twenty years old, it was easy to tell this was the same man. The man in this photo had a fuller head of hair, fewer lines cutting across his face, but the look in his eye was the same. Defiance. Anger.

"There's no scar," I said. "When I saw Benjamin that night, there was a faint scar on his right cheek. There's nothing like that in this picture."

"Let's see here," Curt said. He clicked a button, then the photo enlarged. Curt highlighted a line below the photo. "Mug shot, dated 1969."

"Probably the last shot taken before he was sent to Attica," I said.

Amanda traced her finger down the man's cheek on the screen. "So if this photo was taken before he went to prison, there's certainly a chance he either got that scar in jail or afterward."

"Yeah, the scar actually did zigzag a little bit, like it had been stitched up by someone who got their medical license at the local butcher shop." I looked at Curt. "This is the only photo on record for this guy?"

"Afraid so," he said. "So what I want to know is how a dude who got busted for armed robbery in the sixties ended up buying a house that got burned down over thirty years later?"

"After he almost barbecued my balls," I added. "And if the house is owned by a three-time loser, why did the inside look fit for the Huxtables?"

"Obviously the house was in his name, but that was to hide whoever actually lived there," Amanda said.

"What I think happened," I said, "is that this guy Benjamin bought the house as a front. I'm not quite sure what the catalyst was, but a husband and wife named Robert and Elaine Reed have actually been the ones living on Huntley."

"They weren't in the fire though," Amanda said.

"No, no bodies found. Not that Russian doctor or anyone else," Curt said.

"So the papers are in this guy Benjamin's name, but he sublets it to the Reeds. Only there's no paperwork or documentation. The Reeds have a young son, Patrick, but according to receipts from a local toy store they'd been purchasing gifts for a young girl within the past month. I think very recently, the Reeds added a young girl to their family. Only I don't think they did it through conception or adoption."

"In vitro?" Curt said.

"No."

"Adopted a kid from Zaire?"

"Uh-uh. I think they kidnapped a child, and until that house burned down they'd been holding the girl just like whoever took Daniel Linwood and Michelle Oliveira had done. Amanda, you saw all the toys in the room you were held in. This wasn't some medieval torture chamber, this was a home. A place for a family to live."

Amanda reluctantly nodded. "Actually reminded me a little of my room when I went to live with Lawrence and Harriet Stein," she said. She turned to Curt. "I was adopted. My parents died when I was young, then I went from orphanage to orphanage until the Steins took me home. I remember my room feeling not really like an actual room a young girl would live in, but the kind of room parents *thought* a girl would want to live in. Too many floral patterns, too many dolls. Just overkill to the extreme."

"That's why the Reeds racked up a hefty bill at Toyz 4 Fun," I said. "They were pampering this kid like she was their own."

Curt said, "So why kidnap a kid if you're not holding her for a ransom? What, you just pamper her for a few years and then let her go? I mean, you're comparing this Girl X to Danny Linwood and Michelle Oliveira. Both those kids wound up returning home unharmed. If what you're saying is true, the Reeds planned to eventually let this kid go. Why go through all that trouble?"

"So she'd feel like a part of their family," I said. "When I interviewed Danny Linwood, he made a brief reference to his 'brothers.' I didn't think much of it at first, but combined with this, I think all three of these kids were taken with the intent of ingratiating them into their 'new' families."

"But why?" Amanda said. "If the kidnappers knew they were going to let them go, why bother?"

"I'm not sure," I said. "But what scares me is that the Reeds somehow knew Raymond Benjamin. He owned the house they used. So how did a supposedly regular family, a loving father and mother with a young son, wind up in bed with a career criminal, and end up stealing someone else's child?"

None of us had the answer.

"So what else can I do?" Curt said.

"We need to confirm that the Reeds did in fact kidnap another child. And if we do that, and we can find out who that child is, hopefully we can find the Reeds and they can answer all these questions."

"It'll be tough," Curt said. "I can submit a request for a breakdown of all children reported missing within the past two weeks, but unless we can narrow down where the child was from we're basically looking in every town in every city in the country."

I thought for a moment. Then I said to Curt, "Cross-check your records with Yardley Medical Center, the pediatrics unit. I have a feeling whatever child was taken was born in Hobbs County, and was a patient of Dr. Petrovsky's, just like Daniel Linwood and Michelle Oliveira."

"How can you be sure?" Amanda said.

"Thiamine levels," I said. "I spoke to Jack's doctor at Bellevue and asked what might cause a child to go through what Daniel and Michelle did. According to him, it's likely they both suffered from a severe case of anterograde amnesia, exacerbated by depleted thiamine levels. He said that it was technically a form of short-term brain damage, but when thiamine and vitamin B1 levels dropped in patients whose thiamine levels were low to begin with, it could cause exactly what afflicted Daniel and Michelle. I think whoever has been kidnapped was born with low thiamine levels, and Dr. Petrovsky supervised it all."

Amanda said, "That would have to mean the kids were preselected based on their medical histories. Which means Petrovsky knew which kids to look out for."

"I think there's a strong chance he did just that. So this new Girl X was chosen for the same reasons Dan and Michelle were years ago—they were susceptible to having their thiamine levels tampered with to a far greater degree than a normal child. With the right—or wrong—nutrition and care, you could almost literally give a child short-term brain damage and harm their memory receptors."

"Which would explain why Daniel and Michelle didn't remember a thing about their time missing," Amanda said. "And it means the Reeds are expecting the same thing from this kid. Girl X."

"Find her," I said to Curt. "I'm tired of this bullshit, like one lost kid doesn't matter. What, because Hobbs County and Meriden got a few extra bucks, a few of the houses got a nice coat of paint, this is all swept under the carpet? These kids are giving their lives for some awful cause I don't understand."

"I hear you, man. Give me some time," Curt said. "I'll need to get medical records from Petrovsky's office, which won't be easy, especially since the dude's disappeared."

"He's dead," I said. "There's just no body to bury."

"Either way, the guy won't be answering his phone. Give me a day. I'll get an answer."

"Thanks, Curt, every second counts. Benjamin wasn't expecting us to follow Petrovsky, and who knows if the Reeds are even still alive. There's a chance that, like Petrovsky, they 'disappeared' the Reeds so nobody could ask questions. We need to see if we can find the Reeds before Benjamin takes desperate measures. And this is a guy who seems to be redefining the term."

32

Raymond Benjamin dialed the number of the motel. He'd made the reservation for the Reeds just before he'd told them what was going to happen to their home. He'd broken it to them matter-of-factly. He'd told them they might have to leave at a moment's notice, but didn't really believe himself it would ever come to that. Elaine seemed pretty unnerved but agreed to cooperate. Like always. Bob stayed silent, nodded at his wife's approval. But now it was Ray who was unnerved.

When the receptionist picked up, he said, "Yes, can you connect me to the room of Robert and Elaine Reed?"

"Hold a moment, sir." Ray heard typing in the background. "Sir, we don't have any record of anyone by that name checking in."

"But you do have a reservation, right?"

"Yes, sir, Mr. and Mrs. Robert Reed, weekly rates, supposed to have checked in yesterday, but according to this they haven't."

"Fuck me," Ray said.

"Excuse me, sir?"

"Nothing. You're sure about that?"

"Yes, sir. Would you like me to have a message waiting for them when they do check in?"

Ray slammed the phone down on the cradle so hard the plastic receiver broke in half. It took him far too long to jimmy open the door to the pay phone booth, and finally he cracked the glass when he kicked it inward with his foot. Vince was leaning up against the car, an errant toothpick sticking out of his mouth. Either it was lodged between two teeth or the man had simply forgotten it was there. Ray had a sudden desire to smack the thing out of his mouth. But he restrained himself.

This wasn't going as he'd hoped. Things had taken a drastic turn once Parker and the girl had arrived at the house on Huntley, and that necessitated burning the place down. Of course, doing that meant relocating the Reed family, which was an ordeal in and of itself.

He'd begun to worry about Bob and Elaine from nearly the moment they took the girl home. There was something in their eyes that was different from the other families, a sense of sorrow that worried him from the start. He'd told them from the first time he met them that they'd have to be strong. Keep everything in perspective. Look at this as short-term pain for a long-term solution. They were doing it for the right reasons, and years from now they'd be happy they did it.

Now he wasn't so sure.

Bob and Elaine had a motive. There was a reason they were chosen. The same way there was a reason Ray was good at his job, he expected the Reeds to live up to their end of the deal. Looking back on that one week that shaped Raymond Benjamin into what he'd become, he knew how fast one moment could change everything.

Few people knew the truth about Raymond Benjamin.

That all of the violence, everything that had occurred during the horrific, bloody days from September 9 to September 13 was because of him. While the riots started because the Attica prisoners were tired of being treated like animals, there was one spark that started the explosion.

The week of September 2, 1971, a small metal bucket was placed inside Ray's cell. It contained about a gallon of water. The guard told him it was his weekly supply of water to shower with. On September 8, during mess hall, Ray mouthed off about the food. He didn't remember his exact words, but it boiled down to the meat loaf tasting like it had been some poor guy's meat. That got him one cigarette burn behind his knee.

The next morning, on September 9, Raymond Benjamin thought he was in for the worst day of his life. The previous night, one of the guards came by, dropping a single roll of toilet paper into Ray's cell. *Hope you got a clean ass, 'cause this is the last one you're getting until the end of the month.*

Frustrated, Ray threw the roll back at the officer, hitting him in the head. It barely stunned him, but soon all of 5 Company was laughing their ass off. The guard turned red, told Ray he'd see him in the morning and walked off. While his fellow inmates hooted and hollered at the newly christened "Officer Shithead," Ray sat in his cell, shivering as if death itself was waiting for him. And for all he assumed, it was.

The next morning, September 9, all of 5 Company's cells opened, the sign for morning roll call. All cells except for Ray Benjamin's. As his friends walked past, they saw him still in the cell, sitting on the edge of his bed, knees quaking. Ray had never been so scared in his life. He could hear the footsteps of the guards as they did morning rounds, could hear the clomps as his friends walked past, knowing their buddy was about to face the worst beating of his life. Perhaps the last beating of his life.

Ray sat there and prayed. He apologized to the Lord for what his life had become. He apologized for his sins and promised that, if he was given another chance, he would make the most of it. He would right those wrongs. Ray's eyes were squeezed shut, tears pouring out the sides. He hoped it would be quick, if anything. That would be something to be thankful for.

Then Ray heard something odd. Footsteps coming back his way. But they weren't the loud *thump-thump* of the guards', they were the soft, muffled steps of the prisoners. Then Ray heard a man yelling, and damned if it wasn't Officer Shithead himself.

"You assholes get back here, right now!"

The 5 Company prisoners didn't go back to roll call. Instead they walked right back to their cells and sat down. Possum, a big black man from Alabama, said, "Fuck you. You gonna take one man, you gonna take all the men."

Possum was talking about Ray.

Soon Officer Shithead was marching down the cell block, nightstick unsheathed.

Officer Shithead didn't live another minute.

After they'd beat him to death with his own baton, Ray's brothers in 5 Company managed to get his cell open. Several minutes later, a guard heard a commotion down A Tunnel, went to see what the hell was taking 5 Company so long, and that's when the devil unleashed hell.

Ray survived the riots with his life, his sanity, and just one small scar on his cheek obtained on September 13 when the cops finally opened fire. A glass pane shattered, carving out a chunk of Ray's face. William "Billy Buds" Moss, a surgeon in lockup for raping a patient, stitched it together with a spool and tweezers stolen from the nurse's office, moments before it went up in flames.

Raymond Benjamin would be ejected from the penal system two years later. Thirty-nine people died in those riots. Most of them were buried. Officer Shithead, Ray later learned, had been burned beyond recognition. There was barely enough of him left to bury.

Leaving Attica, Ray Benjamin was a changed man. Not so much in deeds. He was still prone to violence, still had the temper of a pissed-off Viking, but now he had a cause. Not to mention a massive nicotine addiction. He told friends that after all the pain cigarettes had caused him in prison, he might as well get a little pleasure out of them.

Several times a month Ray would wake up at night, remembering that morning sitting in his cell, praying for forgiveness. Waiting for a death that, with mercy, decided to pass him over. He never forgot that. Never took it for granted. And every act of violence, everything he did that "society" wouldn't approve of, was going toward making things right. It didn't matter if people couldn't understand it. *He* knew it was right.

The Reeds were part of that plan. They were doing the right thing.

But now they were gone, and Ray Benjamin felt concern for the first time in a long time. If the Reeds lost their will, they could give up everything. Ray would go down. So would the big man. And everything Ray had worked for over the past thirty years would be lost.

Ray thought about the Reeds. Where could they have gone? And why would they suddenly decide to disobey such simple fucking directions?

They weren't at the motel. Elaine wasn't picking up her cell phone. He'd given them the address, a newly cloned phone, and now he couldn't find them. It was like they'd looked him in the eye and lied to him.

"This isn't good," he said to Vince. "The Reeds have disappeared."

Vince snorted a laugh, managed to keep the toothpick in his mouth. "Ain't that ironic."

Ray looked at him, then said fuck it. He couldn't help himself.

He slapped Vince across the face, the toothpick doing a little spiral before landing in a puddle of sludge several feet away. That made Ray smile.

When Vince recovered, he was holding his jaw, a thin trickle of blood at the corner of his mouth.

"Ow, man, what the fuck?"

"Couldn't take that stupid toothpick anymore."

"Christ, you could have asked me to throw it out!"

"Consider this an apology. Come on, let's go."

They got into the car, Ray shaking his head as Vince started the engine.

"What is it?" Vince said, mopping up his lip with a handkerchief.

"The Reeds," he said. "I don't trust them anymore. They don't realize this thing is bigger than them. They're being selfish, not realizing they're putting years of work at risk. I thought they could be trusted, that they had their family's best interests in mind. I guess I was wrong."

"What are you saying, boss?" Vince asked.

"I think when we find them, we need to make them gone."

"Gone like the kids? Or, like, *gone* gone?"

Ray looked at him, didn't say a word. Vince nodded solemnly. Ray patted the kid on the back. That was his answer right there. Then they drove away.

33

"According to DMV records," Curt said, "the Reeds drive a 2002 silver Ford Windstar, license plate JV5 L16. I don't think it'll come as a huge surprise to anyone that their current address is listed as 482 Huntley Terrace."

We were still at the 19th Precinct, corralled in a conference room on the second floor. Curt had already had to shoo away three other officers who tried to reclaim the room. When they couldn't offer concrete reasons for needing the space—the excuses ranged from "It has the only good coffee machine in the building" to "Fuck your mother"—I quickly figured out the cops simply didn't want us there. And that was fine with me. The more roadblocks were put up in our effort to find out the circumstances surrounding these kidnappings and Petrovsky's murder, the more insolent I became. Though I didn't think Curt would go so far as to have my back if I lost control and tried to pick a fight. And I was getting pretty damn close to that.

Amanda said, "So at least we have direct legal proof that ties the Reed family to this guy Benjamin. But we still don't know why the hell they have anything to do with a criminal."

"What if," I said, "the Reeds weren't linked directly to Benjamin?"

"Not sure I follow," Curt said.

"We're forgetting about Petrovsky. He knew Daniel Linwood and Michelle Oliveira. His career was based around children. Bob and Elaine Reed have one son, Patrick, and we suspect they might have kidnapped another child, too."

"I'm still waiting for the search on that," Curt said. "I'm hoping you're wrong."

"Anyway, isn't it possible that somehow the Reeds became linked to Benjamin *through* Petrovsky?"

"Like some sort of middleman?" Amanda asked.

"Exactly. I'm willing to bet Petrovsky knew Benjamin, and Petrovsky knew the Reeds, as well. Amanda, is there any way you could get information about Patrick Reed? I have a feeling we might see Dmitri Petrovsky's signature on his delivery forms as well."

"I'm on it," Amanda said. She gathered up her coat and purse and stood up. "Good luck, guys." She spent an extra moment looking at me, then she left.

Curt waited until the door had closed, then he said, "So what's going on with you two?"

"Nothing," I said. "Absolutely nothing."

"You sound like you're as happy with that situation as I am with my mortgage."

"Just don't know what to do. I broke up with her, but not a day goes by I don't regret it. In my mind I can erase that mistake, but expecting her to… I wouldn't expect that."

"You think maybe part of the reason you're working this story so hard is to be close to her?"

"I don't know."

"That's not a no."

"No, it's not."

"Part of me don't feel right letting her do some of the dirty work on this. I mean, look at you, man. Seems like every few months you get beat up. You really want her that close to you?"

"That's why I broke it off in the first place," I said. "I took the decision out of her hands. But she's been with me every step of the way on this. Relationship or not, she wants to be here. And it's not my place to tell her not to."

"That's a selfish way to look at the world, especially if she might be in danger."

"I'd kill myself if anything happened to her, Curt," I said. "But she's a hell of a strong woman, and I know that anything I can take, she can, too. Probably more so. She works with kids every day, and she's seen some of the most terrible cases of abuse you can imagine. She doesn't talk about it much, because, well, who wants to bring that kind of work home with her? But don't be fooled into thinking she's in this for me, or for the adrenaline. This is a cause for her. And I respect that."

"So if it's a cause for her, and it's about my job for me, what's it about for you?"

I thought about that for a moment, then said, "The truth, man. It's about the truth. That's *my* job."

"So since we're both on the job," Curt said, "how the hell do we find the Reeds? They obviously jetted from Huntley before smokey the pyromaniac got his hands on the house. They're registered with Verizon, but the phone's going right to voice mail. No luck tracking it down just yet. There are no known family members for either Robert or Elaine Reed, and we're checking their phone records for friends and acquaintances."

"They won't be at a friend's house," I said. "Benjamin got them into the house on Huntley so they could keep private. That place was like a fortress. You don't go through all that trouble only to have Elaine spill the beans to someone in her knitting group. You said they have a minivan, right?"

"Yeah, a Windstar."

"Nobody buys a minivan for one kid. I'm getting more and more sure that they've kidnapped another child. Anyway, I'm betting they're staying at a motel somewhere. A place where nobody knows them, and nobody knows where they are except for Benjamin and his crony."

"There's a lot of motels in this country, man. You can't expect us to cover all of them."

"No, but if you're a parent with two bawling kids in a minivan, do you really think you're driving ten, fifteen hours for the same kind of motel you can get within a few miles? My bet is they're still in the state. Say a four-hour drive, make it an even two hundred and forty miles, and that's your radius from Huntley Terrace. They'll stay away from major cities and metropolitan areas."

"There's still a shitload of fleabag motels in that range, Henry."

"Christ, Curt, you're a cop. Don't you guys do this all the time?"

Curt smiled at me. "I'm on it. Go run some more of your magic. I'll give you a ring if we get any more info on the Reeds or other missing children."

"Thanks, Curt, appreciate it. You want to sock me in the eye once, gain a little street cred among your fellow boys in blue?"

"Tempting, but tell you what. Leave the building like I broke you down into tears, we'll call it even. Deal?"

"Deal."

I left the 19th Precinct with a sullen look on my face, as if Curt Sheffield had just ripped the head off my favorite teddy bear. Rounding the corner onto Lexington, I called the *Gazette* from my cell phone. I asked to be connected to Wallace Langston's office, and the editor-in-chief picked up immediately.

"Wallace, it's Henry."

"Henry, good to hear from you. What's the latest?"

"I'm in the middle of tracking down a family that I'm ninety-nine percent sure is part of some sort of weird kidnapping ring that involves the Linwood and Oliveira children. There's a link between the Reed family and this psycho Benjamin who mistook me for an ashtray. I'm running down the link, and when I have that I'll let you know. How's Jack doing?"

Wallace sighed. "They released him yesterday. He's got the rest of the week off for some R and R and detox. I've never seen the man like this before. It worries me."

"What do you mean?"

"Jack has been with this newspaper since he was a young man, Henry, younger than you are now. He's worked himself to the bone for his profession. He's a legend in this field, and he's paid his dues to become that. But Jack's not a young man anymore. You can't go with that same kind of drive, that kind of passion at his age, without compensation. I wonder…God, I can't believe I'm saying this…but I wonder if his career isn't beginning to wind down."

I felt like I'd been punched in the gut. But rather than a sensation of pain emanating from it, I felt anger. How could Wallace even begin to question the longevity of Jack's career? Things were looking bad now, but everyone was entitled to fall off the wagon once or twice. It was a divot in the road, not a full-blown earthquake. And it pissed me off to hear Wallace insinuate otherwise.

"He'll be just fine," I said through gritted teeth. "Give it a week or two, he'll be tracking leads and breaking stories like he's a new man."

"I sincerely hope you're right, Henry. But it worries and saddens me to think you may not be. Listen, my friend, keep pushing on this story. I've gotten three calls from Gray Talbot's office since your detainment up in Hobbs County. Our friend the senator is no doubt perturbed that we've ignored his requests. I expect a hate-o-gram to arrive any moment in the mail, but until you see me led away in handcuffs, keep pressing."

"That's what I do," I said. "Talk to you later, Wallace." I hung up.

It took a moment to register that my stomach was growling. I stopped at a deli and wolfed down a bagel with lox spread and a large coffee. When that was polished off, I had half a blueberry muffin for dessert. My natural reaction to that would be to run it off the next day, but my legs were beat. I hadn't put in for vacation time in ages. I didn't think Wallace would be all that surprised to see my paperwork cross his desk in the near future.

When I finished the meal, I took a cab back home, sat down on the couch and waited. This was the worst part of the game, and as a reporter the most frustrating part of the job. The waiting.

So much of my work was dependent on sources getting back to me, but every moment that phone didn't ring there was a fear that the story was slipping through my fingers. I worried that Curt's searches would turn up empty. That Amanda would discover Patrick Reed was born in Idaho and not Hobbs County like I suspected. Not to mention cigarette boy Benjamin wandering the streets somewhere, and I had a little more anxiety at that moment than I liked.

I had to distract myself. Music, that would do it. Calm, soothing music.

I turned my computer on, opened iTunes and started to play Dylan's "Not Dark Yet." The melody calmed me.

I thought about Daniel Linwood, Michelle Oliveira. Two children with their lives once laid out in front of them, yet forevermore they would be outcasts. They would always live with that stigma, never fitting in. The beauty of a child, the pain from a life stolen away.

And just while those lyrics had begun to burrow their way into my skull, my cell phone rang. If there was ever a time to be jostled out of morose thoughts.

The caller ID read "Amanda cell." I answered it without hesitating.

"Hey, wondering what happened to you."

"Seriously? It's been, like, fifteen minutes. What the hell do you expect?"

"Sorry, just a little antsy here. I feel like things are starting to become clearer."

"Well, your feelings might be real. Turns out that Patrick Reed, son of Robert and Elaine Reed, was born on May 29 four and a half years ago at Yardley Medical Center in Hobbs County."

"You're shitting me."

"Nope. And I'll give you three guesses at to who signed the delivery certificate."

"I'll take Dmitri Petrovsky for one thousand, Alex."

"Ding ding ding. I'm actually out of cash, so I hope you'll take your winning either in an IOU or a Sweet'n Low packet I just dug out of my jeans pocket."

"Amanda, you know what this means, right? The Reeds knew Petrovsky. Their son was born at the same hospital as Daniel Linwood and Michelle Oliveira. That's their link to Raymond Benjamin. Somehow he found out about these kids through Petrovsky."

"Wait," Amanda said. "Patrick Reed wasn't kidnapped, he's the Reeds' biological son. What gives?"

"Patrick isn't the issue, I just needed a connection so we could figure out how the Reeds came in contact with Benjamin. Petrovsky is the middleman. Benjamin the facilitator. The Reeds—I'm not quite sure what they are."

"So we have three pieces to the puzzle, but the three pieces are blank right now."

"Yeah, pretty much. We need to find the Reeds. Petrovsky is dead and Benjamin will kill us before he talks." I heard a beeping sound on my phone. I looked at the display. It read "Curt cell."

"Amanda, Curt's on the other line. I need to take this."

"Call me right back."

"Will do." I hung up. My palms were sweating. This was all coming together. The bigger picture was still invisible, but it would come. Benjamin. Petrovsky. The Reeds. What the hell were they all involved in?

"Hello?" I said, answering the call.

"Hey, man, I got a ton of info for you." It was Curt. He was talking fast. "We might have found your girl. Two weeks ago, Caroline Twomey, age nine, was taken from her parents' home in Tarrytown. She was reported missing the next day, but the Tarrytown PD haven't turned up any leads. I did a background check on Caroline's parents, a Mr. and Mrs. Harold and Phyllis Twomey. Harold works construction but hasn't made more than thirty-five grand a year in his whole life. Phyllis is a part-time schoolteacher. And by part-time, I mean she hasn't worked in nearly five years."

"Really? Why is that?"

"Five years ago, Phyllis Twomey was arrested for shoplifting. The store decided to press charges, and Phyllis was fined five hundred bucks and sentenced to fifty hours of community service. She hasn't worked a day since."

"What store did she rob?"

"A Healthwise pharmacy just three miles from their house. They caught her on the security camera, cops met her at her house fifteen minutes after it was called in."

"Curt," I said. "What did she steal?"

"Says here she tried to steal two dozen vials of insulin."

There it was. I knew the link. I knew why Benjamin had come to Petrovsky. I knew why Daniel Linwood, Michelle Oliveira and Caroline Twomey had been chosen.

"Curt," I said. "Daniel Linwood is a diabetic. So is Caroline Twomey. When I spoke to Michelle Oliveira's violin teacher, Delilah Lancaster, she mentioned noticing needle marks on the girl's skin. She thought it might have been drugs, but it was because Michelle is a diabetic. They're all diabetic."

"So Dmitri Petrovsky was feeding Raymond Benjamin information about diabetic children that were born in his pediatric ward. For what purpose?"

"Diabetics are more susceptible to lower thiamine levels," I said. "If they don't get proper nutrition, it can result in both short-term and long-term brain damage. One of the side effects of short-term brain damage is Korsakoff syndrome, which prevents the brain from processing certain compounds, and prevents the brain from retaining long-term memory."

"That would explain why Michelle and Dan Linwood had no recollection of their years missing."

"Right," I said. "But whoever took Dan and Michelle, and now this Twomey girl, knew about their conditions. And they were prepared for it. They didn't want to kill these children, they just needed to get them away from their families for a period of time."

"Why?" Curt asked.

"I don't know yet," I said. "But I'm sure the Reeds can answer that question for us."

"Well, that was my next piece of information. You owe me a steak dinner after all this, Henry."

"Come on, cough it up."

"You're lucky it's a slow day. I had a dozen cops calling every hotel and motel within a two-hundred-and-fifty-mile radius of that house on Huntley Terrace. We got an affirmative for a Mr. Robert Reed at a Sheraton in Harrisburg, Pennsylvania. About two hundred miles from Hobbs County."

"Holy shit, Curt, you're a godsend." I checked my watch. It was six o'clock. With any luck I could be in Harrisburg by nine. "Listen, I need to call Amanda. I'm driving up there right now."

"Like hell you are," Curt said. "You have no idea what's up there. Hell, that's not even my jurisdiction."

"Lucky for me I don't have to worry about jurisdiction," I said. "News is interstate. Sorry about that, bro."

"You asshole," Curt said. "All right, screw it. I'm coming with you. You got a car, right?"

"Sure do."

"Then count me in. And I call shotgun."

"Bitch, please. You think there's any chance in hell you're riding shotgun over the girl I'm still in love with?"

Curt laughed. "No, guess not, but at least you finally admitted it."

"What do you want, a cookie? Meet me here in half an hour." I hung up. Called Amanda. Set the meeting time. Wondered if somehow Robert and Elaine Reed expected some company.

34

"Hello, miss, are you still there?"

"Yes, Mr. Benjamin, I'm processing your information as we speak."

"Thanks a lot, dear. And just to be sure, you got that the car was loaned to a Mr. and Mrs. Robert Reed?"

"Yes, sir, I heard you the first three times. Now, can you give me Mr. Reed's date of birth and social security number?"

Raymond Benjamin repeated both numbers to the woman on the other line. He was standing at a pay phone at Eighty-First and Columbus in New York City. Vince was Uptown. He'd called frantically ten minutes ago, saying Parker, the girl and some black guy had gotten into the same car they'd been driving the other night and sped away. Vince said they looked like they were in a hurry. And that made Ray Benjamin nervous. He had a feeling somehow Parker had found the Reeds. And if he had, Benjamin would be in a world of trouble.

No, there was still time. But it meant Ray had to get creative.

The Ford Windstar had been bought in his name. He'd never used that stupid Pioneer system, since the last time he trusted a computer for direction he ended up somewhere with cows and silos. Not exactly what he was looking for.

The one thing he did have to be thankful for was reading the damn machine's instruction book. Just in case. He remembered reading that, in case of an emergency, you could call a Pioneer technician and receive help in either starting or locating your car.

When he signed the papers, he'd made sure to authorize Robert and Elaine Reed, as well. They'd be the ones driving it, and he didn't need them to be pulled over and have to explain their relationship. Thankfully he knew everything about Robert and Elaine Reed, from social security numbers to their son Patrick's birthday.

"Mr. Benjamin, how did you say you lost the car again?"

"Lost it?" Ray said. "Actually, we think our son took it out for a spin last night, got drunk and got a ride home from a friend. When he sobered up he couldn't remember where he left it. I'd really rather not get the police involved unless we have to. All I want is my car back."

There was a moment, and then Raymond heard the woman say, "Mr. Benjamin, according to our tracking system your car has been located in Harrisburg, Pennsylvania. On Lindle Road, right by the entrance to I-283 North. It looks like it's right off of exit 2. Sir, you're sure you don't want us to contact the police? Our caller ID shows you're phoning in from New York City. That's quite a drive."

"No worries," Raymond said. "I'm a fast driver."

35

The Harrisburg Sheraton was right off of the Interstate, about a hundred yards down Lindle Road and a few miles east of the Oberlin College campus. Though the night sky had descended on the city, I could see that the trees were full, the grass lush. The town had a wonderful, old-America feel. And we were less than ten miles from Hershey Park. Unfortunately, this wasn't the best time to check out the chocolatey goodness.

Some terrible techno music was playing on the radio, but I hadn't been paying attention for the past hour. Every minute that passed we were closer to finding the Reed family and getting to the bottom of this bizarre triangle.

Dmitri Petrovsky.

Robert and Elaine Reed.

Raymond Benjamin.

Three groups of people that would never have any sort of interaction in a normal world, yet for some reason they'd become intimately involved in one another's lives and businesses. I hoped Curt's boys had done their homework at the precinct, and I hoped that, if this was the place, that the Reeds hadn't already packed up ship.

My eyes were weary. A three-and-a-half-hour trip

doesn't sound like much, but after a full day's work in addition to the other stresses involving Jack and this story, it was all I could do to keep focus. I had to keep telling myself what the opportunity was here, both the truth to be revealed and the benefits for the *Gazette*. Things would be tough with Jack out. I liked Wallace, and the man had been almost endlessly supportive, but he was hardly a mentor. I was on my own at work. Thankfully the two people in the car were my backup.

The Harrisburg Sheraton was a fairly quaint hotel, the low-slung roof lined with hanging plants out front. Lamps in the grass lit up a trail that went from the parking lot to the entryway, and the guest rooms, about eight floors of them, were just a few yards beyond.

I parked the car, turned off the ignition.

"How you all feeling?" I said as we exited the car. Curt stretched, his long limbs raised into the sky. I noticed the gun by his hip. He'd come in plainclothes. There wouldn't be much love for an NYPD cop in PA. Amanda had on a nice purple blouse. She wrapped her arms around her chest, looked slightly worried.

"I'm good," she said. "Could use a bathroom break."

We walked into the hotel. The floors were covered in beige tiles, and half a dozen overstuffed chairs surrounded tables. A few hotel guests were seated, reading books and newspapers, sipping coffee.

Curt said, "They're not just going to give us the room number. I thought about this. We need a way to find out what room the Reeds are in without alerting them to the fact that we're here."

"Oh, man," Amanda said, sighing. "You guys are seriously like troglodytes. Does everything have to depend on me?"

She walked up to the reception desk as Curt and I

watched, curious, scared and feeling a little emasculated. We trailed behind Amanda just enough that we could hear, but far enough behind in case her ruse specifically did *not* include us.

"Hi," Amanda said, sprawling her arms across the desk. "Lissen, I need to see my boh-friend. He's staying in your ho-tel. I think he might be with his wife, so I guess this really is a ho-tel."

The receptionist, a guy with acne scars and a badge that read "Clark," who looked like his first day on the job was tomorrow, said, "I'm sorry, ma'am, what can I help you with?"

"My boh-friend," she slurred. "Robert Reed. He's in this ho-tel. I need to know what room he's staying in."

"Ma'am, we're not supposed to give out guests' information. If you'll just…"

Amanda dug into her purse, then slapped something down on the desk. Clark's eyes bugged open. Curt and I leaned in closer. When I saw what it was, I had the exact same reaction as Clark.

"M-Ma'am," Clark said, stammering now. "That's a condom."

"You're damn right. Robert promised me a good time tonight, so if you don't tell me where I can find him, I'm jus' gonna have to find someone else at this ho-tel to do what he can't." She looked around, a lascivious grin on her face. "Do you have a bar in this hotel?"

Clark gulped, then ran some digits into his computer. He looked at Amanda as though to make sure she hadn't started propositioning guests. She hadn't, though she was licking her lips. I had to close my mouth, look away.

"Mr. Reed is staying in room 602. Now, if you'll please, just go find him. We don't need anyone causing a scene."

"Much obliged," she said, leaning over. *"Clark."*

Amanda headed for the elevators. We waited a moment before following her. When the doors closed, I said, "You sure you weren't trained at Juilliard?"

"God, you guys could use a set of balls sometimes. Come on."

The door dinged open. We followed the signs toward room 602. The halls were lined with seashell-shaped lights, and the carpet was a zigzagging pattern of red-and-black squares. A few pieces of standard hotel art hung on the walls. Men fishing off piers. A windmill across a bay. I had no eye for art. For all I knew these pieces could have secretly been worth millions.

When we came to 602, we stopped in front of it. Curt and Amanda stood to either side of me.

"I'll do the talking," I said. "Curt, if we need you…"

"I have my badge on me, Henry."

As I got ready to knock, I heard the *ding* of another elevator opening onto the sixth floor.

"Hold on a second," I said. "Just make sure they're going in another direction. Nobody needs to see three people hanging around the hallway."

They didn't respond. The footsteps appeared to be heading our way. No big deal, I thought. Hotel guests going back to their hotel room. Even if they were heading this way, they'd enter their room and be done with it. We'd be talking to the Reeds before anyone had a chance to get suspicious.

I leaned back against the wall, pretended to fiddle with my cell phone. When I saw a shadow appear at the other end of the hall, I turned to look at the guests that were coming.

I nearly dropped the phone when they came into view.

I recognized the first man immediately, and I dove for Amanda just as Raymond Benjamin pulled a gun from his coat and opened fire.

I heard Amanda scream as bullets smashed into the wall above us. I thought we were safe, but then I heard another, deeper yell, turned to look, and saw Curt Sheffield on the ground, blood pouring from his leg.

"Curt!" I screamed.

I pushed Amanda toward the other end of the hall where an exit door was visible, and by that time Curt had taken the gun from his hip holster. Benjamin was reloading when Sheffield emptied three bullets into the hallway. Ray Benjamin managed to dive for cover, but two of the bullets struck his sidekick square in the chest. The younger man went toppling backward, his back smacking against the wall, where he slid down, leaving a bloody smear.

Benjamin was gone. I heard footsteps running toward the elevators. He was getting away.

I knelt down by Curt. His hand was pressing down on the wound, hard, but blood was still seeping through his fingers.

"Benjamin," Curt said, the pain evident in his voice. "Don't let the fucker get away."

Amanda appeared beside us. She'd taken off her fleece, then rolled it up and tied it around Curt's leg. He howled in pain as she pulled the loop together, trying to stem the flow of blood.

I looked at them both. Amanda had taken her cell phone out. She said, "I called 911. Make sure he doesn't hurt anybody else."

I nodded, then sprinted for the exit door. My pulse raced as I looked for the stairwell. A diagram of the floor plan was on the wall; the stairs were just to my left. I ran for them, banged the door open and hurtled down the stairs as fast as I could.

By the time I got to the first floor I was out of breath. When I shoved open the stairwell door, I could hear panic in the lobby. Several people were screaming, a rolling cart was overturned and an elderly man looked to be unconscious. I ran toward the lobby exit, but then another thunderous gunshot exploded in the night, and I dove behind a marble wall for protection. I waited a minute, unsure of what to do, then took a few quick breaths and ran for the exit.

As I ran into the warm evening air, I heard a car's ignition turn on and a pair of brake lights come on at the other end of the parking lot. I ran for it, saw a dark BMW peeling backward. It backed up into a pool of light cast by a lamp, and I read the license plate numbers, punched them into my cell phone.

I couldn't chase Benjamin's car. The fight was over. I had to see how my friends were.

Just as I ran back into the lobby, the elevator door opened and out came Curt Sheffield, hobbling, leaning on Amanda for support. The fleece was soaked through with blood. I heard sirens approaching from outside. I ran to Curt.

"Christ, man, how is it?"

"I'll live," he said through gritted teeth. Then he took one hand from Amanda's shoulder and grabbed my shirt. "The Reeds," he said. "They're gone."

"But we found this," Amanda said. She pulled a man's leather wallet from her pocket. "It was down at the other end of the hall, through a set of double doors. I thought I heard another noise, like several people running down the stairs. It's Robert Reed's. They must have been approaching the room. He was going for his room key, then dropped it when he heard the gunshots. The key is still inside."

"I saw them," Curt said, the pain evident on his face. "Damn it, if only I could run…"

Amanda helped him sit, kept pressure on his wound.

I took the wallet, opened it. The key card was nestled inside one of the slits inside. I went through the rest of it. Credit cards. Driver's license. And a small slot for photos.

I opened it up. There was a picture inside that looked awfully familiar.

The shot was of a young boy. It was taken from behind, from a close distance. There was nothing special about the shot. The boy's face was turned away and he was in midstride.

I slipped the photo from the wallet and turned it over. On the back of the photo was written one word.

Remember.

36

Curt had seen the Reeds approaching from the other end of the hallway. The family looked happy. Curt recognized Robert from his driver's license photo. And when he saw that Robert was with a woman and two children, he knew for sure that this was the family we'd been searching for.

I confirmed with the hotel restaurant that the Reeds had finished a late supper just a few minutes earlier. Then they'd gone upstairs. They must have seen Curt lying outside their room, blood everywhere. That's when they'd run.

On the way to the hospital, Curt said they'd likely seen the body at the other end of the hall, as well. If so, they probably recognized the dead man. If they knew Raymond Benjamin, chances were they'd met his flunky. And with all that death and blood, they must have known Ray Benjamin had come for them.

We followed Curt to the Harrisburg hospital, the primary hub for all the medical centers in the Harrisburg area. They'd taken Curt right into surgery. Amanda and I sat in the waiting room as a doctor explained that the bullet had nicked his femoral artery. Luckily the bullet had missed severing the vessel by half a centimeter, otherwise, he said, we'd be having an entirely different conversation.

I'd given the license plate number to the Harrisburg chief of police, a burly man named Hawley who had a look on his face that said as soon as they found Benjamin, the three of us would have hell to pay. An APB was put out on a dark BMW with New York plates, but an hour later the license plate was found abandoned in a gas station in Bethlehem. Raymond Benjamin was gone.

Curt would be laid up for several days. Amanda and I slept in the hospital that night, occasionally shifted positions in the waiting room. Amanda waking up on top of me, then moving; me waking up leaning on her shoulder, not wanting to move.

When morning came and the doctors confirmed that Curt was out of danger, we went in to see him.

Our friend was heavily sedated. His leg was swathed in bandages. We approached his bed, cautious, unsure if he could hear us or understand what happened.

As I got closer, I heard Curt whisper, "Henry."

"I'm here, buddy." I took Curt's hand in mine. Amanda stood beside me. I noticed her absently rubbing her hands on her jeans.

"The Reeds," he said. Curt swallowed, with some difficulty. Then he licked his lips. "The Reeds, man. They recognized Benjamin. They were scared."

I nodded, squeezed his hand.

"Find them," he said. "Now, get out of here before somebody else shoots me instead of you."

Amanda and I walked out of the hospital like two zombies who hadn't slept in weeks. Her eyes were bloodshot, her tank top caked with sweat and dirt. Her blouse was in some medical waste bin. Now she wore a gray sweatshirt, two sizes too large. The only thing that had survived the night physically and emotionally intact was our car.

We began the drive back to New York in silence. Amanda turned on the radio. Found some talk station that neither of us listened to, but it at least punctured the quiet. When we saw a rest stop, we pulled in and got a few fast-food burgers for the road. We ate without talking, arrived in New York three hours later barely having said a word.

When we pulled onto the Harlem River Drive in Manhattan, I turned to Amanda.

"Where does Darcy live again?" I asked.

Amanda shook her head. "Just take me home."

"Where do you mean..." I began to say, but when Amanda looked at me I realized what she meant.

I parked the car on the street, then walked back to my apartment, finding Amanda's arm intertwined with mine. I found an old pair of shorts that were too small for me, and a Cornell T-shirt. Amanda put both on. The T-shirt fit like a nightgown, drooping down to her knees. I turned off all the lights and climbed into bed.

Amanda lay down next to me. I could hear her breathing, could feel my heart beating next to hers.

She turned onto her side, nuzzling her head into the nook between my head and shoulder. Her arm wrapped around my waist. And there she lay, soon drifting into sleep. I watched Amanda for as long as I could, staring at that face, knowing how hard it would be to spend one more minute without it next to mine at night. I thought about Curt and prayed he'd recover completely, thanked whoever it was that watched over us that we'd escaped with his life.

I prayed that Caroline Twomey was still alive and healthy, and that we would find her soon. I thought about all of that, and then my muscles quit on me and I drifted to sleep.

37

I woke at seven-fifteen, like I did most mornings. My alarm was set every day to go off at seven-thirty on the dot, but my internal alarm had a wicked sense of humor, always screwing me out of fifteen minutes of shut-eye a day.

Blinking the sleep from my eyes, I leaned over to see Amanda rolled up in my comforter like a pig in a blanket, only if the pig were a beautiful woman and… I decided to just stop that train of thought before I accidentally said it to Amanda and wound up with my head shoved up my ass. She was still wrapped in my clothes, her eyes shut, snoring lightly. I leaned over and shut off the alarm clock, then rolled out of bed, picked some clean clothes out of my dresser, went into the living room and got dressed there so as not to wake her.

I left the apartment, picked up two Egg McMuffins and two large cups of coffee, and was setting up breakfast on my meager dining room table when Amanda appeared in the doorway.

"Morning," she said, rubbing her eyes. She looked at her finger—likely identifying a smudge of eye gunk—then flicked it away. She offered a goofy smile and noticed the setup. "You got breakfast?"

"Straight from the kitchen at Mickey D's."

"Yum. Just like Mom used to make."

"Your mom worked the fry-o-lator."

"All right, enough out of you, smart guy. What do you have?"

I unwrapped the sandwiches, opened the coffees. I had ketchup waiting for her, knowing she liked to slather her eggs with the stuff. She took a seat, her eyes still red, and began to pick at the food.

"How'd you sleep?" I asked.

"Better than you'd think after a day like yesterday," she said. "Guess your brain trumps all, tells you you're too tired to stay up all night thinking about things. Like Curt lying on the floor bleeding everywhere."

"Yeah," I said.

"That's all you can say?" Amanda said, looking at me as if I'd just committed to invading Iran by myself.

"Don't know what else to say. It's just overwhelming. You know, seeing Curt injured like that. Seeing Jack in the hospital the other day. Two of my best friends have nearly died over the past week. I'm sorry if I'm not as articulate as usual."

"I didn't mean to suggest you didn't care," Amanda said. "But…do you wonder, ever, if it's worth it? I mean I'm not a reporter, I haven't spent a lot of time in the 'field'…but unless you're in Afghanistan, I've never heard of any journalist being subjected to this much violence in such a short period of time. So either you happen to chase down these stories that inevitably lead to ruin, or…"

"Or what?" I said.

"Or you go looking for them on purpose."

"You know that's not true. Wallace assigned me to this story. He set me up to interview Daniel Linwood."

"And so you interviewed him. You wrote a terrific story about it. Then what?"

"That wasn't the end of it," I said. "Once I knew something was being hidden, I had to go deeper. It's what I do. If it leads to this, it leads to this, but I never want anybody to get hurt. Fact of the matter is, I don't want you coming along with me. I didn't want you to come last night."

Amanda looked hurt, confused. "So why did you let me come, then?"

"Because the last time I made a decision for you, it was the worst decision of my life."

Amanda took the bottle of ketchup, unscrewed the lid and peered inside.

"What are you doing?"

"Just making sure I'm comfortable with the amount of congealed tomato paste in here." She screwed it back on, squirted a dollop onto her sandwich. "Doesn't look too bad."

She took a bite, munched, then put it down. Looked me in the eye.

"So, what, you've grown over the past few months? All of a sudden things are clear?"

I didn't know how to respond to that. I felt my feelings for her were clearer than they'd ever been, and I'd been worse at hiding it than a silverback gorilla playing hide-and-seek. "Yes. Sort of. I mean, personally things are clear."

"Really," she said, in a manner that stated she didn't believe me.

"We were good together," I said.

Amanda chewed. "So that's your great introspection? As far as I know, we didn't break up because things were going badly. We broke up for other reasons. Do those not matter now?"

"They matter, but I know that this…thing…it's a two-person thing."

"Eloquent."

"What I'm saying is, I shouldn't have made the decision for you. And I understand how it would put you in a position where you'd be afraid to get hurt again."

"Hurt?" she said incredulously. "You're worried about me? Henry, you've cornered the market on that front. I'm not saying this to be funny, but when things happen like yesterday, I worry that you're not going to live to thirty. So you can worry about me being hurt emotionally, while I'm going to be the one at night wondering if you'll be coming home. Or if I'm going to get a call from Curt one day, and I'll hang up before he can say a word because I'll just know."

"I'm trying," I said. "I swear. But this Linwood story, I have to see it through. Especially now. One of my friends could have died yesterday. I have to find out what Ray Benjamin, Petrovsky and the Reed family are involved in. I need to know what Benjamin is going through all this trouble for. He strikes me as a career thug. The kind of guy you hire for muscle. Not the kind of guy who orchestrates a series of kidnappings spanning a decade."

"What's he been doing since he got out of prison?" Amanda asked.

"That's a good question."

"Ya think?" she said, taking another bite.

"I mean, he's had a massive house in his name, a minivan in his name. Where's his income coming from?" I looked at her sandwich. She had one or two bites left.

"What, you want me to leave because you have work to do?"

"No. I was just wondering if you were going to finish that."

She mocked throwing the last piece at me, then shoved it all in her mouth and swallowed.

"I'll walk out with you," she said. "You heading to the office?"

"Yeah. But I need to make a few calls and see if I can track down Raymond Benjamin's employment records. If the Reeds knew what was good for them, they'd be in Arizona by now."

"What about Benjamin?"

"If yesterday was any indication, he'll follow them into hell if he needs to. He was there to kill the Reed family. His gun was already drawn when he came into the hall at the hotel. If we don't find out what's going on, it won't just be another kidnapping to investigate, or having to deal with at least two people who have already been killed, but we'd have to live with the murder of an entire family."

38

Raymond Benjamin sat in the black Ford Escape and finished his third pack of the day. He rolled down the window and flicked the butt into the wind, where it landed among a pile of a dozen other butts that had come from the same vehicle.

Ray's heart had been racing for nearly twenty-four hours straight. Vince was dead. And though he had no love lost for the bumbling idiot, there was a huge difference between thinking someone a dolt and wishing them dead. He still couldn't figure out how Parker, the girl and the black guy with the gun had found the Reed family. It should have been quick, easy and relatively painless. At least for him and Vince. They'd both loaded their guns with dumdum rounds—hollow-point bullets. There were four targets: Robert Reed, Elaine Reed, Patrick Reed and the girl. Caroline Twomey. They didn't want to take any chances that one or more of them might have gotten away or fought back. He'd met Robert Reed before, and the man had some athletic genes.

The dumdum rounds were specially designed to expand upon impact, the bullets deforming when they entered the skin, causing a maximum of trauma. That way even if they didn't get off a kill shot, the wound would have been devastating enough to keep the target down. With four targets, you couldn't take chances.

Now Vince was dead. He'd worked with the man for going on seven years, and while Raymond never would have asked him to be on his team for Trivial Pursuit, he had developed an odd affection for him, like an owner with a three-legged dog.

When Parker began to investigate Petrovsky, Ray knew the plan had encountered serious problems. Reporters didn't just go away. If anything, resistance made them dig deeper. And especially after he looked into Parker, he realized that this guy would never quit, wouldn't back down, even when facing down the barrel of a gun. And to compound that, Bob and Elaine clearly left the house on Huntley in an effort to disappear, or at least hide out until they could figure out how to untangle themselves from the mess. Raymond had never fully trusted Elaine Reed. It took too long. Too much effort. When they ran away in that tin can of a minivan, to Raymond that's when the answer became clear. It wasn't something Raymond wanted to do, but it was necessary.

He'd run it up the flagpole. Nothing happened without the say-so of his employer. And, like Ray, his employer wasn't thrilled with the option but realized there was no choice. The Reeds had to disappear, along with Caroline Twomey.

As far as Ray knew, the Windstar was still in play. The Reeds were hardly versed in espionage. Hell, he'd be surprised if Elaine even knew how to use e-mail. Soon he'd have the car's location, and if the Reeds were there he would correct everything that had gone wrong.

He raised the window and turned on the engine. He

found a good jazz station with John Coltrane's quartet playing "Pursuance." He sat and listened to the entire song, felt the rhythm swim through his head. He reached into the glove compartment, closed his hand around the gun, and felt like everything would even out.

This time had been a mistake. It was unfortunate for Caroline Twomey. The next time, though, they would make things right.

39

I left the apartment with Amanda. We said our goodbyes outside. She hailed a taxi. I watched it pull away, for a second hoping that her window might lower, her head drifting out like in an old movie, where the cab would pull over and all sorts of romance would ensue. 'Course, that didn't happen. The cab pulled up to the light, then turned out of sight when it became green.

I trudged to the subway, feeling like the whole story had begun anew. We'd found the Reeds once, and that was almost out of blind luck. The next time, neither I, nor they, would be so lucky.

The Harrisburg police believed every word I said, and were more than happy to step up their patrol and look for this man Benjamin. It was maddening that we were facing such resistance in Meriden and Hobbs County, the cities that preferred to keep their heads stuck in the sand.

I got onto the subway, flipping through the *Gazette* to pass the time. As much as I was reading the paper for the articles, I also felt somewhat obligated to advertise our paper, make sure fellow straphangers were well aware of the newspaper of choice. Given the fact that I'd probably slept a total of five hours in the past two days and my eyes were totally bloodshot, they might have assumed the *Gazette* was a paper for strung-out junkies. Not exactly the target market for our reporting skills.

I got to the office at a quarter past nine. When I stepped off the elevator, I was greeted by a sight that cheered me up immediately.

Sitting at his usual desk was Jack O'Donnell. And he looked no worse for wear.

Hardly able to contain my excitement, I half walked, half sprinted through the newsroom and perched myself by Jack's desk. He was wearing one of his patented suit jackets with patched elbows, and pants that looked like they'd survived a horrific gardening accident. He smelled like Old Spice, and his beard was neatly trimmed. He looked exactly like what you'd expect a seasoned reporter would look like. The old newsman turned to me, a weary smile spreading across his lips.

"Hey there, if it isn't the boy who saved an old man's life."

"Come on," I said, "stop it." I felt like a schoolgirl complimented by the starting quarterback.

"Seriously, Henry, I owe you a great deal of gratitude. I've been on this earth for a long time—maybe I've outstayed my welcome considering some of the things I've done—but if not for you there's a good chance I wouldn't be here right now. So thank you."

"You don't need to thank me, Jack," I said. "You'd have done the same for me."

"Saved your life?" he said. "An old bag of bones like me can barely muster up the strength to get dressed in the morning, let alone go around saving lives. I appreciate the gesture, but you're the hero here."

"If you remember," I said, "you saved my life a few years ago. You know, that whole thing where they thought

I'd killed John Fredrickson? After Amanda, you were the only one that helped me. So get off this modesty kick, it doesn't suit you."

Jack smiled smugly. "Okay, I'll take it. But I promise, that's the last time you'll have to go picking me up off a floor. Unless I'm break-dancing, but then all bets are off. Speaking of bets, Wallace tells me you're in the middle of a pretty tense story. What's the deal?"

I recounted everything that had happened since I first interviewed Daniel Linwood. I told him about the discovery of Michelle Oliveira's disappearance, our attempt to follow Dmitri Petrovsky and the doctor's murder. About the Reeds and how I believed they'd kidnapped a girl named Caroline Twomey for reasons I still didn't know. And about Raymond Benjamin, the career thug who was somehow mixed up in all this.

Jack sat there, resting his head on his hands, his eyes betraying a sense of worry. When I was finished he stayed seated for another moment, took a breath, closed his eyes, and said, "It's not supposed to be this difficult, Henry. You can't put your life in danger on every story."

"That's not fair, Jack. I didn't choose for this to happen. I was assigned to the Linwood story, and then—"

"And then what? That should have been the end of it. Your piece on the Linwood boy was terrific. Case closed. So what happened?"

"Life happened," I said, feeling my blood pressure rise. "I can't speak for you, Jack, but I can't just let things go. As soon as I knew there was more to the Linwood story, as soon as I realized there were people who didn't want me digging, it's like…it's like someone turned on a switch inside me. And I can't stop until I know everything."

"You know what they call someone who needs to know everything?" Jack asked.

"A good reporter?" I replied.

"Dead," Jack said. "Every trail leads somewhere. Very few stories simply end. And if you keep playing Indiana Jones, at some point your luck's going to run out, and some very bad people are going to shut you up."

"Thanks for the pep talk," I said. "I'll take it under advisement." I stood up.

"Where are you going?" he asked.

"This story isn't finished," I said. "I have to go make some bad people upset at me."

I walked back to my desk, happy that Jack seemed healthy and vibrant, but annoyed that he was still questioning me. He had to know I couldn't just give this up. I needed to know why Raymond Benjamin got involved with the Reeds. And if, somehow, through all this he was connected to Daniel Linwood.

Rule number one in journalism: always start with the money.

Specifically, where did Raymond Benjamin get it?

I logged in to our LexisNexis terminal and ran a search for Raymond Benjamin. More than a thousand hits came up. I narrowed it down by adding search terms like "criminal," "jail" and several others. A few hits came up relating to the 1971 riots at Attica. Raymond Benjamin was named in several newspapers as one of the inmates involved, though none of them named him as having taken part in violence or murders. I scrolled down through several entries, and found one that piqued my interest.

It was printed in the *Buffalo News* out of Buffalo, New York. It was an in-depth article, four pages long, and incredibly detailed. It went on record about the horrific abuses suffered by the prisoners in Attica, and how the shoddy treatment was the catalyst for the riots.

One of the most damning pieces of evidence, the article stated, was the discovery by Dr. Michael Baden that all twenty-nine of the prisoners and all ten of their prison-guard hostages were killed by Attica guards themselves. This was a huge blow to the penal system, which for years had been spreading stories that the hostages had been killed by the prisoners, who had slit their throats. That the guards resorted to lethal measures so quickly and brutally was yet another blow to the system.

According to the article, a prisoner by the name of Raymond Benjamin was treated for facial lacerations, as well as severe dehydration and malnutrition. When asked about his conditions inside the prison, Benjamin stated he'd eaten only one meal a day the week before the riot, hadn't showered more than three times a month the prior year, and had repeatedly been subjected to other forms of torture and brutality. Strangely, though, Benjamin refused to blame the prisoners or the guards for his wounds. Benjamin was quoted as saying, "I got nobody to look at besides myself, where I come from. Sometimes you make your own choices, sometimes where you come from makes 'em for you. Me, my fate was set long before I had any say in it."

All of this seemed to jibe with what I remembered of Benjamin. He'd brought up Attica that night I was held in the basement on Huntley. And I distinctly remembered that long, thin scar running down his cheek.

I went through every article I could find pertaining to Raymond Benjamin and the riots. Then, in a small item in the *Journal News,* a paper that served Westchester, Putnam and Rockland counties in New York, I found a short item in which Raymond Benjamin was named. It was accompanied by a photograph, as well. I recognized Benjamin immediately.

The photo was taken at a ribbon-cutting ceremony at the opening of a new shopping mall in Chappaqua, New York. Chappaqua was a pretty tony suburb, and I wondered what Ray was doing there. In the photo he was wearing a hard hat. And he was clapping. The caption read, "Workers from Powers Construction celebrate. Raymond Benjamin of Hobbs County among those proud of this state-of-the-art development."

Right there, two things leaped out at me. Raymond Benjamin was from Hobbs County. Just like Daniel Linwood and the Reed family. Not to mention Dmitri Petrovsky. No doubt that's how Ray met the good doctor.

And second, according to the article, Benjamin was employed by a company called Powers Construction. I couldn't picture the man who pressed a lit cigarette to my skin working on a job site, holding a jackhammer under his gut. It didn't seem right. This was a guy whose job was to hurt, to kill, not to build.

Unless it was a sham.

I logged off the machine and went straight to Wallace's office. He was on the phone, but when he saw me enter he said, "I'll call you back," and hung up. He turned to me, pressed his palms on the desk.

"Henry," he said. "How's your friend Sheffield?"

"He'll pull through," I said. "A centimeter in another direction and it would have been a different story. He'll have a tough recovery, but he's a tough guy."

"I'm glad to hear that. And you saw Jack out there— the place wasn't the same without him."

"No, sure wasn't."

"And how are you holding up?"

"Can I use up my daily allotment of 'I've been better'?"

"Consider it done."

"Great," I said. "What do you know about an outfit called Powers Construction?"

Wallace shook his head. "Doesn't ring a bell. Why do you ask?"

"I've been doing some research on the man I think is behind these kidnappings, and he's named in a New York paper as working with this Powers Construction company. It just doesn't seem to make sense. The guy I saw seems to be more handy with a gun than a screwdriver."

"I'm sorry, off the top of my head I don't know."

"You think it could be a front? He's employed there for legal purposes, maybe does his wet work on the side? You know, waste-management consulting?"

Wallace chuckled. "It's possible," he said. "But then why would Powers Construction employ the man if he's got a record—which he would have to disclose—and to top that off, he's hardly a model employee?"

"Until now, he hasn't been in any trouble since the seventies. Something just feels off here."

"Do some looking into this Powers Construction," Wallace said. "Are they a legit outfit? And where are they based out of?"

"Putnam County," I said. "They've done work all over the surrounding towns. Including Hobbs County, which as it turns out is the birthplace of our very own psychopath Benjamin."

"You know, now that I think about it," Wallace said, "I remember reading somewhere that Powers Construction was responsible for some pretty major jobs. Not just commercial, but residential, too. If I remember correctly, a congressman who recently retired had a mansion built by Powers."

"I'll check it out," I said. "But if you're right, it definitely seems like these might be some big-time players in real estate development."

"Strange times for that market," Wallace said. "Millions of people's lives are being ruined by the subprime mortgage mess. Government's doing what it can to help, but it can't help everyone. You're going to have a lot of foreclosures over the next few years. And that means a lot of business for a company like Powers. People buy up those foreclosed homes, then either gut and renovate or simply tear them down and rebuild."

"Strange," I said, thinking. I felt like a piece of the puzzle might have just become clearer. "I spent a lot of time in Meriden and Hobbs County recently. And in both places it was obvious they'd seen more work than Joan Rivers. Each town was like a tale of two cities—one old and decrepit, one new and rebuilt."

"I'm sure if part of the town was rebuilt, it's only a matter of time before the rest catches up."

"Maybe," I said. "Even the Linwoods' house looked like it had been carved out of marble recently. When I read up on Daniel Linwood's kidnapping, the family received thousands of dollars in donations, public and anonymous. No idea if that went into their house, but I'll tell you, it wasn't the only one on the block that looked new. I'm wondering if Powers Construction has held the scalpel over Hobbs County. And if so, maybe they're tied into the mess somehow."

"Even if you think it's not about the money," Wallace said, "it's about the money."

Obviously there was a strong motive for Powers Construction to want to be a part of some major rebuilding projects in Hobbs County, as well as other towns and cities across the Northeast. I still felt like I was missing something. Follow the money, Wallace said. That's what I decided to do. I had to talk to Reggie Powers.

40

The home office of Powers Construction was located at Twenty-Third and Fifth in Manhattan. Before calling over, I decided to do a little research on the company. Their Web site had one of those incredibly flashy designs, and I could picture Reggie Powers grimacing as he handed over thousands of dollars to some tech geeks who'd likely never seen a working construction side. The company logo was an intersected *P* and *C*. Both letters looked like they were made out of curved steel, bolts and all.

Powers was, according to the site, one of the leading commercial and residential contractors in the entire Northeast. Their projects ranged from billion-dollar properties, from several financial institutions, to smaller homes and houses. They were credited for having essentially rebuilt several small towns, and were even one of the contractors called in to evaluate the Gulf Coast after the devastation of Hurricane Katrina. Whatever the size of the project, it looked like Powers Construction was the bidder to beat.

It was no secret that the construction industry had some shady underpinnings, since the majority of contracts were doled out to the lowest bidder. The problem therein was that the lowest bidders often miscalculated their budgets, necessitating a six-million-dollar property costing north of seven million. Yet the smarter, or shadier companies (amazing how often the two went hand in hand), worked out sweetheart deals to rig bids. The contractor would offer a bid far lower than any of his competitors, which was of course accepted. If they ran over budget, which was almost guaranteed, the bill would be settled under the table. This meant projects were bid on for far less money than they actually cost, keeping other companies out of the loop, but allowing the illegal parties to get rich based on the sheer number of developments they partnered on.

Reggie Powers himself had quite an interesting story. According to his online biography, he was the most influential black construction owner in the entire country. Born in Crown Heights in 1959, Powers had little formal education and had worked various construction jobs throughout his formative years. Then after the Crown Heights riots of 1991, Powers decided he was tired of seeing his neighborhood torn apart by violence, and was tired of seeing good men and women live in housing that was akin to inhumane treatment. Within five years, Powers had taken his own earnings, and with the help of lenders, bought out a company known as TBC—Thomas Blakeman Construction—renaming it Powers Construction. One of his first rebuilding projects was tearing down a number of projects in which drugs and violence were rampant. These buildings were replaced with low-income housing. According to Powers, it was the end of the dark days, and the beginning of a new Brooklyn.

Within a few years, Powers had become known not only as one of the wealthiest and most influential private contractors on the East Coast, but one of its biggest philanthropists. He donated time, money and manpower to numerous towns, and was credited with helping to lower crime rates across the board.

Of course, official biographies often swept more than their fair share under the carpet. Not to mention that Powers's relative inexperience made his volcanic rise even more shocking. I had to think that simply due to the sheer size of Powers Construction, it would be strange if they didn't have some sort of bid-rigging system going on.

Once I'd done some digging around regarding the company profile, I decided it was time to meet the man face-to-face. Reggie Powers. See what, if anything, he knew. And whether he was aware that one of his employees, Raymond Benjamin, was a murderer.

I called the main switchboard at Powers Construction, and a pleasant secretary picked up the phone. She sounded as if she'd been there a long time, even had a cadence nailed down.

"Po-*wers* Con-*struct-ion,* how may I direct your call?"

"Well, first I was wondering if you could give me the extension for one of your employees. The name is Raymond Benjamin. And after that I'd like to be transferred to Reggie Powers's office."

"One moment, sir," the woman said. I heard typing on the other end. Then I heard her mutter, *Hmm, that's odd.*

"Ma'am? Are you still there?"

"Yes, sir, sorry about that. According to our database, we do employ a Raymond Benjamin, but he doesn't have an office or an extension."

"Is there any contact information for him?"

"I'm sorry, sir, not that I have access to. You'd have to speak to our human resources department."

"That's all right. Can you transfer me to Mr. Powers's office?"

"Sure thing, just a moment."

She put me on hold. A minute later, a young man's voice came over the line.

"Mr. Powers's office."

"Hi, my name is Henry Parker and I'm a reporter from the *New York Gazette*. I'd like to come in and speak with Mr. Powers today. It's a pretty urgent matter."

"Mr. Powers has a very busy schedule today. He's not in the office right now, but if I can pass a message to him, I'll see if he has some free time."

"Absolutely," I said. "Tell him I want to speak to him about Raymond Benjamin and Dmitri Petrovsky."

"Can you spell those for me, sir?"

"Just remember the names."

"Um…okay. I'll call Mr. Powers right now. Is there a number where I can reach you?"

I gave the secretary my cell phone number. He said he'd get back to me ASAP. I hung up the phone and began to play the waiting game again.

I tried to think how Reggie Powers might be connected to all of this. Powers Construction employed Raymond Benjamin, though the fact that he was a ghost at the office pretty much confirmed that he was there to do dirty work, collect a W-2, and that was all. But why would Reggie Powers want anything to do with Dmitri Petrovsky? He seemed like the least likely person on earth to want to have anything to do with a kidnapping, especially given his background. The more the pieces came together, the more trouble I had making them all fit.

Ten minutes later, my cell phone rang. I picked it up.

"Mr. Parker." I recognized the voice as Powers's secretary. "Mr. Powers is at a job site all day today, but he said if you can meet him there at six o'clock, he'd be happy to speak with you."

"Where's the site?" I asked.

"He's overseeing the construction of a mall in Hobbs County, New York, today."

Hobbs County. Why was I not surprised. I checked my watch. It was three-thirty. I had plenty of time to drive up to Hobbs County.

"Give me the address," I said. I jotted down the information, thanked the secretary and hung up. I chewed on the tip of my pen. I had no idea what Reggie Powers would know. I sure as hell had a few questions he needed good answers to.

I put my tape recorder and notebook into a small backpack, stopped in to Wallace's office to tell him where I was going. He told me to check in once I was done with Powers. I got the sense Wallace understood how big this story was getting. And that scared me.

I took the subway Uptown to my apartment, got in the rental car and began the drive up to Hobbs County.

41

"Tomorrow," Paulina said. She was sitting at her desk, leaning back in her desk chair, the one the assistants commonly referred to as the "bitch throne." She'd caught James Keach referring to it as such one day, but rather than admonish the boy, she merely laughed and told him not to be shy about it. From that day on, James commonly referred to the chair with that moniker, using the slight whisper of a child who can't believe his parents permit him to curse in the house.

The copy was set. The pictures had been laid out. She'd pored over every inch of the article with greater focus than any story she could remember. She couldn't say for sure whether this piece would be her crowning moment as a journalist—in fact, she wasn't sure she'd want it to be—but in many ways it meant the most to her. It represented a clear turning point in her career, and would mark perhaps the first official shot of the war. To this day it had been the newsprint version of Russia versus the U.S. No casualties, lots of trash talk and hidden agendas everywhere they turned.

Paulina's article would change all of that. So while nobody quite knew just who fired that first shot at Lexington and Concord, in the future they could pin this one to her blouse. The Parker stories had been small potatoes. Going after a baby fish as though people would care. To this point, Henry hadn't been in the game long enough for people to truly care. Like Stephen Glass and Jayson Blair, the sting would have been worse if they had the tenure of, well... Paulina laughed.

A bottle of Dom was waiting in her fridge. Myron's phone number was on her cell phone. At first she debated calling him again—the last thing she needed tonight was another pity party—but ending the night with a good drink and a great lay would be the perfect capper. The end of the beginning, the beginning of the end.

And even though she hadn't seen him in many months, Paulina rather wished she'd be able to see the look on Henry Parker's face in the morning.

42

The sun bathed Hobbs County in a beautiful mélange of reds and golds. This could be such a breathtaking town, I hated to think so much evil had taken place here. When I parked the car in the lot by the construction site, I took a moment to take it in, to breathe it in. You didn't get many views like this in the city, one of the trade-ins you had to make to live there. I didn't mind so much. Spending my whole childhood growing up way out West, I'd seen enough sunsets to quench a lifelong thirst. Living amid the steel and bustle of New York didn't quite feel like home yet, but it was getting there.

I turned off the car and parked outside the site.

The mall was coming up well. Steel beams were exposed everywhere. Tools and wheelbarrows and mixers were scattered about. I had no idea where I was supposed to meet Reggie Powers. I figured there would be some sort of office structure set apart, or he'd just be waiting for me outside. Yet as I took a quick look around, there was no sign of him.

As I walked through the construction area, dipping under low beams, peeking around corners, I felt a queasy sensation in my stomach when I realized there wasn't a single person in sight.

Powers's secretary had told me Reggie would be at the site all day. But there were no other cars on the lot. No discarded papers or bags. No sign that any human beings had even set foot here today. Why would Reggie be here all day if nobody else was?

A terrible suspicion grew that I was alone here. Or even worse, not as alone as I thought.

"Hello?" I called out. My voice echoed through the structure. A chill ran through my body, and I held the backpack tighter. "Mr. Powers?"

Still nothing.

I exited the structure, walked around the exterior.

Several cranes were standing tall over the skeleton, long steel beams lying at their feet. The cement trucks were quiet, side elevators dark.

"Reggie Powers!" I called again. When again there was no answer, I decided it'd be best to get the hell out of there.

I began to jog back toward the car, winding my way around the side of the building. As I passed a blue van, I saw something that made me stop in my tracks. My breath caught.

Beside the van I could make out a human hand splayed out on the ground. As I crept closer, I could see the fingertips coated with blood. The hand belonged to a black man.

The body was on the ground in an awkward position. The right hand was splayed out above the man's head, the left arm at a ninety-degree angle. The legs were crumpled, one stuck beneath the man's torso. A single hole was in the center of his head, and a pool of blood had begun to dry.

I didn't need to check the wallet to know that Reggie Powers had been murdered.

I whipped around, looking for something, anything.

He'd clearly been dead a little while, so whoever had done it had either fled the scene, or was waiting for me.

I took the cell phone from my pocket. Dialed 911. I felt panicked as I waited to be connected, every second not knowing what the hell was happening. Was Powers already dead when I called his office? Or had he come here with the intent to meet with me, then was murdered by someone who knew…

Then I knew it. Powers meant to set me up. He knew nobody would be at the construction site. He must have told somebody before he arrived. And that somebody took him out. Somebody who'd begun to think Powers was better off dead. Somebody who felt he'd become a liability.

And when I heard the click of a gun safety being removed, I knew immediately that Raymond Benjamin had killed him.

"Step away from the van, Parker."

I put the cell phone in my coat pocket. Every muscle in my body was numb.

I recognized the voice. I'd heard it that night at the house on Huntley, as this man tried to torture information out of me.

I slowly turned around. Hands above my head.

Raymond Benjamin was standing ten feet away from me. He held a gun in one outstretched hand. The scar on his cheek seemed to glisten in the darkening sky. His face was a mask of anger and frustration.

"I didn't want it to come to this," he said. "Killing is an ugly, ugly thing. If you'd just let it be, Parker, this wouldn't be happening."

"Petrovsky. Powers. You killed them both, and for what? To hide your dirty secret? I know what all this is," I said. "All this by your hand."

Benjamin took a step closer. "Parker," he said. "I'm sorry you won't have a chance to know any better."

The sky exploded, a yellow blast echoing in the night, and I shut my eyes and waited to die. When after a moment I felt no pain, felt nothing at all except the wind on my face, I opened them. Raymond Benjamin was dead on the ground. Smoke wafted from a bullet hole in his back, right where his heart had beat its last breath. And standing there, smoking gun in his hand, was Senator Gray Talbot.

43

"It was you all along," I said, staring into the senator's cold eyes. "You were behind the kidnappings. Hobbs County and Meriden were your pet projects so you could look good come voting season. That way you could come off looking like some great savior, when in reality you were feeding people the same poison you claimed to be eradicating. You and Raymond Benjamin found children who were born with diabetes, whom you could subject to these sick experiments to rob them of years of their lives. You take them away, then use their disappearances as leverage to get good press, gentrify the towns. The crime rate plummets. Property values go up. In come landowners who are more willing to vote for you. You bring in Reggie Powers to rebuild the town. You steal lives for political gain, you fucking monster."

Talbot shook his head like a teacher whose student was too stupid to understand a simple equation. "That's the black-and-white version," Talbot said. "But who's really losing here? These kids lose a couple years of their lives, but when they come back their towns aren't criminal beehives anymore. Their schools aren't run-down. Drugs aren't sold on their blocks. It's a small sacrifice for a lifetime of happiness, for them and their families."

"So one life is worth shattering if it saves another, is that right? The ends justify the means?"

"They always do," Talbot said. "And if I'm reelected because of it, if this leads me to the governor's mansion or, heaven look upon me, the White House, it will be because I take steps weaker men aren't willing to take. If you can sacrifice one life to save others, don't you have to do that? As a human being?"

"I don't buy that," I said. "Reggie Powers contributed thousands and thousands of dollars a year to political campaigns. Want to bet if we looked up his history of donating to your fund, we'd find a little more than 'Good Samaritan' money?"

"Reggie had a good heart," Talbot said, and I detected a hint of real sadness. "He was a true hero. But he was compromised. Just like the Reed family, it was only a matter of time before Reggie's heart got the best of him."

"So you're tying up your loose ends," I said. "Dmitri Petrovsky. Reggie Powers. Ray Benjamin. Everyone who knew about this is dead. And if we hadn't found them first, the Reeds would be, too. All those lives, you're actually trying to say these people's deaths are worth furthering your demented cause?"

"Without a doubt, absolutely. You cannot put a value on one life, Henry. But I can tell you that a hundred lives, a thousand lives, are worth more than a simple few. The tree of liberty must be refreshed from time to time, with the blood of patriots and tyrants. Those children, these men, were our patriots. They gave their lives to prevent others from suffering in the future. Men like Raymond Benjamin are our tyrants. He represents everything wrong with our culture. And so while he was a means to an end, so, too, did his blood need to water the ground."

"And Daniel Linwood," I said. "Michelle Oliveira. Caroline Twomey. Their blood funds your campaign, too."

"If my platform must stand on a column these children have provided, so be it. I can live with that. I am sorry, Henry. Consider yourself a patriot. Your death will save lives."

"One thing before I, you know, go," I said.

"Yes, Parker?"

"The blood might choke the ground," I said, taking my still-connected cell phone from my coat pocket. "But with my plan I get a signal pretty much anywhere."

Talbot looked at me with horror, and right as he raised the gun to fire, I heard the sound of several sirens approaching. Talbot turned around to see a police cruiser pull into the construction site, followed by half a dozen more along with two ambulances.

A dozen cops leaped from their vehicles, guns raised, pointed at the silver-haired senator.

"Drop your weapon!" a cop yelled. "Drop it now or we will take you down!"

Talbot looked at me, and for a moment I saw a fear and confusion in his eyes that brought terror to my heart. He raised the gun an inch, aiming straight and true at me, and for a moment I believed the senator would end my life along with everything else.

Then he lowered the gun, his eyes dropping to the ground, and the gun clattered on the gravel.

Instantly he was pinned down by three police officers, who handcuffed him and then picked the man up. Standing by one of the cruisers were the two detectives who'd questioned Amanda and me after we'd escaped from Huntley. Their faces were blank, unbelieving, as they watched Senator Gray Talbot pushed into the back of a police car, which then pulled away.

I stood there in the waning daylight, looked up at the sky and took a long, sweet breath. There was one more task to be done. One more terrible question that needed to be answered.

44

The money trail was there. A spot-check of Gray Talbot's campaign finance reports showed a yearly influx of $50,000 dollars from a company called Shepherd Incorporated. Shepherd was owned by Reggie Powers, a shell company set up separately from Powers Construction. Yearly withdrawals from Shepherd, Inc. were being matched to Gray Talbot. And everyone knew what they would tell us.

Finally the story came together. Several of the players, I knew, had to believe the bullshit Gray Talbot was spewing. Several of them had to feel that what they were doing was right. That to destroy evil, you had to commit evil. That getting your cause noticed was justification for it all.

It was easy to be cynical. Both Amanda and I came from broken homes, where we could never believe a parent would go to such lengths to allegedly protect us.

Gray Talbot hired Raymond Benjamin to be his eyes, his ears, his gun. All orders went through Benjamin, nothing went to Gray. Benjamin was his wall of protection.

Benjamin, a Hobbs County native, approached Dmitri

Petrovsky in order to obtain hospital records of infants born with childhood diabetes. They screened children who would be most susceptible to Korsakoff syndrome. Once Petrovsky came back with a name, a plan was put in motion.

The child would be kidnapped. Petrovsky would develop a nutritional plan that would keep the child's thiamine levels at a level dangerous enough to cause minor brain damage, enough to bring an onset of Korsakoff, but not so severe that it would endanger the child's life.

When the child was gone, when the police search turned up fruitless, that's when Gray Talbot stepped in. He would trumpet his concern for the welfare of the community. Talk about how crime rates were unacceptable. That children were being snatched from their families.

Millions of dollars would be pumped into the communities through donations, federal and state funding. Police forces would be bolstered. Neighborhood watches on patrol. Broken streetlights fixed. Homes made safe again.

And real estate would slowly creep up.

That's when Talbot would enlist the help of Powers Construction. Reggie would come in with his trucks and his men, level the homes consumed by crack, rebuild houses that would attract more money than the neighborhood had ever seen.

Talbot would gain a wealthier, more affluent constituency. Powers would make millions from the sweetheart deals. And the communities would be better off.

Everybody won.

Except the children.

Amanda sat in the seat next to me, the radio turned to a soft rock station. The music they played was unthreatening, wouldn't offend any sensibilities, lyrics that couldn't harm a fly. That's all we wanted at that moment. Serenity. Emotionlessness.

The next few hours would be difficult. We didn't want it to start until it absolutely had to.

After I'd gone on record with the police, handed over my cell phone and explained everything that had happened, I called Amanda immediately. I told her what we had to do. I wasn't sure how the night was going to end, but if we didn't ask that one final question, I didn't know if I'd ever sleep again.

I steered the car, unable to help but think about Danny Linwood, how in some ways we both had lost years from our childhood. The difference was I had a choice. My memories and experiences helped mold me into what I was now. Danny would need time, years perhaps, to even know who he was.

We arrived at the house shortly past ten o'clock. The porch lights were out. The street was dim save a few lampposts. Turning the engine off, I walked up to one, felt the metal, inspected it. It was well cared for. No graffiti. No damage. It was doing its duty without any interference. Illuminating a world that was, for better or worse, now a safer place.

"You think they're asleep?" Amanda asked.

"No way. At that age I fought tooth and nail for every extra minute. I'd sneak an AM/FM radio into bed so I could listen to ball games, maybe a book and a flashlight. I hope kids haven't outgrown that."

"Not outgrown it," she said. "They just have more options now. Portable video games, iPods, televisions the size of a quarter. It's a miracle they don't spend half their time choosing which one to watch."

We stepped up to the porch. I saw the wind chimes again. In a moment they'd be ringing their tune.

I pressed the doorbell, heard a chime go off inside the house. There were footsteps, a woman's voice shouting something. Then the screen door opened, and Shelly Linwood was standing right in front of us.

She was wearing a terry-cloth bathrobe, her hair done up in rollers. I saw a child run past behind her. Tasha, if I remembered correctly.

"Henry? Henry Parker?" she said, unsure of what to make of this late-night visit.

"Mrs. Linwood," I said. "I need a minute of your time."

"I was just doing my hair," she said. She looked eager to get back to that, but the look on my face told her we weren't leaving anytime soon. Resignedly, she said, "Come on in."

She held the door open for us, and we walked inside.

"Mrs. Linwood, this is Amanda Davies. She works for the New York Legal Aid Society. She's a good friend of mine, and I just thought it would be good for her to meet Danny. Danny might have some questions she can answer. And if not, he'll make a new friend."

I saw a mop of hair peek from behind a doorway. Shelley turned around, said, "Danny, come in here. You remember Henry, right?"

Daniel Linwood tentatively stepped into the room. He'd gained a few pounds since I last saw him, his hair a little longer. His eyes seemed more frightened, his gait more awkward.

"Danny," I said. "This is Amanda."

She stepped forward, knelt down slightly so she was at his level.

"Hey there," she said. "I'm Amanda. Mind if we chat for a bit? I'd love to see your room."

"Show her your Xbox," Shelly said. Danny nodded reluctantly, led Amanda past us and up the stairs.

"Can we sit?" I said. Shelly nodded.

We went into the living room, sat on the same couch where I'd interviewed Danny not too long ago.

"How is he?" I asked.

Shelly sighed, scratched her neck.

"I get a call from his school almost every day. Kids picking on him. Giving him wedgies. Stealing his lunch money. It wasn't like this before."

"He's a different person now," I said. "It's going to take a long time for him to find himself."

"I know," she said. "God, I know."

"Mrs. Linwood," I said. "I want you to hear this from me. And only from me. I want you to know what I know."

She looked up, her eyes big and brown and watery. "Yes?"

"You knew about Daniel's kidnapping. You knew it was going to happen. You knew he would be taken. And you probably told them when they could do it. Know that I know. Because you'll have to live with that. Live with everyone knowing what you did."

Her mouth fell open. She stared at me, shaking her head, openmouthed.

"No," she said. "My Danny, I didn't—"

"Shelly," I said. "You've been lying too long. I know why you did it. I know you met Raymond Benjamin."

Shelly just sat there, her lower lip trembling.

"When I spoke to Danny, you even brought him a tray of food. Vegetables that would help replenish the thiamine levels that were so low in his brain. Food high in vitamin B1. Did Petrovsky tell you to do that?"

Shelly sat there, stone silent.

"Did he come to your house? Raymond Benjamin."

She continued to stare, then a tear streaked down her cheek as she nodded.

"Yes," she said.

"What did he say?"

"He told me," Shelly said, sucking in air and wiping her face, "that this town was tearing itself apart. That he'd grown up here, and there were only two options for boys Danny and James's age. Prison or the grave. Raymond said he'd been to prison, but that's only because he got caught."

"And he offered you a deal," I said. "Right? He would take Danny away for a few years. He would be gone, but he would be safe. And by doing that you would give your children a chance to grow up in a neighborhood where they'd be safe. Where they could make something of themselves."

Shelly nodded. Then she stood up. Went over to the mantel, and took down a framed photograph. She handed it to me.

It was an odd picture. I'd noticed it during my interview with Daniel. And now I thought about the photo I found in Robert Reed's wallet and it all made sense.

The photo was of Shelly's younger son, James. The shot had been taken from about five feet behind him. He was wearing a knapsack, baggy jeans. He was unaware of the photographer.

I turned the frame over and removed the knobs that held it in place. When the backing came off, the back of the photo was visible. One word was printed on it.

Remember.

"Raymond Benjamin gave that photo to me," she said. "He told me he'd taken it himself. He said if he could get that close to James, others could, too. People who meant him more harm than he did. He said it was a fair trade. A few years of Daniel's life would guarantee the safety of my whole family forever. Daniel would, in a way, be a hero. I never understood how my son could be a hero giving his life for a cause he didn't understand or even know about. I just wanted to believe in some way he was doing it for the future of James and Tasha. And he said that anytime I began to doubt myself or what I'd done, to look at that photo and remember what could happen to the rest of my family."

"What did you do, Shelly?" I asked.

Shelly began to weep. She held her head in her hands. I felt a modicum of remorse for this woman, but it soon went away.

"I told Benjamin the route Danny took to get home from practice," she said. "Six-thirty every night. I made him promise not to hurt my baby. He told me he wouldn't."

"What else did Benjamin say?"

"He promised me a family would take care of him. They knew about his diabetes and they would care for him," Shelly said through bloodshot eyes. "And I believed him. At least I wanted to. I needed to know my babies could grow up and lead full lives. I've seen what this town can do to people. I wanted my sons to have something better."

"Is that what Danny has now?" I asked. "Something better?"

"I don't know," she said. "But if he can get out of here and ends up in a safe office, making money, starting a family instead of rotting behind bars or in the dirt, then yes. He has something better. I know you can't possibly understand that, Henry. Wanting your child to not just survive but live a life. Maybe one day you will. But you can't right now."

"No," I said. "I can't."

45

I woke up the next morning, pleasantly surprised that sleep had come so easily. I think it was more due to the complete lack of energy in every one of my muscles, the utter exhaustion I felt, than any sort of blissful conscience.

As soon as we returned from the Linwood residence, I'd gone straight to the *Gazette* to write up my story. Amanda had given me a long, deep hug, and for the first time since we'd started speaking again, a hug was all I wanted.

The story was difficult to write. That so many people had been so deceitful, purposefully putting so many lives at risk, it was hard to fathom how any of them could have felt they were doing the right thing. I heard over the wire that the police had apprehended Robert and Elaine Reed in a suburb just outside Chicago. Caroline Twomey was in the process of being returned to her family. The police had reopened the kidnappings of both Danny Linwood and Michelle Oliveira. They still didn't know who kidnapped them, and they believed Gray Talbot had inoculated himself from that knowledge. It was Ray Benjamin who was the button man. And Gray had killed him to seal off the investigation. There was a chance those families who held the children would never be found, never be prosecuted. We got lucky with Daniel Linwood.

The Reeds were found at a hotel outside Chicago. They'd driven halfway across the country after fleeing Harrisburg. The manager became suspicious when all of the family's credit cards were declined, and Elaine Reed attempted to use an expired driver's license as identification.

They claimed, like Shelly Linwood, that they were doing it to protect their son, Patrick. That Benjamin had threatened them, as well. And now Patrick would likely spend most of his childhood in foster care, and his parents would have to deal with the legal ramifications of what they'd done.

The children's lives would go on. But they would never be the same.

It's always the innocent who are forced to suffer.

Like Shelly said, maybe in a few years I would understand. When I had a family of my own, children I would do anything to protect, maybe that kind of sacrifice would feel justified.

But not right now.

I looked forward to seeing the paper, so when I rolled out of bed the first thing I did was go to the front door to get my morning delivery.

My neighbor down the hall, the lovely Ms. Berry, all eighty nightgowned years of her, must have been thrilled to see me standing there topless in my boxers. I waved hello. She retreated back inside. Maybe she wasn't so thrilled.

I took the paper inside, laid it on the table and read.

When I was through, my emotions were mixed. I was happy with the story, but not the outcome. All I could say is that Gray Talbot's operation would be shut down, and the man would certainly spend years behind bars.

Caroline Twomey was returned to her family. It remained to be seen what would happen to her parents. I assumed they were accessories, like the Linwoods. And it was only a matter of time before the Oliveira case was reopened, as well.

So many lives shattered by greed and fear. And I still wasn't quite sure who the villains were.

I took a hot shower, feeling like a year's worth of crud had built up, caked my skin an inch thick. I let the water run in and out of my mouth, felt the steam coat my face. It felt good.

When I washed up, I packed the paper, got my stuff together and headed to the newsroom. Though the story was a difficult one for me to write, I knew Wallace and the crew would be thrilled. It was a huge get, the kind of story that would not just have people talking today, but would ripple for months if not years. It made me glad that Wallace would be proud. Though I secretly hoped Jack would be, too. I still resented what he'd done to himself, resented that he might have jeopardized his legacy, but his validation meant more to me than he likely knew.

I took the train down to Rockefeller Plaza, remembering I'd have to return the rental later that day.

The plaza was already crowded by the time I walked over. Tourists were perched on the benches, taking pictures of the grandness of the area. People stood outside the shops waiting for that first door to be cracked open.

I'd never been much of a sightseer when I was younger. Wonders never really amazed me like they did most folk. I chalked it up to my profession, where everything had to come with some sense of detachment. If you got too personally involved in a story, it could come back to haunt you in more ways than you could imagine. I thought about my last few major stories, beginning with being sought for a murder charge a few years ago, to hunting William Henry Roberts after that. And now, with Gray Talbot behind bars and the lives of several families never to be the same, I wondered if I'd mistakenly forgotten all that. If I'd gotten too close, whether by chance or by choice.

Once this was over I wanted to step back, reevaluate my situation. I loved my job, and that wouldn't change until they dragged me out of the newsroom, kicking and screaming while I tried to beat off Security with a legal notepad. There was room to grow. Personally and professionally. And with all the time spent chasing murderers, liars and politicians (who managed to encompass both), it was time to take stock.

The wall clock read 9:05 when the elevator opened on to the newsroom floor. I expected some sort of jubilation, maybe a pat on the back or two. I'd cracked a huge case that would have ramifications potentially all the way to the top. A man considered a potential front-runner for the biggest job in the land would now be spending at least eight years behind bars. There was something sad about ruining a career. Ending a life. And I wondered where Hobbs County would be today if Gray Talbot had never thought of a boy named Daniel Linwood.

I walked to my desk looking for my colleagues, looking out for Wallace. The pride quickly turned to fear when I noticed all the reporters were sitting at their desks. They were silent. Their faces ashen gray. Some were at work, but it was perfunctory.

Evelyn Waterstone passed by. She gazed up at me for a moment, her mouth opening. For the first time I could remember, Evelyn Waterstone looked sad. She said two words to me, "Sorry, Parker," and walked on.

I didn't know what to do, but something had bitten the newsroom of the *New York Gazette*. I had to find out. The only person who didn't look like they were drowning in their own sorrows was Frank Rourke.

There was no love lost between Frank Rourke and me. We'd had a pretty intense falling-out over the shit bag incident last year, and since then never really attempted to patch things up. I never felt the need to gain his approval. My work would accomplish that in my stead.

Rourke was yapping away on his desk phone—something about preseason football—so I walked over when he hung up and stood over his desk, waiting to hear what he said.

Rourke didn't notice me at first. He just sat there drinking coffee out of a Thermos the size of my head. Then when he turned around and saw me standing there, the smile disappeared. My stomach dropped when I realized he had the same look on his face Evelyn had minutes earlier.

"Parker," he said. "Listen, man…I don't know what else to say. But I'm sorry. This sucks majorly."

"What does?" I said. "I just got here, *please,* everyone else looks like they have one foot in the grave."

Rourke said, "Oh, man, you didn't see it?"

"See what? Speak to me, goddamn it."

Rourke spun around, looked at the desk across from him. Then he stood up, went over and began rifling through the garbage can. I wondered what the hell he was doing, but then when I saw him take a newspaper out of the can, that queasiness returned. He handed it to me, front page out, and said, "Like I said, this sucks."

I unfolded the front page and held it up. It was a copy of this morning's *New York Dispatch*. When I read the headline, in huge bold print, I nearly threw up.

The headline read: A Lush Life: Jack O'Donnell and All the Booze That's Fit to Print.

The byline was credited to Paulina Cole.

The two *l*'s in *all* were liquor bottles. Below the headline were two pictures. And both made me sick to my stomach.

The first picture looked to have been taken in some sort of storage room. It was about the size of a walk-in closet, with three rows of shelves traversing the space.

Every single space was lined, front to back, with empty bottles. Wine. Beer. Whiskey. Bourbon. The caption below the photo read: Jack O'Donnell Downs in One Year What Most People Drink in a Lifetime!

The second photo, the one that made me clench the paper into a wad in my hands, was of Jack. Lying in the hospital. Tubes running through his veins.

I recognized the setting. It was taken after I'd brought Jack to the hospital after he nearly choked to death on his own vomit. Somebody had snuck into the hospital and photographed Jack while he was unconscious and recovering from alcohol poisoning. I couldn't imagine the kind of black heart needed to do such a thing.

I took the paper without saying another word to Frank and took it to my desk. There I read the entire article, every single word. And when I was done, I crumpled it up, took it to the incinerator on our floor and chucked it into the darkness.

Paulina Cole had done one of the worst hatchet jobs on Jack I'd ever read. Somehow she'd gotten one of the porters in Jack's building to collect the liquor bottles from the recycling bin every morning. Easy, since he occupied the entire floor himself. The bottles were then brought straight to Paulina Cole. Every single one was finger-printed to confirm that Jack had in fact drunk them himself. No other fingerprints were found on any of the bottles. And there must have been several hundred in the photograph. And he'd drunk them all himself over the span of one year.

The article described how much alcohol must have been absorbed by Jack's bloodstream over that year. It also made mention of every correction in every story that Jack had written that same year, comparing it to his previous work. It portrayed Jack as a man whose profes-sional life was now ruled by one of the most aggressive bouts of alcoholism ever seen in the newsroom, whose work had depreciated to the point where his stories were filled with more holes than an O. J. Simpson alibi.

Then the story took a more macro perspective, going into great detail about how the *Gazette* promoted Jack as one of the legends of New York journalism. Paulina ended her story with the following paragraph:

"It can be said that a news institution can be judged on one thing, and one thing only: the reputation of the men and women who report the news. Jack O'Donnell is a man whose reputation, built over years more through joviality and cronyism than true journalistic integrity, has opened a window into the true nature of this black-and-white beast. And what an ugly, ugly creature it is."

The next thing I knew I was going straight for Jack's desk. It was unoccupied. But worse than that, it was empty. The computer was off. There were no odds and ends on the countertop. There was nothing.

I marched to Wallace Langston's office and threw open

the doors. The editor-in-chief was on the phone. His face was ashen. I knew the feeling. He motioned for me to take a seat. I declined.

When he hung up the phone, I said, "Wallace, what the fuck is going on? Where is Jack?"

Wallace sighed and leaned back in his chair. I knew my anger was misplaced, but my mind was going a thousand miles an hour in a hundred different directions. "Jack is on leave," he said.

"On leave? What the hell does that mean?"

"I assume you saw the story in today's *Dispatch*," he said.

"I just finished it."

"Well, word came down from Harvey Hillerman himself that Jack had two choices. An extended personal leave to deal with his demons in a treatment center. Or the termination of his employment with the *Gazette*." Harvey Hillerman was the president and CEO of the *Gazette*. If it came from him, it meant Jack had no way out.

"And?"

"And as of this morning, Jack O'Donnell is no longer an employee of this newspaper."

I felt as if a cannonball had hit me square in the stomach. My knees went weak, and I fell into the chair across from Wallace.

"He can't do that," I said. "Jack *is* this newspaper."

"No, he's not, Henry. Jack has done more for this paper than any employee in its history. But we are not one and the same. You've seen Jack over the past few months. You know things have been going downhill. He was hospitalized just last week."

"Yeah, and I know that damn picture is out there for everyone to see."

"You need to think about Jack," Wallace said. "The man needs help. More than what you or I can do. If he chooses to do it on his own, so be it. My take is that he didn't want to be forced into doing anything. That doesn't surprise me. It's always been the way he's worked."

"So what now?" I said. "We just keep working like nothing ever happened?"

"That's impossible," Wallace said. "Jack's been here so long some of his blood does run through this paper's veins. But we have to move on. You've done some amazing work in your time here, Henry. Jack has put down his mantle for now. And I expect you to be one of the people to take it. To carry it with pride."

"You don't take that because it's been thrown down," I said. "You earn it. I can't just take Jack's place. Nobody can."

"That's true. So just do your job to the best of his ability. Learn from his mistakes. Don't let your problems overwhelm you. Because at the end of the day, you're remembered for the end of your career, not the beginning. And the saddest part of all this is a generation might only know the Jack O'Donnell on the cover of today's newspaper."

I couldn't listen to any more. I slammed the door to Wallace's office and left the building. Hailing a taxi, I instructed the driver to take me to Twenty-Seventh and Park. The offices of the *New York Dispatch*.

I left the cab, throwing the fare at the driver, and entered the building through the revolving door, feeling as if I could tear the walls apart with my bare hands. A security guard stopped me as I approached the turnstiles. He said, "Sir, you'll need to check in and show your ID."

I went to the security post. Another guard sat there looking bored. "Who are you here to see?"

"Paulina Cole. *New York Dispatch*."

"Do you have an appointment with Ms. Cole?"

"No."

"Does she know you're coming?"

"No."

The guard looked confused. "Sir, can you state your business with Ms. Cole?"

"That's between me and her."

The guard eyed me suspiciously. Then he said, "I'm going to have to pat you down." I let him. He found nothing. "Let me call upstairs."

He picked up the switchboard phone and dialed a few buttons. I was growing impatient. I needed to see that bitch face-to-face.

The guard put down the phone and said, "Sir, Ms. Cole is not picking up her phone. I can leave a message that you stopped by."

"I can wait for her upstairs."

"No, sir, I can't let you do that."

"Listen, asshole," I said. "I'm seeing Paulina Cole today. Whether you let me upstairs or not."

Just then I heard a commotion by the revolving door. Several voices were congratulating someone. A throng of people surrounding one person.

Then they parted and Paulina Cole continued walking toward the turnstiles.

She saw me and stopped. She was startled for a moment, then a slow smile spread across her face.

"Hi, Henry," she said. "It's been so long. Have you been keeping up with the news?"

"You fucking bitch," I said, starting toward her. I didn't take more than two steps before I felt a pair of hands grab my arms and pull me backward. The security guards were holding me. I thrashed and struggled to get free. "He was a friend to you," I spat. "How could you?"

"It was easy," she said, stepping forward. "And you know what probably angers you the most, Henry? That every word of it is true."

I tried to pull free, but then the two guards began dragging me outside. We passed by Paulina. She raised her hand, waved a sarcastic *goodbye* before the guards shoved me through the doors and out onto the street.

I tumbled onto the sidewalk, then scrambled to my feet. The guards stood there with their hands across their chests.

"Sir," one of them said, "if you don't leave the premises, we will be forced to call the authorities."

I took one step forward, hatred boiling inside me, but then I stopped. Jack had been broken. Defeated. Getting arrested would affect nobody but myself. Jack had been an idol to me for years. I owed him more than that.

I left the *Dispatch* and took the train up to Jack's apartment. The whole way I sat there shaking, not knowing what to say, what to think. After everything with Daniel Linwood, now that Amanda and I seemed to be on good terms, I'd finally felt like things were on the right track. No more days drinking at bars by myself. No more nights sleeping at the office because I couldn't face my own bed.

Then, I wondered, how many nights had Jack O'Donnell had just like that?

When I got to Jack's building, I buzzed his apartment, dying to see that grizzled face in the hopes that it would all make sense. There was no answer. I buzzed again. Still nothing.

I took out my cell phone and rang his house line. It went right to voice mail.

"Jack," I said. "This is Henry. Please call me back. I need to speak to you. Please tell me you're all right."

I clicked off the phone and took one last look at the building. Then I turned around and went back to work.

The old man stood by the window for a long time, watching the boy walk away until he'd disappeared from sight. When Henry Parker turned the corner, he stepped back into his apartment. His body was racked with convulsions, the sobs like mortar rounds. Then Jack O'Donnell slid down the wall until his frail, arthritic knees were tucked up under his chin, and he began to cry.

46

Though I hadn't been a reporter that long, I can honestly say I'd had some long days on the job. The longest weren't the ones where I was on deadline, typing page after page or sifting through an entire casebook worth of notes. The longest days were those where nothing happened. I wasn't waiting for a source to call back. I wasn't waiting for Legal to approve a story. I wasn't waiting on anyone or anything. The day just *passed*.

Today was perhaps the longest of my career. Every few minutes I would turn around to look at that empty desk, wishing upon nothing that Jack would appear magically and just start writing. There would be no story written by Jack O'Donnell in tomorrow's edition, or next week's papers, or any for the foreseeable future.

I was merely a soldier who, until today, had been following the example set by Wallace Langston and Jack O'Donnell. But our ranks had been broken. And who knew if it would ever be repaired.

I left the *Gazette* at five o'clock on the dot. The first day I could ever remember leaving on time. The train ride home was lonely. More so when I saw people reading the very paper that had changed the landscape of my world.

When I stepped off the train, the sun was already beginning to set, and any day now the summer sun would begin to fade into fall. I walked down the street, my bag heavy, not caring where I stepped, my eyes looking no more than two feet in front of me.

Rounding the corner onto my block, I was surprised to hear a voice call out, "Careful, there, I see a hydrant with your name on it."

I looked up to see Amanda standing in front of my building, her hair rippling lightly in the wind, her face golden in the orange haze. If there was one sight that could melt away a man's sorrows, it was that one.

She was wearing tight jeans and a red sweater. Walking closer, I recognized the sweater. I'd given it to her on our six-month anniversary. That seemed like ages ago.

"What are you doing here?" I said, silently chiding myself for the impatient tone in my voice.

"I thought you could use someone to talk to tonight," she said. "I saw the newspaper."

I nodded, only because there was nothing else to say. Amanda approached me, put her hand on my shoulder; the other hand tilted my chin upward.

"I'm sorry," she said. "I know what Jack meant to you."

"He'll get things together," I said softly. "He has to."

"I hope he does. I guess at some point everyone needs to take stock of their life."

"I've been doing a little of that," I said.

"Me, too."

I looked up at her. "Why you?"

"I don't know," she said, brushing a strand of brown hair from her eyes. "At this point in my life, I want to think about what I have. What I want. What I have that I don't want. What I want that I don't have."

"What do you want?" I said.

She smiled demurely. "I'm not a hundred percent sure," she said. "I didn't say it happened all in one day. But I wanted to wait for you. I thought it might be a nice way to end what must have been a pretty crappy day."

"You have no idea," I said.

"How's Curt doing?" she asked.

"He's going home this weekend. I sent a few Olsen twins movies to his apartment as a joke. Figured if Ashley and Mary Kate can't cheer him up, the guy's hopeless."

Amanda smiled. "You're a true friend."

"He's lucky to have me," I said. "So you came here because you wanted to talk about things? About us?"

"Not so much talk," she said. "I had an even better idea. I hope you're okay with it."

"Yeah? What's that?"

"I'm going to take you out tonight. Dinner and a movie. There's an Italian place on Eighty-Third that's supposed to serve the best gnocchi in the city."

"Wait," I said, "this sounds an awful lot like a date."

"I could be coy and play hard to get, but what's the point? Henry Parker, I would love to take you out on a date tonight."

My heart swelled. It was probably from the huge emotional swing, but suddenly I found myself hugging Amanda, pulling her as hard as I could into my chest. Then her hands were on me, pushing me away. Confused, I stepped back, looked at her.

"Are you kidding?" she said, smiling. "This is a first date. You don't get to hug before the movie popcorn."

"Wait, a first date?" I said. "Was I imagining, you know, our whole relationship?"

"Uh-uh. But when I thought about it, I realized we'd never really gone on an actual first date. Meeting when you were on the run for your life and all. So I thought let's go back, start where we never got the chance. Dinner and a movie, sport."

"Shouldn't I pay, then?"

"This is the twenty-first century, Henry, get real. Besides, I think I make more money than you."

"I can't say no, can I?"

Amanda smiled "Do you really want to?"

"Not in the slightest."

"Just a date," she said. "Then we'll go from there."

"Just give me one more chance," I said, "and I promise it will be worth it."

* * * * *

Coming in March 2009
The next Henry Parker novel
THE FURY
by Jason Pinter

1

At nine in the morning, the offices of the *New York Gazette* were usually quiet as reporters read the morning papers, got ready to call their sources and blinked off hangovers. Today, however, it was a different kind of quiet. The "something must be wrong" kind of quiet.

I'd exited the elevators onto the ninth floor, expecting the usual quiet walk to my desk. Yet when I navigated the mess of chairs and debris and entered the cubicle farm, I noticed the other journalists who shared my row were nowhere to be seen.

I put my coffee and muffin down on the desk, debated simply pulling up the little plastic tab, sitting down and enjoying my breakfast. But to ignore the strange stillness of the office would have been going against every bone in my body. So I took a lap around the news floor to see what the hell was going on.

I didn't have to go far.

Half a dozen reporters were huddled around the desk of Evelyn Waterstone, the *Gazette*'s Metro editor. They were talking under their breaths, worried looks in their eyes. I wondered if there were going to be layoffs. If some of my colleagues—perhaps even myself—would be out of a job. That Evelyn had seemingly replaced the water cooler as the center of office scoop was itself noteworthy. Evelyn stayed as far away from gossip as those who gossiped stayed away from her. Whatever had happened had to be big. I walked up casually, inserting myself into the conversation through proximity alone.

"Morning, Parker," Evelyn said. She held a black Thermos between her fleshy hands, and took a long, drawn-out sip. "Another beautiful day at your local newspaper."

"Morning, Evelyn," I said, nodded hello to the other reporters, who offered the same. "What gives? One of the windows on the seventeenth floor fall out again?"

Jonas Levinson, the *Gazette*'s science editor, said, "As a matter of fact, something has died this morning. Something precious that needs to be mourned as long as we're employed by this godforsaken newspaper. As of today, my young Henry, good taste has kicked the bucket."

I stared at Jonas, waiting for some kind of explanation. Levinson was a tall man, balding, who wore a different bow tie to the office every day. He very seldom exaggerated his feelings, so at Jonas's remark a flock of butterflies began to flutter around in my stomach.

"I'm not following you," I said to Jonas. "Good taste? Evelyn, care to explain?"

"Just follow the eyes, Parker," Evelyn said. "Follow the eyes."

I opened my mouth to ask another question, but then I realized what she was saying. The eyes of every member of our group were focused on two individuals making their way across the *Gazette*'s floor. They were stopping at each desk, popping into each office, where it looked as if some sort of introductory ritual was taking place.

One of the two men was Wallace Langston, editor-in-chief. The other I didn't recognize.

"Is Wallace," I said, "introducing a new reporter?"

"Reporter? Hardly," Jonas replied.

Frank Rourke, the sports editor, said, "I never met a damn person until my first staff meeting. I got as much of an introduction to my colleagues as my stove has to my cooking pot."

"Same here," I said.

Wallace was still too far away to make out who he was introducing around the office or what his beat was, but I got the feeling Wallace would prefer if he didn't have to do the ritual en masse.

"I'm going back to my desk," I said. "Jonas, if you see good taste anywhere, I'll get the electric paddles and we'll resuscitate the bastard."

"Thank you for the offer, Henry, but I do believe time of death has already been established as—" he checked his watch "—8:58 a.m."

I walked back to my desk, trying not to think about what this could mean. The *Gazette* had been on a recent hiring freeze. We were in a war with our rival, the *New York Dispatch,* over circulation rates, advertising dollars and stories, and our efforts were taking a toll. If Harvey Hillerman, the president and owner of the *Gazette,* had hired a new reporter, he or she had to be a big enough name to cause a stir. Not to mention someone who would be approved of by the other reporters whose pay raises had been nixed last holiday season.

I sat down and was about to pick up the phone when I heard the sound of footsteps approaching my desk. I looked up to see Wallace Langston. And standing next to him, his mystery hire.

"Henry Parker," Wallace said, hand outstretched, "meet Tony Valentine."

Tony Valentine was six foot three, svelte to the point of gaunt, with the plastic smile of a cruise ship director. His hair was bleached blond, his teeth glistened and his cheekbones looked artificial. When he extended his hand to shake mine, I noticed that his palms were much paler than the rest of his bronze skin. The beauty of spray-on tans. Valentine wore a designer suit, a red pocket square neatly tucked into the pocket. The initials *T. V.* were embroidered in white script on the cloth.

His sleeves were held together by two gold cufflinks. Also monogrammed with *T. V.*

Clearly this man did not want his name to be forgotten.

"Henry Parker," Valentine said, gushing insincerity. "It's just such a pleasure to finally meet you. I've been following your career ever since that nasty business a few years back. All those guns and bullets, and now here I am, working with you. Sir, it is an *honor.*"

I shook Valentine's hand, then looked at Wallace. The name Tony Valentine sounded familiar, but I couldn't quite place it....

"Tony is our new gossip reporter," Wallace said enthusiastically. "We were able to pluck him from *Us Weekly.* Today is his first day."

"And not a day too soon," Tony said, pressing the back of his hand against his forehead, as though diagnosing a strange malady. "As much as I admire your paper—and, Wallace, please don't think otherwise—it's lacking a certain *pizzazz.* A certain *panache,* if you will. A certain sexiness."

"Let me guess," I said. "You're here to bring sexy back."

Tony pursed his lips and smiled. "You're a clever one,

Henry. I'm going to have to keep an eye on you. Maybe both if you misbehave. So guess the name of my new column."

"Do I have to?"

"You most certainly do." Tony waited a moment, then blurted out, "Valentine's Day. Because at the *Gazette*, Valentine's Day comes five days a week. Isn't that a riot?"

"Yeah, just like L.A. and Crown Heights."

Tony said, "Listen, Henry, it's been a pretty pleasure. We'll *have* to go out for a celebratory cocktail one of these nights. I want to hear *all* about what you're working on. Okay?"

"I'll check my calendar right away."

"Terrific. Wallace, on with the show?"

As Tony and Wallace walked away, I saw Wallace turn toward me. There was a remorseful look in his eye. Immediately I knew Tony's hire was at the behest of Harvey Hillerman. Gossip was a commodity in this town. I knew it, had been the subject of it. For the most part, the *Gazette* had kept its beak clean, relegating society and gossip stories to the weekend Leisure sections. Now, though, times were changing. I wondered how much an embroidered pocket square cost.

I left the *Gazette* thoroughly exhausted. Crossing through Rockefeller Plaza, I checked my cell phone. One message, from Amanda. We'd been seeing each other steadily over the past few months, trying to start over on a relationship that broke from the gate too fast. I didn't want to screw things up this time, so I was more than happy to take it slowly.

As I put the phone to my ear, I heard a strange voice call out, "Henry Parker?"

I turned to see a man approaching me. He was dirty and

disheveled, wearing rags that looked about to fall off his deathly skinny and pallid frame. His eyes were bloodshot, fingernails dirty. He looked to be in his early thirties. I'd never seen the man before in my life, yet for some reason he looked oddly familiar.

"Are you," he said, the words coming out through rotted teeth, "Henry Parker?"

I picked up the pace. I had no idea how this man knew my name, but from the looks of him I certainly didn't want to find out.

"I am," I said, speeding up as I walked through Rocke-feller Plaza. The man kept pace. His sneakers were falling apart, and the gray overcoat he wore was tattered and soiled.

"Please, Henry, I need to talk to you. Oh, God, it's important."

"Call the *Gazette* tomorrow," I said. I gave him the switchboard number. He didn't seem to care. I walked faster, a slow trot, but my heart began to race when I saw that the man was matching my pace.

"Henry," he said, his eyes now terrified, "please stop. It'll only take a minute. I'm begging you, man!"

"Sorry, don't have time," I said. I broke into a jog, crossing the street just as the light turned red. As I reached the other side, I looked back. The man looked prepared to race through the oncoming traffic, but then thought better of it.

Our eyes met for one moment. His were pleading, scared, and for a moment I debated crossing back over to see what he wanted. Then I saw him reach into his pocket, put something to his nose and take a quick snort. That was all I needed to see.

I turned around and headed toward the subway. If he

really needed to reach me, he could call. I'd been through enough over the past few years to know there were some people you needed to turn your back on.

2

I stopped to pick up some pasta for dinner on my way home, got up my laundry and managed to check the mail before collapsing under a pile of errands when I entered the apartment. I peeled off my clothes, put the food in the fridge and stepped into a hot shower. The day seemed to rinse right off me. I thought about the man who'd confronted me, how there was a look of genuine terror in his eyes. I began to regret turning away. Maybe he would call the next day. I wondered what he needed to talk to me about that was so urgent.

When I got out of the shower, I threw on a pair of shorts and a T-shirt and put the spaghetti in the microwave. I sat down and began to eat, washing the food down with a glass of iced tea. I splayed a few newspapers in front of me and read while I ate. The *Gazette*'s pages looked naked without the familiar byline of Jack O'Donnell. I hoped wherever he was, Jack was getting the treatment he needed.

Dinner was a long affair. I made the pasta last, and savored every word in the newspapers. I was fascinated at just how many stories there were within this small city, and excited at how many were out there waiting to be uncovered.

When I finished dinner, I got up to put my dishes in the

sink and my cell phone rang. I put the plate down and picked it up. Didn't recognize the caller ID.

I clicked Send and said, "This is Parker."

"Henry Parker?" the voice on the other end said.

"Yes. Who may I ask is calling?"

"Henry, this is Detective Makhoulian with the NYPD. Are you busy tonight?"

I looked at my watch. It was nearly ten o'clock. What the hell did the cops want with me at this hour?

"Detective, can I ask what this is about?"

"Let me ask you a question, Mr. Parker. Does a man fitting this description sound familiar? About six-two, thin as a bone. Brown hair, hazel eyes, the look of a serious drug problem, among other things. That ring a bell?"

I felt my pulse quicken. "Actually, a man fitting that description was waiting for me outside my office tonight when I left. He tried to speak to me, but from the look of things he wasn't the kind of person you want to get close to."

"Interesting," Makhoulian said. "Listen, Mr. Parker, I'm going to need you to come down to the medical examiner's office right away. You know where it is?"

"Thirtieth and First. I've been there before. I'm a reporter."

"I know who you are, Mr. Parker. I'm going to need you to meet me there in one hour. Will that be a problem?"

"No, but I would like to know what all this is about."

"This man I'm speaking of, he was found an hour ago in an apartment in Alphabet City, dead from a single gunshot wound to the head. We have reason to believe you were the last person to see him alive."

"Okay," I said, my stomach beginning to turn. The last thing I wanted was to get tied up in the murder of a homeless junkie who happened to have seen my name in the newspaper. "Listen, Detective, no disrespect, but this guy probably saw one of my stories and figured a reporter might be more inclined to listen to a junkie than a cop. And now he's dead, and while it really is a shame, I don't think there's much I can offer to help your investigation."

"I disagree," Makhoulian said. "This man's name was Stephen Gaines. Does that ring a bell?"

"No, Detective, it doesn't."

"That's interesting. I'm going to need you to meet me at the ME's office right away. Because according to his medical records, Stephen Gaines was your brother."

A legal thriller by acclaimed author
KATE WILHELM

Twenty-two years ago, while attending the University of Oregon, David Etheridge and Robert McCrutchen were investigated in the death of a young coed. The case was never solved, and now old stories have resurfaced when Etheridge returns to Eugene, Oregon. Tied by the past, McCrutchen, now a senator, is his grudging host—until the senator is found shot dead.

Once again Etheridge is suspected of murder. Only this time he's facing a double charge.

Barbara must battle the prosecution and the court of public opinion. As the pressure mounts, Barbara ties the past and present together, risking her own life to protect a client and preserve justice.

Cold Case

More Praise for
Gay Talese and
THY NEIGHBOR'S WIFE

"A report (the result of no less than nine years of work) on just how far some of us have willingly, gladly strayed not from nineteenth-century morality, but from the kind that most of the twentieth-century has taken for granted . . . We are given, really, a number of well-told stories, their social message cumulative: a drastically transformed American sexuality has emerged during this past couple of decades."
The New York Times Book Review

"Every man who reads it will recognize himself. Every woman will discover, perhaps for the first time, the secret fantasies and public privations, the loneliness and passionate lusts, of most men."
Chicago Sun-Times

Also by Gay Talese:

HONOR THY FATHER*
THE KINGDOM AND THE POWER*
THE BRIDGE
FAME AND OBSCURITY*
NEW YORK—A SERENDIPITER'S JOURNEY
THE OVERREACHERS
UNTO THE SONS*

Published by Ivy Books

THY
NEIGHBOR'S
WIFE

Gay Talese

IVY BOOKS • NEW YORK

Ivy Books
Published by Ballantine Books
Copyright © 1980, 1981 by Gay Talese
Foreword © 1993 by Gay Talese

ISBN 0-8041-1059-X

Note to Reader
The names of the people in this book are real, and the scenes and events described on the following pages actually happened.

Manufactured in the United States of America

First Ballantine Books Edition: March 1993

for Nan

AUTHOR'S FOREWORD

This book explores the private lives of many ordinary Americans in the era before AIDS, probing in particular the liberating 1960s and '70s that reverberated with the loud voices of marchers who, in protesting the United States' military involvement in Vietnam, had urged their fellow citizens to "Make Love, Not War."

But while this advice was widely endorsed on college campuses and in the homes of married couples across the country, it so infuriated the sensibilities of America's sexually puritanical President, Richard M. Nixon, that he appointed a six-foot four-inch moral vigilante to help eliminate what he saw as the obscene behavior that was undermining the family values of an entire nation.

President Nixon's appointee, an attorney and business leader from Cincinnati named Charles Keating (whose background and activities are described in Chapter 22 of this book), was known among his admirers as "Mr. Clean." In 1992, however, he is better known to Americans as the manipulator who sits in prison today after being convicted for his role in the multi-billion dollar Savings and Loan scandal that may continue to burden taxpayers throughout the decade. And so while this book concentrates on the sexual permissiveness that reached its peak in the 1970s, converting America into what writer John Updike calls in his latest novel, "the paradise of flesh," it deals as well with the hypocrisy of such moral crusaders as Charles Keating and some of his successors in the 1990s who trace the tolerances introduced during the '60s to America's present-day problem with AIDS. Indeed, this is not strictly the opinion of the so-called moralists; it has also been expressed by such outspoken defenders of sexual freedom as the essayist and academician Camille

Paglia, who was a student and an activist during the '60s, but who writes in her latest book published earlier this year *[Sex, Art and the American Culture]*:

> The Sixties attempted a return to nature that ended in disaster. The gentle nude bathing and playful sliding in the mud at Woodstock were a short-lived Rousseauist dream. My generation, inspired by the Dionysian titanism of rock, attempted something more radical than anything since the French Revolution. We asked: why should I obey this law? and why shouldn't I act on every sexual impulse? The result was a descent into barbarism. We painfully discovered that a just society cannot, in fact, function if everyone does his own thing. And out of the pagan promiscuity of the Sixties came AIDS. Everyone of my generation who preached free love is responsible for AIDS. The Sixties revolution in America collapsed because of its own excesses.

But did it really collapse? Like everyone else, I've read numerous newspaper accounts in recent years based on poll-takers' surveys indicating that, due to AIDS, single's bars are no longer so promising as preludes to sex, that married couples are less prone to adultery, that sexy novels are less successful commercially, that a New Puritanism is pervading the consciousness of the country. But I also wonder if people are telling the poll-takers one thing, and doing another; in any case, the flagrant openness that was a hallmark of the 1960s remains quite evident today. We see the advertised solicitation of prostitutes on cable television; the total nudity allowed on Broadway stages and in general-audience films, the display of hardcore sex magazines and cassettes on store shelves in small towns as well as cities. There are also the multitudes of unwed mothers to say nothing of extra-martial dallances indulged in by some highly respected people who, one might assume, would reflect the New Puritanism if it did indeed exist.

And I read in *The New York Times* on this very morning, in early November of 1992, that the chief judge of New York's highest court, a 62-year-old family man with a renowned reputation for high moral values and professional opinions, became so distressed after his inamorata had replaced him with another lover that he tried to blackmail her and to harass her in other ways as well. Arrested by the F.B.I., the judge later in the day announced his resignation. In recent years there have been priests accused of sexual acts with young men, TV evangelists cited for their extramarital acts with young women, and male members of Congress identified as indulging in pleasures provided both by young women and men.

All that I am suggesting, essentially, is that contrary to publicized opinion garnered by poll-takers, I doubt that the America of the '90s—with all due respect to the trepidation and fear over AIDS—is subjecting itself to a New Puritanism that is curbing the temptations and prerogatives that seemed so shocking when they went public a generation ago.

More true, I think, is what was defined as novel in the '60s has today become so integrated into the mainstream that it remains "new" only to those news editors who are new to their jobs—or who are so guided by the daily pressures of their profession that they're driven to pinpoint as "trends" aspects of personal behavior that have long been the practice of people in private. And so, in one sense, this is a book about the sexual revolution of the 1960s and 1970s. It is about the men and women who personified that revolution. It is specific to certain people and certain places. But in another sense the book is timeless and placeless. For what can it tell about temptations and tempests between men and women that has not been told before, and lived before, eons ago back to the Dark Ages and companionship in caves? Since men and women first co-mingled, there has been an on-going struggle between the sexes, an eternal love-hate relationship that predates the Babel over languages; for men and women always have (and always will) speak and understand separate languages. These languages are beyond translation and interpretation—whether spoken in a law office occupied by the current Supreme Court Justice, Clarence Thomas, and his ex-colleague, Anita Hill, or spoken in a garden occupied by Adam and Eve.

And so there is nothing new in *Thy Neighbor's Wife*.

Nor is there anything old.

1

SHE WAS NUDE, lying on her stomach in the desert sand, her legs spread wide, her long hair flowing in the wind, her head tilted back with her eyes closed. She seemed lost in private thoughts, remote from the world, reclining on this windswept dune in California near the Mexican border, adorned by nothing but her natural beauty. She wore no jewelry, no flowers in her hair; there were no footprints in the sand, nothing dated the day or spoiled the perfection of this photograph except the moist fingers of the seventeen-year-old schoolboy who held it and looked at it with adolescent longing and lust.

The picture was in a photographic art magazine that he had just bought at a newsstand on the corner of Cermak Road in suburban Chicago. It was an early evening in 1957, cold and windy, but Harold Rubin could feel the warmth rising within him as he studied the photograph under the streetlamp near the curb behind the stand, oblivious to the sounds of traffic and the people passing on their way home.

He flipped through the pages to look at the other nude women, seeing to what degree he could respond to them. There had been times in the past when, after buying one of these magazines hastily, because they were sold under the counter and were therefore unavailable for adequate erotic preview, he was greatly disappointed. Either the volleyball-playing nudists in *Sunshine & Health*, the only magazine showing pubic hair in the 1950s, were too hefty; or the smiling show girls in *Modern Man* were trying too hard to entice; or the models in *Classic Photography* were merely objects of the camera, lost in artistic shadows.

While Harold Rubin usually could achieve some solitary fulfillment from these, they were soon relegated to the lower levels of the stacks of magazines that he kept at home in the closet of

his bedroom. At the top of the pile were the more proven products, those women who projected a certain emotion or posed in
a certain way that was immediately stimulating to him; and,
more important, their effect was enduring. He could ignore them
in the closet for weeks or months as he sought a new discovery
elsewhere. But, failing to find it, he knew he could return home
and revive a relationship with one of the favorites in his paper
harem, achieving gratification that was certainly different from
but not incompatible with the sex life he had with a girl he knew
from Morton High School. One blended with the other somehow. When he was making love to her on the sofa when her
parents were out, he was sometimes thinking of the more mature
women in the magazines. At other times, when alone with his
magazines, he might recall moments with his girl friend, remembering what she looked like with her clothes off, what she
felt like, what they did together.

Recently, however, perhaps because he was feeling restless
and uncertain and was thinking of dropping out of school, leaving his girl, and joining the Air Force, Harold Rubin was more
detached than usual from life in Chicago, was more into fantasy,
particularly when in the presence of pictures of one special
woman who, he had to admit, was becoming an obsession.

It was this woman whose picture he had just seen in the magazine he now held on the sidewalk, the nude on the sand dune.
He had first noticed her months ago in a camera quarterly. She
also had appeared in several men's publications, adventure magazines, and a nudist calendar. It was not only her beauty that
had attracted him, the classic lines of her body or the wholesome
features of her face, but the entire aura that accompanied each
picture, a feeling of her being completely free with nature and
herself as she walked along the seashore, or stood near a palm
tree, or sat on a rocky cliff with waves splashing below. While
in some pictures she seemed remote and ethereal, probably
unobtainable, there was a pervasive reality about her, and he
felt close to her. He also knew her name. It had appeared in a
picture caption, and he was confident that it was her real name
and not one of those pixie pseudonyms used by some playmates
and pinups who concealed their true identity from the men they
wished to titillate.

Her name was Diane Webber. Her home was along the beach
at Malibu. It was said that she was a ballet dancer, which explained to Harold the disciplined body control she exhibited in
several of her positions in front of the camera. In one picture in

the magazine he now held, Diane Webber was almost acrobatic as she balanced herself gracefully above the sand on her outstretched arms with a leg extended high over her head, her toes pointed up into a cloudless sky. On the opposite page she was resting on her side, hips fully rounded, one thigh raised slightly and barely covering her pubis, her breasts revealed, the nipples erect.

Harold Rubin quickly closed the magazine. He slipped it between his school books and tucked them under his arm. It was getting late and he was soon due home for dinner. Turning, he noticed that the old cigar-smoking news vendor was looking at him, winking, but Harold ignored him. With his hands deep in the pockets of his black leather coat, Harold Rubin headed home, his long blond hair, worn in the duck's-ass style of Elvis Presley, brushing against his upraised collar. He decided to walk instead of taking the bus, because he wanted to avoid close contact with people, wanted no one to invade his privacy as he anxiously anticipated the hour at night when, after his parents had gone to sleep, he would be alone in his bedroom with Diane Webber.

He walked on Oak Park Avenue, then north to Twenty-first Street, passing bungalows and larger brick houses in this quiet residential community called Berwyn, a thirty-minute drive from downtown Chicago. The people here were conservative, hardworking, and thrifty. A high percentage of them were descendants of parents or grandparents who had immigrated to this area from Central Europe earlier in the century, especially from the western region of Czechoslovakia called Bohemia. They still referred to themselves as Bohemians despite the fact that, much to their chagrin, the name was now more popularly associated in America with carefree, loose-living young people who wore sandals and read beatnik poetry.

Harold's paternal grandmother, whom he felt closer to than anyone in his family and visited regularly, had been born in Czechoslovakia, but not in the region of Bohemia. She had come from a small village in southern Czechoslovakia near the Danube and the old Hungarian capital of Bratislava. She had told Harold often of how she had arrived in America at fourteen to work as a servant girl in a boardinghouse in one of those grim, teeming industrial towns along Lake Michigan that had attracted thousands of sturdy Slavic men to work in the steel mills, oil refineries, and other factories around East Chicago, Gary, and Hammond, Indiana. Living conditions were so overcrowded in those days, she said, that in the first boardinghouse where she worked there were four men from the day shift renting four beds at night and four other men from the night shift renting those same beds during the day.

These men were treated like animals and lived like animals, she said, and when they were not being exploited by their bosses in the factories they were trying to exploit the few working girls like herself who were unfortunate enough to be living in these towns at that time. The men in the boardinghouse were always grabbing at her, she said, banging on her locked door at night as she tried to sleep. When she related this to Harold during a recent visit, while he sat in the kitchen eating a sandwich she had made, he suddenly had a vision of what his grandmother must have looked like fifty years ago, a shy servant girl with fair complexion and blue eyes like his own, her long hair in a bun, her youthful body moving quickly around the house in a long drab dress, trying to elude the clutching fingers and strong arms of the burly men from the mill.

As Harold Rubin continued to walk home, his school books and the magazine held tightly under his arm, he remembered how sad yet fascinated he had been by his grandmother's reminiscing, and he understood why she spoke freely with him. He was the only person in the family who was genuinely interested in her, who took the time to be with her in the big brick house in which she was otherwise nearly always alone. Her husband, John Rubin, a former Teamster who made a fortune in the trucking business, spent his days at the garage with his fleet of vehicles and his nights with a secretary who, if referred to at all by Harold's grandmother, was referred to as "the whore." The only child in this unhappy marriage, Harold's father was completely dominated by *his* father, for whom he worked long hours in the garage; and Harold's grandmother did not feel sufficiently close to Harold's mother to share the frustration and bitterness she felt. So it was mainly Harold, sometimes accompanied by his younger brother, who interrupted the prevailing silence and boredom in the house. And as Harold became older and more curious, more remote from his parents and his own surroundings, he gradually became his grandmother's confidant, her ally in alienation.

From her he learned much about his father's boyhood, his grandfather's past, and why she had married such a tyrannical man. John Rubin had been born sixty-two years ago in Russia, the son of a Jewish peddler, and at the age of two he had immigrated with his parents to a city near Lake Michigan called

Sobieski, named in honor of a seventeenth-century Polish king. After a minimum of schooling and unrelieved poverty, Rubin and other youths were arrested staging a holdup during which a policeman was shot. Released on probation, and after working at various jobs for a few years, Rubin one day visited his older married sister in Chicago and became attracted to the young Czechoslovakian girl then taking care of the baby.

On a subsequent visit he found her in the house alone, and after she had rejected his advances—as she had previously done with men when she had worked in the boardinghouse—he forced her into her bedroom and raped her. She was then sixteen. It had been her first sexual experience, and it would make her pregnant. Panicked, but having no close relatives or friends nearby to help, she was persuaded by her employers to marry John Rubin, or else he would go off to prison because of his prior criminal offense, and she would be no better off. They were married in October 1912. Six months later they had a son, Harold's father.

The loveless marriage did not greatly improve with time, Harold's grandmother said, adding that her husband regularly beat his son, beat her when she interfered, and devoted himself mainly to the maintenance of his trucks. His lucrative career had begun when, after he had worked as a deliveryman on a horse and wagon for Spiegel, Inc., a large mail-order house in Chicago, he convinced management to lend him enough money to invest in a truck and start his own motorized delivery service, thus eliminating Spiegel's need for several horses whose performance he said could not match his own. After buying one truck and fulfilling his promise, he bought a second truck, then a third. Within a decade John Rubin had a dozen trucks handling all of Spiegel's local cartage, as well as that of other companies.

Over the futile protests of his wife, his son was summoned as an adolescent into the garage to work as a driver's helper, and although John Rubin was amassing great personal wealth at this time and was generous with his bribes to local politicians and the police—"If you wanna slide, you gotta grease," he often said—he was a miser with the family budget, and he frequently accused his wife of stealing coins that he had left around the house. Later he began deliberately to leave money here and there in amounts that he precisely remembered, or he would arrange coins in a certain way on the bureau or elsewhere in the house in the hope that he could prove that his wife took some or at least touched them; but he never could.

These and other remembrances of Harold's grandmother, and similar observations that he made himself while in his grandfather's chilly presence, gave Harold considerable insight into his own father, a quiet and humorless man of forty-four resembling not in the slightest the photograph on the piano that was taken during World War II and showed him in a corporal's uniform looking relaxed and handsome, many miles from home. But the fact that Harold could understand his father did not make living with him any easier, and as Harold now approached East Avenue, the street on which he lived, he could feel the tension and apprehension, and he wondered what his father would choose to complain about today.

In the past, if there had not been complaints about Harold's schoolwork, then there had been about the length of Harold's hair, or Harold's late hours with his girl, or Harold's nudist magazines that his father had once seen spread out on the bed after Harold had carelessly left his door open.

"What's all this crap?" his father had asked, using a word far more delicate than his grandfather would have used. His grandfather's vocabulary was peppered with every imaginable profanity, delivered in tones of deep contempt, whereas his father's words were more restrained, lacking emotion.

"They're my magazines," Harold had answered.

"Well, get rid of them," his father had said.

"They're *mine*!" Harold suddenly shouted. His father had looked at him curiously, then began to shake his head slowly in disgust and left the room. They had not spoken for weeks after that incident, and tonight Harold did not want to repeat that confrontation. He hoped to get through dinner peacefully and quickly.

Before entering the house, he looked in the garage and saw that his father's car was there, a gleaming 1956 Lincoln that his father had bought new a year ago, trading in his pampered 1953 Cadillac. Harold climbed the steps to the back door and quietly entered the house. His mother, a matronly woman with a kindly face, was in the kitchen preparing dinner; he could hear the television on in the living room and saw his father sitting there reading the Chicago *American*. Smiling at his mother, Harold said hello in a voice loud enough that it would carry into the living room and perhaps count as a double greeting. There was no response from his father.

Harold's mother informed him that his brother was in bed

with a cold and fever and would not be joining them for dinner. Harold, saying nothing, walked into his bedroom and closed the door softly. It was a nicely furnished room with a comfortable chair, a polished dark wood desk, and a large Viking oak bed. Books were neatly arranged on shelves, and hanging from the wall were replicas of Civil War swords and rifles that had been his father's and also a framed glass case in which were mounted several steel tools that Harold had made last year in a manual-arts class and which had won him a citation in a national contest sponsored by the Ford Motor Company. He had also won an art award from Wieboldt's department store for his oil painting of a clown, and his skill as a woodcraftsman was most recently demonstrated in his construction of a wooden stand designed to hold a magazine in an open position and thus permit him to look at it with both of his hands free.

Placing his school books on the desk and taking off his coat, Harold opened the magazine to the photographs of the nude Diane Webber. He stood near the bed holding the magazine in his right hand, and, with his eyes half closed, he gently brushed his left hand across the front of his trousers, softly touching his genitals. The response was immediate. He wished that he now had the time before dinner to undress and be fulfilled, or at least to go down the hall to the bathroom for quick relief over the sink, holding the photograph up to the medicine-cabinet mirror to see a reflection of himself exposed to her nude body, pretending a presence with her in the sun and sand, directing her dark lovely lowered eyes toward his tumescent organ, and imagining that his soapy hand was part of her.

He had done this many times before, usually during the afternoons when it might have seemed surreptitious for him to close his bedroom door. But, despite the guaranteed privacy behind the locked door of the bathroom, Harold had to admit that he was never completely comfortable there, partly because he really preferred reclining on his bed to standing, and because there was insufficient room around the sink on which to lay down the magazine if he wished to use both hands. Also, and perhaps more important, if he was not careful the magazine might be stained by drops of water bouncing up from the sink, since he kept the faucet running to alert the family of his presence in the bathroom, and also because he occasionally needed additional water for lathering when the soap went dry on his fingers. While the water-stained photographs of nude women might not offend the aesthetics of most young men, this was not the case with Harold Rubin.

And finally there was a practical consideration involved in his desire to protect his magazines from damage: Having read in newspapers this year about the more zealous antipornography drives around the nation, he could not be sure that he would always be able to buy new magazines featuring nudes, not even under the counter. Even *Sunshine & Health*, which had been in circulation for two decades and populated its pages with family pictures including grandparents and children, had been described as obscene this year at a California judiciary hearing. Artcamera magazines had also been cited as "smut" by some politicians and church groups, even though these publications had attempted to disassociate themselves from girlie magazines by including under each nude picture such instructive captions as *Taken with 2 1/4 x 3 1/4 Crown Graphic fitted with 101 mm Ektar, f:11, at 1/100 sec.* Harold had read that President Eisenhower's Postmaster General, Arthur Summerfield, was intent on keeping sexual literature and magazines out of the mails, and a New York publisher, Samuel Roth, had just been sentenced to five years in prison and a fine of $5,000 for violating the federal mail statute. Roth had previously been convicted for disseminating copies of *Lady Chatterley's Lover*, and his first arrest, in 1928, came after the police had raided his publishing company and seized the printing plates of *Ulysses*, which had been smuggled in from Paris.

Harold had read that a Brigitte Bardot film had been interfered with in Los Angeles, and he could only assume that in a city like Chicago, a workingman's town with a tough police force and considerable moral influence from the Catholic Church, sexual expression would be repressed even more, particularly during the administration of the new Irish-Catholic mayor, Richard J. Daley. Already Harold had noticed that the burlesque house on Wabash Avenue had been closed down, as had the one on State Street. If the trend continued, it might mean that his favorite newsstand on Cermak Road would be reduced to selling such magazines as *Good Housekeeping* and *The Saturday Evening Post*, a happenstance that he knew would provoke no protest from his parents.

In all the years that he had lived at home he had never heard his parents express a sexual thought, had never seen either of them in the nude, had never heard their bed creaking at night

with love sounds. He assumed that they still did make love, but
he could not be certain. While he did not know how active his
grandfather was in his sixties with his mistress, his grandmother
had recently confided in a typical bitter moment that they had
not made love since 1936. He had been an unskilled lover anyway, his grandmother had quickly added, and as Harold had
pondered the statement he wondered for the first time if his
grandmother had secret lovers. He seriously doubted it, never
having observed men visiting her home, or her often leaving it;
but he did recall discovering to his surprise a year ago in her
library a romantic sex novel. It had been covered in brown paper, and on the copyright page was the name of a French publishing house and, under it, the date, 1909. While his
grandmother had been taking a nap, Harold sat on the floor
reading once, then twice, the 103-page novel, enthralled by the
tale and amazed by the explicit language. The story described
the unhappy sex lives of several young women in Europe and
the East who, after leaving their small towns and villages in
despair, wandered into Morocco and became captives of a pasha
who secluded them in a seraglio. One day, when the pasha was
away, one of the women noticed through the window a handsome sea captain below and, luring him upstairs, made passionate love to him, as did the others in turn, pausing between acts
to reveal to the captain the sordid details of their past that had
eventually led them to this place. Harold had read the book
during subsequent visits so often that he could practically recite
certain passages. . . .

Her soft arms were wound around me in response, and our
lips met in a delicious and prolonged kiss, during which my
shaft was imprisoned against her warm smooth belly. Then
she raised herself on tiptoes, which brought its crest among
the short thick hair where the belly terminated. With one hand
I guided my shaft to the entrance, which welcomed it; with
my other I held her plump buttocks toward me. . . .

Harold hear his mother calling him from the kitchen. It was
time for dinner. He put the magazine with its photographs of
Diane Webber under his pillow. He replied to his mother, waiting momentarily as his erection subsided. Then he opened his
door and walked casually toward the kitchen.

* * *

His father was already seated at the table with a bowl of soup in front of him, reading the paper, while his mother stood at the stove talking airily, unaware of the minimal attention she was receiving. She was saying that while shopping in town today she had met one of her old friends from the Cook County tax assessor's office, which is where she had once worked, operating a Comptometer. Harold, who knew that she had left that job shortly before his birth seventeen years ago, never to work again outside the house, commented to his mother on the fine aroma of the cooking, and his father looked up from his paper and nodded without a smile.

As Harold sat down and began sipping the soup, his mother continued to talk, while slicing beef on a sideboard before bringing it to the table. She wore a housedress, little makeup, and smoked a filter-tipped cigarette. Both of Harold's parents were heavy smokers, smoking being their only pleasure insofar as he knew. Neither of them was fond of drinking whiskey, beer, or wine, and dinner was served with cream soda or root beer, purchased weekly by the case.

After his mother had seated herself, the telephone rang. His father, who always kept the phone within reach at the dinner table, frowned as he grabbed it. Someone was calling from the garage. It happened almost every night during dinner; and from his father's expression it might be assumed that he was receiving unwelcome news—perhaps a truck had broken down before making its delivery or the Teamsters' union was going on strike; but Harold knew from living in the house that the grim, tight-lipped look of his father did not necessarily reflect what was being said on the telephone. It was an inextricable part of his father's nature to look sullenly upon the world, and Harold knew that even if this phone call had come from a television game show announcing that his father had just won a prize, his father would react with a frown.

Still, despite whatever genuine aggravation was inherent in managing the Rubin trucking business, his father got up diligently at five-thirty each morning to be the first on the job, and he spent his days dealing with problems ranging from the maintenance of 142 trucks to the occasional pilferage of cargo, and he had to deal as well with the irascible old man, John Rubin, who personally wanted to control everything, even though the operation was now too big for him to do so.

Harold had recently heard that several of Rubin's drivers had been stopped by the police for driving without license plates, which had infuriated the old man, who ignored the fact that his stinginess had caused this: Trying to save money, he had purchased only 32 sets of license plates for his 142 trucks, requiring that the men in the garage keep switching the plates from vehicle to vehicle or risk making deliveries without plates. Harold knew that sooner or later this scheme would result in a court case, and then his grandfather would try to bribe his way out of it, and, even if he was lucky enough to do so, it would probably cost him more than if he had paid for the proper number of plates in the beginning.

Harold vowed that he would never work full-time in the garage. He had tried working there during the summer but had soon quit because he could not tolerate the verbal abuse from his grandfather, who had often called him a "little bum," and also that of his father, who had remarked sourly one day, "You'll never amount to anything." This prediction had not bothered Harold because he knew that the price of appeasing these men was total subjugation, and he was determined that he would not repeat the mistake of his father in becoming subservient to an old man who had sired a son he had not wanted with a woman he had not loved.

After his father had hung up the telephone, he resumed eating, revealing nothing of what had been said. A cup of coffee was placed in front of him, heavy with cream as he liked it, and he lit up an Old Gold. Harold's mother mentioned not having seen their neighbors from across the street in several days, and Harold suggested that they might be away on vacation. She stood to clear the table, then went to check the fever of her younger son, who was still sleeping. Harold's father went into the living room and turned on the television set. Harold later joined him, sitting on the other side of the room. Harold could hear his mother doing the dishes in the kitchen and his father yawning as he listlessly watched television and completed the crossword puzzle in the newspaper. He then stood, yawned again, and said he was going to bed. It was shortly after nine o'clock. Within a half hour, Harold's mother had come into the living room to say good night, and soon Harold turned off the television and the house was soundless and still. He walked to his bedroom and closed the door, feeling a quiet exuberance and relief. He was finally alone.

He removed his clothes, hung them in the closet. He reached for the small bottle of hand lotion, Italian Balm, that he kept on the upper shelf of his closet, and he placed it on the bedside table next to a box of Kleenex. He turned on the bedside lamp of low wattage, turned off the overhead light, and the room was bathed in a soft glow.

He could hear the wind whipping against the storm windows on this freezing Chicago night, and he shivered as he slipped between the cool sheets and pulled the blankets over him. He lay back for a few moments, getting warm, and then he reached for the magazine under his pillow and began to flip through it in a cursory way—he did not want to focus yet on the object of his obsession, Diane Webber, who awaited him on the sand dune on page 19, but preferred instead to make an initial pass through the entire fifty-two-page issue, which contained thirty-nine nude pictures of eleven different women, a visual aphrodisiac of blondes and brunets, preliminary stimulants before the main event.

A lean, dark-eyed woman on page 4 attracted Harold, but the photographer had posed her awkwardly on the gnarled branch of a tree, and he felt her discomfort. The nude on page 6, sitting cross-legged on a studio floor next to an easel, had fine breasts but a bland expression on her face. Harold, still on his back with his knees slightly raised under the blankets, continued to turn the pages past various legs and breasts, hips and buttocks and hair, female fingers and arms reaching out, eyes looking away from him, eyes looking *at* him as he occasionally paused to lightly stroke his genitals with his left hand, tilting the magazine in his right hand to eliminate the slight glare on the glossy pages.

Proceeding through the magazine page after page, he came to the exquisite pictures of Diane Webber, but he quickly skipped over them, not wanting to tempt himself now. He moved on to the Mexican girl on page 27 who sat demurely with a fisherman's net spread across her thighs; and then to the heavy-breasted blonde reclining on the floor next to a small marble statue of "Venus di Milo"; and on to a lithe, lovely blonde standing in the shadows *1/25 sec. at f:22* of what appeared to be an empty stage of a theater, her arms crossed under her chin and above her upturned breasts, which were gracefully revealed, and, in the very subtle stage lighting, Harold was quite certain that he could see her pubic hair, and he felt himself for the first time becoming aroused.

If he were not so enamored of Diane Webber, he knew he could be satisfied by this willowy young blonde, satisfied perhaps more than once, which to him was the true test of an erotic picture. In the stacks of magazines in his closet were dozens of nudes who had aroused him in the past to solitary peaks, some having done so three or four times; and some were capable of doing it again in the future as long as they remained unseen for a while, thereby regaining their sense of mystery.

And then there were those extremely rare pictures, those of Diane Webber, that could fulfill him constantly. He estimated that his collection contained fifty photographs of her, and within a moment he could locate every one of them in the two hundred magazines that he kept. He would merely have to glance at the cover and would know exactly where she was within, how she was standing, what was in the background, what her attitude seemed to be during that special split second when the camera had clicked. He could remember, too, first seeing these pictures, could reconstruct where and when he had bought them; he could practically mark a moment in his life from each of her poses, each being so real that he believed he knew her personally, she was part of him, and through her he had become more in touch with himself in several ways, not merely through acts which Victorian moralists had defined as self-abuse, but rather through self-acceptance, his understanding the naturalness of his desires, and of asserting his right to an idealized woman.

Not able to resist any longer, Harold turned the page to Diane Webber on the dune. He looked at her, lying on her stomach, her head held up into the wind, her eyes closed, the nipple of her left breast erect, her legs spread wide, the late-afternoon sun casting an exaggerated shadow of her curvaceous body along the smooth white sand. Beyond her body was nothing but a sprawling empty desert—she seemed so alone, so approachable and available; Harold had merely to desire her, and she was his.

He pushed the blankets off his body, warm with excitement and anticipation. He reached under his bed for the wooden stand he had made in school, knowing that his manual-arts teacher would be astonished to learn what use would be made of it tonight. He placed the magazine on the stand in front of him, between his widely spread legs. Raising his head, supporting it on two pillows, he reached for the bottle of Italian Balm, poured lotion into his palms and rubbed it between his hands momentarily to warm it. Then, softly, he began to touch his penis and testicles, feeling the quick growth to full erection. With his eyes half closed, he lay back and gazed at his glistening organ towering in front of the picture, casting a shadow across the desert.

Continuing to massage himself up and down, up and down, back and forth across his testicles, he focused sharply on Diane

Webber's arched back, her rising buttocks, her full hips, the warm, moist place between her legs; and he now imagined himself approaching her, bending down to her, and determinedly penetrating her from the rear without a word of protest from her as he thrust upward, faster faster, and upward, faster, and suddenly he could feel her buttocks pounding back against his thighs, her hips moving from side to side; he could hear her sighs of pleasure as he tightened his grip around her hips, faster, and then her loud cries as she came in a series of quick convulsions that he could feel as fully as he now felt her hand reaching back to hold his tight testicles exactly as he liked to have them held, softly, then more firmly as she sensed the throbbing, shuttering start of sperm flowing upward and gushing out in great spurts that he grabbed in both hands as he closed his eyes and felt it squirt through his fingers. He lay very quietly in bed for a few moments, letting his muscles relax and his legs go limp. Then he opened his eyes and saw her there, as lovely and desirable as ever.

Finally he sat up, wiped himself with two pieces of Kleenex, then two more because his hands were still sticky with sperm and lotion. He rolled the tissue into a ball and tossed it into the wastebasket, not concerned that his mother might recognize it in the morning when she emptied the baskets. His days at home were numbered. In a matter of a few weeks, he would be in the Air Force, and beyond that he had no plans.

He closed the magazine and placed it on the top of the pile in his closet. He put the wooden stand back under the bed. Then he climbed under the covers, feeling tired but calm, and turned out the light. If he was lucky, he thought, the Air Force might send him to a base in Southern California. And then, somehow, he would find her.

2

IN 1928 THE mother of Diane Webber won a beauty contest in Southern California, sponsored by the manufacturers of the Graham-Paige automobile, and one of the prizes was a small part in a silent film directed by Cecil B. De Mille in which she portrayed the coy and pretty teenaged girl that in real life she was.

She had come to California from Montana to live with her father, who, after the bitter breakup of his marriage, had quit the Billings Electric Company and found work as an electrician in Los Angeles with Warner Bros. studios. She was much closer to her father than her mother, and she also wanted to escape the harshness of the rural Northwest where her parents had so often quarreled, where her grandmother had been married five times, and where her great-grandmother, while swimming in a river one day, was killed by an arrow shot into her back by an Indian. She had arrived in Southern California convinced that it would offer more fulfillment than the limited horizons of the big-sky country.

And it did, in most ways, even though she would never achieve stardom in the several films in which she appeared in the late 1920s and early 1930s. Her satisfaction came rather from a sense of serenity she felt in Los Angeles, a sunny detachment from the grim girlhood she had known in Montana. In Los Angeles she felt free to pursue her whims, to revive her early interest in religion, to walk in the streets without wearing a bra, eventually to marry a man who was almost thirty years older and then, seven years later, to take a second husband who was five years younger. Southern California's characteristic disregard of traditional values, its relatively rootless society, its mobility and lack of continuity—the very qualities that had been a burden in her family's past in Montana—were accepted easily by her in

15

Los Angeles, partly because she was now sharing these newly accepted values with thousands of her own generation, pretty young women like herself who had left their unglamorous hometowns elsewhere in America and had migrated to California in search of some vaguely defined goal. And while very few of these women would succeed as actresses, or models, or dancers—more likely they would spend their best years working as cocktail waitresses, or receptionists, or salesclerks, or as unhappily married women in San Fernando Valley—nearly all of them remained in California, and they had children, children who were reared in the sun during the Depression, who played outdoor sports the year round during the 1940s, who matured in the period of great California prosperity that began with World War II (when American defense investments poured millions into West Coast aircraft plants and technological industries); and by the 1950s there had emerged in California a new generation that was distinguished for its good looks, its casual style in dress, its relaxed view of life with an emphasis on health, a special look that on Madison Avenue, throughout the nation, and overseas was regarded as peculiarly American—the California Look. And among those who possessed this look in the 1950s, though her mother was among the last to recognize it, was Diane Webber.

Diane's problems with her mother began after her parents were divorced. Diane's father, twenty-seven years older than her mother, was a writer from Ogden, Utah, named Guy Empey. He was a short, stocky, imperious, adventurous man who had joined the United States Cavalry in 1911, and, because his country was late in becoming involved in World War I, he joined the British Army. He saw frontline action in Europe, earning battle scars that he would proudly wear on his face the rest of his life, and in 1917 he wrote a best-selling book about his experiences called *Over the Top*, which sold more than a million copies. It also became a film, which he directed and in which he played the lead.

Guy Empey wrote other books during the next decade, though none nearly as popular as the first, and by 1930 he was reduced to writing pulp fiction for magazines, often under pseudonyms. It was around this time, at a social gathering in Hollywood, that he met the small, spry, twenty-year-old actress from Montana whose short dark hair, large brown eyes, and infectious smile reminded him of the silent-screen star Clara Bow. He quickly courted her with bouquets of flowers, took her for rides in his

Cadillac touring car, and soon he had proposed marriage—and she accepted, although at forty-six he was as old as her father.

Unwisely, he moved his bride into the home he shared with his beloved mother and sister, to whom he had dedicated *Over the Top*. Both were cultured, sophisticated women from New York—his mother's uncle, Richard Henry Dana, had written *Two Years Before the Mast*; and his widowed sister, who had been married to a top executive with W. & J. Sloane, read *The New Yorker* each week and had filled the Los Angeles house with fine furnishings and a wonderful library that she had brought with her from across the country. These two women, and particularly Guy Empey's strong-willed mother, were not overly impressed with the little actress from Montana, and he was unable or unwilling to resolve a growing marital conflict that was only briefly interrupted in the summer of 1932 by the birth of their only child, who was named, after a song then very popular, Diane.

When Diane was two, her mother separated from her father; when she was five, after a brief reconciliation, her parents were divorced, and Diane spent the ensuing years dividing her time between two households. During the week she lived with her mother, who in 1939 married a handsome man of twenty-four who had worked as a photographer for the International News Service and had modeled in a cowboy outfit on billboards advertising Chesterfield cigarettes. At the time of the marriage he owned a small restaurant on Sunset Boulevard, and Diane's twenty-nine-year-old mother suppressed whatever lingering movie ambitions she still had, as she joined her new husband and worked as a waitress.

On weekends Diane would ride the trolley from the Hollywood Hills over to Echo Park, where her grandmother would meet her and escort her to her father's house; there, with the music of Handel softly playing on the phonograph, she would dwell in the intellectual presence of her aunt and grandmother, who encouraged her to read widely, who took her to proper films, and who were forever using words that sent her searching through the dictionary. As the women took their daily afternoon naps, and as her father worked at his typewriter—with a minimum of success—Diane would sit alone in her room quietly reading everything from *Anthony Adverse* to the plays of Shakespeare, from the *Arabian Nights* to *Gray's Anatomy*, acquiring gradually a strong if erratic background in the classics as well as an intense sense of fantasy.

Her fantasies were formed more clearly one afternoon after

she had been taken to the ballet *The Nutcracker*. From then on, in her dreams, Diane saw herself as a glamorous girl in tights, twirling alone onstage in a graceful pirouette. She began taking ballet lessons once a week after school, but this was a privilege that her mother granted on the basis of Diane's personal behavior and how well she performed various chores around the house. Her stepfather, with whom she felt uncomfortable, would often watch her as she practiced at home, would sometimes gently tease her as she held on to the mantel in the living room and pointed a leg high into the air. This sight did not please her mother, who, having already objected to her young husband's attempt to display Varga pinups in the hallway, certainly was no less amused by the attention he was now giving to her budding twelve-year-old daughter. Late one afternoon, in a moment of petulance that shattered Diane, her mother remarked that it was most unlikely that Diane's beauty would ever match her own.

The situation at home quickly worsened for Diane later that year when her mother gave birth to a son and, two years later, to a baby daughter. Although Diane was approaching her teens, was becoming curious about boys and dating, she was expected to return home after school each day to help care for the children. This routine had continued more or less until she graduated from high school, whereupon she left home to live temporarily in the apartment of her mother's sister, earning money for her keep and dancing lessons by working as a gift wrapper in the Saks department store on Wilshire Boulevard. Months later, not wishing to further intrude upon the privacy of her maternal aunt, who was then dating a married man who worked in the office of the Beverly Hills Hotel, Diane moved into the Hollywood Studio Club, where her mother had once lived, a residence for women in the movie industry. It was there that Diane learned of an audition for chorus dancers willing to work in a nightclub in San Francisco, and while this was a dubious opportunity for an aspiring ballet dancer, she had concluded that she was probably already too old, at eighteen, and far too undertrained, ever to master the delicate physical art that she performed with such perfection in her fantasies. So she appeared at the audition and passed the test. When she approached her mother to ask if she could accept the position, her mother replied, ''Don't ask me. Make your own decision.'' Diane left for San Francisco not knowing whether her mother had granted her independence or was expressing indifference.

Diane earned eighty dollars a week for doing three shows a

night, six nights a week, dancing in the chorus behind such headline talents as Sophie Tucker. She wore a modest costume that revealed only her bare midriff, but while changing backstage she became exposed for the first time to group nudity, and she could see how her body compared to those of other women. It compared very well, and she was therefore not surprised when a friend in the chorus suggested that Diane might earn extra money as a figure model and gave her the name of an art professor at Berkeley who had paid other dancers twenty dollars for a brief photographic session in the nude.

Timidly, Diane appeared at the professor's residence, but his detached, formal manner soon put her at ease. She removed her clothes and stood nude before him. She watched him back away and heard the camera click. She heard it click again and again, and without any instructions from him she began to move like a ballet dancer, her arms slowly reaching, her body turning, twirling on her toes as she heard interior music and the camera click, and she was no longer aware of the professor's presence. She was aware only of her body as an inspired instrument that she artfully controlled, and with which she could rise beyond her limitations. Though nude, she did not feel naked. She felt internalized as she danced, private, alone, deeply involved with emotions that might be projected externally in her movements or expressions, but she did not know, she did not contemplate, what effect she was having on the professor behind the camera. She could barely perceive his fuzzy gray figure in the distance. Diane had her glasses off, and she was quite myopic.

Returning to Los Angeles after completing the nightclub engagement, Diane took the initiative and telephoned various fashion photographers who were listed in the classified directory, asking for an appointment. She called such men as David Balfour and Keith Bernard, Peter Gowland and Andre de Dienes, William Graham and Ed Lange, among others. Nearly all were attracted to her and were impressed by the fact that a young woman of such wholesome appeal would so willingly pose in the nude—she was at least ten years ahead of her time.

By 1954, when she was twenty-one, her photographs began to be seen in nudist and camera magazines all over the country. And in 1955, after a series of color photographs of her were sent to *Playboy* magazine in Chicago, the young publisher, Hugh Hefner, examined them in his office and he was immediately impressed.

3

HEFNER WAS TWENTY-EIGHT years old when he first saw the pictures of Diane Webber, and his magazine was in its second year of publication. He had edited the first issue of *Playboy* in 1953 on the kitchen table of an apartment he shared with his wife and infant daughter, but now he and a staff of thirty occupied a four-story building near downtown Chicago, and he sat in his large office on the top floor behind a modern white L-shaped desk, the photos of Diane Webber before him.

As he casually examined each picture he gave no indication of how embarrassed he had once been by any sign of nudity, or by his erotic dreams in the boyhood bedroom of his puritanical home. Now as a prosperous publisher of a sex-oriented magazine, separated from his wife, and sleeping with two young women on his staff, Hugh Hefner's fancied eroticism had achieved reality. The magazine that he had created had re-created him.

He virtually lived within the glossy pages, slept in a small bedroom behind his office, and worked all hours of the day and night on *Playboy*'s color and design, the cartoons and captions, the fact and fiction, reading every line as carefully as he was now examining, under a magnifying glass, the photographs of Diane Webber.

In the first picture, she was dancing bare-breasted in a ballet studio, wearing opaque black tights that revealed the strength and grace of her thighs, her calves, her round buttocks. Her stomach was flat, her smooth, strong back was not marred by the knotty muscles that dancers often develop; and, although she was in motion, her skin did not glisten with perspiration. This impressed Hefner, who during his youth perspired freely,

particularly when his hand touched a girl's waist at school dances
or when his arm was around her shoulder in movie theaters.

Slowly, he followed the line of Diane Webber's breasts, which
were large and firm, and her nipples, which were pink and erect.
He marveled at their perfect size and shape and imagined how
they would feel in his hands, a thought that he knew would occur
to thousands of other men once these pictures had been published and circulated in his magazine.

Hefner identified strongly with the men who bought his magazine. He knew from the letters he received, and from *Playboy*'s
soaring sales figures, that what appealed to him was appealing
to them; and at times he saw himself as a fantasy provider, a
mental matchmaker between his male readers and the females
who adorned his pages. Each month, after a new issue had been
completed under his personal direction, he could predictably
contemplate the climactic moments of solitary men all over
America who were aroused by his selections. They were road
salesmen in motel bedrooms, soldiers on bivouac, college boys
in dormitories, airborne executives in whose attaché cases the
magazine traveled like a covert companion. They were unfulfilled married men of moderate means and aspirations who were
bored with their lives, uninspired by their jobs, and sought temporary escape through sexual adventure with more women than
they had the ability to get, or the time to get, or the money to
get, or the power to get, or the genuine desire to get.

Hefner understood this feeling, had experienced it in the early
years of his marriage when he would slip away from his sleeping
wife at night to take long walks through the city. Along the lake,
he would look up at the luxurious towering apartment houses
and see women standing at the windows, and imagine that they
were as unhappy as he was; he wanted to know all of them
intimately. During the day he would mentally undress certain
women he saw walking in the street, or in parks, or getting into
cars, and although nothing was said or done, not even a glance
was exchanged, he nevertheless felt a quiet exhilaration, and he
could revive the impression of these women weeks later in his
mind, could see them as clearly as he was now seeing the photographs of the nude dancer on his desk.

Squinting through the magnifying glass, he focused on Diane
Webber's upraised chin, her sensuous lips, and her large hazel
eyes which looked back at him with an expression both inviting
and distant. This intrigued him, her way of looking directly at
him and yet remaining remote from the response she was in-

spiring. It was as if she were appearing nude for the first time, was still naïve about men, which was exactly the attitude that Hefner wanted nude women to convey in his magazine, although few playmates so far had achieved this look. Beginning with Marilyn Monroe in the first issue of December 1953, all of the *Playboy* centerfolds had been professional models, and they had the look of self-assurance and experience; they were women who had been around. Still, they had lured new readers to the magazine each month to a degree that had astonished even Hefner, and it was likely that *Playboy*'s early success had less to do with the actual magazine than it did with the men who bought it.

Prior to *Playboy*, few men in America had ever seen a color photograph of a nude woman, and they were overwhelmed and embarrassed as they bought *Playboy* at the newsstand, folding the cover inward as they walked away. It was as if they were openly acknowledging a terrible need, a long-repressed secret, admitting their failure to find the real thing. Although the Kinsey report revealed that nearly all men masturbate, it was still a dark deed in the early 1950s, and there had been no indication of its association with pictures; but now the strong connection was obvious with the success of *Playboy*, a magazine that had climbed in circulation within its first two years from 60,000 copies sold per month to 400,000. Little of this interest could be attributed to the articles, which were unexceptional, or to the cartoons, the satire, or the reprints of stories by Ambrose Bierce or Sir Arthur Conan Doyle. It was rather that Hefner, in founding a magazine that each month presented a nude woman who appeared to be sexually approachable, had discovered a vast audience of suitors, each privately claiming her as his own.

She was their mental mistress. She stimulated them in solitude, and they often saw her picture while making love to their wives. She was an almost special species who existed within the eye and mind of the observer, and she offered everything imaginable. She was always available at bedside, was totally controllable, knew the perfect touch in personal places, and never said or did anything to disturb the mood before the moment of ecstasy.

Each month she was a new person, satisfying the male need for variety, catering to various whims and obsessions, asking nothing in return. She behaved in ways that real women did not, which was the essence of fantasy, and was the primary reason for the prominence of Hugh Hefner, the first man to become rich by openly mass marketing masturbatory love through the illusion of an available alluring woman. It was a convenient way to carry on a relationship. For the price of the magazine, Hefner gave thousands of men access to an assortment of women who in real life would not look at them. He provided old men with young women, ugly men with desirable women, black men with white women, shy men with nymphomaniacs. He was an accomplice in the imagined extramarital affairs of monogamous men, supplied the stimulus for dormant men, and was thus connected with the central nervous system of *Playboy* readers nationwide, men whose passions were preceded by the preliminary wooing that Hefner did through a magnifying glass at his desk in Chicago, the erection center of the ultimate service magazine.

For himself, Hugh Hefner had more grandiose goals. He wanted not only to have the nude pictures but also to possess the women who had posed for them. His sexual appetite, long frustrated, was now insatiable. Not content with merely presenting fantasy, he wished to experience it, connect with it, to synthesize his strong visual sense with his physical drives, and to manufacture a mood, a love scene, that he could both feel and observe.

With him it was not so much a case of divided attention as it was his dual state of mind. He was, and had always been, visually aware of whatever he did as he did it. He was a voyeur of himself. He acted at times in order to watch. Once he allowed himself to be picked up by a homosexual in a bar, more to see than to enjoy sex with a man. During Hefner's first extramarital affair, he made a film of himself making love to his girl friend, a 16mm home movie that he keeps with cartons of other personal documents and mementos, photo albums, and notebooks that depict and describe his entire personal life.

From his early boyhood, though he was most unattractive and shy, he nevertheless had a high sense of self-esteem, believed he was somehow special, and regarded his existence as a potentially public event that he should scrupulously take note of. He saved his childhood drawings, kept snapshots from grade school through the Army, from college to his marriage to the founding of *Playboy*. He continues to update this material, saving letters, notes, photographs, preserving them with the care of a curator confident of their historical worth.

What Hefner did not document on film or in writing he witnessed with such attentiveness that he still remembers the texture of his surroundings and sees himself at the center. When he was thirteen, while attending a Boy Scout meeting one evening, he saw through the half-raised shade of a window next door a young girl getting undressed. It was the first time he had seen an undressed female, and he was mesmerized. Decades later, he could still recall exactly how he felt, what he had seen.

Hefner had never seen nudity at home. His mother was always fully clothed around the house, was careful to change her clothes behind closed doors. When he and his younger brother were taken to the public swimming pool in summer, his father would turn his back to them in the men's locker room while putting on his bathing trunks. Hugh Hefner attributes much of his own early shyness to the discomfort conveyed by his parents at the pool, where the mass display of flesh was an affront to their traditional modesty. Adding to Hefner's self-consciousness about the pool was the fact that he could never learn to swim. He had developed an early phobia about water when, after an older boy had coaxed him to jump into the pool at a depth over his head, he nearly drowned. Although his father, a competent swimmer, had tried to help him overcome the fear, young Hefner stubbornly refused, and one day his father became so frustrated and angry that he hit him.

It was a rare and almost welcome display of emotion from his father, a remote, repressed man who seldom revealed his feelings to his family and spent most of his time working quietly as an accountant in a large Chicago firm. The elder Hefner worked six days a week, sometimes seven, and considered himself fortunate to have a job during the Depression, particularly as an accountant. Hugh and his brother Keith, who was three years younger, were reared almost entirely by their mother, Grace, a petite, soft-spoken woman of rigid propriety. Like her husband, she had been born on a Nebraska farm before the turn of the century, and was raised in an atmosphere of pious fundamentalism that she sought to preserve in twentieth-century Chicago.

In her home there was no drinking or smoking, swearing or card playing. She occasionally took her young sons to a Saturday movie, but Sunday was strictly a day of worship in the Hefner household, and even the radio was silenced. If the boys became restless indoors, they were permitted to sit at the workbench in the backyard where they could draw pictures or sculpt with the colored clay that she provided. Hugh Hefner, who was facile in drawing and sculpturing, was more than diverted by these activities—he often seemed entranced by the clay figures of his creation, relating to them with a special intimacy, and if at such times his mother called to him from the back door, he would not hear her.

In school he daydreamed and doodled, ignored the classroom proceedings, and caused his teachers to send home complaining notes that upset and embarrassed his mother. She had been a schoolteacher herself in Nebraska before her marriage, and, while she was convinced that Hugh was intellectually capable, she was bewildered by his listlessness. She had first noticed him retreating from his surroundings when, as a four-year-old suffering from a mastoid condition, he would become absorbed in forming tiny odd shapes from the cotton he pulled out of his infected ears. Later, he became totally preoccupied with his drawings of monsters and mad scientists, spacemen and supersleuths; and when the telephone rang in the house, he seemed unaware of the sound, though he had perfect hearing. When riding in the family automobile he became carsick. He chewed his fingernails. Occasionally he stuttered. His near drowning at the swimming pool seemed to drive him more deeply into himself, and finally his mother took him to the Illinois Institute for Juvenile Research to be examined by child psychologists. Following a series of tests they concluded that his problems were rather special. Hugh Hefner was a genius. His I.Q. was 152. But, the doctors added, he was emotionally deficient, was socially immature for his age, and they suggested that it might help if Mrs. Hefner displayed more warmth around the house, more love and sympathetic understanding.

For Grace Hefner, who was so sexually demure that she had never even kissed her sons on the mouth—she later explained that she feared spreading germs—the doctors' recommendations were indeed a challenge. But encouraged by the report of Hugh's intellectual superiority, and also being a conscientious mother, she did attempt to be more supportive and understanding at home, never dreaming that this understanding would in a few years extend to her tolerating on Hugh Hefner's bedroom walls the sight of nude pinups.

The pinups were the highly stylized drawings by Alberto Vargas and George Petty that appeared in *Esquire*, which in the 1940s was published in Chicago and was the most risqué men's magazine in America. Hugh Hefner had first seen *Esquire* while visiting the home of an elementary school classmate whose father, a commercial artist, subscribed to the magazine. Everything in *Esquire* excited young Hefner—the romantic and adventurous stories by such writers as Fitzgerald and Hemingway, the photographs of classic cars, the sophisticated cartoons, the travel articles about glamorous places, the fashion layouts, and the foldout that each month offered an exquisite color drawing of a beautiful woman.

Hefner was able to decorate his room with such voluptuaries, with his mother's acquiescence if not approval, because his schoolwork had suddenly improved and he also now seemed determined to pursue certain vaguely artistic goals that his mother was reluctant to discourage. His drawings and cartoons, which had once merely cluttered the house, were now appearing in the grammar school newspaper that he edited and in the large illustrated personal diary that he meticulously kept up to date with facts and observations about himself and his classmates. Inactive in sports and still shy around girls, Hefner remained socially close to his contemporaries by becoming their chronicler.

He progressed in this passive way through his first two years in high school, after which he gradually began to assert himself, to emerge as a personality, to participate as well as observe. He acted in class plays and satires that he also helped to write. He became president of the student council, vice-president of the literary club. He did radio broadcasts for the Board of Education, and contemplated becoming a network broadcaster or a movie star. He learned to dance well, to relax more around girls. One of the girls that he dated had recently been photographed in the school newspaper, following her election as the student most representative of Steinmetz High School. While she had not greatly appealed to him before the contest, her triumph quickly affected him, made her enticing to him—she symbolized the desires of the student body, she was an object of adoration, and he was lured by her limelight. He dated her often, and one night in the darkness of a movie theater he began to touch her, to reach up under her skirt and feel between her thighs. This was his most aggressive sexual moment in high school, one that he would always remember, even though he got no further.

In 1944 he graduated from Steinmetz High in the top quarter of his class of 212 students, and was voted the third most likely to succeed. His plans for college were postponed because he soon would be called into the Army. World War II was more than a year away from ending in Europe and Asia. His mother, who knew that she would worry incessantly about Hugh's safety if she remained inactive at home, got a job in the research laboratory of a Chicago paint company. While Hugh was also somewhat apprehensive about the Army, he welcomed the opportunity for travel, having so far not ventured beyond Chicago. But two weeks before his induction, while attending a party, he met a girl who suddenly made him wish that he had more time left as a civilian.

She was a pretty brunet with large brown eyes and a slender, graceful figure. She wore her long straight hair with bangs, and she had a friendly manner that put him quickly at ease. Her name was Mildred Williams, and, though she had been in his graduating class at Steinmetz, they had never really met, which seemed incredible to Hefner, who was particularly attracted to her kind of wholesome good looks. He danced with her many times at the party, escorted her home, and dated her in the time he had left before his induction.

He wrote her often during the summer of 1944 from Fort Hood, Texas, where he took basic training and was alternately bored and appalled by his life as a soldier. A rather idealistic young man of eighteen who neither drank, smoked, nor swore, and whose limited sexual experience had so far precluded even masturbation, Hugh Hefner quickly found himself surrounded by the vulgarity and cynicism of a typical military barracks. While he adjusted to it, he did not indulge in it. He went to service club dances but did not pursue the women around the base. He spent his free time going to the movies, drawing cartoons or sketches, and writing long reflective letters to Mildred Williams, who, though he hardly knew her, had become intimately involved in his fantasies and his future expectations.

On furloughs he came home to see her, and she did not disappoint him. Although her standards of sexual propriety kept him at a distance, this merely added to the challenge and mystery that she represented. As a practicing Catholic she did not believe in premarital sex, and as a practical young woman in her freshman year at college she was wary of complications that might detract from her studies. Though she possessed the carefree look of the All-American girl, Mildred had been reared in an unhappy overcrowded home with an autocratic father who could not adequately support his five children on his salary as a Chicago bus driver, and a religious mother who was sustained by her faith that life would somehow get better. But it never did. Mildred thus acquired an early belief in self-reliance, an assumption that any improvements she sought would most likely come through her own initiative. She was never lazy. She studied hard in school and also held jobs in the late afternoons and on weekends to earn money for college. At the University of Illinois she worked during the evenings at the library, planning to become a teacher. She did not join a sorority, had no time for dating. During the summers she worked without a vacation, even refusing to take time off from her job when Hefner was in town on furlough. While he fretted and sulked, he privately admired her dedication, it being comparable to his own mother's efforts many years ago in achieving a higher education without the help or encouragement of her rural parents in Nebraska.

Hefner was no less aspiring about himself, and following his discharge from the Army in 1946 he enrolled at the University of Illinois and planned to take the maximum number of courses each and every term, including the summer terms, so that he could complete the four-year curriculum in two and a half years. He wanted to make up for the two unproductive army years during which he had lingered in various bases in the United States as the war ended overseas. As a twenty-year-old student on the G.I. Bill he was anxious to regain his personal momentum, to define his life's goals, and to resume the almost Victorian courtship of Mildred Williams.

His understanding of her so far, aside from their limited time together during furloughs, had been acquired largely through the mail in the many letters she had written, nearly all of them highly idealistic in tone, discreetly affectionate, encouraging— letters that relieved his loneliness in the barracks and convinced him that she was indeed the embodiment of the romantic image that he had created.

But even his high expectations were exceeded in 1946 after he had rejoined her on the Illinois campus, and began dating her every weekend, and meeting her each night on the library steps, walking slowly with her hand in hand through the most glorious autumn of his life. He was enraptured, thrilled by her looks and manner, and excited too by the world around him, the new freedom of college life, the deferential treatment accorded him by other students as a returning veteran, and the sense of overwhelming optimism and confidence that inspired so many Americans at that time, the first year after the triumphant war.

Hefner took up stunt flying as a weekend diversion at an airport near the campus, and within a year he had earned his pilot's license and was maneuvering his biplane through startling turns, stalls, and loops. He sang with a student dance band, imitating the style of Frankie Laine. He started a college humor magazine, earned excellent marks in class, majoring in psychology, and he felt for the first time that he was physically attractive. His cartoons and articles were published in *The Daily Illini*, and as an intellectual exercise he wrote a play about a scientific discovery proving that God did not exist; the play ends with the government vigilantly suppressing the information because it thought the public could not live with the truth.

When Hefner wrote this he was an agnostic, which he would remain thereafter, departing from his fundamentalist Methodist background. But he believed that his rejection of his family tradition was just part of a larger social revolution that he saw developing all around him. He had read in the newspapers that the industrialist-filmmaker Howard Hughes had challenged the Hollywood moral code by releasing his movie *The Outlaw*, in which a voluptuous actress named Jane Russell climbs into bed with a man. Hefner's favorite magazine, *Esquire*, which the Post Office wished to ban from the mail as obscene, had won its case before the Supreme Court and was free to distribute without harassment. The recent discovery of penicillin as a cure for venereal disease had suddenly lessened the inhibiting fear that for centuries had been associated with sexual profligacy. And the Kinsey report on men, based on data accumulated after more than 12,000 interviews, revealed that, despite much puritanical posturing in America, its citizens were secretly very sexual. Fifty percent of all married men had slept with women other than their wives while married, Kinsey stated, and 85 percent of all men had experienced intercourse before marriage. Nine out of ten men masturbated, and, in a statistic that shocked many readers, 37 percent of the male population had achieved an orgasm through at least one homosexual act.

These and other findings resulted in the condemnation of Dr. Kinsey by clergymen, politicians, and editorial writers, but Hugh Hefner was greatly impressed with the book, and in his review of it in *Shaft*, the magazine he began in college, he wrote: "This study makes obvious the lack of understanding and realistic thinking that have gone into the formation of sex standards and laws. Our moral pretenses, our hypocrisy on matters of sex have led to incalculable frustration, delinquency and unhappiness."

This last statement could have applied to Hefner himself, for in spite of his various achievements on the campus during his first two years, he was sexually frustrated. At twenty-two he still had not experienced intercourse. He had repeatedly tried to seduce Mildred, but each time she had pleaded, sometimes tearfully, that they wait a while longer. It was not only her religion and the fear of pregnancy that influenced her thinking but also her wish that their first lovemaking be a splendid occasion, a private celebration in romantic surroundings, and not, as was the case with most students, a furtive hasty happening in a borrowed car.

Hefner at first agreed with her and admired her attitude. She was, like his mother, uncommonly idealistic, a serious, strong, and trustworthy young woman who in marriage would become, as he wished, exclusively his own possession. But as the months passed, Hefner could no longer contain his sexual drive and curiosity, and during weekend dates in Chicago their heavy petting in his father's Ford gradually extended to mutual masturbation, and then fellatio. On a Sunday night as they were returning to the campus on a Greyhound bus, and after their kissing and caressing in the darkened vehicle had become increasingly passionate, he urged her to perform fellatio on him right there at their seat, under a blanket. As surprised as she was by his request, she was even more surprised by her willingness to accede to his wish without reluctance or awkwardness, so eager was she at that moment to please him, as well as being herself excited by doing this act so daringly behind the backs of unsuspecting passengers. As she lowered her head in the darkness and took his penis in her mouth, she felt not only love for him but a dramatic awakening of her own liberation.

Though she no longer attended Mass regularly, she did not interpret this as a sign of declining morality but rather an increasing commitment to the man she would one day marry and from whom she was now learning much about the art of giving and receiving pleasure. She marveled at how much Hefner seemed to know and care about sex. He was endlessly reading marriage manuals and erotic novels, nudist magazines and books about sex laws and censorship. From him she heard for the first time such phrases as "erogenous zones," and with him she experienced her first orgasm, through cunnilingus.

During an afternoon in Chicago when his parents were not at home, he took her to his bedroom on the second floor and pulled down the shades; then from the closet he brought lights and a camera, and, after a minimum of coaxing, Mildred slowly removed her clothes and stood nude before him. Quietly, excitedly, he began to take photographs of her on the bed and against the wall where the Petty pinups had been, and soon she responded as naturally as she had on the bus, striking her own poses, appreciating her graceful body as much as he, though nonetheless amazed by her willingness to do what months before would have been inconceivable and wildly shocking.

Though she never saw the pictures and had no idea what use Hefner made of them, she continued to have positive feelings about her sexual episodes with Hefner even after she had reflected upon them; since she was now a senior in college, she believed she was more than ready for these experiences—as she was ready, too, after her final examination in the spring of 1948, to join Hefner in a hotel room in Danville, Illinois, and spend the night making love.

Convinced of their compatibility and planning soon to become engaged, Hefner returned to the Illinois campus during the summer of 1948, while Mildred accepted her first teaching assignment at a small high school in the northwestern part of the state. Since neither of them had cars, and both were very involved with schoolwork, they did not see one another every weekend. When they did meet it was usually in Chicago, where their relationship and future wedding had already been acknowledged and approved by their parents, although in attaining this harmony Hefner had compromised to a degree his views on religion. He had at Mildred's request agreed to take religious instructions from a priest and to allow their children to be raised in the Church. It was not Mildred so much as her mother who felt strongly about this, and Hefner was at first opposed because he regarded Catholicism as a tyrannical force against sexual freedom and the rights of personal privacy. He had often expressed this opinion in letters to Mildred, in which he questioned the infallibility of the Pope, disagreed with the Church's policy on birth control and abortion, and denounced the Church's history of censorship, from the Middle Ages to the present, of thousands of erotic books, pictures, films, and other forms of expression. But while his feelings about Catholicism were unchanged as the wedding plans were made, he was too preoccupied at the time with college to make an issue of it; and also, knowing how far Mildred had privately departed from the dictates of her religion, he foresaw no problems with her after their marriage.

So he concentrated instead on what currently mattered most to him—completing college by February 1949, marrying Mildred during the following June, and quickly establishing

himself as a successful cartoonist, writer, or editor. In college
he had demonstrated a talent as all three, in addition to gaining
much personal self-confidence and also an awareness that young
women were attracted to him. But he did not exploit this. He
remained faithful to Mildred after she had left the campus, and
while he had once regarded bachelorhood as an idyllic state, he
now was anxiously anticipating marriage to Mildred, particularly when he began to perceive some tentativeness on her part
after they had become formally engaged during their Christmas
vacation in 1948.

He had no idea what was causing it, but sometimes when they
were together on weekends after the holidays she seemed a bit
tense, tight, and without the enthusiasm she had shown for him
since they had first become sexually intimate during the previous
spring. Hoping that she was just temporarily distracted by the
new pressures of teaching, he attempted to conceal his own mild
irritation and to show her instead much understanding and patience. When they were alone he occasionally tried to engage
her in long personal conversations that might reach the source
of her discomfort, but his soft probing revealed nothing and his
more direct questioning elicited only denials from her that anything was wrong.

One cold weekend in Chicago, after borrowing his father's
car and picking up Mildred at her parents' home, the couple
drove downtown to see a movie called *The Accused*, starring
Loretta Young. In this film Loretta Young portrays a beautiful
but inhibited teacher at a university who, after one of her male
students comes to her saying that he desperately needs advice
and guidance, agrees to go out to dinner with him. Later in the
evening, the student drives her to a secluded spot and attempts
to seduce her and, failing that, to rape her. But she fights him
off with a steel object, only to discover after he has stopped
attacking her that she has killed him. Panicked, she runs from
the scene and stumbles to a highway, where she manages to
hitchhike a ride with a truck driver. Composing herself, and
revealing nothing of what has happened, she returns safely home
and the next day resumes teaching. But in an attempt to alter her
appearance to avoid being identified as the woman who had been
with the student on the night of his death, she begins to dress
more fashionably and changes her hairstyle, and soon she begins
to feel more glamorous and desirable than she has ever felt before. As a result, after the criminal investigation has begun, even
the truck driver who had picked her up on the highway does not

recognize her, and both the homicide officer and the attorney for the deceased become enamored of her.

But eventually her own guilt prompts her to tell the truth, and at this point in the film Mildred, who had been watching with tears in her eyes, began sobbing and asked Hefner to take her home. As they got into the car, Mildred cried uncontrollably, becoming hysterical when Hefner put an arm around her and sympathetically sought an explanation.

Finally Mildred regained control and, turning toward him in the front seat, her tears reflected in the dim light of the car, she admitted that in the town where she now lived she was having an affair with a man on the faculty.

Hefner listened with disbelief. It was as if this astounding moment was too unreal to accept, was still part of the movie he had just seen. He sat behind the wheel of the parked car feeling stunned, betrayed, very alone. Mildred had suddenly become an intimate stranger, a lover he no longer knew, though she now tried in a quivering voice to explain how it had happened. She said that she had first gotten to know the man after he volunteered to drive her to the railroad station on a Friday evening when she was taking the train to Chicago. They enjoyed talking, she said, and after she had returned from the weekend in Chicago they began playing bridge together on certain weeknights in town with other teachers from their school, and one evening in his car he reached over to kiss her and she immediately responded, and they had not stopped until they made love.

They had repeated it since then, she went on, adding that she now felt unworthy of Hefner and assured him he was under no obligation to marry her. As remorseful and embarrassed as she was in recounting this, she also felt great relief, even freedom, but when she looked into Hefner's eyes she saw that he was beginning to cry. She reached toward him and embraced him. She said that she loved him, though she repeated that he should choose someone else for a wife.

But Hefner shook his head. No, he said, he wanted only her. Though he did not admit it, he wanted her now more than he ever had before, being very alarmed by the competitive presence of another suitor. He pleaded with her to stop seeing the other man; and Mildred, filled with confusion and guilt, agreed to do so. She wanted to believe that her brief affair was uncharacteristic of her true nature, and she was grateful to Hefner for wanting to proceed with their wedding plans.

They were married on June 15, 1949, in the Saint John Bosco

Rectory in Chicago. Mildred wore a white gown, and smiled as she later posed for pictures with Hefner and their families. Their gray-haired mothers wearing orchids, their fathers in dark-suited sobriety, stood together outside the church, squinting in the sun, affecting expressions of forced familiarity.

After the ceremony, Hefner in his father's car drove with Mildred to Hazelhurst, Wisconsin, for a brief honeymoon at Styza's Birchwood Lodge. Then they returned to Chicago to begin a life together that would never be as romantic as it had once been.

Among their problems was Hefner's failure, after graduation from college, to find a job that he liked. His various ideas for a cartoon series were rejected by the newspaper syndicates, and the only job that he could find was in the employment office of a carton company. When he realized that the firm would not hire blacks, he quit in protest. Since the job market was then overcrowded with war veterans, and since Hefner preferred remaining at home working on new cartoons rather than accepting unsatisfying employment, they lived off the money that Mildred earned from various jobs, including that of teaching in a Chicago grade school that Hefner had once attended.

To minimize expenses they stayed in the house of Hefner's parents, a move that they thought would suit them temporarily until Hugh Hefner could begin to sell his cartoons or establish himself in a suitable career. But more than two years later they were still there, occupying a bedroom next to the elder Hefners' on the second floor of the small two-story brick house on a quiet street on the outer edge of Chicago's Northwest Side. The house had been built for $13,000 in 1930 when Hugh Hefner was four years old, and it was the only home that he had ever known, though now as he occupied its tight quarters he felt the loss of the expansive dreams of his youth, and the loss, too, of much sexual interest in his wife.

But Mildred blamed herself for this. She rarely felt like making love to him in that house, knowing that their bed sounds could easily be heard by his parents in the adjoining room, and she also believed that her indiscretion with the other man had diminished Hefner's romantic fervor, as well as resurrecting some of her own Catholic girlhood guilt feelings about sex and pleasure. She had enjoyed sinful sex, she reasoned sardonically, and now she was being punished. Her penance was in living a passionless married life in the claustrophobic home of her in-

laws, where her husband drew cartoons in his room all day, as
he had as a boy, except now she was noticing a degenerate trend
in his drawing. He was producing for his own amusement pornographic cartoons of Dagwood and Blondie. He was also
bringing home sex magazines and making no attempt to conceal
them from her, as he undoubtedly once had, and still did, from
his mother.

His mother, who was too polite to pry, was no comfort to
Mildred during these years, nor would it have occurred to
Mildred to discuss her marital problems with either of Hefner's
parents. As close as they all lived physically, they remained
emotionally remote. The elder Hefners each day quietly went
their own way, out to their respective offices in the morning,
returning in the evening to use the kitchen at a time when it was
not being used by Mildred and Hugh. It was a home of tight
routines and tidiness, order and control. In her years there,
Mildred never saw either of Hefner's parents lose self-control,
even for an instant. She never heard them yell or cry, argue or
stomp their feet; she also did not witness signs of their affection,
such as a soft greeting kiss at the door, or a tender touch, or a
word of endearment. Mildred did not assume from this an absence of caring, but rather a rigid resistance to showing it. Compared with her own expressive and frequently combative parents,
the Hefners were extraordinary examples of restraint and repression.

While Mildred had no idea how such behavior had affected
the Hefners' second son, Keith, who was now away at college,
she believed she could measure much of its influence on her
husband. Like his parents, Hugh Hefner wanted tight control
over his surroundings, was most comfortable with orderliness.
From his pietistic Swedish mother he inherited his idealism and
standards, and like his German accountant father he was precise
and pragmatic. But unlike them he revealed emotion. Mildred
had sensed his anger, she had seen him cry. She identified his
pornographic cartoons and magazines as signs of rebellion
against his upbringing, and, perceiving the depth of his depression after their marriage, she suggested that he leave home for
a while, forget temporarily about a career, and perhaps return
to the place where he had last been happy, the college campus,
and seek a master's degree.

He did as she suggested in 1950, registering at Northwestern
as a graduate student in sociology. But his only achievement
there was a lengthy term paper on American sex laws, most of

which he thought should be abolished because they were antiquated and too private for government intervention, such as the
law that still existed in many states against oral sex even between
a husband and wife. Though Hefner received high marks for his
extensive research, his conclusions were not enthusiastically
shared by his professor, and after one semester, feeling restless,
Hefner left the campus and attempted to reinterest himself in
the outside world.

He found work as an advertising copywriter in a Chicago
department store, then in a small advertising agency; he quit the
first job and was fired from the second. He was next hired by
the promotion department of Esquire, Inc., which published the
men's fashion magazine and also a sophisticated pocket-sized
monthly called *Coronet*; and Hefner quickly conjured up images
of himself working in a creative atmosphere surrounded by ur-
bane editors and Vargas girls. But after working there he found
the setting sedate, the female employees dowdy and prim, and
the men living unadventurous lives with none of the verve reflected on the illustrated pages. One afternoon when Hefner
removed from his pocket a photograph of actress Carmen Mir-
anda twirling on a dance floor with her skirts high and wearing
no panties, and showed it to a *Coronet* executive, the latter
turned away, seeming unamused.

In 1951 the company announced that it was moving the
Esquire-Coronet promotion offices to New York City, but Hefner, who had just been refused a five-dollar raise, resigned and
remained in Chicago. He liked Chicago, and was feeling better
about himself there after he had arranged with an independent
printer to publish five thousand copies of a book of drawings
and cartoons he had done characterizing the city. While the book
was not financially profitable, its press reviews brought Hefner
local attention, and he foresaw the day when he might be able
to launch a slick magazine devoted to Chicago urban life.

In the interim he found a job at eighty dollars a week, twenty
more than his *Esquire-Coronet* salary, as the promotion manager for a Chicago magazine magnate named George von Rosen, a shrewd and prescient man who, having failed to gain
employment on *The Christian Science Monitor*, and having
worked as a circulation manager for several music magazines
and one that catered to Protestant ministers, decided after World
War II to become his own publisher and hopefully prosper in
the increasingly popular market of the girlie magazine.

* * *

A fortune had already been made during the war by such New York publishers as Robert Harrison, whose many magazines—with titles like *Flirt, Titter, Wink* and *Eyefull*—had greatly appealed to lonely servicemen at home and overseas. But Harrison, who was personally offended by nudity and would in 1952 devote himself to exposing scandal in his new publication *Confidential*, limited his sex magazines to black-and-white photographs of young women wearing bathing suits, negligees, and undergarments only slightly more immodest than might be found in the ladies' lingerie ads of the New York *Times* Sunday magazine, which was one of the nation's principal stroke books *sub silentio*.

Among other magazines offering masturbatory possibilities before George von Rosen entered the market were movie magazines that displayed starlets in bikinis, adventure magazines that occasionally depicted scantily clad beauties in distress, the nudist-family magazine *Sunshine & Health*, and such large circulation magazines as *Life* and *Look*, which, in beguiling ways, sometimes surpassed all other publications in presenting sexually arousing photographs.

Life and *Look* in the late 1930s justified as photojournalism the controversial pictures they printed of actress Hedy Kiesler swimming in the nude with a nipple exposed, from a scene in a Czechoslovakian movie called *Ecstasy*. So sensational was the reaction to the film, and to the publicity surrounding it, that *Ecstasy* was later banned or cut by censors everywhere; and when Hedy Kiesler moved to Hollywood to work on other films, she sought a new identity by changing her name to Hedy Lamarr.

In 1941 *Life* published perhaps the most famous pinup picture of the war years, that of Rita Hayworth in a lacy satin slip kneeling on a bed; her stilted but oddly sensual pose—unrivaled in popularity except for a studio publicity photo of the rear view of Betty Grable in a tight-fitting bathing suit—was later reported to have been attached to the atomic bomb dropped on Hiroshima. *Life*'s photograph in 1943 of a smiling blond model, Chili Williams, whose polka-dot swimsuit seemed to be tucked inward at the crotch, received 100,000 "feverish" letters, according to the magazine, as well as a screen test for Chili Williams that led to small parts in Hollywood.

While some publishers thought that the pinup craze would subside after the troops had returned home, George von Rosen believed that these filaments of fantasy had permanently infiltrated the erotic consciousness of the returning veteran; and during the postwar years he circulated assorted magazines that emphasized what he considered three essential elements—guns, guts, and girls. The laws at this time regarding girlie photographs were not clearly defined, pending the final outcome of such lengthy litigation as that fomented by church groups and postal authorities against *Sunshine & Health* magazine, which persisted in selling on newsstands and sending through the mail its monthly editions containing unretouched nude photographs. Total nudity was lewdity, the Post Office claimed, but members of nudist associations which supported *Sunshine & Health*, and saw themselves as cultists and not pornographers, believed that the First Amendment guaranteed their right to accurately portray the nudist movement, including its pubic hair, in their official magazine.

Similar rights were claimed by unofficial nudist magazines, one of which—*Modern Sunbathing & Hygiene*—was published by George von Rosen. While he obeyed the postal policies banning pubic hair, he featured breasts and nipples almost exclusively on the young bodies of buxom women, some of whom violated nudist tradition by posing alone indoors, far from the bucolic family gatherings celebrated in *Sunshine & Health*— thus lending credibility to the rumor that when Von Rosen was unable to find attractive photos of legitimate nudists, he was not averse to using strippers.

Women who could easily have passed for strippers appeared regularly in Von Rosen's *Art Photography* magazine, but, as if to assure the censors of their lofty purpose, they stood nude in statuelike repose, muted as the undraped marble maidens of classical sculpture, their expressionless faces and innocuous eyes avoiding direct contact with the potentially lustful lens of the camera.

Such delicacy was neither expected nor desired by Von Rosen in his more flamboyant girlie magazines because, inasmuch as the models wore some semblance of clothing, he felt that they deserved concomitant freedom of expression, such as the option to wink at the camera, to leer, swing their hips, and smile with their mouths open.

The most successful of his girlie magazines was started in 1951, not long before Hugh Hefner had joined his staff. It was called *Modern Man*, and its first cover girl was actress Jane Russell smiling as she sat on a rail fence, wearing frayed shorts, a tight-fitting jersey, and leather boots. While the pictorial focus of *Modern Man* was voyeuristic, Von Rosen saw himself not as a salacious man but a businessman now bringing to a market craving photogenic females the same detached efficiency that had characterized his career when he was selling *Etude* to piano students and *The Expositor* and *Homiletic Review* to preachers. His initial editorial problem with *Modern Man* was not in determining what men wanted to see but rather what men wished to read, if anything. At the same time he had to attempt to appease the censors by providing in his magazine editorial matter of hopefully redeeming social value to counterbalance the breasts and buttocks that so fulsomely filled his pages.

Von Rosen decided to refrain from publishing any word or idea bordering on the pornographic or politically controversial, and the editorial content of *Modern Man* became similar to what might have been acceptable in the essentially asexual outdoor men's magazines such as *True* and *Argosy*. In the first issue of *Modern Man* there was an article on the lure of mountain climbing, an interview with actor Dana Andrews on his boat with advice on how to sail, a feature on such stylish custom-made cars as the 1913 Jaguar, a photo essay on Paris' Place Pigalle, a shopping guide for collectors of classic guns. The reader response to this last item, and to subsequent articles on gun collecting and hunting, prompted Von Rosen to eventually start other magazines devoted entirely to these subjects. If there was anything innovative in *Modern Man*, it was perhaps Von Rosen's decision to print in this one magazine both the photographs of jovial seminude pinups and the solemn totally nude art models, a combination that would later be imitated by Hefner in *Playboy*.

Wishing to present the most respectable examples of art nude photography, Von Rosen spent thousands of dollars during the first year of *Modern Man* to buy the work of a distinguished Hungarian named Andre de Dienes, who in the 1930s had specialized in photographing European art and sculpture exhibited in the Tuileries Gardens, the Louvre and other great museums. Many of De Dienes' photographs of classical nude sculpture had appeared in *Esquire* before the war, but at the time Von Rosen was starting *Modern Man* the editors of *Esquire* were deemphasizing the titillation that had tinged their magazine since its inception in 1933. Not only did the *Esquire* editors think that girlie magazines would soon become anachronistic in postwar America, as so many veterans advanced educationally through the G.I. Bill, but the magazine had also become weary of defending its rakish image in the courtroom. Though it had won the major obscenity case brought against it by Postmaster General Frank Walker, a prominent Catholic and Democratic National Committee chairman, the litigation had been costly and time-consuming for the magazine, lasting from 1942 to 1946.

Even before this, the *Esquire* management had been intimidated by members of the Church: In an article in one of *Esquire*'s subsidiary magazines, *Ken*, there had been unflattering references to the Catholic Church's support of General Franco in the Spanish Civil War, and as a result of the article, written by Ernest Hemingway, the Catholic hierarchy encouraged priests in their Sunday sermons to denounce *Esquire*'s publications, and soon there was extensive boycotting at the newsstands of *Esquire*, *Coronet*, and particularly *Ken*, which hastened the latter's discontinuance. And so in 1951 the nude photography of Andre de Dienes appeared not in *Esquire* but in *Modern Man*, and the most daring publisher in America at this time was undoubtedly George von Rosen, who remained so until Hefner would surpass him after 1953 with *Playboy*.

Hefner and Von Rosen were in some ways similar. Both had been reared in puritanical homes in the Midwest and were the sons of fathers who were accountants of German-American ancestry; and both were orderly, ambitious, and self-absorbed. Von Rosen, eleven years older than Hefner, was a lean, lively, green-eyed man with the taut tidy features of a navel commander, and he controlled his magazines like a fleet of vessels. He demanded strict punctuality from his subordinates, cleanliness in their cubicles, and formality in their dealings with him. The ambience within the company was sterile, and the conservative midwestern men and women that he employed were emotionally detached from the nude photographs and layouts that they handled—as was Von Rosen himself, being in this sense quite different from Hugh Hefner. To Von Rosen, the magazines represented an efficient, profitable operation; to Hefner, magazines were a personal passion.

If this distinction was not so apparent to Von Rosen, it was because he did not really know Hefner well during their time together, and what Von Rosen did know left him unimpressed. He considered Hefner's cartoons mediocre, refusing to publish even one of them in his magazines, and he was mildly shocked one day when Hefner arrived at the office carrying a package and announcing that it contained an excellent pornographic movie. Hefner's amiable offer to screen it for the staff was peremptorily refused by Von Rosen, who had no desire to see such a film himself and was irritated that Hefner would suggest showing it on company time. Although Hefner performed adequately in the promotion department, he somehow conveyed the impression that he was engaged in several outside interests and adventures, and that his destiny would never be determined by a single employer. This attitude was not gratifying to George von Rosen. Had Von Rosen known the full extent of Hefner's preoccupations, he would have been more bewildered than perturbed, and possibly convinced that there was something about Hefner that was sexually bizarre.

At this time Mildred Hefner was pregnant, and they had finally moved out of his parents' home into a charming apartment in the Hyde Park section of Chicago; but Hefner's marriage was still unsatisfactory, and he was having an affair with a nurse with whom he would soon make a sex movie. This film, which would be shot in the apartment of a male friend and collaborator of Hefner's, was a private venture that he did strictly for the fun and experience of doing it, having no illusions that he would ever become a professional maker of films, even sex films. However, he did believe that his future career would somehow be related to sex, for this was the subject that more and more dominated his thinking. He began to broaden his curiosity and to be almost as intrigued with other people's sex lives as he was with his own. He continued to read books about sex laws and censorship, about the social mores and rituals of the ancient past, the attempts by kings, popes, and theocrats like Calvin to control the masses by declaring certain private acts of pleasure to be forbidden and punishable. He read the scurrilous classic tales of such writers as Boccaccio and the banned books of Henry Miller that many G.I.s discovered in Europe during World War II and smuggled into the United States. Hefner examined in art books the reproductions of nude paintings by the masters, the works of Leonardo da Vinci and Raphael, Titian, Ingres and Renoir, Rubens, Manet, Courbet, and many others who often portrayed the body with the genitals uncovered, the breasts grandly revealed, the eyes focused more directly on the observer than Von Rosen would have permitted in his photographic art magazine. It was doubtful that Von Rosen's magazine had yet presented anything as suggestive as Manet's painting in 1865 of an almost leering young nude woman, or Courbet's two voluptuous naked ladies embracing in bed, or Goya's naked maja reclining on pillows with her hands clasped behind her head, her eyes staring at the spectator, her dark pubic hair exposed.

Of course the difference between this and what appeared in men's magazines was characterized by one word—art; and yet what was defined as art, and what was condemned as pornography, often changed from one generation to the next, depending on the audience for which a work was intended. The nude art that hung in the great museums was created for the nobility and upper classes that commissioned it, while the photographs that appeared in the magazines were printed for the common man in the street, whose museum was the corner newsstand.

And it was this latter group that the censors wished to protect from indecency, and to control as well, when in 1896 the United States Supreme Court sustained a conviction against a publisher named Lew Rosen, whose periodical *Broadway* contained photographs of women defined as lewd. This was the first federal conviction under the Comstock Act, named in honor of the most awesome censor in the history of America, Anthony Comstock.

4

ANTHONY COMSTOCK WAS a vengeful, evangelical man born in 1844 on a farm in New Canaan, Connecticut. The death of his mother when he was ten left him extremely morose, and throughout his life he idolized her and later dedicated his purification campaigns to her memory.

As one who had masturbated so obsessively during his teens that he admitted in his diary that he felt it might drive him to suicide, Comstock was terrifyingly convinced of the dangers inherent in sexual pictures and literature, and was aware that legal authorities were very lax in dealing with the problem. Though a federal law had been passed in 1842 banning the importation of French postcards, Comstock had often seen these small erotic pictures circulated among soldiers while serving with a Connecticut regiment in the Civil War. And he was equally appalled in New York after the war by the prevalence of prostitutes on lower Broadway and the sight of sidewalk vendors selling obscene magazines and books.

There were no federal laws at this time against obscene publications, although in the state of Massachusetts there had been antiobscenity statutes as early as the 1600s. These statutes, however, defined obscenity not in sexual terms but rather as words written or spoken against the established religion—for example, in the Puritan colony of Massachusetts until 1697, the penalties for blasphemy included death, and even later the statute stated that offenders could be tortured by such methods as boring through the tongue with a hot iron. The laws in Puritan-dominated Massachusetts also opposed the distribution and possession of religious literature expressing Quaker opinions, and in 1711 there were additional sanctions against the singing of irreverent songs, with the offenders sometimes locked in a pillory.

It was not until 1815, in Pennsylvania, that a man was cited for sexual obscenity—he displayed for sale a picture of an "indecent" couple; but since this violated no American law, the arrest was supported by an existing English law dating back to 1663, the case of *Rex* v. *Sedley*, in which Sedley was fined and jailed for a week after exposing himself naked from the balcony of a tavern, drunkenly shouting obscenities and pouring urine from a bottle on other customers. While this blatant behavior appears to have little relevance to the case of the American caught showing a sexual picture, the Pennsylvania law enforcers regarded both acts as examples of public indecency contrary to common law as well as to the moral strictures of religion.

The first erotic book banned in America was the illustrated edition of the English novel by John Cleland, *Memoirs of a Woman of Pleasure*, sometimes called *Fanny Hill*. This book, published in London in 1749—and prosecuted in Massachusetts in 1821, following a similar order in England—described the social and sexual life of a young prostitute, and among the early Americans who owned a copy was Benjamin Franklin.

It was not unusual to find in the libraries of colonial American leaders books that might have been defined as sexually obscene, by such writers as Ovid and Rabelais, Chaucer and Fielding. But since the reading of books in those days was largely limited to the well-educated minority, the need for literary censorship was not considered so important as it would be in succeeding generations, when the common citizen became more literate, printing presses became more numerous, and religion in the expanding nation ceased to dominate daily life as it had among the early settlers. As more schools opened, including the first public high school in 1820, there was increasing concern in government over the type of books that should be available to students; and it was a similar concern for youth, and a desire to protect it from corruptive influences, that Anthony Comstock expressed in the 1860s when he sought to justify his censorship campaigns in New York.

At this time, after the Civil War, Comstock was working unenthusiastically as a New York grocery store clerk and later as a dry-goods salesman, but he was an inspired member of the YMCA, and it was with the help of this organization that he persistently petitioned public officials to strengthen and enforce the laws against immorality and sexual expression. He strongly believed that erotic books and pictures were the plague of the young and also drove adults to degeneracy through masturbation and fornication, abortion and venereal disease.

While many politicians agreed with Comstock's conclusions, there was some reluctance to support him because his corrective methods—which included the use of informers, spies, and decoys, as well as tampering with the mail—threatened constitutional freedoms in America and were more like the repressive practices that then existed in England in the interest of combating immorality. In 1864 the English government, hoping to eliminate venereal disease, had passed a law that forced women suspected of spreading the disease to submit to medical examinations and to wear yellow clothes until they had been cured. In hospitals the women were segregated in special sections known as canary wards. This practice continued for more than twenty years, until the protests of feminists successfully led to the repeal of the law.

Also in England at this time were several presumed cures for masturbation, including a sort of chastity belt that parents could lock between their son's legs each night before he went to bed. Some of these gadgets were adorned with spikes on the outside, or came equipped with bells that would ring whenever the youth touched his genitals or had an erection.

Citizens' antivice societies were now abounding in England, baiting not only prostitutes, adulterers, and alleged pornographers but also the publishers of certain instructional sexual manuals. These groups had actually existed in one form or another for centuries in England, being particularly conspicuous during the mid-1600s as Oliver Cromwell's Puritans overthrew the monarchy and abolished a putrid source of profanity, the theater. But in the mid-1800s, during the righteous reign of Queen Victoria—when the joy of secret sex possibly reached its zenith and pornography proliferated—the antivice societies became fanatical, and their attitude was reflected in a series of oppressive laws that were passed at this time.

There was a law allowing the government to conduct searches of private shops to see if obscene material was held for sale, and in 1868 the Chief Justice in England defined obscenity in such restrictive terms that Queen Victoria's enforcers could prohibit adults from reading anything that seemed inappropriate for children. Obscenity, according to the Chief Justice, was whatever might "deprave and corrupt those whose minds are open to such immoral influences and into whose hands a publication of this sort may fall." This law also permitted the courts to declare an entire book obscene even if it contained but a few sexual paragraphs and the author's motive in producing these paragraphs was deemed irrelevant.

Even more remarkable was the fact that this Victorian law of 1868 would not only outlive England's most enduring governess, who died in 1901 after more than sixty years on the throne, but would continue to influence obscenity convictions in both England and the United States until the mid-1950s. An American nation that had audaciously rebelled against the mother country over economic and political issues remained nonetheless subservient to English laws on sex, and no man was more successful at reinforcing America's puritanical roots than Anthony Comstock, who referred to himself as a "weeder in God's garden."

Undeterred by those who opposed him, Comstock and his followers from the YMCA vigorously appealed to the New York State legislature and to federal officials in Washington to combat immorality with strong antivice laws, and it was a propitious time for such a proposal. The federal government, following the turmoil of the Civil War and continuing street crime and poverty—and the scandals of the wealthy robber barons—welcomed any excuse to divert attention from its own ineptitude and corruption and to gain greater control over the restive population; additionally, several business leaders and industrialists, believing that sexual permissiveness diverted workers' energy from the job, also favored tighter regulation over the common morality. Church groups, too, being aware of the prostitutes in the streets and the vendors of controversial literature, felt that reforms were overdue, that writers had become excessively impious, including the poet Walt Whitman, who had recently been dismissed from his government position in the Interior Department for writing an "indecent book" called *Leaves of Grass*.

Far worse was being published without punishment, Comstock claimed, and as proof he displayed before congressmen cartons of marriage manuals, erotic pamphlets, and revealing pictures that he collectively described as a "moral vulture which steals upon our youth, silently striking its terrible talons into their vitals"; and with the support of such influential citizens as the soap manufacturer Samuel Colgate and the banker J. P. Morgan (who had his own collection of pornography), Comstock finally persuaded Congress in 1873 to pass a federal bill banning from the mails "every obscene, lewd, lascivious or filthy book, pamphlet, picture, paper, letter, writing, print or other publication of an indecent character." The bill, signed by President Ulysses S.

Grant, included an amendment that appointed Comstock a special antiobscenity agent of the Post Office Department. Two months later, an organization that Comstock had founded, the New York Society for the Suppression of Vice, was endowed with police powers by the state legislature, and Anthony Comstock was given the right to carry a gun.

During the years that followed, Comstock and his Society terrorized publishers, arrested hundreds of citizens caught with questionable literature, and caused fifteen women accused of immorality to commit suicide rather than face the humiliation of a publicized trial. The various charges against the women included prostitution, performing abortions, selling birth-control devices, and—in the case of Ida Craddock—writing a marriage manual called *The Wedding Night*.

A New York publisher named Charles Mackey was hand-cuffed, sent to jail for a year, and fined $500 for having in stock nothing more lascivious than Ovid's *Art of Love*. A bookstore owner on Canal Street received a similar sentence for selling a copy of Dr. Ashton's *Book of Nature and Marriage Guide*, which had been routinely sold in New York stores for twenty years. A young news vendor on Chambers Street, enticed by a persistent customer eager to pay handsomely for erotic pictures, was shocked after he had procured the pictures to learn that he had sold them to a Comstock informer, resulting in a jail term of one year.

Most of Comstock's convictions in New York were attained through entrapment. Either he or his associates personally posed as customers or wrote registered letters under pseudonyms, enclosing money for certain books and pamphlets that later served as Comstock's evidence in court. Since the sale or dissemination of birth-control information was illegal, many unsuspecting pharmacists served prison terms for selling condoms or even the rubber syringes that many women used strictly for hygienic purposes.

Photography studios were often raided and the files searched for erotic pictures, and an exhibitor of stereopticons was investigated, and later arrested, after he had shown to an audience interested in art a few photographs of classic nude statuary. One night in 1878, Comstock and five male associates from the Society visited a brothel at 224 Greene Street and, after inducing three women to strip naked for fourteen dollars, Comstock pulled out his revolver and arrested them for indecent exposure.

There was relatively little protest against Comstock's tactics in the major newspapers, most of whose publishers felt, as did the politicians, that opposing Comstock might be interpreted as tolerating crime, as well as perhaps subjecting their own private lives to Comstock's scrutiny. A few smaller publications, however, representing the underground press of that time, were vehement in their coverage of Comstock, particularly one paper with offices on lower Broadway called *The Truth Seeker*. This weekly was owned and edited by an unremitting skeptic and Bible-debunking agnostic named D. M. Bennett, whose inspiration was Thomas Paine and whose editorial policy favored birth control, the taxation of church property, and a respect for freedoms that Comstock would deny.

In his writings, D. M. Bennett compared Comstock to Torquemada, the inquisitor general of fifteenth-century Spain, and to the seventeenth-century witch finder Matthew Hopkins. "Hopkins," wrote Bennett, "was clothed with a species of legal authority to prowl over several of the shires of England, seizing his victims wherever he could find them, and Comstock had been clothed with a similar sort of legal authority to prowl over some of these American states, hunting down his unfortunate victims in the same kind of way."

Since sexual obscenity was now a federal offense in America—punishable by fines as high as $5,000 and imprisonment as lengthy as ten years—Bennett insisted that it should be so clearly defined by the government that every citizen would understand its meaning as well as citizens understood the meaning of such crimes as murder, homicide, rape, arson, burglary, and forgery. But regrettably the crime of obscenity was imprecisely defined, and was therefore interpreted variously by different citizens, judges, juries, lawyers, and prosecutors, thus remaining on the lawbooks to be exploited by powerful people whenever they felt the need, for whatever reason, to create criminals.

If the circulation of sexual material was to be excluded from the mail primarily for the moral protection of the young, as Comstock claimed, then Bennett suggested that all mail being sent to homes and schools be inspected by parents, teachers, or guardians, and not by government censors and religious fanatics. Bennett believed, as did many prominent skeptics of his time, that organized religion was oppressive, anti-intellectual, and contrived to control and deceive people with its promises of posthumous paradise for those who obeyed its doctrines, and threats of eternal hell for those who did not; and its liturgy, based on myth, went unchallenged by the government because it mollified great masses of people who might otherwise be rebelling in the streets against the injustices of life on earth.

Bennett saw the major churches and the government as partners in the perpetuation of a compliant public, and they thus maintained their privileged status. The churches, which were exempt from taxation and therefore amassed enormous wealth and property, refrained from condemning the sometimes barbarous acts of a government at war; and the government often provided policemen to support the church's invasion of people's privacy. Religion's presumption that it had the right to regulate what people did with their own bodies in bed, that it could pass judgment on the manner and purpose of sex, could control how sex was portrayed in words and pictures, could prevent through censorship the sinful specter in a parishioner's mind of an impure thought—thereby justifying thought control—incensed the agnostic passions of D. M. Bennett, who regarded it as a violation of the antitheological basis upon which the founding fathers had established the American Constitution.

Being endlessly vituperative on this subject, and having the temerity to express it in print, made inevitable Bennett's confrontation with the law, which did occur on a wintry day in 1877 when Anthony Comstock himself, accompanied by a deputy United States marshal, appeared at Bennett's office with a warrant for his arrest. Comstock, stern and solemn, charged Bennett with having sent through the mail two indecent and blasphemous articles, both having appeared in *The Truth Seeker*. One article was called "How Do Marsupials Propagate Their Kind?"; the second was "An Open Letter to Jesus Christ."

As Comstock stood before him, Bennett quickly defended his right to publish the articles, adding that neither was indecent nor blasphemous. The piece about marsupials, written by a contributor to the newspaper, was a specific article that answered precisely and discreetly what the title asked. The letter to Christ, which Bennett had composed, did question the veracity of Mary's virginity, but Bennett believed that he was legally entitled to ponder this miracle.

If Comstock was looking for obscenity, Bennett said, there was much of it in the Bible, and he suggested the tale of Abraham and his concubine, the rape of Tamar, the adultery of Absalom, the lustful exploits of Solomon. Comstock, impatient, told Bennett to get his coat. Comstock wanted no more of this irreverence, and so Bennett did as ordered, and was taken as a prisoner to the office of the United States commissioner in the

Post Office building, on Broadway and Park Row. There his bail was set at $1,500 and a pretrial hearing was scheduled for the following week. Comstock hoped to make Bennett the first victim of the federal law against defiling the mail.

After obtaining bail, Bennett immediately began to campaign for his defense, and he published new attacks on Comstock and the law. Many people were inspired to support Bennett, including his distinguished friend and fellow agnostic, the lawyer Robert G. Ingersoll. Ingersoll, who like Bennett had been reared in Illinois, had served valorously as a colonel in the Union cavalry, being greatly motivated not by the war itself, but by his opposition to slavery. His parents had both been outspoken abolitionists more than twenty years before the war, causing his father, a Presbyterian minister, to shift from one congregation to another, spending more time in disagreeable debate with churchgoers than in communal worship, a situation that contributed to the younger Ingersoll's early skepticism of Christian virtue.

After the war, Robert Ingersoll practiced law and frequently defended the radical causes of his day, and his abhorrence of censorship made him a natural enemy of Comstock. If the government intended to support Comstock by censoring such articles as had appeared in *The Truth Seeker*, then Ingersoll was anxious to defend Bennett's cause up to the Supreme Court, and he so informed the Postmaster General in Washington.

The evidence against Bennett, being neither lewd nor lascivious, and no doubt protected by the First Amendment, was not a case that Comstock was likely to win at the highest level of the law; and it was perhaps a belated recognition of this, following Ingersoll's intercession, that prompted the Postmaster General to quietly drop the case against Bennett.

Most citizens in this situation, having just thwarted the government and the formidable Comstock, and perhaps anticipating the censor's wish for revenge, might have thereafter pursued life more prudently; but not D. M. Bennett. He celebrated the occasion in his newspaper by accelerating his criticism of Comstock, urging the repeal of postal censorship, and calling for the legalization of contraceptive instruction and devices. He also wrote and published a lengthy diatribe on Christianity, describing its history as a holy massacre, bloody conquests in the name of Christ, while its popes indulged in acts of debauchery, incest, and murder.

Bennett portrayed the apostle Paul as an impious proselyte, a hypocrite, and a woman hater who initiated the antifeminist tradition in the Roman Church. Bennett described Paul II as a "vile, vain, cruel, and licentious pontiff, whose chief delight consisted in torturing heretics with heated braziers and infernal instruments of torment." Bennett saw the Jesuits as henchmen of secret horrors, and called Martin Luther a man of "insane violence" and John Calvin a "calculating, cruel bigot." Pius IV "filled the papal palace with courtesans and beautiful boys for the purpose of satisfying his sensual passions and assuaging his lubricity"; Pius VI "was guilty of sodomy, adultery, incest and murder"; and Sixtus V "celebrated his coronation by hanging sixty heretics." After similarly describing dozens of other popes, saints, reformers, evangelists, and Puritans, Bennett concluded that Anthony Comstock "has proven himself equal to almost any of his Christian predecessors in the work of arresting, persecuting, prosecuting, and ruining his fellow beings."

Bennett published this in 1878. In that year he was again arrested by Comstock, but the religious critique was not mentioned in the warrant, for even a work as vitriolic as that might be considered defensible under the free speech amendment. Comstock had something better, a strictly sexual pamphlet called *Cupid's Yokes* that advocated free love, denigrated marriage, favorably described people living in an erotic commune devoid of restrictions, and boldly asked: "Why should priests and magistrates supervise the sexual organs of citizens any more than the brain and stomach?"

While Bennett had neither written nor published this pamphlet—it was the work of an already imprisoned Massachusetts freethinker named E. H. Heywood—Bennett had reportedly been selling it, in addition to other controversial literature, at a convention near Ithaca, New York; and Comstock was confident that responsible people would be less eager to openly support Bennett now than they had been after his first arrest.

But there was rising public sentiment against Comstock at this time, it being the fifth year of his antivice crusade, and Bennett was again able to arouse through his newspaper considerable support and financial aid for his defense. The case did go to trial, however, and a severe judge—introducing to American jurisprudence the illiberal English law of 1836 that declared an entire literary work obscene if any part of it was obscene and was inappropriate for youthful readers—achieved a guilty verdict against Bennett for selling the pamphlet. The judge then sentenced Bennett to thirteen months of hard labor at the penitentiary in Albany.

Thousands of citizens soon petitioned President Rutherford B.

Hayes to pardon Bennett, and there was talk of appealing to the Supreme Court; but these efforts were diminished when Comstock, who had somehow obtained love letters written by the sixty-year-old Bennett to a young woman, publicly condemned Bennett as a lecherous adulterer. Bennett's admission from prison that he had written the letters did not help his cause with some people, including Mrs. Bennett and the wife of President Hayes; and it was reportedly Mrs. Hayes who urged her husband to ignore the Bennett petition.

Bennett served the full term at hard labor and was greatly debilitated by the experience. After his release he traveled in Europe, leaving the editorship of his paper to an associate who had run it during his imprisonment. In 1881 Bennett published a book called *An Infidel Abroad*, a collection of his own typically irreverent articles and comments that had established him in the free-thought movement of nineteenth-century America, a movement that in succeeding generations would include such publishers as Emanuel Julius, whose controversial Little Blue Books in the 1920s commenced the nation's mass-market paperback industry; Samuel Roth, who was often imprisoned between the 1930s and 1950s for dealing in books banned by the government; and Barney Rosset, who would eventually impede the postal censors in a celebrated court case.

D. M. Bennett, who died the year after publishing *An Infidel Abroad*, was long survived by his eminent tormentor, Anthony Comstock. Before Comstock's own death in 1915 he sent many other men to jail, being particularly gratified in 1896 when the United States Supreme Court upheld the conviction of Lew Rosen, whose publication *Broadway* had traveled through the mail featuring pictures of provocative women partially covered in lamp black that could easily be erased by the subscriber at home. Although Rosen's energetic attorneys had contested the lower court convictions with various arguments—including the fact that the copy of *Broadway* used in evidence had been mailed in response to a government decoy letter, and also that Lew Rosen himself had not been aware of the ease with which the photographed women could be deprived of their carbon covering— the Supreme Court supported the Comstock Act and Lew Rosen was forced to serve thirteen months at hard labor.

The death of Comstock did not lessen the prosecution of pornography; it was continued by postal censors and church leaders, by the antivice society in New York and similar organizations in other cities, such as the Watch and Ward Society of Boston and the Chicago Law and Order League.

The Chicago league was directed by Arthur B. Farwell, a descendant of New England Puritans whose own missionary zeal had been intensified by the disheartening news when he was younger that his father, a political leader, was financially and socially involved with certain Chicago swindlers, rogues, and a prominent madam. From then on the younger Farwell was decidedly aloof from his father, and was equally intolerant of any citizen who profited from political schemes, gambling, or sought pleasure from immoral sex.

Most Chicago brothels were closed temporarily in 1912 after constant petitioning by Farwell's league, and it succeeded in 1915 in having Chicago's saloons shut down on Sundays. If Farwell's league had little success during Prohibition in curbing the profitable partnership between politicians and gangsters that produced the speakeasies and whiskey wars, it was partly because Chicago after the Volstead Act of 1919 was under the strong influence of ethnic groups—mainly the Irish—who did not share the prohibitionists' view of whiskey as a vice, although on matters of sex the Irish were possibly more puritanical than the Puritans.

In fact, by the 1920s—as Hugh Hefner's sober Methodist parents from Nebraska had settled into Chicago—the Irish-Catholics had more or less replaced the Farwell-type bluenose Protestants as the enforcers of sexual morality in the city. The great Irish immigration of the mid-1800s had imported into Chicago a fierce brand of Catholicism founded on sexual regulation and orthodoxy, and the city gradually reflected these values politically and socially, becoming less tolerant of unorthodox thought and behavior. Even when the Irish did not control the mayor's office—which they did regularly since the 1920s—the orthodox Catholic view on morality and sexual censorship was reinforced by the preponderant number of Irish-American state legislators, aldermen, ward leaders, state's attorneys, police officers, and politically connected clergymen. The Irish were more quickly successful than other immigrants because they arrived in the new land with an ability to speak the language, were united in their religious beliefs, and were politically hardened and organized as a result of their shared struggle back home against the English. Fortified by their interfaith marriages and political cronyism, they slowly shaped a Chicago Democratic machine from their South Side shanties, blue-collar bungalows, and tenements that excluded blacks, and from such a neighborhood came not only Mayor Richard Daley but also the two Irish-Catholic mayors who had preceded him, Ed Kelly and Martin Kennelly.

Daley's neighborhood was not so different from other ethnic white areas largely populated by the Polish, or Czechoslovakians, or Italians, or Russian Jews; nearly all were inhabited by socially conservative Chicagoans tightly tied to their families and trade unions, and they were more enduringly insular and immutable than the ethnic Americans living in more liberal cities, where the neighborhoods were not so formidably preserved as blocs of votes. Chicago was well organized, solid, stolid—a town of regulars who were shocked less by political chicanery and extreme racism than by an attempt of a neighborhood theater owner to show a sexy movie.

The films that Hugh Hefner had seen as a teenaged usher at the Rockne Theater, and as a patron of other cinemas, had been screened beforehand by a police censor board, whose reviewers usually included five housewives married to policemen. When Hefner was working in Von Rosen's promotion department, Chicago's main distributor of magazines refused to carry Von Rosen's products because they were sexually oriented and might provoke the displeasure of City Hall and church leaders. Von Rosen's magazines were therefore circulated circumspectly to newsstands by drivers working for a smaller, hungrier, more daring firm known within the trucking trade as a "secondary" distributor.

In almost every large American city there was a primary distributor that circulated the socially acceptable mass-market magazines, like *Reader's Digest* and *Ladies' Home Journal*, and a "secondary" distributor that took what the primary preferred not to touch. In Chicago the secondary was the Capitol News Agency, and, like such firms in other cities, its warehouse was located on a remote side street and had bricked-up windows so that snoopers on the sidewalk could not see what was stored within. An arriving driver with a truckload of new magazines from the printing plant, before gaining entrance to the warehouse, had to first ring a buzzer at the side door and identify himself through the intercom; then the big sliding door was elevated, the truck entered the warehouse, and, after the door had been lowered and locked shut, the shipping clerks helped the driver unload the merchandise along the interior docking area. The cartons of magazines were counted and checked against the invoice. Some of these cartons had been sent from such distant points as Los Angeles and New York, being transported by carriers who traveled the secondary routes through America, dropping off cartons along the way in places like Denver and Des Moines, Cleveland and Columbus. After the big truck had left the Chicago warehouse, smaller panel trucks owned by Capitol would deliver within the city prearranged numbers of magazines to specific news dealers, some of whom would sell the magazines under the counter or in plain brown wrappers.

Although Capitol's merchandise was transported as cautiously as was bootleg whiskey in an earlier era, and was perhaps driven by some of the same drivers, not all of the cartons handled in the Capitol warehouse contained erotic publications. Capitol also distributed a few academic and literary magazines, such as *The Partisan Review*, that did not sell well enough in Chicago to interest the primary distributor. Also in the Capitol warehouse were certain political publications that were offensive to Chicago's municipal and religious leaders, such as the Communist *Daily Worker*. And Capitol handled all the black publications—*Ebony* magazine, *The Negro Digest*, *Tan*, as well as the newspaper the Chicago *Daily Defender*.

The Capitol News Agency was founded in the mid-1930s by a Chicago horseplayer named Henry Steinborn, who in the beginning circulated mostly tip sheets, but he also included in his truck a few magazines then considered indecorous or obscene—*Sunshine & Health*, *The Police Gazette*, *The Hobo News*, film fan magazines featuring "starlets" in swimsuits, and certain women's confessional magazines. Although no erotic photographs appeared in the confessional magazines, many priests in Chicago and around the country believed that their sin-centered content and private disclosures aroused lustful thoughts, and parishioners were urged to avoid reading these magazines. (Interestingly, the historic case of 1868 in England that first defined obscenity—known among lawyers as the *Hicklin* decision—evolved out of the prosecution of a pamphlet describing how priests were often so sexually aroused while hearing women's confessions that they sometimes masturbated and even copulated with their repentant subjects in the confessional.)

With the popularity of the girlie magazines during World War II, Capitol's business, along with that of other secondaries around the country, greatly increased. Capitol circulated within Chicago the Robert Harrison publications (*Wink, Flirt, Whisper, Eyefull*) and also those of another New York publisher named Adrian Lopez (*Cutie, Giggles, Sir, Hit*). After the war, when paper rationing was lifted, there were newer magazines like *Night and Day*, *Gala*, and *Focus*, all of which featured a tall, blond California bathing beauty named Irish McCalla and an attractive, somewhat devilish, dominant high-heeled brunet from Florida named Bettie Page. These two women, more than any other photo models, were the masturbatory mistresses for many thousands of men during the postwar years, and they remained popular through the 1950s as Diane Webber emerged, increasingly nude, in *Sunshine & Health* and the Von Rosen magazines.

As Von Rosen's publications became more daring, revealing everything but pubic hair, Henry Steinborn of Capitol News became concerned about police raids of his warehouse. He moved to a new location, obtaining a larger warehouse but displaying a smaller company sign above the door. Steinborn was making money for the first time in his life, he had ten trucks operating in the city, and more newsstands than ever were now quietly accepting girlie magazines. With the sale of each fifty-cent magazine, the newsstand owner earned a dime, and so did Henry Steinborn. Thousands of magazines were selling each month in Chicago, and various publishers were hiring lawyers as advisers, hoping the lawyers knew how much of the female body could legally be shown in pictures. Some lawyers expressed opinions, others shrugged and said that a definition of obscenity depended on which judge was defining it; and so Steinborn's panel trucks pluckily continued their deliveries to various newsstands, and eventually to a small bookshop located first on Dearborn Street, later on Van Buren Street.

In the front window of the store was a selection of current hardcover and paperback books that could be found in an ordinary bookshop, but near the back of the store, and under the counter, were books and magazines that could only have been supplied by a secondary.

In time, many customers became aware of the full variety of the merchandise, and they stopped in often, eventually getting to know the counter clerks well enough to gain flipping privileges with the girlie magazines without having to buy one. But most customers bought at least one magazine, tucking it into their coat or putting it into a bag; and two customers, perhaps the best patrons of the store, purchased copies of nearly every girlie magazine that was available for sale. One of these customers was Hugh Hefner. The other, a younger man, was named Harold Rubin.

5

As Hugh Hefner sat at his desk in the *Playboy* office on this wintry day in 1955 deciding which of Diane Webber's nude photographs would be the centerfold in the May issue, he could hear a church bell ringing from the Holy Name Cathedral across the street. It was the 6 P.M. Angelus bell reminding the faithful, as it did thrice daily, of the angel Gabriel's announcement to the Virgin Mary that, through a miracle of sexual uninvolvement, she would become the mother of the Messiah.

Thus did Catholicism dishonor sex by denying its necessity to those most virtuous; and this doctrine of denial would continue for centuries during which the Church demanded celibacy of its clergy, expected chastity of its unmarried parishioners, sanctified conjugal copulation mainly for the propagation of the faith, and canonized such women as St. Agnes because, rather than submit to male lust, she preferred death as a virgin martyr.

This asceticism was, to say the least, substantially at variance with the life-style being advocated across the street at *Playboy* magazine, and had Hefner initially given more thought to it, he might have located his offices further from the gigantic Gothic cathedral that dominated the block and cast a disapproving shadow down upon the gray four-story Playboy building at 11 East Superior Street.

But since great cathedrals cannot be constructed and maintained without great sinners to justify them, perhaps Hefner belonged where he was. Like most unrepentant sinners, however, he could expect no benediction from the believers, and he had already aroused the cardinal's wrath months before by reprinting in *Playboy* a medieval tale from Boccaccio's *Decameron* that describes the carnal life of a convent gardener constantly seduced by sexually aggressive nuns.

The Church that had condemned this story in the mid-1500s had no higher opinion of it following its reappearance in the *Playboy* issue of September 1954, and after a recriminating call from the chancellery Hefner asked his distributors at Capitol to withdraw the issue from the Chicago newsstands, although these magazines were redistributed in other cities. Hefner did not want to escalate religious opposition so early in his publishing career, being overworked as he was with normal business problems and also having previously experienced negative signs that might have been induced by complaints from church members.

The Chicago postmen, for example, often delayed for several days delivering the mail to the Playboy building, stalling the magazine's incoming subscription orders, and the Postmaster General in Washington denied *Playboy* the less costly second-class mailing privileges customarily granted to publications, because he considered *Playboy* obscene. The police enforced parking regulations in front of the Playboy office more vigilantly than elsewhere in Chicago, ticketing and towing away cars whenever possible—which one day prompted a Playboy employee named Anson Mount to call a policeman's attention to an illegally parked car on the opposite side of the street, the limousine used by the Archbishop of Chicago, Samuel Stritch.

The policeman thought at first that Anson Mount was kidding; but when Mount insisted that parking laws in Chicago should be equitably enforced, the policeman asked Mount if he wished to register an official complaint. Mount said that he did, and after the form was prepared Mount signed it and listed his address. A week later, while Mount was at his apartment, his landlord knocked on his door saying that there were two visitors from the police department. They were plainclothesmen, and after Mount had invited them in and the landlord had left, one of the men asked abruptly, "What do you have against the cardinal?"

Mount replied that he had nothing against the cardinal, but before he could say much more the other plainclothesman, suddenly enraged, lunged at Mount, slapped him across the head, and banged him against the wall. Then the men left, leaving Mount stunned and confused. His first instinct was to bring assault charges against them, but later he thought it would be unwise to do so. The consequences might be worse than he had received already, and a court case against the Chicago police seemed futile, time-consuming, and would undoubtedly produce newspaper publicity of no benefit to the magazine.

* * *

In spite of the opposition, *Playboy* was doing extremely well—it was, in fact, the fastest growing magazine in America. So suddenly had it succeeded that newsstands across the nation could barely keep it in stock, and advertisers that had once considered *Playboy* an improper medium for the promotion of their products were now reconsidering their position, never imagining that if they approached Hefner with ads he might have rejected them.

Hefner would not print any advertising that focused on male problems or worries, such as baldness, physical frailty, or obesity. Having made a small fortune at the newsstand by selling a magazine that emphasized pleasure, that linked naked women with dapper young men who drove sports cars and lived in bacchanalian brown leather bachelor apartments, Hefner did not intend to desecrate this dream with advertisements reminding male readers of their acne, halitosis, athlete's foot, or hernias. Hefner believed in health through hedonism; he was an optimist and positive thinker. Had he been otherwise, he would never have achieved what he had during the last two years.

He had started *Playboy* in 1953 with a personal investment of only $600. He had obtained this money from a bank loan, using as collateral the furniture in his Hyde Park apartment. He was then twenty-seven years old, was living with his sexually unresponsive wife and crying baby daughter, was driving a dilapidated 1941 Chevrolet, but he was propelled by golden fantasies.

He had quit his $80-a-week position with Von Rosen's firm the year before to accept a higher-paying, less interesting job with a children's magazine that allowed him more free time to plan his own magazine. As one who for years had read and analyzed every magazine from the pulpiest pinups to the most slickly sophisticated, Hefner was convinced that what he had in mind was different from the rest, even from the girlie magazines that Von Rosen was distributing.

The articles in Von Rosen's *Modern Man*, for example, as well as those in men's publications like *True* and *Argosy*, were written for the action-oriented male readers interested in hunting and fishing, gun collecting and deep-sea diving, mountain climbing and other outdoor adventures and activities that reinforced the feelings of male camaraderie that so many men had experienced during World War II. These magazines ignored the reading interests of indoor urban types like Hefner who disliked hunting and fishing, and dreamed of one day dwelling in a modern bachelor apartment with a gleaming high-fidelity set and having a new girl and a new car. Hefner associated romantic adventure with upward mobility and economic prosperity, believing that men who were successful in bed were also successful in business; and while this was merely theory on Hefner's part, he intended to promote it in his magazine as no other publisher was now doing.

Sex in other magazines was usually presented unwholesomely as a vice or scandal. One men's magazine, called *Male*, printed each month an article entitled "Sin City," in which it ruefully reported the night life in various American cities or towns with their burlesque houses, nightclubs, and brothels—a magazine that never failed to accompany the text with several photographs of exotic dancers or strippers.

The girlie magazines of Robert Harrison portrayed sex as bizarre behavior, and his high-heeled heroines with whips and frowning faces were, in the best Puritan tradition, offering punishment for pleasure. The women's magazines wrote about sex as a problem, hiring doctors or family counselors to provide solutions or solace. The magazine that most appealed to Hefner, *Esquire*, was now ignoring sex, and the magazines that were saturated with sex—the cheaper pulp magazines and *Enquirer*-style tabloids—presented it as an abomination to be endlessly explored with such headlines as: "How Wild Are Small-town Girls?" or "The Lowdown on the Abortion Business" or "The Multimillion-dollar Smut Racket."

"Smut" was also a favorite headline word with the desk editors of large metropolitan newspapers, including the New York *Times*, because it fit easily into their space restrictions, it aroused reader interest, and it suggested editorial disapproval. Nothing pleased editors more than news that allowed them to express moral indignation while satisfying their prurient interest. A classic postwar example of this was the relentless coverage given to the affair on the island of Stromboli between director Roberto Rossellini and the married movie star, Ingrid Bergman, which prompted her self-imposed exile from Hollywood for seven years.

As Hefner planned his magazine, the headlines were devoted to more recent sexual revelations, including the sex-change operation of Christine Jorgensen, the café-society prostitution ring of the oleomargarine heir Mickey Jelke, and the 1953 Kinsey report on American women. Kinsey's statistics stated that about 50 percent of all women, and 60 percent of female college graduates, had experienced intercourse prior to marriage, and about

25 percent of all wives indulged in extramarital sex. More than half of the female population masturbated, 43 percent performed oral sex with men, and 13 percent of the women had at least one sexual experience with another woman that resulted in an orgasm.

While the national press reported Kinsey's findings at great length, several editorial writers viewed Kinsey as little more than a pornographer, and the conservative Chicago *Tribune* denounced Kinsey as a "real menace to society." A few newspapers, feeling that the facts would offend their readers, decided to censor the report from their news columns—the Philadelphia *Bulletin* was one such paper—and other newspapers that planned installments on the report were dissuaded from doing so by protesting religious groups. Despite the controversy, Kinsey's research was respectfully acknowledged within the scientific and academic communities, and it inspired one obstetrician, named William Masters, to begin his own research on human sexual response.

For Hefner, the report confirmed what he had long suspected—women were becoming increasingly sexual, and the postwar generation of which he was a part was quietly rebelling against the standards that had prevailed when his parents were young. Almost wistfully, Hefner saw his parents as loving relics of the Victorian era, monogamous and predictable, and his mother was perhaps among the last plurality of virgin brides. Hefner's wife did not possess the virtue, or limitation, of his mother, and Hefner himself was somewhat ambivalent about the female trend toward greater sexual adventure. In a way he welcomed it, had already enjoyed it, and intended to take full advantage of it whenever he could; and yet he was still saddened by Mildred's affair during their engagement—it had made her less special to him, she had become tainted by the lapse, and partly because of this their marriage had not fulfilled for him the romantic promise of their campus courtship, and now a divorce seemed inevitable.

Hefner was not alone in his disillusionment with marriage—Mildred shared his view, as did several young married couples that they had known from college and who were now also becoming divorced or separated. So many couples of Hefner's generation seemed restless and bored, unhappy in their gray flannel suits and suburban homes, and too young to settle down in the conformist fifties and join a country club and become inspired by the presidential leadership of an old general who patrolled golf courses in a cart.

Many young men who had survived World War II had been spoiled by its glory and become its romantic victims. For them the war had been a great adventure as well as a hardship, an escape from a neighborhood to an international event. But they had been disappointed after their return to civilian life by the dullness of their jobs, and they were unexcited by the women whom they had perhaps hastily married during a furlough, or had married as the culmination of a long and dutiful caring correspondence that had relieved the barracks loneliness but had created a false sense of familiarity and compatibility.

But for women during the war it would have been almost unpatriotic not to regularly write V-mail expressing encouragement and hope and loving lies, suggesting a sexual fidelity at home that was often as fictional as that of their lovers overseas. The war was sexually liberating for women, particularly those who ventured into the expanded American job market and worked in factories or offices far from the restrictive influence of their parental homes, their relatives and neighborhood churches. These women were among the first of their sex to earn equitable salaries, and with it they rented their own apartments, and dated different men, and learned much about themselves that would have astounded their domestic mothers, if not Dr. Kinsey. While they wrote letters to men they loved, they made love to men they didn't, and along with this varied experience and experimenting they developed a tolerance and understanding that would one day contribute to their permissiveness as parents, a permissiveness that would be condemned by moral critics of the sixties.

But in the 1940s the overwhelming popularity of the war effort, and the social upheaval that it imposed and allowed, temporarily exculpated in America the expedient adventures and sexual dalliance of an entire generation. The war manufactured its own morality as it did its bombers and battleships. So righteous seemed the Allied cause that Cardinal Spellman of New York sprinkled holy water on American military planes before their raids on enemy cities, and so destitute were foreign women in these war zones that they eagerly traded their bodies to invading G.I.s for canned goods and cigarettes. So omnipotent was the government in Washington that, in the name of national security, it made propagandists of the press, which portrayed the Hiroshima bombings as a holy holocaust, and many years would pass before the press would fully rise above its belief in government and skeptically analyze the Capital's cold war intrigues and Asiatic interventions.

But the end of World War II quickly terminated the conquering roles that had been assumed by several thousand Americans from small towns and city tenements—young men who, no longer able to personally identify with historical headlines, slowly retreated into the relatively petty problems of peacetime and their own private battles. They stored away their uniforms as souvenirs of the sweet seductions and salutations attained overseas, and the respect accorded them on Main Street, and they returned to the classroom as average students, or reclaimed jobs that during the war had perhaps been done only too well by women.

For these men it was a time of readjusting to a demobilizing nation applying pressure on them to settle down, obtain a home loan, raise a family. Many men adapted to this quickly and eagerly, and fortified by the do-it-yourself gadgets and status symbols of the postwar economy, they sallied into suburbia and exurbia and familiarized themselves for the first time with lawns and commuter trains and the numbing delights of a dry martini. But men like Hefner wanted something more, something different, an alternate route through civilian life away from the commuter tracks and the wandering road that would be charted by Kerouac. Hefner wanted not to move ahead with the masses but back into himself, and begin life again in a style that was peculiarly his own.

He saw his life so far as a mistake. He had played by the rules and lost. Shaped by a conservative home, he had conformed in school, had become a joiner. After the Army, he had efficiently completed college in two and a half years, had married his campus sweetheart, had sired a child. Unable to succeed as a cartoonist, he had accepted a series of conventional jobs with a carton company, an advertising agency, a department store, and three magazine publishing companies. And now in 1953, at the age of twenty-seven, he had a failing marriage and a 1941 Chevrolet.

While his contemporaries seemed headed for premature grayness in quiet corporations, Hefner reread stories of the jazz age by his favorite writer, F. Scott Fitzgerald, and pondered the richness of life and glittering things and various women with whom he could share again and again the nectar of new love. He wanted wealth, power, and prominence without the restrictions that usually accompanied the attainment of these goals. He contemplated limitless adventure in business and romance, and during his nocturnal walks through the city, while looking up at Chicago's tall luxurious apartment buildings along the lake, and seeing again his women in the windows, he felt himself soaring with the optimistic emotions of youth that he used to feel as a summertime usher at the Rockne Theater while engrossed in a movie and all things seemed possible.

But not even the most high-spirited moments during these walks could have suggested to him the possibility that within a little more than a decade, one of Chicago's most magnificent skyscrapers would be his—that a Playboy bunny symbol would be perched atop a thirty-seven-story building towering over the golden cross of the nearby Holy Name Cathedral. Such thoughts were beyond his imagination because, when he designed the first layout of *Playboy* magazine during the summer of 1953, he had no idea that so many men of his generation shared his dreams and desires. He initially saw *Playboy* as having an audience of perhaps 30,000 readers, and he had estimated this after being greatly encouraged by his acquisition of the rights to publish the famous nude photograph of Marilyn Monroe.

This picture was one of several pinups—and three nudes—that she had posed for in 1949 when she was an impoverished actress in Hollywood. After Hefner had read in *Advertising Age* that the pictures were owned by a calendar manufacturer in suburban Chicago, he quickly drove to the plant and, without an appointment, got in to see the proprietor and to purchase for $500 the photograph he considered the most sexual. It showed her stretched out on a red velvet backdrop looking immodestly up at the camera with her mouth open, her eyes partly closed, and with nothing on, as she later recalled, "but the radio."

While the $500 price seems in retrospect a great bargain, Hefner's offer at the time was the only one the calendar manufacturer had received, possibly because Hefner alone was then willing to assume the risk of publishing in a magazine a full-page color photograph of a movie actress whose eroticism clearly went beyond the sedate standards of the nude models in the art-photography magazines. As it was, the purchase of the Monroe picture left Hefner with only $100 from his $600 bank loan; but it did give him a sensational focal point around which to create his magazine, and this, together with his infectious enthusiasm, quickly produced additional revenue from other investors.

One of the first investors, who bought $2,000 worth of stock in Hefner's new corporation, was a former Air Force pilot and close friend named Eldon Sellers, who had previously collaborated with Hefner in the making of the sex movie. At the time of the film, Sellers had been separated from his wife, and was working as a credit investigator for Dun and Bradstreet; but after the stock purchase he became Hefner's business manager, and it was Sellers who suggested that the magazine be called *Playboy*, remembering that many years ago his mother had driven a stylish automobile by that name. Hefner, who had already announced that his magazine would be called *Stag Party*—and might have held to it had he not received a threatening letter from a lawyer representing the pinup magazine *Stag*—immediately accepted Sellers' suggestion, believing that the name *Playboy* evoked the buoyant spirit of the twenties and the Fitzgeraldian era with which he strongly identified.

Another early investor, contributing $500, was Hefner's younger brother, Keith, who perused girlie magazines as avidly as Hugh. Their mother, though quietly appalled by the career her eldest son had chosen, nevertheless gave him $1,000, and his father would one day serve as the magazine's accountant.

Prior to the actual publication of *Playboy*, Hefner had collected close to $10,000 from the stock sale, and a few writers, illustrators, and an engraver accepted stock in lieu of payment for their contributions to the magazine. After reading Hefner's prospectus and his description of the Monroe photograph, dozens of secondary magazine wholesalers around the country, many of whom he had known while working with Von Rosen, decided to place large orders for the first issue. By the summer of 1953, these orders had exceeded the 30,000 goal that Hefner had hoped for. By the fall, the figure was close to 70,000. While all the magazines could be returned if they failed to sell on the newsstand, the impressive number of advance orders was an indication of future success, and this enabled Hefner to gain generous credit from the printing company that would produce *Playboy* at a plant about eighty miles northwest of Chicago.

The first issue, which had a picture of Marilyn Monroe wearing clothes on the cover, was forty-eight pages in length and, predictably, was edited for the urban indoor male who, like Hefner, saw bliss in bachelorhood and was skeptical of marriage. The lead article, in fact, was entitled "Miss Gold-Digger of 1953," and it sympathized with divorced men who were forced to pay unjust amounts of alimony. There was also a reprint of a Boccaccio story on adultery; risqué illustrations inspired by the Kinsey report on women; and a photo feature showing young couples undressing in a living room while playing a game called "Strip Quiz," which, according to Hefner's caption, was a perfect pastime for people who were "bored and blasé." Hefner himself had tried this game with Mildred and other couples at their apartment, but the stripping had not gone far enough to excite him. Recently he had thought of mate-swapping with Mildred and another couple, and while he had not yet proposed it to her, he knew that his willingness to share her with another man marked the end of his possessiveness of her, his jealousy and deep caring.

In addition to the color nude of Marilyn Monroe, which illuminated the centerfold, the issue contained a cartoon by Hefner; a page of party jokes; a black-and-white picture layout showing nude women sunbathing in California; an article about football, and another article on the musical Dorsey brothers, whose great fame had first been achieved during Hefner's days in high school. The most professional writing in the issue was that of authors long dead—Sir Arthur Conan Doyle and Ambrose Bierce, whose stories Hefner did not have to buy because both were in the public domain, having been copyrighted before 1900.

It was not merely the tight budget that forced him to reprint the old work of well-known writers; he would have welcomed stories by more modern writers, but their agents and publishers rejected him. When seeking permission from *The New Yorker* to reprint James Thurber's "The Greatest Man in the World," he was rebuffed because his was not a magazine of "established reputation." Scribner's refused his request for Hemingway's short story "Up in Michigan" because *Playboy* had not yet "demonstrated its character." When he approached Random House for the reprint rights to John O'Hara's "Days," the publisher demanded $1,000, well beyond what Hefner could pay—although, when he later prospered, he would offer more money to writers for their work than any magazine in America, with the possible exception of *The New Yorker*.

Prior to his first issue, however, Hefner shared with the established publishers much of their uncertainty about his magazine, particularly what the legal response and public reaction to it would be; and this no doubt influenced his decision to omit his own name from the masthead of the publisher's page, and he also deleted the date from the cover. If the magazine did not sell during the first month, he hoped it would linger on the newsstands for a second month, until most of the copies were bought.

Playboy was ready to be printed in October 1953, and Hefner, Eldon Sellers, and Art Paul—who accepted stock in place of a salary to design the magazine—drove to the plant in Rochelle, Illinois, to make the last-minute corrections and to watch the first of the 70,000 copies roll off the presses. Hefner was in a frenzied state caused by elation and fatigue—and he was depressed: The magazine was now completely out of his control. The man in charge of distributing it around the nation, a onetime Von Rosen employee named Jerry Rosenfield—who had also advanced money to Hefner—expressed optimism that it would sell, but he no more than Hefner knew exactly what to expect. If only 10,000 or 15,00 copies sold, and more than two-thirds were returned, it would put Hefner into immediate bankruptcy and terminate *Playboy* after one issue. Hefner would have to find a job. It would take him years to repay personal loans, and the bank would claim his furniture. Hefner returned that night trying not to think about it.

He had to assume there would be a second issue, and, in his apartment during the rest of the week, he worked on the new layout. He already had a color nude of a reasonably attractive, though obscure, model who would be the next centerfold. He also had obtained several black-and-white art nudes from Andre de Dienes. He had a wide selection of fictional stories in the public domain, a few nonfiction pieces that were competently done, and, of course, an endless supply of his own cartoons.

Mildred was very encouraging and tolerant at this time; she never complained, though the living room floor of their apartment was littered with nude pictures, and her husband's co-workers went in and out of the kitchen each day discussing sex and women while she tried to care for the baby.

Within the month, the first issue had arrived on the Chicago newsstands, and Hefner left the apartment to drive around the city surveying the business activity at the sidewalk stalls. Parking his car, he walked from one stand to another, watching the browsers from a discreet distance. Approaching a stand, he would pick up a copy of *Playboy*, examine it as if for the first time; if the vendor was not looking, he would move his magazine to a better position, closer to the front, or next to the copies of *The New Yorker* or *Esquire*, and further from *Modern Man*. He wished that he could personally promote his magazine to the people passing, could make a sidewalk speech heralding its arrival. Occasionally he observed a man picking up a copy and thumbing through it. If the copy was bought, Hefner felt a surge of silent excitement.

After a week on the stands, it seemed to Hefner that the stacks of *Playboys* were getting lower on most of the newsstands he visited. After two weeks, he received an enthusiastic call from Jerry Rosenfield saying that the issue was selling fast around the nation and that Hefner should definitely proceed with the second issue. Hefner then learned that both *Time* and *Newsweek* had favorably commented on the first issue, and *The Saturday Review* reported that the new magazine "makes old issues of *Esquire*, in its most uninhibited days, look like trade bulletins from the W.C.T.U." By the end of the month, with more than 50,000 copies already sold, Hefner's old automobile collapsed; but feeling suddenly rich, he purchased a sleek new Studebaker, and when he delivered the second issue to the printer in Rochelle he inserted the date on the cover—January 1954—and printed his name on the masthead. He was *Playboy*'s editor and publisher, a fact that he now wanted everybody to know.

The meteoric rise of his magazine carried Hefner away from his marriage and into the alluring escape and challenging demands of monthly deadlines. Mildred saw him infrequently after the fourth issue was published, when he moved his staff of seven into the building across from the Cathedral. He was clearly obsessed with the magazine, worked through the day and night, and slept at odd hours in the bedroom behind his office. When Mildred informed him that she was again pregnant, he seemed barely interested, although he did arrange for the rental of a large new apartment in a building near the lake. But he did not move in with her.

He no longer walked the streets at night, remaining within the Playboy building for days and weeks. He kept his clothes there, had food sent in, girls sent in, made love in the office bedroom, and then returned to his desk to read manuscripts, compose captions, write headlines, and examine the color transparencies of a prospective playmate.

A photographer one day took a snapshot of him at his desk scrutinizing pictures, and Hefner seemed pale and undernourished, his high-cheekboned face was thin, there were circles under his dark eyes, and it appeared that he had been up all night. Though his dark hair was cut short in the style of young executives in the 1950s, his clothes were ill-fitting, and, while in this instance he wore a necktie, his office attire usually consisted of a sports shirt, dark trousers, loafers, and white wool socks. Some staff members assumed that the loafers and socks were his way of prolonging the carefree look of his college days, but the white wool socks were worn because of a foot fungus, a condition acquired in the Army. While the snapshot of Hefner made him a poor representative of a magazine hoping to attract men's fashion advertising, it nevertheless appeared in *Playboy*'s first anniversary issue of December 1954, an occasion he celebrated by printing 175,000 copies.

The reclusive Hefner was now beginning to reveal himself in his own pages, not only in the snapshots that would be printed, or the opinionated columns that he would write, but later—as the magazine doubled again in circulation and wealth—by inserting evidence of his existence in the backgrounds of nude photographs that were shot exclusively for *Playboy*. In a picture of a young woman taking a shower, Hefner's shaving brush and comb appeared on the bathroom sink. His tie was hung near the mirror. Although Hefner was now presenting only the illusion of himself as the lover of the women in the pictures, he foresaw the day when, with the increasing power of his magazine, he would truly possess these women sexually and emotionally; he would be realizing his readers' dreams, as well as his own, by touching, wooing, and finally penetrating the desirable Playmate of the Month.

But first he had to make them more desirable to himself, to create within the centerfold a look and attitude that would appeal to his own special fondness for virgins, an admission that he immediately recognized as a contradiction, for it linked him curiously to those cathedral dwellers across the street who disapproved of him. And yet such contradictions and complex passions were part of him; while he espoused a philosophy of sexual liberation, he was also afflicted with a Madonna complex, and in this sense he was typical of many men of his time.

They wanted women who were virginal, devoted, eternally faithful, and yet they went through life wondering about other women, watching them on beaches, in parks, on the streets, mentally molesting them; or peering at them from across courtyards or in the windows of buildings, framing them in fantasies of eccentric fulfillment. Hefner had grown up in an America that had divided young women into two categories—"good girls" who were not sexual, and "bad girls" who were; and while he lusted for the latter he could not imagine becoming romantically involved with them. But during his campus courtship of Mildred he had been forced to redefine the sexual nature of modern women. He knew that a modest comely co-ed could—as Mildred did—pose in the nude, perform fellatio in a bus, and conduct a secret sexual affair with one man while being engaged to another.

This was the new 1950s woman, wholesome in appearance but sexually unpredictable, and he hoped to reveal her pictorially as Kinsey had done statistically—he wanted *Playboy* to unveil the ''good girls'' and to dispense if possible with the struggling starlets, professional models, and demimondaines. Despite its success, the Monroe photograph had been viewed by many critics of *Playboy* as a desperate act by a destitute actress; and during the next fifteen issues of *Playboy*, Hefner rarely acknowledged the names of the centerfold models, though he usually knew who they were. One of them was Jayne Mansfield, a voluptuous platinum blonde vying to become the next Monroe. Another was Bettie Page, who wore her dark hair in bangs like Mildred but who was more established in Hefner's mind from the underground photographs he had once seen and had masturbated to in private.

But now he wanted the type of playmate who could be part of his public life, that he might enjoy socially as well as sexually. The only problem was in finding the average young woman with the right look who would disrobe for *Playboy*. The California outdoor look that Diane Webber possessed in abundance was the best he had found so far, and she would be featured in the May centerfold together with her name and a brief biographical sketch. But Hefner knew that Diane Webber had already been in other magazines; she was not the camera virgin he was looking for.

Hefner wanted to discover someone new, to convince her to pose after winning her trust, and then, if necessary, to refashion her in a way that would be identified with his taste. Like the Gibson girl of the 1890s, the Ziegfeld girl of the 1920s, the Goldwyn girl of the 1930s, and the Powers model of the 1940s, he now hoped to create the Hefner girl of the 1950s. She would be unpretentious, healthy, and unintimidating, the normal pretty girl that men saw each day in large cities and small towns: the smiling secretary, the airline stewardess, the banker's daughter, the college cheerleader, the Sweetheart of Sigma Chi, the girl next door—and he wanted to feel that she belonged to him.

After her debut as a *Playboy* nude, he did not want her to pose for other publications. He wanted her to be monogamous with his magazine, for which he would pay handsomely; but in order to guarantee her exclusivity he devised a plan for paying each new playmate in monthly checks sent over a two-year period. During this time she, and others like her, would remain associated with *Playboy*, would perhaps earn extra fees for making public appearances in front of advertisers and subscribers, and would lend credibility to the rapturous life-style that Hefner was trying to establish around himself.

For his first personally chosen playmate, he already had someone in mind. She was one of his new employees. She worked on the second floor, in the circulation department. A twenty-year-old blonde with blue-green eyes and creamy complexion, she was cheerful and alert, and though she dressed modestly, it was obvious to Hefner the first time he saw her that she had a magnificent body. Her name was Charlaine Karalus. She had joined *Playboy* earlier in the month, answering an ad placed by the business manager, Eldon Sellers. Following her interview with Sellers, Hefner introduced himself and quickly communicated his personal interest. He made a dinner date and later drove her to a restaurant in a bronze-colored Cadillac convertible that he had just purchased for $6,500 in cash.

They enjoyed one another's company and began dating regularly, and also making love in his office bedroom. Charlaine was eager to help the magazine in every way, and she particularly wanted to please Hugh Hefner, being flattered by his attention, awed by his success, and reluctant to disappoint him when he asked that she be his playmate in the July issue. He in turn promised to personally supervise the photo session, and to permit both Charlaine and her mother to see the pictures before publication. He also gave her mother a job in the business department, and said he would not use Charlaine's name in the picture caption. He would identify her instead as "Janet Pilgrim," a subtle thrust at the Pilgrim Fathers who had arrived on the *Mayflower* and brought puritanism to America.

In the introduction to her picture in the July issue, Hefner wrote: "We suppose it's natural to think of the pulchritudinous Playmates as existing in a world apart. Actually, potential Playmates are all around you: the new secretary at your office, the doe-eyed beauty who sat opposite you at lunch yesterday, the girl who sells you shirts and ties at your favorite store. We found Miss July in our own circulation department, processing subscriptions, renewals and back copy orders. Her name is Janet Pilgrim and she's as efficient as she is good looking. Janet has never modeled professionally before, but we think she holds her own with the best of the Playmates of the past.''

In the centerfold she was shown seated at a bureau in a bedroom, her negligee open in the front so as to reveal her large pink-nippled breasts. In the background, standing out of focus with his back to the camera, was a man wearing a tuxedo and holding a top hat. He was Hugh Hefner.

Several hundred approving letters greeted the pictorial debut of Janet Pilgrim, and Hefner quickly urged her to pose again for the coming Christmas issue. She was more hesitant this time, not only because her relatives had expressed embarrassment after seeing the magazine but also because she herself had been unsettled by the very personal tone of certain letters sent by strangers. But Hefner's charm and persuasiveness were formidable, and she was induced to appear once more.

This time Hefner posed her under a Christmas tree, and he embellished her nude figure with gleaming jewelry and highlighted her breasts with a white mink stole that she wore loosely around her shoulders. He also printed several candid black-and-white photographs of her relaxing alone in an apartment, playing Frank Sinatra records, reading *Marjorie Morningstar*, undressing for bed, and Hefner reported in the text that Janet Pilgrim preferred wearing men's pajamas—but only the tops, having thrown the bottoms away.

After this fact had been published, the magazine began receiving several pajama tops that male readers wished to exchange for her bottoms, and she also was approached with modeling assignments, television offers, and an opportunity to appear in a Broadway show. But she chose to remain with *Playboy*, which in 1957, partly due to her promotional activities, increased its press run from 600,000 copies per month to 900,000.

As part of a *Playboy* sales gimmick, she made a personal telephone call to each man who paid $150 for a lifetime subscription, and she also traveled around the country representing the magazine at business conventions, fairs, sports-car races, and special events on college campuses. She spent a weekend as an honored guest at Darmouth College, where she participated in a student variety show and autographed her Playmate pictures, having a much more pleasant time than she normally did when appearing before groups of older men at business conventions. The latter group assumed, because of her pictures, that she was sexually available, and they followed her through hotel lobbies and corridors propositioning her, or they pressed hard against her body after she had agreed to dance. If she posed for a picture and acceded to a kiss, they sometimes tried to force their tongues into her mouth.

Adding to her displeasure at this time was the knowledge that, while she was traveling for the magazine, Hugh Hefner was in Chicago attracting new women into his office bedroom. She was infuriated and crushed after learning of this from an office friend; having been reared in an unhappy home of separated parents, and having escaped at eighteen into her own brief hapless marriage, she had mistakenly assumed that her romance with Hefner would provide her for the first time with security and stability. Instead she felt more vulnerable, and so she tried behaving indifferently toward him, and did not answer her telephone at night—only to be disturbed by his loud pounding outside her apartment door until she let him in. He wanted to be certain that she was not with another lover. One afternoon at the East Inn tavern, near the office, where she sat having a drink with a young man, Hefner suddenly appeared, held her arm, and pulled her away. She was, like her new name, a product of his creation, and he assumed the right to repossess her whenever he wished.

Twice she quit the magazine, but each time she was lured back by his persistence. She even posed again for the centerfold, both loving and hating the joy she seemed to give him as he watched her in the studio. He was a selfish, disturbing yet innocent adolescent, a Pepsi-drinking tycoon in white socks who was building an empire out of a baffling sense of reality. While he did not lie to her, he confused her by the way he lived. After telling her that his marriage had ended more than a year ago— and the couple were indeed living apart—she heard that his wife had just produced his second child, a son. In a newspaper column one day Janet read that she had dined with Hefner the night before at a hotel restaurant, but in fact she knew he had been with a blonde who greatly resembled her and who had just appeared on the *Playboy* cover, dressed as a college cheerleader.

Soon after this, Janet Pilgrim, who had been part of Hefner's erratic world for two years, left it with a resoluteness that she had never before demonstrated. She had met a successful young businessman whose values were more compatible with her own, and, after his divorce, she married him and eventually moved with him to New York, and raised their children in an elegant suburb.

Hefner, who was now thirty-one, continued to pursue one woman after another, nearly all of them associated with the magazine as cover girls or staff members; and these office affairs, far from distracting him from his work, rejuvenated him, bolstered his ego, inspired him to take greater business risks that enlarged his fortune and advanced him as a public figure. Influenced by his promotion director, a debonair twenty-nine-year-old divorcé named Victor Lownes—who had first entered Hefner's world as a model in a *Playboy* picture layout on young executives—Hefner dressed more carefully and expensively, abandoned his white socks, and bought a white Mercedes-Benz.

Hefner was interviewed by national newsmagazines and appeared on television smoking his pipe and refuting the Puritan notion that great success was fostered by the denial of pleasure. As he traveled across the country, he could see not only that *Playboy* was selling but that it was no longer an under-the-counter item, and that men seemed less awkward as they carried it away from the newsstand—they did not so quickly fold it inward or conceal it within a newspaper; they were possibly comforted by the fact that close to one million people each month were now buying *Playboy*, in addition to several similar magazines, and that Americans everywhere were becoming increasingly tolerant of, if not preoccupied with, various forms of sexual expression.

In this Freudian age, Americans were opening up, acknowledging their needs, and, because of automation and the shorter workweek, they had more time in which to ponder and seek their pleasure. The newly developed birth-control pill was being anticipated by women. The bikini bathing suit, imported from France, was beginning to appear on American beaches. And there were newspaper stories about the existence of mate-swapping clubs in several suburban communities. Jukeboxes across the nation were throbbing with the music of the pelvic-thrusting Elvis Presley, and audiences gathered in nightclubs to hear a shocking new comedian named Lenny Bruce.

Bruce's uniqueness was in mentioning the unmentionable, describing certain private acts and attitudes that people blushingly recognized as their own. While Bruce and Hefner both in their own way, and through their own initiative, extended the limits of sexual expression, neither man would have been able to reach such large audiences had not the law itself become more liberal during the late 1950s. But the individual who was most responsible for this change, and whose rebellious life was a precursor to the sexual revolution of the 1960s, was relatively unknown in America, except to the authorities who now held him in jail as the nation's most incorrigible literary outlaw.

His name was Samuel Roth.

6

Samuel Roth was born in an Austrian mountain village to
Orthodox Jewish peasants who had an instinctive reverence for
the printed word. On sabbath afternoons his mother would read
to him about the miracles of the rabbis, hoping that it would
inspire him to a religious life; but the likelihood of this was
diminished by an incident that occurred while he traveled in the
steerage section of a New York-bound ship with his family and
two hundred other immigrants in the spring of 1904.

Samuel Roth, then nine years old, was in a bunk reading a
Yiddish pamphlet that had been given him by a stranger along
the loading dock at Hamburg, a pamphlet describing a Jewish
prophet who was more brilliant than all the rabbis and who,
though later crucified, rose from his death to resume his spiritual
mission. This was a tract from the New Testament, and young
Roth became so enthralled as he read it that he began reading
aloud to the passengers near him, causing religious discussions
and debates that could be heard on the deck above.

Suddenly, a tall red-bearded rabbi appeared at the top of the
stairs, and in an ill-tempered voice he demanded to know who
had been reciting from "heathen scrolls." The boy was pointed
out, and as the rabbi descended into the dark and fumy dungeon
there was total silence, except for one man who, recognizing
the interrogator, whispered in awe, "the great Rav from Pinsk."

The rabbi approached the boy, quickly grabbed the pamphlet,
and damned it as a sinful work forbidden to Jews. He tore it into
several pieces and threw it out a porthole into the sea. Roth
watched, shaken and humiliated, wincing as he again saw the
rabbi's condemning eyes and heard further warnings on the evils
of false knowledge. Finally, after the rabbi had returned to his
quarters above, Roth felt hatred for the holy man and his de-

75

structive act; and he would that night, and many nights in the years that followed, remember the damnation and never again abide by any literary judgment but his own.

Roth was a precocious student in the public schools of the Lower East Side. His teachers, however, were rarely impressed with him and his argumentative nature, and were intolerant of his habit of bringing to class books that were not part of the curriculum. Often reprimanded, he was finally suspended, which incensed his humble father, a pants maker in a sweatshop, who had little sympathy for a son who challenged authority.

Roth recognized himself as a rebel, if not an anarchist, when he became a follower of Emma Goldman and Alexander Berkman, whose radical lectures he regularly attended at a lyceum on East Broadway. He read the anarchist magazine *Mother Earth*, and he befriended many dissident young men from the tenements who would one day gain power through the unions and fame during strikes. But Roth was also too individualistic to remain harmonious for long with any group, including his own family, which was why at fifteen he was banished from home by his father, and why he failed to complete any school that he ever attended. "I was," he later observed in his journal, "too much in love with books to make a good student."

During his many scholastic interruptions, he held a variety of jobs for brief periods of time. He sold newspapers along the East River to commuters using the Brooklyn ferry, worked as a waiter in a small restaurant, and, as a drugstore clerk, he filled bottles, typed labels, and occasionally sold condoms to red-faced rabbis. At night, if lacking access to a sofa in a friend's apartment, he slept in the sheltered halls of buildings, using newspapers as pillows, and he bathed in the public washrooms of parks or terminals. He felt at home only in a library, particularly the one on East Broadway and the Bowery, where he read and reread the works of Keats, Shelley and Swinburne, Spencer and Darwin, and also wrote poetry and articles that he always sent, and sometimes sold, to Anglo-Jewish weeklies.

After a friend had shown examples of Roth's published work to an influential professor of English at Columbia University, Roth received in 1916 a faculty scholarship; but, as in the past, he was an unsuccessful student, being less committed to the classroom than to editing the campus poetry magazine and joining the student protest movement against American involvement in World War I.

Roth's defective eyesight made him ineligible for the draft, but he was too restless to remain in college longer than a year. In 1918, after he had married a young woman he had known from the Lower East Side, he opened at 49 West Eighth Street a small bookshop made quickly popular by the illegal distillery that he kept in the back room. Along the walls of the shop he permitted Greenwich Village painters to display their canvases, and he also functioned as a kind of pawnbroker to local writers and artists. In exchange for small loans, which were rarely repaid, he accepted unsold manuscripts and portraits, unsalable trinkets and heirlooms, old books that were not rare, and rare books that nobody seemed to want.

Pleased to be in the book business, but selling few books, Roth closed his shop after Christmas in 1920 to accept, at the suggestion of an editor he knew on the New York *Herald*, the assignment of interviewing literary celebrities in London. But this opportunity dwindled to another of his misadventures when the articles that he sent back proved to be more candid than the *Herald* had bargained for. Describing the Georgian poets as "nibbling on the dry bones of Keats," and writing that Arthur Symons "is a torch blazing in the vacuum," and suggesting that George Moore was impotent, was not what the *Herald* had in mind when it made Roth its literary correspondent; and so at the age of twenty-six, just as he was cultivating a British accent and becoming accustomed to the daily use of a walking stick and a fur-collared coat that lent distinction to his lean six-foot frame, he was ignominiously recalled to New York, where during the next few years his skill with words was limited to the Jewish immigrants to whom he taught basic English at a special school on the Lower East Side.

Fortunately for his finances, his wife was now prospering as a milliner, a trade to which she had been apprenticed as a teen-ager, and she would undoubtedly have enjoyed ever greater success had she not, in 1925, agreed to join her voluble husband in a venture he considered more intellectually rewarding, that of founding a literary magazine and a mail-order book business that specialized in the lightly libidinous nineteenth-century fiction of such writers as Zola and Balzac, De Maupassant and Flaubert.

The Roths' magazine was called *Two Worlds Monthly*, and its early editions featured excerpts from the condemned *Ulysses*, offending not only the American censors who had banned the book but also its author in Paris, James Joyce, who, though offered by Roth the double rate of $50 per installment in deference to his "seniority in genius," claimed that Roth had not received permission to serialize the book.

Roth argued that permission had been granted him by Ezra Pound, who had represented himself as Joyce's agent, and this led to additional controversy in Europe between Pound and Joyce. Roth meanwhile continued to excerpt the book in *Two Worlds Monthly*, deleting some of Joyce's explicit sexual language; but after several issues, Roth was ordered by the court to discontinue the serialization, which by this time had bored most of its readers into abandonment, leaving Roth and his wife nearly bankrupt.

Throughout his life Roth took pride in being the first American publisher to challenge the censors on *Ulysses*, and he accepted as a croix de guerre his sixty-day imprisonment for later distributing unexpurgated editions of the entire book in 1930—three years before it would be elevated from obscenity to art in the celebrated ruling of Federal Judge John M. Woolsey. While Random House would accept full credit for the legal triumph, and would profit grandly from the American distribution rights it acquired directly from Joyce, Roth believed that it was his intransigence that had goaded Random House into its noble, belated defense of a classic. In his journal, Roth noted: "The rich publisher lets the poor one set precedents in moral standards."

Having perhaps had enough of moral standards and poverty for a while, and wishing to redeem himself after the loss of his wife's savings, Roth ventured more boldly into the literary underworld by including among his enterprises—under a fictitious name and a temporary address—a mail-order subsidiary that he hoped would thrive by selling such books as a fourteenth-century Arabian ritualistic love volume called *The Perfumed Garden*, which contained illustrations depicting 237 possible positions for men and women "in congress." Roth had gained access to this book when he was approached one day by another underground publisher who, having just been arrested for circulating *Memoirs of a Woman of Pleasure*, was now anxious to dispose of three hundred copies of *The Perfumed Garden* that he had hidden in a warehouse on Fourth Street. The book, printed in Paris, was priced at $35 a copy, but the desperate seller said that Roth could have the copies for only $3 each, meaning that Roth could possibly earn $10,000 from the transaction.

Long before Roth had earned anything close to that amount, however, his mail-order operation had been infiltrated by spies from the New York Society for the Suppression of Vice, which had been watching him closely ever since the serialization of *Ulysses*. The Society not only obtained incriminating copies of *The Perfumed Garden* through the use of decoy letters but also raided a store on East Twelfth Street that Roth and his wife had rented for an art auction and book sale, and there the investigators discovered a book by Boccaccio and a series of figure drawings that the Society's leader, John Summer—Anthony Comstock's successor—considered obscene. For these transgressions, Roth was sentenced to three months of hard labor at Welfare Island in New York.

After his release, unrehabilitated and certainly unrepentant, Samuel Roth resumed immediately his career in precarious publishing. Because of his arrests and the arrogance with which he defended his principles, he was now endowed with a certain cachet along the side streets of the book business, and he was often propositioned by smugglers from Europe wishing to sell him pornographic novels and erotic classics, and by collectors eager to purchase from him almost any risqué rarity. Photographers made available to him their private prints of nudes, and writers presented him with manuscripts that, for a variety of reasons, no other publisher would print.

One of the manuscripts that Roth arranged to have printed and bound had been written by an Englishman named John Hamill, and it was a pernicious biography of President Herbert Hoover that newspapers later refused either to review or advertise; and yet Roth sold close to 200,000 copies, and it became a best seller in Washington, Boston, and St. Louis. Another of Roth's books, by Clement Wood, was entitled *The Woman Who Was Pope*, in which it was alleged that from the years 853 to 855, between the reigns of Leo IV and Benedict III, the Vatican had been ruled by a female vicar; and while this book did not become a best seller, it did add to Roth's infamy within the New York archdiocese and the local police department.

Roth also reprinted and sold several underground editions of *Lady Chatterley's Lover*, as well as an ancient Hindu sex manual known as the *Kama Sutra*, and a book entitled *Self-amusement*—"a handbook on the harms and benefits of the universal custom sometimes called self-abuse." In addition Roth published books written by himself, including a favorable biography on the controversial writer Frank Harris, best known for his lickerish autobiographical volumes entitled *My Life and Loves*, a smuggler's gem that titillated or shocked nearly everyone who read it except Mrs. Frank Harris, who believed that her husband had greatly exaggerated his sexual adventures, and she was quoted as saying after his death in 1931: "If Frank did the things he says he did, he did them on the running board of our car as we drove across France together."

While many civil libertarians in the early 1930s believed that censorship was subsiding in America, particularly after Judge Woolsey had lifted the ban on *Ulysses*, Roth was not inclined to such optimism, being influenced by the fact that his office on East Forty-sixth Street was being watched from a hotel window across the street by men standing behind a telescope. Roth also learned confidentially from a postal employee that the mail to and from his office each day was being intercepted by federal inspectors who, after steaming it open and perusing it, visited his customers and sought to convince them to testify against him. Roth wrote a letter of complaint to the Postmaster General, James A. Farley, which went unanswered, but shortly thereafter Roth did receive an indictment charging him with defiling the mail with obscenity. Among the books listed in evidence were *Lady Chatterley's Lover* and *The Perfumed Garden*.

After a trial, Roth was convicted; and in 1936 he began serving a three-year term at the federal penitentiary in Lewisburg, Pennsylvania. That his plight caused no great protest or lamentation within the literary community did not surprise him, for he dismissed most other publishers as cautious men not drawn to unpopular causes. In the autobiographical writing that he did in jail, Roth recalled in particular how Alfred A. Knopf had reacted after being warned by the Society for the Suppression of Vice not to publish Radclyffe Hall's *The Well of Loneliness*: "Knopf did what he always does under these circumstances," Roth wrote. "He yielded his fealty to letters to fear of the censor. He destroyed the type of the book and relinquished his contract for it."

Roth's opinion of literary lawyers, especially after his latest conviction, was also not flattering. "Substituting one lawyer for another is not like changing doctors or jewelers," he wrote. "Every lawyer you talk to finds additional difficulties (however imaginary in your case), bills you for them, and, since they all work in unison, like the witches in *Macbeth*, manages to raise the price of the services of the one you finally chose to defend you."

* * *

Roth served the full term in Lewisburg, and then returned to New York to the livelihood that inevitably could lead him only back to jail. A friend of his once speculated that Roth possibly liked being in jail, or sought beatification as a literary martyr. But Roth denied this. His prison record, he said, was easily explained—"I am at war with the police"—and by this he meant not only patrolmen and detectives but also district attorneys, FBI agents, postmasters and clergymen and their confederates in the antivice societies and on the judicial bench—anyone who sought to restrict what could be read or written was at war with Roth, and as such he was resigned to a lifetime of rifts and reprisals.

He became accustomed, after leaving Lewisburg, to being followed through the New York streets by plainclothesmen, who soon learned of his new office address at 693 Broadway. Working in his office at this time, in addition to his wife and a few fanciful employees, were his daughter and son, scholarly teenagers who, though grieved and sometimes embarrassed by his legal difficulties, shared his commitment to free expression. Roth's daughter translated from the French the first book that he published after his prison release—Claude Tillier's novel *My Uncle Benjamin*—and Roth's son, until called into the Army, worked part-time in the firm's sales department.

Hoping to confuse the postal inspectors and to protect his books from the notoriety of his name, Roth used a variety of business aliases on his office stationery and on the packages containing the books he mailed out; some labels indicated that his books were being published by a company called Coventry House, others by Arrowhead publishers, still others by the Avalon Press, or Boar's Head publishers, or the Biltmore Publishing Company. Roth occasionally arranged to have books left in the metal lockers of New York bus terminals or train stations, with the keys later provided to special customers. These books—by such writers as Henry Miller, Frank Harris, and the anonymous Victorian author of *My Secret Life*—were usually expensive editions that had been smuggled in from France, although during World War II the professional smuggler was being outdone by amateurs from the United States Army. With so many veterans returning from overseas with duffel bags concealing contraband books, the literary black market in America seemed threatened by saturation; but the government after the war, as if to exorcise what remained of an unconquered enemy, intensified its drive against pornography, and not only Roth's books were affected but also some of the more sensual works of modern authors published by distinguished houses.

Among the better-known novels prosecuted after the war were Lillian Smith's *Strange Fruit*, Erskine Caldwell's *God's Little Acre*, and Edmund Wilson's *Memoirs of Hecate County*. The campaign against Wilson's book in New York had been led by the Society for the Suppression of Vice, and after the New York State courts sustained a lower court decision that the novel was obscene, Edmund Wilson's publisher, Doubleday & Company, took the case to the United States Supreme Court. This resulted in a four-to-four deadlock because Justice Felix Frankfurter, a friend of the author, disqualified himself; and thus the rulings in New York against the book were upheld.

Among the books seized by the police in Philadelphia during an antipornography raid in 1948 were William Faulkner's *Sanctuary* and James T. Farrell's *Studs Lonigan* trilogy; and these books might have lingered for years in the literary underground had it not been for the surprising legal opinion of a judge in Pennsylvania named Curtis Bok.

In condemning the Philadelphia raid, Judge Bok declared that books were obscene only if they provoked readers into criminal behavior; but he doubted that it could be proved that books alone had this negative power because readers are also influenced by factors not on the page. "If the average man reads an obscene book when his sensuality is low, he will yawn over it," Judge Bok wrote. "If he reads the *Mechanics Lien Act* when his sensuality is high, things will stand between him and the page that have no business there."

This benign assessment of pornography was shared by few other judges in 1948. The great majority of them viewed an obscene book as a criminal entity, even if it did not directly drive a reader into crime; and since this legal thinking prevailed through the 1940s into the 1950s, Samuel Roth was prosecuted for every possible offense.

After being cited for selling the allegedly obscene *Waggish Tales of the Czechs*, he was accused by postal inspectors of having salaciously advertised through the mail two books that were *not* salacious. One book, entitled *Self-defense for Women*, was advertised in a way that might have appealed to male masochists. The other, advertised as a pulsating romance, was a passionless novel called *Bumarap* that Roth himself had written in jail. For his advertising deceptions, Roth was charged with "fraud."

While appealing these rulings to higher courts, Roth was visited by FBI agents who, having heard that he had volunteered to testify in behalf of Alger Hiss, warned him against doing so. Roth was not personally acquainted with Hiss, the former State Department official then suspected of espionage, but he had known Hiss's accuser, Whittaker Chambers, during the 1920s in Greenwich Village when Chambers was an aspiring poet. In those days Chambers had submitted poetry to Roth under the pen name "George Crosley," the same name that Hiss later claimed Chambers had used when subletting Hiss's apartment in Washington.

When Chambers testified that he could not recall ever having used that name, Roth contacted Hiss's attorneys with his recollections about "Crosley" that could have damaged Chambers' credibility as the star witness for the House Committee on Un-American Activities and its prosecutor, Richard Nixon; and Roth would have taken the stand, despite the FBI warning, had not Hiss and his attorneys decided finally that the help of a highly publicized pornographer was of dubious value.

Alger Hiss later conceded, however, after his conviction and imprisonment, that perhaps a mistake had been made in not calling Roth. By the time Hiss admitted this, Roth had become an even more discredited celebrity.

He was denounced on network radio as a smut king by Walter Winchell, who was angry with Roth for having published an anti-Winchell biography written by Lyle Stuart. In 1954, on the day after Winchell had concluded a broadcast with the suggestion that Roth be jailed again for obscenity, the police were at Roth's apartment door at 11 West Eighty-first Street. They had a search warrant stating that Roth and his wife were engaged in a possible conspiracy and, despite Roth's protests, the lawmen forced their way in and began to scrutinize the entire apartment, opening bedroom closets, bureau drawers, and overturning furniture. Roth was prevented from telephoning his attorney, and when he later ran out of the apartment toward a telephone booth downstairs, two policemen assaulted him.

Roth and his wife were driven downtown to the office of the Manhattan district attorney, Frank Hogan, where Roth saw some of his employees in the waiting room and heard from them that his publishing office had also been raided—all the filing cabinets, desks, and books had been removed in police vans, all the mail had been opened, and the telephones were now being answered by the police. The raid was under the supervision of

Hogan's assistant, Maurice Nadjari, who, when asked by one of
Roth's employees about the future of the firm, replied, "As far
as I'm concerned, your boss is out of business."

In night court, Nadjari demanded that Roth and his wife each
be held on $10,000 bail, saying that thirteen vans containing
more than fifty thousand obscene books had been confiscated.
For the next few days, the raid was major news; but months
later, as a higher court ruled that the search and seizure of the
Roths' property had been illegally conducted, the news coverage was minimal. The district attorney's office consented to dismiss the case if Roth promised not to sue the city. He reluctantly
agreed, being too preoccupied at this point in 1955 with federal
cases pending against him, and also a subpoena that he had
received compelling him to appear before a Senate subcommittee hearing on pornography and juvenile delinquency, headed
by Senator Estes Kefauver of Tennessee.

Senator Kefauver, a Democratic presidential candidate who
had achieved national recognition as a crime fighter during his
televised interrogation of Mafia leaders in 1951, was privately
known to some members of the press as an eminent womanizer,
and on at least one occasion this restricted his campaign against
organized crime. In Chicago, where he had scheduled a public
hearing on gangster influence, Kefauver had been secretly photographed in his hotel bed with a young woman connected with
the underworld. After he learned of the photographs—according
to later reports in the New York *Times*—he cancelled the public
hearings in Chicago.

But his investigation of pornography was not compromised
by such senatorial circumstances, and during the hearings in the
federal court building in New York he was very accusatory
toward Roth, whose business he called "slime," and whose
influence he partly blamed for the existence of juvenile delinquency in America.

Roth denied this, alluding to the fact that his own children,
who were not delinquents, had grown up around him and had
worked in his office, and he suggested that juvenile delinquents
as a group were perhaps the least affected by books because they
rarely read them. While Roth had a cogent reply for every question, his self-assured manner and his retorts delivered in his mild
British accent suggested a tone of condescension that irritated
Kefauver. After Roth had attributed literary value to most of
what he had published, Kefauver noted that Roth had once tried

to negotiate a contract with the prostitute Pat Ward of the Mickey Jelke case.

"Why would you like to have a book about a person who had just been in a notorious trial?" Kefauver asked.

"I believe," Roth said, "that the New Testament rotates around just that kind of woman."

Kefauver paused, but soon recovered; and in his concluding remarks he repeated that Roth's business was "reprehensible," an opinion seconded by Senator William Langer. Then Kefauver permitted Roth to have a final word before the committee.

"I believe the people who have criticized me are wrong," Roth said; and looking at Kefauver: "I believe you are a great deal more wrong than they are, because you are sitting in judgment on me, and I believe that I will someday within the very near future convince you that you are wrong."

"It will take a good deal of convincing," Kefauver said.

"I will do it," insisted Roth.

When Roth left the federal building, he believed that he had made an impressive showing, and he expected to pay dearly for it. But he was nevertheless overwhelmed when he later learned from his lawyer that the government had amassed a twenty-six-count obscenity indictment against him, and was planning to bring him to trial almost immediately. The most prominent items that he had been accused of sending through the mail were several issues of a pocket-sized magazine called *Good Times*, which displayed photographs of airbrushed nudes, and a single edition of the hardcover quarterly *American Aphrodite* that had reprinted "Venus and Tannhäuser," written and illustrated by Aubrey Beardsley.

While Roth did not believe that a jury would be offended by either *Good Times* magazine or Beardsley's frolicking drawings and esoteric erotica, he still asked the court to postpone the date so that he might prepare himself more fully for the trial and also devote some time to his floundering business and interrupted homelife. But his request was denied, and in January 1956 he found himself in court facing a jury and a large red-faced judge who had once been an assistant district attorney.

The trial lasted for nine days, and during that time Roth did not testify in his own behalf, accepting the advice of his family that his interests would be better served if he remained silent. Roth did telephone Dr. Alfred Kinsey to ask if he would serve as a defense witness, but Kinsey firmly refused, saying that he could not support obscenity. Those who did testify for Roth tried to present him to the jury as a defender of individual rights and an appreciator of literature, but the prosecution was more effective in portraying him as a profane and lurid peddler.

After twelve hours of deliberation, and a cursory examination of the material Roth had distributed, the jury found him guilty on four counts—one for reprinting Beardsley's "Venus and Tannhäuser" and three others for the sexually suggestive advertising circulars that he had mailed. Though dejected by the decision, Roth believed that since he had been exonerated on twenty-two of the twenty-six counts, his punishment would not be more than a ninety-day sentence. But his attorney, reacting to information received from a source in the Justice Department, told him to prepare for something much worse. "You're an old offender entitled to the limit," the attorney said. "And your enemies include a member of the United States Senate."

This grim assessment of the situation proved to be prophetic when on February 7, 1956, Roth stood before the judge and was told that his sentence would be five years in a penitentiary and a fine of $5,000. Samuel Roth, sixty-two years of age, felt the ebbing of his existence—a life that had begun in a Carpathian mountain village would probably end in an American dungeon. Before he could turn to speak to his family, two guards had grasped his arms, led him from the courtroom through a side door, and hastened him to a room where he was locked behind bars.

While his attorney appealed the ruling to higher courts, Roth's guilt was affirmed at every stage, although one federal judge named Jerome Frank did recommend that the United States Supreme Court review the case and modernize the legal meaning of "obscenity." The definition as it now existed in 1957 was still influenced by the English law of 1868, the *Hicklin* decision, which stated: "The test of obscenity is whether the tendency of the matter charged as obscenity is to deprave and corrupt those whose minds are open to such immoral influences and into whose hands a publication of this sort may fall."

Judge Frank doubted that a publication could "deprave and corrupt" anyone, young or old, and in the extensive research he had done before writing his opinion he found no evidence that could convince him otherwise. He did concede that erotic literature was often stimulating, but the same could be said of perfume and dozens of other commercial products that were sent through the mail and were displayed in stores; and while photographs of nude women undoubtedly aroused men, men could as easily be aroused by newspaper advertisements showing women in bathing suits and lingerie—indeed, well-dressed women in public stimulated men every day, Judge Frank added, quoting a psychiatrist's opinion that he possibly shared: " 'A leg covered by a silk stocking is much more attractive than a naked one. A bosom pushed into shape by a brassiere is more alluring than the pendant realities.' "

But what most appalled Judge Frank about the present obscenity law was its capacity to invade a citizen's privacy in an attempt to legislate morality. "To vest a few fallible men—prosecutors, judges, jurors—with vast powers of literary or artistic censorship, to convert them into what J. S. Mill called a 'moral police' is to make them despotic arbiters of literary products," Judge Frank wrote. "If one day they ban mediocre books as obscene, another day they may do likewise to a work of genius. Originality, not too plentiful, should be cherished, not stifled. An author's imagination may be cramped if he must write with one eye on prosecutors or juries; authors must cope with publishers who, fearful about the judgments of government censors, may refuse to accept the manuscripts of contemporary Shelleys or Mark Twains or Whitmans. Some few men stubbornly fight for the right to write or publish or distribute books which the great majority at the time consider loathsome. If we jail those few, the community may appear to have suffered nothing. The appearance is deceptive. For the conviction and punishment of these few will terrify writers who are more sensitive, less eager for a fight. What, as a result, they do not write might have been major literary contributions. 'Suppression,' Spinoza said, 'is paring down the state till it is too small to harbor men of talent.' "

The case of *Samuel Roth* v. *United States of America* was heard by the Supreme Court in April 1957. It was the contention of Roth's attorneys that the federal mail statute, the Comstock Act of 1873, was unconstitutional, and that the controversial literature that Roth had distributed was permissible under the First Amendment. The government attorneys, however, declared that "absolute freedom of speech was not what the founding fathers had in mind, at least where the interest in public morality was at stake," adding that society had "competing interests of its own in granting the individual freedom of speech and press."

After the nine justices had listened to both sides, they pondered the issue among themselves, and two months later their published opinions revealed that they had mixed feelings about Samuel Roth.

Justice William O. Douglas felt that Roth should be freed because if Roth was guilty of anything it was for merely provoking readers' "thoughts" and not "overt acts" or "anti-social conduct"; and Douglas added: "I have the same confidence in the ability of our people to reject noxious literature as I have in their capacity to sort out the true from the false in theology, economics, politics, or any other field." Justice Hugo L. Black agreed with Douglas that pornography was protected by the First Amendment and supported Douglas' warning that "the test that suppresses a cheap tract today can suppress a literary gem tomorrow."

While Justice John M. Harlan was less concerned about suppressed literary gems and favored certain legal controls in obscenity cases, he voted on the side of Black and Douglas.

But Chief Justice Earl Warren endorsed Roth's conviction, being particularly piqued by Roth's "conduct" in the way he advertised his books and magazines. Even if the material itself was not obscene, Warren would punish any defendant who pandered to the public with tasteless advertising, and he felt that this is what Roth had done. The five other justices—William J. Brennan, Felix Frankfurter, Harold H. Burton, Tom C. Clark, and Charles E. Whittaker—also affirmed Roth's guilt, believing that obscenity, like libel, was not protected by the First Amendment. Obscenity, according to Justice Brennan, who wrote the majority opinion, "was utterly without redeeming social importance," and Brennan's test for obscenity was: "whether to the average person, applying contemporary community standards, the dominant theme of the material taken as a whole appeals to prurient interest."

Since six of the nine justices saw no reason to vindicate Roth, he was directed to serve the full five-year prison term, and this news was applauded by religious groups and antivice agencies around the nation. The National Office for Decent Literature issued a statement saying that "the cause for decency has been strengthened," and President Eisenhower's Postmaster General, Arthur Summerfield, pleased that the Court had not infringed upon the Comstock Act, announced: "The Post Office Department welcomes the decisions of the Supreme Court as a forward step in the drive to keep obscene materials out of the mails."

But many defense attorneys, after carefully reading the opinion of Justice Brennan, saw in it a historic change in the legal attitude toward sexual expression, one that suggested hope for many books now banned. In having defined obscenity for the first time, the Supreme Court had finally severed all connections with the illiberal English definition as expressed in the *Hicklin* case of 1868.

In *Hicklin* the English court had ruled that an entire book could be condemned if it contained one lewd paragraph, whereas in Justice Brennan's wording the "dominant theme" of a book had to be obscene in order to ban it. In *Hicklin*, a sex book might be disallowed if inappropriate for juveniles, whereas Justice Brennan wrote that it had to offend "the average person." Since Brennan also defined obscenity as being "utterly without redeeming social importance," he might have meant that a book or film offering even a minimum of "social importance" could evade censorship; and if this were true, the Roth decision was a favorable omen for advocates of greater freedom. Whatever the trend, defense attorneys had to wait until the next major obscenity case had reached the Supreme Court, and then to search for clues in the judicial opinions. Such a case reached the High Court in the fall of 1957.

It involved an imported French film entitled *The Game of Love*, which had been closed in Chicago because it displayed nudity and presented an allegedly decadent story. The film opened on a bathing beach where a teenaged boy, completely nude after a boating accident, appeared in view of young girls. Later he met an attractive older woman who seduced him and educated him sexually for the erotic episodes he would soon experience with a girl of his own age. While the film contained no hard-core scenes, intercourse was clearly implied, and the Chicago case was upheld by an intermediate federal court. But when the Supreme Court heard the case and saw the film, it found sufficient social importance in the screenplay to determine, under the new *Roth* definition, that the film was not obscene.

The Supreme Court also quoted *Roth* in overturning subsequent obscenity cases against a homosexual magazine called *One* and the nudist magazine *Sunshine & Health*. The homosexual publication had been barred from the mails by a Los Angeles postmaster; and, though the district and appellate courts had sustained the ruling, the Supreme Court contended that *One* represented a viewpoint, a way of life, that was constitutionally protected under the free speech amendment. The High Court ruled similarly for *Sunshine & Health* against Postmaster General Summerfield, and as a consequence it established for the first time that even pubic hair and genitals were representative of an "idea" essential to the nudist movement, and therefore mailable under the law. Adding to Summerfield's displeasure over this ruling was his seeing in one issue of *Sunshine & Health* a postal employee sunbathing at a nudist camp in Florida. The employee was dismissed.

Gradually, as one obscenity conviction after another was reversed by the Supreme Court, as banned novels and erotic art films were suddenly redeemed by *Roth*, the name became more easily recognized as an italicized legalism than as a reminder of the man now residing in prison at Lewisburg; and ironically, while serving out his term that extended into the 1960s, Roth could have received through the mail into his cell most of the books that had contributed to his being there.

7

He slipped out of bed with his back to her, naked and white and thin, and went to the window, stooping a little, drawing the curtains and looking out for a moment. The back was white and fine, the small buttocks beautiful with an exquisite, delicate manliness, the back of the neck ruddy and delicate and yet strong. . . .

He was ashamed to turn to her, because of his aroused nakedness. He caught his shirt off the floor, and held it to him, coming to her.

"No!" she said, still holding out her beautiful slim arms from her drooping breasts. "Let me see you!"

He dropped the shirt and stood still, looking toward her. The sun through the low window sent in a beam that lit up his thighs and slim belly, and the erect phallus rising darkish and hot-looking from the little cloud of vivid gold-red hair. She was startled and afraid.

"How strange!" she said slowly. "How strange he stands there! So big! and so dark and cock-sure! Is he like that?"

The man looked down the front of his slender white body, and laughed. Between the slim breasts the hair was dark, almost black. But at the root of the belly, where the phallus rose thick and arching, it was gold-red, vivid in a little cloud.

"So proud!" she murmured, uneasy. "And so lordly! Now I know why men are so overbearing! But he's lovely, really. Like another being! A bit terrifying! . . ." She caught her lower lip between her teeth, in fear and excitement. . . .

"Lie down!" he said. "Lie down! Let me come!"

He was in a hurry now.

And afterwards, when they had been quite still, the woman

91

had to uncover the man again, to look at the mystery of the phallus.

"And now he's tiny, and soft like a little bud of life!" she said, taking the soft small penis in her hand . . . "And how lovely your hair is here! quite, quite different!"

"That's John Thomas' hair, not mine!" he said.

"John Thomas! John Thomas!" and she quickly kissed the soft penis, that was beginning to stir again.

"Ay!" said the man, stretching his body almost painfully. "He's got his root in my soul, has that gentleman! An' sometimes I don' know what ter do wi' him. Ay, he's got a will of his own, an' it's hard to suit him. Yet I wouldn't have him killed."

"No wonder men have always been afraid of him!" she said. "He's rather terrible."

The quiver was going through the man's body, as the stream of consciousness again changed its direction, turning downwards. And he was helpless, as the penis in slow, soft undulations filled and surged and rose up, and grew hard, standing there hard and overweening, in its curious towering fashion. The woman too trembled a little as she watched.

"There! Take him then! He's thine," said the man.

And she quivered, and her own mind melted out. Sharp soft waves of unspeakable pleasure washed over her as he entered her, and started the curious molten thrilling that spread and spread till she was carried away with the last, blind flush of extremity.

THIS SCENE AND other intimate passages in *Lady Chatterley's Lover* caused the book to be labeled "obscene" in America for thirty years; but in 1959 a federal judge, influenced by the new definition of obscenity as written by the Supreme Court in the 1957 Roth case, rescinded the ban against *Lady Chatterley's Lover* and conceded that the book's author, D. H. Lawrence, was a man of genius.

Had Lawrence been alive he would have undoubtedly concurred in this opinion, although after completing the novel in 1928, two years before he died, he was more accustomed to hearing himself referred to as a rancid pornographer, a sex fiend, and the source of what one English critic called "the most evil outpouring that has ever besmirched the literature of our country. The sewer of French pornography would be dragged in vain to find a parallel in beastliness."

Lady Chatterley's Lover was Lawrence's tenth and final novel, and it told the story of the frustrated wife of an imperious, impotent aristocrat who had been injured during World War I, and of her affair with a gamekeeper by whom she became pregnant and for whom she left her husband, her home, and her social class. Despite its adulterous theme, Lawrence was convinced that he had written an affirmative book about physical love, one that might help to liberate the puritanical mind from the "terror of the body." He believed that centuries of obfuscation had left the mind "unevolved," incapable of having a "proper reverence for sex, and a proper awe of the body's strange experience"; and so he created in Lady Chatterley a sexually awakened heroine who dared to remove the fig leaf from her lover's loins and examine the mystery of masculinity.

While it has long been accepted as the prerogative of both artists and pornographers to expose the naked female, the phallus has usually been obscured or airbrushed, and never revealed when erect; but it was Lawrence's intention to write a "phallic novel," and often in the book Lady Chatterley focuses entirely on her lover's penis, strokes it with her fingers, caresses it with her breasts; she touches it with her lips, she holds it in her hands and watches it grow, she reaches underneath to fondle the testicles and feel their strange soft weight; and as her wonderment is described by Lawrence, thousands of male readers of the novel undoubtedly felt their own sexual stirring and imagined the pleasure of Lady Chatterley's cool touch on their warm tumescent organs and experienced through masturbation the vicarious thrill of being her lover.

Since masturbation is what erotic writing so often leads to, that was reason enough to make Lawrence's novel controversial; but in addition, through the character of the gamekeeper, Lawrence probes the sensitivity and psychological detachment that man often feels toward his penis—it does indeed seem to have a will of its own, an ego beyond its size, and is frequently embarrassing because of its needs, infatuations, and unpredictable nature. Men sometimes feel that their penis controls *them*, leads them astray, causes them to beg favors at night from women whose names they prefer to forget in the morning. Whether insatiable or insecure, it demands constant proof of its potency, introducing into a man's life unwanted complications and frequent rejection. Sensitive but resilient, equally available during the day or night with a minimum of coaxing, it has performed purposefully if not always skillfully for an eternity of centuries, endlessly searching, sensing, expanding, probing, penetrating, throbbing, wilting, and wanting more. Never concealing its prurient interest, it is a man's most honest organ.

It is also symbolic of masculine imperfection. It is unbalanced, asymmetrical, droopy, often ugly. To display it in public is "indecent exposure." It is very vulnerable even when made of stone, and the museums of the world are filled with herculean figures brandishing penises that are chipped, clipped, or completely chopped off. The only undamaged penises seem to be the disproportionately small ones created perhaps by sculptors not wishing to intimidate the undersize organs of their patrons. In religious art, the penis is often represented as a snake, a serpent crushed by the feet of the Blessed Virgin; and priests since the eleventh century, adhering to the vows of celibacy, have rigidly resisted its covetous temptation. Masturbation has always been considered sinful by the Church, and cold showers have long been recommended to unmarried male parishioners as a means of dampening the first simmerings of rising passion.

While the moral force of Judeo-Christian tradition and the law have sought to purify the penis, and to restrict its seed to the sanctified institution of matrimony, the penis is not by nature a monogamous organ. It knows no moral code. It was designed by nature for waste, it craves variety, and nothing less than castration will eliminate the allure of prostitution, fornication, adultery, or pornography.

Pornography is especially appealing to the penises of men who cannot afford prostitutes or mistresses, or who are too shy or ugly to entice women, or who are temporarily isolated from women (as when incarcerated in prisons or hospitals), or who wish to remain conjugally faithful in every way except when indulging in an orgasmic fantasy with a magazine or when, during marital intercourse, they imagine that their wife is another woman. This is called "superimposition." It is the most common, and private, form of infidelity in the world, and it does not depend upon pornography for its stimulation.

Each day the penis is prey to sexual sights in the street, in stores, offices, on advertising billboards and television commercials—there is the leering look of a blond model squeezing cream out of a tube; the nipples imprinted against the silk blouse of a travel-agency receptionist; the bevy of buttocks in tight jeans ascending a department store's escalator; the perfumed aroma emanating from the cosmetics counter: musk made from the genitals of one animal to arouse another.

The city offers a modern version of a tribal fertility dance, a sexual safari, and many men feel the pressure of having to repeatedly prove their instinct as hunters. The penis, often regarded as a weapon, is also a burden, the male curse. It has made some men restless roués, voyeurs, flashers, rapists. It is what conscripts them into military warfare and often sends them to a premature death. Its inane seductions can lead to marital discord, divorce, child separation, alimony. Its profligacy in high places has provoked political scandals and collapsed governments. Unhappy with it, a few men have chosen to rid themselves of it.

But most men, like the gamekeeper, admit that they cannot deliberately kill it. While it may typify, in Lawrence's words, the "terror of the body," it is nevertheless rooted in a man's soul, and without its potency he cannot truly live. Lacking it, Lord Chatterley lost his lady to a social inferior.

The fact that Lord Chatterley had been a war victim, paralyzed while serving his country on the battlefields of Flanders, made the story of his wife's departure with a lusty gamekeeper all the more tragic and obscene to many Englishmen; and after Lawrence had completed the final draft of *Lady Chatterley's Lover* in 1928, his publisher and agent both refused to be associated with the book.

When other publishers also rejected it, Lawrence took the manuscript to Florence, where, with the help of Italian printers who did not understand a word of English but who reacted nonchalantly to Lawrence's verbal translation of the sex scenes—"But we do it every day," said one printer—he produced a limited hardcover edition of one thousand copies. Each copy, printed on creamy hand-rolled Italian paper and handsomely bound, bore his autograph and was priced at ten dollars. The books were then smuggled into England and distributed through his friends to many readers who, curious about the work that critics were calling an "abysm of filth" and "the foulest book in English literature," were possibly more anxious than ever to read it.

The first edition quickly disappeared, and a second printing followed. Soon the book became exceedingly scarce in England as agents from Scotland Yard began raiding the homes of Lawrence's friends in search of copies to confiscate. Censors were also alerted in the United States, where customs officials in New York intercepted several shipments and, according to Lawrence, resold many books to black marketeers. Underground publishers made facsimile copies of the Italian edition and sold them by the thousands. Some of these books were cheaply bound unfocused editions copied photographically; others were expensive black-bound volumes designed to resemble Bibles or hymn books.

While Lawrence was as irritated by the pirates as by the censors, being deprived of royalties by both, most of his admiring readers were thankful to the pirates for making available to them what Lawrence's Italian printers could not efficiently provide; and while large profits were made in the underground by such distributors of the books as Samuel Roth, these men usually paid a price for selling the words that Lawrence had written. Twice during the 1930s Roth went to jail for trafficking in the novel, and these and his other dealings in illegal literature all contributed to the five-year term that Roth received in 1956 and was still serving after *Lady Chatterley's Lover* was declared legal in the United States during the summer of 1959.

The liberation of *Lady Chatterley* was achieved after the United States Post Office had been sued by a rather romantic young radical named Barney Rosset, a man who knew Roth and who owned an avant-garde publishing house in Greenwich Village called Grove Press. Had Rosset been born a decade sooner, he might have become a fellow prisoner of Roth's, since he shared Roth's passion for independence and abhorrence of censorship. But it was Rosset's good fortune to have published many erotic books at a time when the nation itself was becoming more sexually permissive about literature and life; and Rosset's business success was additionally enhanced by the fact that, unlike Roth, he had been born wealthy and he thus had the resources to formidably defend in court such books as *Lady Chatterley's Lover*, Henry Miller's *Tropic of Cancer*, and other sensuous novels and films that would be distributed by Grove Press from the late 1950s through the 1960s.

The initial source of Rosset's affluence was his father, an ambitious Chicago banker and businessman who, descendant from a hapless Russian Jewish patriarch who made corks for champagne bottles, celebrated his prominence and patriotism during World War II by bequeathing his yacht to the United States Navy. Rosset's mother, who married the banker in 1921 after she had won a beauty contest and attracted his attention, was the daughter of a militant Irish-Catholic exile from Galway who worked as a sewer contractor in Michigan, spoke Gaelic, and felt such contempt for the English that he would not allow the color red to appear in his house because he associated it with red-coated British soldiers. Barney Rosset, the only child of the marriage, was also aware of anti-Semitic comments made by his mother in private about her Jewish neighbors in Chicago, and at times he could not help but wonder if at least part of her disapproval of Jews might be directed toward him.

As an adolescent he was sensitive, hyperactive, and rebellious. In private school, he coedited a newspaper entitled *Anti-Everything*, and he once joined a picket line outside a theater showing *Gone With the Wind* because the film seemed demeaning to blacks. Though he was diminutive and wore thick glasses, he became a star halfback on the high school football team, and dated perhaps the prettiest girl in the class. He was also the senior class president, the first among his group to drive a car, a new beige Packard convertible, and the first to buy an illegal copy of *Tropic of Cancer*.

At Swarthmore College in 1940 he wrote a freshman English paper on Henry Miller, receiving a B minus; and the following year, restless under the school's Quaker influence, he transferred to the University of Chicago. Three months later, still dissatisfied, he moved to Los Angeles and attended UCLA. Within the year, in October 1942, he had enlisted in the Army, eventually becoming a lieutenant in the Signal Corps assigned to photographic missions in China, where he sometimes had to be restrained by fellow officers from venturing beyond the approved perimeters.

After the war Rosset returned home, earned a bachelor of philosophy degree from the University of Chicago, co-owned a small plane in which he flew over the city's skyscrapers, and had an affair with a blond socialite who wanted to become a painter. At a time when it was considered scandalous to do so, the couple lived together openly without being married, first in New York, later in France; and when they finally did marry, in Provence in 1949, the romance was essentially over.

Upon returning to New York she gradually left Rosset for a struggling Jewish-American abstract expressionist painter, and Rosset soon met and later married a young woman employee of Brentano's bookshop whose father had been a German intelligence officer in World War II. Rosset was thirty when he remarried in 1953, a year after he had acquired Grove Press and began to publish the work of talented writers who were as yet too uncommercial, unconventional, or shocking for the major

American publishers, but who appealed to Rosset's own eclectic taste.

Among the writers that signed contracts with Rosset were Jean Genet, Samuel Beckett, Eugene Ionesco, Alain Robbe-Grillet, Simone de Beauvoir, and other Europeans and literary exiles who were living in Paris, which was then still the capital of Western culture. Rosset spent considerable time in that city not only in negotiating with French agents and publishers for the American rights to novels and plays that he admired but also in acquainting himself with many young Americans who were editing literary magazines in Paris, or writing first novels there, or merely living the café life along the Left Bank and discovering for themselves what Hemingway meant when he called Paris a Moveable Feast. There was a social and artistic freedom in Paris peculiar to that time and place, and largely due to the presence of one man, an audacious publisher named Maurice Girodias, Americans in Paris could buy English-language books that were as yet too outrageous or realistic to be sold legally in the United States.

Maurice Girodias was, like Rosset, the son of a Jewish father and Catholic mother, and soon after Rosset had met him in Paris there developed between them a kinship and professional admiration. Girodias' firm, the Olympia Press, founded in 1953, was the first to publish in English Vladimir Nabokov's *Lolita*, J. P. Donleavy's *The Ginger Man*, Pauline Réage's *Story of O*, William Burroughs' *Naked Lunch*, and *Candy*, by Terry Southern and Mason Hoffenberg. Like Rosset, Girodias was impulsive and daring, influenced by what he called "individualistic anarchy," and was resentful of *l'esprit bourgeois* in all its manifestations. While a portion of what he published in Paris was conventional—Girodias printed books of political essays, Russian classics in French, even a journal devoted to the art of knitting—his name was inextricably linked to libertinage, and among his more carnal contributions to letters were such novels as *With Open Mouth*, *The Chariot of Flesh*, and *White Thighs*.

The last novel, written under the pseudonym of Frances Lengel, was actually the work of a talented Italo-Scottish writer named Alexander Trocchi, the editor of a Paris-based English literary quarterly called *Merlin*. Girodias also published an adventure thriller entitled *Lust*, by the British poet Christopher Logue, under the Girodias-inspired nom de plume of Count Palmiro Vicarion. Girodias attributed the authorship of *Candy* to "Maxwell Kenton" because its American coauthor, Terry Southern, felt that if his true name were associated with this tale of an uninhibited young wench from Wisconsin it might reduce his chances of selling to an American publisher a children's book that he had just submitted for consideration.

Other writers who wished for various reasons to conceal their identity wrote for Girodias under such names as "Marcus Van Heller," "Miles Underwood," and "Carmencita de las Lunas." When Girodias was short of cash, which he frequently was because of his casual management, he would mail out to his vast clientele of readers in France and overseas advertising blurbs that seductively summarized a new sex novel that he urged everyone to buy; and after he had received a sufficient number of replies with money, he would hire a writer to produce a novel that more or less conformed to the plot that he had concocted.

"It was great fun," he later recalled in a memoir about his rampant career in postwar Paris. "The Anglo-Saxon world was being attacked, invaded, infiltrated, outflanked, and conquered by this erotic armada. The Dickensian schoolmasters of England were convulsed with helpless rage, the judges' hair was standing on end beneath their wigs, black market prices in New York and London for our green-backed products were soaring to fantastic heights."

In directing his "erotic armada" from Paris, Maurice Girodias, though adopting the French surname of his Catholic mother, was following a course charted years before by his father, Jack Kahane, an English Jew who until his death in 1939 had been an expatriate writer and publisher in Paris of English-language books often considered obscene.

Jack Kahane had been born in Manchester, and as a young British soldier in World War I he had suffered lung damage from German gasses in the battle of Ypres. But his contempt for the Germans was matched after the war by his disenchantment with Britain, its stringent conformity and enduring Victorianism, and long before the government had instituted its tirades against D. H. Lawrence, Kahane had abandoned England and returned with his piquant French wife to the Continent, where he eventually established the Obelisk Press in Paris, and befriended Henry Miller, and became the first publisher of *Tropic of Cancer*.

In addition to his own immodest novels, Kahane published works by Cyril Connolly and Anaïs Nin, Frank Harris' *My Life and Loves*, Joyce's poetry and excerpts from *Finnegans Wake*, and Lawrence Durrell's first novel, *The Black Book*. But shortly after completing his *Memoirs of a Booklegger* in 1939, Kahane died, leaving to his twenty-year-old son, Maurice, along with several unpaid bar bills, the challenge of continuing the Obelisk Press.

For a time the business survived partly through the presence in Paris of American G.I.s who purchased in abundance the works of Miller and Harris and the "Memoirs" of Fanny Hill. But Maurice Girodias made political enemies in Paris after he had published an exposé written by a French Resistance figure charging collusion between public officials and business leaders; and while Girodias was vindicated of libel by a French court, he felt thereafter more conspicuous and vulnerable as a publisher, and in time he began receiving visits from inspectors inquiring about obscenity.

First he was questioned about the works of Miller, which had gone unchallenged for years, and then Nabokov's *Lolita* was declared obscene many months after it had been published. Next there were objections to Genet's *Our Lady of the Flowers* and to the Victorian tale *Under the Hill*, written and illustrated by Aubrey Beardsley.

Suddenly it seemed to Girodias that the liberal tradition of France, the legacy of a bloody revolution, was being subverted by reactionary forces within the government, and his feelings were shared by several political observers and correspondents then residing in France; one of them, David Schoenburn, believed that the nation's military frustrations in Indo-China and Algeria had convinced many prideful patriots that France lacked discipline, that excessive permissiveness had drained the nation's resourcefulness, and that what was needed was a restoration of order, obedience, and old-style morality.

As the purge of pornography often signals the rise of a righteous, illiberal regime—one of Hitler's first acts in the early 1930s was to ban nudist camps and the instructional sex book *Ideal Marriage*—the harassment of Girodias during the latter 1950s presaged the elevation to power of General Charles de Gaulle and his dour and pious wife. Under De Gaulle, the Catholic Church and the military enjoyed increased prestige and influence, and soon Maurice Girodias fell victim to what he called the "priggish virtues" of bourgeois extremism, and about France he would write in his memoir: "All the fun and gaiety have left this nation; the Algerian war chased the last colonies of young artists and loafers away from Paris; in this hygienic-looking city, white-washed by government decree, the spirit is dead, the secular feast is ended.''

Girodias closed the Paris office of the Olympia Press and spent much time in America, where the new definition of obscenity that Roth had provoked helped to transfer a blithe semblance of the literary Left Bank to New York's Greenwich Village, to San Francisco's North Beach, to Los Angeles' Venice, and to the Near North Side of Chicago. Espresso coffeehouses were flourishing in major cities, beatnik writers and poets were prospering, paperback books by Genet and Beckett were selling well in university bookshops, and *Lolita*, still banned in France, was considered legal in the United States and published by G. P. Putnam's in 1958, one year before Barney Rosset's Grove Press would release *Lady Chatterley's Lover*.

While the French were following their antiquated hero, Americans were becoming increasingly weary of *their* aging general, were mimicking Eisenhower's garbled statements to the White House press, and were offended and embarrassed when, after he had set aside Russian charges in 1960 that American spy planes were patrolling over Soviet territory, his deception was exposed by the confession of an American U-2 pilot who had just been shot down and captured by the Russians.

This was one of many incidents that contributed to growing public doubts about the integrity and supremacy of American leadership, and it also served to symbolize a younger generation's departure from the policies and practices of the past. As the U-2 pilot had violated military tradition in confessing to the enemy—an unthinkable act during Eisenhower's army days—so were multitudes of younger Americans now disregarding the codes and inhibitions that had influenced their parents, and they thus were contributing to the foundation of a new society that would be less secret, more open, less conformist—a society that would soon be demanding free speech on campuses, denouncing racism, burning draft cards during the Vietnamese war. While most of these and similar acts of defiance would be associated historically with the mid-sixties and later, the initial tremors were felt years before when Eisenhower was still the President; and many early signs of this schismatic trend were sexual.

In 1959 a moviemaker named Russ Meyer, once a cheesecake photographer for men's magazines, produced a film called *The Immoral Mr. Teas* that displayed the bare breasts and buttocks of attractive Hollywood starlets. Taking advantage of the recently liberalized obscenity law, Meyer was able to exhibit his film in several art theaters around the nation, reaching an audience much larger than the usual crowd of lonely men, and, on a total investment of only $24,000, Meyer's film earned a million-dollar profit. This quickly inspired dozens of imitating films that featured nudity, and it launched the multi milliondollar ''skin flick'' market in America.

Although Lenny Bruce's nightclub routines continued to be raided by the police, the obscenity charges against him were often overturned on appeal, allowing him to continue (until his death from drugs in 1966) his harangues against American hypocrisy, his defense of pornography as free speech, and his sardonic speculations on the sexuality of censors and clergymen.

While the photographs of nude women had heretofore appeared almost exclusively in men's magazines, *Harper's Bazaar* in 1960 printed a picture by Richard Avedon of a bare-breasted blond socialite, Christina Paolozzi, that prompted her expulsion from the Social Register but established her as a media celebrity and promoted the *Bazaar* as a trend-setter in flaunting fashion.

Throughout the country average middle-class citizens were becoming less squeamish about nudity in films and magazines, and more accepting of brief bikinis on beaches. An influencing factor was no doubt *Playboy* magazine, which, now in its seventh year as an advocate of greater freedom and an irrepressible promoter of the bikini, was selling copies openly and prodigiously not only at urban newsstands but also in small-town drugstores. The magazine also appealed to national advertisers because it had captured a large portion of the affluent youth market—25 percent of all copies were sold on college campuses. Many older Americans who were still repulsed by *Playboy*'s content were nevertheless impressed by the magazine's commercial success, and juries now seemed less likely than before to convict the purveyors of similar periodicals, even in Mayor Daley's Chicago.

In 1959, after a Chicago vice squad had arrested fifty-five independent news vendors for selling girlie magazines, a jury of five women and seven men—uninfluenced by a church group that sat in the courtroom holding rosary beads and silently praying—voted to acquit the defendants. After the verdict had been announced, the judge seemed stunned, then slumped forward from the bench and had to be rushed to a hospital. He had had a heart attack.

By 1960 the multiplying fortunes of Hugh Hefner permitted him to purchase for $370,000 a forty-eight-room Victorian mansion near the exclusive Lake Shore Drive, and to spend an additional $250,000 on renovations and such furnishings as a large circular rotating bed that would become the center of his expanding empire. Hefner also opened during this year in Chicago the first Playboy Club, which featured a new black comedian named Dick Gregory and was decorated by wall posters displaying such centerfold inamoratas as Janet Pilgrim and Diane Webber. Among the first customers, having just turned twenty-one, and currently between jobs, was Harold Rubin.

As if to separate itself officially from the grandfatherly era of Dwight D. Eisenhower and to acknowledge the inevitable ascendance of a new generation, the nation in November 1960 elected to its highest office the youngest American President in history, the handsome forty-three-year-old senator from Massachusetts, John F. Kennedy.

During his brief, dramatic term in office—one that would involve him in a failed attempt to invade Cuba, a triumphant nautical confrontation with the Russians, various crises in the Congo and Berlin and Southeast Asia as well as in Mississippi and Alabama—he nonetheless found time to inaugurate the Peace Corps, to promote national physical fitness and body awareness, to go sailing off Newport, to appear on a California beach in bathing trunks surrounded by admiring women, and to embellish the White House with a glamour and glitter that, for those fortunate people who shared it with him, was unforgettable.

Almost everything he said in speeches, or did in public, or read in private had an awesome influence during these trendy times. His publicized admiration for Ian Fleming's spy novels boosted their sales; he lent distinction to cigar smoking; even his special rocking chair, prescribed for his aching back, became a celebrated design quickly imitated by furniture manufacturers.

His personal popularity was of course enhanced by his fashionable young wife, Jacqueline, who became the most photographed woman in the world and, parenthetically, the masturbatory object of numerous male magazine readers. Never before in American history have so many men privately craved a President's wife; but as enticing as she appeared to be, it did not curb her husband's interest in other women. Though a Roman Catholic, he was not monogamous; he was an elitist member of that religion, a wealthy worshiper who, like his father before him, consorted with cardinals and was unaffected by the joyless philosophy that stifled the sex lives of the poor parish regulars.

While his infidelities were not reported in newspapers, the rumors were constant, and various journalists assumed that his lovers included, among others, two Hollywood actresses, a young Radcliffe graduate living in Boston, an attractive secretary on the White House staff, the genteel sister-in-law of a communications executive, and a lovely divorcée residing in Los Angeles. If the name of no particular mistress emerged in the 1960s to personalize or scandalize his secret fervor, it was because he, unlike a few previous Presidents, had no desire for a mistress; he preferred variety, and, according to one correspondent who knew him well, he could make love as casually and quickly as he could swim the length of a pool—which is not to denigrate his fondness for the women who shared his bed, but rather to suggest that sexual intercourse for him was not a clinging complicated act of commitment. It was an indulgence in pure pleasure, a healthy exercise that relieved tension and produced a delightful sense of being alive. Kennedy was—as D. H. Lawrence might have described him—a phallic President.

However representative of the sixties his sexual style may have been, there were White House aides and political associates who were quietly appalled by it, or who, having so long associated the presidency with much older men, were unprepared for the youthful lusty drives exemplified by Kennedy and other New Frontiersmen.

One comely young woman, a campaign worker in 1960 who thought that she had gained a White House job because of her intelligence and idealism, was disappointed to discover that what Kennedy and a few of his men found most desirable about her was her body. Another White House secretary, who also traveled with the President and spent many private hours with him when Jacqueline was away, gradually by 1963 became consumed with anxiety because she feared that soon the press would expose the *dolce vita* and her own participation in it; and later, hearing the disastrous news of his death in Dallas, her first reaction was a sense of relief. Now his image as a good and gallant leader would be preserved, she thought, untarnished by an exploitative inquiry into his private life.

Hugh Sidey, *Time* magazine's Washington correspondent, had

before Kennedy's death written about the libertinism in the White House, but Sidey's account was a confidential memorandum meant only to inform his editors in New York. In the memo, Sidey suggested that at times the sensuality and sumptuousness of the Kennedy administration evoked thoughts of the hedonism of ancient Rome, and this made Sidey's reportorial job more difficult since he often could not reach government spokesmen at night or during weekends because they all seemed to be socially involved in Washington or elsewhere. During one weekend when Kennedy and his staff were in Palm Beach, the memo added, even the President's aging mother, Rose Kennedy, was part of the high life, attending a party with an escort that Sidey had overheard being referred to as her "gigolo."

Although the *Time* staff alone was to have access to this memo, Hugh Sidey was later astonished to discover himself in the office of the Attorney General, Robert Kennedy, hearing the latter say in an enraged voice: "We could sue you for slander." Robert Kennedy had on his desk a copy of the memo. When Sidey demanded to know how Kennedy had gotten it, the only answer was that someone had sent it to him. Sidey now became angry, and while apologizing for the flippant reference to Rose Kennedy's escort, he would not retract anything else he had reported, saying that what was going on was "disgusting" and "I don't think that this is the way the government should be run, or the way you people should encourage it to be run."

Had *Time* magazine published the contents of Sidey's memo, it would perhaps have prompted many favorable replies from readers, particularly those residing in smaller cities and towns away from the eastern seaboard, for despite the Kennedy-inspired excitement and welcomed changes there was increasing sentiment among middle-class Americans that things were moving too fast, that there were too many sit-ins in the South, and that there were too many parties in Washington to which they had not been invited. The Kennedys inspired a clannishness, an "in" crowd of beautiful people and movie stars, Harvard professors and rich liberals who wanted to democratize every place except their well-policed city neighborhoods and exclusive beaches in New England and the Hamptons.

The emphasis on youth made many Americans in their thirties feel older, particularly those junior executives who, having identified with corporations and having associated wisdom with seniority, now felt suddenly uncertain and outmoded in this age of new personalities and vacillating values. College graduates of the 1950s, revisiting their schools in the 1960s, were astonished by the new freedom on campus. Unmarried co-eds, some of them pioneering with the Pill, lived openly with young men, taking for granted liberties that years ago would have caused their predecessors' expulsion. The male students of the sixties seemed almost devoid of formality, lacking neckties and a traditional respect for elders, and they suggested an easy confidence inspired perhaps by an assumption that with their knowledge of the new technology, and the accelerating obsolescence of the older generation, they could anticipate careers characterized by shortcuts to the top.

While older graduates were often irritated by this attitude, they also envied those who were part of the new freedom, and wished that they were younger and more available to indulge in it. One individual who felt this way, whose emotions were typical of thousands of other men in their early thirties—and who would later be lured into a voluptuous experience that would exceed his desires—was a normally cautious insurance executive in Los Angeles named John Bullaro.

8

JOHN BULLARO WAS a compactly built man, just under six feet, with hazel eyes and even features, who arrived each morning at the insurance office in downtown Los Angeles wearing a suit and tie and exuding a pleasant, outgoing manner. His clothes were in the style of Brooks Brothers, and his light brown hair, cut short and neatly trimmed, would have pleased his conservative Italo-American father, who had once operated a six-chair barbershop in the Hearst building in Chicago.

While Bullaro had voted for Kennedy and had mourned his death, he was aware that the Kennedy influence had widened the wedge between the ways of fathers and sons, creating an atmosphere out of which would come the "generation gap"; and John Bullaro was personally offended after the Berkeley campus riots of 1964 when one student made headlines by saying: "You can't trust anyone over thirty." Bullaro was thirty-three, and he felt at least as trustworthy and idealistic as any caviling self-righteous campus radical.

Since graduating in 1956 from New York University with a master's degree in educational administration, having resisted inclinations toward medical school, Bullaro spent years in youth work as a director with the Boys' Club of Hollywood in Los Angeles; and in 1960, following his marriage to Judith Palmer, a pretty blonde who was training to become a nurse at the Beverly Hills Clinic, he shifted his career to a higher-paying position in the insurance business, which he saw as being somewhat related to social work and community assistance and, by extension, to the national welfare.

Without the underwriting and risk-taking of the great insurance companies, Bullaro believed, the United States could not have achieved the economic miracle of the past century, and as a young agent in its Los Angeles office he read with pride the history of the New York Life Insurance Company, which since 1845 had shared in the grief and glory of American adventure. New York Life helped to finance the Industrial Revolution, it insured the lives of wagon-wheeled travelers to the California gold rush, it invested many millions in government bonds to support American military efforts in Europe and Asia.

While John F. Kennedy had not been a policyholder, the company had insured the lives of nine earlier Presidents, including both Roosevelts and two victims of assassination, Garfield and McKinley, as well as such venturing individualists as Harry Houdini and the astronaut Virgil Grissom, Charles Edison and Walter Chrysler and General George Custer, whose last stand in 1876 at Little Big Horn had been insured by New York Life for $5,000.

When Bullaro joined it, the insurance company was established as one of the nation's five largest, maintaining 360 offices around the country with nearly ten thousand full-time employees, and an equal number of independent agents working on commission; but Bullaro nonetheless felt personally involved with the firm, being by nature an organization man who could identify with corporate goals, and he soon was cited for promotions. In 1962, having fulfilled the company's highest sales standards, he was made an assistant manager. In 1964 he was appointed to a regional managership, was given a large raise, and purchased a spacious home in the Los Angeles valley suburb of Woodland Hills. He was a member of the local Rotary Club and the Junior Chamber of Commerce, a fundraiser for United Way, and an adviser to the Boys' Club of Hollywood where he had once worked. He was also on the board of the Valley Oaks Church of Religious Science, having abandoned the casual Catholicism of his Italian father and the stronger traditions of his Jewish mother.

As a teenager in Chicago, living in a lower-middle-class neighborhood where anti-Semitism was prevalent, he had never revealed to his friends his mother's Russian-Jewish heritage. Fearing social ostracism, and hoping to blend in with the Christian majority, he had once belonged to a neighborhood youth club affiliated with the Episcopal Church. But after his family had moved to Los Angeles in 1951 at his mother's insistence, she having grown weary of Chicago's cold winters and the crowded urban apartment house in which they lived, Bullaro became more accepting of himself.

He felt less self-conscious and ethnic in the sprawling open atmosphere of Southern California, where there were no insular neighborhoods dominated by the Irish or Italians or Slovaks or Germans, feuding factions united only in their animosity toward the blacks and Jews. Los Angeles was a relatively young and rootless city unconnected to Old World ties and traditions; here the settlers had not come from Europe but from other cities in America—they were native-born, secure in their national identity, and they did not seek shelter or strength in ethnic alliances. Their reliance on the automobile made them a very mobile society, less circumscribed and entrenched than most Chicagoans or New Yorkers, and in the balmy Los Angeles climate even the slums, the white rows of palm-shaded shacks, seemed vastly preferable to the dark, dank tenements of Chicago in winter.

As with thousands of other westward-moving people who were establishing California as the fastest-growing state in the nation, Bullaro saw the shift as rejuvenating and emancipating for both himself and his family. His father, who had initially been reluctant to leave the prospering barbershop in Chicago, soon found work at M-G-M studios and was cutting the hair of Clark Gable, Fred Astaire, and Mario Lanza. His mother, who after eighteen years had recently had another child, was now joyfully preoccupied in California with her infant daughter and was less intrusive into her son's personal affairs. Though she had sought to discourage him from leaving Los Angeles in 1955 for New York University, and was later disappointed when he stopped seeing the young Jewish woman that he had been dating, she did not object to his courtship of Judith Palmer, and in 1958 she attended the wedding, conducted by a Congregationalist minister.

Bullaro's marriage to Judith Palmer greatly advanced his quest for assimilation. He felt that her acceptance of him was almost tantamount to his admission into a desirable club to which a majority of citizens belonged, and it was no longer necessary for him to think of himself as a member of a minority group, a fractional American. Her father, a top executive with a Los Angeles aeronautics firm, had personal connections in the military-industrial complex that was investing billions in the California economy, and in him Bullaro saw an ally in the corporate hierarchy to which he himself aspired.

From the moment he met her, Bullaro had been attracted to Judith's wholesome good looks, and her fair complexion, cheekbones, and short blond hair reminded him of the actress Kim

Novak. While at parties Judith drank more than any woman he had previously known, he attributed this to her liberated background and possibly to the influence of her convivial father, whom she adored. Since the drinking did not detract from her poise in public, Bullaro was not unduly concerned, although he was aware that it had an invigorating effect on their sex life. After parties and much drinking, she became extremely responsive and uninhibited in bed, and on such occasions she performed fellatio with uncommon skill and ardor.

Otherwise she was sexually passive, and this seemed to be increasingly prevalent as their marriage moved through the 1960s. It was as if the illicit premarital passion that they had enjoyed with one another in the 1950s had languished with legality, and it now required added stimulation for revival. Also, as they had children, first a son, then a daughter, Judith was often tired in the evening, and Bullaro sometimes welcomed this because, with his increased responsibilities at New York Life, he was able to work at home late at night while the family slept.

He enjoyed living in the Woodland Hills house, it being the first house that he had ever owned after a lifetime of dwelling in apartments. It was a beige ranch-style house with a heavy shake roof, and in the front were planted pine trees, sycamores, and a pepper tree. A semicircular driveway cut through the dichondra lawn, and in the garage were two cars, Bullaro's new Oldsmobile and an older Thunderbird that had been a gift to Judith from her father. The interior of the house suggested a Spanish influence, and there was a brick fireplace and an oval table which served as a bar and on which were bottles of California wines.

On weekends the couple sometimes had dinner out with Bullaro's colleagues from New York Life and their wives, and they would all return home for an after-dinner drink. One evening they were joined by a man from the John Birch Society who showed a political film on the Conservative party and was anxious to solicit Bullaro's help on the formation of a Birch chapter in Woodland Hills.

Although Bullaro had become more conservative politically since the death of Kennedy, he was far from ready to become a Birch activist; and while Bullaro was as surprised as his friends by the recent race riots in the Watts section of Los Angeles, and was affronted by the recurring disturbances on campuses, he also recognized within himself a grudging fascination with the way young people were now expressing themselves. He was impressed by their openness and their assertiveness in defending minority groups and opinions, and by the ease with which they found time to indulge in sexual freedoms that Bullaro could only envy.

On Sunday mornings, after telling Judith that he was going off with his bicycle-riding club on a cross-country trip, as was his custom, Bullaro would sometimes pedal alone for fifteen miles to Venice Beach, where large numbers of students and hipsters and artists and dropouts gathered in the coffeehouses or along the waterfront, sitting in the sun conversing among themselves, or reading avant-garde paperbacks that Bullaro had never heard of. As he slowly rode his ten-speed bicycle along the palm-lined path, wearing his NYU sweat shirt and sneakers that he knew were too white, he could see the colorful plastic Frisbees spinning softly in the sky and the long-haired couples strolling along the beach, and sometimes as he rode past the open windows of seaside apartments he caught glimpses of young people walking around casually in the nude. Bullaro often smelled the fragrance of marijuana in the air, and from the cafés he heard guitar music and folk songs making a mellow mockery of his materialistic world, and at such times he was tempted to step down from his bike and politely approach these tranquil strangers at their tables and try to reason with them and perhaps convince them that he was a part of them, that he too was skeptical of the system, and was personally unfulfilled despite his seeming success. But he continued to pedal onward rather than subject himself to what he foresaw as their ridicule, and he perceived his Sunday bike rides through Venice for what they probably were, an exercise in self-pity, a search for a solution to a problem he could not define. He knew only that, in his thirties, he felt old and very alienated.

But on Monday mornings, as if the Sundays had never existed, Bullaro was back in his suit and tie and driving his new car with enthusiasm toward his office—or, as on this September morning in 1965, he was a passenger on an airplane flying to Palm Springs to attend an insurance conference over which he would partly supervise. Among those invited were several dozen newly hired California agents of New York Life, and, for three days and two nights at a modern hotel in the desert, they would listen to speeches by senior executives, participate in seminars, and learn about the future goals of the company. The invited agents had already in their brief careers with New York Life proved by their records that they could sell insurance, which is a rare and special talent, for the agent must sell a product that the public subconsciously associates with death and disaster, and the natural resistance to it is so strong that agents initially confront repeated rejection.

One consequence of this, Bullaro believed, was that it made insurance selling less tolerable to women than to men; women tend to avoid situations that could lead to face-to-face rejection, whereas men become accustomed to it early in life when they begin to make sexual advances, and they soon accept rejection as a natural if not pleasant part of life. Bullaro noticed during the first day at the conference that there were only four women among the seventy new agents; one of the women, however, had surpassed nearly all of the men in sales, and Bullaro had already heard of her by reputation before meeting her in the cocktail lounge that first evening.

He had been sitting with three other executives when she entered the crowded room alone, and, after one of the men who knew her asked if she would join them, she did. Her name was Barbara Cramer. She was a petite, bespectacled woman in her mid-twenties with short blond hair and a well-proportioned body clothed in a dark tailored business suit; though somewhat plain, she was attractive in a boyish way. She sat next to Bullaro and, after refusing a cigarette and ordering a drink, she listened quietly but attentively as the men resumed their conversation. They were talking about the Keogh plan, a tax-free pension program for self-employed citizens that Congress had just passed, and, without abruptly interjecting herself, she nonetheless conveyed the impression that she knew as much as they did about the complexities of the plan.

The business discussion went on for an hour and two more rounds of drinks, after which the men stood to say good night and left Bullaro at the table with Barbara Cramer. Though she made no move to leave, she did complain of a mild headache, and Bullaro offered to get her an aspirin. The bar was crowded and so Bullaro walked across the lobby toward his room, which was nearby on the second floor. As he opened his medicine cabinet, he heard the door to his room close behind him. Turning, he saw that Barbara Cramer had followed him. She was standing next to the bed, and was smiling.

"I've decided," she said, "that I probably need more than an aspirin. I need a good lay."

He knew that he had heard her correctly, but even so he was astonished by her directness. His first concern was whether she had been seen by any of his associates as she entered his room. The regional vice-president was next door, and other executives were across the hall; but before he could say anything she had removed her jacket and her shoes, and was beginning to unbutton her blouse.

"Well," she asked, as he continued to stare at her in silence, "are you going to join me?"

Bullaro was as excited as he was confused by the suddenness of what was happening. She looked at him inquiringly, her fingers on the buttons of her blouse.

"I guess we know what we're doing," Bullaro said finally, putting the aspirin on the bureau and walking toward the closet. He took off his shoes and undid his tie, though keeping his eyes fixed on her as she resumed undressing. She hung her blouse carefully over the back of a chair, placed her jewelry and glasses on the desk, and removed her skirt. She unhinged her brassiere, and Bullaro saw her large breasts, and then her firm thighs and buttocks as she turned, completely nude, toward the bed. She climbed under the covers, waiting as he removed his trousers and shorts. He was fully erect, and as he walked self-consciously across the room he was aware that she was now watching him.

She said nothing as he got into bed, but he quickly felt her hands moving across his chest and stomach and down to his penis. He lay on his back, doing nothing as she stroked him, and then moved on top of him. She was the aggressor, the manipulator of every move, and he was enjoying her sense of domination. She seemed so different from his wife and other women—she did not seek comfort in words, or try to embrace him, or kiss him, or ask to be kissed. It was as if she wanted him in a purely physical way, free from emotional distractions, and soon she had straddled him and had inserted him in her; and for several moments she moved up and down with her eyes closed until, her grip tightening on his hips, she sighed softly, and stopped.

"That's better," she said.

"Better than an aspirin," he added, seeing her smile. Then she turned over, indicating that she was ready to satisfy him, and he moved on top of her and he came quickly.

They were in bed together no more than ten minutes. They remained there awhile longer, then she got up, put on her glasses, and began to dress. Her figure, Bullaro noted, was voluptuous and mature, and yet so incongruous with her small boyish face and her gamin hairstyle. Sexually she was like a man—the first hit-and-run female he had ever met.

"Tomorrow night," she said, as she finished dressing with her back to him, looking at herself in the mirror, "you can come to my room."

She turned toward him, and he nodded from the bed. Then she walked to the door, opening it slowly to be sure that no one was in the corridor, and, waving to him, she left, pulling the door softly behind her.

9

Barbara Cramer, born on a Missouri farm, perceived as an adolescent that she had been an unwanted child. Her mother, who was thirty-nine at Barbara's birth, had produced two other daughters nearly two decades before, when her marriage offered hope if not always happiness; but the unexpected arrival of Barbara in 1939 in a remote farmhouse that still had no interior plumbing promised only more drudgery and a continued commitment to a dismal domestic ritual.

Since Barbara shied away from her mother's sullenness, and since her older sisters had both left home early to marry, escaping to lives only moderately less grim, Barbara grew up with a minimum of female influence. When she was not attending the one-room Osage County schoolhouse—within which the sixth- and seventh-grade students sat in the front rows, to which the lessons were directed, while the younger ones sat in the back, absorbing whatever they could—she was helping her father on the farm, hoeing the garden, feeding the chickens, even driving a tractor through the wheat and corn fields.

The farm was seven miles from the closest town of Chamois, and Barbara's social life was restricted to a few friends on adjoining farms, most of them young boys with whom she played sports and from whom she soon learned about sex in an open, natural manner. One day when she was ten, she saw two boys she knew standing inside a barn moving their hands in front of them; and, after one of the boys called for her to join them, she approached closer and saw that each was stroking his penis.

Though she had sometimes seen her father nude when he bathed in a galvanized tub near the kitchen, she had never before seen an erect penis, and she reacted with unflinching curiosity. When the older boy, who was thirteen, asked if she would like to touch it, she did; and when he showed her how he wanted her to massage it, she obliged and she was more surprised than shocked later when she felt the throbbing and saw a creamy substance seeping up through her fingers.

As the younger boy masturbated himself to a climax, the older one kissed her, and she felt not abused but warm and wanted. After this, she and the older boy often masturbated one another in the hayloft; but, without ever discussing it, they sensed the peril of additional exploration and went no further.

Sex was never discussed in the Cramer household. When Barbara began to menstruate, her mother merely provided her with several small pieces of white sheets, told her to line her panties with them, and to burn the sheets later. It was the custom of farming women in that region to save old sheets and rags for this purpose, since modesty more than economy prevented them from buying the Kotex sold in the general store.

Barbara found the plain country women collectively unattractive, and it was not until she attended high school in Chamois that she met someone of her own sex that she considered physically appealing. Her name was Frances, and she was tall, dark-haired, and stylish, as popular with the boys as she was envied by the girls, all except Barbara, who, contented with her role as the class tomboy, did not feel competitive with feminine beauty. The two young women became quick friends, largely because they complemented one another: Frances was graceful and poised, Barbara driving and audacious. Barbara was unintimidated by boys, was quick to retort to their rowdy comments, and even sipped Bourbon from the bottles they occasionally sneaked into the school yard. The two girls were inseparable except during the summer months when Barbara worked full-time earning money for her support.

One summer she was employed in a country store that had a gas station in front and a dance hall in the back, and, in addition to pumping Phillips 66 and selling household supplies, she served beer in the back to the farmers and local boys, some of whom had their hair cut in the current Mohawk fashion—heads shaved bald except for a strip of hair extending down the middle.

During the following summer, wanting to be further from home, she traveled fifty miles to Jefferson City, lived in a rooming house owned by a classmate's aunt, and worked behind Woolworth's soda fountain, idling away many lonely afternoons listening on the radio to Elvis Presley singing "Heartbreak Hotel." Later she found a higher-paying job in a pants factory where, surrounded by cranky middle-aged seamstresses, she spent the day fingering crotches, zipping flies up and down, and thinking often of sex.

She was now sixteen and had recently lost her virginity to a Chamois student whom she thought she loved. He was more intelligent than most and was always careful to use condoms when they made love in his jalopy. Among their common interests was an abhorrence of farm life, and he spoke often of becoming a commercial airlines pilot. Though she did not consider herself sufficiently pretty or subservient to become a stewardess, she nevertheless applied to several airlines and asked to be based in St. Louis, but she was neither surprised nor disappointed when none accepted her.

While she did not know what she wished to do with her life, she was determined to avoid the hapless routine of rural poverty and childbearing that she had seen all around her. After graduation, she returned to Jefferson City as an X-ray technician in a hospital, and then moved to St. Louis with Frances to share an apartment. Frances had found a clerical job in an insurance office, while Barbara worked in the billing department of a cardboard manufacturer, a position she soon came to deplore. The female employees were segregated from the males, and in Barbara's department were fifteen doleful, pinch-mouthed women totally lacking in humor and spirit.

Barbara had yet to meet a woman who seemed happy with her work. In her reading of books and magazines she had never read a story about a businesswoman, a career woman who was successful, respected, prosperous, sexually free, not dependent on a man—and yet this was the sort of woman that Barbara vaguely hoped to become, if not in Missouri, then somewhere else; and when Frances one night suggested that they move to Los Angeles and live with her aunt, Barbara was ready to leave. Barbara's parents by this time were divorced, and her boyfriend had gone to Texas for flight training; she was leaving nothing behind.

Arriving in Los Angeles, she responded immediately to the mild climate, the palm trees, the cordiality of the new people she met. Here there seemed to be the perfect blend of work and pleasure, an emphasis on health and sports as well as productivity and materialism, and Barbara was confident that this was where she belonged.

Following a few weeks' stay with Frances' aunt, the two young women found an apartment of their own in Hollywood, held secretarial jobs that they considered temporary, and explored the city on weekends in a newly acquired used car. After months as a typist for the *Encyclopedia Americana*, Barbara found a better job in the contract department of a large automobile dealership, and it was here that she had her first affair with a married man, the boss's son-in-law.

She accompanied him to motels during lunchtime and occasionally in the evenings, and since she liked the sex and was not interested in marriage it was an agreeable arrangement that could have continued indefinitely had he not become so emotionally involved and possessive. One afternoon in bed, after he had tearfully revealed to her his frustrations with his wife and his domineering father-in-law, Barbara knew that their affair should end before it became too complicated.

She found a new job in the insurance department of another auto dealership, where she met a tall, rugged salesman who during the basketball season played in the National Basketball Association. She communicated her interest in him and he quickly reacted, but when they went to bed he proved to be a careless lover, a big, aggressive, insensitive bull who came quickly and then wanted to sleep. But she was nonetheless attracted to his athletic body, and she tolerated in him things that she would never have condoned in another man, partly because he was something of a celebrity, a man with a name, pride, an ego, as well as boyish charm that he effectively used to sell cars to the short, flabby men who were his fans.

She herself was doing well in her work, demonstrating an extraordinary efficiency that was appreciated by her employers and resulted in salary raises and increased responsibility. On weekends when she was not working she went water skiing, or snow skiing, or spent the time reading; and the only disturbing event in the otherwise auspicious move to Los Angeles was Frances' decision during their second year of living together to marry a man that she had been dating. Though her affection for Frances had never been sexually expressed, Barbara was strangely panicked by this news, saddened and confused; and later, when Frances moved out of the apartment, Barbara felt both abandoned and betrayed. She did not attend the wedding, nor did she ever see Frances again.

But she was fortunate in having befriended during this period a supportive and interesting man who, at seventy, was still very vigorous and debonair. He was one of the city's auto kings, selling fleets of vehicles each week, and he had hired Barbara

Cramer to help manage his insurance department. While he was shrewd and hard in his business dealings, he was always kindly toward her, and she saw in him the father she never had. He took her to expensive restaurants, convinced her that she was special, and encouraged her to pursue her ambitions without concern for the feminine tradition of restraint.

After a year with his firm, she was eager to find a job that offered more independence, and that was when she became an agent with New York Life. After buying from several retail stores the lists of their top customers, as well as compiling the names of people she had met through the automobile business, she spent endless hours on the telephone trying to arrange appointments; and then, in the new red Mustang convertible that she had just bought, she drove to all parts of the city to speak to people personally about the benefits of buying more life insurance. Although she encountered as much resistance as any other agent, she succeeded where others failed because she was more persistent and also because she concentrated on groups of people that had been largely ignored, such as career women, particularly nurses, who, being in daily contact with death and accidents, were very susceptible to her lectures on the importance of being adequately insured.

During her first two years at New York Life, when she was totally preoccupied with insurance and was earning close to $30,000 a year, she had no real interest in men; and so, in the relaxed atmosphere of the cocktail lounge on the first night at the Palm Springs convention, it came as a surprise to her that she suddenly felt a strong urge for sex.

When she was introduced to John Bullaro, she found him attractive and was aware of his strong body. But after sitting next to him for an hour at the table, she sensed that he was not the type to take the sexual initiative—and therefore, when he volunteered to get her an aspirin, she decided to follow him.

10

JOHN BULLARO'S AFFAIR with Barbara Cramer, which continued through the fall and winter into the spring of 1966, was characterized by quick midday sex in motels convenient to the office, followed by her driving off to business appointments while he lunched alone pondering erotic pleasure and also feeling at times a dyspeptic aftertaste induced by mild guilt and rising anxiety.

He feared that sooner or later his liaison with Barbara would be discovered by someone from the office and provoke a scandal that would jeopardize his career and his marriage; but so far nothing had happened to justify his trepidation. On the contrary, his life had improved since knowing Barbara Cramer—the sexual stimulation that she aroused in him had extended to his marriage, reviving his dormant interest in Judith and gaining her reciprocation. His career was also proceeding smoothly and he had recently learned that he would soon be sent by the company to New York City to receive top executive training in the home office.

Barbara was as pleased by the announcement as she had been professionally encouraging throughout their affair, and he was always impressed by her capacity to restrict their relationship to sex and shop talk without becoming emotionally involved with him and making demands on his marriage. She never telephoned him at home or complained about his unavailability at night and on weekends, and she revealed no curiosity about his wife except once to express interest in the fact that Judith was trained as a nurse.

Barbara's demeanor toward Bullaro in the office was flawlessly formal, even on days when they had gone earlier to a motel. Though they did not often have dinner together at night, when they did go out she occasionally picked up the check, and she sometimes paid their motel expenses. Once after he had been reluctant to accompany her to a particular motel because it was rather close to his home in Woodland Hills, Barbara had him wait in the car while she registered alone at the desk, and then she rejoined him with the room key in her hand.

She was the most independent, self-sufficient woman he had ever known, and while she intrigued him she also piqued him by her sometimes cool dispassionate manner in bed; it was as if their lovemaking meant no more to her than pumping gas into the red Mustang that she hastily drove to each business appointment. Still, if she were to become suddenly romantic, he knew that he would probably panic, and therefore he did not complain to her about the style of their relationship—it provided good extramarital sex that required little of his time and energy, did not threaten his job or marriage, and during the past year he had become accustomed to it and perhaps even dependent upon it.

And yet Bullaro's uneasiness about it persisted. He could not overcome the feeling that eventually it would cost him dearly, and he was rather relieved by the fact that he would be leaving Los Angeles in the fall to attend the executive training program in New York. But a few months before his departure, the relationship with Barbara Cramer abruptly ended in a way that he had not anticipated.

After not seeing her for weeks—she had complained of being preoccupied with interviews—Barbara telephoned him one afternoon to say that she had recently met a man who fascinated her; and in a voice that sounded uncharacteristically timid, she admitted that she might be in love. The man was an engineer, she went on, a brilliant technician who had worked on the rockets that had launched the astronauts; and while Bullaro congratulated her on her choice, he had the uncomfortable feeling that he was being unfavorably compared.

He quickly tried to persuade her to go out with him that night, but she politely refused. He called her a week later, but she repeated that she was now seeing only the engineer, adding that they were contemplating marriage. Bullaro finally conceded to himself that the affair was over, and that realization made him somewhat depressed.

He worked at the office through an uneventful summer, then took a short vacation with Judith and the children, and began anticipating his months ahead in New York. Though he would be in New York during most of the winter, he would be commuting regularly to Los Angeles on weekends, and as Judith drove him to the airport in September she said that she would miss him but took pleasure in the fact that this trip marked his rise to higher management. Judith seemed very cheerful and hardly sentimental as she said good-bye, and Bullaro boarded the plane feeling oddly disquieted.

It was a decade since he had last seen New York City as a student at NYU, and the company's skyscraper on Madison Avenue and Twenty-seventh Street was within walking distance of his old apartment in Greenwich Village. Though he spent his first Sunday afternoon strolling through Washington Square listening to the folk songs being sung by students around the fountain, and admiring the young women in miniskirts with their nipples protruding through their T-shirts, he was not as drawn to them as he had been enticed by the image of youthful freedom along the beaches in California. He was now more committed to the company, was conscious of the honor of being one of eleven New York Life insurance men selected from around the nation to be trained as a general manager. After completing the course, Bullaro and the ten others would return to their regions to preside over staffs of assistants and agents in a general office of New York Life. It would mean for Bullaro and the others more money and prestige, and an opportunity to move closer to the top.

The men stayed at the Roosevelt Hotel on Forty-fifth Street off Madison, and each weekday morning they took the subway or shared cabs to the New York Life building, except for Bullaro, who got out of bed earlier so that he could jog the eighteen blocks downtown as a way of staying in condition. While the sidewalks were not crowded at this hour, a few pedestrians stopped to observe him trotting past them in his dark suit and tie, his leather briefcase sometimes held under his arm like a football, and he half expected to hear a mock cheer or a comment that would reveal the impression he was creating, but all he ever heard above the noise of motor traffic was the rhythmic clapping of his heavy cordovans against the pavement.

Approaching the home office, Bullaro slowed to a walk and tucked in his shirt. The building was a gray Gothic skyscraper that soared thirty-four stories through a series of setbacks and terraces to a pyramidal roof topped by a golden lantern. On entering, Bullaro passed between ornamental bronze gates into a high-vaulted marble corridor that led to the ornate embossed doors of the elevators. The elevators moved quietly, and since the ceilings of the inner offices throughout the building were covered with noise-absorbing felt, the sounds of conversations and typewriters were muted. Bullaro felt like a parishioner in a cathedral, and his reverential attitude increased as he became more familiar with his firm and the history of insurance, which he perceived as a secular religion that offered value to life after death and catered to man's natural fear of the hereafter.

Visiting the archives of New York Life during his first week in the building, Bullaro saw in glass cases the famous signatures of entombed policyholders: General Custer, Rogers Hornsby, Franklin D. Roosevelt; and there were also on display the photographs of disasters that had been costly to the company—the Iroquois Theater fire in Chicago in 1903 in which nineteen policyholders burned to death; the San Francisco earthquake of 1906, which included in its devastation a branch office of New York Life; the supposedly indestructible *Titanic*, which sank in 1912 with eleven policyholders aboard, and the liner *Lusitania*, which was torpedoed in 1915 by German submarines, causing the death of eighteen passengers who had been insured by New York Life.

While various forms of maritime insurance had existed within seafaring nations since the Renaissance, Bullaro read that the practice of insuring human life in Europe after the seventeenth century had offended many church leaders, who denounced the underwriters as conjurers, death gamblers, and tamperers with the divine will. In several countries, including France, life insurance was banned until the late eighteenth century; but in the major nautical nations such as England, where it had long been the custom to insure ships and cargo against storms and pirates, there was little resistance to extending the protection to include inland property and people.

Bullaro read that it had been the English who introduced insurance selling to America, but as a business it floundered through most of the eighteenth century partly because the majority of citizens in the agrarian economy of the time lacked the surplus funds or disposition to pay in advance for an imagined emergency. With the coming of the Industrial Revolution, however, American insurance firms began to thrive as the guardians of materialism, and as Bullaro read the current pamphlets and figures he learned that the top insurance companies had now become, in the mid-1960s, among the wealthiest private enterprises in the land, exceeding even the leading oil companies in assets.

The preeminent insurer, Prudential Life, with $35 billion worth of assets, was $10 billion more affluent than Exxon, while the second largest insurer, Metropolitan Life, was $7 billion richer. Bullaro's firm, worth nearly $14 billion, was fourth among the insurers, being behind the $20 billion Equitable and ahead of the $13 billion John Hancock. More than thirty other American insurers were worth at least $1 billion each, and every day of the week the insurance industry took in $120 million, or more than forty cents from every man, woman, and child in the nation, while paying out only half that amount in such items as death claims and annuities. Ten percent of the nation's gross national product was spent on insurance.

But despite the industry's prominence, the men who ran the giant corporations remained largely anonymous, and if a newsmagazine wished to publish a lead story on the insurance business it would be unable to select a single recognizable face with a familiar name to put on the cover. Insurance seemed to cultivate among its leaders a quality of diffidence, and as Bullaro toured the executive tower in the New York Life building and looked up at the large oil paintings of past presidents that lined the walls—bewhiskered Victorians of the 1800s, bespectacled conservatives of the 1900s—he was impressed by the similarity of their expressions, their pervasive shyness and serenity: They were timid tycoons, and Bullaro wondered if his own personality and talent made him compatible with these eminent stewards of the public trust.

While he believed that he was sufficiently diligent and self-effacing to eventually qualify for the hierarchy of New York Life, he was never unaware of that deepest part of him that rebelled against corporate conformity, that was lured by fantasies of freedom, although, while in New York, he firmly repressed any expression of this. Each day at the home office, in manner and appearance, he was a model of the young executive on the rise. He seemed totally absorbed in the policies and theories of the company and in becoming knowledgeable about its newly structured major medical programs and group insurance plans. When he left the office, he often went out with his colleagues to dinner, but, unlike them, he did not stay out late drinking and he conserved his sexual energy for his weekend visits with Judith in Los Angeles.

* * *

The time away had a salubrious effect on their marriage, and each visit home was a renewed honeymoon. Judith, smiling at the airport gate, very blond and comely and distinguished in the crowd, embraced him warmly and conversed with him enthusiastically in the car, and later, after seeing the children, they made love with a fervor reminiscent of their courtship.

But when he returned permanently to Los Angeles and accepted his position as a general manager with his own office in Woodland Hills, presiding over a staff that included nine underwriters, his relationship with Judith gradually reverted to the predictable routine that it had been before his trip to New York. After a domestic day of caring for the children, Judith went to bed early, while he occupied himself in the living room with the increased work produced by his promotion.

Though he had not spoken to Barbara Cramer in months, he had heard that she was now married to the engineer John Williamson, had kept her job with the company, and was maintaining her established sales standards. Bullaro had thought of writing her a note or calling her to say hello, but before getting around to it he met her one afternoon near the elevator in the main office. She was very cordial and Bullaro felt more casual about being seen speaking with her now that she was married; it never occurred to him, as they made a date for lunch later in the week, that their relationship might again become sexual.

But during lunch, in her inimitable manner, Barbara suggested that they go to a motel. Bullaro thought at first that she was kidding, but when she repeated it, adding that he could wait in the car while she registered for the room, he called for the check and left the restaurant with her. He was as awed as ever by her impulsiveness and boldness, and also excited as he anticipated their lovemaking; but after they had pulled into the motel parking lot and she got out to register, he waited uneasily in the driver's seat, sitting lower than usual behind the wheel, questioning the wisdom of being here with a married woman while wondering whether she would sign her husband's surname in the registration book. He said nothing, however, as she returned to the car with the room key, preferring at this moment to avoid any mention of her marriage.

In the room she hastily removed her clothes, and Bullaro saw again her remarkable body, and soon felt her aggressive touch as he lay naked on the bed and she mounted him. The ease with which she achieved her satisfaction, and the agile manner with which she pulled him on top of her without disengaging him, reminded him of a tumbling act in a circus, and confirmed as well that her marriage had neither altered her sportive style nor diminished her desire for supplementary sex.

After they had finished and were relaxing on the bed, Bullaro asked if she was happily married. She answered that she was, adding that her husband was the most remarkable man she had ever known; he was sensitive and self-assured and was not intimidated by her individuality. In fact, she went on, he was encouraging her to become more independent than she was already, hoping that as she attained higher levels of fulfillment and self-awareness she would reinvest these assets into their marriage. A marriage should promote personal growth instead of limitations and restrictions, she went on, and as Bullaro listened with a certain cynicism he assumed that she was paraphrasing her husband. He had never heard her speak this way before, and while he was still bewildered by her husband's motives, and pondered what her husband would do if he knew what had just transpired in this bedroom, he remained silent as Barbara Williamson continued to explain for his benefit, and perhaps for her own, the kind of marriage she now had.

Most married people, she said, had "ownership problems": They wanted to totally possess their spouse, to expect monogamy, and if one partner admitted an infidelity to the other it would most likely be interpreted as a sign of a deteriorating marriage. But this was absurd, she said—a husband and wife should be able to enjoy sex with other people without threatening their primary relationship, or lying or feeling guilty about their extramarital experiences. People cannot expect all of their needs to be satisfied by a spouse, and Barbara said that her relationship with John Williamson was enhanced by their mutual respect for freedom, and they both felt sufficiently secure in their love to admit openly to one another that they sometimes made love to other people.

Hearing this made Bullaro nervous, and he quickly interrupted to say that he certainly hoped that she was not planning to tell her husband about this motel visit. She laughed, and replied casually that such an admission would not in the least upset John Williamson because he was not the jealous type. Bullaro suddenly felt panic and fury rising within him, and he jumped out of bed and was about to scream when she quickly held up her arms, shook her head, and told him to relax, calm down, she would say nothing to her husband. Bullaro was barely pacified; and though she repeated her promise, he did not completely trust her.

He decided after leaving the motel that he would never go to bed with her again. Her libertine life with her new husband and her ridiculous philosophy about sexual honesty was guaranteed to boomerang, and when it did he wanted to be nowhere in sight. Having read enough newspaper stories about the murders of wives and paramours by husbands considered not the jealous type, Bullaro knew that he had better be wary of Barbara Williamson. At the very least his continuing involvement with her, now that she was experimenting with her new-fangled freedom, could scandalize his marriage and abruptly terminate his promising career. As an insurance man, he assessed his current situation as too risky.

Two days later, when his secretary buzzed his office to announce that Mrs. Williamson was on the line, he was ready to tell her that he was permanently unavailable for lunch and whatever else she had in mind; but when he picked up the phone, she greeted him with a rather urgent question about an insurance problem, and her tone was strictly business throughout their discussion. She also informed him that there was an outstanding woman who wished to apply to New York Life for a job as an agent, and Barbara requested that he conduct the interview and give the company's customary evaluation test. Bullaro, whose responsibility included recruitment, arranged the time on his calendar for the following afternoon, and Barbara thanked him and hung up.

The applicant that Barbara escorted into his office was a lissome woman in her late twenties with long dark hair, angular features, and expressive eyes that focused warmly upon him throughout the interview. Her name was Arlene Gough, she had been born in Spokane, and she now lived in Los Angeles with her husband, an engineer. She said that she had worked as an interior decorator and also as a secretary at Hughes Aircraft, but she expressed confidence in her ability to sell insurance. She was conservatively dressed in a well-tailored gray suit, and Bullaro was impressed by her articulateness and poise as well as by her sensuality, and he hoped his attraction would not be too obvious to Barbara, sitting across from his desk.

When his secretary came in to say that the test papers were ready, Barbara waved good-bye and left, and Arlene Gough was shown into the conference room. It was now late afternoon, and before Mrs. Gough had completed the examination most of the staff had gone, and the office was about to close. She seemed confident as she reentered Bullaro's office and asked him when the results would be known. He said that it would take a few days and that he would keep her informed. She asked if he would mind if she remained in the building while he finished his work, and if he would then drive her home—her husband was away on business and Barbara had been unable to wait. She lived not far from Bullaro, and he said he would be happy to drive her.

In the car she sat very close to him, was convivial and attentive, and when they arrived at her home she invited him in for a drink. The house was quiet as they entered, and after she had returned from the kitchen with ice she stood near him at the bar and looked into his eyes as if waiting to be kissed; and when he did, she responded immediately and placed her body firmly against his. He felt her arms around his neck, and then her hands moving slowly down his back to his hips and thighs, and finally she whispered that they should go into the bedroom.

Whatever influence Bullaro's normally cautious character might have exerted over the passions of his penis were now nonexistent, and he unhesitatingly followed her and quickly undressed. Soon he saw her lovely nude body that was as graceful and sinewy as a dancer's; and later, when he entered her, he felt her long legs wrap around him, her cool heels pressing against the lower part of his back. Bullaro was ecstatic, and as he came he heard her sigh, felt her movements quicken, and he could hardly believe what was happening in his life—Arlene was as sexually voracious as Barbara, and he could only conclude that there must be something quite bizarre or lacking in their marriages.

Since Arlene's husband was due home in the evening, Bullaro left shortly after 7 P.M., feeling pleasantly exhausted as he drove through the quiet suburban streets into Woodland Hills. He saw Judith on the lawn as he turned into the driveway, and getting out of the car he immediately apologized for his tardiness, explaining that he had been obliged to have a few drinks with an agent who was having personal problems. If Judith was skeptical, she did not show it, and as he went into the house with her he was spared further explanation by the interrupting noise from the television set and the cries of his children.

The next day Barbara telephoned him at the office to ask how he had liked Arlene, indicating that she might be aware that they had gone to bed; but Bullaro replied formally that he was reserving his opinion until he knew the results of the examination.

Bullaro was anxious to get off the phone, and when Barbara suggested lunch, he quickly agreed to a date later in the week and hung up.

An hour later, Arlene Gough telephoned to say how much she had enjoyed being with him and expressed the hope that after she knew her husband's travel schedule for the following week she might call him and arrange to see him again. She quickly added that she wanted to see him regardless of the results of the test, and Bullaro was relieved to hear this, for he had just decided that it would be a grave mistake to hire her.

During the next two months Bullaro visited the Gough residence several times on his way home from work; and, against his better judgment, he also resumed seeing Barbara Williamson. Resolutions to the contrary, he found it difficult to resist Barbara's persistence, partly because he enjoyed the brief erotic rendezvous and he also thought it unwise to reject her now that he was also seeing her friend Arlene. Though neither woman ever made sexual inquiries to him about the other, he assumed that they were confiding in one another, but this possibility did not bother him as long as he believed that their husbands were unsuspecting.

Barbara's constant reassurance had finally convinced him to stop fretting, to worry less and enjoy more; no one was being hurt, she reasoned, and much pleasure was being exchanged. He had to agree, and he was also aware that his intrigues with Barbara and Arlene had revived his sexual interest in his wife; and since he was functioning efficiently in the office, he saw no reason why this happy blend of circumstances should not continue unabated.

But on a rainy Monday morning in the early winter of 1967, as Bullaro arrived at his office, his secretary informed him that she had just received two calls from a persistent man named John Williamson. A sudden queasiness penetrated Bullaro's stomach, and he felt a feverish chill. The secretary, who apparently did not realize that the caller was Barbara's husband, said that he had left no message except that he would soon call again.

Bullaro nodded, entered his office, and closed the door softly. He lowered himself slowly into his red leather chair, rubbed his forehead, and attempted to remain calm. On his desk facing him were photographs of Judith and the children, and on the walls were hung sales awards from the company, his diploma from NYU, a plaque commending his support of the Boys' Club of Hollywood. Quickly his whole life seemed unhinged, about to crack into pieces, and he hated himself for his foolishness and he blamed Barbara, too, for misleading him. He was sure that if he had been guided by his true instincts he would not be in this situation, although at this moment there was nothing he could do but wait and prepare for the confrontation. The worst that could happen would be a physical threat to his life, or a scandalous highly publicized court case that would embarrass Judith and the insurance company. Even if Williamson turned out to be, as Barbara suggested, an unpossessive man, he might nonetheless seek some financial compensation, blackmail, a personal loan or business favor, or perhaps he would request something unusual and extraordinary.

Bullaro heard the phone ring, then his secretary buzzing to inform him that Mr. Williamson was on the line. With all the jauntiness that Bullaro could summon, he said hello. The voice on the other end was low and resonant, so soft that Bullaro could barely hear it.

"I'm John Williamson, Barbara's husband," he began, "and I was wondering if we might have lunch."

"Yes, of course," Bullaro quickly replied, "how about today?" Though Bullaro already had an important business luncheon scheduled, he decided to cancel it rather than prolong the agony and suspense.

"Fine," Williamson said. "May I come by and pick you up around 12:30?"

Bullaro agreed, and Williamson thanked him and hung up.

For the rest of the morning Bullaro went through the motions of management, fingering documents on his desk, watching the clock. He tried calling Barbara at her office, but there was no answer, and he did not want to try her at home and risk being greeted by her husband's voice.

At precisely 12:30, Bullaro's secretary buzzed and announced that Mr. Williamson was waiting in the reception room. Bullaro left his office at once, and, with a hand extended in greeting, he walked toward a large broad-shouldered man wearing a dark suit, white shirt, and tie; he was in his mid-thirties, had very blond hair and a strong leonine face dominated by pale blue eyes that were heavy-lidded and somber. Forcing a smile, Williamson shook hands and, in a soft voice that seemed southern, he thanked Bullaro for making himself available on such short notice.

Outside it was overcast but no longer raining. In the parking lot Williamson suggested that they take his car, a beige Jaguar

XKE, which Bullaro quickly admired. Climbing inside, Bullaro noticed that there was an air-conditioning unit that had not yet been fully installed, and Williamson explained that he had just bought it, adding that he liked doing all his own mechanical work.

Williamson drove fast, shifted gears abruptly, and Bullaro saw through the tight-fitting suit that he had heavy biceps and forearms, and his ruddy freckled hands were strong and had thick fingers. Although Williamson never turned to look at him, concentrating on the road as he drove, Bullaro sensed that he was under intense observation, that his every nervous twitch might be perceived by Williamson's peripheral vision. Bullaro could think of nothing to say but felt compelled to speak, and he ventured a comment about Williamson's mild southern accent. Williamson answered that he had been born in Alabama, but added that he had not lived there since finishing high school. Bullaro waited for Williamson to continue, but only silence followed until Bullaro asked where he had gone to college. Williamson curtly replied that he had not gone to college. Bullaro wished that he had withheld that question.

As they drove on, the silence seemed increasingly foreboding, but rather than risk another awkward question Bullaro kept quiet and tried to relax by looking out the window and affecting an attitude of nonchalance. They were driving through Canoga Park in the Valley over roads with which Bullaro was quite familiar—he had sold insurance in this community, had ridden through it on his bicycle, had patronized its restaurants. As Williamson turned off the main road and directed the car up the street toward the Red Rooster Restaurant, Bullaro's anxiety increased—this was where he had often gone with Barbara, and the choice of this place for lunch now struck Bullaro as darkly contrived.

Saying nothing as he got out of the car, Bullaro followed Williamson into the main room, where, after a few moments' wait, they were escorted to a table near the back. The restaurant was crowded and noisy, but a waiter was mercifully available so that Bullaro could quickly call for a drink. Williamson sat with his hands folded, hesitating. He seemed either shy or troubled. Bullaro leaned forward in his chair. Finally, Williamson spoke.

"I know about you and Barbara," he said quietly.

Bullaro, looking down at the table, said nothing, but he felt completely trapped, and he hated Barbara for having betrayed him.

"I know about it," Williamson went on, "and I think it's a good thing."

Bullaro looked up with disbelief, doubting that he had heard correctly.

"You think it's a good thing?" Bullaro repeated, his voice rising with incredulity.

"Yes," Williamson said. "You are good for her. You fulfill certain needs in her life. She thinks a lot of you. I think it's wonderful and," he added softly but decisively, "I'd like it to continue."

Bullaro was now even more confused, and he thought that Williamson might be taunting him with a twisted sense of humor. As he studied Williamson's face, however, and saw the blue eyes regarding him gently, he was convinced of Williamson's sincerity, although he still had no idea how he should react, what he should say, or what was the motivation behind Williamson's request that the affair with Barbara be continued.

The waiter arrived with the drinks, allowing Bullaro a few extra seconds in which to think before speaking. He certainly wanted to say nothing inappropriate now, but he had momentarily lost all sense of rationale. He had entered this restaurant expecting to be threatened or blackmailed by a vengeful husband; instead, he had been complimented by Williamson, and was being encouraged to continue sleeping with his wife. Under these peculiar circumstances, Bullaro was not sure he wanted to; but he wanted even less to risk offending this unusual man who might, if affronted, resort to vindictiveness.

As the waiter left, Bullaro quickly decided that he had better go along with Williamson for the time being, avoid all arguments and debates, and perhaps flatter him if possible. Bullaro did feel an inward exhilaration because his job and marriage were apparently not in jeopardy, at least for the present; and wishing to celebrate his sense of relief, he held up his glass in a toast, thanked Williamson for his kind words, and expressed admiration for Williamson's emancipated marriage.

"It's really wonderful that you and Barbara have been able to reach the place where you are," Bullaro began.

"Yes," Williamson agreed, "but there are other places we're now trying to reach."

Bullaro nodded, acknowledging that he had already heard from Barbara about Williamson's conviction that marriage should not encourage feelings of ownership, that couples ideally should be able to have sexual relations with other people without inspiring guilt or jealousy.

Williamson accepted Bullaro's summary, but said it was more complicated and ambitious than that. There was a group of people, Williamson said, who met regularly at his home to discuss and explore ways of achieving greater fulfillment in marriage. The American marriage was in trouble, he said, the traditional roles of the sexes demanded redefinition, and the therapists and psychologists were too aloof professionally, and unprepared personally, to deal with the problem.

But Williamson's group was making remarkable progress, he suggested, because the members were willing to use themselves "as instruments for change in others." The group was largely composed of average middle-class people who held responsible jobs in the community, were integrated in the social system, but, being cognizant of certain limitations and flaws within their surroundings and themselves, they sought improvements. Williamson mentioned that his group included a woman in whom Bullaro had already shown interest, Arlene Gough.

"Yes," Bullaro said, surprised to hear that she was involved, "but it's becoming too complicated and I'd like to cool it."

"Well, then it will be cooled," Williamson replied casually.

Bullaro was impressed by Williamson's easy confidence, and he wondered if perhaps it had been Williamson who sent Arlene Gough to the insurance office that first day with Barbara. The whole arrangement seemed somewhat eerie, a sexual scheme of some sort that disturbed Bullaro; and yet, as Williamson continued during lunch to describe the interesting men and women who gathered at his home, where they sometimes conducted their meetings in the nude, Bullaro felt himself increasingly curious, lured against his will.

As the lunch ended, Williamson said that he hoped Bullaro would visit his home and meet his friends. Bullaro said that he would be happy to do so.

"Good," Williamson said, "tomorrow night at eight o'clock."

Bullaro, alarmed at how quickly things were moving, fearful as he saw himself being drawn closer to Williamson's erotic world, concealed his uneasiness and said that he would be there.

11

History is but an invention of man to bring order to his past. Evolution is not an invention but the real fact and master; when man understands this fully, in the context of his being, he will bring order to his future and finally comprehend his past.

—JOHN WILLIAMSON

WILLIAMSON'S PAST BEGAN during the Depression in an Alabama swampland south of Mobile, an indolent nameless place of piney woods and cypress trees, of log cabins and clannish families, of birds and squirrels and rabbits that were stalked each morning for food by men who, like their prey, were guided by the primal demands of their nature.

The men killed with slingshots as well as rifles, and the women cooked on wood-burning iron stoves that provided the only heat within the cabins, which during winter were often rained upon by sleet and surrounded with ice. Summers in the backwoods were hot and humid, with so little breeze at times that the leaves did not rustle, the birds sat silently in the trees, and the only sound around the water was an occasional pop of a bubble on the stagnant surface made by an unseen creature nibbling below.

At night the woodlands crackled with crickets and locusts and crawled with snakes, but the two dozen people who occupied the six cabins that were clustered in the clearing—the family and kin of John Williamson—walked fearlessly through the familiar paths of this dubious paradise, preferring it to the subtler uncertainties of outer civilization. Even if the men could have found full-time jobs in the farming region and mills beyond, they would have remained in the woods where they understood the sounds and echoes of isolation, and had learned to survive as hunters

and fishermen and makers of moonshine, which they later sold
to the bootleggers who serviced the hamlets and towns where
liquor was outlawed.

The stills were sheltered in the swamps, and the boiling of
the corn and sugar was done by one of Williamson's uncles,
while Williamson's father, Claud, who had one arm, drove the
whiskey to the bootleggers at night in an old car that was rusty
and battered but mechanically perfect.

Claud Williamson was a wiry, dark-haired, ill-tempered man
who during his youth had crushed his left arm against a moving
freight train that he had been attempting to climb. Though he
learned to compensate physically, the mental adjustment was
more difficult, and long after the injury he imagined pain in the
place where his left arm and fingers had been, and he sometimes
dreamed that the missing limb was being consumed by insects
invading the burial box, and he was also convinced that the arm
had been buried in an awkwardly bent position and that this was
contributing to his discomfort. Finally he dug up the box and
saw that his preconceptions had been right; and after he had
rearranged the arm in a straighter position and had sealed a
slight opening in the wood against the infiltrating insects, he felt
the lingering pain leave his body.

John Williamson's mother, Constance, born in the Midwest,
had settled in the Alabama woodlands with Claud almost as an
act of rebellion against her own mother, whom she despised.
Her mother was a buxom traveling show dancer from Chicago,
a wandering libertine who left Constance's father for a handsome gambler, and then, after that romance ended, had a series
of affairs with other men while Constance, an only child, was
usually left alone at night or was entrusted to casual acquaintances for sometimes weeks and months.

As a young girl, Constance grew up very lonely but adjust-
able, independent-minded, and introspective, studious in the
several schools she attended and an omnivorous reader. Unlike
her flamboyant mother, who dressed with a flapper's flair and
sought constant attention from men, Constance cared little about
how she looked in clothes or the impression she was creating.
She was a plain, round-faced blonde with expressionless blue
eyes who as a teenager, and throughout her life, was overweight.

After her mother had settled in Mobile with a new husband,
a Nash automobile dealer, Constance, who was then fifteen, ran
away from home. When her mother next located her, Constance
was living with the group in the woods, was pregnant, and had

married nineteen-year-old Claud Williamson. Resisting all attempts by her mother and stepfather to reclaim her, Constance remained with Williamson in the woodlands, where her daughter was born in 1924; and eight years later, after Constance had twice left the heavy-drinking Claud but each time returned, a son was born to them in 1932: This was John Williamson.

While the primitive living conditions with Claud rarely seemed idyllic, Constance nevertheless found comfort in the communal intimacy, a sense of family among rustic strangers. The vegetables that were grown, the game and fish that were caught, were exchanged within the group, and there was also a spirit of sharing in each other's personal problems and difficult chores. The men helped one another in the building or enlarging of their homes and storage shacks, and the women served as midwives during the birth of children. Everyone's children roamed freely in the outdoors, and when a child was injured or frightened he ran not necessarily to a parent but to the nearest adult.

When the children reached school age, they walked together each morning, sometimes without shoes, through a mile-long path to a dirt road where a bus stopped and took them an additional ten miles to a country schoolhouse. Later in the afternoon they returned to help the adults with the cleaning and preparing of food and the chopping of logs for firewood. During leisure hours, in the privacy of trees and bushes, there was considerable sexual adventuring among teenagers, and because of the insularity of their families, sexual contact between young boys and girls who were cousins was very common. John Williamson had intercourse for the first time at the age of twelve with a slightly older cousin, but the incest taboo was adhered to by all members of an immediate family.

Many people within the settlement were of French extraction and had been baptized Catholic, and on Sundays the faithful among them traveled to a small roadside church, attended also by Creoles, to hear Mass celebrated by an old Jesuit priest who had driven the twenty miles from Mobile. Constance Williamson, a Catholic convert, played the organ and sang, but no other member of her family was influenced by religion, and her sensuous daughter, Marion, a dark-eyed brunet with a voluptuous figure, was believed by the more righteous women to be under Satan's sway, for there was no other explanation for Marion's wild and rampant behavior.

Marion Williamson wore the tightest clothes she could find,

and from the time she was fourteen there was not a man in the woods who did not lust for her body. Her awareness of this made her even more flirtatious, being endlessly pleased with the effect she could arouse in the opposite sex; but she sensed early in life that none of these men were worthy of her charms, nor could they provide her with what she really wanted—an escape from stagnation and the claustrophobic cabin of her surly father and her serene and vegetating mother.

She regarded her mother almost as a lost survivor of some secret tragedy, a wolf child in the wilderness, and Marion felt far less identity with her mother than she did with her maternal grandmother, that aging flapper who on rare occasions she was taken to visit in Mobile. Her grandmother was an attractive perfumed woman with dyed dark hair and large breasts pressing up against her well-made gowns, and she lived in a comfortably furnished home and owned a big car provided by the hefty German who was her second husband but would not be her last. She drank martinis and chain smoked Chesterfields, had a sense of humor and exuded energy, and as Marion compared this worldly woman with her own pale and frumpy mother, she was seeing evolution in reverse, and there was no doubt in her youthful mind as to which woman had so far been the wiser.

Marion's desire for escape was also prompted at this time by her awareness that the entire Mobile area was being invaded by thousands of free-spending pilots and naval men who were being mobilized for possible action in an upcoming war. It was 1940; the radio news spoke of Japanese and German aggressions, and each day the skies over the Mobile swamplands roared with military planes flown from the nearby Brookley Air Base or from the Pensicola Naval Training Station across the bay in Florida. The shipyards of Mobile were now busy with defense contracts, and soon there would be such a demand for workers that even the men in the woods would be recruited, and among those hired, despite his having one arm, was Marion's father.

On weekends the sidewalks of bayside cities were crowded with airmen and sailors cruising for women, and one that they would soon see, looking older than her age, and smiling, was Marion Williamson, who had run away from home. Before her parents would again hear from her, she would marry a serviceman, becoming a bride at fifteen.

But the marriage did not curb her restlessness, and within a few months, with the cooperation of the military, the relationship was dissolved. At the age of sixteen, however, she was married again, this time to a naval pilot who was ten years her senior. His name was John Wiley Brock, and he took her from Pensicola to Norfolk, where a son was born to them in February 1941.

When Brock was assigned to duty in Pearl Harbor, Marion and the baby moved in with Brock's parents in Montgomery, but after the Japanese raid on Pearl Harbor in December 1941, which Brock survived, Marion left with the child for California, explaining to her in-laws that she wanted to be closer to her husband while awaiting his return. But in California she met another man and began having an affair, placing her infant in a children's home; and soon her in-laws in Alabama received an angry message from Brock aboard the carrier *Enterprise* informing them of her behavior and asking that they fly to California to retrieve the little boy. This they did, bringing the child back to Montgomery and eventually becoming, despite Marion's protests, her son's legal guardians. Ensign Brock meanwhile rewrote his will and military insurance policy in an attempt to deprive his wife of certain claims as his beneficiary, and he also established a trust fund for his son, which was one of his final acts before Japanese antiaircraft fire hit his torpedo plane during the battle of Midway and sent him crashing to his death.

In 1943 Marion became the wife of a naval officer named Richard McElligott, an Annapolis graduate with whom she would have two sons and a daughter; but this relationship, too, did not diminish her drive for adventures with other men. In time she left the naval officer for a public relations man from Columbia Pictures with whom she had another son, only to leave this husband later for a Brazilian rancher.

During her endless odyssey out of the woods, like a beautiful vagrant bird in tireless flight, she settled briefly in dozens of cities in the United States, Europe, and South America, and held a variety of jobs—a tour guide in Rio de Janeiro, a barmaid in Taramolinas, an assistant buyer in the children's department of Saks Fifth Avenue in New York, a cashier at a Hawaiian restaurant in Beverly Hills called the Luau; and periodically, and always unannounced, she returned to Alabama to see her parents and also her grandmother. Her last visit with her grandmother before the latter's death was spent in a honky-tonk on the Alabama-Mississippi state line where the two women, together with Marion's pot-smoking daughter, spent the evening dancing to jukebox music and playing the slot machines.

* * *

Of all the men who knew Marion, perhaps the one who most understood her nomadic nature, and emulated it, was her brother John, who was also obliged to her for providing him with his first glimpse of the larger world beyond the trees. As a schoolboy he twice was invited to other sections of the country to stay with her and her third husband, the naval officer, Richard McElligott. On the first occasion, in 1943—when McElligott was assigned to a cruiser in Boston—the eleven-year-old Williamson lived in their apartment in Cambridge for six months and attended a Boston public school. In 1947, when Williamson was fifteen, he spent the summer with the McElligotts in Alhambra, California, near Los Angeles, where he met a group of teenaged drivers of modified racing cars and hot rods and helped them with the maintenance of their engines. Even at this age, John Williamson was a skilled mechanic.

In Alabama he had spent many hours after school working as a mechanic's apprentice at a roadside garage not far from where his parents during the war had moved their house by rolling it on logs to a clearing beyond the woods. Williamson was a quiet tinkerer, a lean brooding boy with blond almost-white hair and soiled fingers invariably fiddling with the parts of failing farm trucks, malfunctioning hunting rifles, broken record players. He had an instinctive sense of mechanical relationships, could feel his way through a repair. As a twelve-year-old he had built his own radio, using wire and discarded metal he had found in the woods, including a piece of copper he had stolen from one of the moonshine distilleries, resulting in a brutal beating from his father.

In the country high school he attended, he was an excellent student in science and mathematics and very poor in history. There were eighteen students in his class, but he was not particularly friendly with any of them. The presence of his irascible father inhibited him from ever inviting a classmate home after school, and he also preferred being alone much of the time so that he could read books, work on machinery, or communicate with the voices of distant strangers via his ham radio set.

While there were farm girls nearby that he occasionally slept with, and one who allowed him to photograph her in the nude, Williamson was never seriously involved, and his fantasies focused mainly on his solitary escape from all that he had known in the rural South. After he completed high school in 1949, his sister wrote that she had arranged for him an appointment to Annapolis; but the idea of rigid academic confinement was unappealing, and he enlisted instead in the Navy. After boot camp in San Diego, and training in electronics at naval schools in northern California, Williamson was sent thousands of miles further west to join American occupational forces on a series of small primitive islands in the South Pacific that would be his home for the better part of the next four years.

During this time he developed into one of the Navy's most versatile electronics technicians, being adept in the maintenance and repair of all types of equipment from teletype machines to radar and sonar. Assigned first within the Marshall Islands to a bleak, almost treeless atoll called Kwajalein, on which a thousand sailors and airmen dwelled in a state of unflagging tedium, his status as a maintenance specialist soon allowed him to travel on naval patrol planes to several other islands on which he met not only a variety of military and civilian personnel, including women, but also the native inhabitants, which to him were far more interesting.

One of his favorite places was the island of Ponape in the Carolines, a volcanic elevation of lush land with beautiful jungles and rain forests, waterfalls and streams, and a few thousand friendly natives who, like the inhabitants of most other islands, spoke their own language and had their particular culture and customs. Williamson eventually learned their language and was invited into their homes, became familiar with their artifacts and participated in their ceremonies; he also drank their kava, a potent liquid made from the root of pepper plants, and at times this remote island seemed hauntingly reminiscent of the backwoods boyhood that Williamson thought he had left behind.

As the military forces gradually abandoned several islands in the early 1950s to the trusteeship of the United States Interior Department, which supervised them under a United Nations charter, John Williamson accepted a premature discharge from the Navy in exchange for agreeing to become a civilian government employee assigned to help maintain all the navigational and communications equipment necessary for the United States to continue its watchful contact within the South Pacific.

Assisted by both American and native technicians, Williamson made his office on the island of Truk, but he traveled thousands of miles each week checking the facilities at other outposts. One day while visiting an island in the western Carolines called Yap, he met an attractive blond German woman three years older than himself who was living alone in a Quonset hut and was employed in the records department of the American hospital at Yap. Her name was Lilo Goetz and she aspired to becoming an anthropologist, an expert on native culture in the South Pacific, which was a part of the world that had fascinated her ever since as a little girl in Berlin she had seen the first movie version of *Mutiny on the Bounty*. She read all the library books available on the South Pacific during her early school days, and in 1950, leaving her parents' home in the American sector of Berlin, she flew to Honolulu and spent the next two years studying at the University of Hawaii.

After that she traveled widely through the Pacific and lived briefly on several islands before settling in Yap, and she knew she was adjusting successfully to her new environment when she finally became comfortable at making love to a Yapese man in the sitting and squatting positions most islanders preferred. Such positions required fine balance and strong legs, which in her case had been developed through years of athletic exercise and a love of dancing, and it was her appearance of conspicuous good health that greatly appealed to Williamson when he first met her in 1953 at a party given by one of the staff directors of her hospital.

Overcoming his usual reticence with women he did not know, Williamson engaged her in conversation and asked if she would have dinner with him when he returned to Yap on the following week. She accepted graciously and, while she did not mention it at the time, she was already somewhat familiar with him, having recently made inquiries after noticing him from her office window one day during a hurricane while he stood on a nearby tower, seeming oblivious to the raging wind and rain as he took weather photographs. She had enjoyed watching him, his drenched and buffeted figure reminding her of the storm-swept sea captains she had seen in movies, perched bravely and defiantly on their masts; although, after dining with him, she discovered to her satisfaction that he did not seem in the least bit bold, reckless, or carefree. Instead, she found him reserved and pensive, an attentive listener and extremely well read, a little melancholy perhaps—and, where sex was concerned, quietly persistent. Though clearly disappointed when she refused to sleep with him after their first few dinner dates, he continued to telephone her and arrange to see her after each flight in from Truk; and as an indication of his desire to please her—after she had reacted negatively to the tattoo on his left arm, calling it the mark of a ruffian he was not—he went to a doctor and had it removed.

Soon Williamson was not only her lover but had also persuaded her to join him in Truk, which was eight hundred miles from Yap. He had hastened her departure by convincing her that the natives of Yap were becoming increasingly unhappy with the presence of Westerners, an opinion she was willing to accept after she observed one evening two unsmiling Yapese men loitering near her living quarters, brandishing machetes. In Truk, staying with Williamson, she felt secure and contented, and in March 1954 they were married on that island, spent their honeymoon there, and she considered this period of her life quintessentially romantic.

But in November, when she was six months pregnant, she developed a case of pernicious anemia, and Williamson thought that they should finally leave the Pacific to live on the mainland of America, not only for Lilo's benefit but for his own as well. He was no longer challenged by his work and was also tired of the transitory existence at sea, the flying and floating from place to place, the flimsy housing on tropical islands. He had heard, too, that there now were opportunities for engineers and technicians on the eastern coast of Florida, in and around Cape Canaveral, where the government was embarking on a missile program that, it was hoped, would one day launch satellites into space. Several major corporations were committed to spending large sums of money on space research and development; and American scientists, together with Wernher von Braun and other transplanted German missile men now employed by the American military, were designing larger, more powerful versions of the V-2 rockets used by the Nazis during World War II.

Since Lilo was not only willing but eager to live in the United States, they left Truk as soon as she was well enough to travel; and in late February 1955, a month after they had arrived in Florida, and Williamson had been hired by Boeing, a son was born to them. Lilo named him Rolf. Having a child diverted her from the disappointment she felt at having to live in a small dank motel that was isolated on an oceanfront wilderness a few miles from the military base at Cape Canaveral. This was not the Florida she had read about in travel magazines—here it was all desolate dunes and scrawny palms backed by swamps and dominated by mosquitoes. Located more than a hundred miles down the coast from Daytona Beach, with an even longer drive southward to Fort Lauderdale, Cape Canaveral was as yet unprepared to accommodate the women and children who had followed the missile men and technicians to this sequestered seaside rocket range. The closest grocery store, in the town of Cocoa Beach, was three miles away. The nearest movie theater was fifteen miles; the hospital where Rolf had been born was twenty miles; and for a good restaurant or a modicum of night life it was necessary to drive sixty miles inland to Orlando.

Nostalgic as she sometimes was for the picturesque islands of the South Pacific, Lilo was also aware that her husband seemed happy with his work, although military regulations prevented him from discussing much of it with her. Each morning he drove their small black Ford convertible to the air base and joined other engineers and technicians in the hangars where their offices and laboratories were, and in the evening he returned to the motel to have dinner in their two-room apartment. Nearly everyone in the motel, as well as the people occupying the rickety frame houses on the edge of the highway, was somehow connected with the military mission at Cape Canaveral, and it seemed ironic to Lilo that these pioneers in futuristic technology would be living and working in such antiquated, ramshackled surroundings.

But this began to change in 1956 as new homes and motels were constructed back from the beach and along the lagoons; and in 1957—after the Soviet Union's *Sputnik* had shocked America—there suddenly seemed to be an unlimited amount of government funds available for the space race with the Russians. Each day military planes landed at the Cape with high-ranking officers and scientists from Washington, and von Braun and his retinue commuted regularly from Huntsville. Taller towers, more launching pads and hangars were built along the waterfront, and the number of missile workers doubled and tripled. Real estate developers and speculators exploited the swampland around Cocoa Beach; stores, saloons, fast-food places opened and were joined by the operators of vending machines, gas stations, Laundromats, and pharmacies as well as insurance agents, doctors, clergyman, and bar girls.

Just before the land boom, Lilo and John Williamson built a small house on two acres of Cocoa Beach lagoon property for less than $10,000, a value that soon quadrupled. Williamson left Boeing for a better job at Lockheed, and was now among the engineers working on the X-17, the Polaris, and other missiles, and he was also sent out of town on unexplained trips. When at the Cape, he sometimes worked through the day and night, and the frequent failures and malfunctions of the early rockets kept

Williamson and his co-workers in an almost constant state of fatigue and depression. They all felt the pressure of having to catch up to the Russians, whose larger rockets were now equipped to carry a dog and even a man into orbit; and the increasing presence of the press at Cape Canaveral meant that no American mishap would long remain a secret.

At home with Lilo and his son, Williamson was tense and remote. He slept irregularly and spent many hours in the middle of the night reading technical manuals or science fiction novels, or preoccupying himself with the design or maintenance of some mechanical gadget. He demonstrated little interest in his son, who was now close to three years of age; and on a Sunday morning in August 1958, while Williamson was on the front lawn adjusting the propeller on a swamp buggy, the little boy fell over the side of the wall into the lagoon. The splash could not be heard because of the noise from the propeller, and when the child became entangled under a docked sailboat, he could not rise to the surface.

When Lilo, who had been in the kitchen, came out to look for him and did not find him, she ran toward the beach. Williamson searched along the lagoon, dived into the water, but failed to see the trapped body. Later, after the police had arrived, the dead child was discovered. Lilo collapsed and required sedation for the next two months. John Williamson assumed his full share of guilt for the negligence, and, after the burial, he left Florida with Lilo for Germany, where they stayed with her sister and brother-in-law.

Returning home six weeks later, in October 1958, Williamson welcomed a year of detached duty from Lockheed so that he could work as a military consultant in California and later at the Wright Air Force base in Dayton. Lilo accompanied him, lived with him in motels and furnished apartments, kept busy with outside employment, and in late 1959 was gratified to discover that she was again pregnant.

After they had gone back to Florida, however, Lilo was often alone when John made overnight trips to missile tracking stations in the Caribbean; and one evening he urged her to revisit her sister in Germany—he said he was now involved in an important confidential assignment, adding that he would soon join her in Europe and they would probably be moving to Pakistan. He seemed excited and pleased by these events, and she was just as eager to be leaving forever this place in which she had mainly felt loneliness and despair.

But while in Germany, Lilo received a message from him saying that their plans had abruptly been canceled. He would not be meeting her in Europe, they would not be moving to Pakistan; she was to return to Florida. When Lilo rejoined her husband in Cocoa Beach, she was so shocked by how haggard-looking and dispirited he was that she did not immediately press him for an explanation about Pakistan. He had deep circles under his eyes, he had put on weight, he was chain smoking, drinking heavily, and seemed almost in a coma or under the influence of some drug. Months would pass before she could guess why he had not joined her in Europe before moving to Pakistan.

From the little he revealed, and from rumors she heard around the Cape, she understood that her husband had been working as an engineer on U-2 spy planes—one of which, in 1960, had been announced shot down by Russian artillery, resulting in the capture of the pilot, Gary Powers, who disclosed the American espionage mission. The protesting Russians also announced that some U-2 flights had been made from a base in Pakistan.

While this incident made world headlines for weeks and greatly embarrassed President Eisenhower and American military leaders—and suspended the U-2 project—the political clamor eventually subsided; but her husband remained endlessly morose, conveying at times a deep bitterness toward certain unnamed government and military officials. Lilo could only speculate that he had become embroiled in some lasting internal dispute over the communications equipment or the operational capabilities of the U-2, which was apparently expected to fly at such a high altitude that no Soviet ground weapons could hit it. In any case, the Russians had once more proved their technological skill, and, if her husband's mood was any indication, there was much misery within the secret ranks of American spy pilots and their civilian collaborators.

John Williamson continued to go to his office each morning at Lockheed, but Lilo doubted that he could rise above his sullenness and boredom to function satisfactorily as an instrumentation engineer. When she once hinted that a psychiatrist might be helpful, he reacted coolly. He expressed only mild pleasure after the successful suborbital flight of the astronaut Alan Shepard in 1961 and the space launching of John Glenn in 1962—two events that inspired outbursts of joy and revelry among the thousands of spectators lined along the beach and the hundreds of technicians and officials at the Cape. While he escorted his wife to the postlanding celebration parties attended by other engineers, politicians, and astronauts, he did not appear to be having a good time. He drank a lot and said little. He had become, at least with Lilo, almost unapproachable, so different from the romantic figure she had seen standing on the wet, wind-lashed tower years ago during the Pacific hurricane. She conceded the possibility that he might be involved with other women, of which there were several attractive ones now living near the Cape and working in the offices of the space administration, or the stores of Cocoa Beach, or the restaurants and bars of the new motels. If he was not having sex with at least one of these women, he was doing without it, because his sex life at home was almost nonexistent.

When he returned from the office in the evening usually late and with a whiff of liquor on his breath, he seemed to be internalized, dwelling within himself, detached from his surroundings. He was no more interested in his infant daughter than he had been in his son. After dinner, he stayed up late reading books on philosophy, religion, psychology, and science fiction paperbacks, which he devoured by the dozens.

Shortly before Christmas in 1962, he became completely engrossed in a long novel that suddenly and inexplicably seemed to revive his spirit. The novel was *Atlas Shrugged*, by Ayn Rand, and after he had finished it and Lilo expressed curiosity about it, he discussed some aspects of it with her. The main characters are strong-willed American industrialists and idealists who are opposed by a group of Washington politicians and bureaucrats anxious to reduce them to government-approved standards of mediocrity and conformity, and thereby control them. The individualists not only rebel against this pressure but finally remove themselves and their considerable talent from the nation and form their own idealized community in a place that only they can recognize. The hero of the book is a strange, elusive, intellectual misfit named John Galt; the heroine is a dynamic railroad heiress named Dagny Taggart; and the book's cynical view of the federal bureaucracy is in harmony with the way Williamson had been feeling for at least two years.

Like the hero of the book, Williamson felt that one way to change society for the better was to become temporarily removed from it, to carefully create a more idealized mode of life in a private place, and then gradually to enlarge that place and its purpose by luring into it certain people who are not only willing to change but are worthy of change. Williamson had long been eager to change and be changed, but so far he saw himself as merely a misdirected migrating man who had moved from the Alabama woods to the Pacific islands to the technical tribes of Cape Canaveral in search of a compatible place he had yet to find. Perhaps he would discover, as did the hero in the book, that the place could not be found; it had to be created. Though he had no idea how to begin, he decided that he could no longer work for the government.

He resigned his position at Cape Canaveral and planned to leave within the week for Los Angeles, where for the time being he would accept a high-paying job that had already been offered him as an engineer with a firm that manufactured magnetic recording equipment. He told Lilo that he hoped she would follow him to California within the month, driving at a leisurely pace with the child, and that he would have a house waiting for her when she arrived. She wondered to herself what she should do, doubting that the marriage could last; but having no reason to remain in Florida, nor the desire to find one, she agreed that she would join him.

Lilo arrived with their two-year-old daughter in February 1963, spent a quiescent year living with Williamson in the Los Angeles suburbs, and was more relieved than surprised when he finally recommended that they get a divorce. Where there was no passion there was also no hostility. She quietly agreed with him that they should go their separate ways and she had no quarrel with the divorce terms he suggested. She would continue for the present to live in the Los Angeles house and acquire the rent-producing property in Florida, and also receive $650 a month in child support. Williamson said, too, that he wanted to provide her with a better life insurance policy, and one day before the divorce was final, he brought home an agent to explain the terms. The agent was Barbara Cramer.

12

Barbara Cramer had first met John Williamson while attempting to sell a group-insurance policy to the Los Angeles electronics firm where he worked as the general manager. He was remote, almost rude to her after she had arrived; having forgotten about their appointment, and irritated that she could not reschedule it for the following day, he relegated her to the reception room for a long wait before finally admitting her into the grim, sparsely furnished office where he sat behind a steel gray desk, chain smoking and barely attentive, as she proceeded to explain the particulars of the policy.

It was early afternoon and, despite his aloofness, she was very relaxed and confident. She had driven here from a pleasant motel meeting with Bullaro, and she had also enjoyed the ride later alone through the Valley, humming in the car to music from the radio, her body still refreshed from the shower. She often found automobile driving a sensual experience, an opportunity to be briefly removed from other people to ponder private thoughts while moving with music over smooth wide roads, and she had no doubt that thousands of other Californians also sought daily solace and the benefits of self-reflection from behind the windshields of their cars—Los Angeles was a city of motorized meditators, of interior travelers fantasizing along freeways, and the blissful mood that had encapsulated her on this sunny afternoon could not be disturbed by the ungracious atmosphere of Williamson's office.

If anything, she was merely curious about this man who seemed to be trying hard to create the impression that he did not care what impression he was creating. His office was so conspicuously austere as to suggest that he had carefully arranged it. Instead of personal mementos or photographs on his

148

desk, there were two ashtrays filled to the brim with his cigarette butts. There was no rug on the floor, the chairs were uncomfortable. The gray office walls were completely bare except for the one large picture behind his desk that showed two empty roads extending through a desert and converging in the distance, going nowhere. His replies to most of her questions were monosyllabic; his comments were always brief, his attitude indifferent. And yet she sensed that close to his surface there was an almost desperate need. He was perhaps a man who had built a wall hoping that someone would climb it.

When she had finished explaining about the policy, he abruptly stood, signifying that their meeting was over. He said that if she would leave the documents he would study them and telephone her within the week with his reaction. After a week had passed and he had not contacted her, she called him asking if he would have lunch with her. He said that he was not interested in lunch; instead he proposed that they have dinner. She accepted and, contrary to her expectations, she had a delightful evening.

They dined at an oriental restaurant in the Hollywood Hills, later going to a nightclub. They drank a good deal, spoke easily and openly about their private lives, and she could not believe that this interesting, soft-spoken man was the same disgruntled individual that she had met in the office. Either he had a dual personality or she had merely encountered him on an unusually bad day. Now she sensed that he was completely relaxed with her; he seemed to be compatible with her background: They were both country people living in the nation's largest city, they were exiles from white rural poverty trying to succeed in corporationland without the usual credentials and connections— although Williamson acknowledged during the evening that he was about to quit his firm to begin a smaller business of his own. While Barbara quickly saw that he would now be of no use to her in pushing her insurance policy with his colleagues, she did not really care. Her interest in him was suddenly strictly personal, and when they left the club together, arm in arm, he impulsively suggested on this Friday evening that they go away for the weekend.

She agreed, and three hours later, somewhat fatigued but still exuberant, they were in San Francisco, standing in front of a hotel registration desk.

"Two rooms," Williamson announced to the clerk, who, after looking at the couple, asked, "Why two rooms?"

"Because," Williamson said, "we're two people."

Sleeping separately the first night was a decision that Barbara found very romantic, and it was one of several small and pleasant surprises that would make John Williamson more intriguing to her. They abstained from sex on the second night, too, and when they finally did make love, after they had returned to Los Angeles and spent the evening in her apartment, it was an exciting culmination to a weekend of deepening familiarity and intensified desire.

His effect upon her was immediate and agreeably bewildering. With him she felt oddly coy, unaggressive, feminine, yet no less liberated. She felt as free as ever to pursue her whims and aspirations, and she knew from their conversations that he perceived and admired her independent spirit and style, and that it had been his awareness of these qualities that had quietly attracted him to her, despite his curtness, during their first meeting. Submissive and dependent women did not appeal to him, he told her, nor did the double standard that exists between the sexes, nor the conventional roles that predominate in nearly all marriages, including his own failed marriage. If he married again, he told Barbara, he wanted not a subservient wife but a strong equal partner in a relationship that would be advanced and adventurous.

As Barbara spent more time with him in Los Angeles, seeing him nearly every evening and sometimes visiting his bachelor apartment in Van Nuys, she gradually realized that the many books he owned dealing with psychology, anthropology, and sexuality represented not only intellectual curiosity on his part but also a growing professional interest.

John Williamson's career ambitions seemed to be shifting from mechanical engineering to sensual engineering, from the wonders of electronics to the dynamics of cupidity, and although his concerns were with contemporary society, his knowledge extended back to ancient times and early religions, to the first prophets and heretics, the scientists and dissenters of the Middle Ages as well as the freethinkers and founders of rural utopias in the industrial age. He was particularly interested in the work of the controversial Austrian psychiatrist Wilhelm Reich, who was opposed to the double standard between the sexes but recognized it, and the general repression of women, as society's venal way of preserving the family unit that it considered necessary for the maintenance of a strong government. In a male-dominated world, Reich suggested, there was an "economic interest'' in the continued role of woman as "the provider of children for the state'' and the performer of household chores without pay. "Owing to the economic dependence of the woman on the man and her lesser gratification in the processes of production,'' Reich once observed, "marriage is a protective institution for her, but at the same time she is exploited in it.''

The average woman's early social conditioning was described by Reich as "sex-negating'' or at best "sex-tolerating''; but in view of the conservative morality advocated by governments and religious institutions, this sexual passivity made women more faithful wives if not more daring lovers. Men meanwhile indulged their unfulfilled lust in what Reich called "mercenary sexuality'' with prostitutes, mistresses, or other women that respectable society held in low esteem. Largely from the lower classes, these women were the sexual servants in a system that scorned them and punished them, but could not eliminate them because, as Reich wrote: "Adultery and prostitution are part and parcel of the double sexual morality which allows the man, in marriage as well as before, what the woman, for economic reasons, must be denied.''

While Reich himself did not personally favor prostitution or promiscuity, he did not believe that the law should seek to prevent acts of sexuality between consenting adults, including homosexuals, nor would he restrain expressions of sexual love between adolescents. "The statement is made,'' he wrote, "that the abstinence of adolescents is necessary in the interest of social and cultural achievement. This statement is based on Freud's theory that the social and cultural achievements of man derive their energy from sexual energies which were diverted from their original goal to a 'higher' goal. This theory is known as that of 'sublimation.' . . . It is argued that sexual intercourse of youth would decrease their achievements. The fact is—and all modern sexologists agree on this—that all adolescents masturbate. That alone disposes of that argument. For, could we assume that sexual intercourse would interfere with social achievement while masturbation does not?''

Throughout his professional career, which began in the 1920s when he worked as a clinical assistant to Freud in Vienna, Wilhelm Reich's daring defense of sexual pleasure brought misery to his life and would finally lead him into the American prison where he died in 1957. Departing from Freud's exclusively verbal analysis, Reich studied the body as well as the mind, and he concluded after years of clinical observation and social work that signs of disturbed behavior could be detected in a patient's musculature, the slope of his posture, the shape of his jaw and mouth, his tight muscles, rigid bones, and other physical traits of a defensive or inhibiting nature. Reich identified this body rigidity as "armor."

He believed that all people existed behind varying layers of armor which, like the archaeological layers of the earth itself, reflected the historical events and turbulence of a lifetime. An individual's armor that had been developed to resist pain and rejection might also block a capacity for pleasure and achievement, and feelings too deeply trapped might be released only by acts of self-destruction or harm to others. Reich was convinced that sexual deprivation and frustration motivated much of the world's chaos and warfare—the 1960s' slogan of the Vietnamese war protestors, "Make Love, Not War," reechoed a Reichian theme—and he blamed the antisexual moralism of religious homes and schools, along with the "reactionary ideology" of governments, for their part in producing citizens who feared responsibility and savored authority.

Reich further believed that people who cannot achieve sexual gratification in their own lives tended to regard expressions of sexuality in society as vile and degrading, which were the symptoms of Comstock and other censors, and Reich also suggested that the religious tradition of sex as evil had its origin in the somatic condition of its celibate leaders and early Christian martyrs. People who deny the body can more readily develop concepts of "perfection" and "purity" in the soul, and Reich deduced that the energies of mystical feelings are "sexual excitations which have changed their content and goal," adding that the God-fixation declined in people who had found bliss in sex.

Such sexually satisfied people possessed what Reich called "genital character," and he considered it the goal of his therapy to achieve this in his patients because it penetrated the armor and converted the energy that nourished neurotic numbness and destruction into channels of tenderness and love that released all "damned-up sexual excitation." An individual with genital character, according to Reich, was fully in contact with his body, his drives, his environment—he possessed "orgastic potency," the capacity to "surrender to the flow of energy in the orgasm without any inhibitions . . . free of anxiety and unpleasure and unaccompanied by phantasies"; and while genital character alone would not assure enduring contentment, the individual at least would not be blocked or diverted by destructive or irrational emotion or by exaggerated respect for institutions that were not life-enhancing.

Partly because Reich suggested healthy sexual intercourse as an antidote to many ailments, his critics often saw him as espousing nothing but pleasure, whereas in fact Reich claimed that his purpose was to allow his patients to feel pain as well as pleasure. "Pleasure and *joie de vivre*," he wrote, "are inconceivable without fight, without painful experiences and without unpleasurable struggling with oneself"; although he asserted that the capacity to give love and gain happiness is compatible with "the capacity of tolerating unpleasure and pain without fleeing disillusioned into a state of rigidity."

Reich assuredly did not believe, as did many therapists who had followed Freud, that culture thrived on sexual repression, nor would he quietly condone what he saw as a church-state alliance that sought to control the masses by denigrating the joys of the flesh while presumably uplifting the spirit. Control, not morality, was the central issue, as Reich perceived it; organized religion, which in Christian countries fostered among the faithful such traits as obedience and acceptance of the status quo, strived for conformity, and its efforts were endorsed by governments that passed illiberal sex laws that reinforced feelings of anxiety and guilt among those lawful God-fearing people who sometimes indulged in unsanctioned sex. These laws also gave governments additional weapons with which to embarrass, harass, or to imprison for their sexual behavior certain radical individuals or groups that it considered politically threatening or otherwise offensive. The writer Ayn Rand went even further than Reich in suggesting that at times a government hoped that citizens would disobey the law so that it could exercise its prerogative to punish: "Who wants a nation of law-abiding citizens?" asks a government official in Rand's novel *Atlas Shrugged*; "What's there in that for anyone? . . . Just pass the kind of laws that can neither be observed nor enforced nor objectively interpreted—and you create a nation of lawbreakers and then you cash in on guilt. . . . The only power any government has is the power to crack down on criminals."

Among those upon whom it cracked down, making him a martyr of the sexual revolution, was Wilhelm Reich, whose words and ideas aroused conflict in every country in which he lived and worked. As a Communist in Germany, Reich was expelled from the party for his writings on sexual permissiveness and "counter-revolutionary" thinking, while the Nazis denounced him as a "Jewish pornographer." In Denmark the attacks on him by orthodox psychiatrists in 1933 hastened his departure for Sweden, but the hostility he encountered there led him in 1934 to Norway. In 1939, after two years of adverse publicity in the Norwegian press, he left for the United States, where he resumed his psychiatric practice in New York, trained other psychiatrists, and lectured at the New School for Social Research. In 1941, a week after the raid on Pearl Harbor, the FBI, which had a dossier on Reich as a possible enemy alien, held him on Ellis Island for three weeks before releasing him.

After the war, following the publication of magazine articles that acerbically reported his claim to have discovered "orgone energy"—a primal force found in the living organism and in the atmosphere that could be absorbed by a patient sitting in one of Reich's "orgone boxes," which resembled telephone booths— he came under investigation by the Food and Drug Administration. Ignoring the fact that his patients, before using the boxes, had signed affidavits stating that they knew the treatments were experimental and guaranteed no cures—although there was often hope on their part that the energy might cure everything from impotence to cancer—the FDA proceeded to prohibit the orgone box as a fraud, and it also banned all of Reich's books containing his socio-political theories on health and sex.

In the McCarthy atmosphere of the early 1950s, few people were eager to defend Reich's civil liberties, and he did not help his own cause by ignoring a court date and writing instead to the judge saying that the courtroom was an inappropriate place for adjudicating questions of science. Sentenced in 1956 to a two-year term for contempt of court as well as for violation of the Food and Drug Act, Reich was sent to the federal penitentiary at Lewisburg, Pennsylvania (where the prison population would soon include Samuel Roth, following his 1956 obscenity conviction); but after Reich had served eight months, he suffered a fatal heart attack.

The death of Wilhelm Reich in November 1957 was not considered major news by the media—his brief obituary appeared near the bottom of page 31 in the New York *Times* of November 5—and, except for dissenting academics and Reichian therapists and young Americans who identified with the "beat" movement (Kerouac, Burroughs, and Ginsberg were adherents of

Reich), relatively few people were interested in the underground copies of his work that the FDA had banned and, in many instances, had burned.

But all this was changed by the mid-1960s, as biographies and articles about Reich by former colleagues and friends, as well as the legal reissue of his books—including *The Mass Psychology of Fascism*, *Character Analysis*, and *The Sexual Revolution*—found a receptive audience among college students and activists who, through him, understood more clearly the connection between sex and politics.

Had Reich lived long enough to witness the radical sixties, he undoubtedly would have seen much that would have confirmed for him his predictions made long ago that society was "awakening from a sleep of thousands of years" and was about to celebrate an epochal event "without parades, uniforms, drums or cannon salutes" that was no less than a revolution of the senses. The churches and governments were gradually losing control over people's bodies and minds, and while Reich conceded that the shifting process would initially produce confrontations, clashes, and grotesque behavior, the final result, he believed, would be a healthier, more sex-affirmative and open society.

The Berkeley Free Speech Movement in 1965, which forged its slogan with the initials of a four-letter word ("Freedom Under Clark Kerr"), as well as the civil rights protests in the South and the subsequent antiwar demonstrations and marches on Washington—the sit-ins, teach-ins, love-ins—all were manifestations of a new generation that was less sexually repressed than its ancestors and also less willing to respect political authority and social tradition, color barriers and draft boards, deans and priests. It possessed more of what Reich called "genital character" and less of what another Freudian radical, Géza Róheim, called "sphincter morality."

But while the blasphemous, braless, peace-beaded young counterculturalists received most of the attention in the media during the sixties, multitudes of quiet middle-class married people were also involved in this quest for free expression and more control over their own bodies. Like the draft-age demonstrators who defied the law in refusing to risk their bodies in Vietnam, church-going women disobeyed their religion in preventing the birth of unwanted children through abortion or various forms of birth control. A reported 6 million women, many of them practicing Catholics, were using the Pill in 1967; and in this time of

topless bars, miniskirts, and long-haired lawyers and businessmen it seemed clear that the governing forces of society had
limited influence over what clothes should be worn or how the
hair should be shorn. Pubic hair made its film debut in Michelangelo Antonioni's *Blow-Up*, and penis-shaped plastic body vibrators for women were displayed for sale in drugstore windows
in many cities, although the New York *Times* censored them
from its advertising columns.

The sexual satisfaction of the body—pleasure, not procrea-
tion—was generally accepted now in the middle class as the
primary purpose of coitus, and in an attempt to more fully comprehend and rectify unresponsiveness among pleasure-seeking
patients, the Masters and Johnson researchers in St. Louis pio-
neered in the use of an eight-inch plastic phallic "coition
machine," employed a number of former prostitutes among its
co-experimenters, and later also provided "surrogate wives" as
sex partners for dysfunctional men.

A lawsuit against the Masters and Johnson center by a husband of one of the surrogates, as well as snide speculation in
public print about the performance of the machine, contributed
to the researchers' decision to eliminate these features from their
laboratory work, although female surrogates would continue to
find employment at several other sex-therapy clinics that would
be established around the nation as a result of Masters and Johnson's fame and success. At some of these clinics, couples would
be tutored in the art of giving erotic massages and would also
be shown instructional films on fellatio, cunnilingus, and the
joys of mutual masturbation that were more sexually explicit
than what was passing for pornography in theaters on Forty-
second Street.

The number of mate-swappers in America, most of them
middle-class married people with children, were now estimated
by some swing-trade periodicals to exceed 1 million couples;
and in a speech to the American Psychological Association, Dr.
Albert Ellis, a psychologist and author, said that marriages can
sometimes be helped by "healthy adultery." Group nudity could
also be personally beneficial, according to psychologist Abraham M. Maslow, who believed that nudist camps or parks might
be places where people can emerge from hiding behind their
clothes and armor, and become more self-accepting, revealing,
and honest.

Mixed nude bathing and massage became popular during the
sixties at such "growth centers" as the Esalen Institute in North-

ern California, a lush retreat nestled in rocky cliffs overlooking the Pacific where the spirit of Reich seemed alive in the faculty that supervised dozens of sensuous seminars attended by thousands of predominantly middle-class couples that made Esalen a million-dollar-a-year enterprise. Most of the new forms of therapy that had been at least partly inspired by Reich's work— bioenergetics, encounter, sensitivity training, primal therapy, rolfing, massage—were available at Esalen, where the most prominent therapist was Dr. Frederick S. Perls, a German refugee who had been one of Reich's patients in Europe before the war.

Like Reich, Perls had become dissatisfied with Freud's "talking cure" as well as with many of Freud's rigid practitioners who, in Perl's view, were "beset with taboos"—it was as if "Viennese hypocritical Catholics had invaded the Jewish science"—and Perl's therapy emphasized instead new methods for achieving freer body movement, more awareness, fuller expressiveness, and "life feeling." Too many people were obsessed with their heads and were alienated from their bodies, Perls believed, adding: "We have to lose our minds and come to our senses."

Much of what was being advocated at Esalen and elsewhere was in harmony with John Williamson's own attitude, although he wanted to go further than Reich's followers in altering the sociopolitical system through sexual experimentation—he hoped to soon establish his idealized community for couples wishing to demolish the double standard, to liberate women from their submissive roles, and to create a sexually free and trusting atmosphere in which there would be no need for possessiveness, jealousy, guilt, or lying. Now was the perfect time for such a venture, Williamson felt; society was in turmoil, and people were responsive to new ideas, particularly in California, where so many natural trends and styles had started.

If successful, his project could be financially profitable—like Esalen, or the Synanon drug program founded by a onetime alcoholic; or at least heavily funded and solvent, like the Kinsey Institute and the Masters and Johnson clinic—as well as becoming a contributing force toward a healthier, more egalitarian society. But first he had to organize his core group, those intimates who would help him initiate the process and ultimately serve as the "instruments for change" in other people's lives. He already had several candidates in mind, people he had befriended since moving to California three years ago. Most of

them were in their late twenties or early thirties, were employed
in large corporations, were divorced or unhappily married, were
restless and searching. Several of the men were engineers, conservative individuals whose livelihood was linked to the fortunes
of the defense industry in California but who admitted to extreme boredom with their work and home lives and seemed
ready for radical alternatives.

Among the women Williamson had in mind were Arlene
Gough, with whom he had enjoyed a brief affair after meeting
her at Hughes Aircraft, and with whom he was still friendly. He
was also close to two other women who worked at his electronics
firm, one of them an extremely attractive individual who had
been an airline stewardess. But the woman he considered most
essential to his program—which he would call Project Synergy—was Barbara Cramer.

In the months he had spent with her since their trip to San
Francisco, he gradually realized that she already possessed many
of the qualities that undoubtedly would be the goals of women
in Project Synergy: She was professionally successful, independent, and self-assured, was sexually liberated and aggressive
when it suited her, and was not intimidated by the possibility of
rejection. In some ways she reminded him of Dagny Taggart,
the heroine in *Atlas Shrugged*, although Barbara Cramer was
thankfully not a female elitist and would therefore serve as a
more representative role model to the young middle-class women
that Williamson hoped would be drawn into Project Synergy.
He saw Barbara as the prototype of the new woman of the changing middle class; and, in a synergistic sense, she ideally suited
him—her assets complemented his deficiencies, and vice versa.
She was verbal and active while he was theoretical and introspective; she was more direct and efficient if less calculating
and visionary. She did not procrastinate, she knew what she
wanted. She had already decided, at twenty-seven, that she
would never have children, being aggrieved by recollections of
her hapless mother and other child-rearing women she had
known since leaving rural Missouri. But Barbara nonetheless
wanted to become more feminine than she was, more gentle and
sensitive, and she also admitted to Williamson that she sometimes felt sexually attracted to certain women. Williamson urged
her not to repress this, but to explore it in the interest of greater
self-awareness; and shortly after their marriage in the summer
of 1966—a conventional act that they both agreed would create
a socially acceptable facade for their unconventional life-style—

John Williamson decided to fully test Barbara's tolerance of sexual variety within their marriage.

Hours before they were to leave Los Angeles for a restful weekend at Lake Arrowhead, he informed her that they would be accompanied in the car by a young woman from his office named Carol, the former airline stewardess that he had dated prior to his meeting Barbara. When Barbara seemed unenthusiastic, he assured her that Carol was very feminine and charming, adding that it would be both beneficial and enjoyable for Barbara to have her as a friend.

Barbara had heard him discuss Carol before, always fondly but never hinting that he was still seriously involved with her, if he ever was; and Barbara imagined Carol to be, like the receptionist she was, a lovely frontispiece for a faceless corporation, a naïve young individual who had found a father figure in John and had, like so many other women, been drawn to him because, unlike so many men, he would *listen* to a woman, would really listen to what she was trying to say.

Late that afternoon after she had met Carol, Barbara amended some of her assumptions about her. A tall, angular blonde with dark eyes and a graceful body, Carol seemed hardly naïve and quite composed, although there was nothing haughty or affected in her manner. She appeared to be genuinely happy to meet Barbara, and remarked on how impressed she had been by John's description of Barbara's career; as they rode in the car toward Lake Arrowhead, Carol was careful to include Barbara in all the conversations with John about their office and their mutual friends.

Still, despite these efforts, Barbara felt uneasy with Carol, and she recognized this as characteristic of the way she had nearly always felt toward women in social situations; though she privately was attracted to them, she could not easily relate to them, having had limited experience with her own sex during her tomboy adolescence and the years that followed. The one time that she had cultivated a female friendship with her schoolmate Frances, it had ended sadly and bitterly, and Barbara still could not explain her own strange, hostile reaction to Frances after Frances had announced that she was getting married and moved out of their apartment.

Barbara also felt somewhat disconcerted in the car because she sensed that she was the odd woman in this threesome with Carol and John, and that they had arranged this weekend behind her back. Barbara had pondered her husband's intentions as soon as he had mentioned that Carol would be joining them, and she now anticipated being put in the position of possibly having to accept or reject Carol as a bed partner with John at Lake Arrowhead, or perhaps being left with the choice of remaining on the sidelines while her husband embraced Carol as a way of proving, as he often said he could, that wholesome, open sex with friends need not disturb the deeper meaning of marriage.

When they arrived at the lake, it was early evening and Barbara was relieved to discover that their cabin had two private bedrooms. But before they unpacked their luggage, John suggested that they quickly go out to dinner before the restaurant closed. After a few drinks, a good meal, and much amiable conversation and laughter, Barbara felt more at ease; but later, on returning to the cabin, she saw Carol and John place their luggage in the same bedroom, and soon they began to casually undress.

Barbara remained in the living room, stunned, silent, waiting for an explanation that was not forthcoming. Too proud to reveal her discomfort, too shocked to even think clearly, she sat on the couch staring at the open door of the bedroom. She heard them hanging their clothes in the closet, speaking softly. The open door was no doubt John's way of saying that she was welcome to join them, but he would not be coaxing her, the decision would be entirely her own.

It was confusing, harsh, and frightening, and all the earlier talk on John's part since their marriage about the merits of open sexuality did not now alleviate Barbara's uncertainty; it was one thing to agree with John's theories and quite another to employ them in moments like this, with a woman she had just met, and the longer Barbara hesitated the more she knew that she was unable or unwilling to move toward the door.

She felt numb, dizzy, and it took all her resources to stand and walk into the other bedroom. She closed the door. It was after midnight and she was very tired and cold. She realized that she had left her suitcase in the living room but she did not want to get it. Slowly undressing and folding her clothes over the back of a chair, she got into bed and tried to sleep; but she remained tearfully awake until dawn, hearing the sounds of their lovemaking.

The next day, shortly before noon, she was awakened by the soft touch of her husband and his gentle kiss. Carol was smiling behind him, holding a breakfast tray, and soon they both were

sitting on the bed, stroking her and comforting her as if she were
a young girl recovering from an illness. Barbara felt strange and
embarrassed. John said that he loved her and needed her; Barbara, forcing a smile, did not reply. He suggested that after
breakfast they all go swimming and skiing on the lake, but Barbara said that she preferred remaining in bed awhile longer, and
told them to go on ahead, she would join them.

She spent part of the afternoon in the cabin, then took a long
walk in the sun and crisp air, regaining her composure. She was
not angry with John or Carol, though she conceded that this
weekend surely was the beginning of a new phase in her marriage; but instead of feeling panicked or threatened, she felt
oddly contented and free. Her husband had freed her of certain
indefinable fears and romantic illusions about sex and body
pleasure, as distinguished from the meaning of marital love. Her
awareness that her husband had been sexually engaged the previous night with another woman, after she had recovered
from the shock, not really so shocking; and when John had
announced his love for her in front of Carol this morning, Barbara believed him, for now there was no reason for lying. Their
relationship had become more honest and open, had expanded
not only for him but for her. She knew that now she could do
as she wished, with whomever she pleased, without risking his
rancor, or so she assumed. His railing against covert adultery
and senseless sexual possessiveness and jealousy had culmi-
nated last night in a defiant act against a centuries-old tradition
of propriety and deceit, and she admitted to being both stunned
and stimulated by what had just transpired in her life. She was
married to an uncommon man, mysterious, unboring, unpredictable, a quiet man who said he loved her and needed her.

Soothed by the walk, she returned to the cabin, took a bath,
and changed her clothes; then she left for the restaurant-bar
looking for John and Carol. John smiled and waved as he saw
her, and both stood to embrace her as she arrived, and Barbara
soon felt almost as comfortable with Carol as she did with her
husband. Though the bar was crowded and noisy, there was a
special warmth among the three of them as they sat drinking
and talking, and the dinner with wine that followed in the restaurant represented to Barbara an almost celebratory conclusion
to all the preceding hours of anguish and anxiety; and the last
thing she expected at this time was that the complexity of her
life would be compounded.

Shortly before eleven o'clock, at the end of dinner, she was

surprised by the sudden arrival at their table of a man to whom
she had been attracted in the past. The man was a friend of her
husband's named David Schwind, an engineer; about thirty years
of age, he was one of the few men her husband knew in Los
Angeles who had not been married at least once. Barbara had
met him earlier in the year while water-skiing with John and
others at Pine Flat Lake, near Fresno, and she had then been
drawn to his strong but delicate features, his athletic body, and
his somewhat shy, aloof manner. David Schwind was employed
at Douglas Aircraft, and John had seen signs of his mechanical
skill during the weekend when David had quickly repaired the
motor of a malfunctioning skiboat. Since then, in various ways,
John had recruited David's friendship, taking him to lunch, seeing him socially after work. Now at Lake Arrowhead, as David
joined their table and sat next to Barbara, unannounced but obviously expected by her unsurprised husband, Barbara had no
doubt that David's presence was attributable to a telephone call
made by John earlier in the day. While the purpose of this visit
was not entirely clear to her, it was a foregone conclusion on
her part, knowing her husband, that it had a purpose, and would
in time clearly reveal itself.

In the meantime, in a mood of blithe resignation, Barbara
ordered another drink and responded amiably toward David,
although she detected within him a certain discomfort and reticence. Sipping his drink, saying very little, listening absently
while John and Carol did most of the talking, of which little
could be heard over this increasingly noisy Saturday night crowd,
David Schwind seemed to be debating within himself the wisdom of being where he was. A half hour later, after John had
paid the bill and rose to leave, David reacted by suggesting that
perhaps he should be on his way; but John urged that he return
with them to the cabin, and Barbara smiled at David in a way
she hoped was reassuring.

It was well past midnight as they returned, and, after they had
sat for a while in the living room, Barbara volunteered to make
a pot of coffee and asked David if he would mind igniting the
small stove in the corner. While waiting for the water to boil,
Barbara and David stood talking together, soon becoming so
engrossed in one another that they were unaware of the fact that
John and Carol had quietly left the room. When David turned
and noticed the unoccupied sofa, he seemed startled.

"Where's John?" he asked.

Seeing that the bedroom door was closed, Barbara replied

with newfound nonchalance, "He's with Carol." As David looked at her quizzically, she hastily added, "It's okay. There's nothing to worry about."

"But shouldn't I be going?"

"No, please don't," she said quickly. "I'd like you to stay." She moved closer to him, put her arms around him, and told him that her husband was counting on his staying overnight, and so was she. After reaching behind him to switch off the living room lights she took his hand and led him into her bedroom. She closed the door and immediately began to remove her clothes.

Making love to David that night, and again at dawn, was for Barbara a source of great release and unabashed pleasure; and far from having any misgivings about it, or feeling romantically detached from her husband, she felt quite the opposite. She believed that she had now achieved a new level of emotional intimacy with John, and that they had both shared during the night, in different rooms with different people, a gift of loving trust.

Instead of loving him less after sleeping with another man, she was sure that she loved him more; and when she got up for breakfast, leaving David asleep beside her, she was greeted in the living room by her husband's approving smile and kiss.

13

JOHN BULLARO, WHOSE extramarital affair with Barbara Williamson had been incredibly sanctioned by her husband—who had also taken Bullaro to lunch and urged that the affair be continued—knew that he had no choice but to comply with John Williamson's astonishing request, and this he diligently did during the winter of 1967 through the spring of 1968.

Bullaro had also agreed to visit the Williamsons' new home in Woodland Hills and meet a few of their liberated friends, an obligation that he anticipated with trepidation until he arrived one night to find the group very congenial and attractive, particularly a petite dark-eyed brunet who greeted him at the door with a serene smile and wearing only a negligee. Her name was Oralia Leal, and in the light of the doorway he could see her upturned breasts and dark nipples through the delicate material, and as he followed her through the foyer he observed her graceful hips and the fact that under the negligee she was completely nude.

While Oralia Leal went to get him a glass of wine, Barbara and Arlene Gough came forward and kissed him, and then escorted him into a large dimly lit living room in which a half-dozen people sat fully clothed on the rug and on chairs listening attentively as John Williamson in a soft voice discussed the work of the Indian spiritualist Krishnamurti.

Seeing Bullaro, Williamson stood and thanked him for coming, and then introduced him to the others in the room. Williamson was informally dressed in a sports shirt, slacks, and slippers, but the other men were in business suits and ties, as was Bullaro, and the women wore dresses and jewelry and moderately high-heeled shoes. Only Oralia's attire suggested a preparedness for bedroom frolicking, or hinted at the possibility of her later stag-

164

ing an erotic solo performance that the others would watch. But
when she returned to the living room with Bullaro's wine, she
seemed to be exceedingly shy and modest, even embarrassed
by her appearance, and soon she sat curled up on the floor at
Williamson's feet as if seeking his protection, and she said very
little during the rest of the evening.

Bullaro sat on a sofa between Barbara and Arlene listening as
the discussion was resumed about Krishnamurti, a man he had
never heard of, nor did he know much more about Maslow and
the other names that figured prominently in the exchanges between Williamson and his friends. Feeling intellectually inadequate, Bullaro petulantly reminded himself that he must revive
and broaden his education, must read more books, must expand
his interests and not allow himself to be so circumscribed by
the narrow demands of the insurance business. It seemed that
whatever scholarly drives he had once possessed had ended when
he received his master's degree in education, and now he was
forced to sit ignorantly in a room dominated by a burly blond
man who had not gotten beyond high school. Bullaro studied
this man at whose feet sat the feline Oralia, and begrudgingly
acknowledged that Williamson exuded an air of effortless authority and demonstrated a carefree command of facts and figures and people; and Bullaro also conceded with a certain
irritation that there was much he could probably learn from him.

But one thing that Bullaro was apparently not going to learn
tonight was the real purpose of this evening, and the sort of
relationship that existed between these people and the Williamsons. After having sat for more than an hour and drunk a second
glass of wine, and having cogently replied to one of Williamson's questions about the rising cost of medical malpractice insurance after the discussion had shifted to the recent heart
transplant performed by a surgeon at Stanford University, Bullaro was obliged to say that he had to be getting home. So far
the scene in this living room was, except for Oralia, typical of
what could be found in any suburban home; and while much
might transpire in the hours ahead, Bullaro knew that time was
against him tonight. His wife, Judith, was waiting up for him,
he having explained that he would be only briefly delayed by a
late business meeting. John and Barbara Williamson also said,
as they escorted him to the door to wish him good night, that
they hoped he would soon return and stay longer, adding that
they had visitors every night and he was always welcome. Bullaro nodded and thanked them, and knew that he would return

if for no other reason than to see again the svelte figure of Oralia
Leal and to satisfy his curiosity about these people Williamson
called liberated.

During the following week, early one evening, Bullaro appeared at the Williamsons' door and was greeted by Barbara.
He apologized for not telephoning in advance, but explained
that while driving through the neighborhood on his way home
he noticed the many cars parked in the driveway and thought
that he would stop in for a brief visit. Barbara said that she was
pleased that he did and, taking his arm, accompanied him
through the foyer toward the living room. There he suddenly
stopped, held his breath—sitting in the living room were several
people who were completely nude, just sitting on the furniture
or on the rug sipping wine and talking among themselves with
an unselfconsciousness that amazed Bullaro almost as much as
the sight of their naked flesh.

Although he had been forewarned about the possibility of
nudity during his memorable lunch with John Williamson, as
Bullaro now entered the living room with Barbara he felt his
pulse quickening, his palms moistening, and a stirring in his
groin. He turned toward Barbara for an explanation, a mere
word or a gesture that might reduce the tension and awkwardness he felt, but Barbara casually led him toward a sofa on which
sat a buxom red-haired woman whose large freckled breasts
were covered only by a strand of pearls.

"You remember John Bullaro from the other night, don't
you?" Barbara asked, and the woman nodded and smiled, and
as she extended her hand up toward him, her breasts also rose.
Bullaro blushed. Barbara guided him around the room to meet
other people, but all he saw in furtive glances were dangling
breasts and hairy chests, bare buttocks and white thighs, pubic
hair of various colors, penises that were large and small, cir-
cumcised and uncircumcised, and, remarkably, unerect.

In the corner Bullaro recognized the familiar body of Arlene
Gough, who was talking to a couple who were fully clothed, for
which Bullaro was grateful. Kneeling next to them, near the
stereo, was the well-proportioned presence of David Schwind,
the engineer Bullaro had met during his first visit. Sitting in the
center of the room, surrounded by a small circle of people who
seemed to be listening raptly to his words, was the burly figure
of John Williamson, broad-chested with a potbelly and small
penis, a blond Buddha whose right foot was being massaged by

the dazzling olive-skinned Oralia, a nude Nefertiti whose perfect body, Bullaro assumed, was the envy of every woman in the room.

Williamson called for Bullaro to come join him, and Bullaro, leaving Barbara with David Schwind, stepped carefully over assorted torsos and limbs to settle himself on the rug next to his host and Oralia, who smiled at him demurely and said hello. She continued to massage Williamson's foot. Though Bullaro tried to focus only on the faces of the people around him, and to suggest by nodding his head often that he was paying attention to what they were saying, his eyes kept darting back toward the contours of Oralia, and he was aware that her dark skin was unblemished, her breasts did not sag, her stomach was smooth, her black pubic hair was a neatly trimmed triangle, and he was tantalized by the sight of it. He felt his penis stalking within his shorts. Lifting up his knees, he sipped the wine that someone had handed him.

Looking upward, trying to avoid an obsession with Oralia's enticements, Bullaro studied the heavy wooden beams of the high slanted ceiling, which he estimated to extend about thirty feet above the floor. It was an unusually designed house, perched on a mountain peak overlooking the Valley, and during his earlier visit he had observed from its spacious patio, after dark, a spread of glowing lights from the houses below. Except for a small staircase in the living room, which led up to an elevated kitchen, the house's entire living area was restricted to the main floor; and from where Bullaro now reclined on the rug he could see the closed doors of what he guessed were two bedrooms, one of which suddenly opened to reveal a nude couple walking out, arm in arm, to rejoin the party.

Whatever was going on privately in this house, or indeed what he could see with his own eyes, was clearly beyond his comprehension, especially while reeling in his present state of fettered agitation. He felt unconnected with this group, frustrated with himself. He hated being an outsider, even among these people, and that was certainly what he was tonight, a clothes-bound prisoner in a liberated circle of nudists. While the quest for adventure that had long plagued him now tempted him to remove his clothes, an even more persuasive force within him prevented him from doing so, mainly because he feared revealing for the first time in front of so many people that unpredictable organ he assumed was every man's burden—although, as was apparent from the number of flaccid phalli he saw all around him, no man seemed burdened tonight except himself.

If only Williamson had suggested before Bullaro had sat down that he perhaps would be more comfortable wearing fewer clothes, Bullaro might have impulsively complied; but without such prompting, it seemed impossible. It was probably typical of Williamson to let people untangle themselves from their own inhibitions while he remained detached, quietly observing, and Bullaro suddenly saw this whole house as a kind of maze into which Williamson had lured people, stimulated them with un-defined promises, and then allowed them to shift and scramble for themselves, all justified as a learning experience.

Hearing laughter behind him, Bullaro turned toward the foyer to see Barbara and Arlene merrily greeting a newly arrived cou-ple, and Arlene, covering her pubis with a cocktail napkin, was wiggling her hips and batting her lashes in an exaggerated imi-tation of a stripper. Barbara, who had presumably remained fully dressed this evening because she was responsible for an-swering the doorbell, looked at Bullaro and waved toward him. Grasping this opportunity to separate himself from Williamson's little seminar and the seemingly unobtainable Oralia, he got up and joined Barbara and the others near the doorway, from where he knew he could soon make his inconspicuous retreat.

He was restless, resigned to having spent an evening he could not account for. He had seen everything and nothing. He had been confounded by visual bombardment. It was also getting late, close to midnight, and, if his wife was still up, he did not want a confrontation at home. He kissed Barbara good night, and she walked him to the door, reminding him that they had a lunch date on the following day. She suggested that they meet here at the house instead of going out, and he agreed, saying he would see her shortly before one o'clock.

Judith was asleep when he arrived home, sparing him the effort of having to lie about where he had been. But in a way he was sorry that she was asleep, for his sexual energy was now very high, and he would have enjoyed making love in the dark to the image of Oralia, which he considered vastly preferable to, and quite distinct from, masturbating Oralia out of his sys-tem. Bullaro had never greatly enjoyed masturbation, even as a Chicago schoolboy growing up around his father's barbershop that had its share of girlie magazines. As an aspiring member of the Amundsen High School football team, he was influenced by the spartan philosophy of the coaches of that era who believed that masturbation was debilitating and dispiriting, that it drained combative drives; and when Bullaro himself coached the Hol-

lywood Boys' Club football team in the early fifties, he was still
influenced by such thinking. Intercourse, however, was an entirely different matter, at least where he was concerned, even
though he did not know exactly why, or if, intercourse was less
ravaging to the body than masturbation; but he dismissed the
entire issue as academic tonight because he was not going to
indulge in either.

Fixing himself a scotch and water, and taking a book to the
sofa, he decided to read himself to sleep; and that is how he slept
on this night, on the sofa, his chest covered by a large American
Heritage edition of a book on the Civil War by Bruce Catton.

At dawn, Bullaro awakened and quietly went into the bathroom, shaved and dressed for the office. Leaving a note for
Judith saying that he had a breakfast meeting to attend, he got
into the car and was safely gone before Judith was up.

He felt uneasy and a bit guilty during the morning at the
office, and he knew he should telephone Judith later in the day,
although there was little that he could tell her except more lies
about where he had been and what he had done. It was absurd
and pathetic; he was reacting once more like the schoolboy he
had been, covering up the truth, fearing exposure, misrepre-
senting part of his ethnic background to his neighborhood friends
in Chicago, appeasing his Jewish mother by telling her the lies
she wanted to hear so that they could both go on pretending he
was what she admired in a son. But what was even more sickening in this instance with his wife was that, though he acknowledged feeling guilty about last night, he had done virtually
nothing to warrant this guilt. If he had at least gone to bed with
Oralia, or been drawn into a debauched bacchanalia on the Williamsons' living room rug, then all the lying to Judith would
seem worthwhile. As it was, his deceptions merely concealed
his failure to fulfill his latent longings in that jaded and prurient
parlor, and the whole evening also confirmed the wisdom of
John Williamson's argument that lying about sex was a waste of
time and energy.

Bullaro marveled at the Williamsons' marriage, that sybaritic
scene in their living room, and the fact that Barbara was casually
greeting guests at the door while Oralia was sprawled nude on
the rug massaging John Williamson's foot and later who knows
what else. Bullaro spent much of the morning ruminating on such
matters while also concentrating on the prosaic paper work of
New York Life, sitting in his red leather chair in an office on the

walls of which were hung framed degrees and decrees testifying to his achievements and virtuous deeds in the community—none of which would delay for one moment his departure from the office at 12:30 for his erotic lunch with Barbara Williamson.

Eagerly anticipating his satisfaction as he drove up the winding, hilly roads of Mulholland Drive toward the Williamsons' house, he was not disappointed when he arrived. Barbara, who was alone in the house, greeted him at the door with a prolonged kiss and warm embrace, and she accepted unhesitatingly his suggestion that they delay lunch and go straight to the bedroom.

Though he was surprised at first by the presence of various mirrors affixed to the walls and ceiling, he soon became an avid appreciator of these accoutrements after he lay nude on the bed and watched Barbara crawl toward him, with a coquettish smile and hanging breasts grazing his chest, to take his penis in her mouth and arouse him in a way that he could see from different angles. It was a rare visual experience to watch her voluptuous figure and bowed blond head, multiplied in the mirrors, stimulate him kaleidoscopically, fondle with many hands and mouths the profusion of penises that were all his to feel and see, near and afar, as an optic orgy.

Soon he felt the familiar convulsions rising within him, and as his whole body shuddered he lay back and luxuriated in his orgasm for several moments before he again opened his eyes and saw all around him his reflected stillness. He remained in bed with Barbara for more than an hour, an uncommon length of time in their history of brief encounters, but on this day they both were more ravenous for sex than food, and they exhausted one another in fulfilling their desires.

Shortly before three o'clock, driving back to his office down the curving roads deeper into the Valley, he felt as light-headed and free as if he were gliding; but after returning to the subdued quarters of the insurance firm and telephoning his wife, he was again confronting the shifting gravity of his life.

He called Judith to suggest that they have dinner that night at their favorite restaurant, but she refused, although there was no indication in her voice that she was upset by the hours he had been keeping of late; on the contrary, she was calm and even cheerful on the phone, saying that she had already planned their dinner at home, but added that she had arranged something for them to do later in the evening. John Williamson had called earlier in the day asking for him, she explained, and she had introduced herself over the phone. After a cordial conversation in which Williamson had expressed much admiration for Bullaro, he suggested that the Bullaros stop by for a drink after dinner; and Judith, who had not gotten out of the house in days, had gladly accepted the invitation, saying that they would be there around nine o'clock.

John Bullaro was speechless and petrified. His grip tightened on the telephone, his mind flashed with images of nude people in the Williamsons' living room, and while he could not believe that John Williamson would subject a woman he had never met to such a scene, he knew that with Williamson he could be sure of nothing. He remained silent. Judith asked if he could hear her; when he said yes, she asked him not to be late for dinner because she wanted to be out of the kitchen before the girl next door came over to baby-sit, and then she went on with other details that Bullaro did not hear, so impatient was he for her to hang up so that he could call the Williamsons. He wanted an explanation for the call to Judith, an indication of what might be expected during the evening ahead, although as he dialed the Williamsons' number he reminded himself that he should not seem too irritated or abrupt, particularly if John Williamson should pick up the telephone; Bullaro still believed that all dealings with that man should be conducted with extreme caution.

But there was no answer at the Williamsons' home. Bullaro dialed the number again several times during the afternoon, and tried Barbara's office, but he was still unable to reach them. As he later drove home he knew that he had no choice but to prepare Judith for the possibility of surprises during the evening.

At dinner, after the children had gone to bed, he told Judith that he perceived the Williamsons to be an unusual couple, saying that he had heard in the office that they were involved with a kind of encounter group that occasionally held meetings at their home in the nude. While Bullaro said that he could not personally vouch for the accuracy of this information, he thought that Judith should be prepared tonight for almost anything, adding that if she felt uneasy about going, there was still enough time to cancel.

She looked at him strangely; and then, seeming confused and irritated, she asked what exactly he was getting at, and she also demanded to know why he had waited until the last minute to raise this issue. Quickly apologizing for upsetting her, he explained that he merely felt he should tell her what he had heard; to which Judith replied that the whole idea of nude encounters seemed ridiculous to her, but as long as *she* was not expected to remove her clothes, she saw no reason to cancel the evening.

Bullaro said nothing more about it, although privately he was surprised by her tolerant attitude.

In the car along the way, however, Judith said very little, and he suspected that she now shared his anxiety. Pulling into the Williamsons' driveway, he noticed three cars parked in front of the house, and the lights were on in all the rooms. Hearing voices inside, he pressed the bell and waited. Oralia opened the door, and, he was relieved to notice, she was modestly dressed in a skirt and sweater. Barbara and John then came forward, also fully dressed, to be introduced to Judith, and in the living room other people were similarly clothed, including Arlene Gough and David Schwind.

After Judith remarked on how she admired the house, particularly the high ceilings and antiques, Barbara led her out to the patio with its view of the Valley. Wine was poured, music was coming from the stereo, and soon the Bullaros were settled comfortably in the living room involved in a general conversation that seemed to be continuing indefinitely until unexpectedly, Judith herself introduced the subject of nudity, saying that she had heard of the Williamsons' participation in nude encounter groups.

John Williamson nodded, and Barbara smiled, while John Bullaro blanched.

"But what do you people in these nude groups *do*?" Judith asked rather insistently.

"We do people things," John Williamson replied.

"My husband gives me the impression that you sit around talking to one another," Judith went on, "but why in the nude?"

"Have you ever tried it?" Williamson asked.

"I've never seen the need for it."

"Taking off one's clothes can be a first step in breaking down barriers," Barbara explained. "In our group we're trying to relate honestly and openly with each other. So many of the problems all of us have are the result of our inability to be honest and . . ."

"Yes," Judith interrupted, "but you don't have to be nude to achieve honesty."

"You're right," John Williamson said. "You don't have to take your clothes off. But for *many* people, having their clothes off does remove certain psychological barriers that can ultimately lead to a higher level of honesty." As Williamson continued to elaborate, John Bullaro sat silent and tense among the other people and wished that there was some way he could change the subject of this conversation. The wine had gotten to

Judith, he thought; it had no doubt accentuated the uneasiness she had felt in coming here, and now she seemed defensive and almost hostile. But he knew that there was nothing he could do now but try to avoid becoming involved in this discussion, and he might have managed it had Barbara not suddenly turned toward him and said in a voice loud enough for everyone to hear: "Well, *you're* being very quiet tonight, John."

"Oh," Bullaro said, "I'm just listening." He sipped his wine, and looked idly out toward the patio. But Barbara persisted.

"John, do you think that you and Judy are honest with one another?"

Bullaro turned slowly back toward Barbara with the expression of a man in slight pain. The room was completely silent now as everyone waited for his answer. Finally, he nodded and said in a softer voice: "Yes, I think we're honest."

"We're *very* honest with one another," Judith added.

"You mean John tells you everything?" Barbara asked Judith.

"Yes, he does."

"Does he tell you about the time he spends with me?"

Judith turned hesitantly toward her husband who, looking downward, slowly began to shake his head.

"I'm not sure I know what you mean," Judith replied to Barbara.

"Yes," John Bullaro said, looking up in anger, "what the hell are you getting at?"

"I was just wondering if you ever told Judy about us?"

"What *about* us?" he demanded.

"Well," Barbara went on easily, "did you tell Judy about *us* this afternoon?"

Everybody in the room edged forward in their seats, and Bullaro saw his wife looking from one to the other, and asking anxiously, "What happened this afternoon?"

"Nothing happened!" Bullaro yelled. "I just came here this afternoon and had lunch with Barbara."

"Oh, come on, John," Barbara interrupted, "is that what you call honesty?"

"Yes," said Oralia, "*you* know you had more than lunch here today."

Bullaro was stunned that Oralia, who until now had seemed so demure and delectable, would rise against him, and as he looked around the room the other people also seemed accusatory, even Arlene Gough, who sat on the sofa regarding him as if he were a complete stranger. Turning toward Judith, he noticed that there were tears in her eyes, and sitting on the rug at her feet was the quiet instigator, John Williamson. The silence continued until Barbara, her eyes fixed on Bullaro, challenged him once more.

"What *else* did we do today, John, besides have lunch?"

Bullaro saw no way out. He knew it was pointless to continue his pretense, for Barbara would grill him to the bone.

"All right, for God's sake," he finally shouted, "I went to bed with Barbara this afternoon! Is that what you all want to hear?—*I went to bed with Barbara this afternoon!*"

"Just *this* afternoon?" Barbara quickly asked.

"No!" he answered, almost screaming, addressing the entire group and not caring what he said anymore. "I slept with her before!"

Nobody said anything, or even moved; and in the stillness of the room Bullaro sat with his head lowered, his heart pounding heavily. He felt empty, almost nauseated. Hearing Judith sobbing, he looked up to see John Williamson leaning toward her, speaking quietly, and with his hands he was softly massaging her ankles. This odd gesture seemed at first to offend her, causing her to frown, but as she did not voice an objection Williamson continued to touch her, and soon the others in the room had also gathered around to comfort her, leaving Bullaro on the outside feeling alone and condemned.

For several moments Bullaro sat watching, inert, mesmerized, as the whole group, including Barbara, performed this strange rite of consolation around his wife. But after she had stopped crying, she abruptly sat upright and waved them away, and with surprising petulance she declared: "I think that what you have all done to Johnny tonight is terrible!"

Everybody remained silent, and John Williamson stopped massaging her ankles as Judith directed her attention toward her husband.

"Tell me," she asked in a tone that was firm but not condemning, "have you had affairs with other women besides Barbara?"

"Yes," he admitted.

"Who else?"

"Well," he said, nodding toward the lean, impassive woman sitting next to Barbara, "Arlene Gough."

Judith studied Arlene Gough momentarily without comment, then turned back to her husband.

"Did you ever sleep with that dark-haired girl that lived in our apartment house on La Peer?"

Though it had been more than a decade since he had seen her, Bullaro had no difficulty in remembering his affair with Eileen, a divorced art teacher and native of Chicago who had occupied the apartment behind the Bullaros' at 145 North La Peer in Beverly Hills. Eileen had walked like a ballerina, had muscular thighs and dark exotic features. . . .

"Yes," he said.

"Oh, I *knew* it," Judith said, seeming perversely pleased by his admission. "All that time I thought I was going crazy with suspicion, and I hated myself for those thoughts I had, and now it turns out that I was right! I remember once mentioning her, and you seemed so offended and indignant . . ."

"Now wait a minute . . ."

"No, *you* wait a minute. You had me feeling hysterical for months, always wondering about that woman in the back apartment, seeing her come and go, even hearing her on the phone sometimes, through the wall when I was in the laundry room, speaking to you at your office—though I still couldn't believe it. I remember one weekend you said you were going off camping with your friends from the health club, and I *knew* you were with her—I even went to the club to see if you'd left your car there, as you said you were going to do, and you didn't. Later, on Sunday night, after I heard her coming home, *you* came home, and you had both driven in from the same direction! I knew because I was watching from the window. And when you walked in I saw that you weren't wearing your wedding ring. I think that was when I approached you about her, and you swore that I must be crazy, that I was imagining things . . ."

"Dammit, Judy, in those days you were imagining me going to bed with everybody. And unless you'd been drinking, you didn't want sex anyway. So what did you expect me to do?"

Judith said nothing, for now she was aware of the avid interest everyone was showing in the intimate disclosures of her marriage, and she was embarrassed. The awkward silence continued until John Williamson slowly rose to his feet, and, after walking over to place a hand on the shoulder of John Bullaro, who sat slumped forward with his head in his hands, Williamson faced Judith and optimistically predicted that the wrenching events of this evening would eventually prove to be very beneficial to herself and her husband. A new level of honesty had been attained, Williamson announced, and this would allow their relationship to continue and grow without the usual deceptions and illusions. The admissions of sexual infidelity had been painful for her, Williamson conceded, but the Bullaros were still basically the same compatible couple that they had been when they arrived here earlier in the evening—things were now merely out in the open, but nothing about them as people had greatly changed.

While Bullaro listened cynically, imagining that Williamson had made this speech many times before, Judith seemed impressed with Williamson's comments, and she interrupted him to say that she *did* feel changed by what had transpired tonight. For one thing, she said, she felt personally vindicated in knowing that her past suspicions about her husband had been well founded and were not merely the hallucinations of the crazy housewife that he had portrayed her as being. She said she also now realized that she had degraded herself by becoming so possessive, by snooping at windows and magnifying her own insecurity, and feeling often like a shrew; this was not her true nature, she asserted, and Williamson nodded in agreement, saying that she had become a victim of "ownership problems," a common condition in marriage. Judith admitted that for most of her life she had clung too tightly to those around her, possibly because her mother had died when Judith was ten, and she felt threatened by the women her father later dated. But now, with her husband, Judith wanted to overcome this problem, and Williamson said that he and his group could help her if she were willing to deal with it openly; and then he made a suggestion: She should return to the Williamsons' home and actually watch her husband walk off to a bedroom with another woman to make love, and perhaps in this way she would realize that an open act of physical infidelity was less threatening than one that she might suspect and embellish with emotion.

While Judith contemplated Williamson's suggestion, her husband, who was appalled by it, quickly looked up and said: "We're not ready for *that!*"

"Speak for yourself!" Barbara abruptly replied.

Finally, after looking somewhat timidly at her husband, Judith said to Williamson: "I'd like to try it."

Bullaro sat almost stupefied in the chair, amazed by what was happening. He could not believe that this woman to whom he had been married for nearly a decade and thought he understood could suddenly become so sporting and reckless with their private life.

14

DURING THE NEXT few weeks, accompanied by Judith, John Bullaro visited the Williamsons' home on several occasions, and it was surely the most bizarre period of his life. Even years later, when he reflected upon these erotic adventures, it was difficult for him to believe that they had actually happened, and that he had allowed them to happen, even though he had remained throughout a reluctant participant, or so he preferred to think.

Judith, however, was anything but reluctant, for it had been she who insisted that they accept Williamson's challenging test of open infidelity, hoping that it just might be the therapy she needed to overcome her lifelong feelings of dependence. She knew she did not like the woman she had become, the suspicious wife in the suburbs, but until the fortunate meeting with Williamson's group she had never met anyone who seemed willing or able to help her change. While she did not express it in quite this way to her husband, she saw the group as a catalyst in her own self-liberation, and just as her husband had been forced to admit his deceptions, she, too, hoped to unburden herself of certain personal secrets that had caused her much anxiety and guilt. She would like to reveal, for example, that she had also been unfaithful during her marriage; and in the car on the way home from the Williamsons' that first night she had been strongly tempted to tell her husband about it. But she had lacked the courage, possibly because her sexual affair was somewhat unusual, involving as it did a young man who was black.

His name was Meadows, and he had been an orderly at the veterans' hospital in Los Angeles where Judith had worked during her final year in nursing school. Since all the patients were male, the student nurses were accompanied at all times by orderlies, and Meadows, who was tall and attractive, was the first

177

black man Judith had ever become acquainted with. During recreational periods, after the patients had been escorted out to the
hospital lawns to play ball, Judith and Meadows would sit on
the grass watching and talking; and one day, after their conversations had gradually become more intimate, Meadows suggested that they meet privately after work.

Although Judith at this time had been married for only a year,
her sex life with Bullaro had become an uninspired weekend
routine, for which she felt largely responsible but could in no
way alter; she simply had not enjoyed sex after marriage as she
had when she and Bullaro—and her earlier lovers at college—
had been surreptitious about it, had sneaked in and out of motels
and borrowed apartments, and had cavorted in bedrooms at
home while parents and guardians were away or unaware. Sly
sex for Judith had been exciting, wondrously wicked, a challenge to her strict religious upbringing: but once sex had become
legal with her marriage in February 1958, she gradually began
to regard it as just another household chore, like cooking and
shopping, and she continued to feel this way about it throughout
the years that followed, except for the brief fling she had with
Meadows between the winter of 1959 and the spring of 1960.

She and Meadows would go from the hospital to the nearby
apartment of another black orderly, usually on days when her
husband was working late; and for hours they would indulge in
uninhibited lovemaking that gratified and thrilled her—it was
absolute pleasure, uncomplicated by the possibility of an emotional commitment, for she knew that she could never marry
Meadows; he was to be forever associated with her most unacceptable self, a dark fantasy that was fulfilled and then, just as
impetuously, terminated. Her affair had reached the point where
she could no longer face her husband at night, nor pretend she
was asleep when he entered the bedroom, nor justify her resistance to his infrequent advances. As Judith recognized her duplicity, she also realized she wanted children, believing that they
would bring joy and purpose to her life, and eventually they did.

But during the ensuing years of monogamy, her sexual passion
remained subdued, and while she occasionally longed for the
kind of illicit romance she had enjoyed with Meadows, she feared
that it would jeopardize the security of her marriage and family
life, and the mere thought of it accentuated within her the rising
insecurity she had begun to feel about her husband's possible
infidelities.

She had never been able to quell her suspicions, and so she

had welcomed John Williamson's suggestion that such feelings
were unnecessary and should be eliminated. She was surprised
that she had not been more upset by her husband's confessions
during the first evening at the Williamsons' and she looked forward to this second visit as she sat in the car next to her husband,
who seemed rigid and almost haunted behind the wheel.

When the Bullaros arrived, they joined the group in the living
room, and Judith recognized each of them from before, with
one exception. An attractive, shapely young woman named Gail,
who had red hair and dimples, was introduced to the Bullaros,
but she avoided looking directly at Judith, causing Judith to
wonder if she had been selected as her husband's bed partner
later that evening. Quickly, Judith felt her confidence wane. And
at the same time she noticed her husband perk up as Gail smiled
at him, and made room for him next to her on the rug and
devoted her attention completely to him.

Judith sat on the sofa next to David Schwind and Arlene
Gough, sipping wine but inattentive to the conversations around
her because of her own anxiety; and then John Williamson
walked over and kneeled at her feet. He was tender and solicitous, making her feel that he knew exactly what she was thinking, and when he placed his hand on her ankle and began his
peculiar massage, she did not resist his touch, but in fact welcomed it. While she was not physically attracted to him she felt
drawn to those unusual qualities that made him seem special,
mysterious, even indiscreet; and she was also impressed by the
influence he obviously had over the people in this room. Without
apparent effort he had interlaced their lives with his own; and
instead of feeling threatened by him, Judith sensed from the way
he spoke that he was sincerely concerned with her welfare and
personal growth. When he asked if she now felt strong enough
to test the overpossessiveness that she had talked about the last
time, she hesitated for a moment, and then, wanting his approval, replied firmly that she was.

Soon Williamson waved for silence in the room, and, after
explaining to the group that Judith Bullaro now sought their
cooperation in coping with her ownership problems, he turned
toward Gail and asked if she would escort John Bullaro into one
of the bedrooms. Gail immediately stood and extended her hand
to Bullaro, who became self-conscious as everyone turned toward him, including Judith. Although Judith nodded her head,
reaffirming her approval, he felt his heart flutter and knees
weaken as he climbed to his feet. But as he followed Gail toward

the bedroom, watching her hips move, he eagerly anticipated being in bed with her.

She led him into a room that Bullaro had not seen before, faintly lighted by a small lamp on the bureau. After she had closed the door, she stood motionless at the side of the bed for a moment as if suddenly undecided and reluctant, and Bullaro feared that this visit to the bedroom might merely be Williamson's way of testing Judith's jealousy without actual sex taking place. But then Gail pulled back the bedspread and began to unbutton her blouse, remarking at the same time on how strange she felt: Until a few years ago, she said, she had been a twenty-seven-year-old virgin in the Midwest, a victim of her Irish-Catholic background; but now, as she unhinged her brassiere, she remarked on the fact that she was not only about to go to bed for the first time with a married man, but his wife was sitting no more than forty feet away in the next room!

Bullaro smiled and tried to think of an appropriate comment, but as he undressed he remained silent, watching with feverish desire as she climbed nude into the bed. Soon he was lying next to her, kissing her softly, stroking her large breasts and red pubic hair, and gradually becoming aware that though she remained motionless on the bed she was beginning to glisten with perspiration. All at once she seemed shy, nervous, and unknowing; yielding but unresponsive. Her eyes were closed, as if not wanting to witness what was happening. Though she lightly returned his kisses, she did not touch him with her hands. He wondered how a woman so unaggressive could become involved with Williamson's group, and then it occurred to him that perhaps she, like Judith, was now undergoing some private test—Williamson, the sexual problem-solver, might be helping Gail to overcome frigidity, and Bullaro was her surrogate. He whispered in her ear, asking if she was all right, and she nodded with her eyes still closed. But when after considerable difficulty he finally penetrated her, Gail suddenly came alive under him, bolted forward to meet him, wrapped her legs around him and began to cry out, softly at first then louder and louder as he accelerated his thrusting until she was almost screaming, and Bullaro wished that he could somehow silence her. Having never before made love to a noisy woman, he did not know how to react, what to say, what to do except to continue his thrusting and try not to think about the people gathered in the living room who surely could hear.

Then, astonishingly, Bullaro heard high, hysterical howling

coming from the living room, and he recognized the voice as Judith's. He tried to block out her cries and drive himself on to orgasm, but he was unnerved by this conflicting counterpoint: Gail's ecstatic sighs and moans, and Judith's desolate wailing and shrieking; and quickly he lost his erection.

Gail opened her eyes, saying nothing. He lowered himself to his elbows and buried his perspiring face in the pillow. For several moments they both lay motionless and listened as the crying in the living room eventually subsided, and Judith was comforted by other voices. Then the bedroom door slowly opened. It was Arlene Gough, whispering that everything was all right. After briefly watching them lying in bed, Arlene came in and sat next to them and, with a smile, asked if they wanted a threesome. Bullaro thanked her, but shook his head, saying that a twosome was all he could handle tonight.

When Arlene had gone, Bullaro was able to revive his erection and complete the lovemaking with Gail, though it was not nearly so vigorous as it had been. They both felt the inhibiting presence, if no longer the anguished sounds, of Judith; and while they were getting dressed, Bullaro again heard Judith's voice, though now she clearly was no longer distraught—she was laughing; and when Bullaro opened the door he saw her sitting on a chair close to Williamson seeming very comfortable and contented.

Just Judith and John Williamson were in the room, the others having apparently gone off to other bedrooms, and Judith appeared to be so interested in Williamson that she did not notice her husband until he leaned down to kiss her. She smiled but did not get up; and while she assured him that everything was fine, she gave the impression that she wished to be alone with Williamson. As Bullaro moved away and rejoined Gail, he felt for the first time in his marriage that Judith was no longer his.

This feeling persisted in the car as they drove home, and it continued for the rest of the week. Though she was cheerful and dutiful around the house, and kindly toward the children, she seemed preoccupied with her private thoughts, and at night instead of going to bed with him she stayed up late reading the books Williamson had loaned her by Alan Watts, Philip Wylie, and J. Krishnamurti. One night she insisted on going alone to the Williamsons', and when she returned at three o'clock in the morning she seemed charged with energy and a sense of self-discovery, and though he had waited up for her, wanting to talk, she pleaded that she be left alone so that she could sit at the desk and compose the poetry she felt stirring within her.

Having overcome her possessiveness, Judith now seemed unpossessible; and the more distant she became, the more desperate he was to reclaim her. Suddenly and ironically, she was becoming the kind of woman he had long idealized in his fantasies—the daring, carefree woman he had searched for while bicycling through Venice Beach; the impulsive, sexually liberated woman best personified by the art teacher who had once occupied the rear apartment on La Peer.

Since it was apparent that Judith now envisioned Williamson's group as a source of her stability and enlightenment, Bullaro knew that he, too, had to remain closely involved with the group; and when on the following day she suggested that they join the Williamsons for a weekend at Big Bear Lake, he reluctantly agreed, fearing that if he did not she would go with them anyway, perhaps accompanied by another man.

During the eighty-mile ride in the Williamsons' car on Friday night, Bullaro sat in the back holding Judith's hand and hoping that a leisurely weekend would restore some harmony and unity to their relationship. The conversation between the four of them in the car was relaxed and friendly, and after dinner the Williamsons brought wine back to the cabin, and, until midnight, they all sat in front of the fireplace exchanging stories about their youth.

Bullaro did most of the talking because the Williamsons, who seemed very interested in what he was saying, asked several questions; and as he continued to reminisce and drink wine, he gradually began to describe things he had never discussed before. He spoke of his anti-Semitic neighborhood in Chicago and how he had feared being exposed as half-Jewish, and he remembered the many injuries he had sustained on the football field while trying to escape the unathletic image often associated with being Jewish. He remembered his conflicts with his Jewish mother, his uncomfortable visits to Christian churches, and the many lies he told around the neighborhood in the hope of gaining greater social acceptance, most of which now caused him to cringe with embarrassment and self-loathing; but he also felt much pity and compassion for the lonely boy he had been—and suddenly, as the Williamsons and Judith waited for him to continue, he began to tremble. He then stood and walked into the bedroom.

Barbara followed him, closing the bedroom door behind her.

She saw tears in his eyes and offered him a handkerchief and put her arms around him. As he sat silently on the bed, his head lowered, she kissed him and soothed him with soft words, and began unbuttoning his shirt.

After she had completely removed his clothes, and her own, she asked him to lie back on the bed, which he obediently did, and then she lay next to him and gently massaged his body. Though they had previously spent uncountable hours in bed together, this was the first time that he had felt her tenderness.

After they had made love, Bullaro felt his anguish dissolve, and he briefly fell asleep in her arms. But he was awakened by odd sounds coming from the other room, and when he got up and opened the door, he saw, lying on the rug in front of the glowing fireplace, two naked bodies together.

The woman was on the bottom, lying on her back with her eyes closed, her blond hair touching the floor, her legs spread wide and held high with her toes pointed to the ceiling. She was sighing softly and edging her hips forward as the broad-shouldered man who hovered over her was penetrating her with a penis that in the firelight looked like a burning red rivet.

Having never before observed from a distance two people making love, Bullaro was stunned and awed; and for moments he watched with fascination as the interlocked bodies moved in the changing light amid the crackling sounds of burning logs, and for the briefest moment he regarded the sight as beautiful. But then he recognized the familiar shape of his wife's thighs and saw the foreign fetid penis oozing in and out of her, provoking her pleasurable sighs, and pounding back her buttocks, and ripping into Bullaro's guts with such violent force that he suddenly felt disemboweled.

Bullaro fell back, stumbling as he turned quickly toward the bedroom. He felt Barbara reaching out to him, trying to embrace and comfort him, but he abruptly slapped her hands away, no longer wanting to be touched by her, or by anyone, as he slammed the bedroom door behind him and collapsed crying on the bed.

15

CONVINCED THAT THE balance and order of his life had been destroyed, a vengeful John Bullaro quietly plotted the murder of John Williamson and also contemplated his own suicide. Williamson's death could be easily achieved with a few quick pistol shots in the back while Williamson was in the bedroom with his head buried between Judith's thighs, and if Bullaro was content to spare his wife, it was mainly because she would be needed to care for the children. As for Bullaro, he saw himself sinking into the Malibu surf during the final session of the scuba-diving class he was enrolled in, a romantic exit that he replayed in his mind many times as he drove back and forth to the insurance company.

Listening to the news in his car, Bullaro was somewhat consoled to hear that he was not alone in his turmoil—in fact, the entire nation throughout 1968 seemed preoccupied with acts of violence, insanity, and self-destruction. Martin Luther King, Jr., had been assassinated in Memphis, Robert F. Kennedy was fatally shot in Los Angeles, and, in Bullaro's native city of Chicago, there were gory confrontations between the club-swinging police and thousands of antiwar demonstrators and Yippies who had been lured to town by the spotlight of the Democratic National Convention. Among the many innocent bystanders along the sidewalk who had been shoved and hit by the onrushing swarms of police was a spectator named Hugh M. Hefner.

In Vietnam thousands of American soldiers continued to die in the unwanted war that no one seemed capable of stopping, and President Lyndon B. Johnson was so unpopular that he decided not to seek reelection. As peace activists besieged campuses across the nation, civil rights protesters tried to desegregate a bowling alley in Orangeburg, South Carolina, resulting in the deaths of three black students and injuries to thirty-seven other people in battles with the police. At the Olympic games in Mexico City two black sprinters who won medals and then raised black-gloved fists in the air during the playing of "The Star-Spangled Banner" were dismissed from the American team. In Nevada the most powerful hydrogen bomb ever exploded in the United States sent vibrations from the remote desert to the dice tables of Las Vegas one hundred miles away.

Admirers of Fidel Castro hijacked American commercial planes and diverted them to Cuba. Jacqueline Kennedy, America's most glamorous widow, flew in a private plane to a private island in the Ionian Sea to marry the Greek shipping tycoon Aristotle Onassis. After seven hundred prisoners rioted at the Oregon State Penitentiary, causing $2 million worth of damage, they were assigned a new warden. Indicted by a federal grand jury in Boston on charges of conspiring to counsel young men to evade the draft were the pediatrician Dr. Benjamin Spock and Yale chaplain Rev. William Sloane Coffin, Jr. Twenty-three years after American Marines had captured it in one of the bloodiest battles of World War II, the Pacific island of Iwo Jima was returned to Japan. Narcotics agents on the New York waterfront discovered 246 pounds of heroin, worth $22.4 million, secreted in an automobile shipped from France.

Paper money was suspect and financial investors rushed to buy gold. Arab sheiks, saturated with American dollars from oil royalties, were among the most active traders. The California industrialist and art collector Norton Simon paid more than $1.5 million for a Renoir painting. Nude body-painting studios opened in several cities, and the one in Chicago was managed by twenty-eight-year-old Harold Rubin. The year's best-known character in literature was the chronic masturbator in Philip Roth's novel *Portnoy's Complaint*.

Feminists at the Miss America pageant in Atlantic City burned their brassieres. Largely due to the Pill, the American birthrate was the lowest since the Depression. Male and female frontal nudity was displayed on the New York stage in *Hair* and in the imported Swedish film *I Am Curious (Yellow)*. On the day before the nation elected to its highest office the man who promised to combat sexual lewdity and organized crime, and to restore law and order to the land, there was published in New York City the first issue of a ribald tabloid newspaper devoted entirely to sex and pornography. Its name was *Screw*.

Taking the position that nothing between consenting adults is obscene, and that pornography—no less than any other form of expression—is a way of knowing nature, and that the portrayal of open sexuality principally offends those who are most offended by their own nakedness, *Screw* quickly assaulted the Nixonian bourgeois culture with a view of contemporary American life that no establishment journal would have deemed fit to print.

Each week, at thirty-five cents a copy, *Screw* published photographs of people flaunting their genitals and giving the finger to polite society, and the newspaper's captions and articles contained four-letter words that it believed reflected the anger and frustration of the average man with his government. Its cartoons depicted brutish politicians and judges involved in debauchery, and four-star generals were shown buggering one another after they had dropped their bombs over Vietnam. The FBI director was criticized in a *Screw* article under the headline that brazenly asked what many people had long wondered: "Is J. Edgar Hoover a Fag?"; and while the paper ignored the rhetoric of civil rights leaders it did cover the story of a black man who charged racial discrimination after he had been denied service at several legalized brothels in Nevada.

Although the photographs of nude women in *Screw* were rarely beautiful, it was always the intention of the paper to present unretouched realism, ordinary-looking females with their natural blemishes and faults—the modern-day Molly Blooms and Constance Chatterleys rather than the plastic perfect playmates of *Playboy*. *Screw* chronicled America's increasingly depersonalized society by detailing the escalating sales of vibrators to women and the new male market for artificial vaginas and inflatable rubber sex dolls; and *Screw*'s advertising columns published the solicitations of prostitutes, the longings of lonely spinsters, and the uncommon desires of solitary men: "Handsome foot specialist seeks girls with sensitive soles. Write: Ed, GPO Box 2428, NYC 10001."

Screw's scathing and scatological editorials railed against a meddlesome government that justified war while imprisoning such erotic magazine publishers as *Eros*' Ralph Ginzburg; and after the New York police had closed down the stage production of *Che*, arresting ten cast members along with the theater's floor sweeper because the show included an act of fellatio which was considered morally perilous to theater-goers, *Screw* demanded to know why the police that week had not also closed down the city's streets, on which 145 people had been killed. The frequent police raids against the sex shops, adult bookstores, and porn theaters in New York were reported in *Screw* with cynical alarm, for it saw behind each policeman's angry nightstick a sexually frigid Irish-Catholic mother, a drinking father, and a latent homosexual priest in the confessional deploring fleshly pleasure between men and women. When a parish bordered on a porno district, as did Father Duffy's old Irish neighborhood west of Times Square, there were endless battles between proponents of individual freedom and religious restraint; and while the major daily newspapers endorsed the city's latest antismut campaigns in Times Square (which would eliminate, for instance, the coin-operated peep shows patronized by the hoi polloi but allow the continuance of high-priced sex shows like *Oh! Calcutta!* for patrons of the legitimate stage), the staff of *Screw* defended the pleasures of Dirty Old Men, espoused the sidewalk hooker's right-to-life, and was unappalled by the sight of black devils from the ghetto cruising through the blue-collar neighborhood in Lenten-purple pimpmobiles.

Refuting allegations that Times Square had become less safe and inviting since the proliferation of sex businesses in recent years, *Screw* pointed out that the Square has always been a garish, tawdry part of town dominated by transient talent and tacky tourists, a place where people seek what they would rather not find in their own neighborhoods; and furthermore Times Square was now better-policed and less dangerous than it was in Father Duffy's time, when impoverished youth gangs from nearby Hell's Kitchen overwhelmed the area with their maraudings and murders, and where earlier in the century there were so many prostitutes south of Forty-second Street that a resident bishop claimed they outnumbered the city's Methodists.

In the interest of historical perspective, *Screw* often reprinted the faded nude photographs of ancient prostitutes and show girls that were once the horror of New York's fusty "Little Flower" Mayor Fiorello La Guardia; and in a weekly feature entitled "Smut from the Past," it printed old privately taken hard-core snapshots that it received in the mail anonymously from septuagenarians wishing to will to posterity visible proof of their long-ago lust, no longer caring what the neighbors thought because all the neighbors were now dead.

The first police raid on *Screw*'s offices occurred after the issue of May 30, 1969, printed a composite picture of New York's Mayor John Lindsay displaying a hefty penis, and the accompanying text suggested that the mayor's political ability was no match for his agility in bed, limited though it was to the missionary position. Although *Screw's* top editors were charged with obscenity, were fingerprinted at the police station and held briefly behind bars, the paper continued to appear each week, shameless as ever, because its sudden financial success allowed it the luxury of hiring top lawyers to defend its First Amendment rights in court and win the freedom of its editors. After one year of publication—though the police continued to round up sidewalk news vendors who openly sold *Screw*, including some vendors who were blind—the paper's weekly circulation reached 140,000 and the novelist Gore Vidal hailed it as the only newspaper in America that properly serviced its readers.

Assuming that a majority of its readers were very curious about, if not always participants in, the assorted sexual subcultures that existed in New York, *Screw* described and listed the addresses of bars that catered to swinging couples, lesbians, homosexual males, and the leather fetish set; and the reader also learned where to find the best buys in dildoes and French ticklers, superior condoms and aphrodisiacs. Knowing that many people who bought "marital aids" through the mail might be too defensive or shy to complain if they received faulty or worthless merchandise, *Screw* took it upon itself to purchase and test the mail-order gadgets in its office laboratory and to publish negative stories if the items proved to be fraudulent, such as a reputed penis enlarger, or over-priced, such as the erection-sustaining salves that were no more effective than several desensitizing lotions sold in drugstores at one-tenth the cost.

Aware that newspaper advertisements of porno movies invariably exaggerated the film's erotic content, *Screw's* critic noted in his review of each new sex movie the number of erections he had while watching it, a fact that was calibrated in the "peter meter" rating *Screw* gave to each film. The paper conducted investigations of certain swindling lonely hearts clubs and deceptive dating bureaus; and it not only reviewed novels and nonfiction books that were explicitly sexual but conveyed a sense of the writer's style and candor by quoting at length from the book's most passionate passages.

Screw was the only newspaper that, when reviewing the new Viking paperback edition of *The Selected James Joyce Letters*, quoted liberally from the raunchy correspondence between Joyce and his wife, Nora, when he was away from home for an extended period—letters that perhaps shocked the more prim journals because they revealed Joyce's interest in sexual masochism (*I would love to be whipped by you, Nora*) as well as fetishism and anality: *The smallest things give me a great cockstand—a whorish movement of your mouth, a little brown stain on the seat of your white drawers . . . to feel your hot lecherous lips sucking away at me, to fuck between your two rosy-tipped bubbies, to come on your face and squirt it over your hot cheeks and eyes, to stick it up between the cheeks of your rump and bugger you.*

"This is fairly standard fuck fantasy fare," *Screw* commented, although it welcomed the Viking publication, which confirmed what H. L. Mencken had stated long ago: "The great artists of the world are never Puritans, and seldom even ordinarily respectable."

The individual most responsible for the content and philosophy of *Screw* was its executive editor and co-founder, Alvin Goldstein, a man who did not aspire to influence society so much as to reflect the world as he knew it was being lived each day and night by thousands of unnoticed people like himself. At thirty-two, Goldstein was shy, overweight, sexually frustrated, and restless. His first marriage to a Jewish princess, which had been opposed by her parents from the start, had ended bitterly; and his second marriage, to a comely airline stewardess taking flight as a feminist, was not destined to endure. Since he had dropped out of Pace College in New York, where he had majored in English, Goldstein had been an insurance agent, a taxi driver, a glass packer, a welfare recipient, a carnival pitchman at the New York World's Fair, an industrial spy for the Bendix Corporation, and a creator and writer of bizarre tales for a sensational weekly tabloid called *The National Mirror*. The stories that he wrote described acts of pleasure followed by punishment and pain, in the best Judeo-Christian tradition, and the fact that he was so prolific a producer of them was due less to his imagination than to his memory of the past.

Born and reared in a tough ethnic neighborhood in Brooklyn where youthful cruelty was rampant and the favorite game was shoplifting, Goldstein was a stuttering, flabby, fearful adolescent who wet his bed until almost reaching his teens. Intimidated by the dour Jewish women who taught public school, he kept his eyes lowered in class, trying to avoid their glance as he concentrated on drawing endless pictures of World War II fighter pilots shooting one another down in dogfights. He flunked the fifth grade and was sent for treatment to a child psychologist assigned by the Board of Education; but his schoolwork did not improve and his morale worsened. He was humiliated at being left back with the younger students and at being rejected and ignored by his peers, and his alienation became fused with hostility, and after school in the street he was regularly beaten up by older boys, particularly the blacks. Soon he almost began to like it; he was at least getting their attention and, in a strange way, their respect as he subjected himself again and again to their punishment. He would see gangs standing on the corner, the school athletes, the muggers, the super-shoplifters, and he would provoke them with gestures, and they would predictably pounce on him and pummel him with their fists as he fought crazily back, cursing them and challenging them to hit him again.

His mother, who stuttered as badly as he did, was a compassionate but unassertive woman, the daughter of Russian immigrants; and his father, who had dropped out of grade school on the Lower East Side to become a motorcycle messenger with International News Photos, and eventually a photographer with that Hearst-owned organization, seemed lost and almost cataleptic when he was not harnessed with camera straps and running with a pack of news hounds chasing a story. On those occasions when the family would dine at a Chinese restaurant, his father would sit meekly at the table, addressing the Chinese waiter as "sir"; and in the house he was either quietly disapproving or uninvolved with family activity. The only thing that aroused any curiosity in Al about his father was the fact that he kept hard-core pictures of nude women in his bureau drawer, some of them of Orientals that he had photographed during the war while he was a Hearst photographer in the Pacific, and others that he had obtained from friends in the New York Police Department after there had been a porno raid on Times Square.

The only male figure in the Goldstein family that Al admired was his Uncle George, his mother's brother, a large and personable Damon Runyon character who was divorced and lived in a hotel apartment off Broadway in the theater district, where he operated a busy parking lot and was constantly behind the wheels of some very important cars. While he would never know the owners as intimately as he did their vehicles, he nonetheless conveyed to his nephew a convincing familiarity with most of Broadway's top producers and stars, gamblers and pimps; and his persuasiveness was such that when he expressed dismay over the fact that his nephew was still a virgin at sixteen, Al's humble parents wearily conceded that this might represent yet another problem in their son's troubled life, and they welcomed George's offer to resolve it. Soon Al received a call from his uncle instructing him to appear in his hotel suite on the following evening at ten, where a woman would be awaiting him.

Dressed in his bar mitzvah suit, Al Goldstein arrived at the hotel a half hour early. His uncle greeted him, poured him a drink of whiskey, and then took him across the street to a drugstore to buy him a condom, an expensive lambskin premoistened Fourex brand that his uncle considered to be the Rolls-Royce of rubbers. Al was then told to take a long walk around the block before returning to the hotel, by which time the lady should have arrived.

The door to Suite 709 was half opened when Al reappeared twenty minutes later, and in the darkened living room he saw his uncle sitting in front of the television set watching a wrestling match. After waving him in, and asking him to remove his jacket, his uncle pointed to the door of the bedroom and wished him good luck.

Nervously, Al opened the door and heard in the complete darkness a woman's husky voice say, "Hello, I'm Helen. I'm glad you're here." As he held on to the knob, she said, "Come in, close the door. There's nothing to be afraid of." She seemed friendly and gentle and, though he still could not see her, he could distinctly smell her perfume.

"You nervous?" she asked.

"No," he said.

"Would you like to take off your clothes and join me?"

"Yes."

He was beginning to see her now in the unlighted room, sitting up in bed under the covers. She appeared to be a blonde. Carefully he removed his shirt and tie, and heard coins and subway tokens jingling in his pockets as he lay his pants over a chair. Slowly approaching the bed, he felt her hands reaching out to him; and soon she was cuddling him in a motherly way, softly directing his hands around her body, letting him stroke her large breasts, her stomach, and the hair between her legs. She was a very large woman but not fat, and when he pressed his mouth against her breasts, she said encouragingly, "That's right—anything you want is all right."

Then he felt her hands exploring him, touching his penis, exciting him in a way that was strange and wonderful. When she asked if he had brought a condom, he replied that he had; but as he stood up to get it, and saw his erection in the window light from the tall Broadway buildings across the street, he was embarrassed and turned his back to her as he fumbled through his clothing. He searched through his pants pockets, then his shirt pocket, then back to his pants before finally finding it; and after he had climbed back into bed, hesitating, she took the condom from him and opened it, and then expertly slipped the sheath over his penis, again saying, "Everything is going to be fine." He was too excited to speak.

After wetting the tips of her fingers in her mouth, and touching herself between her legs, she pulled him on top of her, inserted him, and then began to move up and down in a rhythm he imitated. He felt totally enclosed in this large woman, comfortably ensconced within her heavy legs and long arms, and when he came she hugged him and said, "Oh, that was nice." He had never felt happier.

Later, relaxing next to her, she asked him how he liked school and other general questions, but she revealed nothing about herself; and he was too shy to inquire. He would have liked to remain longer with her in his uncle's bed, but it was already late, and, since he had school in the morning, he finally said that he should be returning home. As he dressed she remained in bed, and when he said good night and thanked her, she kissed him.

In the living room his uncle, who was still watching the wrestling on television, stood up and asked if everything had gone well, and he seemed genuinely pleased to hear that it had. Al shook his hand and thanked him, and soon he was down the elevator and out in the night air of Broadway, surrounded by people and noise and glowing lights; and he felt older.

Within a few months, having turned seventeen, he dropped out of school and joined the Army. A letter to the Pentagon from one of his father's friends at Hearst was instrumental in getting Al Goldstein into the Signal Corps, where for the next two years at various installations he worked as a photographer, taking pictures of hundreds of military parades and medal-pinning ceremonies—and once, at the request of his sergeant, he photographed the former being orally gratified by a prostitute.

Goldstein was a regular patron of prostitutes in both the United States and Europe while in the Army, and it was not until he had been discharged and began attending Pace College on the G.I. Bill, in the winter of 1958, that he did not automatically expect to pay money for sex—and it was the first time, too, that he did not feel socially and intellectually inferior to nearly everyone around him. He had matured in the Army, had done considerable reading during many lonely nights in the barracks, and at Pace College he was two or three years older than most of his classmates, had traveled more than they had, and he enjoyed a certain status as a returning veteran. In addition to his success with his studies, he wrote for the campus newspaper, and worked each night after class as an apprentice photographer with his father at International News Photos. Having overcome the worst of his stuttering, he joined the college debating team, and was elected its captain.

But the realization that he was now more acceptable did not make him more accepting of other people; if anything his new self-confidence and status encouraged him to express more fully the hostility and frustration he had long felt. Now that his words could be understood he wanted to vengefully compensate for his many years of stifled rage and incoherent muttering that people had often mimicked; and if he should somehow achieve success in life, he knew that his greatest satisfaction would come from knowing that his old teachers and classmates in grade school had failed to perceive his winning potential.

Winning meant everything to Al Goldstein as a college debator, particularly when Pace was challenged by teams from the Ivy League, whose members he saw as socially privileged and rich, and therefore worthy of his scorn. In order to gain points against them Goldstein would do anything: He would falsify facts, would distort and lie in a dozen different ways—none of which disturbed his conscience because in his view Ivy Leaguers *deserved* to be lied to.

Soon, much of his churlishness was directed at Pace College itself. He began to feud with his professors, to write editorials denouncing campus policies, to rebel against the custom of students wearing a jacket and tie to class. As a twenty-one-year-old junior, Goldstein had grown a beard and was recognized as the school's foremost beatnik; and as he neglected his textbooks for the novels of Kerouac and the poetry of Allen Ginsberg, his academic rating declined, although this was also due to the excessive amounts of time and energy he was devoting to an elusive, pretty co-ed who was on the debating team.

Since she represented his very first love experience, his ardor was as romantic as his expectations were naïve, especially since she was a sexually adventurous and popular young lady who had made it clear from the beginning that she did not intend to limit her social life exclusively to his nightly desires. Occasionally with his knowledge, and sometimes covertly, she dated other men—not consistently, but just often enough to keep Goldstein in a constant state of uncertainty and despair. His problem was that he could neither withdraw from her nor control her. She obsessed him physically. On nights when he was not in bed with her he masturbated to her image, seeing with maddening clarity her lean graceful figure and long, slender legs wrapped around the bodies of men he feared were more worthy than he was.

Though he was overweight, he had an aversion to overweight women; and despite the fact that his mother was large-breasted, or possibly because of it, Goldstein was lured by the smaller, firmer breasts of the sort that adorned the girl on the debating team; and while she had caused him much anguish since they had begun dating, reviving his old feelings of self-doubt, she also aroused his new combative spirit, his grim drive to conquer—she was, like the challenge of a debate itself, something he believed that he could finally win with his cunning mind, his quick mouth, and, in this particular instance, his cunnilingual tongue.

If there was a way to her heart, it was possibly through virtuoso performances upon her vulva, a conclusion he tentatively arrived at one night after she had gently pushed his head down between her legs and pronounced this to be her favorite pleasure. Prior to this, he had hardly ever heard of cunnilingus, and certainly never by that name. On the rare occasions when it had been referred to in the Army or in his Brooklyn neighborhood, it had prompted only vile and scrubby descriptions, the most polite of which was "muff-diving," and no self-respecting macho street hoodlum of his acquaintance had ever admitted to indulging in it. It was unmanly, if not unsanitary. It placed a man in a submissive role to a woman. It was primarily for perverts.

Indeed, after Goldstein had done research on the subject in the sex encyclopedias of various libraries, he discovered that cunnilingus, along with fellatio, was officially defined by the government as an obscene act, a form of sodomy, and it was illegal in most of the American states even when practiced in private by married couples. In Connecticut the crime of oral sex could be punishable by a thirty-year jail term. In Ohio it was one to twenty years. In Georgia such a "crime against nature" could lead a practitioner to life imprisonment at hard labor—a penalty far more severe than having sex with animals, which in Georgia was punishable by only five years.

The laws against oral sex evolved of course from ecclesiastical law, which since the Middle Ages had determined these unprocreative acts to be unnatural, even though they had been natural enough to the multitudes who had practiced them since the earliest days of recorded civilization. Pictures showing people engaged in cunnilingus and fellatio could be found on Chinese scrolls dating back to 200 B.C., and also on ancient oriental rice bowls, perfume vases, and snuff bottles. Sculptured figures in erotic oral postures had appeared on early temples in India; and the first-century Roman satirist Juvenal referred often to cunnilingus and fellatio, suggesting that both were common during that time among heterosexuals as well as homosexuals. While the medieval church heavily penalized those who confessed to such pleasures, and created guilt within those who did not admit their sins, the oral predilection continued unabated for centuries in private, though it was rarely described and depicted openly except in forbidden art and literature, such as the eighteenth-century novel *Fanny Hill* and the much-censored work of Henry Miller.

Having read most of Miller's books, Goldstein was not only impressed with the author's vivid description of cunnilingus but was convinced that Miller himself greatly enjoyed bringing pleasure to a woman in this manner—and so did Al Goldstein, after much practice and encouragement from his young lady friend. When he had his head between her legs, and his tongue caressed her clitoris and vaginal lips, and his hands were firmly holding on to her buttocks and moving her at will, he sensed his power over her as he did at no other time. His tongue was a more potent weapon than his penis, or so it seemed to be during this period of his life; it was more reliable, tractable, responsive to his every command—his penis could be limp, unarousable, but his tongue was always capable of thrusting, curling and whirling its way into her good graces; and as his mouth was upon her he was conscious not only of the luxuriance of her loins but also that he was making a literary connection with Henry Miller.

But when he was not in bed with her, she seemed indifferent to him, even more so after she began attending classes at night, and gradually during the fall of 1960 their relationship ended. Soon he found another girl, not quite so sophisticated but more attentive; and he cared for her less.

Having learned all he could from his after-school job as a

photographer's apprentice with the Hearst organization, Goldstein during the Christmas holidays accepted an assignment from a photo agency to fly to Cuba, where the rising tension between the new Castro regime and the American government would soon lead to the termination of diplomatic relations, an inevitable event perhaps hastened a bit by the disruptive presence in Havana of Al Goldstein. Within an hour of his arrival he began taking pictures with a telephoto lens from his hotel window of the female militia marching across the street, and later that afternoon he wandered around the city photographing armed installations and anti-American slogans that appeared on billboards. During the evening, with four cameras strapped around his neck, he attended a news conference presided over by the Cuban leader's brother, Raoul Castro, and after taking more than thirty pictures of the speaker and the other principals on the stage, he discovered that he was being edged out of the room by armed guards who demanded that he turn over his film.

Expressing outrage at being interrupted from his work, Goldstein refused; and as he flamboyantly and futilely waved his press credentials, he was shoved into a vehicle and driven to a military prison and arrested on charges of espionage. He would spend four days and nights in jail before the American Embassy could convince the Cubans that he was not a spy but merely an exuberant student photographer on holiday; whereupon he was released and flown off the island on the next plane to Miami.

While the publicity from his Cuban experience added to his stature as a big man on the campus, it also intensified his desire to leave it, especially since he was about to flunk freshman math for the third successive year and he was bored and restless with student life in general. And so in the spring of 1961, during his junior year, he quit college to become a full-time freelance news photographer in search of a profession and high adventure. But he would be extremely disappointed. His most important assignment during the next two years would be a relatively uneventful trip on a government press plane to Pakistan to photograph the arrival of the First Lady, Jacqueline Kennedy; and his most daring voyage would be his elopement to Great Neck, Long Island, in January 1963 with a young woman he did not love.

He had first met her during her student days at Pace not long before he left the campus; and while he had not been attracted to her—she was overweight and aggressive, the indulged daughter of socially ambitious Jewish parents—he was impressed with the fact that she was impressed with him, and she was the first person who had ever seriously suggested that he would one day become a success. If her parents had not so vehemently objected to the few dates she had with him, the relationship would have become at best a passive, friendly acquaintanceship, but their insistence that he was unworthy of her, and that she should stop seeing him, induced her rebelliousness and infuriated Al Goldstein well beyond the point of pacification. He *had* to marry their daughter. And he did. And he was sorry.

Shortly after the couple had settled into their new apartment on West Fifty-fourth Street, their irreconcilable incompatibility was evident to both of them; and although they remained married for two and a half years, they argued constantly and rarely made love. Rather than have sex with her, Goldstein would often masturbate in the bathroom late at night to the nude photographs of Diane Webber, Bettie Page, or Candy Barr, the pretty Texas stripper who starred in the famous 1953 blue movie *Smart Aleck*; or to the lingerie models in the New York *Times* Sunday magazine; or to the *Life* magazine photos of Marilyn Monroe climbing out of the swimming pool; or to the news pictures of Jacqueline Kennedy in sleek low-cut gowns that he mentally removed.

He also sought erotic stimulation by going to pornographic films off Broadway, where he spent afternoons in the company of other lonely men who, with wishful thoughts and private stirrings, sat separated by empty seats and avoided eye contact with one another when the house lights went on between shows. On nights when Goldstein had an excuse to be out alone, he would often visit one of the many brothels he knew in Harlem, which was not yet completely off-limits to prowling white men, although the Black Power movement and racial fear would soon discourage the sex traffic and result in black hookers being brought downtown in big cars and deposited along Lexington Avenue and the Times Square district.

In one sense Goldstein's married years did fulfill the prophecy expressed by his wife during their courtship: He did become a success, though not as a photographer. He excelled at selling insurance. Eager to earn more money than he thought he ever could earn as a photographer, he answered a help-wanted ad in the *Times* placed by the Mutual of New York insurance company, and within a year of being hired his sales record established him as No. 14 among Mutual's seven thousand agents.

Ambitious and energetic, he traveled swiftly around town on a motor scooter, and he benefited from his verbal skill and his capacity to convince large numbers of people that dire events loomed ahead.

But after two years with the firm, and the dispiriting effect of his wearisome homelife, his sales declined and he suddenly confronted the gloom that he had foreseen for other people. One night when he returned home he found his apartment ransacked, the furniture gone, and his clothing tossed around the room and cut into pieces. His expensive cigars had been broken in half, his stereo was missing, and the bathroom floor was covered with broken glass and smelled of his after-shaving lotion. His wife was nowhere in sight, and she had left behind none of her own personal possessions.

Enraged as he was, he felt completely helpless. He knew that he could never prove that this had been his wife's way of avenging his rejection of her, and if he sued her he also knew that her father, a lawyer, would be a formidable opponent in court. Leaving the apartment as he found it, Goldstein spent the next several nights at his parents' home in Queens, an uninsured insurance man too stunned to speak; and during the ensuing days in New York he was consoled mainly by the friends to whom he had sold policies.

Soon he decided to quit the business, convinced that selling insurance was only reinforcing his depression; and when one of his friends—a man who presided over the Belgian Village at the New York World's Fair—offered him a job managing a dime-pitching concession, Goldstein immediately accepted. Six nights a week Goldstein stood in colorful clothes, bally-hooing behind a microphone, trying to entice people to toss dimes and land them within the small red circles that were etched on wooden blocks, thereby winning a television set. The game was not rigged, and during the summer of 1965 he gave away thirty sets, while earing $250 a week and losing himself in the carnival atmosphere.

But in the fall of 1965 the fair closed, and, owing credit companies more than four thousand dollars in bills incurred by his wife and himself, Goldstein worked at various times during the next year as a rug salesman, an encyclopedia salesman, a taxi driver, and he also sold his blood regularly to a Times Square blood bank. Personally discouraged, and equally disenchanted with the world around him, he became, at the age of thirty, a part-time drifter and full-time fantasizer.

* * *

Though his marital experience made him wary of becoming deeply involved with women, he still craved female company and preferred to think that each night in New York there were many attractive women who were as lonely as he was, and were available for the asking, if he only knew where to ask. But while he could have gone to bars and discotheques, he did not like the drinking or the noise or the inevitable competition with other men for the choice pickups, and he also felt too old and fat for the collegiate singles scene. There were of course always B-girls and street hustlers at his disposal—and for the first time in his life he understood the absolute necessity for such women in society—but on his limited budget he could not in this manner afford his sexual habit. He did subscribe to a computer dating service, which turned out to be fraudulent, and each week he bought *The East Village Other* and scanned the personal advertising columns where women often expressed a desire for male companionship, listing a postal box address. But for every ten ads that he replied to, nine went unanswered, and the tenth was usually a prostitute.

He also became a member of lonely hearts clubs and corresponded with pen-pal organizations and periodicals that offered social introductions through the mail—such as Wally Beach's ''Select'' service in New York; Sharon's ''Exotic'' service in Toronto; the Renaissance Club of Index, Washington; the Happi-Press of Whittier, California—and he eventually composed his own advertisement and circulated it in the lonely hearts press throughout the land. He wrote:

I am thirty, am 5'8½", blue eyes & brown hair. I have been a photo journalist with assignments in Pakistan & Cuba, etc. I am also divorced. I hope that this fact does not dampen your interest. One would hardly know that I am ''used'' merchandise. I prefer to think that I'm now like a comfortable pair of shoes, ''broken in.'' I enjoy everything with an emphasis on reading, movies, theater, outdoors, & good times of a non-selfish nature. I travel in my work and will shortly be spending 2 to 7 days at a nudist colony at Mays Landing, N.J. Well, I do anything *once*.

So drop me a line with your response to this brief one of mine & include your address and phone number, etc.

Yours for future fun,

Al Goldstein

He listed his address and telephone number, and waited for weeks. But no one replied.

It was while in this rejected condition, and also between jobs, that he met on the street one day a young male acquaintance from Pace College who said that he had just heard of a potentially lucrative part-time position that might interest Goldstein; it was with a large company and it paid $200 a week and offered a $10,000 bonus if the work was satisfactorily completed. Goldstein was given the telephone number of a certain labor lawyer in New York who would arrange for an appointment. After Goldstein had called the number and been interviewed in person by the lawyer and another man, he was given the job. Goldstein was now an industrial spy for a subsidiary of the Bendix Corporation.

The subsidiary—the P&D Manufacturing Company of Long Island City, which produced ignition systems and other automotive parts for Detroit—was a profitable firm whose executives feared that the factory workers were planning to defect from their traditional union, which was now management-controlled, and affiliate themselves with the independent and powerful United Auto Workers' union, which would surely demand higher wages and greater workers' benefits. The UAW had already used sound trucks outside the factory gates urging the P&D employees to vote for UAW representation at the next labor meeting, and now the company's executives were interested in knowing approximately how many of its four hundred workers would vote to quit the home union.

Goldstein's assignment was to ingratiate himself with the other workers, to perceive their intentions regarding the UAW, and then to secretly report back to the front office. Goldstein worked as a stock-room clerk and deliverer of auto parts around the factory, allowing him to move freely within all the departments and partake in much socializing and eavesdropping. In less than a month he deduced that the majority of workers favored the UAW; and after consulting with management, he participated in a campaign to spread the rumor that if the UAW was voted in, the company would close down the Long Island plant and move south, meaning that nearly everyone would lose their jobs. Since this had recently happened at another factory in Long Island after a UAW takeover, the rumors were credible; and when the workers voted, the UAW issue was defeated 203 to 198.

Though he initially took a perverted pleasure in the triumph,

Goldstein later began to feel somewhat guilty and loathsome. However foolish or improper he had been during his erratic life, he had always sympathized and identified with the underprivileged and subordinate, and now he was disgusted with his role as a management spy; and while he remained on the job for several weeks and was expected to continue his covert actions, he sensed that even his employers were becoming contemptuous of his position, which was an embarrassing reminder of their own duplicity.

Finally, and without warning, Goldstein left the company one evening and did not return on the following morning, or any morning thereafter. He did not know precisely what determined his decision; he just woke up one day with an irrepressible urge to sever his connection with the company, and the inevitable forfeiture of the $10,000 bonus did not deter him. He stayed home for several days, refusing to answer the constantly ringing telephone, and at night he wandered aimlessly around the city, browsing through bookstores in Times Square and going to all-night movies. He became increasingly dependent on his radio during this time, listening regularly at home to the talk shows of Barry Gray, Long John Nebel, and Jean Shepherd, as well as to the antiestablishment commentators employed by station WBAI, and several other shows that provided compatible company for his misery.

In the summer of 1966, after he had resumed working as a taxi driver, he listened in his cab to his favorite programs on a new German portable radio that cost him most of his savings; it was a $500 Nordmende shortwave model that also allowed him to tune in at any hour of the day or night to words and music from around the world. This radio, which he carried with him everywhere, represented through most of 1966 his main contact with contemporary life, and Goldstein would no doubt have remained remote from human involvement for an even longer period were it not for a fortuitous meeting one day with an insurance agent he had known at Mutual of New York. The agent was very cordial and seemed concerned with Goldstein's welfare, and in the course of their conversation he told Goldstein that he occasionally dated an airline stewardess who had a roommate, also a stewardess, and he suggested that Goldstein call her and ask her out. She lived on East Ninety-first Street and flew with Pan American; her name was Mary Phillips, and she was a pretty blue-eyed ashen blonde from South Carolina.

The description roused Goldstein from his lethargy, and as

soon as he returned to his apartment on West Twentieth Street he dialed her number. There was no answer, but he tried it again one hour later, then again within the next hour, and then with almost desperate persistence he continued to dial through the night into the next day and finally through the week.

Frustrated, and finding it sadly reminiscent of the time when his ads in the lonely hearts press went unanswered, he telephoned his friend at the insurance company who commiserated but encouraged Goldstein to keep dialing—Mary Phillips was probably on an overseas flight or short vacation, the friend said, adding that after she had returned to New York and Goldstein had finally managed to meet her, he would not be disappointed.

Goldstein thanked him, and during the next two weeks he called her number several times each day, while her continued unavailability allowed full play to his fantasies; he was becoming obsessed with her, was convinced that she would ultimately fulfill his romantic need, was jealous of the pilots who traveled with her and the corporate businessmen who propositioned her at 35,000 feet, from one time zone to another—and then one afternoon, after he had dialed and the telephone began to ring, the receiver was picked up at the other end, and Goldstein was suddenly tempted to hang up, but he heard a woman's voice say hello, and when he asked for Mary Phillips, the voice said, ''This is she.''

With a slight stutter, Goldstein introduced himself; he mentioned the name of their mutual acquaintance from the insurance company, and asked if during the coming week she was free for lunch or dinner. She thanked him but said that her travel schedule and other obligations would make lunch or dinner impossible for most of the next month, but after that she would be happy to see him, and she suggested that he call her again. She seemed sincere, and he liked the sound of her voice, which was warm and vivacious, although he quickly reminded himself that she was an airline stewardess and that he might be naïvely responding to what was merely a professionally polite manner.

Nevertheless, he continued to dial her number regularly, but each time he reached her she declined to go out with him—and yet her charm and gentility kept him from becoming irritated or discouraged; her elusiveness seemed to intensify his desires, to heighten his anticipation.

Finally, after five months of trying, Al Goldstein made a date with Mary Phillips. They had brunch at a restaurant off Lexington Avenue near her apartment. As he sat across from her he was so awed by her beauty that he could barely speak or eat. Her blue eyes were exquisite. Her blond hair, her creamy complexion, her sunny disposition suggested to him that she had never known an unhappy day in her life. Her lean figure was exactly to his liking, and, as he sat listening to her and also watching as other people entered the restaurant, he could not help but think that they were wondering what she was doing with him—this golden belle having brunch with a fat Jewish cabdriver.

But she appeared to be unembarrassed, replying easily and at length to the questions he asked about her job and her girlhood in the South, her ancestors who were country doctors and lawyers, her mother who was a musician and her father who taught history at The Citadel military college in Charleston. She seemed to be fond of her parents and comfortable with her past, and as Goldstein listened he realized how little the two of them had in common. And he also knew, though he had no insight into her at all, that she was not the sort of person that he could ever make a pass at. She seemed too ethereal for his rampant coarseness. And then she told him that she had been expelled from college in her junior year for keeping her lover in her dormitory room.

The ease with which she revealed this astonished him as much as the fact itself. There was no remorse in her voice, no change in her angelic presence, as she recalled being summoned before the disciplinary committee of Hood College in Frederick, Maryland, just before the spring holiday, and charged with harboring a male in her room for several nights. Actually, she admitted to Goldstein, the young man had been living with her for nearly a month, and although she knew that this was against the campus rules she also believed that she had a right to privacy in her dormitory. When Mary and her friend left the school and went to Charleston to tell her parents that she had been expelled, her parents reacted with anger. Her father banished Mary's lover from the house, and her mother urged her never to tell anyone in the town why she had left college.

After sitting mournfully at home for several days, Mary read an announcement in the Charleston newspaper that a representative of Pan American had just arrived in the city to interview prospective stewardesses, and Mary saw this as a grand opportunity to escape the continuing disapproval of her parents; so she applied to the Pan Am representative, passed the examination, and was accepted. Weeks later she was attending a training school in Miami, and five weeks after that she graduated and was transferred to New York. During her first year with Pan Am, she flew to the Caribbean, then shifted to the European division. And while she told Goldstein that she did not intend to make a career of flying—her ambition was to become an editor or freelance writer—she liked her work and enjoyed living in New York.

After they had finished brunch, she invited Goldstein back to her apartment. She was very open and friendly, and they spent the rest of the afternoon talking; and later she made it clear, in ways that women can, that she was ready to go to bed with him. He hesitated, unable to fully believe what was happening, but by early evening they were making love.

He saw her often after that, and while he remained somewhat skeptical of her affection, assuming that much of it was inspired by her rebellion against her parents, he did not care to question too closely the source of his pleasure. She moved into his apartment during the spring of 1968, and they were married that summer in Mexico, though he had yet to get a divorce from his first wife. Such technicalities did not greatly concern him during this chaotic year when the government seemed unworthy of consultation, and civil disobedience and dissent was being adhered to across the country; and while Goldstein had never thought of himself as a political activist, he now felt the urge to take an antiestablishment position, and he decided to begin by exposing in the underground press his espionage mission for the Bendix Corporation.

He saw this as a way of assuaging some of his lingering guilt as well as embarrassing a large corporation that fulfilled major defense contracts with the government, and when he proposed his idea in person to the editors of a radical tabloid, the New York *Free Press*, he was pleased to hear that they were eager to print his story. They could only afford one hundred dollars for it, but they promised to begin it on page one and to allow him adequate space in which to describe all the sordid schemes used by white-collar executives against the unsuspecting workers.

It took Goldstein ten days to write his story, and when he delivered it the editors were impressed with its condemning evidence and predicted that its publication would set off traumatic repercussions within the corporate hierarchy of Bendix. But a week after the 10,000 copies of the New York *Free Press* were delivered to the newsstand with Goldstein's story on page one, under the headline ''I Was an Industrial Spy for the Bendix Corporation,'' it was obvious that the editors had overestimated the public's interest in this story, or perhaps the people who read it simply did not believe it.

For whatever reason, the *Free Press* did not receive a single letter or phone call in response to the story, and Al Goldstein, who had been sitting around the newspaper office each day in a state of vaulted anticipation, was visibly deflated by the result. But the assignment with the *Free Press* would prove in time to be beneficial to Goldstein, for it provided him with an introduction to a young staff member who would befriend him and later help him launch his own newspaper.

Jim Buckley was a typesetter and subordinate editor on the *Free Press*, a diminutive dark-haired twenty-four-year-old New Englander who, despite four years in the Navy and a lifetime of misadventure, exuded the starched innocence of an ageless choirboy. He had large doeful brown eyes, a well-scrubbed pale complexion, and a timorous disposition that concealed a restless spirit that drove him from job to job and place to place as a temporary companion of anyone who seemed to have a sense of direction.

Born in Lowell, Massachusetts, and reared in several orphanages while his quarreling and separated parents took turns reclaiming him and abandoning him, Buckley attended schools in New England and Florida, and California and Hawaii, before dropping out to become a full-time hitchhiker, a delicate and meek roadside figure that motorists invariably stopped for. Following his release from the Navy in 1965 after a tour of the Orient, Buckley worked variously as a teletype operator with a San Francisco securities firm, a sidewalk vendor of the Los Angeles *Free Press*, a cook in a Greenwich Village restaurant, a typist with the United Nations, a fudge maker at the New York World's Fair (standing in a glass booth not far from where Goldstein managed the dime-pitching concession), and a porter in a cheap London hotel that catered to $5-a-day tourists.

After living in France with dope-dealing American college boys, and in North Africa with Arab sheepherders, and returning home to have a wayward cross-country romance with James Agee's niece, Buckley felt he was ready to settle down in New York and pursue a career in journalism. But after a few months with the New York *Free Press* he was again ready to quit, planning to invest his limited savings in a newspaper of his own, one that would hopefully be less polemical and more profitable than the *Free Press*, whose forlorn owner discouraged requests for salary raises by walking around the office in bare feet.

This was when Jim Buckley met Al Goldstein, whose spy piece he helped to edit, and whose expressed frustrations he not only identified with but saw as the essence of a viable partnership—or at least some hedge against the probability that neither of them could ever make it alone. While Goldstein's idea of starting a sex tabloid did not immediately appeal to Buckley, who was not yet completely liberated from the years of strict upbringing in Catholic orphanages, Buckley did agree with Goldstein that there was undoubtedly a ready market for the sort of weekly periodical that Goldstein envisioned—a kind of *Consumer Reports* on bodily pleasure and prurience, a newspaper that would unabashedly portray the erotic world that was rising all around them but was being ignored by the squeamish proprietors of the establishment press. Sex was the biggest story of mid-twentieth-century America, Goldstein told Buckley in a burst of pitchman's pride, and their libidinous and frolicsome journal would be a welcome contrast to the dreary palaver of the New Left that dominated the underground press in America.

And so in the late summer of 1968, with each man investing $175, a corporation was formed to publish a newspaper that Goldstein entitled *Screw*, being somewhat inspired by a defunct poetry periodical of the recent past that had called itself *Fuck You—a Magazine of the Arts*. Fearing that his first wife might one day legally claim part of his stock in *Screw*, Goldstein registered his half of the partnership in the name of his second wife, Mary Phillips, who was listed on the masthead as a copublisher with Buckley, though she continued to fly as a Pan Am stewardess. Goldstein identified himself as the executive editor, and placed his name at the top of a long list of staff members, most of whom were imaginary.

In producing the twelve-page first edition of *Screw* in November 1968, and introducing it in an editorial as "the most exciting new publication in the history of the West," Goldstein and Buckley did almost everything themselves: Goldstein wrote most of the articles, Buckley did the typesetting, and they both personally delivered the initial printing of 7,000 copies to the few newsstands in New York that would accept a tabloid whose front page was dominated by a photograph of a bikini-clad brunet stroking a large kosher salami.

The first issue sold more than 4,000 copies, the second issue did better, and after ten issues *Screw* became a twenty-four-page paper selling nearly 100,000 copies. Now *Screw* had the money to advertise for more editors and reporters, and many it hired had the professional skill and educational background to work on almost any publication in New York. *Screw*'s book critic, Michael Perkins, a graduate of Ohio University with postgraduate work at CCNY, had previously reviewed books for *The Village Voice*. The new managing editor of *Screw*, Ken Gaul, a graduate of Seton Hall with a degree in English literature, had worked for Prentice-Hall and other publishers; and *Screw*'s contributing editor, Dean Latimer, had won a creative writing fellowship to Stanford. The art director of *Screw*, Steven Heller, who had worked with Buckley on the New York *Free Press*, would years later become an art director on the New York *Times*. A young photojournalist on *Screw* named Peter Brennan had graduated with honors from Fordham and earned a graduate degree in literature from Harvard.

When Brennan joined *Screw* in January 1971, the paper had recently shifted its operation from overcrowded quarters on Union Square into a more spacious office in a tall loft building less than two blocks away. While the loft building at 11 West Seventeenth Street was dark and grimy, and was located on a shadowed side street west of Fifth Avenue, Goldstein and Buckley considered it an ideal place in which to inconspicuously produce their controversial tabloid, never realizing that this new location was already under the surveillance of the police and the FBI.

16

ALTHOUGH THE TWELVE-STORY brick building into which
Screw moved had been designed in 1907 as a factory loft, it was
architecturally elaborate; it had corniced columns, and curved
front windows, and escutcheoned metal trimming across its facade, and carved on its front wall, above an ornate row of
second-story windows, were the initials of the millionaire realtor who once proudly owned it—E.W.B., for Edward West
Browning, better known in old tabloid headlines as "Daddy"
Browning after he had become scandalously involved during the
1920s with a curvesome, blue-eyed, flirtatious girl of fourteen
named Peaches Heenan.

Browning had first noticed Peaches at a high school dance
one night at the Hotel McAlpin on Broadway; and though he
was then a gray-haired man of fifty, it was not considered unusual for him to be among such young people because he was
renowned in New York as a leader in youth work and a philan-
thropist who donated generously to underprivileged students,
hospitalized children, and orphans.

In 1919, having no children of his own after three years of
marriage, Browning and his wife had adopted a little girl. A
year later, after adopting another girl, Browning built for their
pleasure, over one of his large apartment houses on the Upper
West Side, a luxurious rooftop residence that was surrounded
by a garden with Japanese lanterns and temple bells, fountains
and songbirds, and a lake large enough to allow a boat to be
rowed about. The celebrated largess of Daddy Browning, extolled in newspapers throughout the nation, possibly lent inspiration to the cartoonist who in 1924 created the comic strip
characters of Daddy Warbucks and Little Orphan Annie.

In 1925, however, Browning's wife had divorced him, taking

their older adopted daughter with her to Paris, and leaving him with the younger child, named Sunshine; and while he received favorable publicity and thousands of letters after he had advertised in the press for a "girl of 14" to become a companion to the eight-year-old Sunshine, Browning's altruism suddenly became suspect after he had met, and later began to date, young Peaches Heenan, who would be seen smiling along Fifth Avenue in the back of his peacock blue Rolls-Royce surrounded by gift boxes containing toys, expensive clothing, and jewelry. In 1926, with the consent of her separated parents, who had reared her in a tenement building in Washington Heights, Peaches Heenan became, on her sixteenth birthday, the second Mrs. Browning.

At this time Edward Browning was worth more than $20 million. Born in Manhattan to solvent Victorian parents who had schooled him in the Bible and the virtues of hard work, Browning advanced into manhood with a limited knowledge of youthful frivolity. With his marriage to Peaches, however, he vowed that he would devote less time to business and more to leisure, and he adjusted rather quickly to his new public image as a debonair rake. Suddenly he was part of the Jazz Age, and as he escorted the ermine-cloaked Peaches into fashionable restaurants, he paused patiently on the sidewalk in the flashing light of photographers. He provided Peaches with a chauffeured limousine, and underwrote her buying sprees along Fifth Avenue with her mother, a hospital nurse who had encouraged the relationship with Browning from the start and had received in turn cash gifts during the courtship.

In his office, Browning kept a large scrapbook filled with news clippings that mentioned his name, and he never turned down an opportunity to be interviewed—even when, ten months after the marriage, he was sadly forced to admit to a noisy gathering of newsmen that Peaches had run away. The servants had reported seeing her leaving the Long Island house with her mother and a moving van loaded with everything he had given her. Though bitterly disappointed, Browning announced that he still loved her, and through the press he pleaded with her to return.

But Browning's next glimpse of his wife was in a crowded New York courtroom where her lawyers demanded a divorce with a huge settlement, and where Peaches herself took the stand and charged him with mental cruelty and immorality. She said that he liked to see her in the nude at the breakfast table, and that he had once given her a book of nude photographs, and she hinted that he was a gentleman of unnatural desires.

When Browning's attorneys cross-examined her, however, they elicited the information that prior to the marriage Peaches had kept an erotic diary containing the names of other men with whom she had made love—a fact that she tearfully admitted above the sighs and groans in the courtroom and the judge's banging gavel. Although the final settlement was far less than Peaches Browning had hoped for—she received $170,000 in cash and eventually six West Side buildings—she capitalized on her publicity by becoming, under her mother's guidance, a vaudeville personality and aspiring actress. But she was professionally unsuccessful, and during the ensuing decades the news about her was restricted mainly to her remarriages—she would marry and divorce three more men after Browning—and finally, in 1956, there was the headline that the former Peaches Browning had taken a fatal fall in a bathroom at the age of forty-four.

Edward Browning, who died in 1934 shortly before his six-tieth birthday, had spent his final years concentrating on what he knew best, the real estate business; and long before most of his contemporary tycoons, he foresaw the Depression and profitably sold off the bulk of his West Side property prior to the crash, including the loft building at 11 West Seventeenth Street.

Decades after his death the exterior of the building remained pretty much as he had left it, retaining its embellished turn-of-the-century facade and his deeply carved initials; but the interior soon showed signs of deterioration and neglect. The paint peeled, the cracks widened in the walls, and the city soot settled so thickly on the windowpanes that it dimmed the daylight. The various small dress factories and milliners that had traditionally rented space in the narrow twelve-story building, south of the Garment Center, gradually moved out due either to their bankruptcy or to dissatisfaction with the building's outmoded fixtures and the fact that its single small slow-moving elevator often broke down.

Between the 1930s and the 1960s the property was sold and resold to several owners, none of whom found it profitable, and by the 1970s the upper floor space was rather indiscriminately rented out to tenants who, in grander times, would have been deemed undesirable. In addition to *Screw*, which occupied the eleventh floor, there was on the tenth floor the headquarters of the American Communist party; and on the top floor there was a homosexual commune consisting of young men who had converted Browning's old business office into living quarters. On the floors below, most of the tenants were, if not socially or politically deviant, at least quaintly unconventional, somewhat mysterious, or borderline bizarre.

One tenant was a metal craftsman who made brass knuckles. There was a group of middle-aged men who on certain evenings each week gathered to tinker with their model trains and run them around the miniature tracks that encircled the room. There was the editorial staff of a science fiction horror magazine called *Monster Times*, and on another floor was the office of a scandal tabloid entitled *Peeping Tom*. A divorced New York socialite, a descendant of Cornelius Vanderbilt Whitney, used his floor as an atelier and romantic retreat. There was also in residence a reclusive red-haired lady bookbinder who was often visited at night by her twin sister. Two floors below was an Israeli repairman who worked in an office surrounded by several tapping typewriters with nobody behind them—all the machines were automatic. Shortly before Christmas in 1970, two men who had been in the fast-food business rented space on the ninth floor and opened a massage parlor.

They concealed the cracked walls with brown Formica paneling and installed wall-to-wall carpeting that covered the floorboards between which were thousands of rusty pins and needles dating back to the days when garment workers were employed there. They built a reception room near the elevator entrance, furnishing it with a Danish modern desk and cushioned swivel chairs, a stereo and a large coffee table on which were copies of *Playboy* and *Penthouse*. In the rear they built a shower room and a sauna, and also four small private massage rooms. Each room was equipped with a massage table and a bedstand containing bottles of rubbing alcohol, oil, talc, and boxes of Kleenex.

Then they placed ads in *The Village Voice* and other newspapers seeking female employees to work as "figure models" or "masseuses." They hoped to hire at least eight or ten women who would coordinate their daily schedules so that at least four of them would always be on duty to keep the four massage rooms in operation during the expected busy hours of noon, 5 P.M., and 11 P.M. Since massage parlors were still relatively new to New York, and were not yet identified by the police as fronts for prostitution, dozens of unsuspecting young women applied for work thinking that the job was in a photographer's studio or perhaps a health club; and when they realized that they would be rubbing the nude bodies of men, and confronting erections and sexual propositions, they sought employment elsewhere.

But other women, more liberated products of the sixties, were unappalled by this kind of work. They were not discomforted by the nudity of strangers, nor were they restrained by moral definitions that in the early fifties had inhibited their mothers. Among those hired were students working their way through New York colleges, as well as dropouts and aging flower children; and also less-educated females who considered massage work preferable to, and far more lucrative than, toiling as a waitress or a secretary. One applicant, a secretary who had been fired by a *Monster Times* editor on the seventh floor, walked up two flights and gained employment as a masseuse, and soon she had more than doubled her income to $350 a week.

The quick success of the massage parlor brought into the building as customers a new social element—nervous middle-class businessmen whose furtive entrances and hasty exits intensified the building's already portentous atmosphere. The Communists on the tenth floor, most of them gray-haired Old Left radicals whose revolutionary zeal had reached its peak during the great riots and rallies in Union Square during the Depression, were particularly unnerved by the presence of the massage parlor, not only because they were sexual Puritans but because they knew that having a quasi-brothel located one floor below would inevitably add to the notoriety of the building and soon lead to frequent disruptive visits by the police as well as city inspectors who thrived on harassment. Having already heard rumors circulated through the building that the FBI had considered renting space on the ninth floor, and being regularly taunted over the telephone by anti-Communist bomb threats and hostile pickets along the sidewalk, the aging party members were undoubtedly the most paranoiac tenants on the premises, and they could not be sure that the quiet, tight-lipped conservatively dressed men seen in the elevator were not in fact federal agents.

The only tenants who welcomed the massage parlor were the male members of *Screw*'s staff, who were allowed to use the sauna whenever they wished and, at reduced rates, to be oiled and stroked to orgasm by a topless lady of their choice. The staff in turn published favorable articles about the parlor—which called itself "Experience One"—and *Screw* also began to print paid advertisements in which the parlor listed its telephone number and business hours, and boasted of the magical fingers and rapturous pleasures guaranteed by the masseuses.

Such exalted claims were quickly matched in *Screw*'s advertising columns by other parlors in New York, some of which also exhibited photographs of bare-breasted women, a winking, alluring covey of co-eds and hippy courtesans who suggested that they were totally available to the customer for the price of the massage. But *Screw* soon received complaints from its readers that the advertising was often deceptive, and that certain masseuses, after sexually titillating a customer who had already paid twenty-five or thirty dollars for a half-hour massage, would refuse to fellate or even masturbate him unless they were promised a tip of at least fifteen dollars; and there were also complaints that a few masseuses adamantly refused to touch a man's genitals, no matter how much money was offered, on the grounds that it was against the law.

The law was variously interpreted around the city, and across the nation, with regard to what was morally permissible in the privacy of a massage room. While there had once been specific city and county ordinances prohibiting a professional masseur or masseuse from working on a body of the opposite sex, these Victorian restrictions declined during World War II as nurses and other female medical aides increasingly performed physical therapy on injured G.I.s, and as the massage profession itself asserted its right to treat patients and customers regardless of their sex. It saw no reason why a licensed specialist in massage, whose school training included neurology and pathology as well as a complete knowledge of musculature, could not minister to the opposite sex as ethically as, for example, a podiatrist or psychiatrist; and in such cities as New York it had for years resented the fact that its massaging practitioners—many of them members of the respected American Massage and Therapy Association, or the New York State Society of Medical Masseurs—were licensed by the city Health Board, which also licensed barbers and cosmeticians, and not by the New York State Department of Education, which issued licenses to all categories of doctors and nurses.

By 1968, however, after much lobbying by the professional massage associations, this policy was changed—the massaging professionals became reclassified as medical personnel, with their licenses issued by the Department of Education in Albany; and each massage student, prior to receiving his degree, had to undergo a five-hundred-hour program of study at special schools and then to pass a comprehensive state examination that scrutinized his massaging technique and evaluated his working knowledge of the body's muscular and nervous systems.

The examiners also made certain that the student was aware of the proprieties of the profession, which included the practice of always covering the genitals of the person on the massage table with a towel or sheet, and also avoiding direct physical contact with the female breast. Such admonitions, to be sure, were not overemphasized by the examiners since the reported instances of personal misconduct by a masseur or masseuse had been exceedingly rare during the many postwar years in which opposite-sex massaging had been considered acceptable in the United States.

This is not to say, however, that improprieties on the massage table had not at times transpired; in fact it had long been privately known within the profession that certain licensed practitioners, including some matronly masseuses whose hefty figures might not be expected to inspire romantic illusions, had regularly favored requests for sexual intimacy with male clients and patients who were considered trustworthy and prudent. Since the extent of this was primarily masturbation, which some veteran masseuses of Scandinavian origin in particular regarded as a healthy culmination to a relaxing massage, and since it was always privately performed at the client's solicitation—and added both to his satisfaction and proffered gratuity—the massage associations, while never officially condoning genital gratification, were nevertheless no more eager to publicly expose their colleagues' misdeeds than were the associations of doctors and nurses when hearing of occasional transgressions within *their* circles. It had certainly been no secret to the medical associations that for decades certain distinguished physicians had arranged illegal abortions for privileged patients, or that psychiatrists sometimes indulged in tepid trysts on the couch with lady patients, or that night nurses and female therapists often brought manual relief to the genital frustrations of hospitalized male patients who were long restricted to restless confinement.

Such merciful acts of masturbation, in fact, were often remembered by grateful men as high points in their recuperation, and it was perhaps not surprising that a few of these Florence Nightingales of massage were among the pioneering women in the first "parlors" that began to inconspicuously flourish in smaller West Coast cities and towns in the late 1950s and early

1960s. These parlors were actually massage offices and they were usually located in commercial buildings that specialized in renting space to physicians, dentists, podiatrists, dermatologists, and others in the healing profession. In appearance, the massage office closely resembled a medical office—it had a white door with the upper half inset with frostlike glass, across which was printed in small black lettering the words "Physical Therapy" or "Massage" and the name of the practitioner. The interior of the office was hygienic if not antiseptic, and tidily furnished; and hung on the walls were framed parchment massage licenses and physical therapy diplomas, of sometimes dubious authenticity, that were bordered with tiny ink-drawn curlicues and seraphs. In the rear rooms, in addition to the massage table and showers, the stacks of white towels and bottled emollients of the trade, there was often a whirlpool bath, a sauna, and weight-reducing equipment.

Visitors were admitted by appointment only, and the masseuses, invariably refined-looking women, often wore starched nurses' uniforms that they covered with a white smock while administering a massage to a naked man on the table. To be fully massaged and finally masturbated by one of these white-gowned professionals was, to many men, a highly erotic experience, placing as it did a traditionally guilt-ridden act in unsullied surroundings while also catering to certain adolescent male fantasies of once-imagined intimacy with childhood nannies, or school nurses, or Dominican nuns, or other women whom one would not expect to see working in a massage office with oily fingers adroitly stroking an erect penis until it ejaculated into a small towel or Kleenex kept readily within reach.

Dozens of men became once-a-week customers of these massaging amorettas, and for years the practices prospered without legal difficulty partly because politicians and law-enforcement officials were among the satisfied regulars, and also because the masseuses conducted their businesses fairly and discreetly. For a complete massage they rarely charged more than fifteen dollars per half hour, and often refused gratuities. They restricted their advertising in the local press to a few agate lines under "Massage" in the classified columns, listing only office hours and telephone numbers. Their customers, too, were protective of their practices; indeed, many men believed that they alone were the recipients of a masseuse's *spécialité*, and even those customers who were less naïve would not loudly boast or gossip around town about their massage visits. While men might ju-

bilate after a wild evening in a brassy bordello, or discuss with
their male friends their extramarital activities, a midday appointment with a nurse-*manqué* for the primary purpose of being
masturbated was quite a different matter. Such an admission
might be interpreted as pathetically desperate or kinky; and there
certainly was nothing adventurous about it. It might even be
considered foolish to pay money to a woman for a service that
a man could as easily perform on himself, although the habitué
of the massage office would not agree with this reasoning. Unlike the millions who casually masturbate in solitude while looking at girlie pictures in *Playboy* and similar magazines, the
massage man preferred an accomplice, an attendant lady of respectable appearance who would help him reduce the guilt and
loneliness of this most lonely act of love.

The massage man was typical of many secret survivors in the
enduring world of marital monotony: He was competent at his
job, reasonably contented with his wife and family, and, as he
approached middle age, he sought the spice of sexual variety
without wishing to become entangled in romantic involvements
or complications, which he could support neither financially nor
emotionally. Too old for the singles scene, too slow for the fast
amateur action often available at neighborhood bars patronized
by other men's discontented wives, he also eschewed the scab-
rous and possibly disease-infected flophouses of street hustlers
and even the more elevated boudoirs of call girls and other
women who capitalized each night on what Balzac called the
fortune between their legs.

For such a man, distracted almost daily by the conflicting
forces of lust and guilt, restlessness and caution, a soothing
sexual massage represented an almost perfect panacea; and by
the 1960s there was hardly a major city in America that did not
have at least one of these masquerading medical offices in which
could be found a white-gowned manual therapist who would
satisfy a man's desire to be touched in ways that he could not
get, or did not want, from his wife at home.

By 1970, however, things began to change in the massage
world as this private service went public: Young entrepreneurs
from the counterculture moved in to build—along with head
shops that sold pot pipes and yoga books and other marketable
nirvanas—funky massage parlors and nude photography studios
that they operated conspicuously along city streets. Above the
front doors of these massage parlors, or in the windows, they
blatantly displayed such signs as "Girls of Your Choice—Live

Nude Models,'' and additional offerings were often hinted at by the long-haired men who stood along the sidewalk handing out leaflets to male pedestrians.

While these leaflets did not promise orgasmic satisfaction, they did guarantee a "sensuous massage" by a "topless masseuse''; and such offers initially prompted no adverse response from law-enforcement authorities because sensuous massaging and the display of nude bodies had gained conditional acceptance and legality in much of America by 1970. Total nudity had been permitted on the Broadway stage in *Hair* and *Oh! Calcutta!*; and topless and bottomless bars were allowed to exist in several cities, at least for the present. The famous Esalen massage, administered in the nude by attractive suntanned masseuses and masseurs to oil-slick patrons of the California spa, was described and extolled in illustrated books and manuals sold around the nation; and on television talk shows, Reich-influenced therapists and authors recommended the erotic massage as a means to a smoother relationship between couples. In sex clinics, female surrogates massaged and aroused to orgasm "dysfunctional" men; while sexually dissatisfied female patients were trained to stimulate their lovers with artful genital stroking and acts of mutual masturbation, as well as to masturbate themselves often when alone, sometimes with the aid of vibrators or dildoes. In sexual education classes in most American schools, perhaps for the first time in history, autoeroticism was not presented as a sad or shameful act.

Although the licensed massage associations were quietly displeased by the neon lights and psychedelic signs that identified the new parlors, they were slow to condemn them because they knew what had long been the private practice of certain nurse-*manqués*. The police, too, had reason to ignore the parlors; after years of club-swinging confrontations with young people, followed by charges of police brutality in court and notorious publicity in the press, the police had become wary of impulsive behavior and were not eager to raid the parlors while the massage laws remained as vague as they appeared to be in 1970.

Thus the time was propitious for the young entrepreneurs; for in addition to the legal confusion and the expanding market for pleasure, there was an abundance of sexually liberated women, unemployed free spirits from the sixties revolution, who had no compunction about earning money through the masturbation of men; and for the young owner, his initial financial investment was small—merely the monthly cost of renting a second- or third-story floor above a store in a business district, and the hiring of amateur carpenters to erect beaverboard walls that would subdivide the floor space into a reception room and several smaller private rooms for massaging and, occasionally, nude photography. The entire place could be inexpensively furnished with junk shop sofas, chairs, and an old reception desk, second-hand massage tables and army cots covered with Indian print bedspreads. The walls could be adorned with psychedelic posters or verdant oil paintings done perhaps by a hippie masseuse who had recently returned to urban living after a prolonged stretch of salubrious stagnation in a rural commune. While some of the young men who opened the first studios in 1970 had themselves lived briefly in communes and identified with the peace movement, their mellow manner and embroidered blue denim shirts belied their mercenary zeal: They were Easy Riders who during their campus days had frequently dealt in minor drugs as casually as they would now deal in minor sex.

One of the first parlors to openly flourish in New York was called the Pink Orchid, located at 200 East Fourteenth Street off Third Avenue, and founded by two former City College students, Alex Schub and Dan Russell. Schub, an aspiring rock musician who was pensive and shy, was also a fine carpenter, and he employed this skill in building the studio, while the more extroverted Russell, the son of an attorney and nephew of a rare-book reprint publisher, was the studio's main manager and promoter.

With the immediate success of the Pink Orchid, which averaged forty customers a day during the summer of 1970, the two men hired extra people and expanded their business with other studios—the Perfumed Garden on West Twenty-third Street, and the Lexington Avenue Models studio near Fifty-seventh Street; and Alex Schub also hired himself out to other young men to help build their studios.

For one of his friends, a former student of literature at Fairleigh Dickinson College, Schub designed the four dimly lit mauve rooms of the Secret Life Studio, on Twenty-sixth and Lexington; and for another acquaintance, a onetime Columbia student who owned a pair of uptown studios called Casbah East and Casbah West, Schub enclosed the massage rooms with white rounded plastic walls with jagged edges, evoking the atmosphere of an ultramodern cave, or suggesting the splintered parts of a demolished space capsule. On Third Avenue near Fifty-first

Street, Schub built the Middle Earth Studio, owned by a student dropout who was an aficionado of Tolkien's fiction. It conveyed the feeling of a hippie commune, having beaded curtains, madras pillows, and incense burning in the rooms.

Competing with these parlors for business were such places as the Stage Studio, at 12 East Eighteenth Street, which advertised private sessions with "young actress models"; and Studio 34, at 440 West Thirty-fourth Street, which promised: "Five Beautiful College Girls—the kind you would like."

For a salary, the masseuses in all the studios received about one third of the cost of each session, plus their tips, and they could average between $300 and $500 a week, depending on how many days and hours they chose to work. Each parlor had an afternoon shift and night shift, and the women's schedules were flexible. Aspiring actresses and dancers frequently switched their hours with other masseuses, or called in sick, on days when they wished to attend auditions. They also maintained regular contact with their agents through a coin-box telephone installed in the rear of the studio, near the masseuses' private dressing room.

The masseuses who were still attending college—at such schools as NYU, CCNY, and Hunter—often read their textbooks in the reception room when not busy with a customer; while the other masseuses—the adventurous young divorcées, the drifting dropouts, the *grisettes* with an aversion for "straight" office work, the Belle du Jour wives, the girl friends of the owners, the pretty lesbians and bisexuals for whom the parlor provided introductions to certain sister masseuses—idled away the waiting hours in the reception room by conversing among themselves, or reading magazines, or practicing their yoga on the floor, or meditating in a corner despite the constant sound of music coming from the radio and the ringing telephones on the manager's desk.

If the manager was temporarily out of the reception room, and a masseuse picked up the phone, she would sometimes be greeted by the sound of heavy breathing or a man's voice sputtering obscenities—which was why in most parlors only the male manager was supposed to answer the business phones. In addition to collecting money from the customers, and assigning each customer to a private room, and buzzing those rooms twenty-five minutes later to alert the masseuse that the half-hour session was nearly over, the manager could also serve as an occasional bouncer; but there was not much need for this, for it was a rare

customer who was obstreperous. Nearly all the men who patronized massage parlors were well mannered and diffident, and
a large percentage of them arrived wearing suits and ties. As
they walked in, sometimes carrying the leaflets that they had
been handed on the sidewalk, they were welcomed by the manager seated behind the desk and received smiles from the assembled gathering of masseuses. After the customer had paid the
fee to the manager, and selected the masseuse of his choice, she
escorted him through a hall into one of the private rooms, carrying over her arm a starched sheet she had gotten from the
linen closet.

Closing the door and spreading the sheet over the table, she
waited until the man was completely nude before she began to
remove her clothing. It was the belief of most studio managers
that, if the customer happened to be a plainclothes police officer,
the masseuse could not be prosecuted for immorality if the policeman had preceded her in exposing himself; and while this
assumption had yet to be tested in court, it was nonetheless
adhered to in most parlors.

Although the majority of customers were old enough to be
the masseuse's father, there was a curious reversal of roles after
the sexual massage had begun: It was the young women who
held the authority, who had the power to give or deny pleasure,
while the men lay dependently on their backs, moaning softly
with their eyes closed, as their bodies were being rubbed with
baby oil or talc. For these men it was possibly their first intimate
contact with the sexually emancipated youth movement that they
had read and heard so much about, the world of Woodstock and
the Pill; and as they became better acquainted with certain masseuses through frequent visits to a parlor, they often gained insight into the alienated generation that they had helped to sire.

The masseuses in turn learned much about the frustrations of
middle-aged men, their marital difficulties, their job problems,
their fantasies and insecurities. Some men were so nervous as
they lay on the table that their bodies shook and they perspired
excessively. Others could not ejaculate, or maintain their erections, unless the masseuses expressed a personal interest in them,
flattered them on the condition of their bodies, and reassured
them that their penises were as large as, or larger than, other
men's. There were men so guilt-ridden that they could not experience maximum pleasure unless the masseuse, complying
with their requests, verbally admonished them as she mastur-

bated them, berated them and scolded them as if they were
schoolboys caught during moments of "self-abuse."

There were customers who had recently left the priesthood
and were trying to acclimate themselves for the first time to a
woman's touch; and there were Orthodox rabbis who covered
their penises with condoms or plastic sandwich baggies so that
they could be masturbated *without* fleshly contact. There were
distinguished stockbrokers and bankers who negotiated with
masseuses for fellatio, explaining that this was something their
wives refused to do; and there were blue-collar workers who
were similarly satisfied by masseuses but admitted that this was
something they would never ask their wives to do.

Old men carrying canes, widowers and divorcés, modern-day
Daddy Brownings, had regular appointments at certain parlors,
and they sometimes kept bottles of their favorite whiskey in the
linen cabinets; and there were also vigorous younger men so
brimming with energy that they paid double rates for two masseuses at once, and enjoyed three orgasms during the half-hour
session. An extremely shy individual named Arthur Bremer,
wearing a suit with a vest, arrived one day at the Victorian Studio
on Forty-sixth and Lexington, but he was too tense during the
massage to have an orgasm. A month later, at a political rally
in Maryland, Arthur Bremer shot and paralyzed the governor of
Alabama, George C. Wallace.

There were many romantic men who frequented massage parlors. Occasionally one fell in love with a masseuse and became
clearly upset on days when he arrived early for an appointment
and discovered that she was in a room with another man. At the
Secret Life Studio, on Twenty-sixth and Lexington, a frequent
customer was a Harvard graduate and recent divorcé who practiced psychiatry in Manhattan, and his regular masseuse was an
attractive blonde who had graduated from Louisiana State University and had worked for *Look* magazine. After many sexual
sessions in the parlor, the couple began to date on the outside,
and within a year they were married and later moved to Florida.

In time, a few businessmen who had patronized massage parlors—but were dissatisfied with the fact that these undercapitalized establishments rarely possessed even such basic facilities
as a shower room—began to build parlors of their own, larger
places with molded plastic chairs, air conditioning, new massage tables, steam rooms, saunas, sun lamps, Muzak, and credit
card billing. The first of these franchise-modern studios was
Experience One, on the ninth floor of Daddy Browning's old

loft, owned by the men from the fast-food business; but within a year this studio would be surpassed in comfort and gadgetry by several others, all of which would eventually be visited by *Screw*'s top editor, Al Goldstein, who began publishing in his newpaper a weekly connoisseur's column on the booming massage business—and thus claimed that each of his joyful orgasms was a tax deduction.

It was Goldstein's intention to visit, unannounced, each parlor in the city, the new and the old, paying the same price as any other customer; and after experiencing the manipulative skills of the various masseuses, and keeping mental notes on the cleanliness of each establishment as well as the courtesy of the management, he would then write a brief description of each parlor in *Screw* and assign to each a rating of from one to four stars.

When Goldstein began the assignment in 1971 there were not more than a dozen parlors, but by late 1972 the number in New York had exceeded forty, and Goldstein learned that the services and prices varied from place to place, and sometimes from day to day, depending largely on the mood of the masseuse and her compatibility with her customer. At the Pink Orchid on Fourteenth Street, which was hot and overcrowded when he arrived, and still had neither showers nor air conditioning, Goldstein paid fourteen dollars to be massaged by a sullen brunet wearing hot pants; and for a promised fifteen-dollar tip, she masturbated and fellated him perfunctorily, while looking mainly at her wristwatch. Goldstein gave the Pink Orchid one star in the next issue of *Screw*, describing it as ''not recommended.''

At the Mademoiselle Studio on Fifty-eighth and Lexington, owned by three Israelis who equipped their air-conditioned seven-room layout with a refreshment bar and a movie projector that flashed erotic color slides on the walls of the reception room, Goldstein was able to buy, with a twenty-dollar massage charge and a subsequent tip of twenty-five dollars, intercourse on a water bed with an attractive divorcée of twenty-six who said that she had two children in the Connecticut suburbs and that she sold real estate there on weekends. She was amiable and fun to be with, and Goldstein awarded Mademoiselle three stars— ''recommended: the best of its kind available.''

At the Middle Earth Studio, on the second floor of a brick building at 835 Third Avenue, Goldstein paid the manager eighteen dollars and selected as his masseuse a blue-eyed brunet with long straight hair and pure complexion who wore a Rosicrucian cross around her neck. She was serene and graceful, and in the private room she easily aroused him. She had beautiful hands with long fingers and she seemed to enjoy what she was doing, never once taking her eyes off his erect penis as she fondled it, knowing no doubt that most men loved to watch a woman caressing this strange object with familiarity. He wanted almost desperately for her to put it in her mouth; but when he asked if she would do it, she politely refused, saying that the policy at Middle Earth strictly forbid this—only "manual release" was allowed, and this service was automatically provided with the massage. No extra tipping was required. She then confided that the small mirror on the wall of the massage room was made of one-way glass, permitting the manager to peek in to make certain that the rules were being observed. This disclosure suddenly upset Goldstein, disrupting his feeling of intimacy with the masseuse; and while he enjoyed her masturbatory massage, he gave Middle Earth only two stars.

The many mirrors that he later saw as he visited the larger studios, mirrors that sometimes extended across the entire walls and ceilings of the private rooms, continued to discomfort him, not only because he half suspected that a voyeuristic manager might be watching but also because *he* did not want to be exposed to the corpulent reflection of himself as he lay nude on a table.

At the multimirrored Caesar's Retreat, however, a plush mock-Roman studio at 219 East Forty-sixth Street, Goldstein was sufficiently diverted by a toga-clad masseuse and her extraordinary pampering to overcome his self-consciousness; and he bestowed upon Caesar's a four-star citation. Nothing in New York yet compared to Caesar's Retreat, where thousands of dollars had obviously been spent by its owner—a Bronx-born onetime stockbroker named Robert Scharaga—in decorating the many private rooms, the sauna, the circular baths, the plaster-cast Romanesque statuary and fountain. The customers could drink free champagne in the reception room while waiting for their half-hour massage sessions done with warm herbal oil. A proper massage cost twenty dollars, but more money could buy more, and for one hundred dollars a customer could have a champagne bath with three liberated ladies.

After Goldstein had surveyed the parlors of New York, he traveled around the country and discovered that erotic massaging had become a national preoccupation—it was the fast-food business of sex, a nutrient for the libido. In the Washington suburb of Falls Church, Virginia, the ten-room Tiki-Tiki massage parlor was located in a shopping center. There were parlors in Charlotte, in Atlanta, in Dallas; and in the strongly Catholic, Daley-dominated city of Chicago, there was a downtown parlor on South Wabash Street that was decorated to resemble the interior of a church. The manager's small reception desk was enclosed within a six-hundred-pound wooden Gothic confessional that had been purchased from a wrecking company that had demolished a South Side church; and there were prayer benches and other ecclesiastical objects in the parlor, as well as ornate dark-wood bookcases in which were displayed hard-core sex magazines and dildoes.

Hoping to protect the parlor against infiltration by the police, the owner established his business as a private club that customers could join only after they had produced verifiable identification papers and had signed a document stating that they were not affiliated with any law-enforcement agency—a statement that customers were not only required to sign but also to read aloud in front of the confessional, unaware that their voices were being recorded by a hidden microphone, and their faces were being filmed by a camera peering through the folds of the purple velvet draperies that hung within the confessional. The cautious owner of this parlor was named Harold Rubin; and when Goldstein walked in requesting a massage, Rubin eagerly introduced himself as an avid reader of *Screw* and insisted that Goldstein take a session with two masseuses at the management's expense.

In Los Angeles, Goldstein saw dozens of parlors located along Santa Monica Boulevard and Sunset Strip, some of which were open twenty-four hours a day. Los Angeles' most prominent parlor—owned by forty-two-year-old Mark Roy, a former Arthur Murray dance instructor who later prospered as a director of several ladies' weight-reducing salons—was called Circus Maximus and occupied a spacious three-story house located a half block south of Sunset on La Cienega Boulevard. The house had a parking lot large enough for eighty cars. Like Caesar's Retreat in New York, Circus Maximus' decor sought to suggest Roman hedonism; its thirty masseuses wore mini-togas of purple, gold, or white crepe, and its advertising proclaimed: "Men haven't had it so good since the days of Pompeii."

A half hour's drive from Sunset Strip, in the quiet hills of Topanga Canyon high above Malibu Beach, Goldstein visited a nudist "growth center" called Elysium, seven acres of lovely land hidden from public view by trees and tall fences behind which nude members could massage one another, or be massaged by staff professionals. Like the Esalen Institute in Northern California, Elysium offered its visiting members and guests a varied schedule of "awareness" seminars and psychotherapy programs; but unlike Esalen, Elysium was pleasure-oriented, having in addition to pools and saunas, tennis courts and riding horses, semi-private rooms in the main building where people could go to have sex.

Goldstein had previously published in *Screw* photographs taken at Elysium, but he was even more impressed when he saw the place in person and interviewed its founder, Ed Lange, a tall, well-built former fashion photographer with an elegantly trimmed gray beard. Lange had been born fifty-two years earlier into a conservative German family in Chicago and had become an outstanding school athlete, but had recognized within himself a strong inclination toward a less regimented, more creative lifestyle. Ever since purchasing his first under-the-counter copy of *Sunshine & Health* magazine as a teenager in the late 1930s, Lange had been fascinated with nudism; and when he moved to Los Angeles in the 1940s, working as a Hollywood set designer and freelance photographer for such magazines as *Vogue* and *Bazaar*, he joined a pioneering nudist club that was sometimes raided by the police. In the mid-1950s at this club he met an extremely attractive young married couple, Joseph and Diane Webber, and it was Lange who during the next fifteen years took most of the nude pictures of Diane Webber that appeared in magazines around the country. Later these and other nude pictures were reprinted in magazines that he began to publish; and the purchase of the land for Elysium was the fulfillment of Lange's longtime fantasy.

At the time of Goldstein's visit, Lange was engaged in a dispute with Los Angeles County officials who were trying to close his commune under a local zoning ordinance which they interpreted as prohibiting nudist groups from assembling within the district. It was not only Elysium that was being cited but also a neighboring "growth center" located higher in the hills of Topanga Canyon, Sandstone Retreat. Sandstone was a fifteen-acre estate occupied by several nude couples who were living in open sexual freedom and seeking to eliminate possessiveness and jealousy. The owner of Sandstone was named John Williamson; among the couples were John and Judith Bullaro.

17

NOT LONG AFTER John Williamson had become the lover of
Judith Bullaro, he resigned as a partner of his electronics firm,
sold his company stock for nearly $150,000, and put a down
payment on the secluded mountain retreat that would become
his love community. The property was located 1,700 feet above
the Pacific Ocean on the upper ridge of the Santa Monica Mountains, eight miles from Malibu Beach and an hour's drive from
downtown Los Angeles; to reach it most directly from the Pacific Coast Highway a motorist had to drive up narrow, winding
roads that presented a dazzling view of danger and beauty, a
frightening route that climbed through the hovering haze of the
valley and over slanted treetops, rimming the edge of steep cliffs,
swerving inward toward the yellow stone of the mountainside,
curving out again toward the unguarded edge of the road, cutting
in sharply toward the mountain, then back to the open sky and
the risk of a precipitous fall—it was a zigzagging, vertiginous
ride made tolerable only by the contemplation of sexual pleasure
that was waiting at the end of the journey.

Sandstone Retreat, built on the south side of the mountain,
was entered by way of a private drive marked by two stone
pillars; and its main residence, which stood one-quarter mile
beyond the gate, was a large white two-story house perched on
a concrete slab and surrounded by eucalyptus trees and ferns, a
fish pond with a cascading fountain, and a manicured front lawn
so smooth it could be used as a putting green. From the second-
story redwood sun deck of the house could be seen the Pacific
coastline, white specks of distant sailboats, and the misty sil-
houette of Catalina island. Behind the courtyard of the house,
where the rocky land rose higher, there were smaller stucco
houses reached by wooden steps, and also a large glass-doored

building with a beamed ceiling that sheltered an Olympic-sized pool in which people swam in the nude.

Many years ago Sandstone's fifteen acres, and the adjoining land that extended for miles across the mountainside, were owned by wealthy ranchers and such Hollywood figures as Lana Turner; but when Williamson first inspected the area with a realtor in 1968, he saw only signs of isolation and decay, dust-covered buildings and bumpy dirt roads obstructed by fallen boulders and mounds of sun-baked mud. The nearest grocery store was miles below in the canyon, where the rustic Topanga shopping center was a rendezvous for dope-dealing hippies and leather-jacketed motorcycle gangs, and where dozens of under-nourished dogs wandered listlessly across the main road and with reluctance yielded to honking motorists.

When Williamson first showed the Sandstone property to those who were to be part of the commune, they were far from impressed; they considered the site to be too remote and decrepit, and they knew that it would take many months of hard labor to make the houses habitable and to repair the broken roads.

But Williamson nevertheless bought the property and, after appealing to their adventurous spirit and their often expressed desire to escape the frenzy and smog and confinements of the city, he gradually persuaded them that this was an ideal setting for their sensual utopia. Williamson was stubborn and convincing. Like the founding fathers of other utopian settlements in the past, he was unhappy with the world around him. He regarded contemporary urban life in America as destructive to the spirit, organized religion as a celestial swindle, the federal government as cumbersome and avaricious; he saw the average wage earner, who was excessively taxed and easily replaced, as existing only with detached participation in a computerized society.

Williamson's followers, with few exceptions, shared his dismay. Like him, they had worked within the system and found it limiting, and each welcomed an escape from the tedium of their private lives and marriages. Most of them had been divorced at least once and had grown up in families that had been oppressive or unstable. Oralia Leal, the first of seven children born into a Mexican-American family in southern Texas, had fled familial poverty and the sexual molestations of older male relatives to work her way through a junior college in Los Angeles, only to become ensnared in a dreadful marriage and a series of boring jobs as a corporate secretary or receptionist. Arlene Gough, an "army brat" born in Spokane, the daughter of a career sergeant, spent her girlhood traveling from base to base with her parents, became pregnant at sixteen, and was married two more times before she was thirty. The red-haired Gail, reared in an ascetic Irish-Catholic home in the Midwest, experienced sex for the first time at the age of twenty-seven with her fiancé, after which her mother sent her to a priest to seek forgiveness. The engineer David Schwind, who worked at an unfulfilling job at Douglas Aircraft, was a product of remote and conservative parents in small-town Ohio, where his main relief from monotony was found in the pages of *Playboy* or during his nocturnal prowls outside the neighboring bedroom window of an attractive older woman.

The others in Williamson's clique came from similarly unexalted backgrounds; they were people in their late twenties and early thirties who had passed quietly and uncommittedly through the youth-centered 1960s without experiencing much meaning in their lives or hope for self-improvement until they had met Williamson and had been lured into his love net. With the help of his wife, Williamson had used sexual freedom as a way of linking their lives to his own and including them in a group marriage that he believed would effectively meet their needs for affection, emotional support, a commitment to something larger than themselves, and a sense of familial warmth that they had previously lacked.

At Sandstone he provided them with living quarters and an environment that was more luxurious than anything they could have afforded in the city below; and while everyone had duties to perform on the property, Williamson encouraged the men and women to disregard tradition and share the domestic chores in the kitchen as well as duties in the outdoors. At night, when the day's work was done, Williamson listened with interest and patience to whatever they wished to reveal about themselves and their anxieties; he was a combination therapist and teacher, a leader to the men, a lover to the women.

He had wooed one by one each of the half-dozen women who were now part of his circle, and by sharing his wife with the men, and creating a permission-giving atmosphere that fostered open sexuality within the group, he believed that he was forming the nucleus of a cult that would soon appeal to many other couples who truly believed in coequal relationships.

John Bullaro, however, remained somewhat skeptical of Williamson's intentions; and the main reason he continued to associate with Williamson's group was that his wife, Judith, refused to leave it. She was awed by Williamson, insisted on having sex with him often, and she supported Williamson's plan primarily because it advocated greater freedom for women and denounced the double standard. After years of frustration as a Valley housewife, Judith had finally found a cause that appealed to both her mind and her body, and John Bullaro was resigned to the fact that if he wished to save his marriage—and he now did more than ever, partly in the interest of his own ego—he had little choice but to remain close to the group and hope that Judith's attraction to Williamson was merely a passing fancy, a symptom of her capricious and restless nature.

Meanwhile, Bullaro's involvement with the group was on his own terms: He enjoyed the sexual experiences with the willing women who surrounded Williamson—Barbara, Arlene, Gail, and the exotic Oralia, to whom he had finally made love—but at the same time he did not consider himself answerable to Williamson's wishes. Unlike the other men who had quit or neglected their jobs in order to live and work full-time with Williamson on the restoration of the property, Bullaro continued to appear each day at his office at New York Life, and each night he rejoined his wife and the others at the main house in time for dinner or drinks after they had spent the day scraping floors, painting walls, chopping wood, trimming hedges, and, in the case of Williamson and David Schwind, maneuvering two bulldozers up and down the hilly driveways removing boulders and smoothing out the roadbeds.

Although Bullaro had rented out his Valley home after the purchase of Sandstone, he did not move his family into the estate with the other couples but chose instead to lease a nearby ranch in Topanga Canyon, explaining to the Williamsons that his children were yet too young to be exposed to Sandstone's adult freedom; and while he and Judith had hired an architect to design a house that they would presumably build in the near future on one of Sandstone's higher hills, Bullaro privately had no intention of ever letting matters get that far. He was now marking time, indulging temporarily his wife's newfound feminism, partaking in the group nudity and pleasure often available at the main house, and trying to conceal the deepening hostility and jealousy he felt toward the quiet, robust, blond Williamson, who presently held Judith as a love hostage.

But one evening in the main house, where everyone was relaxing in the nude after a day of hard physical work in the sweltering heat, Bullaro could no longer conceal his animosity. He had driven up the hill from his office earlier in the evening pondering Williamson's power over the group, and he concluded that it had less to do with any great wisdom or dynamism on Williamson's part than to Williamson's capacity to exploit the vast emptiness in these people's lives.

Most people, Bullaro thought, were born followers, wanderers in search of guides, gullible disciples of any theorist or theologian, dictator, drug dealer, or Hollywood maharishi who promised palatable cures and solutions. The trendy, rootless state of California was particularly receptive to novel ideas, and if a visionary man had great drive and determination, and was smart enough to remain sufficiently vague and elusive so that other people could superimpose upon him their ideals and fantasies, he would sooner or later attract his share of followers. Williamson was in this category, Bullaro believed, espousing a philosophy that ignored sin and guilt and celebrated pleasure. Williamson flattered his followers by calling them "change people," attributing to them the power to change other people as they themselves had been changed into pioneering practitioners of Williamson's sex theories. While Bullaro reluctantly acknowledged that Williamson had thus far changed Judith, he doubted that Williamson would be able to sell his lotus life-style to the vast market beyond the mountain—and this is precisely what Williamson had in mind; he eventually intended to merchandise his philosophy, to advertise the Sandstone project in the press and entice couples to pay a guest fee to visit his "change people" and share their pleasure and hopefully become converts. Williamson was a guru of the flesh.

Although Bullaro knew that Williamson would not agree with such a carnal assessment of the purpose and goals of Sandstone, he did not particularly care what Williamson thought about anything on this hot evening as he parked his car and walked into the main house to find Judith reclining nude on the sun deck next to Williamson, with the rest of the nude group talking quietly among themselves in the living room, mostly ignoring him.

After he had removed his clothes and hung them in the closet near the front door, Bullaro headed toward the sun deck, but stopped when he heard Barbara commenting sarcastically about his uncanny knack of arriving at Sandstone only after the group had finished the day's work—to which he suddenly responded, in a loud voice, "Why don't you shove it, Barbara? I don't need any of your crap tonight!"

Barbara smiled, seeming pleased by her capacity to easily

provoke him; but on the deck the supine John Williamson slowly rolled over, got up on his elbows, and, looking at Bullaro, asked with irritation: "Why can't you ever listen to what she's saying without letting your bloated ego get in the way?"

"Because," Bullaro said, "I don't think *she's* any great judge of character. She should be spending her time trying to solve her own problems, which are many, without spending time nagging me."

Williamson quietly shook his head, as if deciding that the issue was really too silly to discuss; but Bullaro, glaring down at Williamson, went on angrily: "And why don't you let her fight her own battles? Or is she is incapable without your great support and guidance?"

As Williamson got to his feet everybody in the living room seemed uneasy, having never before heard Williamson addressed so curtly; and Judith also stood, her hand holding Williamson's arm, allied with him against her husband.

"Barbara can take care of herself a hell of a lot better than you can," Williamson announced firmly, his face red with anger. "You're so constantly worried about failure that you don't know what's going on around you. Everybody has been working hard for months to get this place in shape so we can start making money and support what we think is important, and all you've been worrying about so far is your pathetic fucking ego."

"You're damned right I'm worried about my ego," Bullaro shouted, "because this fucking group under your expert direction has been working full-time to tear it down—along with my family. Your biggest turn-on in life is fucking other men's wives. You don't seem to enjoy fucking your own very much!"

Williamson looked hard at Bullaro and said: "You just can't stand the thought of your wife responding to other people, and growing as an individual. You would rather keep her locked in a closet while you continue your insidious little game of sneaky sex. Isn't that how you got trapped in the first place?"

Before Bullaro could reply, Williamson abruptly strode past him, with Judith a step behind, leaving Bullaro standing alone near the sliding glass doorway of the sun deck. He felt his heart pounding, and a mixture of fear and satisfaction. He had challenged Williamson, something he had previously lacked the courage to do, but now as he stood looking at the night sky he felt uncertain. He walked out onto the deck, where there was a slight breeze, and he sat in one of the low-slung chairs. He could see the distant lights from the coastline, could hear the crickets

along the edge of the lawn. He knew he had lost Judith, at least
for the time being, and while he admitted to being surprised by
her loyalty to Williamson, he still believed that he would win
her back when he wanted to, *if* he wanted to. At this moment he
was not sure what he wanted.

After sitting awhile he heard someone behind him, and, turning, he saw the wife of a pharmacist named Bruce, an assertive
woman with small firm breasts. He thought that she had come
out to console him, but instead she asked, almost in a whisper,
"How could you have said such things to John, after all he's
tried to do for us?"

Bullaro, suppressing his anger, did not reply. But he knew he
could no longer remain among Williamson's absurd idolaters.
He got up, walked toward the closet, and began to dress. He
noticed that Williamson's bedroom door was closed, and he
could hear voices in the room, but he did not call Judith to say
that he was leaving; tonight she would have to get a ride home
with someone else.

The children and the sitter were asleep when he arrived and,
feeling exhausted, he quickly went to bed. The next morning,
a Friday, he awoke early and saw that Judith had still not returned. He was perturbed but not alarmed. At breakfast he told
the children and the teenaged girl that Judith would be home
later in the day, which they unquestioningly accepted. He drove
to his office and remained preoccupied with business throughout
the day; at five o'clock he impulsively decided that *he* would
spend the night away from home and let Judith sit wondering
where he might be.

He drove down the curving canyon roads onto the Pacific
Coast Highway and turned right toward Malibu Beach. As he
paused at traffic lights he watched dark-tanned young men and
women wearing bikinis and surfing suits walking across the
highway in front of the cars—sun peasants balancing sleek, colorful boards on their heads and smiling in a carefree manner at
the long line of motorists. Continuing his drive along the beach,
Bullaro passed hitchhiking hippies, and as he turned off the road
into a motel parking lot and got out of his car, he saw standing
near him a young woman with long blond hair, lovely but disheveled, dust-covered and seemingly fatigued. He approached
her and asked if she would like to join him for something to eat
in the motel coffee shop. She nodded and followed him.

He sat in a booth and ordered her a hamburger and Coke
while she used the washroom. Although she seemed more re-

freshed when she rejoined him, he could smell her rancid odor, as if she had not bathed in weeks, and he resisted the temptation to invite her to his motel room. He slept alone that night, thinking about Judith but enjoying his solitude and the independence in being away from Williamson's retinue. Later in the morning, however, after he had returned home and saw that Judith still had not come back, for the first time he felt mildly panicked.

He was scheduled to take a scuba-diving lesson later that afternoon at the beach with David Schwind and Bruce the pharmacist; and since the sitter was off during the weekend he took the children with him, confident that Judith, eager to see them, would drive down with Bruce and David from Sandstone. Bullaro got there early and, after taking his diving equipment out of the car, he played with the children along the surf.

Soon he saw David Schwind's Cadillac pulling into the parking area; there were three people in the front, but Judith was not among them. In addition to David and Bruce there was the woman who had chided him on the sun deck two nights before, Bruce's untimid wife. The two men nodded toward him as they joined the others in the class, but Bruce's wife turned away when she saw him; and Bullaro could only assume, since she had never before attended the scuba class, that Williamson had sent her along to inhibit the men from socializing with him. She remained close to David and her husband when they were not in the water, and as soon as the instruction was over she asked that they return directly to the car, which they did. Bullaro watched with intensified frustration as they drove away and, not for the first time, he contemplated killing Williamson. It would be easy with a rifle, while hiding in the woods, to hit him as he drove the bulldozer up and down the hill.

After arriving home with the children, and still with no sign of Judith, he could not resist the urge to telephone her at Sandstone, even though he had no idea what to say; he felt embittered and betrayed by her, yet wanted to speak to her. As he listened to the buzz on the phone ringing at Sandstone, he was tempted to hang up, and then he heard Barbara's voice. He asked to speak to Judith, but Barbara said, "I'll see if she wants to talk to you."

"You do that!" he said sharply.

After a short while Barbara returned to the phone.

"She doesn't want to talk to you."

"Tell her I have to talk about the children."

There was another pause, and Barbara said once more, "She doesn't want to talk to you."

He wanted to scream, to issue threats, but he knew that the children in the next room might become frightened, and so he hung up and tried to contain his fury.

Later in the evening, after he had made their dinner, played with them, and put them to bed, he again dialed Sandstone, and when Barbara heard his voice she explained with irritation, "Look, John, Judy just doesn't want to talk to you. She's arranging for the children to be taken care of, but we'd all appreciate it if you'd stop calling. We've had a long day and we're all very tired."

Barbara hung up. Bullaro stood with the silent phone in his hand, shaken, incensed, feeling helpless. There was no one in the entire city that he could turn to—nobody from the insurance company, no family member or friend. Everyone he had come to know intimately in recent years was under Williamson's influence, and they were reducing him to a cuckold, a caretaker of children, a man robbed of dignity and confidence. But as John Williamson had declared on the sun deck, Bullaro could blame only himself for becoming trapped in this situation; he had enjoyed the bodies of many women and had become unhappy only after Judith had begun to assert her own independence.

Bullaro believed, however, that there was a difference between what he had done and what she was now doing; for him, sex with Barbara and Arlene, Gail and Oralia, was merely recreational, joyful, and uncomplicated, unthreatening to his marriage, whereas Judith was clearly becoming romantically attached to Williamson—she was more committed and loyal to this man than to her own husband, which she had reaffirmed in the way she stood by Williamson during the confrontation on the porch, and also in her manner of almost clinging to Williamson ever since they first became lovers. While this did not appear to disturb Barbara, it had lately become increasingly irritating to Bullaro—in fact, the mere sight of the two of them lying nude together that evening on the sun deck, a couple savoring their intimacy, had pained Bullaro more than he cared to admit. What had begun as a group experiment to equalize the double standard had now become, for Judith, a serious love affair. Sexual intercourse with Williamson was obviously not enough for her; she had to embellish it with romance, to establish Williamson as the center of her life, to threaten her marriage and the welfare of her children.

This was so typical of traditional women like Judith, Bullaro thought bitterly; they simply could not enjoy extramarital sex without sooner or later becoming emotionally involved, which is what made such women different from men like himself. The average married man, if he had the energy, could have sex with several women without diminishing the affection and desire he felt for his wife. But women like Judith—unlike *truly* liberated females like Barbara and Arlene—could not simply accept a man as a temporary instrument of pleasure; they wanted soft lights and promises, not just a penis but the man attached to it.

Understanding this, however, was not going to get Judith back home, and Bullaro knew that unless he somehow made his peace with Williamson and regained acceptance at Sandstone, he had little chance of even communicating with Judith. While he was not sure that he still loved her, not after all the anguish and humiliation she had caused him, he conceded after some reflection that he needed her and wanted not to lose her, particularly not to Williamson. Bullaro also missed being part of the group, which, with all its flaws, represented the only close human contact he now had—his boyhood fears of isolation and rejection were haunting him still; and so he decided that he *had* to suppress his pride and anger and go personally to Sandstone to plead forgiveness. It would signify total capitulation on his part but, short of violence, there seemed to be no alternative.

Bullaro telephoned his young unmarried sister and urgently asked if she would spend the night with the children. Shortly before 11 P.M., after she had arrived, he began the uphill drive toward Sandstone, pressing hard on the accelerator, feeling the big station wagon leaning heavily into the mountain curves. He still felt a bit ashamed at what he was doing, but on these narrow roads there was no turning back, and he continued without hesitation until he pulled into the courtyard behind the main house. Most of the exterior lights around the property were turned off, and the draperies were pulled tight across the large windows. He knocked on the front door for several moments before he heard footsteps and Barbara's voice calling: "What do you want?"

"I want to speak to John," Bullaro said.

There was a pause; then the door opened halfway. Bullaro saw John Williamson standing behind Barbara in the darkened living room, and, without waiting for any response, Bullaro said in a quiet voice: "John, I want to apologize for the other night."

Williamson remained silent and dour, resistant to Bullaro's appeal. Finally, Barbara asked, "Do you really mean it?"

"Yes," Bullaro said.

Then Williamson spoke, his voice soft but resolute.

"Are you sure you're not just saying this to reach Judy?"

"Yes," Bullaro replied, "I really *am* sorry for what happened . . . and I want to be a part of you again."

Bullaro waited at the door with his head lowered, starting to believe what he was saying. Then he felt Williamson's hand on his shoulder, and Barbara opened the door wide to admit him. Behind him, in the middle of the darkened living room, gathered around and listening, stood the others, all except Judith. As they stepped forward and embraced him, Bullaro heard Williamson's warning: "Judy does not want to live with your hostility anymore."

"I don't blame her," Bullaro replied.

Soon the attractive blond figure of Judith appeared, seeming both familiar and distant, and she tentatively approached with arms outstretched to receive him. They remained with their arms around one another for several minutes, and Bullaro felt her kisses and his own desire, and one by one the other people departed and left them by themselves in the middle of the large room. Judith then took him by the hand and escorted him toward a bedroom; slowly she helped him remove his clothes, and that night she made love to him with a passion and emotion that he had not felt from her in years.

The next morning they awakened late and had breakfast together—it was like a holiday; everybody was relaxed and cheerful, and when Bullaro saw John Williamson it was as if no ill-feeling had ever grown between them. It was remarkable, Bullaro thought, this style of Williamson's—he could seem sinister one day, saintlike the next, and with no apparent effort his mood altered the atmosphere of the entire house and influenced everyone within it. On this morning Williamson was his most munificent self and did not make Bullaro feel like a penitent, a renegade who would have to slowly regain the group's trust and acceptance. Bullaro felt amazingly at ease with all of them— with Barbara, Oralia, even the pharmacist's wife—and in the days that followed, with no sense of obligation, he spent more time at Sandstone and began to work around the property.

He spent less time at his office at New York Life, confident that the many salesmen that he had personally hired and trained no longer required his constant supervision, and he decided, too, that he would hereafter exercise more independence over his life. The company could survive without him, and he without it; he had perhaps been a company man too long, and now he arbitrarily decided to devote more time to his internal self and to fully test his compatibility with this unusual place.

Being at Sandstone during the daylight hours allowed him to see more clearly the remarkable improvements that had been made throughout the estate. Not only the main house but the smaller ones up the hill were freshly painted and comfortably furnished. The landscaping was nearly done, the roads were smooth, if not yet entirely blacktopped, and the electrical wiring and water pipes had been repaired or replaced. The large glass-doored pool house, in which the water was heated to body temperature, was a favorite gathering place of the group on cool evenings, as was the high hill behind the main house that offered at twilight a magnificent view of the Pacific. The nights were quite and serene—Sandstone's closest neighbor was two miles away—and the only nocturnal intruders were a couple of rummaging raccoons that climbed the western fence of the property and clawed futilely atop the securely covered metal garbage cans that were clustered outside the staircase leading up to the kitchen.

One evening when the group was gathered in the living room after dinner, Bullaro felt compelled to describe the positive effect being back at Sandstone was having on him; and he announced with satisfaction that he had overcome his defensiveness, was now liberated from the confining forces that had bound him in the city below. Williamson listened silently, then suggested that Bullaro test his emotions by driving off into the desert and spending time in absolute solitude.

"Oh, I could do that," Bullaro quickly replied, almost boastfully.

"Then *do* it," Williamson said firmly.

"I'll do it this weekend," Bullaro said.

"Why not *now*?" Williamson asked. Bullaro was stunned by Williamson's challenge, and looking around the room he saw that everyone was watching him and waiting to see how he would react. It was close to 11 P.M., a ridiculous time to be driving into the desert; but Bullaro saw no way to avoid it. Attempting to seem casual, he said, "Okay, I'll do it."

Williamson reached for a set of car keys on the mantel and handed them to Bullaro. The keys belonged to Williamson's Jaguar convertible. Bullaro took them without comment, wondering if this was Williamson's way of preventing him from spending the night in his own station wagon rather than sleeping in the desert sand.

After putting on a pair of shorts, a shirt, and hiking boots, Bullaro loaded the sports car with a sleeping bag, cans of food and water, logs, and a large switchblade knife. Judith helped him, while the others stood watching from the porch near the courtyard. Bullaro felt a tingling sense of excitement at being the center of attention and, for reasons he did not precisely understand, he was looking forward to this trip. In his adolescent fantasies he had often seen himself as an explorer, a quixotic adventurer, but in real life, prior to meeting Williamson, he had been guided by caution and conventionality. After kissing Judith, Bullaro climbed into the car and started the engine. Before pulling away, he turned and waved at the group that surrounded Williamson, and he noticed that Williamson was smiling.

Driving through the valley, Bullaro headed north toward the city of Lancaster, and two hours later he was heading east into the Mojave Desert. It had been a hot night when he had begun, but now the air was cold and he stopped to put up the top. There were no other automobiles on the road, and the arid flatland on either side of him was dark and barren. He drove for another hour, thinking of Judith and the children and the people at Sandstone, and reminding himself, as he rolled through the night, that he was sitting behind the wheel of a moving vehicle with no specific destination in mind; it was an imprecise journey into his own interior.

He continued to drive until he felt himself nodding with fatigue; the he slowed down, and, after flicking on the high-beamed lights, he carefully turned off the road and directed the car over the hard sand toward a large clump of desert brush. He decided that this would serve as his shelter against the breeze. Spreading out his sleeping bag, he lay down and fell asleep almost immediately.

At 7 A.M. he awakened to a glaring sun, and, looking around, he saw nothing but miles of vacant land, scrub, rock, and a pale blue sky. He had never before been so alone, and he was excited by the vast clarity and tranquillity; he felt well rested and relaxed, and looked forward to beginning this day that expected nothing from him, nor he from it.

After drinking from his canteen and opening a can of food, he walked a few hundred yards away from the car, then stopped to dig a hole in which to defecate. Although he was far from the road, and probably many miles from any human contact, he still felt strange about loosening his belt and dropping his shorts in the bright outdoors, and if there had been a bush nearby he would have used it for privacy. Nevertheless he squatted over the hole, balancing himself with his arms forward, and he was beginning to feel comfortable in that position when, suddenly, he heard a grinding sound in the distance. Turning, he saw nothing. But the sound persisted, seeming louder and closer; and as Bullaro looked up he saw a small plane descending upon him, piloted no doubt by someone who thought he was lost or in distress. Embarrassed, Bullaro quickly stood and pulled up his shorts. The plane swished over him, then it circled around for a second pass. Bullaro waved at it in a casual manner. Soon, after the plane was gone and silence had been restored, Bullaro dropped his pants and resumed his squatting position.

Later in the morning, back on the main road and driving deeper into the desert, he stopped for gas at a rickety roadside station and then proceeded in the direction of Death Valley. Other vehicles were on the road now, most of them large trucks speeding along the concrete, kicking sand up into his windshield. By noon, the temperature had risen to one hundred degrees and he felt his shirt sticking to his back and his skin itching, and he imagined that he was beginning to smell like the blond hitchhiker he had recently met outside his motel in Malibu. It made him wish for a swim in the Sandstone pool and the sight of the nude bodies of Judith, Oralia, and the others. He thought of returning to Sandstone before nightfall, but decided that he had to spend another evening in the desert, although he was beginning to feel restless. He had responded to Williamson's challenge, which was why he was now sweltering in this wasteland, a foolish victim once again of his ego, but he sought satisfaction in knowing that he could still accept a dare, was open to new experiences, and was not, like most men his age, resistant to change.

Bullaro reflected on Williamson and the group throughout the afternoon and early evening as he camped on a desolate stretch of land not far from China Lake, along the western edge of Death Valley. It was colder now than it had been on the previous night and, after gathering logs and small dead branches that had been blown by the wind along the sand, he built a fire and then lay in his sleeping bag looking up at the stars. In the distance he heard the howling of coyotes, and the sounds were unsettling. He had read somewhere that coyotes were courageous in packs but cowardly when alone, and he suspected that this was perhaps true of himself. He was an interdependent man, assertive within a crowd but deficient when alone, like a solitary log unable to sustain a fire. He could not sleep that night, and at dawn he packed his things in the trunk of the car and began the long drive back to Sandstone.

When he arrived at the top of the mountain and passed through the stone gates toward the familiar trees that surrounded the main house, he was impressed as never before by the beauty of the place and he rejoiced in being a part of it. Parking the car and beginning to unpack, he saw David Schwind waving at him from a bulldozer on the upper roadway; and, turning, he saw a smiling John Williamson walking down the path to greet him.

Williamson extended both arms and, when Bullaro did likewise, Williamson embraced him in a way that a man would not in the city below. Then they stood talking for a few moments, and Bullaro described the trip, telling Williamson where he had been, what he had felt, and finally conceded that the time spent in solitude had clarified and reinforced his commitment to Williamson and the establishment of the love commune.

Williamson nodded, saying nothing; but before Williamson had turned away and headed back toward the house, Bullaro noticed with astonishment that there were tears in Williamson's eyes.

18

SANDSTONE, AND WHAT John Williamson was attempting to create there, was not unlike the idealized community described in *Stranger in a Strange Land*, the science fiction novel by Robert Heinlein in which a group of men and women lived in isolated comfort, swam nude together in a warm pool, made love to one another shamelessly and guiltlessly, and defied the Ninth Commandment because, as the main character in the book explained, "There is no need to covet my wife. Love her! There's no limit to her love. . . ."

But while Williamson would concede a thematic similarity between the novel and his own ambitions at Sandstone, he dismissed the book as an inspirational source, regarding it mainly as one of many simplistic renderings and evocations of a real and powerful desire that has consumed certain men for centuries: namely, the hope of reviving within Western culture the spirit of festival love and joyful coupling, derived from the pagan fertility rites, that existed among early Christians prior to the darkening influence of the medieval church, with its emphasis on sin and guilt.

A man with whom Williamson *could* identify was the fifteenth-century Dutch painter Hieronymus Bosch, a leader among a group of libertines known as the Brothers and Sisters of the Free Spirit, an erotic sect that considered itself directly descendant from Adam and Eve; they worshiped in the nude in secret churches they called Paradise, and while they indulged in group sex they regarded it as an experience in shared love rather than an impersonal orgy. Citing the celibacy of priests and nuns as contrary to nature, and disagreeing with the notion that sexual pleasure was a source of original sin, the freedom-seeking Brothers and Sisters, sometimes called Adamites, were eventually destroyed during the Inquisition, although a remembrance of their nude gatherings survives in the paintings of Hieronymus Bosch.

Closer to Williamson in time and place was the nineteenth-century utopia in Oneida, New York, established by a radical theologian who, with his wife, practiced free love with his closest friends and for thirty years pursued a policy of "perpetual courtship" with myriad lovers on a blissful secluded estate that he identified as heaven on earth. In the center of the estate was an impressive mansion that he and his followers had built, large enough for one hundred people; and surrounding it were other buildings that served as dormitories and schools for the Oneida community's many children, and factories where the community members conducted several prosperous businesses—one of which, the Oneida tin-plated spoon company, begun in the 1870s, would endure and expand into a multimillion-dollar twentieth-century corporation.

The founder of the Oneida settlement, John Humphrey Noyes, was a dignified autocrat with a neatly trimmed red beard who had studied for the ministry at the Andover Theological Seminary and the Yale Divinity School during the 1830s; but his many differences with his ecclesiastical superiors over his interpretation of the Bible precluded his ordination and relegated him to a lifetime as a renegade preacher.

Most upsetting to the church leaders in New England were Noyes' views on sex and marriage and his assertion that the Bible advocated communal love and physical intercourse between all true believers in God. Instead of monogamous marriage, which Noyes saw as a manifestation of selfishness and possessiveness that minimized one's capacity to extend love to others, he envisioned "complex marriage," an arrangement in which harmonious groups of men and women lived and worked together and made love to one another regularly, though never exclusively, and were the collective parents of all children born among them. In an effort to limit the births to a number that the community could financially support, and also in the interest of enhancing women's enjoyment of sex without fear of unwanted pregnancies or the dangers of childbirth, Noyes exhorted his men to withhold ejaculation during intercourse *except* on those occasions when he had previously approved a couple's desire for children, or when he himself had selected a willing couple for propagative purposes.

Noyes' venturing into eugenics, and his persuasive power over the sexual acts of other people, was possible only because his followers accepted him as an inspired medium of God's will—he was their messiah, a majestically aloof and erudite man who promised them salvation from sin as well as continued prosperity, salubrity, and sexual joy with several partners. Life was supposed to be happy, he reassured his cohorts—"the happiest man is the best man, and does the most good." Referring to the prudery that prevailed in the outside world, he declared: "To be ashamed of the sex organs is to be ashamed of God's workmanship," and he added: "The moral reform that arises from the sentiment of shame attempts a hopeless war with nature."

But John Humphrey Noyes' approval of pleasure did not mean that he tolerated unstructured hedonism or laziness. All his men and women were expected to work six days a week on the community farm, or in the mansion, or in the school, or in one of Oneida's many business enterprises; and all the money earned through the manufacture and sale of community-made products—in 1866 Oneida's animal-trap factory alone earned $88,000—went directly into the common treasury that supported Oneida's high standard of living.

Free medical and dental care was provided by Oneida's resident doctors; all clothing was made and repaired by the community's tailors and dressmakers, milliners and cobblers; two and sometimes three meals a day were served in the mansion's huge dining hall. In the basement of the mansion there was a Turkish bath, and on the spacious lawns of the 275-acre estate there were croquet courts and baseball diamonds. There was sailing and boat fishing on Oneida Lake, swimming in the pond, and musical and stage entertainment offered by Oneida's twenty-two-piece orchestra and its drama company, and on weekends communal dances were held in the mansion's ballroom.

Each child was required to attend the community school until the age of sixteen, and some of the more ambitious students were sent on to Yale and Columbia, where they were trained as physicians, lawyers, and engineers, and after graduation some of them returned to live and work within the expanding community. When Noyes believed that certain of Oneida's young people were mature enough for their first sexual experience, community women volunteered to share their beds with teen-aged boys, while Noyes or other older men of his choosing would indoctrinate the female virgins. In addition to pleasing the older people, Noyes believed that this system offered the young the benefit of more experienced lovers—and, since the older males had already proven themselves faithful to Noyes' policy of "male continence," there was little chance of unwanted pregnancies. Although the younger members would also be permitted to enjoy sex within their age group, there was constant community pressure against any sign of "exclusive" love. Like everything else in the community, one's body was to be shared; possessiveness of any kind was considered contrary to the community spirit and the will of God.

In the nurseries and playrooms, young children learned early that they had no proprietary claim to any specific toy; all the toys were to be shared, and after it was noticed by the supervisors that several little girls were becoming attached to certain dolls, preening them, talking to them, and taking them to bed at night, efforts were made to repress the infant mimicking of the traditional role of motherhood. The girls were reminded that dolls were false fabrications of life and that such preoccupations did not honor the ideals of Oneida womanhood.

The leading women of Oneida did not regard a female's primary purposes in life to be childbirth and domesticity; agreeing with Noyes that married women in the outside world too often became "propagative drudges," the Oneida women saw their goals as spiritual growth, personal emancipation, and intellectual improvement. They were encouraged by Noyes to attend the adult education classes conducted nightly at the mansion, and to make use of the community's 4,000-volume library. They wore short skirts and pantalets, bobbed their hair, and assumed a coequal status with the male members concerning community roles and duties. They took turns in factories, as did the men in the kitchen, and while they shared equally in the attention and affection shown to all the children of Oneida, they believed that the little girls' predilection for dolls, those frilly wax figurines with painted faces whose costumes reflected the style of the outside world, advanced an undesirable spirit that should somehow be exorcised.

One woman, a teacher, recommended as a solution that all the dolls be gathered in a pile, stripped of their clothes, and laid on the fiery coals to be "burned up with a merry blaze." After this suggestion was considered by the committee in charge of the children's nursery and school, the children themselves were assembled to respond to the problem—and, with some encouragement from their elders, the little boys unanimously voted to burn the dolls, while the girls, though reluctant, finally concurred. One of the girls who surrendered her doll would recall, in a memoir written many years later, the scene of that dreadful day in 1851: "At the hour appointed, we all formed a circle round the stove, each girl carrying on her arm her long-cherished favorite, and marching in time to a song. As we came opposite the stovedoor, we threw our dolls into the angry-looking flames, and saw them perish before our eyes."

John Humphrey Noyes had personally consented to the burning—"the doll-spirit," he asserted, "is a species of idolatry, and should be classed with the worship of graven images"; and Noyes would have as easily banished from the community any human being who persisted in demonstrating acts of "exclusive" love, be it a mother toward her child or a romantic couple toward one another. "The new commandment," Noyes wrote, "is that we love one another . . . not by pairs, as in the world, but *en masse*." An obedient, God-fearing member of Oneida should not be deprived of love and attention because of the selfish bonding of blood relatives or the possessive passions of a particular couple; Noyes insisted: "Hearts must be free to love all of the true and worthy." After a man had confessed to Noyes that he was hopelessly in love with one woman, Noyes impatiently commented: "You do not love her, you love happiness."

John Humphrey Noyes' unorthodox views on love and marriage were not the result of an unconventional boyhood, for the prominent and prosperous Vermont family to which he was born in 1811 in Brattleboro was in no manner eccentric. Noyes' mother, Polly Hayes, was a gently reared, intelligent woman who descended from the New England family that would produce the nineteenth President of the United States, Rutherford B. Hayes; and his father, John Noyes, Sr., who had successively been a teacher (he had tutored Daniel Webster), a minister, and a successful businessman, was elected to Congress by the voters of southern Vermont when John Humphrey Noyes was four years old.

As a boy Noyes was popular with his peers, was vigorously drawn to outdoor living and sports, and was also a diligent student who, like his father, graduated with honors from Dartmouth College. Leaving the campus in 1830 intending to study law, Noyes became attracted instead to the dramatic flair and conviction of certain revivalist ministers who, near his home and throughout New England, in the name of God, were challenging the traditional interpretation of the Bible and were confronting in particular the Calvinistic doctrine on human unworthiness and the prevalence of sin and predestination. Some new ministers went so far as to suggest that people could, after a true conversion, rise above sin and achieve perfection on earth, a condition that not only appealed to vast audiences but also seemed feasible in this post-Revolutionary War period when all things seemed possible. It was a time of great enthusiasm and optimism in America; the young nation, having severed its official ties to the mother country, was now free to expand and explore deeper into its own wilderness and consciousness, reappraising its Puritan past and seeking control of its own destiny.

A man named Joseph Smith, the son of a poor New England farmer, had in 1827 claimed to have communicated with the angel Moroni, and as a result of this and other revelations Smith founded Mormonism and espoused polygamy—until in 1844 an angry mob broke into the Illinois jail where he was being detained, and killed him. Smith was succeeded as the prophet by a onetime house painter and glazier named Brigham Young, who moved the Mormons westward into Utah, where the religion flourished and allowed Young to support twenty-seven wives.

A Lutheran minister, George Rapp, had years before in Pennsylvania revealed a visit from the angel Gabriel, and he was thus inspired to gather around him more than eight hundred followers who lived and worked unselfishly and contentedly, while practicing celibacy, within an agricultural haven called Harmony.

Frances Wright, a female communitarian and abolitionist of prosperous Scottish parentage, founded in 1826 near Memphis a community called Nashoba, a 2,000-acre farm on which blacks and whites worked together and were allowed to sleep together—and many did until word of their sexual mingling spread through the countryside and provoked controversies that, together with the continued unprofitability of the farm itself, induced the group to disband in 1830. In addition to her opposition to slavery, Frances Wright was also known for her lectures and writings critical of organized religion and the institution of marriage. "In wedded life," she declared, "the woman sacrifices her independence and becomes part of the property of her husband."

Similar views on marriage were often expressed during the mid-1800s by other female activists as well as by ordinary women who dwelled in small free-love communes that existed in New York State and New England, and in such towns as Berlin Heights, Ohio. Freedom between the sexes was sometimes also encouraged within the "Fourieristic" settlements, which were gatherings of people who sought utopia not through communism, but through capitalism, being inspired by the writings of a whimsically idealistic but almost impecunious French aristocrat named Charles Fourier.

Before his death in Paris in 1837, Fourier had lectured and published works asserting that nineteenth-century man's inherent greed and destructive nature could not be curtailed and made compatible with the highest goals of world capitalism unless the system of Western civilization was radically altered. Fourier proposed that national leaders divide the populations of their lands into separate groups numbering approximately 1,600 people, each group living and working within a kind of grand industrial hotel, or "phalanstery," that would fulfill all of a citizen's private and professional needs.

Ideally each phalanstery would be six stories high, cheerfully decorated and comfortably furnished, with separate wings for work enterprises and other wings for social or domestic activities. While regents would supervise the income earning within each phalanstery, individuals would perform at jobs that they did best, though they periodically would be rotated to avoid boredom; and everyone would receive a minimum wage and possibly a higher wage commensurate with their greater productivity or talent. The cost of renting apartments in the phalanstery would vary, depending on the size of the apartment and the luxuries it contained; and if tenants wished to occupy the more expensive apartments but could not afford the higher rent, they could make up the difference by working longer hours. While upward mobility through greater production was encouraged, no member of a Fourieristic community could be socially ostracized for a lack of industriousness, nor was any member expected to feel sexual frustration or deprivation: Even the least physically attractive were guaranteed a "sexual minimum" by the "erotic saints" who would make themselves available in private suites set aside for such purposes.

Monogamy among couples was discouraged by Fourier, who also felt that the nuclear family was a detriment to utopianism because it promoted possessiveness, nepotism, inward-thinking, and a narrow view of life that blurred the grander vision of mankind. Although Fourier was unable during his lifetime to raise sufficient capital to construct even a single phalanstery, certain of his ideas were considered meritorious and even practical by such influential Americans as Albert Brisbane, who had met Fourier in Paris and whose book *The Social Destiny of Man* brought Fourier to the attention of the editor of the New York *Tribune*, Horace Greeley, who in turn invited Brisbane to use the columns of the *Tribune* to popularize the theories and fantasies of Charles Fourier; and thus did Fourierism become a minor fad in America.

During the early 1840s, dozens of Fourier-inspired experiments were begun by various utopians, escapists, and advocates of free love. Occupying large rambling houses on remote farms or in the outer thickets of towns and villages in the Northeast, the Midwest, and as far west as Texas, people sought to earn a collective livelihood through horticulture, small businesses, crafts, and light industries; but few of these associations survived for more than two years because they were undercapitalized, hastily organized, and soon splintered by disruptive factions.

Perhaps the best known of these settlements, though it was relatively discreet sexually, was the Brook Farm Institute of Agriculture and Education, a six-year venture begun in 1841 ten miles from Boston in West Roxbury, and historically remembered mostly for having among its early members an aspiring young writer who had recently lost his job at the Boston Custom House—Nathaniel Hawthorne.

Earning his room and board by working on the farm, Hawthorne was at first enthralled by the rural experience and transcendental atmosphere, and even after spending a day in the field, which was largely devoted to the spreading of manure, he was able to write in a letter to a friend: "There is nothing so unseemly and disagreeable in this sort of toil as thou wouldst think. It defiles the hands, indeed, but not the soul. This gold ore is a pure and wholesome substance; else our Mother Nature would not devour it so readily, and derive so much nourishment from it, and return such a rich abundance of good grain and roots in requital of it."

But soon, within six months, Hawthorne had abandoned Brook Farm, convinced that the community was diverting him from his literary ambitions. "Romance and poetry," he later wrote, ". . . need ruin to make them grow." And in his novel of 1852, *The Blithedale Romance*, which was inspired by Brook Farm, he suggested that in communal living people tended to become *too* close, *too* aware of one another's vibrations and personal piques: ". . . an unfriendly state of feeling could not occur between any two members, without the whole society being more or less commoted and made uncomfortable thereby. . . . If one of us happened to give his neighbor a box on the ear, the tingle was immediately felt on the same side of everybody's head. Thus, even on the supposition that we were far less quarrelsome than the rest of the world, a great deal of time was necessarily wasted in rubbing our ears.''

Although John Humphrey Noyes was familiar with the Fourieristic movement, and had also visited during the 1830s free-love communes in such places as Brimfield, Massachusetts, he preferred to believe that he had little in common with the sexual radicals and social reformers of his day; he felt instead that he was divinely directed, was a spiritual messenger appointed to assist God on earth to establish a religion that would inspire people to love their neighbors truly and completely. Unlike the fanciful Fourier, or the itinerant intellectuals and writers who had visited Brook Farm—a group that included Thoreau and Emerson, Henry James and Margaret Fuller, Brisbane and Greeley—Noyes was not a theoretical utopian or advocate of individual freedoms; he was a committed communist, an absolutist, a theocrat who wished to purge the sin of selfishness from the souls of men and to convert them to what he called "Bible Communism." While he denounced egotism in other people, Noyes' own ego was monumental; and yet he invariably justified his many preferences and pronouncements, including his interdiction of monogamous marriage, as being in concert with the teachings of the Bible.

"In the Kingdom of Heaven," he wrote, "the institution of marriage which assigns the exclusive possession of one woman to one man does not exist [Matt. 22:23–30] for in the resurrection they neither marry nor are given in marriage but are as the Angels of God in Heaven. . . . The abolishment of sexual exclusiveness is involved in the love-relation required between all believers by the express injunction of Christ and the apostles and by the whole tenor of the New Testament. . . . The restoration of true relations between the sexes is a matter second in importance only to the reconciliation of man to God. Bible Communists are operating in this order. Their main work, since 1834, has been to develop the religion of the New Covenant and establish union with God. . . .''

Noyes' reference to 1834 was significant; it was in that year that he became convinced of his spiritual perfection, a state of sinlessness that had been evolving within him for nearly three

years—since he had first received a God sign after attending a
fiery and frenzied four-day revivalist rally held near his home
in Putney, Vermont. At the time of the rally, in 1831, he was
twenty years old, an ambitious and driven law student, though
uncertain about his purpose; but after the rally he recalled:
"Light gleamed upon my soul in a different way from what I
had expected. It was dim and almost imperceptible at first but
in the course of the day it attained meridian splendor. Ere the
day was done I had concluded to devote myself to the service
and ministry of God."

He enrolled at the Andover Theological Seminary, but quit
after one year because he believed that the seminarians lacked
seriousness; he then registered at the Yale Divinity School,
where he studied intensely, argued often with his peers and the
faculty over biblical interpretation, and revealed a passion about
religion that one contemporary likened to "an acute fever."
Soon some of his privately expressed theories at Yale were interpreted by other students as symptoms of a neurotic and he-
retical temperament—such as his belief that the Second Coming
of Jesus Christ was not a future event but had already happened
during the destruction of Jerusalem in A.D. 70, at which time
mankind had been saved from sin. Thus, in Noyes' view, the
Kingdom of God had at that time been established on earth and
was still omnipresent in the atmosphere, and was viable in the
souls of true believers, and, like the traveling evangelists that he
had heard in New England advocating Perfectionism, Noyes was
convinced that a person could, after a religious conversion, be
spiritually perfect and answerable not to mundane moral laws,
but to the mind of the Lord—and Noyes further believed that
such a person was himself.

This he publicly acknowledged one day in February 1834
while preaching in the New Haven Free Church, causing a scandal and resulting almost immediately in the revocation of his
license as a Congregationalist minister. Without a church at his
disposal, Noyes wandered through New England and upstate
New York preaching in the outdoors and recruiting followers.
Hoping to attract distinguished colleagues and perhaps financial
support to his cause, Noyes approached, without success, such
men as the abolitionist and editor of the *Liberator*, William
Lloyd Garrison, who had recently been attacked and almost
lynched by a proslavery mob in Boston; and the controversial
though well-endowed Presbyterian clergyman Lyman Beecher,
father of Harriet Beecher Stowe, author of *Uncle Tom's Cabin*,

and the Reverend Henry Ward Beecher, whom Lincoln would call "the greatest orator since Saint Paul" but who would be better remembered as the defendant in the celebrated adultery trial involving Mrs. Elizabeth Tilton.

In addition to Noyes' personal proselytizing, he promulgated his religious ideas in a magazine that he cofounded called *The Perfectionist*, where he attracted the readership of many free-thinkers, antinomians, and other rebels against convention, including an earnest and well-to-do young Vermont woman whose grandfather had served as the lieutenant governor of the state. Her name was Harriet Holton, and she had first become aware of Noyes through his writings about the Second Coming of Christ.

Soon she began a correspondence with Noyes and later donated substantial sums of money to his movement. Since her parents were dead, her grandparents and family friends sought to discourage her involvement with Perfectionism, but she was intrigued with Noyes' philosophy and became attracted to him personally after their first meeting, being neither discouraged nor disturbed by his views on marriage and monogamy even when he warned her in a letter: "We can enter into no engagement with each other which shall limit the range of our affections as they are limited in matrimonial engagements by the fashions of the world."

Noyes further emphasized his opposition to monogamy in a letter published in a free-thought journal that described his concept of an ideal marital relationship:

> I call a certain woman my wife—she is yours, she is Christ's and in Him she is the bride of all saints. She is dear in the hand of a stranger, and according to my promise to her, I rejoice. My claim on her cuts directly across the marriage vows of this world and God knows the end.

> When the will of God is done on earth as it is in heaven, there will be no more marriage. The marriage supper of the Lamb is a feast at which every dish is free to every guest. Exclusiveness, jealousy, quarreling, have no place there. . . .

Harriet Holton understood and accepted Noyes' doctrine, and in 1838, after their marriage in Putney, they began to invite to their home other religious couples who were interested in the Bible and might become future converts to Perfectionism. Within a few years they had befriended a half-dozen couples who subscribed, at least in theory, to Perfectionism; and of this group the most fervent and physically attractive were Mary and George Cragin.

Before moving to Putney in 1840, the Cragins had associated with free-love cultists in upstate New York, and had earlier served as evangelical workers in the congregation of the famous revivalist Charles G. Finney. Finney was a tall, energetic preacher with an exuberant manner and wide-ranging choral voice; and as he traveled through New York State piously flagellating from the pulpit, he often provoked his audiences to outbursts of tears and distemper, shrieking and fainting—and violent threats and brandished fists directed at Finney himself. Though his methods were deplored by many of his colleagues in the Presbyterian ministry, Finney was nonetheless credited with converting great masses of sinners throughout the western area of the state, and his appeal was no less compelling after he arrived in New York City in the early 1830s to preach at a new church especially designed for him, the Broadway Tabernacle.

It was there that George Cragin, as a member of the Tabernacle congregation and one of Finney's sabbath school teachers, became acquainted with another of Finney's volunteers, a slim and lovely young woman from Maine named Mary Johnson. After a year's courtship, they were married in 1834 at a festive ceremony in New York attended only by devout believers, after which the couple drove off in a horse-drawn mail coach to a honeymoon in Newark. Although Mary and George Cragin had both come from prosperous New England homes, their religious fanaticism limited their family ties, and parental misfortune had greatly reduced their expected inheritance; and, since George Cragin lacked business ambition—and had also rejected a promising job as a European agent for a New York firm because he regarded his would-be employer as an infidel—the Cragins were forced to live frugally in New York and to seek solace mainly in spiritual comfort.

But this, too, was disrupted after 1837 when their temporal leader, Charles Finney, left New York for Oberlin, Ohio, where he founded a theological department at the new college, and eventually became Oberlin's president. The Cragins drifted with diminished enthusiasm to other revivalists, failing to recover their religious zeal until, while in Vermont in 1840, they came under the influence of John Humphrey Noyes, whose religious commune was in an early stage of formation.

Among Noyes' first converts had been members of his own family—a younger brother, two of his sisters and their husbands. While Noyes' mother and the rest of his family and relatives openly disapproved of Perfectionism, no attempt was made to deny Noyes, or his subservient siblings, the $20,000 in cash and various properties that were left in a will after their father's recent death. These assets, along with the $16,000 patrimony of Noyes' wife and the contributions of the other followers, permitted the community members to concentrate on their Perfectionist indoctrination and to recruit new members.

The group did, however, derive some income from working in a general store that Noyes had acquired; and on the two Noyes farms that were inherited, the members grew much of what was eaten at the communal table. All the members and their children lived either in Noyes' home or the homes of his two sisters, and on Sundays everyone gathered to hear Noyes preach in a small chapel that they had built. At Noyes' insistence, each adult was required to devote three hours each day to religious meditation and reading the Bible; and if an individual persistently demonstrated signs of selfishness or possessiveness, or otherwise strayed from the communal spirit, he was summoned by Noyes to appear before the group and submit to stringent criticism. The accused member was expected to sit silently and humbly in the center of the room while the others took turns articulating their disapproval, and at times this experience was so excruciating that the individual abandoned the group in horror or fury.

But there was no sense of disharmony when George Cragin made an introductory visit to the Noyes homestead; and during the ensuing years little would occur to alter Cragin's rapturous first impressions of that day. "The little circle of believers I found there appeared so different from any I had ever met before," Cragin noted in his journal. "All were so kind, so quiet, so thoughtful and studious and yet, in spirit, so free. . . . Providence had now compensated me with a heaven upon earth."

The birth in 1841 of the Noyeses' first child, a son named Theodore, added to the joy and optimism of the group, since the event had followed two stillborn babies produced by Mrs. Noyes during their first two years of marriage. But when two more Noyes children were born dead in 1843 and 1844, John Humphrey Noyes determined that he could never again subject his wife to the physical risk and mental anguish of "propagative love," and from then on he practiced what he called "male continence." Soon he established this as a sexual policy within the settlement, not only because it reduced the dangers of childbirth and helped to control the communal population but also because it allowed Noyes to pursue his plan to further unite his followers in the bond of complex marriage.

With the approval of his wife, Noyes in the spring of 1846 decided to approach Mary and George Cragin and invite them to become their first partners. Noyes had for years been attracted to Mrs. Cragin, and his wife had expressed an affinity and an affection for Mrs. Cragin's courtly husband; and after Noyes' proposal had been privately tendered, the Cragins accepted without hesitation. In her diary, before the appointed evening, Mary Cragin wrote of Noyes: "In view of his goodness to me and of his desire that I should let him fill me with himself, I yield and offer myself, to be penetrated by his spirit, and desire that love and gratitude may inspire my heart so that I shall sympathize with his pleasure in the thing, before my personal pleasure begins; knowing that it will increase my capability for happiness."

The happy consummation of the comarital relationship between the Noyeses and the Cragins was followed in subsequent weeks by other couples exchanging marital partners; and while the members were also free to abstain, the practice of sexual sharing soon prevailed among Noyes' Perfectionists. But in 1847, after rumors of bacchanalian revelry had been circulated by the citizens of Putney throughout the state of Vermont, there was a warrant for Noyes' arrest.

Surrendering without contrition to the legal authorities, Noyes was booked on charges of adultery and, after posting a $2,000 bond, was released awaiting trial. But soon his attorney informed him that a group of moral vigilantes in Putney was planning to capture him and punish him in their own fashion; and being aware of what similar citizens in Illinois had done to the imprisoned Mormon leader, Joseph Smith, Noyes decided to jump bail and hide out temporarily in New York City.

This he did in November 1847, remaining in seclusion for several weeks until the furor in Putney had subsided. Then in early 1848 he informed his followers by mail that he had acquired a new site for their settlement—160 acres of good meadowland in upstate New York, in a quiet valley on the Oneida Creek halfway between the cities of Syracuse and Utica. On the land there were two small farmhouses, a shed, a sawmill, and also two log cabins that until recent years had been occupied by a dispersed band of Indians. While the accommodations were inadequate for the nineteen adults and their children in the Putney settlement, Noyes had fortunately befriended and converted a young architect from Syracuse named Erastus Hapgood Hamilton, who agreed to design a large chateau and, with the aid of Perfectionist labor, to supervise its construction.

The enthusiastic response to this proposal in Putney was promptly followed by the arrival in Oneida of the new settlers; and from the early spring of 1848 through the summer and fall, the men, women, and teenaged children worked indefatigably at clearing the land, sawing the forest timber, carting rock for the foundation and cellar, erecting and stabilizing the support beams and walls, the floors and ceilings, and finally painting the three-story structure that comprised sixty rooms and was topped by a cupola.

Except for the architect and another new convert who was a skilled stonemason, all the construction work was done by people of very limited experience; and yet the large house was ready for occupancy during the winter of 1849, and it sturdily survived for two decades until it was later replaced by a grander hundred-room brick mansion.

After completing the main residence, the Oneida communitarians built a two-story children's house, and also a school that was under the supervision of Mrs. Cragin, a former teacher. They then built smaller structures that sheltered Oneida's many activities—the machine shop and blacksmith's shed, buildings for clothing and shoe repair, the stables and poultry pens, a greenhouse, storage bins, and even beehives. There was also erected a building used entirely for the washing of the community members' clothes—a task performed by men as well as women, and determined each week by the drawing of lots.

While farming was initially Oneida's principal business, Noyes suspected that his settlement could never flourish if dependent on agriculture. This had been the problem of the Fourieristic communes like Brook Farm—their founders had placed too much faith in the land—and Noyes, who sensed the decline of the farmer and the rise of the industrial state, was soon to convert Oneida primarily into a manufacturing community.

By the early 1850s, as Oneida's auspicious atmosphere and beautifully landscaped estate drew to it nearly one hundred new members who were anxious to contribute their talent and time to the cause of Perfectionism, Noyes was overseeing a variety of manufacturing ventures. Brooms were being made from corn husks and sold in nearby towns and villages, as well as in Syracuse and Utica. Rustic outdoor chairs fashioned from cedar were also distributed for sale, as were palm-leaf hats, carpet traveling bags, spokes for wagon wheels, and steel animal traps. The trap business, which had been introduced to the community by a rugged convert who had worked in the area as a hunter and blacksmith prior to meeting Noyes in 1848, would become Oneida's most lucrative enterprise in the mid-1850s as the fur market expanded nationally, creating a demand for Oneida traps from wholesalers in New York City and Chicago.

Converts not only shared their skills but also were expected to yield their worldly possessions at the time they joined the community, and it was in this way that the Oneidans acquired in 1850, from an affluent convert, a large sailing vessel—which led certain Oneida optimists, with Noyes' blessing, into the business of freighting limestone along the Hudson River. But during a voyage on a July afternoon in 1851 near Kingston, New York, while the ship was being guided by an Oneida helmsman who had more trust in God than a knowledge of seamanship, a squall suddenly arose and caused the rock-laden boat to capsize. Among the passengers who had come along for the trip and did not survive it was Mary Cragin.

The event brought grief and despair to the entire community, and most New York City newspapers that reported the accident were sympathetic in their coverage; but a few upstate journals and religious publications that had long been critical of Noyes seized the opportunity to suggest that the drownings might be a sign of heavenly punishment against the licentious practices of the community. These articles, and similar criticisms from the pulpit and a few civic leaders, encouraged a small but vocal group of vigilantes who resided in towns near the Oneida settlement to approach the county magistrate and register a complaint that Noyes was fomenting "Mormonism," "Mahometanism," and "Heathenism."

But Noyes, who had much more invested in Oneida than he had earlier in Putney and had no intention of leaving the area, vigorously defended his beliefs in a series of public statements, and in his community newspaper he wrote:

A scrutiny of the household habits of the Oneida Community during any period of its history would show not a licentious spirit but the opposite . . . it would disclose less careless familiarity of the sexes—less approach to anything like "bacchanalian" revelry—vastly less unregulated speech and conduct than it found in an equal circle of what is called good society in the world.

That we disclaimed the cast-iron rules and modes by which selfishness regulates the relation of the sexes is true; but . . . proof of our morality [can] be found in the broad fact of the general health of the association. No death of an adult member has ever occurred at Oneida . . . many who joined us sick have become well . . . and the special woes of women in connection with children have been nearly extinguished. The increase of population by birth in our forty families, for the last four years, has been considerably less than the progeny of Queen Victoria alone. So much for the outcry of "licentiousness and brutality."

Because the Oneida community also had many influential friends among the citizens of the nearby towns, individuals with whom it had established good business relations—and because Noyes made a concession to the magistrate to abolish complex marriage—the charges against himself and his followers were never pressed.

Soon, however, Noyes decided that the imperfect men who sat in judgment of society had no authority over God's paradise at Oneida, and thus the free-love system was reinstituted; but at the same time Noyes warned his followers that their only safeguard against a "barbarian" invasion of their land was in the greater worship of the Lord, and he urged that they spend more time with their Bibles and deepen their commitment to Perfectionism. "We shall escape the rod only by ceasing to need it," he wrote, "and we shall invite prosperity only by being able to bear it without glorying."

While Noyes had at first been gratified by Oneida's progress in business, he was now concerned that his Bible communists might be developing capitalistic tendencies, a pride in profit making, a propensity for possessiveness and individual achievement. "The Lord alone shall be exalted," Noyes warned; and during the 1850s and early 1860s, as the community's earnings and donations continued to increase, Noyes directed his factory foremen to reduce the work schedule to a six-hour day, which was half the time demanded in most outside industries, and to reemphasize the communal goals of spiritual growth and self-improvement. To this end no moment went undirected. Even while the communists gathered in groups to stitch handbags or to braid palm-leaf hats, a member sat among them reading aloud from an inspirational volume or a book of historical importance or literary merit—a novel by Dickens, a biography of Jefferson. All adults were encouraged to attend the education courses held each evening in the mansion, conducted by converts who had once been teachers; and members with talent in music, or art, or playing chess, were expected to offer instruction to anyone interested in learning.

The principle of sharing extended to the nursery and school-room, where children were told to never say "me" or "mine" but always "we" and "ours." On the farm, in the factories, and in the craft shops, each senior worker trained a young apprentice; and each task, no matter how menial, was to be regarded not as a burden, but as an offering. Music accompanied many of these efforts: A clarinetist tooting melodiously on the front lawn was a signal to all who had free time that volunteers were needed to work on a special project—it might be a berry-picking bee, or a corn-cutting bee, or a vegetable-canning bee, or a road-repair bee. After the volunteers had gathered, and the required number were chosen by the project director, they were lined up and were enthusiastically paraded off toward the work site behind a fife and drum.

When the day's work was completed, everyone from the bees, the factories, the shops, and the farmlands reconvened at the mansion and went to their rooms to wash and dress for supper, which began at 5:30 in the main dining room that seated 110 people. As the members arrived, they walked automatically to the back of the room, occupying whatever seats were available at the dining tables extending through the center of the room, or at the oval tables lined along the walls. Here there was a free spirit of mingling, devoid of cliquishness, with no pairing off between Oneida's senior or junior members, males or females, blood relatives or spouses. Except for the adolescents under twelve, who ate in the children's house, and the teenagers, who were taking turns as kitchen helpers and table waiters, the community's youths were accepted in the dining room as adults, and were expected to conform in all ways to the decorous dining atmosphere.

After dinner, if there was not an outdoor concert or a children's play or poetry recital in the auditorium, some members gathered in the parlor to talk or play chess, while others went into the library to read books, magazines, and such newspapers as the New York *Tribune* that regularly arrived by mail. While Oneidans were only peripherally connected to the outside world through their businesses, regarding themselves as "peaceful foreigners" in their native land, they were nevertheless interested in the headline events and polemics of their time, which rotated around the questions of slavery and suffragism, unionism and temperance.

Since Noyes neither drank nor smoked, both of these habits were considered vices at Oneida; and since the community's religious beliefs taught that all humans were equal in the eyes of the Lord, there was unanimous support for women's rights, the freedom of slaves, and the humane treatment of laborers. Although the community paid taxes, its men chose not to vote in elections; and for reasons never understood by Noyes, nor did he ever seek an explanation, no Oneida man was summoned by the Union Army during the draft act of 1863. It was possible that the military conscriptors felt that the presence of Oneida men might instill an immoral or quirky influence on other soldiers; or it was also possible that the location of the Oneida settlement, which straddled two congressional districts and two county draft boards, was considered by each to be in the domain of the other.

The Oneida businesses that had declined during the war were revived after the restoration of peace; and by 1866, as many army veterans returned to their civilian jobs as fur traders and trappers, the community's factory was selling more than $1,000 worth of traps each week; and the bag factory, the flour mill, and the other enterprises were busy enough to justify for the first time in community history the hiring of outside help to fulfill some of the less skilled labor requirements.

The community enlarged many of its older buildings and added new ones; it expanded its landholdings to 275 acres, and supported not only the two hundred members dwelling within its boundaries but also other converts at its branch commune in Wallingford, Connecticut. Some of the children of Oneida's first settlers were now old enough to be attending college or to be assuming management responsibilities within the community. Noyes' son, Theodore, was a medical student at Yale. George Cragin's son, Charles, also an alumnus of Yale, was temporarily employed far from home studying the modern methods of silk thread production, which was to be one of Oneida's future enterprises.

* * *

By 1869 Noyes believed that his community was sufficiently affluent and spiritually ready to venture beyond the realm of "perpetual courtship" and "male continence" and to attempt to create, through a committee-approved program of selective coupling, a special breed of Perfectionist children.

Prior to 1869, going back twenty years to Oneida's founding in 1849, only thirty-five children had been born in a community that each year was inhabited by at least one hundred sexually active adults. While several of these births had been accidental—despite Noyes' preaching, not all of his men proved to be flawless practitioners of continence—an equal number had been born with Noyes' permission to women who feared that if they became much older they would be unable to conceive.

In addition to the thirty-five children, many other children had been brought to Oneida by their parents, who then surrendered their parental responsibility to the community and also sought to adjust to the community's prevailing atmosphere of free love. In the free-love system at Oneida, any man wishing to go to bed with a certain woman had to first submit his request to a Noyes-appointed intermediary, a senior woman who then relayed the "invitation" to the desired woman and ascertained whether or not the latter was willing. While any woman could refuse the propositions of any and all men, such rejections were generally not the rule in Oneida's sex-affirmative society; and the sexual records kept by Oneida's intermediaries indicated that most community women had an average of two or four lovers a week, and some of the younger women had as many as seven different lovers in a week. The purpose of the intermediary's ledger was not to discourage the frequency of sex, for at Oneida a bountiful bed-life was considered healthy and proper, but instead it served as a check against those couples who might be overindulging in "special" affections for one another and not sharing their bodies with other Perfectionists. Any tendency toward "exclusive" attachments was discouraged by the intermediary, and Noyes had no intention of altering this policy even after he introduced his plan for selective breeding.

After informing the membership that Oneida now had enough money in its treasury to afford the addition of more children, and after asking for female volunteers who would lend their bodies to the procreative program, Noyes made it clear that he would influence the choice of each sire and that the women would have no exclusive maternal rights over the children they produced. Despite these restrictions, Noyes received more than fifty applications, all of which were affixed with the women's signatures that affirmed the following resolution: "That we do not belong to ourselves in any respect, but that we belong first to God, and second to Mr. Noyes as God's true representative . . . that we will put aside all envy, childishness, and self-seeking, and rejoice with those who are chosen candidates; that we will, if necessary, become martyrs to science, and cheerfully renounce all desire to become mothers, if for any reason Mr. Noyes deems us unfit material for propagation."

After reviewing the submissions, Noyes rejected nine applications due to the person's physical condition or to other unspecified reasons. The selected females, who were on the average twelve years younger than the chosen sires, were in some cases virgins—and, not surprisingly, the man most favored by Noyes to impregnate these women was Noyes himself.

Of the fifty-eight live children born of this program, which continued through the 1870s, five boys and four girls were fathered by Noyes, and they carried his surname. The other fathers were senior Oneidans who, in Noyes' view, were not only of superior mind and health but also adhered most faithfully to Noyes' religious philosophy. One of Noyes' appointed sires, however, was not a popular choice in the community, and this would eventually contribute to the schism that would shatter Oneida toward the end of the decade. The man in question was Noyes' son, Theodore, a brooding and indecisive intellectual who had abandoned his career in medicine, remained skeptical of the Bible, and frequently exhibited signs of extreme selfishness and mental instability. And yet the elder Noyes clearly had a softness for this boy, the only one who had lived of the five children born to his wife in their early years of marriage; and Noyes' continued permissiveness toward Theodore was the most flagrant mark of weakness and fallibility in this otherwise stern and righteous autocrat.

The complaints against Theodore included charges of orgasmic carelessness in his sexual relationships, a jealous attachment to a certain young woman, and a somewhat cavalier attitude toward the community's business enterprises. After Theodore had gained access to a $3,500 trust fund that had been left to him by a Vermont relative, he vacated Oneida for New York City, leaving most members with the impression that he would never return. But once his resources had evaporated in ill-advised investments, and after his letters home indicated that his spirit

had been chastened, Theodore was permitted to return to
Oneida, where he was welcomed by his father like a prodigal
son.

Forgiving as John Humphrey Noyes was of his son's
transgressions, he remained firm and inflexible toward anyone
else who seemed to challenge his authority, and this was particularly true in the case of a convert named James W. Towner.
Towner was an articulate and impressive man who had practiced
law in his native Ohio, had been prominent politically, but was
suddenly the object of scandal when it was disclosed that he and
his wife were members of the Berlin Heights free-love community. After the community's love center had been set afire by
a group of incensed townsmen, who also destroyed the printing
press of the sect's libertine newspaper, Towner hastily moved
with his family and some friends to New York State, where he
eventually met Noyes and was accepted into the Oneida community.

For a time at Oneida, James Towner was seen as a positive
presence; he worked cheerfully and energetically at whatever
task was assigned to him, and his intelligence and self-assurance
soon commanded the admiration and respect of other members.
Being that he was in complete accord with Noyes' philosophy
of selflessness and sharing, Towner did not anticipate that there
would be a day when he would have ideological differences with
Oneida's revered mentor.

But in 1875 the sixty-three-year-old Noyes, feeling his age
and sensing his mortality, astonished the community by announcing that the thirty-four-year-old Theodore would in the
future become his successor; and while most Oneidans did not
dare to question their founder's judgment, a small faction did
declare their doubts about Theodore's worthiness, and perhaps
the most loquacious of the dissident voices was that of James
Towner.

Suspecting that this forthright and untimid convert from Ohio
might himself be secretly aspiring to one day rule Oneida, Noyes
was thereafter wary of Towner, and in the years ahead he made
certain that neither Towner nor the other dissenting men would
ever be chosen for the role of "first husband" to the new cluster
of nubile virgins soon available for sexual congress. Unjust as
this decision seemed to James Towner, it was even more outrageous to a few older men who, having been faithful for decades to male continence and Perfectionism, were now being
denied the pleasures of propagation mainly because they had

been unenthusiastic about the proposed elevation of a young scion whose *own* spiritual failings would in no way bar *him* from the bedrooms of Oneida's virgins. Indeed, Theodore would become a sire on three occasions—and, when added to the nine newborn children of his father, it would appear that Noyes *père* and perhaps even Noyes *fils* had instituted the program in the interest of everlastingly establishing their seed as the dominant root in the rich Oneida soil.

But if there was ever a time when the Bible communists could least afford internal squabbling, it was now, in the latter 1870s, for beyond the Oneida gates intensified displeasure was being expressed by clergymen and lawmen on learning that Oneida women were producing dozens of children out of wedlock, and Noyes was condemned on editorial pages as justifying in the name of eugenics the "ethics of the barnyard" and of creating a monstrous Darwin-inspired system whose ulterior motive at Oneida was "to kill off their sickly children."

After a statewide gathering of Protestant clergymen had convened to organize a unified front against the Oneidans, the nation's most powerful censor, Anthony Comstock, joined the campaign against Noyes, declaring that the community's religious pamphlets and literature on free love—much of which had been sent through the mail—had violated the antiobscenity postal statute of the federal government, for which the punishment was imprisonment. Comstock himself had lobbied this act through Congress in 1873, and it had provided him, and his zealous minions within his Society for the Suppression of Vice, with a far-reaching whip with which to beat into line anyone who strayed from his straight and narrow view of morality.

In addition to incarcerating numerous vendors of French postcards, madams and prostitutes, and such irreverent freethinkers as the editor D. M. Bennett, Anthony Comstock had indicted—or would indict—museum dealers of nude art, pharmacists who sold condoms, publishers of marriage manuals and books on birth control by Margaret Sanger. Comstock railed against George Bernard Shaw's play *Mrs. Warren's Profession*, and he was instrumental in getting Walt Whitman fired from the Interior Department for writing *Leaves of Grass*. Comstock's appeal to the United States District Attorney prompted the imprisonment of the radical feminist Victoria Woodhull, who, as the presidential candidate of the Equal Rights party in 1872, had advocated free love, women's voting rights, lenient divorce laws, and birth control; and who later, in her weekly newspaper, exposed the sexual hypocrisies of the Reverend Henry Ward Beecher, for which Comstock had her punished on charges of disseminating obscenity.

But as awesome and vindictive as Comstock was, the censorious crusader was not the worst of John Humphrey Noyes' worries during the disruptive months of the late 1870s: Noyes had heard horrifying rumors that some Oneida defectors of the recent past were now being persuaded by government prosecutors to come forward and testify in court that Noyes had indulged in sexual intercourse with a number of young community women who were legally under age; and since this was true, Noyes knew that he could be charged with statutory rape.

With such pressure mounting against him, and with lawmen now arresting Mormon polygamists throughout the land, Noyes concluded that he had no alternative but to abandon his community. If he were to disappear, perhaps the enemies of Perfectionism would soon lose interest in retribution, as had been the case years ago in Putney.

And so on the night of June 23, 1879, without a word to most of his confidants, including Theodore, John Humphrey Noyes and an elderly colleague climbed aboard a horse-drawn carriage and passed through the Oneida gates, through which he would never return alive. Traveling westward through New York State, Noyes crossed over to the Canadian side of Niagara Falls, where he eventually settled himself in a small home and would in time be joined by his wife and a few old-time loyalists. He was disheartened and enfeebled, but still hopeful that he would one day return to Oneida. In the meantime, he appointed a committee of caretakers—which included Theodore, but excluded Towner—to deal as best they could with the spiritual and business life of the three-hundred-member community; and his emissaries commuted regularly between Canada and Oneida, carrying his spirited letters of instruction and advice to be read aloud in the mansion auditorium, where a majority of the residents still believed in his wisdom and supremacy.

His enforced absence, however, did not diminish the determination of Oneida's outside opposition to destroy what he had created; at the very least, the clergy and lawmen demanded that Oneida's propagative program be abolished, and that the pregnant young women and unwed mothers sanctify their sinful acts by marrying the men who had impregnated them—a proposal complicated by the fact that many of the men were already married to other women. An unmarried woman who had borne one of John Humphrey Noyes' recent sons, for example, had also produced a child with another married man as well as a third child with an Oneidan who could not positively be identified. Such issues as questionable paternity had previously been of minor importance in this once-blissful haven where complex marriage had been heralded as the highest form of union, and where the communal businesses had promised sufficient funds to eternally support all the brides of Christ and their distinctive progeny.

But while prosperity still prevailed at Oneida, and while the community's new silverware enterprise seemed likely to contribute even more money to its half-million-dollar treasury, Oneida's economic situation depended largely on the public's continued goodwill and patronage; and if the highly publicized campaign against Oneida continued unabated, it could ultimately induce an economic boycott of Perfectionist products and finally convert the beautiful estate into an infamous landmark of poverty and social isolation.

Were John Humphrey Noyes still residing at Oneida, his forceful leadership and intrepidity might have given strength to his followers; but no amount of inspirational mail written by him in exile could allay Oneida's uncertainty and consternation, nor could it prevent within the community the gradual emergence of three distinct factions that each offered different solutions to the problems everyone now shared.

One faction, which included Theodore and several of the younger business-oriented members, believed that the community should become more secularized and capitalistic, perhaps reorganizing into a joint-stock company and deemphasizing its identity as an esoteric religion. Hoping to appease its outside critics, it would discontinue Oneida's controversial sex practices, at least temporarily, and would publicly announce that it was encouraging marriage among its young people.

A second faction, headed by James Towner, was still militantly committed to Bible communism and all of its sexual freedoms; it was convinced that if the Perfectionists would replace its aging and exiled leader with Mr. Towner, and conform to his vigorous guidance, it could boldly stand fast against the outside agitation. To the suggestion that Oneida soften its position about monogamous marriage, Towner remained unalterably opposed. "I believe in communism of love as much as I believe in communism of property," he said. "I do not believe that marriage and communism can exist together."

A third group, whose one hundred members nearly doubled the combined total of the other two, consisted of Noyes' loyalists who, having accepted him as God's only true representative on earth, could not even imagine the presence of another man in his place, especially since they knew that Noyes was still alive and perhaps destined to reappear at any moment. Among the leading members of this faction were some elders who had been converted to Perfectionism more than thirty years ago at Putney, such as Noyes' sister, Harriet Noyes Skinner; Noyes' first male partner in complex marriage, George Cragin; and the architect of Oneida's first mansion, Erastus H. Hamilton.

But on the fringe of this faction and the others, there were some Oneidans who were maintaining their neutrality, or were shifting their alliances from day to day, or were just feeling rooted like trees to the property, but stymied without a source of support or sustenance beyond the communal walls, and quietly praying that they would not be invaded by the mobs that Mr. Noyes had often identified as "the barbarians."

Particularly prone to such feelings of insecurity were several unmarried women with children, and many nubile virgins, too, who were now less eager to offer up their bodies in the blithe spirit of free love when they no longer felt the pervasive presence of freedom and love extending through the community. Many women abstained from sex during this time, to the chagrin of the men, while other women began to insist on something more than just bodily pleasure and praise from the men they favored—they wanted to be possessed, and to possess in turn, and to extract from the objects of their affection the promise of eventual marriage.

These inclinations, and others that were contrary to the ideals of Perfectionism, were described in many letters that Noyes received from his loyalists at Oneida, and he was saddened and perturbed by what he read. The young university students and teenagers seemed to be particularly rebellious to the traditions of Oneida: They were going off by themselves and becoming romantically attached as couples; they were ignoring the Bible and the criticism of their elders; a number of young men had somehow acquired their own horses, defying Oneida's longtime rule against private ownership; and a few of the younger women were now letting their hair grow longer, and were also tending toward the longer dresses that were the fashion of the outside world.

The teachers and governesses who formerly exercised complete and unquestioned authority over each and every child were now being challenged by the natural mothers; and one result of the new maternal attention was increased childish unruliness, quarreling over toys, and a general deterioration of discipline.

In addition to the negative reports from Oneida, Noyes was sent clippings from big-city newspapers that, with few exceptions, reflected the condemning views of the nation's legal and moral establishment and portrayed the Oneidans as prurient eccentrics in a state of disarray. Typical of the news coverage was a feature story in the New York *Times* bearing the headline: "Oneida's Queer People; Trouble in the Community of Socialists."

With the unceasing exposure and ridicule from without, and the deterioration from within, Noyes, after weeks of pondering and deliberating with his most trusted advisers, decided that in the interest of saving Oneida from a long and costly legal battle that might bankrupt its businesses and further demoralize its members—to say nothing of the constant threat of bodily harm from the mobs—he must announce the discontinuance of complex marriage and propagative free love. He knew that this would be interpreted in the press as an unconditional surrender to his enemies, but in his public announcement in August 1879, and in his subsequent statements to the press, he was typically unrepentant, and he even hinted that the day might come when his people would again indulge in the joyful rites of perpetual courtship.

The official statement declared: "We give up the practice of Complex Marriage, which has existed for thirty-three years in the community, not as renouncing belief in the principles and prospective finality of that institution, but in deference to the public sentiment which is evidently rising against it." In another statement, he reiterated his position: "The community has no regrets for the past; it, on the contrary, considers itself fortunate in having been called to such pioneer work; it rejoices in the general results of its reconnaissance; it abandons no previous convictions, it is simply persuaded that it is best for all interests, including those of social progress itself, that it should give up the practice of Complex Marriage and place itself on Paul's platform, which allows marriage but prefers celibacy." Finally, as if presenting a historical assessment of the Perfectionists' primary purpose and contribution to nineteenth-century America, Noyes observed: "We made a raid into an unknown country, charted it, and returned without the loss of a man, woman, or child."

But in allying himself with St. Paul in recommending celibacy as the most desirous of virtues, Noyes was not subjecting himself to any great personal sacrifice, for he was at this time in life a sexually satiated man of sixty-eight who had taken full advantage of the free-love system while it lasted, and he could now relax in his Canadian retirement and rejoice in the health and growth of the nine young Oneida-born children who would bear his name and honor his memory through the twentieth century. Indeed, one of his progeny, an industrious adolescent named Pierrepont B. Noyes—whose mother, Harriet Worden, had been brought to Oneida as a girl of nine—would emerge in the late 1890s as Oneida's leader, and, with the help of *his* heirs, he would develop the Oneida silversmith business into an international corporation that in the 1970s would be worth close to $100 million.

This multiplied fortune, however, could in no way be attributed even by free-love advocates to the regenerative energies of sexual variety because the libidinal luxuries of old Oneida would never be restored within the community following the founder's pronouncements of 1879—although it must also be added that few Oneidans were greatly persuaded by John Humphrey Noyes' belated leanings toward celibacy. After he had issued his dictum, which did pacify his foes in the outside world, a majority of Oneida's eligible bachelors accepted the lesser of two evils and succumbed to matrimony.

Thirty-seven marriages were soon performed, many conducted by fellow Perfectionists on the lush mansion lawns, but other Oneidans—including twelve women under forty years of age who had children—remained unmarried, and whether or not they adhered to celibacy and whether the married couples remained monogamous were facts unrecorded by Oneida's social historians. Most of the newly married couples chose to stay at Oneida, living in the fully occupied mansion or in smaller dwellings nearby, and they continued to work at various jobs within the communal complex.

In 1880 Oneida converted itself into a joint-stock company, and all of its remaining 226 residents became stockholders of the Oneida Community, Limited. The division of stock, which gave to the most senior Perfectionists amounts worth $5,000 or more, and lesser shares to the newly arrived and younger members, was a source of contention within the community; and, not unexpectedly, the members most dissatisfied with the distribution of stock—and also with Noyes' continued insistence on the abolition of complex marriage—were James Towner and his thirty followers.

In 1882, four years before John Humphrey Noyes' death in Canada at the age of seventy-four—his body would be returned to Oneida for burial—James Towner and his faction quit the community, converted their shares to cash, and, with a horse-drawn caravan, began a long westward trek toward the more clement atmosphere and loosely federated lands of Southern California. The group resettled in the township of Santa Ana, south of Los Angeles, where in time they gained acceptance and achieved contentment and prosperity—and where James Towner was later to be elevated to county court judge.

19

The winds attack the ego, send it whimpering
and screaming, to leave a bare and frightened soul.
Follow the wind and know godliness.
Draw the shutters of fear and lose eternity
and the bright, dancing flame of self . . .

Seek then to ponder and comprehend infinity.
Go to its door and boldly knock for meaning.
The path is long, cluttered with grasping
vegetables aching to give you roots with theirs.
Pass them by, for they will die with summer . . .
                                        —John Williamson

As John Williamson began in 1970 to recruit new members for Sandstone Retreat, he was not alone in his belief that alternate-life-style communities were finally coming of age in America; in fact, according to a survey published in the New York *Times*, it was estimated that there were now in the nation approximately two thousand separate settlements of various sizes and distinctions, located in farmhouses and city lofts, hillside manors and desert adobes, geodesic domes and ghetto tenements; and they were occupied by hippie horticulturists, meditating mystics, swingers, Jesus freaks, ecological evangelists, retired rock musicians, tired peace marchers, corporate dropouts, and devotees of Reich and Maslow, B. F. Skinner, Robert Rimmer, and Winnie the Pooh.

In Oregon, a few miles west of Eugene, there was an eighty-acre settlement founded by sexually liberated Midwesterners who operated a beef-cattle business. In Berkeley, California, couples lived together connubially, if not always compatibly, in a large house called "Harrad West" that was inspired by one of Robert Rimmer's novels on sexual utopianism. Within a secluded residence in the woodlands of Lafayette, a suburb of Oakland, lived a thirty-four-year-old advocate of "responsible hedonism" named Victor Baranco, who, having made money in real estate developing, now had several mini-communes throughout California and in other states; and *Rolling Stone* magazine called Baranco "the Colonel Sanders of the commune scene."

Not far from San Cristobal, New Mexico, was the 130-acre Lama community founded by a New York artist and his Stanford-educated wife; and in the Colorado mountains, near Walsenburg, were a cluster of chalets belonging to the Libre community, whose members worked as painters, potters, and leather craftspeople. Ten miles outside of Meadville, Pennsylvania, was the hippie commune of Oz, established on land inherited by a former merchant seaman; and in central Virginia, near the town of Culpepper, was the 120-acre Twin Oaks community that had been founded by young social theorists who ran a farm, manufactured hammocks, and named their main residence "Oneida."

In New York City there were ashrams located in brownstones that were occupied by spiritually minded communitarians who, when not concentrating on yoga and chanting mantras, hired themselves out as carpenters, plasterers, and house painters. In Putney, Vermont, from which John Humphrey Noyes' group had been expelled more than a century ago, there were now five countercultural communes, the most anarchistic of which—the Red Clover settlement—was largely financed by a privileged scion of a cereal-manufacturing family. Farther upstate was a farming community named Bryn Athyn that was inhabited by many Reich readers who believed that there was indeed a correlation between monogamy, possessiveness, jealousy, and war; but this agricultural community, like so many others that were populated by campus-bred radicals, would flounder financially because its members spent too much time reading quality paperbacks and pontificating around the fireplace, and not enough time in the barn milking the cows.

This was the recurring impression of a writer named Robert Houriet, who between 1968 and 1971—while researching his book *Getting Back Together*—visited dozens of communes in every region of the nation; and while he admired the idealism and efficiency he found in such places as Twin Oaks in Virginia, he could not ignore the fact that many other communitarians lacked the discipline and dedication to practice what they preached—they denounced the pollution and plastic of the outside world, yet created a junk culture of their own in squalid psychedelic shacks and lofts overpopulated by drifters who were high on dope and low on energy. Everywhere that Robert Houriet went in his travels, he heard young people yearning to live in organic harmony with the earth, to inhabit a peaceful place remote from greed and hostility; but Houriet also found himself surrounded in communes by "hassles and marathon encounter meetings that couldn't resolve questions like whether to leave the dogs in or out. Everywhere, cars that wouldn't run and pumps that wouldn't pump because everybody knew all about the occult history of tarot and nobody knew anything about mechanics. Everywhere, people who strove for self-sufficiency and freedom from the capitalist system but accepted food stamps and handouts from Daddy, a corporate sales VP. Sinks filled with dishes, cows wandering through gates left open, and no one to blame. Everywhere, instability, transiency. Somebody was always splitting, rolling up his bag, packing his guitar and kissing good-bye— off again in search of the truly free, unhungup community."

John Williamson was quite aware that communes tended to attract such rootless people, and he was wary of having too many of them at Sandstone. While he wanted countercultural couples to participate in the Sandstone experience—he even placed ads announcing Sandstone's expanding membership in the underground Los Angeles *Free Press*—he deliberately did not reveal the location of the estate, listing instead the telephone number of a small rented office in the city in which his followers could arrange to personally interview the applicants and explain to them the basic requirements and costs of joining Sandstone.

Because Sandstone had no farm or industry to provide income, Williamson decided to accept approximately two hundred dues-paying members who would be charged $240 annually to use Sandstone as a kind of club: They could visit during the day to swim in the pool, sunbathe nude on the deck of the main house, picnic on the lawn; and on certain evenings they could join the "family" for a buffet dinner, where nudity was customary but not obligatory, and after dinner they could venture downstairs into a spacious, dimly lit, red-carpeted room that was sixty-by-twenty feet and was lined with soft mats and large pillows to be used by anyone who wanted to make love, or merely wished to relax and listen to the stereo music, or to converse with other people around the fireplace.

To make certain that all prospective members were forewarned about Sandstone's permissive evenings, each applicant received during his interview a brochure that stated:

> The concepts underlying Sandstone include the idea that the human body is good, that open expressions of affection and sexuality are good. Members at Sandstone may do anything they like as long as they are not offensive or force their desires on other people. There is no structured activity at Sandstone, no programs of behavioral study, no crutches. Members are free to do whatever they wish, whenever they wish, in the spirit of mutuality. . . .
>
> The strength and lasting significance of the Sandstone experience lies in human contact divorced from the cocktail party context with all its games and dodges and places to hide. Contact at Sandstone includes the basic level of literal, physical nakedness and open sexuality. In these terms, the experience goes far beyond any attempt to intellectualize it. This reality of action with its effect of accepting and being accepted in basic terms, without reservation, without cover, is the essence of the Sandstone experience. It transcends fantasy and is creating a new kind of community where a person's mind, body, and being are no longer strangers to each other. In this community, differences between people become a source of delight rather than a reason for conflict.

Among the few rigidly enforced regulations at Sandstone were that no one under eighteen could become a member; no drugs of any kind were to be used on the property; and, in order to maintain an equal balance between the sexes, only couples were allowed to attend the evening activities. While wine was served with dinner, the consumption of hard liquor was discouraged; and efforts were made during the preliminary interviews in the office, and during the follow-up interviews by John and Barbara Williamson in the main house, to learn if the applicants had a past history of alcoholism, heavy drug usage, mental illness, or other problems that might be revived or aggravated by exposure to the highly charged sexual atmosphere of Sandstone, where committed couples might for the first time become fully aware of, and even be witness to, their lover's infidelity.

To whatever degree was possible, John Williamson wanted to assemble a large membership of stable couples, young middle-class sensualists who believed that their personal relationships would be enhanced, rather than shattered, by the elimination of

sexual possessiveness. Williamson also hoped that the membership would include a high percentage of representatives from
the media and academia, leading businessmen, lawyers, physicians, writers, and social scientists—achieving individuals who,
as "change people," might spread the Sandstone philosophy by
word if not by deed to their friends, their associates, and the
consuming public that was becoming increasingly receptive to
new ideas and values.

In the interest of meeting and possibly recruiting influential
people, Williamson sent letters to distinguished university-
affiliated anthropologists and psychologists, inviting them to
spend a day at Sandstone; he hired a public relations associate
and gave interviews to the press; and with his wife, Barbara, he
traveled long distances to attend and speak at seminars dealing
with alternate-life-style communities and the changing modes
of marriage. At one such symposium, held at the Kirkridge
Retreat in the Pocono Mountains of Pennsylvania, Williamson
delivered a lecture explaining Sandstone's goals to an audience
that included Robert Francoeur, a man who had left the Catholic
priesthood to become a writer, a husband, and a professor of
embryology and sexuality at Farleigh Dickinson University;
Rustrum and Della Roy, two chemists at Pennsylvania State
University who were experienced married counselors; Stephen
Beltz, a psychologist who was the executive director in Philadelphia of the Center for Behavior Modification; the novelist
Robert Rimmer; and several others who, after hearing Williamson, became fascinated with his California experiment and expressed a desire to visit Sandstone and observe what was
happening there.

While Williamson was generating enthusiasm in distant
places, his family back home was not ideally coexisting in his
absence; and even when he was present at Sandstone, he seemed
to be looking outward, drifting away from his circle of intimates
as he focused on plans for the future, devoted his time to entertaining important visitors, and directed his beguiling charm and
sexual energy to the courting and satisfaction of new and different women.

The first person to perceive and resent Williamson's changing
character was Judith Bullaro, who, having been ardently pursued by him in the past, and having become accustomed to his
special attention, and even dependent upon it, now felt somewhat ignored and used. For him she had disrupted her family

life, had left her comfortable suburban home to move with her children and her disaffected husband into a rented ranch in Topanga Canyon so that she would be close to Sandstone and be conveniently available to help Williamson and the others with the cleaning, the painting, the remodeling, the landscaping, and the overall restoration of the property that now, in its state of splendid completion, was serving as a showcase for Williamson's ego and expanding ambitions.

Less the romantic guru that he had appeared to be, and more the calculating engineer that had been his true profession, Williamson in Judith's view was now turning Sandstone into a domestic laboratory in which his nude family were exhibited as models to attract new members, new money, and the interest of the academic world with which Williamson wished to associate himself. Lacking a formal education beyond high school, his only means of achieving academic status for Sandstone was through the establishment of an advisory board composed of university-accredited scientists and random behaviorists who, in return for the revitalization of their own physical drives, might be motivated to support Williamson's future efforts to obtain private foundation grants, or even government funds, so that he could continue his research into the root causes of jealousy and possessiveness—problems for which Judith thought there were no cures except if people ceased to deeply care about one another.

Judith believed, in fact, that even John Williamson—while he did not restrain his wife—was susceptible to feelings of sexual possessiveness; he seemed to dislike the fact that his cherished Oralia Leal was now spending increased amounts of time in private with David Schwind, and Judith herself had felt a negative response from Williamson when *she* confessed to being physically attracted to Schwind.

Disregarding Williamson's reaction, Judith had one day invited David to visit her while her children were at school and her husband was at the insurance office; but she told no one about this rendezvous, nor about one that followed. Nevertheless she was unsettled by these clandestine meetings—bothered by the realization that, because she sensed that Williamson would disapprove of her intimacies with Schwind, she chose to conceal from Williamson what was really none of his business; and thus she was acknowledging his enduring influence over her private life. The whole situation was fraught with contradictions: Williamson, the outspoken advocate of open sexuality and unpos-

sessiveness, seemed to be hypocritical in his manner toward
Oralia and herself; and Judith, in resenting Williamson's "infidelities" with women that he had recently met—and quietly
retaliating perhaps in her liaisons with Schwind—was making a
travesty of the liberated status that she thought she had attained
since joining Williamson's group. It was possible, despite her
experience in consentual adultery with her husband, that she
was at heart a conventional woman who was possessive and
guilt-ridden where sex was concerned; and it was while in this
questioning state of mind, restive and perturbed by Williamson's
elusive leverage over her life, that she concluded that she must
somehow separate herself from Williamson and his disillusion-
ing utopia.

What would prove to be conclusive in her decision, however,
was a relatively trivial incident that on the surface had little to
do with her relationship with Williamson, or her sex life, or her
marriage, or her children, or anything that was deeply personal.
The source of provocation in this case was none other than her
pet cat.

One day after discovering that her cat had just produced a
litter of kittens, Judith found herself fascinated by the new ma-
ternity and taking great pleasure in watching the purring tabby
pampering the kittens, licking their fur, and feeding them. In
the afternoon she noticed the mother carrying them in her mouth
from one corner of the room to another, as if looking for a place
that was warmer and more comfortable. But the mother cat
seemed constantly dissatisfied—after gathering her kittens in one
part of the room, she would pick them up and carry them to
another part, and then another; and as Judith watched with curiosity, she began to identify with her cat's restless and searching
nature.

Later that evening, after Judith and her husband had finished
dinner and the children were in bed, she heard an automobile
pulling into the driveway, and through the window she could
see that John and Barbara Williamson had arrived. It was typical
of nearly everyone she knew in California to visit without telephoning in advance, and normally she did not mind; but on this
occasion, still being attuned to the quiet afternoon with her cats
and having given much thought during the day to the need for
closeness within her own family, she considered the Williamsons' presence an intrusion.

Forcing a smile, she greeted them at the door, and, after
warming the coffee, she and her husband sat in the living room

listening while Barbara and John explained that they had been in town on business and were stopping by on their way back to Sandstone. As they continued to chat, commenting that they had not seen much of Judith at Sandstone in recent weeks, Judith noticed that her cat was still pacing back and forth, carrying what seemed to be a kitten; but on second look, Judith saw a long thin tail dangling from the cat's mouth, and she suddenly realized that the cat was clutching between its teeth a large, bloody rat.

Shrieking with astonishment, Judith jumped up and directed everyone's attention to where her cat prowled near the fireplace; she elaborately explained how the cat, which had no doubt been aware all afternoon of the lurking rat—and had tried to protect the kittens by frequently moving them beyond the rat's striking range—had finally decided to confront the dangerous threat, and to eliminate it. This little episode had symbolic meaning for Judith, and so preoccupied was she with pride in her cat that it took her several moments to realize that the Williamsons were sharing none of her enthusiasm.

If anything they conveyed boredom and annoyance that she, a presumably liberated woman, could identify so completely with the maternal instincts of a house cat. While her husband remained silent, Judith found herself feuding with her guests, furiously on the defensive—an attitude that later, on reflection, she saw as rising out of anxieties and doubts she had long felt about her own maternal dedication since she had become involved with Williamson's group.

But no amount of self-examination on her part could lessen the indignation she now felt toward the Williamsons, who, as a childless couple, she considered to be ignorant of parental feelings; and after they left the house that night, Judith told her husband that she was finished with John Williamson and was ready to move out of the area and sever all connections with Sandstone.

At another time and under other circumstances, John Bullaro would have welcomed her decision, would have been glad to cast off Williamson and regain some control over his homelife. But, instead, he hesitated and then admitted to Judith that he was not eager to leave at this time. He explained that he was finally becoming adjusted to the place, was enjoying the company of various people there, was even developing a trusting friendship with John Williamson. Bullaro now saw Williamson as a man from whom he could learn a great deal, and he did not doubt that he had already become more self-aware since be-friending Williamson, more independent-minded and capable of solitude since Williamson had first dared him to go off alone into the desert, a therapeutic venture that Bullaro had subsequently repeated on his own initiative.

What he did not openly admit to his wife, however, was that he had been somewhat pleased that her pride had been recently wounded by Williamson's romantic withdrawal, and Bullaro was not opposed to having her remain on the scene a while longer to absorb more of Williamson's fading passion. It was her turn, Bullaro thought, to suffer as he had suffered when she had first become infatuated with Williamson, had made love to him that memorable night long ago in front of the cabin's fireplace, and had thus greatly altered the course of their lives.

And yet Bullaro recognized an obligation to his wife and he could not ignore the pain she was feeling; nor could he overlook the fact that it had been he who initially brought her into Williamson's world. He also knew that her continued unhappiness could only further erode their marriage, which he did not want to destroy, and it would merely bring grief to the two children whom they shared and loved.

In the days following the Williamsons' visit Bullaro saw added signs of Judith's depression: On returning from his office he could tell that she had been drinking during the afternoon, and at night in bed she was remote, irritable, and unwilling to make love. One night when he approached her, she became suddenly hysterical, awakening the children. The next morning, remorseful, she promised that she would consult a therapist. She again spoke of leaving Topanga Canyon, and Bullaro now agreed that this was the right thing to do. So after work in the days ahead he began to help her with the packing. Soon they were ready to move back to the suburbs of Woodland Hills.

Since their home was still occupied by tenants whose lease had not yet expired, the Bullaros were obliged to find another house with a short-term lease, which they did with surprising ease. Though smaller than the one they owned, it seemed suitable for their temporary requirements and it was located in a tidy, tree-lined neighborhood with trimmed hedges and smooth streets that were a welcome contrast to the hilly, dusty roads and cliff-hanging atmosphere of the canyon. From here it was very convenient for Bullaro to commute each day to his office; and Judith, wanting to be active while the children were in school, found a daytime job as a nurse in a nearby hospital. At night, they usually had dinner with the children and rarely went out. Instead they listened to music in the living room, read books or watched television, and retired early to bed, where, in deference to Judith's wishes, they did not make love.

Sympathetic to her preference, John interpreted it not as a personal rejection of him but as a negative response on her part toward men in general, following her breakup with Williamson; and he believed that things would improve after they had become resettled in their own home and more readjusted to suburban life and to one another. But just as they were about to reacquire their home, Judith astonished him by pleading that he *not* move in with her, that he allow her more time and "space" with which to deal with her uncertain emotions.

Though upset by this request, he nonetheless agreed to rent an apartment of his own for a period of time that he assumed was very temporary. He was willing to do anything that might restore harmony to their relationship, and he was confident that she, too, was seeking this goal. She no longer drank, she was seeing the therapist, and seemed to be diligent and punctual about her job. From his apartment in the nearby town of Encino, he was within close driving distance of the children, and on two evenings a week he took them out to dinner or brought them for visits to his place. Daily he spoke to Judith on the telephone, and during the early weeks of their separation she assured him that she was feeling better, though not yet quite ready for his return.

As he drove to and from his office, he often went blocks out of his way so that he could pass the house, a precautionary act motivated by his concern for his family's well-being, or so he told himself; but as he made these trips with more frequency, driving up and down Aetna Street at all hours of the day and night, he knew he was responding to instinctive feelings about his wife, certain doubts about her sincerity, a fear that she had perhaps wanted him out of the house so that she would be freer to date other men.

It was soon thereafter that Bullaro began to notice, parked regularly in front of the house, a blue Pontiac—a car that did not belong to Williamson or anyone that he knew. Sometimes he would see it parked at the curb early in the morning, gone in the evening, but back again later at night after the children were presumably asleep. After several days of watching it, and unable to repress his anxieties any longer, he confronted Judith with the accusation that she was seeing another man—and, quietly, she confirmed his worst suspicion.

Bullaro's anger was sudden and uncontrollable. He felt betrayed, humiliated, and stunned. He demanded to know who the man was, but she would say only that it was someone she had recently met. When Bullaro insisted that she stop seeing him, Judith, sounding more distracted than defiant, replied that she could make no promises. Further enraged, Bullaro accused her of setting a poor moral example for the children and told her that he wanted them to come live with him; but Judith answered that she could not part with them. When Bullaro threatened her with legal action, she made no response.

During the following evening Bullaro again saw the Pontiac parked at the curb, and he was tempted to get out of his car, knock on the door of the house, and confront his competitor; but not wanting to provoke a potentially violent scene in front of the children, he resisted the impulse. He did, however, note the Pontiac's license plate number, and, with the help of contacts he had made during his years in insurance, he learned not only who owned the car but also details about the individual's personal life. Among other things, Bullaro was told that the man was a member of Alcoholics Anonymous, that he had a history of unemployment and of drifting from place to place, and that he had once been arrested by the police on charges of assault and battery.

When Bullaro told Judith what he had discovered, she became hostile, denouncing him for violating another man's privacy, and adding that she already knew about his background, having been fully informed by the man himself. Furthermore, she told her husband, the malicious snooping that he had engaged in served only to convince her that she was wise to remain apart from him; and no amount of explaining by Bullaro at this time, or in their later conversations, could reduce the distance that now existed between them. She needed a vacation from their marriage, she explained; she wanted to be free without being answerable to a husband. Were it not for her obligation to the children and to her job, she went on, she probably would have already left town with her lover and begun a new life in a different city.

Although Bullaro found it difficult to believe that she meant all that she was saying, that she could have become so quickly involved with another man, he finally gave up all hope of a reconciliation and sullenly cooperated with her in obtaining a legal separation. He agreed to provide money for the children's support, and she set aside certain days each week for him to be with the children; and she also promised not to allow any of her male friends to remain overnight in the house.

In the ensuing months John and Judith Bullaro continued to see one another regularly, though always briefly, when he came for the children. She seemed to be adjusting easily to their separation; she looked well and appeared to be more in control of her emotions. Though she was now seeing less of her lover, there was no sign of regret in her voice when she admitted this. She was now, in fact, dating more than one man, and had a new friend whom she had met at the hospital. If she was not entirely happy with her life, she left no doubt in her husband's mind that she was at least contented—which was more than he could say for himself.

For him the recent months had so far been frenetic and frustrating. He had dated various women but had shied away from even the mildest form of involvement. Though he had twice accepted the Williamsons' invitations to attend parties at Sandstone, and had once accompanied them on a weekend trip for which they had provided attractive female companionship, he still felt largely uncentered and disconsolate. The now unobtainable Judith seemed, more than ever, desirable and irreplaceable.

His job bored him as never before. After a decade with New York Life, and many months of divided attention between his work and his disturbing marriage, Bullaro thought he had better quit before he was fired. With the money he had saved, he estimated that he could live for a year without relying on regular employment; and so he summoned up the energy to resign.

He wanted to take short motor trips, spend more time in the desert, and, daring to acknowledge a remote ambition, he wanted to try writing a novel. It would be unashamedly autobiographical, the story of his marriage. In the past, as he saw himself shuttling back and forth between his office and Sandstone while his wife was being wooed away, he had kept voluminous notes, a kind of diary composed on company stationery and yellow legal-sized pads, that described his impressions and responses to what was going on around him, and within him.

The diary had been consciously produced as a cathartic experience; but now as he reviewed the notes, he winced with embarrassment. Instead of releasing him from despair, reading back on his life was compounding it: The first sexual encounter with Barbara at the insurance convention in Palm Springs, the emergence of John Williamson as a problem solver, the nude evenings in the Williamsons' house on Mulholland Drive, the months that had seemed so exhilarating and liberating, now loomed as a preamble to destruction and chaos. He saw whatever love and order that had been the stability of his life sacrificed to the whim of experimentation and change. He tried to imagine what might have become of his marriage had he not drawn Judith into those evenings in which Oralia and Gail and Arlene Gough had seemed so tempting and available; but he suspected that the results would have been the same even if he had resisted Williamson's promise to release the suffocating bonds of traditional marriage. And while it had been very painful for him to watch Judith respond to other men, Bullaro was not unaware of the many compensations to himself, even though now as he read his own hollow reminiscences it all seemed reduced to fragments of emotion scattered senselessly. He was alone, jobless, and without a sense of hope.

Months passed, and while he continued to see his children, his aimlessness prevailed; and it was while in this state of dejection that he heard about Arlene Gough, with whom he had enjoyed a brief affair but who had dropped out of Williamson's group and had disappeared into the Valley, as Judith had done so recently. Arlene's name was in the newspapers: She had been found dead at home in bed with a bullet in her body. The police also discovered lying dead next to her, her lover, a young newspaper reporter employed by the Los Angeles *Times*. On the table downstairs was a recently fired .38 caliber revolver. Within hours the police had arrested, and charged with the double murder, Arlene Gough's sixteen-year-old son.

20

Early in the evening, as the sun faded behind the mountain, dozens of automobiles climbed the rocky road to Sandstone—foreign cars and convertibles driven by Beverly Hills adventurers in Gucci shoes and tailored denims; station wagons and new sedans carrying coiffed couples from the Valley and Orange County; Volkswagen buses and Toyotas transporting from lower Topanga and Venice Beach long-haired young people who, after parking their vehicles along the western edge of the property, inhaled the last of the fragrant weed they held dangling from their roach clips.

Even before entering the main house, the visitors could see, through a large picture window near the front door, evidence of a party already in progress: Family members and early guests stood talking, drinks in hand, under the cartwheel chandeliers that hung from the beamed ceiling; flames blazed high in the big brick fireplace; and ensconced in his usual place, in the center of the room, surrounded by his retinue, sat the burly blond emperor without clothes.

John Williamson nodded, smiling softly toward the newly arrived people he knew; but nobody approached him until they had first been admitted to the room by Barbara, who stood behind a registration desk, pen in hand, wearing only eyeglasses—plain gold-rimmed spectacles that suited her clerical countenance but accentuated the contrast of the fabulous body that blossomed below her small determined chin.

Barbara was not happy with her job as the keeper of the gate; she would have preferred a more leisurely role befitting her position as the First Lady of Sandstone—but no one could match her efficiency at this delicate task: It required that she tactfully yet insistently turn away all nonmembers and wandering intrud-

ers; that she refuse entrance to members whose dues were in
arrears, or who had arrived at Sandstone unaccompanied by a
person of the opposite sex, or who were temporarily under sus-
pension because they had previously violated one of the club
rules. While the rejected individuals might have reacted vehemently had they been barred by a male family member, or might
have tried to sweet-talk their way past the less formidable Oralia,
Barbara's no-nonsense manner seemed to minimize all confrontations at the door. Though invariably polite, she clearly was a
woman unimpressed by false flattery, manifestations of ma-
chismo, implied threats, or even overt acts of aggression. Her
unflappable nature was emphasized in a story that, while perhaps exaggerated, was circulated with delight by Sandstone
members. Once, while driving through the canyon, Barbara saw
a struggling woman being molested against a car at the side of
the road by a man who was obviously trying to rape her. Barbara
pulled her own car off the road, jumped out, and fearlessly approached the man, shouting: "Let her alone! If you want to fuck
somebody, you can fuck *me*." The man, astonished, was quickly
intimidated, and retreated.

It was also true of Barbara, however, that she could be charm-
ingly feminine when she wished to be, and that while she was
a stern sentinel at the door she was not without flexibility, having
an instinct for welcoming people who, though uninvited, might
be potentially useful to Sandstone, or at least of sufficient stature
to warrant an introduction to her husband. As Sandstone became more prosperous and relaxed about its club operation, a
number of preferred people were even admitted as singles, and
given honorary memberships, because their presence suggested
an intellectual interest in, if not an endorsement of, the Williamsons' research methods and goals.

On some evenings there were gathered around the fireplace,
conversing, in varying stages of dress and sometimes nude, such
individuals as the British biologist Alex Comfort, who would
later write *The Joy of Sex*; the psychologists and authors Phyllis
and Eberhard Kronhausen, who would establish the Museum of
Erotic Art in San Francisco, featuring their own extensive collection; the marriage counselors William Hartman and Marilyn
Fithian, often referred to as the Masters and Johnson of the West
Coast; the New York *Post*'s syndicated columnist Max Lerner;
the onetime Los Angeles Rams football star turned poet and
actor Bernie Casey; the former Rand Corporation employees
Daniel Ellsberg and Anthony Russo, who had already made

copies of the Pentagon Papers and were secretly being investigated by the FBI; the artist and feminist Betty Dodson, whose heroic paintings of sexual passion had dazzled visitors at her one-woman show in New York's Wickersham Gallery; the editor Kent Carroll of Grove Press, which was planning to produce and distribute a documentary film on Sandstone; the scientific writer of sexual studies Edward M. Brecher, a close friend of Masters and Johnson; the editorial director and former publisher of the Los Angeles *Free Press*, Art Kunkin, whose decision in 1969 to print the names and home addresses of Los Angeles' narcotics agents led to litigation and $53,000 in fines, and prompted him to sell his newspaper to a man named Marvin Miller, a publisher of sexual literature whose *own* subsequent conviction in a pornography case would be carried to the United States Supreme Court and would culminate in the landmark 1973 *Miller* ruling. It was this opinion that would threaten to deliberalize all forms of sexual expression across the nation, thus superseding the celebrated *Roth* opinion of 1957 that had countered the legacy of Comstock in America.

But while the Sandstone living room at times resembled a literary salon, the floor below remained a parlor for pleasure-seekers, providing sights and sounds that many visitors, however well versed they may have been in erotic arts and letters, had never imagined they would ever encounter under one roof during a single evening.

After descending the red-carpeted staircase, the visitors entered the semidarkness of a large room where, reclining on the cushioned floor, bathed in the orange glow from the fireplace, they saw shadowed faces and interlocking limbs, rounded breasts and reaching fingers, moving buttocks, glistening backs, shoulders, nipples, navels, long blond hair spread across pillows, thick dark arms holding soft white hips, a woman's head hovering over an erect penis. Sighs, cries of ecstasy could be heard, the slap and suction of copulating flesh, laughter, murmuring, music from the stereo, crackling black burning wood.

As the visitors' eyes adjusted to the light, there was a clearer view of the many shapes, sizes, textures, tones: Some couples sat cross-legged in circles, relaxing, talking, as if picnicking on a beach; others embraced in many positions: women astride men, couples lying side by side, a woman's legs extended above her partner's shoulders, a man in missionary position with elbows pressing into madras pillows, perspiration dripping from a bearded chin. Nearby, a woman held her breath, gasping as the man inside her began to come; then another woman, responding to the sound, arched her body and moved more quickly into her own orgasm, her skin flushed, her face grimacing, her toes clenched.

In one corner of the room, speckled in the spinning light that raced across the wall, were the silhouettes of nude disco dancers. In another corner, supine on a table, was an oil-covered woman being simultaneously stroked by five people who stood around her, massaging every part of her body, while a sinewy man at the foot of the table stretched on tiptoes toward her open thighs to caress her genitals with his tongue.

There were triads, foursomes, a few bisexuals; bodies that could belong to high-fashion models, linebackers, Wagnerian sopranos, speed swimmers, flabby academicians; tattooed arms, peace beads, ankle bracelets, ankhs, thin gold chains around waists, hefty penises, noodles, curly female pubes, fine, bushy, trimmed, dark, blond, red valentines. It was a room with a view like none other in America, an audiovisual aphrodisiac, a *tableau vivant* by Hieronymus Bosch.

Everything that Puritan America had ever tried to outlaw, to censor, to conceal behind locked bedroom doors, was on display in this adult playroom, where men often saw for the first time another man's erection, and where many couples became alternately stimulated, shocked, gladdened, or saddened by the sight of their spouses interlocked with new lovers. It was here one evening that John Williamson saw Barbara being gratified by a handsome, muscular black man, and Williamson felt for a few disquieting moments the boyhood emotions of the rural Southerner that he had once been.

Often the nude biologist Dr. Alex Comfort, brandishing a cigar, traipsed through the room between the prone bodies with the professional air of a lepidopterist strolling through the fields waving a butterfly net, or an ornithologist tracking along the surf a rare species of tern. A gray-haired bespectacled owlish man with a well-preserved body, Dr. Comfort was unabashedly drawn to the sight of sexually engaged couples and their concomitant cooing, considering such to be enchanting and endlessly instructive; and with the least amount of encouragement—after he had deposited his cigar in a safe place—he would join a friendly clutch of bodies and contribute to the merriment.

Admirably surnamed, Comfort was comfortable in a crowd and comforting to individuals who, as novices to group nudity and sex, seemed nervous or awkward. He was a rarity in the medical profession, one who brought a bedside manner to an orgy. He was reassuring, humorous, erudite but never pompous, and it was a measure of Dr. Comfort's poise and diverting effect on the people around him that hardly anyone seemed to notice that the left hand he adroitly used in group-massage sessions consisted only of a sturdy thumb. His four fingers had been blown off during the 1930s when, as a youth of fourteen, in his home-built laboratory in England, he had experimented too friskily with a quantum of gunpowder. While the loss of the fingers initially depressed him and haunted him with "delusions of sin," and greatly limited his virtuosity at the piano, an instrument he nonetheless continued to play, it had little effect on his future career as an obstetrician, poet, novelist, husband, father, wartime anarchopacifist philosopher on the BBC, gerontologist, and participating sex researcher.

In the ten years that followed the accident, in fact, he published ten books. The first, begun when he was fifteen, was a travel volume describing his visit to South America on a Greek ship; the tenth, written when he was twenty-four and already listed in Who's Who, was a novel about the fall of France during World War II. He had also by this time progressed through Cambridge as a medical student; and years later, as a practicing obstetrician, he discovered that his attenuated hand with its mobile thumb was somewhat advantageous in performing uterine inversions.

Comfort's permissive attitude toward the sexual education of youth established him as a controversial figure in England long before he had written *The Joy of Sex*. In 1963, the year the Profumo call-girl scandal shook the Tory government and launched the careers of many moral reformers, Comfort was widely vilified for publicly advocating contraceptives for teenagers; and a schoolmistress later charged that a student, after reading a treatise by Dr. Comfort, contracted venereal disease—a case of contagion that, Comfort was pleased to discover, did not get very far in court.

After moving to Santa Barbara, California, in 1970, where he served as a senior fellow at the Center for the Study of Democratic Institutions, Comfort heard about Sandstone and later made his first of many visits. While he was already a conditioned nudist, being a member of the Diogenes naturist club in England and a frequenter of such retreats as Mont Alivet on the north coast of Bordeaux, he was immediately impressed by

Sandstone's open sexuality, which provided him with an opportunity to observe, in a nonlaboratory situation, the mating behavior of human beings.

Here he could see the multiformity of anatomy, the diversity in foreplay, the lawless acts of tenderness being exchanged between virtual strangers. A seemingly shy woman whom Comfort had met earlier when she arrived with her husband upstairs, where she had appeared to be uneasy about removing her clothes, was now downstairs in the nude with another man, bouncing astride his pelvis like a fearless bronco rider. Nearby could be seen the white buttocks, the suntanned back, and gray blow-dried hair of a Hollywood producer, kneeling like a supplicant between the open thighs of a dominant housewife who sat on a pile of pillows giving him directions.

In the room were the flaccid penises of anxious men who, perhaps as first-time visitors to Sandstone, were not yet able to maintain erections in the presence of a crowd; and there were also exhibitionistic men, human coital machines, lancers locked in a medieval duel of endurance. There were people, too, who seemed amazingly blasé about sex, such as the two middle-aged men who sat with their backs to the wall and, while being fellated by two women, carried on a conversation as casually as cabdrivers on a sunny day chatting through their open windows while waiting for the traffic light to change.

Many couples in the room merely watched the proceedings in wonderment, and to them the visit to Sandstone was a learning experience, a biology class, an opportunity to become increasingly knowledgeable about sex in the way that people traditionally learned about almost everything *except* sex, through the observation and imitation of other people. Comfort believed that visitors could learn more about their sexual selves in one night at Sandstone than they could from all the authoritative sex manuals and seminars conducted by sexologists.

Here they could watch other people's many techniques, hear the varied responses, see the expressions on the faces, the movements of the muscles, the flush of skin, the different ways that some people liked to be held, touched, tongued, tickled, nibbled, pinched, aroused with genital kissing, anal stimulation, scrotum stroking. Special acts of titillation that some visitors privately fancied, but had never requested of their lovers because such penchants might seem "kinky," often were on view in the room downstairs, and thus Sandstone served its visitors as a source of reassurance and self-validation. Women who required considerable time and stimulation in order to achieve an orgasm, and had wondered if this was normal, would discover at Sandstone many women like themselves; and women who had been attracted to other women but had been repelled by visions of lesbianism could watch liberated heterosexual women in triads and foursomes fondling another woman's breasts, caressing the clitoris, happily identifying with female pleasure—and men, too, though more concerned than women by the specter of homosexuality, could in the affirmative ambience of group sex touch other men, massage a male body, kiss a man on the mouth as, decades ago, during the final stage of male adolescence in a Puritan society, they had kissed their fathers.

Couples wishing to overcome the boredom of their marital bedrooms, while preserving their marriages, could become eroticized by contact with other people at Sandstone, and later they could divert this sexual energy back into their own relationships. Men who noticed that their wives aroused other men became in many cases aroused by them themselves and strove to repossess them; while women, particularly those who had been monogamous in long-term marriages, could reexperience with a new man old feelings of being desired, sexually free, unaccountable—indeed, many couples could relive during an evening at Sandstone, in ways that were not always harmonious to their marriages but were individually regenerative, the élan of youthful courtship.

A few women who had recently undergone disturbing divorces, and were not yet ready for another *affaire de coeur*, adopted Sandstone temporarily as their second home, a halfway house to which they could bring dates but also maintain their independence by enjoying sex and companionship with other people. For women who were sexually energetic and at least moderately aggressive, Sandstone was perhaps the only place where they could boldly pursue men as objects of pleasure, could approach any desired stranger in the crowd upstairs and ask, after a minimum of conversation, "Would you like to go downstairs?"

There was no need for coquetry or traditional feminine coyness at Sandstone, no thoughts about one's "reputation" nor the legitimate concerns that most women had about their physical safety whenever conversing with male strangers in bars or other public places. A *Goodbar* scene was impossible at Sandstone, where women were protected by those around them from being victims of one man's hostility. At Sandstone a sexually adventurous woman could experience, if her mind were willing, her body's capacity to exhaust in a single evening the best efforts of a succession of lusty Lotharios.

Anyone who doubted the superior sexual stamina of women over men—a fully erect male, according to Kinsey, averaged only two and one-half minutes of thrusting after penetration— had merely to visit Sandstone's downstairs "ballroom" on a party night and observe in action such women as Sally Binford, an elegant gray-haired divorcée of forty-six whose beautifully proportioned body invariably effused the passions of one lover after another, although her bright dark eyes did not look to any man for a confirmation of her desirability: She was as emotionally secure as she was physically alluring. She was also an adventurer and a feminist dedicated to the establishment of a more egalitarian society between the sexes, a world in which women could be as good as men, or as bad as men, and be similarly judged.

Having spent the first two decades of her life in New York, where she was born and reared, and the next two decades in Chicago, where she acquired four college degrees and three husbands, she moved to California, where during the mid-sixties she participated in, and contributed to, the continuing radicalization of the West Coast.

In the early summer of 1970, after learning of the existence of an unusual commune in Topanga Canyon, she drove alone one afternoon up the hilly roads into the bucolic splendor of Sandstone Retreat, where, after parking her car and looking through the large front window of the main house, she saw in a corner of the living room a blond man sitting nude behind a desk tapping on a typewriter.

John Williamson stopped typing when he heard her knock; and after Barbara had opened the door, and Sally had presented her credentials, she was welcomed. Williamson, impressed with what he saw, invited her to take a swim and introduced her to other members of the family, including a perky young brunet named Meg Discoe who had been a UCLA student in Sally Binford's Department of Anthropology.

From then on Sally Binford became a Sandstone habitué and a sex partner of, among other men, John Williamson.

21

By PROFESSION, SALLY Binford was an anthropologist and archaeologist, a student of extinct civilizations and Neanderthal cavemen; but, unlike many of the prehistoric subjects she excavated and studied, she was adaptable to various climates, atmospheres, and habitations, and was quick to move from place to place whenever she became dissatisfied with her environment and the people who were part of it.

The social and sexual mores that influenced the behavior of most female members of her generation were largely ignored by her from the time of her adolescence in suburban Long Island, where she was reared by wealthy parents in a home with servants, but where—unlike her favored older sister, a conformist whom she deeply resented—Sally Binford had been a rebel, a tomboy, a kind of changeling that her mother tolerated but could never understand.

Sally was no more understanding of her mother, a woman who had earned a law degree from NYU but had neglected her career for a suburban marriage that centered around the home and such diversions as mah-jongg parties and charitable activities with other idle ladies, one of whom introduced her to the preaching of the celebrated network clergyman Msgr. Fulton J. Sheen, under whose influence Sally Binford's Jewish mother converted to Catholicism.

Sally's father, a shrewd and domineering man who had been born in London of German-Jewish parentage, made a small fortune in America during the Depression through the importation of shellac. With money, he cultivated a smooth personal style and sporting habits, enjoyed the private affections of other women, and bought a Cadillac that carried him on weekends to the best country club in Long Island that accepted Jewish golfers.

Sally's awareness of anti-Semitism, racial discrimination, and the class snobbery that cut across every hedge and lawn on Long Island—to say nothing of the double standard between the sexes—ignited in her a drive to be different, untraditional, unaffected by community standards, remote from the decorative domesticity of her mother and closer to the free-wheeling ways of the parent she preferred.

As a daring young equestrian riding out of the Cedarhurst stables, she was excited by her ability to control a large and powerful animal; and as an unbridled teenager in a low-cut gown at school dances, she lured young men with an ease that was the envy of her female contemporaries, who regarded her as bold and shameless. After completing her junior year at Woodmere Academy and getting a summer job as a theater apprentice in a Cape Cod playhouse, she met a Yale sophomore, and equipped with a diaphragm she had obtained from a woman gynecologist on lower Fifth Avenue, she embarked on her first affair.

A year later, in 1942, reacting against her mother's insistence that she attend Vassar College, an all-girl institution that Sally found oppressively dull, she cut classes so often that she was expelled before the end of her freshman year. Cashing in the war bonds that her parents and relatives had given her after graduation from Woodmere Academy, Sally moved to New York, rented a one-room apartment on West Thirteenth Street, and got a job in the psychiatric-treatment clinic of the Children's Court, where she typed case histories that made her own past seem prudent.

She was happy with her life and enjoyed the bistros and bohemian character of Greenwich Village, where, one night in a bar near Sheridan Square, she met a forty-year-old black jazz musician who would introduce her to Harlem, to the serene stimulation of marijuana, and to techniques of lovemaking that were new and sophisticated.

After nearly two years in the Village, which included a brief career as a journalist on the Long Island *Daily Press*, Sally decided that she should return to school; and with financial help from her father she entered the University of Chicago in the fall of 1945, being drawn to that campus because of its undergraduate program and its innovative president, Robert M. Hutchins.

She would not be disappointed by the move to the Midwest, where she distinguished herself as an undergraduate student and later earned a master's and Ph.D. in anthropology, and she would also participate in archaeological expeditions in Europe and the Middle East. In Chicago she lived in the Hyde Park section, a charming neighborhood of Victorian houses near the lake populated by university faculty members, writers, artists, young married couples, and a gaunt dark-haired publisher on whose living room floor was laid out the first issue of a magazine he would call *Playboy*.

Though the city's political system was corrupt and racist—and, in Saul Bellow's words, "No realistic sane person goes around Chicago without protection"—Sally Binford felt safe in the streets and perceived a more civilized representation of the voting public in the rising popularity of Adlai Stevenson of Illinois, whose cause she served as a campaign worker. She took pride, too, in Chicago's cultural life, including its Second City theater club that introduced such talents as Mike Nichols, Elaine May, Severn Darden, and Barbara Harris. Only in one area—marriage—did Sally Binford fail to find fulfillment in Chicago, and in this her quarrel would finally not be so much with the three men she married and divorced as with the male world that they typified. They were, like most men of this generation, unable to accept a liberated female, one who abhorred the double standard and the assumption that, despite her career ambitions and intelligence, she should concentrate on the domestic chores, the child-rearing and cooking. She was a decade ahead of the feminist movement in America; and yet, bright as she was, she had a facility for falling in love with the very men who made the least compatible husbands—male chauvinists like her father.

As a consequence, her marriages were contentious and temporary; and Sally, often alone and restless, unable to satisfy her amorous desires, spent many solitary evenings in bed masturbating to images of vaguely defined men, strangers that she imagined meeting on trains, in airports, or in the streets of unidentifiable cities; men who would follow her and then gently, skillfully coerce and control her, and finally seduce her in scenes similar to the ones that she read in pornographic books that she kept in the bedroom of her Hyde Park apartment.

Nearly all of these books, which were contraband in Chicago during the 1950s, had been smuggled into the United States by faculty members and Fulbright scholars who had visited Paris; and the titles included *Lady Chatterley's Lover*, the *Kama Sutra*, *My Secret Life*, *The Perfumed Garden*, Henry Miller's *Tropics*, and a number of erotic French novels that Sally, who was fluent in that language, read in their original editions. What most aroused her were the descriptions of sexual acts that she personally craved but were not available to her in real life, such as cunnilingus, which one husband disliked doing; or acts about which she was curious but reluctant to try, such as anal sex. In these fantasies she sometimes imagined herself in the center of a luxurious orgy, surrounded by artful lovers who simultaneously catered to her every whim, stimulated her orally, genitally, and gratified every inch of her body, while she in turn aroused them to peaks of orgasmic jubilation.

But in real life, when she and one of her husbands tried to experience group sex by answering an advertisement in a swingers' periodical, the only result was a rendezvous in a restaurant-bar with a portly burgher wearing a Goldwater button on his lapel, and his timid wife, who wore a plastic daisy in her hat. After moments of awkward amiability during which the couple explained that they were not interested in a foursome but wanted to swap partners in private, they all shook hands and the couple disappeared into the balmy summer night.

In this time of marriages and affairs, teaching and traveling, Sally Binford was also raising a disenchanted young daughter who would leave home as soon as she was old enough to do so, and would during the 1960s become a hippie and a dropout. As Sally herself entered the sixties, she was embattled but stylishly slim, wearing tight-fitting blue jeans and rose-tinted granny glasses through which she viewed the world with a rejuvenated sense that her personal liberation was within reach. She had moved to Southern California, transferring to the anthropological department of UCLA, and there became involved with the campus peace movement as a faculty activist.

In her rented beach-front apartment in Venice, she befriended student radicals and other young people who shared, as her contemporaries had not, her anger with the policies and methods of the men who influenced the nation. She participated in the UCLA classroom strike in May 1970 that followed the Kent State incident in which four students in Ohio were fatally shot during a confrontation with National Guardsmen; and she made antiwar speeches and marched in parades. It was during this period that she became reunited with her drifting daughter, who now had a child of her own.

Sally also met, at the home of a UCLA student, a large man with a Fu Manchu mustache and long hair named Anthony Russo. A year later he would be known across the land as the furtive idealist who, with Daniel Ellsberg, had acquired and leaked to the press the Pentagon Papers, thus revealing to the public the American government's history of lying about its political and military dealings in Vietnam. But when Sally first met Russo, there was in his manner no hint of the political desperado; a Southerner in his mid-thirties of Italo-redneck ancestry, he was a recent convert to the counterculture, a man not yet entirely accustomed to his long, shoulder-length hair. After years as a security-cleared corporate thinker, he was now living in Los Angeles on unemployment insurance, and he described himself to Sally as a "Rand dropout." She liked him. And as she became better acquainted with him, and through him met his friend Daniel Ellsberg, she decided to introduce them both to Sandstone.

Of the two men, Ellsberg adjusted more quickly to the place. He had been among nudists before, having visited Elysium in Los Angeles and also the famed Ile du Levant in the South of France; and after rejoining Rand in 1967, following a two-year tour of duty in Vietnam with the Department of Defense, Ellsberg—who was then almost forty and between marriages—had participated in orgies with people whose ads he had answered in the Lost Angeles *Free Press* or whom he had met at a special Los Angeles bar in Studio City called The Swing.

Perhaps the first tavern of its kind in the nation, The Swing was owned by an attractive married couple named Joyce and Greg McClure—the latter, a former movie actor, had starred in *The Great John L*—and Ellsberg befriended the McClures and frequented the bar, introducing himself during 1968 as "Don Hunter." In deference to his position at Rand, Ellsberg did not want his real name to be listed in the address books of people he did not know very well, particularly since nobody was then sure of the legal status of group sex in California. But aside from the pseudonym, he was hardly cautious about the people he associated with in the bar, or the places he later went for sex parties; he was open to suggestions, was as comfortable in large crowds as in threesomes, and he took pride in his energy and style as a lover. Even after he had made copies of the Pentagon Papers, and might have assumed that the FBI would soon be tapping his telephone and tailing him by car, Ellsberg made no attempt to conceal his nocturnal carousing, traveling from swing bar to orgy—and also to Sandstone—as casually as if he were attending a reunion of Harvard alumni.

In retrospect, after he had been indicted for espionage and

conspiracy in 1971, Ellsberg conjectured that it had possibly been his openness about sex that had most aroused the curiosity of the Puritans in Nixon's White House. They perhaps felt that if Ellsberg was so blasé about attending orgies, his real secret life must indeed be kinky and sinister. In any case President Nixon, determined to defame and punish Ellsberg for leaking government documents to the press, authorized a penetrating investigation that would expose the nature of this turncoat who had once been a loyal Marine and a high-ranking hawkish bureaucrat in the Department of Defense. And it was this investigation, conducted by a former CIA agent named Howard Hunt and a onetime FBI agent named Gordon Liddy, that would lead to the break-in of the Beverly Hills office of Ellsberg's psychiatrist.

Eight months later, Hunt, Liddy, and their fellow infiltrators would be assigned to use similar tactics against other enemies of the President, enemies who resided in Washington and had offices in a building called Watergate.

22

RICHARD NIXON HAD come to the White House convinced that the spirit of America was being eroded by domestic radicals, degenerate hippies, and exploitative pornographers; and as part of his campaign to purge the nation of its lurid temptations, and to restore law and order on the campuses and in the cities, Nixon advocated a "citizens' crusade against the obscene." Although most of the sex films and hard-core photographs sold in the nation had emanated from the region of his birth, Nixon neither appreciated nor understood the appeal of such material, nor had he ever identified with the loose, laid-back, self-indulgent lifestyle that had seduced so many other natives of Southern California.

Nixon grew up as an indoor man in an outdoor state, a Puritan born in an impoverished farm town outside Los Angeles that was closer to the Grapes of Wrath than to the hills of Hollywood. His father, a frostbitten streetcar motorman from a barren region of Ohio who had migrated West in 1906 and had failed as a lemon rancher, was a cantankerous, frustrated man and a harsh disciplinarian of his children. Nixon's mother, Hannah Milhous, who had come to Southern California at the age of twelve with her Quaker parents from Indiana, and had been reared in the religious community of Whittier—founded by New England Quakers in the late 1800s at the same time that James Towner's free-love Oneidans were moving into nearby Santa Ana—was a righteous woman of fortitude and faith who, in order to afford the medical care of one of Richard Nixon's tubercular brothers, worked outside the home for three years as a cook and scrubwoman.

Richard Nixon labored after school at various jobs, had little time for laxity or leisure, and grew up to be a dutiful, humorless young man who played the piano in the Friends Church on weekends and was a top student and aggressive debater at Whittier College, a Quaker institution dedicated to the training of Christian leadership. After graduating on scholarship from the Duke University Law School, and serving as an officer in the Navy, he successfully ran for Congress in 1946 against a California Democrat whose liberal views he attacked as sympathetic to communism; and while this scathing campaign, and similar ones that followed, would propel Nixon into the national limelight as a patriot and moral inquisitor, he would rarely feel truly accepted and admired by his constituents, nor would he often be, even in the Oval Office of the White House, secure within himself.

If he could have controlled the nation over which he presided, he would have extended through cities and towns the ethos of Whittier College, a place where order and conformity had prevailed and where there had been respect for hard work, religion, and moral rectitude. As President, he brought to Washington two Californians who shared his view that such traditions should be preserved, and these men became his top domestic advisers. Both were nondrinking, nonsmoking Christian Scientists who had attended UCLA; both were conservative Republicans, patriots, and family men who were appalled by the clamorous counterculture, the spreading sexual permissiveness, and the pornographic trend in films and publications. One of the men, a tall, crew-cut, autocratic former advertising executive named H. R. Haldeman, would become the Chief of Staff of Nixon's White House. The other man, attorney John D. Ehrlichman, a former Eagle Scout and decorated Air Force navigator who flew in twenty-six bombing missions over Germany, would serve as Assistant to the President for Domestic Affairs. After Daniel Ellsberg had leaked the Pentagon Papers to the press, Ehrlichman would retaliate by organizing the "plumbers" brigade that would raid the office of Ellsberg's psychiatrist and the Democratic National Committee headquarters in the Watergate building.

In addition to Haldeman and Ehrlichman, President Nixon would bolster his "crusade against the obscene" by appointing as Chief Justice of the Supreme Court—following the retirement of the liberal Earl Warren—a majestic white-haired exemplar of high-minded Methodist morality named Warren Burger. A former Assistant United States Attorney General and an Eisenhower appointee to the Court of Appeals, Burger was known to be supportive of government wire-tapping privileges against domestic radicals, to be restrictive of freedom of the press, and to be repulsed by pornography.

Soon the President was able to place three more conservatives on the high tribunal, following the deathbed retirements of Hugo Black and John Harlan, and the pressured departure of Abe Fortas in the wake of publicized allegations of financial improprieties. The Nixon replacements were William Rehnquist, a tough-minded, forty-seven-year-old Goldwater Republican from Milwaukee who had been working in the Nixon Justice Department and was known to favor capital punishment and to oppose abortion; Harry Blackmun, a teetotaling, straitlaced Harvard-educated Minnesota resident who had gone to the same grade school and church in St. Paul as Chief Justice Burger, had been the best man at Burger's wedding, and, in response to one of Nixon's questions during a prenomination interview for the Court position, had assured the President that none of the three Blackmun children were "hippie types"; and Lewis F. Powell, a proper Virginian and former ABA president who, shortly after his Supreme Court appointment, was shocked at having to sit in the Court's screening room one day and watch, as relevant evidence in an obscenity case, a nude blond Swedish actress performing lickerishly in a sex movie entitled *Without a Stitch*.

With such sexually prudish justices added to the Court, Nixon anticipated considerable support for his drive against pornography; and he also expected help from the recently established Presidential Commission on Obscenity and Pornography, an eighteen-member group appointed by former President Johnson in 1968 to determine what effect hard-core material was having on American society and, if the situation warranted it, to suggest corrective action. It had long been contended by the FBI director, J. Edgar Hoover, and many congressmen and church leaders, that exposure to hard-core sexual magazines and films prompted crimes of violence and rape; but until the formation of the commission, for which Congress appropriated $2 million for the research that would take two years to complete, there had not been a federal attempt to produce the evidence that would test such claims.

When one member of the commission—the group included distinguished educators, scientists, clergymen, lawyers, and businessmen—resigned in 1969 to accept an overseas diplomatic assignment, Nixon was able to appoint an individual of his own choice, a man he knew was one of the most fanatical foes of pornography in America. He was Charles H. Keating, a lean, blondish, determinedly Catholic, six-foot-four-inch Cincinnati attorney whose many years of lobbying against sex films and books had caused Cincinnati headline writers to call him "Mr. Clean."

As the father of six children, a former All-American intercollegiate swimming champion, a naval fighter pilot during World War II, and a top executive with a large financial company, Charles Keating was a formidable presence in his community; and after he had become offended during the 1950s by the expanding display of girlie magazines and porno paperbacks on the city newsstands, he convinced several civic boosters, business leaders, and churchgoers to join his antismut crusade and to donate funds to the tax-exempt society that he had founded called the Citizens for Decent Literature.

The main goal of the CDL was to apply community pressure on local politicians and lawmen to close down the bookshops and cinemas that exploited sex in Cincinnati, and to inspire letter-writing campaigns and even economic boycotts against the proprietors of general stores that sold sex magazines and against the sponsors of television and radio shows that tolerated sex-oriented programs or other broadcasts that might be construed as inappropriate for a moral family audience. The CDL, in essence, was reviving the prewar tactics of the old Catholic Legion of Decency that had once terrified the Hollywood film industry until boldly challenged by such independent producers as Howard Hughes and Otto Preminger; and while many civil libertarians initially dismissed Keating's CDL as anachronistic, the society nonetheless continued to grow throughout the sixties into a national organization with thirty-two chapters in twenty states, and an estimated 350,000 active supporters of sexual restraint and censorship. Its honorary members included eleven United States senators, four governors, and more than one hundred members of the House of Representatives. It was supported by many municipal leaders, district attorneys, and the Catholic archbishops of Cincinnati, St. Louis, Washington, and Los Angeles. Dozens of big-city daily newspapers, which otherwise would have opposed censorship, endorsed the CDL's "cleanup" programs and agreed to restrict, subdue, or ban entirely the advertising of X-rated sex films. Among the papers that did this were the Cincinnati *Enquirer* (where Keating's younger brother was the company president), the Miami *News*, the San Francisco

Examiner, the Los Angeles *Times*, the Detroit *News*, the New Orleans *Times Picayune*, the Chicago *Daily News*. And eventually, even the New York *Times* would be influenced by the trend.

The CDL's own bimonthly periodical, the *National Decency Reporter*, enthusiastically recounted each new raid against "dirty" bookshops by alert police departments around the country and eagerly announced the courtroom verdicts of pornographers' convictions; it also printed in each issue a flattering biographical sketch and photograph of a law-enforcement official who had recently inflicted punishment upon the "merchants of smut," and this individual was hailed under the headline: "Prosecutor of the Month."

The muckraking editor of the *National Decency Reporter* was a bespectacled, stocky, ruddy-complexioned man in his fifties named Raymond Gauer, who, before being discovered by Keating, had worked obscurely in Los Angeles as an accountant with a milk company and as a systems analyst with a firm that manufactured chain saws. Gauer was exactly the kind of man that Keating wished to recruit into the CDL: He was a political conservative, a Catholic family man with seven children, a naval veteran who had struggled for decades to eke out a modest living for his large family while repressing his resentment against the nation's welfare cheats, the privileged campus radicals, and the sexual degenerates who were committing every imaginable sin against God and nature.

Gauer had come to Keating's attention in a circuitous way. One Sunday evening while walking toward a Chinese restaurant to pick up an order of food to take home to his family, Gauer found himself standing wide-eyed in front of a sex shop that had recently opened in his Hollywood neighborhood. In the window, and on the front cases, he saw racks of paperbacks with lurid titles, arrangements of electric vibrators and rubber dildoes, French ticklers, cock rings, tubes of lubricants, garter belts, and many magazines on the pages of which were full-color photographs of young women posing in the nude with their legs spread, their arms extended, their mouths open. Though Gauer grunted disapprovingly to himself, he felt a stirring of excitement, a loathsome awareness of illicit desire. Immediately he walked away, embarrassed that he had lingered as long as he had.

Later that night, after his wife and children were asleep, the reflections of the evil store window persisted in his mind. Troubled by the images, he was restless, agitated; but he also felt summoned by the spirit of the Lord, a feeling he had not felt since his altar-boy days in his native Chicago, and he recognized within himself a pious passion, a wish to confront and overcome the demonic allure of the despicable pornographers. He got little sleep that night, and the next day he composed an angry letter to the Hollywood Chamber of Commerce, protesting the presence of such a store near his home. Within a week he had received a letter of thanks, promising that the police would be notified. A few days later, he read in the newspapers that the store had been raided by the authorities and was now closed.

Impressed and encouraged, and experiencing for the first time in his life the power to exert his influence within the tawdry world around him, Raymond Gauer proceeded to drive around the city in his spare time and note the names and addresses of other sex shops. In downtown Los Angeles, near City Hall, he counted six places that seemed to be thriving, and he wrote to the mayor questioning how such places could be legally tolerated in the shadow of the mayor's own office and the headquarters of the Los Angeles Police Department. Days later Gauer received a telephone call from an officer with the city's vice squad who said, "Mr. Gauer, watch the papers tomorrow." On the following day the front pages of the Los Angeles press reported a simultaneous raid on the six establishments, the arrests of several salesclerks, and the confiscation of seven tons of obscenity.

Not long after this a representative of the CDL contacted Raymond Gauer, and, during one of Charles Keating's speaking engagements in Los Angeles, it was arranged that he and Gauer should meet. In style and appearance, the two men were strikingly dissimilar. Keating was tall, impeccably neat, commanding. Gauer was plain, craggy-featured, and of sufficient girth to strain the seams of his tight-fitting suits. But in their mutual abhorrence of sinful sex they were kindred spirits; and as the men became better acquainted, Keating perceived in Gauer a loquacious simplicity that he thought could be converted into a convincing voice for the CDL.

Soon Keating's instincts about Gauer were put to a test: Due to a prior commitment, a regular CDL lecturer on sex was unable to accept a lecture date with a Los Angeles service club, and Gauer was persuaded to take his place. Although Gauer was initially very nervous and self-conscious about having to stand before a crowded room, he nevertheless proceeded in plain terms, but with disarming conviction, to express to his audience his objection to the pornographers' public desecration of the private and sacred act of love. He did not deny the appeal of pornography. He admitted, in fact, that he was as vulnerable as most men to its stimulation. But he said it was potentially corruptive, it was a sickening substitute for the genuine affection that sexual union should symbolize. If the sex peddlers were allowed to continue to circulate their filthy material in the future with the freedom they enjoyed at present, their pollution would not only contaminate the deserving victims who consumed it but also spread indiscriminately to the society at large, thus weakening the fiber of family life and the moral health of the nation.

The success of Gauer's first speech was such that Keating urged him to continue as a CDL spokesman, and dozens of other appearances by him followed, not only before service clubs but also on the stages of auditoriums where he and other CDL members debated ACLU lawyers and various First Amendment advocates. By 1967 Raymond Gauer had accepted Keating's offer to head the CDL's Los Angeles chapter and to represent the CDL before school audiences and on radio-television talk shows in California and around the country. On one occasion Gauer flew back to his hometown, Chicago, to condemn pornography on a talk show where the opposing guest was a twenty-nine-year-old local porno merchant and massage parlor owner named Harold Rubin. Gauer and Rubin disliked one another instantly. Gauer viewed the outspoken young man as a vulgarian lacking scruples and standards, while Rubin saw in Gauer signs of his own Chicago-born father, a repressed blue-collar conservative who was more offended by sex than by the war in Vietnam.

In 1968 Raymond Gauer was in Washington as an unofficial CDL lobbyist. There, with the help of DeWitt Wallace of *Reader's Digest*, Gauer and a CDL attorney named James J. Clancy met privately with several congressmen to urge the introduction of stronger antiobscenity legislation. The men were given access to a small room below the Senate floor, and, equipped with a slide projector and screen, they exhibited to the congressmen—among whom were Senators Strom Thurmond of South Carolina, Robert P. Griffin of Michigan, and Jack Miller of Iowa—examples of the type of obscenity that was being sent through the mail and sold nationwide largely due to the liberal standards of the present Supreme Court.

Quite coincidentally, while Gauer and Clancy were in Washington, the Senate Judiciary Committee began public hearings on the nomination of Justice Abe Fortas to replace the seventy-seven-year-old retiring Earl Warren as the Chief Justice of the Supreme Court. Many politicians and special-interest groups, including the CDL, were opposed to Fortas, and during the early summer and fall of 1968 the jeremiads against Fortas would range from the lucrative seminar fees that he had received to the chiding telephone calls he had allegedly made to important people who had been critical of President Johnson's foreign or domestic policy. Several Republicans, led by Senator Griffin, were outraged that President Johnson, who had already announced that he would not seek the Democratic renomination in 1968, would try during his final months in office to elevate his judicial friend to an exalted position that might otherwise go to a man preferred by the incoming President, who might be a Republican.

The CDL's quarrel with Fortas was based on his tolerance of pornography as revealed in several recent obscenity cases, including his vote to legalize the long-banned English novel about the prostitute Fanny Hill (entitled *Memoirs of a Woman of Pleasure*) and his permissiveness in the case of *Corinthe Publications* v. *Wesberry* for such paperback sex novels as *Sin Whisper*. Furthermore, the CDL was aware that the publisher of *Sin Whisper* had once been a client of Fortas' law firm in Washington— indeed, the CDL claimed to have learned from an FBI agent that the publisher had allegedly boasted of his Fortas connection, suggesting that it would protect him from federal prosecution; and the CDL further asserted that its spreading of this FBI notion through the Senate ultimately influenced Minority Leader Everett M. Dirksen of Illinois (who had originally favored Fortas' promotion) to tilt the senatorial momentum against Abe Fortas.

After Richard Nixon had been sworn in as the President in January 1969, and after his Attorney General, John M. Mitchell, had come forth with new evidence against Fortas—the latter had been receptive to a $20,000 fee from a foundation created by a financier who had once been convicted of selling unregistered securities—Abe Fortas was driven to resign altogether from the Court, creating a vacancy that Nixon would fill with a conservative.

A month after the Fortas resignation, there was additional rejoicing within the CDL as Nixon appointed Charles Keating to the Presidential Commission on Obscenity and Pornography, and the CDL newspaper expressed optimism that Keating's forceful personality (though he would be joining the commission a year after it had been set in motion by President Johnson) would soon inspire the other members to discover effective ways and means of excoriating smut. The other members, most of whom Keating saw as representing high moral standards, included Winfred C. Link, a Methodist minister from Hermitage, Tennessee; Irving Lehrman, a rabbi at Temple Emanu-El in Miami Beach; and Morton A. Hill, a Catholic priest who had previously led pickets against pornographers in Manhattan and was president of a censorial organization called Morality in Media, Inc. There was also on the list an ordained clergyman and teacher from Southern Methodist University named G. William Jones; the attorney general of the state of California, Thomas C. Lynch; and two women—an English instructor from South Dakota named Cathryn Spelts and a New York attorney with the Motion Picture Association named Barbara Scott—who might be expected to add more than a touch of womanly resentment to the manner in which female bodies were so often used in the world of pornography.

The other commissioners also appeared to represent a responsible cross section of society: Morris A. Lipton, a professor of psychiatry at the University of North Carolina Medical School; Otto N. Larsen, a professor of sociology at the University of Washington; Edward D. Greenwood, a child psychiatrist at the Menninger Foundation; Joseph T. Klapper, a research sociologist with CBS; Thomas D. Gill, chief judge of the Juvenile Court in Connecticut; Freeman Lewis, president of the Washington Square Press in New York; Edward E. Elson, president of the Atlanta News Agency; Marvin E. Wolfgang, professor of sociology at the University of Pennsylvania; Frederick H. Wagman, director of the University of Michigan Library; and the chairman of the commission was William B. Lockhart, dean of the University of Minnesota Law School.

The commissioners were assisted in their work by more than twenty staff members and several outside research specialists who were assigned to travel around the country gathering the information that the commissioners would later evaluate. During the first year, before Keating became involved, the commission had dispatched research teams to interview and analyze the major manufacturers of hard-core material, the proprietors of the stores that sold it, and the customers who regularly bought it. The researchers sought out the postal inspectors and law-enforcement authorities who were the most knowledgeable about pornography, gaining not only facts and insights into the size and scope of the illegal industry but also an estimation of the Mafia's possible influence in the production and distribution of pornography. The researchers entered prisons in the Midwest and in New York to interrogate the inmates who had been convicted of rape and other sex crimes, seeking to learn about their family backgrounds and the kinds of films, books, or magazines that they had found interesting prior to their difficulties with the law.

One hundred national organizations were consulted by the commission and asked to submit in writing their views on pornography. A commission investigator was even sent to Denmark, where hard-core pornography and live sex shows had recently become legal, hoping to discover what effect this had on the number of Danish sex crimes, the trends in social behavior, and the moral atmosphere of the nation. At the University of North Carolina, a scientific team showed twenty-three male students sex films for ninety minutes a day, five days a week, over a three-week period, in an attempt to determine what effect the films had on the students' personal habits and passions. All of the student volunteers watched the films while wearing robes under which their penises were sheathed in condoms attached with electrodes that gauged penile erection, and they also wore bellows around their chests and electrical instruments in their ears. Prior to each daily film session, the researchers privately asked the students whether or not they had masturbated or had intercourse during the intervening twenty-four hours.

The commissioners themselves saw hard-core movies; in fact, the commission's first official meeting in 1968 was held at the Kinsey Institute in Indiana, where, in addition to being shown Dr. Kinsey's vast collection of erotica and being briefed on the latest national sex statistics, the members were escorted into a screening room to see examples of antiquated "blue" movies as well as an assortment of contemporary sex films done in living color. Perhaps the most mesmerized viewer in the audience, though he blushed after the house lights went on, was Father Morton Hill, one of New York's most knowledgeable and indefatigable enemies of pornography. After that screening and further exposure to such material, Father Hill expressed his concern to the female lawyer on the commission that she was obliged to watch such filth; but when she indicated that the experience did not really horrify her, he was clearly dismayed and said he would pray for the redemption of her soul.

While the commissioners and staff were free to discuss among themselves their reactions to the material brought before them, they were urged by the chairman, William B. Lockhart, never to reveal their personal opinions to the public or to political officials. Lockhart sensed that he was part of a potentially incendiary research project; and if mishandled or prematurely disclosed in fragmentary form to the newspapers before the commission had completed and interpreted all of its research, it could elicit much misunderstanding and controversy that would diminish the impact and importance of the final report and recommendations. Therefore, all interim queries by the press or politicians were to be directed and replied to by Lockhart or his personal staff; and while Lockhart's authoritative posture as a law school dean and his superior role as the commission's chairman were duly respected by his colleagues during the first year of operation, the assertive arrival of Charles Keating in 1969 quickly introduced into the interworkings of the membership an element of tension and confrontation.

The discord began when Keating discovered that most of the fieldwork was not being done by the commissioners themselves but by a staff and researchers largely selected by Lockhart. Keating was further offended when Lockhart's chosen counsel, an ACLU-affiliated lawyer named Paul Bender, was permitted to participate in the commission's sessions while Keating's friend and counsel with the CDL, James J. Clancy, was denied even the right to observe the proceedings. Keating was also disturbed when Lockhart would not allow him to serve on all the committees that he wished to become affiliated with; and when Lockhart persisted in his opposition to the holding of public hearings that in Keating's opinion would have properly publicized the epidemic of erotica and exposed the merchants who were becoming rich through the sales of smut, Keating decided to boycott all future meetings of the commission.

But such haggling between Keating and Lockhart was minor when compared to the wrath and acerbity with which Keating would greet the preliminary conclusions and recommendations that the Lockhart-dominated commission arrived at in the fall of 1970 and were planning to edit and deliver to the government printing office. After all the money, the energy and time spent in investigating the problem of pornography, Keating was stunned to discover that the Lockhart majority had ultimately decided that pornography was not a national problem after all, and that the wisest way to deal with it—at least where adults were concerned—was simply to ignore it.

"The Commission believes that there is no warrant for continued Government interference with the full freedom of adults," the report said, "because extensive empirical investigation, both by the Commission and others, provides no evidence that exposure to or use of explicit sexual materials plays a significant role in the causation of social or individual harms such as crime, delinquency, sexual or nonsexual deviancy or severe emotional disturbances."

Rapists and other sexual delinquents, the report went on—after taking into account the research done in prisons and mental institutions—were less likely to be consumers of pornography than products of "conservative, repressed, sexually deprived backgrounds"; and the people who were most incensed by the popularity of pornography in America, the report added, were the "overzealous" and "religiously active" older citizens who also believed "that newspapers should not have the right to print articles which criticize the police, that people should not be allowed to publish books which attack our system of government, and that people should not be allowed to make speeches against God."

The effect of showing sex movies to the twenty-three college boys in North Carolina resulted largely in their boredom; and not only had the legalization of pornography in Denmark failed to produce the crime wave that some Danes had earlier anticipated, but there had been instead a substantial decline in such offenses as voyeurism, the latter fact suggesting that "Peeping Toms" were less willing to risk being arrested for looking into people's windows since they were able to see more in bottomless bars, porno films, and live sex shows. Contrary to the assumption of many United States citizens, the report went on, the sex industry in America was not controlled by the Mafia or other factions in organized crime; while the pornography business certainly supported many people who had criminal records (which was not surprising since the police were constantly arresting them for trafficking in sex) there was no evidence of a "monolithic 'smut' industry" interlinked with Mafia mobsters. The tycoons in the sex industry—such men as Milton Luros and Marvin Miller of Los Angeles, William Hamling of San Diego, Reuben Sturman of Cleveland, Michael Thevis of Atlanta—were hardly honored members of the Better Business Bureau, but they

were not a national network of Mafia godfathers each ruling a
"family" of hit men. And, the report continued, the majority
of American consumers who spent millions annually in attending porno films, buying "skin" magazines, patronizing massage parlors, and depositing tons of coins into sex-film vending
machines were typically not the reprobates, the rapists, the motorcycle gangs, the assassins or other deranged dregs of society,
but were instead what the Supreme Court might define as the
Average Man, or in the words of the commission report, "predominantly white, middle class, middle aged, married males,
dressed in a business suit or neat casual attire."

The effect of pornography on such men did not, as some
alarmists insisted, drive them madly into the streets to rape or
provoke them into breaking up their homes and abandoning their
families. Instead, if it stimulated them at all, it might lead to
private acts of masturbation; or, if the individual had a receptive
wife or mistress or girl friend, it might add impetus to the desire
to make love. But criminal behavior did not result from exposure
to pornography, the report reiterated, and for this reason the
Lockhart majority advocated that the United States Government—which annually invested many millions of dollars in taxpayers' money to harass and prosecute the pornographers, with
questionable results—should now abolish all laws that sought to
deprive adults of the right to see or read any and all so-called
obscene materials.

Charles Keating was alarmed by this suggestion, and, after
warning Nixon's office about what was forthcoming from Lockhart, he filed a suit in the federal district court in Washington
that temporarily stalled the commission's plans to proceed with
the publication of its report. After the judge had granted Keating
a restraining order, Keating rallied his people in the CDL to
write letters and send telegrams to Washington urging a "prompt
and full Congressional investigation of the Commission." Of
the eighteen members, only Keating and three others were totally opposed to the report that had been drafted by Lockhart's
staff. Keating's fellow dissenters were Father Morton Hill,
Rev. Winfred Link, and the California attorney general, Thomas
C. Lynch. Father Hill was as angered as Keating was by the
report; and the Hill-Link dissenting response began with the
statement: "The Commission's majority report is a Magna Carta
for the pornographer."

Soon, many important people had joined Keating's protest.
Among them were Vice-President Spiro Agnew, the United

States Postmaster General, the leaders of both parties in the Senate, and the head of the National Conference of Catholic Bishops. Attorney General John Mitchell asserted: "If we want a society in which the noble side of man is encouraged and mankind is elevated, then I submit pornography is surely harmful." Finally, after verifying that the report was as unpunitive as Keating had claimed it was, President Nixon declared in a public statement that he would "totally reject" the recommendations of the commission, which he accused of having performed a "disservice" to the nation. "So long as I am in the White House," he added, "there will be no relaxation of the national effort to control and eliminate smut from our national life. . . . The Commission contends that the proliferation of filthy books and plays has no lasting, harmful threat on man's character. . . . Centuries of civilization and ten minutes of common sense tell us otherwise. . . . American morality is not to be trifled with."

Had it been in Nixon's power to shred the report he might have done so, but the commission was operating under a congressional act requiring that it submit in writing its findings and recommendations; and so after a ten-day delay due to Keating's injunction, the commission report was revived and processed through the government printers with the proviso that Keating would be allowed to publish a separate report that would reflect *his* views on the question of pornography.

The Keating report was a 175-page document that condemned Lockhart and his research methods, characterized the commission fact finders as a mixture of naïve "Ivory Tower" academicians and young "green graduates," and reprinted police records and the opinions of commentators that cited sexual immorality and pornography as the most acute problem confronting modern America. Keating quoted Arnold Toynbee's view that the most progressive culture is the one that postpones the sexual experience of its young adults, and Keating added Bruno Bettelheim's observation: "If a society does not taboo sex, children will grow up in relative sex freedom . . . but so far history has shown that such a society cannot create culture or civilization; it remains primitive." Keating also included a paragraph that Alexis de Toqueville had written after visiting America between 1835 and 1840: "I sought for the greatness and genius of America in her commodious harbors and ample rivers—and it was not there; in her fertile lands and boundless prairies—and it was not there. Not until I went to the churches of America and heard her pulpit aflame with righteousness did I understand the secret of her genius and power. America is great because she is good—and if America ceases to be good, America will cease to be great.''

The controversy generated by Keating's report kept the story of the commission's findings in the newspapers for several days; and just when it appeared to be subsiding, another event occurred that would compound the conflict. In November 1970 there was produced in California an unauthorized illustrated edition of the Presidential Report, a large, glossy, $12.50 paperback that contained on its 352 pages not only a full text of the commission's project and Keating's rejoinder, but graphic depictions of the subject matter—photographs and drawings of copulating couples, groups involved in orgies, females masturbating men, men vibrating women, homosexuals engaged in sodomy, lesbians in cunnilingus, medieval nuns fornicating with candles, ancient oriental prints of elaborate debauchery, concupiscent cartoons of popular comic-book characters, salacious engravings by Pablo Picasso, leather-clad high-heeled females flailing manacled men, interracial bacchanalias, spread shots of vaginas, and a red-haired woman caressing with her tongue the penis of a horse. No fewer than 546 illustrations of every imaginable type were included in the book, and their use was justified by the publisher on the ground that this was specifically the sort of material that the commission members had scrutinized and evaluated prior to completing their report.

In addition to publishing a first edition of 100,000 copies and delivering them to ''adult'' bookshops around the country, the California firm also mailed out more than 55,000 advertising brochures that contained selected pictures from the book, told readers how they could order copies of the illustrated edition, and also carried a statement denouncing President Nixon for having rejected the commission's recommendations. ''Thanks a lot, Mr. President,'' read the headline on the brochure, and the text underneath continued: ''A monumental work of research and investigation has now become a giant of a book. All the facts, all the statistics, presented in the best possible format . . . and . . . completely illustrated in black and white and full color. Every facet of the most controversial report ever issued is covered in detail. This book is a *must* for the research shelves of every library, public or private, seriously concerned with full intellectual freedom and adult selection. Millions of dollars in public funds were expended to determine the *precise truth* about eroticism in the United States today, yet every possible attempt to suppress this information was made from the very highest levels. Even the President dismissed the facts, out of hand. The attempt to suppress this volume is an inexcusable insult directed at every adult in this country. Each individual *must* be allowed to make his own decision; the facts are inescapable. Many adults, *many of them*, will do just that after reading this Report. In a truly free society, a book like this wouldn't even be necessary.''

Predictably, a copy of the illustrated report was soon in the hands of FBI agents, who dispatched it to J. Edgar Hoover's office in Washington—where the director, after expressing rage and wonderment that such a book could exist, called it to the attention of the President. Nixon had already seen it, having been sent a copy days earlier by the irate Keating, who had been alerted about the book by Raymond Gauer, who had noticed it while browsing through a sex shop in Los Angeles and had purchased several copies. Nixon was aghast at what he saw, and soon federal prosecutors and agents were discussing the legal strategy that might most effectively punish the publisher, a feisty fifty-year-old named William Hamling about whom they already knew a great deal.

William Hamling had been cited in obscenity cases earlier during the last decade in San Diego, where his firm had made millions through the sale of racy paperbacks and magazines, radical political treatises, science fiction novels, general nonfiction, best sellers like Henry Miller's *The Rosy Crucifixion*, Terry Southern and Mason Hoffenberg's *Candy*, and work by De Sade, Alberto Moravia, and Lenny Bruce. It was Hamling who, as a onetime client of Abe Fortas' law firm, had been quoted by the FBI as allegedly saying he was beyond federal conviction—the memo that had been referred to by Gauer and Clancy in 1968 while they were lobbying in the Senate building against the nomination of Fortas as Chief Justice.

Much of what the government knew about Hamling had in fact been published in the CDL newspaper by Gauer, who had assembled from court records a case history of Hamling's litigious career; and Gauer would later learn much more about Hamling when, in a San Diego television studio where Gauer was to participate in a talk show, he met William Hamling for the first time face to face. Although Gauer was prepared to loathe him on sight, he was oddly disarmed by Hamling in the several minutes they spent backstage in casual conversation waiting for the show to begin. In manner and appearance, Hamling and Gauer were not unalike: They were both middle-aged, gray-haired men wearing nearly the same conservative suit and tie; they were both natives of Chicago, the products of a strict Catholic upbringing; and as they continued to talk, Gauer discovered that they had practically been moving in one another's shadow throughout their lives.

Each had been born in the summer of 1921 in the same North Side neighborhood, each had served Mass as altar boys; they had played ball in the same sandlots, had attended neighboring high schools. Hamling and Gauer had both left Chicago for the first time to serve in the military, and after the war had returned to marry young Chicago women with whom they would raise large families. After a number of oppressively cold Chicago winters, each would move with his family to Southern California, where in time each would establish his identity on opposite sides of the issue of erotica. And now in a television studio in San Diego, as they were introduced to an audience as adversaries in the debate, Gauer felt a reluctant kinship with Hamling, and he was initially in no mood for quarreling and fretting.

But after Gauer in his opening statement had referred condescendingly to the thriving business of tainted literature, Hamling became hostile, defensive—a tender spot had been touched, and the two men were quickly involved in an acrimonious exchange. Hamling insisted that he had the right to personally possess and to professionally publish girlie magazines and sex books, while Gauer challenged that right and argued that such tempting material should be prohibited to adults and adolescents alike because it was socially reprehensible and morally dangerous. For nearly an hour the men confronted one another in a dialogue characterized by interruptions and scorched emotions; and the animosity that the program inspired continued to be felt by the men even when the show was over. After the cameras had stopped and the overhead lights were lowered, Gauer and Hamling shook hands with the moderator and then coolly turned away from one another, leaving the studio with little more than a formal good night.

Gauer wondered afterward what it was, considering all they had in common, that made the two of them so different on this one issue; and he could only conclude that somewhere between the altar of a Chicago church and the bench of a federal courtroom, Hamling had lost touch with the spirit of his religion.

Had Gauer been able to talk more to Hamling, he might have confirmed his assumption, for William Hamling had indeed lost his faith after leaving Chicago and joining the Army in the 1940s; although Hamling might well have argued that it was the *Church* that had lost faith in that it had deviated from many of its traditions during the war, becoming more mundane, less ascetic, less spiritual, and therefore less worthy of the awe and devotion that he had once bestowed upon it.

As a younger man who had contemplated the priesthood, Hamling had felt ennobled within the confines of the Church, secure in its rigid rules and regulations, humbled by the certainty with which it identified and punished sin. Restrictive as it was, Catholicism at least represented a clear position on all human issues, it seemed absolute and omniscient, and a parishioner wishing to achieve eternal salvation was *not* required to find his own way in a world clouded with confusion and alternatives—he had only to follow faithfully the clearly marked path charted by the Church.

But in the Army, Hamling's perspective changed; it was there that he saw the Church, in deference to the war, becoming less celestial, more nationalistic and permissive. Sins that had been called sins for centuries were suddenly no longer condemned as such by the Church. Catholic soldiers could eat meat on Fridays, could miss Mass, could avoid the weekly exhortations of their confessors. Bishops blessed bombers; the officers of the Church were allied with the generals—indeed, the generals outranked the clergymen who, frocked in the drab khaki clothing of chaplains, saluted the stars; and when tons of pinup magazines were transported by the military up to the front as substitute stimulants for the womanless warriors, the Church, once so strict and censorial, was silent, and in its silence was complicitous.

While such ecclesiastical concessions were no doubt unavoidable, given the disruptive circumstances that the war imposed on almost every level of social and family life, Hamling nevertheless believed that the wartime secularization of the Church did undermine the religious fervor of numerous Catholic G.I.s like himself; and after he was discharged and had returned to civilian life in Chicago, he was no longer dominated by his early conditioning, his narrow view of sin, his guilt about unsanctified sex.

In time Hamling found himself working as an editor in a publishing company that distributed a variety of monthly magazines, among them a pinup-adventure magazine called *Modern*

Man and a nudist periodical, *Modern Sunbathing & Hygiene*, which printed airbrushed photographs. Hamling's boss, who owned all the publications, was named George von Rosen; and one of the first employees to befriend Hamling was Von Rosen's young promotion director, Hugh Hefner. Though Hefner was more than four years younger than Hamling, he was far more certain about what he wished to achieve in life, and he had already decided to soon quit Von Rosen's firm and risk his talent and luck on a magazine of his own invention. When Hefner described to Hamling the type of magazine that he had in mind, hoping to entice Hamling as an investor, Hamling listened with interest but he finally concluded that, despite the liberalizing effect of returning veterans on postwar society, not enough men were yet ready to financially support on a national scale such a sexually bold publication as Hefner envisioned.

Years later, with Hefner suddenly rich as the founder of *Playboy* and Hamling still toiling obscurely as an editor and freelance writer for pulp magazines, the two men met one afternoon for a friendly lunch in Chicago; and on their way to the restaurant, Hefner proudly directed Hamling's attention toward a sporty new automobile that was parked at the curb, a bronze-colored Cadillac convertible that Hefner had just purchased. Hamling, who had driven into town in his battered 1941 Hudson, was impressed and mildly envious at how quickly Hefner's circumstances had changed—Hefner was not only an affluent publisher but the personification of *Playboy*'s image; and while Hamling knew that he himself lacked the temperament to truly emulate his friend (Hamling preferred evenings at home with his wife, Frances, to pursuing playmates, while Hefner had recently left his wife, Mildred, in search of eternal bliss as a bachelor), Hamling could not help but berate his own caution in having failed to buy the Playboy stock, which was now soaring. And as a result, during their lunch, Hamling sat across the table listening to Hefner with heightened respect and receptivity; and when Hefner, evincing concern for Hamling's welfare, suggested that Hamling should also start a girlie magazine, adding that the men's field had barely been explored and vast fortunes were waiting to be earned, Hamling decided that he was now ready to disregard his customary reticence.

Within a week, again following Hefner's advice, Hamling contacted the director of the Empire News Company, Jerry Rosenfield, who had initially helped in the financing of *Playboy* and was currently profiting nicely as its national distributor; and

Rosenfield reacted favorably to Hamling's plan for a new magazine, promising to advance the necessary funds for printing it in return for the rights to distribute it. As a result, in November 1955, Hamling produced the first issue of a magazine called *Rogue*; and while it was less slick than *Playboy*, having black-and-white photographs instead of color, it was by late 1956 selling close to 300,000 copies per month and attracting sufficient attention on the newsstands to elicit the disapproval of the CDL—and to be classified as obscene by the Post Office, which sought to annul its second-class mailing privileges.

Hefner's magazine had been ruled obscene by the Post Office; but instead of prosecuting the more prosperous and established *Playboy*, the postal attorneys decided to direct their test case against *Rogue*, no doubt thinking that the latter would be easier to beat in court. But in Washington, Hamling had access to the Empire News' law firm in which Abe Fortas was a partner; and while the defense of *Rogue* in the district court would cost Hamling $13,000 in legal fees, the Postmaster General was ultimately overruled—Hamling was awarded the second-class mailing rate; and Hugh Hefner, without any legal cost to himself, automatically received the same privileges for *Playboy*.

Hamling was thrilled with his legal triumph and the prominence it had earned him in the men's magazine field; and as *Rogue*'s monthly circulation gradually approached 500,000, Hamling expanded in 1959 into the sex-oriented pulp paperback business, employing several talented, indigent writers who pseudonymously and prodigiously wrote quick-reading bawdy novels that Hamling sold in enormous quantities under the imprint of Nightstand Books.

Between 1960 and 1963, by which time he had moved his company to San Diego, Hamling had earned $4 million from his gaudy-jacketed novels, each of which preached a message of raunchy adventure—even though the titles that Hamling used on the covers curiously evoked the spirit of guilt. The words "sin," "shame," and "lust" repeatedly appeared in each new title: *Sin Hooked, Lust Hungry, Shame Shop, Sin Whisper, Sin Warden, Shame Market, Passion Priestess, Sinners' Seance, Penthouse Pagans, Bayou Sinners, Sin Servant, Lust Pool, Shame Agent*—the titles could have come directly from the admonitions of the sex-denouncing nuns and priests in the Chicago parish from which Hamling had, in conscience, not quite escaped; and even in the sybaritic atmosphere of Southern California he personally resisted the temptations that were so fulsomely described in the novels that he dispatched by the truckload to the back racks of drugstores and newsstands around the nation. William Hamling remained, as he had been in Chicago, a devoted husband, a father of six children, a conservatively dressed businessman who could as easily have been manufacturing neckties or air conditioner or auto parts. If he deserved credit for becoming a plutocrat in the pulpy trade of third-rate fiction in the early 1960s, it was because he understood, thanks to Hugh Hefner, that America was on the verge of a sex-publishing boom; and he soon realized that there were millions of conventional men like himself who received vicarious pleasure in reading about wild women who resembled not in the least the wives with whom they chose to live. Hamling's typical book buyers were closet Lotharios, ordinary men with extraordinary fantasies that were rarely catered to in the more subtle sensuous novels distributed by the larger so-called legitimate publishers in New York.

Hamling could not have become rich had the nation's obscenity laws not become more liberal just as he was venturing into the paperback sex business. The Supreme Court's altered definition of obscenity, first alluded to in the *Roth* opinion, not only legalized in 1959 such distinguished fiction as D. H. Lawrence's *Lady Chatterley's Lover* but also the sexually explicit works of many inferior writers and filmmakers, magazine and paperback publishers. In two subsequent Supreme Court cases, the freedoms implied in the *Roth* ruling were expanded still further: In the 1962 case of *Manual Enterprises* v. *Day*, the Court liberated several nude male "body-building" magazines for homosexuals from the restraints of Postmaster General Edward Day; and in the 1964 case of *Jacobellis* v. *Ohio*, the Supreme Court negated a lower-court conviction against a Cleveland theater manager, Nico Jacobellis, who had shown an art film called *Les Amants* that focused on the infidelities of a bored French housewife. In the *Jacobellis* opinion, the Court emphasized what had been merely implicit in *Roth*: that a film or any other form of expression, regardless of its sexual or immoral content, could not be prohibited as obscene unless it was "utterly without social importance." On the basis of that phrase, a federal court in Illinois in November 1964 felt compelled to void a conviction it had recently affirmed against comedian Lenny Bruce. While the Illinois court still insisted that Bruce's nightclub routines were revolting and disgusting, it was forced to admit that some of the topics he discussed on the stage had "social importance."

Finally, in the 1965 case of *Memoirs* v. *Massachusetts* (in which the Supreme Court overruled the Massachusetts attorney general, Edward W. Brooke, who had been adhering to the Massachusetts tradition of continuously condemning the Fanny Hill book that had first been outlawed in Massachusetts in 1821) the prevailing opinion of Justice Brennan declared that a book or film or magazine could be classified as legally obscene only if it was simultaneously guilty of each of three offenses: It had to appeal to the average person's "prurient interest" in sex; it had to be "patently offensive" to the average adult; and it had to be "utterly without redeeming social value."

Since very few works are "utterly without" some redeeming value even if prurient and patently offensive, the greatest bulk of questionable periodicals, photographs, films, and books—including millions of Hamling's Nightstand paperback books—were allowed to be sold in every hamlet of the nation during the mid-1960s. But the tolerant First Amendment tendencies of a majority of the nine justices did *not* mean that the advocates of sexual censorship within the government and the lower courts ceased to harass and prosecute sexual expressionists during this period. On the contrary, the campaigners against "smut" became increasingly stubborn and vigilant; and the federal agents and municipal vice squads (supported by church leaders and citizens' groups like the CDL) became more deliberate and exacting in their methods of marshaling provable evidence against the purveyors of sex, knowing that the latter's well-paid attorneys would probably appeal each lower court conviction to a higher court, and, if necessary, up to the Supreme Court in the hope of gaining a reversal on the basis of some legal technicality, or some inventive interpretation of the malleable wording of the flexible definition of the crime of obscenity.

Thus the Post Office Department bolstered its efforts against the pornographers by increasing its number of inspectors and "decoy" letter writers—postal employees who, using false names and addresses, answered ads for hard-core sexual material in an attempt to trap the pornographers into violating the Comstock law that prohibits the sending of obscenity through the mail. One postal inspector, the dean of decoys named Harry Simon, used dozens of pseudonyms (impersonating shy bachelors, aging widowers, college boys, small-town farmers) in his hundreds of letters of request to the mail-order distributors of hard-core photographs, "marital aids," and kinky books. Many of these letters, which would be mailed from different sections of the country by Simon's confederates, would list as a return address a post office box located in a conservative community in which there were illiberal judges and right-minded, puritanical citizens from which a jury would be drawn—thereby allowing the federal prosecutors to take advantage of the congressional amendment of 1958 that could force a sexual merchandiser to stand trial in any town where his material had been received. A long trial lasting a few months in a distant city could financially jeopardize and maybe bankrupt a sex merchant, even if the government's case was weak, because the merchant was deprived of operating the business that was his source of income and was subjected to the mounting legal fees and travel costs of the attorneys who lived with him and dined at his expense in hotels, to say nothing of the expenses incurred by any of his employees who had been forced to stand trial with him.

Congressmen were kept apprised of the spreading pornography through abundant mail from moral societies and private individuals who complained that their neighborhood drugstores and newsstands were being littered with trashy literature that had no redeeming value whatsoever; and much disparaging mail was also sent to the Supreme Court, which was particularly the target of right-wing Americans because of the Court's permissive rulings with regard to free expression and individual liberties and its seeming disregard for the traditions of conservative families and church groups. During the era of Earl Warren as Chief Justice, which began in 1953, the Court had been vilified by various factions for having outlawed compulsory religious exercises in public schools, for desegregating schools, for curbing wiretapping, for liberalizing residency requirements for welfare recipients while in jail, for denying law-enforcement authorities "unreasonable" searches and seizures, for sustaining the right to disseminate and receive birth control information. On the issue of free speech and sexual expression, no justice received more scornful mail than the Court's most doctrinaire civil libertarian, William O. Douglas.

As Justice Douglas opened and read these letters, a number of which were signed by students, he often recognized a precise similarity in phrases and even punctuation, causing him to conclude that the letters were copied off the blackboards of schools or churches. While most of the letters attacked his legal decisions, a few also criticized his private life and many marriages.

In 1963, while in his mid-sixties, Justice Douglas took as his third wife a woman in her twenties. Three years later, he would marry again—to another bride in her twenties. In the long history of the Supreme Court, beginning in 1789, there had only been three divorces involving justices. All three were the divorces of Justice Douglas.

Since joining the Court in 1939 on the recommendation of President Roosevelt, William O. Douglas had symbolized the cause of individualism against the force of authoritarianism. "The Constitution," he once wrote, "was designed to keep Government off the backs of the people." The enmity that Justice Douglas generated in conservative quarters led to three futile efforts by his adversaries to impeach him. The first occurred in 1953 when, during the anti-Communist hysteria inspired by the witch-hunt of Senator Joseph McCarthy, Douglas issued a stay of execution in behalf of the accused Soviet spies Julius and Ethel Rosenberg—who nonetheless died later that year in the electric chair. The second call for Douglas' ouster followed his third divorce; and another attempt to remove him ensued after the publication of his book *Points of Rebellion*—which, as described in the impeachment resolution of the House minority leader, Gerald Ford, was an invitation to "violence, anarchy and civil unrest." When an excerpt from Douglas' book appeared in Grove Press' *Evergreen Review*, an untimid literary monthly often adorned by erotic illustrations and stories, Gerald Ford stood in the halls of Congress brandishing the *Evergreen* issue that contained Douglas' excerpt; and the resolution also alleged that Justice Douglas had accepted funds from improper sources—charges that in both instances were proved to be false after an investigation directed by a House subcommittee. As Senator William Langer of North Dakota once remarked to the Supreme Court's most controversial Justice: "Douglas, they have thrown several buckets of shit over you—but by God, none of it stuck."

It was equally true that all the impeachment threats and vituperative letters that he received failed to diminish Douglas' commitment to a free press and tolerance of sexual expression even when it *did* lack identifiable redeeming importance. "Whatever obscenity is," Justice Douglas once observed, "it is immeasurable as a crime and delineable only as a sin. As a sin, it is present only in the minds of some and not in the minds of others, and is entirely too subjective for legal sanction." In his

view, the task of properly censoring what is sexually improper
is beyond the wisdom and understanding of the moral societies,
the police, the postmasters, the clergymen, the juries, and the
judges—including the nine honorable sages of law who sat on
the loftiest bench in the land. "With all respect," he wrote of
his Supreme Court colleagues, "I do not know of any group in
the country less qualified first, to know what obscenity is when
they see it, and second, to have any considered judgment as to
what the deleterious or beneficial impact of a particular publication may be on minds either young or old."

But despite Douglas' low estimation of his fellow jurists' erotic
perceptions, and his wish that the courts and the constables stay
away from the nation's keyholes and direct their attention to
what should truly be the legal concern of the state, the Supreme
Court nevertheless continued throughout the 1960s to scrutinize
the sources of fantasy and pleasure of American citizens; and in
two unusual cases, the High Court uncharacteristically decided
that the publishers of sex books were so socially unredemptive
that the two men on trial deserved nothing less than to go to jail.

One of these men was named Edward Mishkin. His case—
Mishkin v. *the State of New York*—was heard by the Court on
the same December day in 1965 that it listened to the argument
of *Memoirs* v. *Massachusetts*; but Mishkin's situation was entirely different from the one that would free the ancient tale of
Fanny Hill. Mishkin had been arrested and convicted in New
York, fined $12,000, and sentenced to three years in prison for
manufacturing, selling, and grossly advertising several pulp paperback novels that seemed to be less obsessed with heterosexual activity than with sadomasochism, fetishism, and other
presumed deviations. When Mishkin's attorneys appealed the
conviction to the Supreme Court, they offered a unique argument that they hoped would liberate their client: They conceded
that Mishkin's books might *be* devoid of redeeming value, and
might even disgust and sicken the average adult reader; but these
books were *not* written for, and certainly did *not* arouse the
prurient interest of, the *average* reader. And thus under the specific definition of obscenity, which required that the average
reader be made vulnerable to arousing imagery, Mishkin's bizarre books could not be classified as obscene.

But this logic failed in the final analysis to impress a sufficient
number of justices to be of benefit to Mishkin. While Justice
Douglas, Potter Stewart, and Hugo Black voted to overturn the
Miskhin sentence on First Amendment grounds (Justice Black,

like Douglas, insisted that the government had no jurisdiction over the nation's printing presses, no matter what kind of immoral or deviant literature the presses produced), the six other Justices felt that the lower-court conviction against Mishkin had been justified and they did not void his fine or prison term.

The second individual to appeal to the Supreme Court at this time was also a New Yorker—Ralph Ginzburg, publisher of a magazine called *Eros*, a book entitled *The Housewife's Handbook on Selective Promiscuity*, and a biweekly newsletter called *Liaison*. The magazine *Eros*, which had provoked the indictment against Ginzburg on charges that he had violated the Comstock postal act, was actually more titillating than sexually obscene: Its color photographs of people did not show genitalia or pubic hair; its articles did not blatantly appeal to prurient interest, and its elegant graphics, its heavy paper, and hard cover marked it as a magazine of uncommon design and quality. A quarterly, it was sold by mail subscription at the rate of $25 per year; and during its first year of publication its pages featured such material as Guy de Maupassant's short story "Madame Tellier's Brothel," illustrated by Edgar Degas; color reproductions of classical nude paintings that can be seen in major museums; and lustful selections from the Bible, embellished by woodcuts of Old Testament figures. There was also an article by psychologist Albert Ellis entitled "A Plea for Polygamy"; another article by Phyllis and Eberhard Kronhausen called "The Natural Superiority of Women as Eroticists"; a reprint of Mark Twain's once-controversial essay "1601"; examples of Shakespeare's poetry that were interpreted to suggest that he was a homosexual; photographs of male prostitutes in Bombay; and a story about the infamous Nan Britton, who caused a national scandal in the early 1920s after claiming that she was the mother of an illegitimate child sired by the President of the United States, Warren G. Harding.

In the fourth issue of *Eros*, mailed out to subscribers during the winter of 1962, there was included a feature that Ginzburg called "Black & White in Color," a series of photographs showing a muscular nude black man intimately engaged with an attractive nude white woman; and while none of the sixteen pictures focused on the genitalia, the couple were clearly depicted as lovers. In some pictures they were seen kissing; in others they were stroking one another and lying side by side; and, in perhaps the most striking picture, they were standing face to face with their arms clasped around one another's backs, their thighs and pelvises firmly in contact, their bodies so tightly together that the woman's left breast was pressed flat against the hard chest of the black man. In the introduction to these pictures, which *Eros* called a "photographic tone poem," it was stated—in deference to the law's "redeeming social value" aspect—that the couple were dedicated to "the conviction that love between a man and a woman, no matter what their races, is beautiful"; and, the text continued: "Interracial couples of today bear the indignity of having to defend their love to a questioning world. Tomorrow these couples will be recognized as the pioneers of an enlightened age in which prejudice will be dead and the only race will be the human race."

When the United States Attorney General, Robert F. Kennedy, first became aware of these pictures, he was reportedly enraged. While many of Kennedy's closest friends and associates believed that he was not a puritanical or monogamous man in his personal life, he was known to be as righteous as J. Edgar Hoover on the subject of pornography for the mass public; and, according to the book *Kennedy Justice*, by Victor S. Navasky, Kennedy had contemplated censoring *Eros* and other sexual publications even before he had seen the pictures of the interracial couple. But, as it was explained to Navasky by Kennedy's deputy in the Justice Department, Nicholas deB. Katzenbach, Kennedy was concerned that such interference might be politically interpreted as a sign of his prejudicial allegiance to Catholicism. The fourth issue of *Eros* with its interracial couple, however, was advertised and circulated throughout the nation, including the Deep South, at a time when there was rioting and tension because of the enforced desegregation of the University of Mississippi and the presence of its first black student, a determined young man named James Meredith. Believing that the *Eros* pictures might have a negative effect on civil rights progress in the South, Kennedy moved quickly to indict Ginzburg, charging him with sending obscenity through the mail.

The criminal proceedings against Ginzburg were arranged so that he would be forced to stand trial in Philadelphia, a city in which the mayor and the police were racially reactionary and strongly disposed to antipornography law enforcement, and where much sexual literature had recently been burned on the steps of a church in a ceremony attended by the Philadelphia superintendent of schools, and at which a chorus of young boys, as the books withered in the heat, sang "Gloria in Excelsis.'' Prior to Ginzburg's trial, a Philadelphia resident wrote in a local library journal: ''Ralph Ginzburg has about the same chance of finding justice in our [Philadelphia] courts as a Jew in the courts of Nazi Germany.''

The trial, which began in June 1963, was presided over by an austere judge who throughout the proceedings seemed embarrassed by the material placed in evidence before him; and at the conclusion of the case, during which the government summoned several witnesses to denigrate Ginzburg's literature, the judge himself declared that he had found in *Eros* ''not the slightest redeeming social, artistic or literary importance or value,'' and he had no higher opinion of the newsletter *Liaison* or *The Housewife's Handbook on Selective Promiscuity*. About the *Handbook*, which was an autobiographical account of a female author's various marriages and infidelities, the judge concluded that it was ''extremely boring, disgusting and shocking to this Court, as well as to an average reader.''

But what was decisive in the final disposition of Ginzburg's case was the testimony in court of two small-town postmasters who recalled that they had received letters from Ginzburg's New York office requesting permission to mail Ginzburg's literature and advertising circulars from their post offices, both of which were located in Pennsylvania Dutch communities having sexually suggestive names. One community was called Blue Ball; the other, Intercourse. After the postmasters had denied the request, explaining that their postal facilities were too small to handle such a large volume of mail, Ginzburg contacted the post office in Middlesex, New Jersey; and after receiving permission from that postmaster, Ginzburg and his staff proceeded to send out from Middlesex *millions* of circulars soliciting subscriptions to *Eros* and his other products—it was a stupendously indiscriminate list of names partly drawn from phone books, and while many recipients responded favorably to Ginzburg's message, many others did not, especially those sexually modest parents whose children had inadvertently opened the mail and read the pitchman's enticing prose promising erotic literary fulfillment. Some of the advertising circulars and the full-page newspaper ads in metropolitan dailies that heralded *Eros* even attributed the magazine's origin to the permissive policies of the United States Supreme Court: ''*Eros* is the result of recent court decisions that have realistically interpreted America's obscenity laws that have given this country a new breath of freedom of expression. We refer to decisions which have enabled the publication of such heretofore suppressed literary masterpieces as 'Lady Chatterley's Lover.' '' While some of Ralph Ginzburg's defenders in Philadelphia thought that he had been unwise in including the Supreme Court in his *Eros* advertisements, and also believed that his idea of sending mail from Middlesex had been a very bad joke, they were nonetheless astonished after the Philadelphia judge had announced the verdict: Ginzburg had been found guilty of defiling the mails with obscenity, was fined $42,000, and was directed to serve five years in prison.

Overwhelmed by the severity of the punishment, Ginzburg and his attorneys immediately filed papers with the Federal Court of Appeals in the Third Circuit, which was also located in Philadelphia; but they were notified eleven months later that their appeal had been denied, and the seventy-two-year-old federal judge who wrote the opinion affirming Ginzburg's conviction announced: ''What confronts us is a *sui generis* operation on the part of experts in the shoddy business of pandering to and exploiting for money one of the greatest weaknesses of mankind. . . .''

Finally in December 1965 the case of *Ginzburg* v. *United States* was heard by the Supreme Court; and among the partisans in the hearing was Charles Keating of the CDL, who had filed with the court an *amicus* brief supporting the government prosecutors and urging that the federal law against obscenity be strictly enforced. Ginzburg's defense continued to be, as it had been in Philadelphia, that *Eros* and his other material were neither prurient, nor patently offensive, nor utterly without redeeming social value. Indeed, in the three years that had passed since the Kennedy indictment, Ginzburg had seen Hugh Hefner and several other publishers far exceed him in sexual candor, without being prosecuted; and Ginzburg was confident that in Washington, unlike in Philadelphia, the law would be interpreted with objectivity and fairness, and that surely his conviction would be reversed.

After the Supreme Court had heard the oral argument of Ginzburg's principal attorney, and also the position of the spokesman for the government, it put the case aside for weeks of deliberation; and three months later, when it handed down its opinion, Ginzburg learned that the Court had ignored the question of whether or not *Eros*, *Liaison*, and the *Handbook* were obscene. Instead, the Court dwelled on Ginzburg's advertising campaigns; and in a five-to-four vote, Ginzburg was found culpable of the hitherto unenforced crime of ''pandering'' in the mail—

and by the slim margin of one vote, Ralph Ginzburg's jail term and $42,000 fine were ruled valid and proper.

Justice Brennan, who wrote the majority opinion, and read it with an air of churlishness that surprised the attorneys and other observers in his audience, noted that "the leer of the sensualist" had permeated Ginzburg's advertising, and Brennan left no doubt that he was angered by Ginzburg's exploitative use of the post office in Middlesex, and the temerity with which Ginzburg had associated the Supreme Court with full-page ads celebrating *Eros*. The liberal Court during the last decade had been blamed for fomenting many things in America, but one thing that Justice Brennan would not allow the court to be blamed for was *Eros* magazine; and no matter whether it was legally obscene or not, Brennan found Ginzburg guilty "of the sordid business of pandering—'the business of purveying textual or graphic matter openly advertised to appeal to the erotic interest of their customers' "; and Brennan added, as a warning to other publishers: "Where the purveyor's sole emphasis is on the sexually provocative aspects of his publications, that fact may be decisive in the determination of obscenity."

Among the four dissenting justices—William Douglas, Potter Stewart, Hugo Black, and John Harlan—Justice Douglas wrote the most articulate opinion in defense of Ginzburg's advertising techniques. "The advertisements of our best magazines," Douglas pointed out, "are chock-full of thighs, ankles, calves, bosoms, eyes, and hair, to draw the potential buyers' attention to lotions, tires, food, liquor, clothing, autos, and even insurance policies. The sexy advertisement neither adds to nor detracts from the quality of the merchandise being offered for sale. And I do not see how it adds to or detracts one whit from the legality of the book being distributed. A book should stand on its own, irrespective of the reasons why it was written or the wiles used in selling it."

Adroit legal maneuverings and endless delays by Ginzburg's attorneys managed to keep him free on bail for years, and eventually they did prevail upon the judicial system to reduce Ginzburg's jail term from five to three years; but inevitably the day arrived when he was forced to deliver himself into the care of federal marshals, in the penal city of Lewisburg, Pennsylvania, where less than two decades before the government had incarcerated such circulators of words and ideas as Wilhelm Reich and Samuel Roth. After Ginzburg had made a final sidewalk speech to the press in Lewisburg deploring his circumstances, and had crumpled a parchment copy of the Bill of Rights and tossed it into a wastebasket at the curb, he turned toward the federal office building in which he was to formally surrender. Later he was seen by reporters walking out of the building wearing handcuffs, linked to a black prisoner convicted of bank robbery and manslaughter, and escorted by federal marshals to a vehicle that would transport him miles away toward the walls and steel gate where a warden was waiting.

The Supreme Court continued to hear the appeals of new violators of old moral questions; and a year after the Ginzburg issue had been disposed of, the Court dealt with a literary outlaw who was neither a publisher, distributor, editor, nor writer. He was a man who had worked as a Times Square newsstand vendor, an unfortunate man who during an afternoon in 1966 had sold two paperbacks—entitled *Lust Pool* and *Shame Agent*—to a customer who also happened to be a plainclothes policeman. The vendor, Robert Redrup, had neither read nor even heard of the paperbacks until the plainclothesman had requested them. In fact, Redrup was not even a regular employee of the newsstand; he had just been filling in that day for another man, an acquaintance, who had taken the day off due to illness. But such circumstances were of no interest to the policeman who, after flashing his badge, took the haggard Robert Redrup into custody, where he was fingerprinted, berated by detectives, and charged with having violated Section 1141 of the Penal Law of the State of New York, which prohibits the sale of any "obscene, lewd and indecent book."

Redrup's bail and legal defense were the responsibility of the publisher of *Lust Pool* and *Shame Agent*, William Hamling of San Diego. And although Hamling had just spent more than $300,000 during a two-month obscenity trial in Houston—in which a twenty-five-count indictment against him and several of his books was subsequently dismissed after a hung-jury verdict—Hamling unhesitatingly committed himself to Redrup's defense, which would extend through the appeals route in New York and finally up to the United States Supreme Court. Defending the two seventy-five-cent paperbacks and their Times Square vendor would cost Hamling $100,000; but he considered it money well spent when, in May 1967, seven justices ruled in his favor, freeing Redrup and ruling that the two salacious paperbacks were not legally obscene. It was a *per curiam* decision, one that did not bear the written opinion of the justices; but the

Redrup case would soon be celebrated by sex publishers as the most liberal ruling yet reached by the Court—for if *Lust Pool* and *Shame Agent* were not obscene, hardly *any* book could be called obscene. These paperbacks were as unredeeming as anything that the convicted Edward Mishkin had previously published, and they were beyond the sexual scope of the material for which Ginzburg had been indicted. The *Redrup* ruling was thus interpreted by First Amendment attorneys and legal scholars as signifying the virtual end of book censorship in America. As long as a book was not advertised in the "pandering" manner of Ginzburg, and was not otherwise foisted upon an unwilling public or sold to a minor, it had the Court's permission to exist and be sold to whoever wished to read it, no matter how erotic, emetic, or unredeeming its contents.

Hamling was ecstatic. As he saw it, the courtroom battle that had begun more than thirty years before in the case of *United States* v. *One Book Called Ulysses*, resulting in a victory for the literary elite, had now ended in 1967 with a triumph for the man in the street. It was no longer necessary for a sexually explicit book to justify itself as a Joycean masterpiece, or even as a novel of redeeming value like *Lady Chatterley's Lover*; now, in *Redrup*, the Supreme Court finally seemed to be relinquishing its role as the nation's literary arbitrator, a task for which it admittedly had neither the time nor talent, and the ramifications were awesome. It suggested that *any* book, a trashy book, a volume of words replete with the most angry expletives and scatological ravings of the least talented novelist in the land, might be published and sold no matter what a policeman thought of it, or a clergyman thought of it, or the CDL thought of it. It meant that the paperback novel *Sex Life of a Cop*, distributed by a California publisher in Fresno named Sanford E. Aday— and prosecuted by the government in Michigan, Iowa, Texas, Arizona, and Hawaii—was now legal, because of the *Redrup* decision.

Nearly thirty other obscenity cases on the Court's 1967 docket were similarly overturned with just one word stamped on each petition—*Redrup*. It also meant that a distinguished publishing firm in New York, Random House, would be able in 1968 to distribute without censorship threats and enormous legal fees the autoerotic novel by Philip Roth, *Portnoy's Complaint*. Hamling now saw the frontiers of free expression in America as not being extended by the literary establishment in New York, but rather by *déclassé* California publishers like himself and Milton

Luros and Sanford Aday—men who spent fortunes in court each year fighting the convictions of city vice squads, federal agents, and southern sheriffs in the Bible Belt, and in so doing they opened up the territory that would later be explored more easily and no less profitably by the reputable publishers of a Philip Roth or Norman Mailer, a William Styron or John Updike.

Hamling's satisfaction with the *Redrup* ruling was quickly counterbalanced by a nationwide backlash sponsored by such groups as the CDL, which besieged Congress and President Johnson with thousands of letters and telegrams protesting the sexual permissiveness of the Earl Warren Supreme Court; and it was in reaction to this protest that two congressmen and honorary CDL members—Senator Karl E. Mundt of South Dakota and Representative Dominick V. Daniels of New Jersey—introduced the legislation that formed the Presidential Commission on Obscenity and Pornography, and ordered it to examine, among other things, "the effect of obscenity and pornography upon the public, and particularly minors, and its relationship to crime and other antisocial behavior." The ACLU and other liberal elements were initially opposed to the formation of the commission, knowing that no liberal congressman would risk his career with the voters by openly defending "smut," and also believing that the commission would inevitably become the tool of the political Right wishing to justify its censorious ambitions in the name of "morality."

And thus the commission's conclusions delivered two years later—the report that Father Morton Hill would denounce as "a Magna Carta for the pornographer"—would pleasantly surprise First Amendment absolutists as much as it would alarm the CDL; and the resultant furor would only be escalated by Hamling's decision to later publish and distribute his Illustrated Report adorned by dozens of orgiastic pictures and drawings. This was the most brazen act of Hamling's career, and among the many people who were upset by his decision was his old friend Hugh Hefner. Hamling first became aware of Hefner's feelings after *Playboy* had refused Hamling's request to publicize the Illustrated Report in *Playboy*'s book-review column, a rejection that was explained in a letter sent to Hamling's editorial director, Earl Kemp, by Hefner's managing editor, Nat Lehrman. Of the Illustrated Report, Lehrman wrote:

Personally, I find it very enlightening, but do not see any opportunity for reviewing it in *Playboy*. . . . We can't write a review which simply congratulates [your firm] for its ingenuity in putting together a great deal of hardcore pornography with a text about its harmlessness. Man, talk about "redeeming social value." I suppose if that Supreme Court guideline ever falls by the wayside, your version of the President's report will be responsible for it.

Indeed, I'm quite sad about what you all have done. The President's report is one of the most important documents ever to be published in the censorship area. It's under tremendous assault and you guys are going to boost the wahoos' case by giving the impression that the government provided the pictures for your text. Do you think the Nixon Administration will sit for that?

In any case . . . I think your ingenuity is going to contribute to your downfall. You ought to have Hamling read up on the Greek concept of *hubris*.

When Hamling was shown Lehrman's letter, he felt betrayed; and he suddenly saw *Playboy* and Hefner as cowardly and hypocritical. Hefner, having made his fortune in the sex industry, now seemed to have become conservative and defensive, perhaps reacting to the fact that Nixon was now in the White House and the antiobscenity campaigns were being endorsed on the editorial pages of most metropolitan daily newspapers. In a letter to Hefner, Hamling wrote:

Whether or not *Playboy* reviews our book is irrelevant, indeed inconsequential. What is relevant, although equally inconsequential, is the impertinent, not to say hubristically insolent attitude [Lehrman] purveys. Since the man holds a titular editorial position, I can only conclude that he speaks for management in his thinking. And since management is you then the records should be set straight for his edification through proper channels.

The Supreme Court guidelines so casually mentioned—and most emphatically established in the early and mid sixties—were, in fact, largely established in decisions on cases our companies brought before the Court. Your junior-style editor was not around when the battle was being fought. He certainly was not present that night in my Evanston home back in '53 when I told you and your lovely wife, Millie, that you couldn't sell sex to the American public. A classic error in judgment before *Playboy* was born, but at the time in keeping with the commercial mores. You fought the battle then, and yet even then *Playboy* was condemned by the post office as an obscene publication and refused a second-class mailing permit until mid '57 when I won a second-class mailing entry for my magazine, *Rogue*, through the Federal Court in Washington, and *Playboy* was granted its own entry without a court fight shortly thereafter, and as a result.

It would appear that somehow your staff feels it sits on some self-attained Olympian height when the fact is that others, and our efforts in particular, materially changed the legal atmosphere through an application of guts and perseverance. What would Mr. Lehrman know about "redeeming social value"? Has he ever sat in a Federal Courtroom where the point was being determined? I have, as you well know. . . .

As to the Report itself, I hardly need Lehrman to inform my company of its importance. . . . Of course the Report is important. Having been a part of it I know, and for that very reason we published it. Far from the pussy-footing facade Lehrman represents we tell it loud and clear. But then that's why freedom of speech and expression are what they are today. Because for some fifteen years my firms' positions have been bold and straight-forward. Where does Lehrman think *Playboy* was spawned—in the namby-pamby conservatism of an *Esquire* back room? . . . Doesn't the guy know you worked in von Rosen's sex-oriented publishing firm at that time (Publishers Development Corporation) and that *Playboy* came out of *that* association?

So please straighten your junior employee out on the matter of the book review. When you personally requested copies from me I sent them, feeling your interest was sincere in the project, realizing its importance in the culture and the controversy it would undoubtedly create. The Report is another milestone on the road to intellectual freedom. We've paved a lot of the road. This is one of the important stones. But we don't need your assistance. We never did. I simply thought at long last you were ready to use some of the leadership your circulation warrants. Sorry I misread you. It won't happen again.

Hugh Hefner did not reply, but among the responses that Hamling would soon receive after distributing his Illustrated Report around the country was a federal indictment brought against him in Dallas and San Diego by the United States Attorney General, John N. Mitchell. Hamling and three members of his staff in San Diego were charged with circulating and selling an "unauthorized" edition of the Presidential Commission Report on Obscenity and Pornography, and depicting the work with sexually obscene pictures.

Within a week of Mitchell's announcement, Hamling bought a full-page ad in the Los Angeles *Times* and the two San Diego dailies in which he criticized Mitchell's act as a "thinly veiled political move" by the Nixon Administration to divert the American public's attention to the "Pornography Menace" and away from "problems like: unemployment, hunger, poverty, growing urban blight, education, crushing taxation and undeclared wars far from home. The taxpayers' money," the ad continued, "should not be wasted on policing the thoughts and reading habits of the American people nor should citizens be punished for criticizing official action. The valuable time of the courts should not be wasted with such matters. The Attorney General, and the Administration, should devote their time and attention to the pressing problems of the day."

Although the government's legal proceedings against Hamling began conveniently in his home city, sparing him the extra expense of starting with a trial in Dallas—where the FBI had purchased his illustrated book—the federal judge Hamling faced in San Diego, Gordon Thompson, had been a recent Nixon appointee; and even before the trial began Hamling felt that he was deeply ensconced in unsympathetic circumstances. First, Judge Thompson denied the defense attorney's request for a one-month trial delay which would have allowed the court's master wheel, from which jurors' names are drawn, to include a recently compiled list of newly registered young voters who might be more sexually tolerant than the older names contained in the wheel that had been unrejuvenated for three years. Then the judge overruled the defense attorney's suggestion that each prospective juror be asked such questions as: "Are you a member of the CDL?"; "Do you consider yourself deeply religious?"; "Have you recently heard a sermon at your place of worship dealing with the subject of obscenity?"

When the trial began in October 1971, it was with a relatively senior jury of nine men and three women; and, to Hamling's discomfort, one of the first government witnesses was a strong CDL sympathizer and a contributor to Keating's minority report, Dr. Melvin Anchell, who denounced Hamling's illustrated book and brochure as examples of worthless "pruriency." The San Diego newspapers covering the trial were equally unimpressed with Hamling's illustrated book, referring to it as the "Smut Report"; and the word "smut" appeared repeatedly in the daily headlines: "Smut Case Snags over Conspiracy Facts"; "Judge Bans Reading of Smut Report"; "3 Experts Testify in Smut Trial." In addition, the San Diego editors gave more newspaper space to the testimony of government witnesses than to the witnesses for the defense; and also disturbing to the defense was Judge Thompson's decision to exclude the testimony of one of Hamling's most supportive witnesses—a young woman who had recently completed a survey in San Diego in which, after showing 718 citizens a copy of Hamling's erotic brochure, she discovered that a substantial majority of them thought the public should not be prohibited from seeing it. The judge dismissed the survey as irrelevant because, since Hamling was on trial for a federal offense—contaminating the mail—the evidence had to relate to the sexual standards of the nation as a whole, rather than merely to the standards of San Diego.

The trial, which lasted more than two months, ended in December 1971, and the jury experienced much difficulty in reaching a verdict. While the illustrations in Hamling's book could not have been more sexually explicit to the jury, the members conceded among themselves that the pictures accurately portrayed what the Presidential Report was about; and the words in Hamling's book consisted almost entirely of the hardly obscene prose and statistics of the commission. The jury was less forgiving, however, of the more than 55,000 advertising brochures that Hamling had mailed. While the brochure reprinted a sampling of the hard-core illustrations that were in the book, it did not include any verbatim excerpts from the commission's text, devoting editorial space instead to an attack on President Nixon for having rejected the commission's recommendations; and this combination had so offended at least a dozen citizens who had received it unsolicited in their mail that they each registered an official complaint with the Post Office. And so after six days of private debate and argument, the jury decided that the brochure, if not the book, was probably obscene; and on the basis of this conclusion Judge Thompson summoned William Hamling before the bench in February 1972 to sentence him somberly to four years in prison and fines totaling $87,000. Hamling's chief editor, Earl Kemp, received a three-year prison term, while two subordinate employees were given suspended sentences and placed on probation for five years.

Hamling was stunned and embittered by the sentencing, but as he gained a conditional freedom on bail he was not completely dejected. He and his attorneys intended to take the case to the Court of Appeals for the Ninth Circuit in California; and, failing there, they would go to the United States Supreme Court, where Hamling's books had been successful in the past.

In June 1973 the Court of Appeals made public its opinion of Hamling; siding with the lower court ruling, it affirmed Hamling's guilt. Two weeks later, however, as Hamling's attorneys were preparing petitions for delivery to the Supreme Court, Hamling received news that he considered more ominous than anything he had heard during all his years in publishing: The Supreme Court had suddenly altered its definition of obscenity in a way that portended gloom for pornographers. In a surprising five-to-four decision largely dictated by the four Nixon appointees—Burger, Blackmun, Powell, Rehnquist; plus Justice White, a Kennedy appointee—the High Court had expeditiously removed from the language of the law the "utterly without redeeming social value" phrase that had long been the favorite loophole for sexual expressionists. As a result of the new law, made public on June 21, 1973, any prosecutor wishing to ban a sexual work no longer had to prove that it was "utterly without" value; it merely had to be lacking in "serious literary, artistic, political or scientific value" to be considered obscene. All the liberal trends of recent years—*Redrup* v. *New York*; *Memoirs* v. *Massachusetts*; *Jacobellis* v. *Ohio*—were now superseded by the new opinion written by Chief Justice Warren Burger; and the case that prompted him and his conservative colleagues to toughen the obscenity law involved a pornographer who had been cited for circulating obscene advertising brochures through the mail.

The convicted pornographer was Marvin Miller of Los Angeles, a man that William Hamling knew well by reputation. Miller had made millions in recent years through the distribution of X-rated home movies, hard-core photo magazines, and pornographic paperbacks; and, like so many other Americans who had been accused of scandalous publishing and trading—like Hamling, Hefner, and Barney Rosset of Grove Press; like David S. Alberts, a convicted Los Angeles mail-order merchandiser, and Ed Lange, a Los Angeles nudist park owner who had been the principal photographer of history's most photographed nude woman, Diane Webber—Marvin Miller had been born and reared in the city of Chicago. It was as if that strongly Irish-Catholic town was destined to produce sexually obsessed native sons, most of whom would eventually exile themselves into more liberal surroundings. Chicago was America's Dublin.

Marvin Miller was the son of a Chicago cabdriver who had died months before Marvin's birth in 1929. After living with his impoverished Russian immigrant mother on welfare for five years, Marvin Miller was arrested at the age of six for breaking into a bakery shop, and was committed to the care of a Jewish juvenile agency. Most of Miller's adolescence was thereafter spent in foster homes and state-operated boarding schools, where his supervisors invariably recognized his superior intelligence, his restless ambition, and—as would be noted years later in a parole report—his "flair for fast business deals."

After dropping out of the University of Chicago during his freshman year, Miller worked variously as a bulk dealer in used silver foil, a salesman of wall-to-wall carpeting, an operator of dry-cleaning plants, a stockbroker, and a manager of a towel and linen supply firm in Los Angeles, where, during the early 1950s, he was convicted in court of falsifying the corporate records and bilking the company of more than $35,000. For these and other offenses, including allegations of arson, Miller would become a frequenter of California prisons, where his behavior was always exemplary but where he would be regarded by penal counselors as a born hustler, a man with a certain charm but also a limited sense of how the social system worked, and even less awareness of what might get him trouble.

Following his release from prison in 1961, he in time gained notoriety in Los Angeles pornographic circles as a literary pirate, a distinction he first earned after privately copying and publishing in serialized form the Victorian classic *My Secret Life*, for which Grove Press in New York had just paid $50,000 to a German collector in acquiring what it assumed to be the exclusive American publishing rights. But Miller, without a word to anyone, serialized the work in ten separate issues of a magazine, selling each copy for $1.25 on the newsstands. When Grove's Barney Rosset brought suit against Miller for infringement, a California judge found himself in the peculiar position of having to settle a dispute between two men both of whom he would have liked to send to jail. But since *My Secret Life* had indisputably been in the public (albeit illegal) domain long before Grove Press had decided in the wake of the *Roth* ruling to release it as an expensive two-volume edition, Miller was technically protected from Grove's litigation; and the only way that Rosset could stop Miller from continuing to print extra issues of the magazines was to pay Miller a substantial sum out of court, which is what Rosset unhappily did.

Marvin Miller's brief good fortune would change when he started sending through the mail thousands of advertising brochures calling attention to several items he wished to sell. Among them was a $3.25 paperback picture book of nude male models called *I, a Homosexual*; a large-sized $10 picture book entitled *The Name Is Bonnie*, which promised twenty-four evocative color photographs of a nude blond woman; another $10 picture book, *Africa's Black Sexual Power*, featuring a dark-skinned couple in congress; a $15 volume, *An Illustrated History of Pornography*, which consisted of 150 reproductions of erotic art works, including some from the classic collections of Somerset Maugham and King Farouk; and an X-rated 8 mm film called *Marital Intercourse* that was available for $50.

The names of the people who received Miller's brochures had been supplied by a Los Angeles mailing-list brokerage—a company that specializes in compiling lists of mail-order customers whose names are grouped according to the type of merchandise they have ordered in the past, which might have included anything from garden supplies to antique auto parts. To safeguard his lists, the broker does not reveal the names of those with various "special interests," but rather assumes all responsibility for the addressing and mailing of the advertising material the manufacturer wishes sent, and he charges the manufacturer as much as $100 per 1,000 names for his service. Marvin Miller requested the use of nearly 300,000 names, costing him almost $30,000; and while all the names were on the broker's so-called "X and Y" list—meaning that the people had purchased "adult" merchandise in the past—there was really no way that the broker could be sure that Miller's mailings would not occasionally get into the "wrong" hands, since the sex lists of brokers throughout the nation are infiltrated by the pseudonyms of postal inspectors and spies from moral societies.

It was therefore not surprising, in retrospect, that Miller's advertising campaign would soon be followed by several complaints to the police—although, insofar as the law was concerned, it made no difference who opened the mail. Miller's material was obscene, according to the verdict of a California court, and he was found guilty of a crime for which he would later be admonished by no less than the Chief Justice of the United States Supreme Court, Warren Burger. In his historic ruling of the case of *Miller* v. *California*, Burger wrote: "Appellant conducted a mass mailing campaign to advertise the sale of illustrated books, euphemistically called 'adult' material," and Burger added in a footnote: "The material we are discussing in this case is more accurately defined as 'pornography' or 'pornographic material.' 'Pornography' derives from the Greek (*pornē*, harlot, and *graphos*, writing). The word now means '1: a description of prostitutes or prostitution. 2: a depiction (as in writing or painting) of licentiousness or lewdness: a portrayal of erotic behavior designed to cause sexual excitement.' Webster's New International Dictionary, *supra*. Pornographic material which is obscene forms a sub-group of all 'obscene' expression, but not the whole, at least as the word 'obscene' is now used in our language. We note, therefore, that the words 'obscene material,' as used in this case, have a specific judicial meaning which derives from the *Roth* case, i.e., obscene material 'which deals with sex.' "

Even before Marvin Miller's case had come before the Supreme Court, Warren Burger had long been past the point of toleration for the manner in which sex was being represented in American books and magazines, films and live shows, not only in the big cities of the East and West Coasts but also in the smaller midwestern communities of Minnesota, where Burger had been reared in a family of moral rectitude and scrupulousness. During the last year nearly every state in the nation had been infiltrated by massage parlors, topless and bottomless bars, and such films as *Deep Throat*—a sixty-two minute feature of which fifty minutes were devoted to scenes of group sex, fellatio, cunnilingus, female masturbation, anal sodomy, heterosexual intercourse, and seminal ejaculation. Not only did millions of men view the movie, but they also brought their wives and girl friends: *Deep Throat* was the first hard-core film that was seen by large numbers of couples, many of whom had been lured, through curiosity, to see this highly publicized production that had been regularly raided by vice squads across the land in a vigorous and futile attempt to completely ban the film.

But now in the case of Marvin Miller, Chief Justice Burger, together with the other Court conservatives, finally had an opportunity to express their outrage about sexual openness in

America, and to exorcise the spirit of permissiveness that had been created by their judicial predecessors during the 1960s. The days were gone when pornographers could justify their obscene works by reprinting on the flyleaf of their tawdry books a "quotation from Voltaire," Burger declared; and, enlarging on this theme, he continued: "Conduct or depictions of conduct that the state police power can prohibit on a public street does not become automatically protected by the Constitution merely because the conduct is moved to a bar or a 'live' theatre stage, any more than a 'live' performance of a man and woman locked in a sexual embrace at high noon in Times Square is protected by the Constitution because they simultaneously engage in a valid political dialogue."

The new obscenity law, Burger emphasized, also meant that what still might be legal in the cinemas and sidewalks of Times Square and Sunset Boulevard need no longer influence the way in which censorship laws were interpreted by the magistrates on Main Street or the sheriffs in the Bible Belt—for now "community standards," instead of "national standards," would predominate in all First Amendment obscenity cases. This meant, more specifically, that a magazine like *Playboy* (whose advertisers always assumed that *Playboy* would be displayed each month on small-town as well as big-city newsstands) and such major erotic art films as *Last Tango in Paris* (which, starring Marlon Brando, anticipated reaching a nationwide audience) might now find their markets checked by censorship in those cities or towns where organized groups of vigilantes could apply pressure on the local politicians and the police to uphold moral "community standards." And finally, in what was a repudiation of the findings of the Presidential Commission on Obscenity and Pornography, Chief Justice Burger wrote: "Although there is no conclusive proof of a connection between anti-social behavior and obscene material, a legislature could quite reasonably determine that such a connection does or might exist."

The Burger opinion, which commanded headlines in newspapers across the nation, was applauded most enthusiastically by congressmen representing conservative districts, and by clergymen and such crusading citizens as Charles Keating, who declared in a statement published in the *National Decency Reporter*: "For more than fifteen years, since I started CDL, the pornographers have run rough shod over the American public, engulfing this nation in a tidal wave of filth and turning her along the path of moral corruption and decay. Their reason was money.

Big money. Billions of dollars. And for money they were willing to sell their country, their fellow-citizens, and our children into the bondage of sexual debauchery. These gutter merchants wrapped their soiled merchandise in the flag of the United States, and cowered behind the Constitution. They tried to use that great document which freed men's minds and spirits as a device to enslave the men and debase the women of America. Those sordid years are now behind us. One day soon we will look back with shock and disbelief at the depths to which we allowed ourselves to be dragged in the name of 'freedom.' '' But, Keating's editorial continued, "now it is our turn. And your turn. The decent people of America, backed by the United States Supreme Court, are going to wage a holy, yes, a *holy* war against the merchants of obscenity. From this day forward I will not rest, and no one connected with CDL will rest, until every pornographer in America is out of business, in jail, or both.''

Among those who disagreed with Burger's ruling were four of his colleagues on the Court—Douglas, Stewart, Brennan, Marshall—and several metropolitan newspaper publishers who had previously supported "antismut" clean-up campaigns, having failed to recognize a direct connection between *their* First Amendment rights and the rights of sexual expressionists. The Burger ruling, the New York *Times* conceded on its editorial page, gives "license to local censors. It may, as Justice Douglas fears, unleash 'raids on libraries.' In the long run it will make every local community and every state the arbiter of acceptability, thereby adjusting all sex-related literary, artistic and entertainment production to the lowest common denominator of toleration. Police-court morality will have a heyday.''

Within days of the Burger ruling, state officials in Utah announced that *Last Tango in Paris*, which had been scheduled to open in Salt Lake City, would be prohibited; and in Hollywood, two studios that had been negotiating to film Hubert Selby's book about working-class homosexuals, *Last Exit to Brooklyn*, abruptly abandoned the project. "We don't want to produce law suits, we want to produce pictures," explained one studio executive. Jack Valenti, president of the Motion Picture Association of America, regretted that the new Court ruling "can create fifty or more fragmented opinions as to what constitutes obscenity," while other industry spokesmen predicted that the major moviemakers, and certainly everyone working in television, will now become less "adult" and more queasy when dealing with censorable subjects.

The upcoming covers of *Playboy*, *Screw*, and other sex-oriented publications were quickly modified by their art directors; and in porno bookshops across the country, customers lined up to buy great quantities of merchandise because they feared that at any moment it would be eternally banished from the shelves. "The immediate effect of this decision," Bob Guccione of *Penthouse* said, "will be to drive a multibillion-dollar industry underground—and that means graft and crime in the real sense. It's the same thing as a return to Prohibition." Linda Lovelace, the star of *Deep Throat*, was quoted in the press as saying: "The last person that started censorship was Adolf Hitler, and the next thing they'll be doing is knocking on your door and taking away your TV and your radio."

Among the novelists who expressed concern over the Burger opinion—a group that included Kurt Vonnegut, Jr., Truman Capote, and John Updike—Joyce Carol Oates saw the ruling as symptomatic of a militant society that was partly frustrated because it could no longer release its aggressions in Vietnam. "When America is not fighting a war," she explained, "the puritanical desire to punish people has to be let out at home."

William Hamling read avidly the responses of other people to the issue of obscenity; but throughout the summer of 1973, as his case moved closer in time, he wondered how specifically the new law would affect him when he took Marvin Miller's place in the great hall of justice in Washington. It had been his hope, since he had initially been sentenced by a San Diego judge on the basis of "national" instead of "community" standards—and since there were authoritative surveys showing that San Diego's standards were more liberal sexually than those of the nation as a whole—that he would have at least gained a retrial due to the *Miller* interpretation. But a petition for rehearing during 1973 and 1974 by Hamling's attorneys failed to win either a new trial or a reduction of the judge's severe sentence of four years and $87,000 in fines.

And so finally on April 15, 1974, on a windy Monday morning in Washington, together with his wife and his daughter, William Hamling climbed the white marble steps of the Supreme Court building toward the main entrance leading to the chamber where the nine eminent men would ponder the case of *Hamling* v. *United States of America*.

23

Awaiting the arrival of the justices, William Hamling sat with his wife and daughter on a mahogany pew in the sixth row of the ornate and crowded sanctuary of the Supreme Court, looking up at the high coffered ceiling, the marbeled columns, the classical statuary; and he felt, as he had decades ago during the High Masses of his Chicago boyhood, a mingling of anxiety and awe, a trembling sense of grandeur. On this morning Hamling's appeal would be heard, his destiny debated. But whether he won or lost, his name and his case, *Hamling* v. *United States of America*, would everlastingly be listed in legal texts, the doomsday books of American jurisprudence. He remained hopeful about the outcome of this hearing. He believed that the lawyer who represented him, a diminutive and crippled man whom he could barely see at the counselors' table near the front of the room, was the nation's most persuasive defender of the indefinable crime of which he was accused.

Hamling's wife, however, did not share his optimism. To Frances Hamling, a strong-willed and discerning woman visiting Washington for the first time, this trip was a meaningless excursion, an interesting spectacle to be observed by the hundreds of tourists and law students in the room, but, for her husband, a pro forma affair that would doubtless affirm the conviction already levied against him by lesser judges. Not that she considered the Supreme Court justices to be superior; they, too, were ordinary men under their magisterial robes, political appointees, biased arbitrators who had already predetermined her husband's fate, even though they had yet to appear on the raised burnished bench that loomed before her like an altar.

As a staunchly supportive wife of a much-prosecuted publisher, and as a woman who had quietly suffered through the many trials of this man who had married her as a widow in 1948, and had lovingly adopted her four young children, she deeply resented the presumption of other men to pass judgment on his moral character; and during the last year, her view of the nation's enforcers of law had become increasingly skeptical and cynical. The United States Attorney General, John N. Mitchell, who had personally had the grand jury indict her husband for distributing the Illustrated Report, was himself now indicted for his role in the Watergate scandal. Vice-President Spiro Agnew, who had seemed so sanctimonious in his condemnation of the Report in 1971, had resigned from office under pressure, following charges of graft and tax evasion. And the nation's peerless moral hypocrite, President Nixon, was now desperately cornered in his Oval Office because of his Watergate deceptions, while news reports on radio and television each day speculated on his impeachment or imprisonment.

Still, she noticed while touring the capital earlier in the week that the huge and cumbersome federal bureaucracy continued to endure and to wield its costly ways upon the tax-paying public, which was the most appalling impression she had of Washington: the sheer size of its bureaucracy, the endless gray buildings housing multitudes of employees, the traffic jams of stately limousines and government sedans transporting hither and yon untold numbers of supernumeraries and factotums who were padding the payroll and undoubtedly contributing nothing to the efficient service of American citizens.

The same seemed to be true within the Supreme Court itself. Everywhere in the building, as she and her husband walked through the corridors, they saw rooms crowded with clerks, guards, receptionists, secretaries, bookkeepers; but after arriving at the marshal's office, where Hamling's attorney had arranged for their special seating in the Court chamber, they were dismayed to learn that the marshal's staff had erroneously left their names off the list. And so instead of being assigned to sit near the front with a full view of the proceedings, they were escorted to a row in the rear half of the chamber, greatly irritating her husband, who, having already invested $400,000 in this case, believed that the courtesy of the Court should have guaranteed him on this special occasion a ringside seat to the final round of the most costly legal battle of his life.

She was also displeased by the officious manner in which the guards had frisked her, together with her daughter and husband, prior to admitting them to the chamber. First they insisted that she remove the new yellow coat, which she had bought for this occasion, and check it in the cloakroom; then they opened and searched through her leather handbag, and, after discovering that it contained a camera, they sternly reminded her that picture taking was disallowed and confiscated the camera with the instruction that she reclaim it after the hearing.

In the chamber, she sat close to her husband, trying to repress the anxiety she felt about his future. Four years in prison and $87,000 in fines were hardly matters of casual contemplation. Since nobody was supposed to speak or even whisper in the chamber, she diverted herself by glancing around at the room's opulent interior, the impressive bone-white columns and red velvet draperies that formed the background behind the polished judicial bench and high black leather chairs. A gold clock hung down from between two pillars, signaling that it was 9:57 A.M.— a few minutes before the justices' scheduled arrival. Along the upper edge of the front of the room, close to the top of the forty-four-foot ceiling, Frances noticed an interesting, voluptuous section of Classical art: It was a golden beige marble frieze that extended across the width of the room and showed about twenty nude and seminude men, women, and children gathered in various poses. The figures symbolized the embodiment of human wisdom and truth, righteousness, and virtue; but the bodies to her could as easily have represented an assemblage of Roman hedonists or orgiasts, and it struck her as ironic that such a scene should be hovering over the heads of the jurists who would be questioning her husband's use of illustrations in the Presidential Report on Obscenity and Pornography.

Abruptly, her musings were interrupted by the sharp sound of the marshal's gavel. As everyone in the room quickly stood, the Court crier began to chant: "Oyez! Oyez! Oyez! All persons having business before the Honorable Justices of the Supreme Court of the United States are admonished to draw near and give their attention. . . ." Suddenly, with a theatrical flourish, the red draperies parted and the nine black-robed men appeared between the openings in the velvet, stepped forward, and took their places, as the crier continued: "The Court is now sitting. God save the United States and this Honorable Court!"

Seated in the center, his solid florid face topped by a carefully combed head of soft lustrous white hair, was the sixty-six-year-old Chief Justice, Warren Burger. To his right, wizened and small-boned, was the most senior of the associate justices, William O. Douglas, seventy-six, a member of the Court for thirty-five years. To Burger's left was the bespectacled, balding, seventy-four-year-old William Brennan, an Eisenhower appointee in 1956 and one of six Catholics to serve on the Court during its nearly two-hundred-year history. Extending out from these aging veterans sat the other justices—a rather chunky, friendly faced Midwesterner of fifty-nine named Potter Stewart; the strong-jawed fifty-seven-year-old Byron (Whizzer) White, a onetime Rhodes scholar and star halfback who now seemed grim under a high-domed head shaped like an old-style leather football helmet; and the broad-chested, sixty-six-year-old mustachioed Thurgood Marshall, the first black man ever to serve on the Court. On the outer edge of the bench were the Nixon appointees: the tidy, horn-rimmed, thin-lipped Harry Blackmun, sixty-five; the lean, somewhat frail-looking sixty-six-year-old Virginian, Lewis Powell; and the youngest member of the Court, forty-nine-year-old William H. Rehnquist, a tall and hefty, cool-eyed conservative with slick, dark hair and long razor-edged sideburns.

In his commanding voice, Chief Justice Burger announced that the first of the two cases to be heard on this morning would be the one involving the Hollywood film *Carnal Knowledge*, which had been declared obscene in the rural city of Albany, Georgia. Frances Hamling relaxed, knowing that since the rival lawyers in the *Carnal Knowledge* case would each receive a minimum half hour to express their differing views, her husband's case would not be heard for at least another hour; and so she listened calmly and unemotionally as *Carnal Knowledge*'s legal representative, the dapper and prominent Louis Nizer, stood behind the podium and declared that the prosecution of the film was an incredible miscarriage of justice—an opinion that had already been expressed repeatedly by editorial writers around the country. Since there had been no hard-core sex scenes in the film, the arrest and conviction of the Georgia theater manager for showing it had astonished the Hollywood industry, the media, and most members of the legal profession. But because of the Supreme Court's "community standards" rule in its recent five-to-four *Miller* opinion, even a mildly erotic intellectual film could be legally challenged by a faction of prudish citizens in a small town—which is what had happened in Albany, and which was later affirmed by the highest court in Georgia, a state which restricted sexual expression between consenting adults more severely than it did the sodomitical acts of Georgia residents upon farm animals.

However, as Nizer dramatically emphasized before the Supreme Court bench, *Carnal Knowledge* was not a sexually explicit film, was not patently offensive, was not erotically arousing, nor did it show genital contact between the actors on the screen. It was, on the contrary, a serious and subtle work that should have been legally acceptable in any community in America; and it was also an artistic achievement by one of the nation's most gifted directors, Mike Nichols, an Academy Award winner. As Nizer continued to praise the film, Frances Hamling looked around the room to see if there were any famous Hollywood faces in the crowd, such as the stars of the film, Jack Nicholson and Ann-Margret. But she recognized no one; and since only attorneys are permitted to speak before the Supreme Court, there would have been no necessity for actors to be present. She did recognize in the crowd the president of the Motion Picture Association of America, Jack Valenti; and she also noticed that Valenti had managed to procure for himself a seat near the front.

As Nizer continued to speak, pausing occasionally to answer a brief question from one of the justices, Frances glanced over at her blond daughter, a college sophomore at San Diego State, who was listening intently. Deborah Hamling, the second child born of Frances' second marriage, was studying to become a nurse. Next to Deborah sat a dark-eyed young woman of nineteen who had dropped out of Bennington—Judy Fleishman, the youngest of the three daughters of the Hamling publishing company's attorney, Stanley Fleishman. Fleishman, who sat at the counselors' table, had previously appeared more than a half-dozen times before the United States Supreme Court; and it was Fleishman who had directed the successful legal strategy of the *Redrup* v. *New York* case that involved the two Hamling paperback novels purchased by a plainclothes detective in Times Square.

At fifty-four, Stanley Fleishman was recognized within his profession as a brilliant and shamelessly committed advocate of the rights of American eroticists and libertines; and after more than twenty years of arguing obscenity cases in countless courtrooms—among his chastised clientele were the exhibitors of *Deep Throat*, the publishers of Henry Miller novels, the distributors of Diane Webber photographs, and the owners of Sandstone Retreat—Fleishman took pride in the fact that none of his defendants had ever served hard time in prison.

The Sandstone litigation had been initiated by a few Los Angeles County officials and a citizens' group after John Williamson had opened his nudist estate to club membership in 1970, a decision that the prosecution charged was in violation of an antinudity ordinance first established in Los Angeles during the 1930s. But after much legal maneuvering and several hearings, Fleishman finally convinced the Intermediate Appellate Court of California that the county ordinance was unconstitutional—it was an invasion of privacy, an infringement upon the Sandstone members' legal rights of free association and assembly; and Sandstone was permitted to continue its operation without further interference.

Fleishman's defense in 1965 of a nude photograph of Diane Webber, in addition to the pictures of other California models who had been featured in magazines owned by Los Angeles publisher Milton Luros, was a more expensive trial than Sandstone's because the government insisted that the case be argued in Iowa, having proven that some of Luros' magazines and erotic paperbacks had been mailed there; and the trial in Sioux City, which lasted three months, was heard by a cranky judge and a jury that consisted almost entirely of farmers' wives. Since the trial coincided with the harvesting season, nearly all the potential male jurors succeeded in avoiding jury duty; and the ten women that Fleishman faced seemed to be a joyless gathering, blushing or frowning at his every reference to sex—and, not surprisingly, they convicted Luros of obscenity at the conclusion of the trial. But Fleishman immediately carried the case up to the Court of Appeals for the Eighth Circuit and succeeded in having the verdict against Luros overturned.

Stanley Fleishman was not a man to be discouraged by temporary setbacks. Though his small body had been ravaged and twisted by polio since childhood, he moved determinedly, with the aid of braces and crutches, into courtrooms throughout the country, overcoming handicaps that only he refused to recognize. Born in 1920 on New York's Lower East Side of immigrant Russian-Jewish parents, he was transported around the neighborhood for years by his mother in an oversized baby carriage. At five, he was enrolled in a home for crippled children in Queens, where his parents moved so that they could regularly and conveniently visit him. At the institution, despite the full-length cast that confined his body, he learned to stand and walk with crutches. He remained institutionalized for nearly ten years with forty other handicapped children and adolescents, receiving his grammar-school education there.

At fourteen, his parents transferred him to a public high school in Queens, exposing him for the first time to students who were not physically handicapped, which intensified his sense of isolation; and the daily proximity of young girls, whose healthy budding bodies he diffidently adored, sent his mind spinning at night with scenes of splendid fantasy. But the woman with whom he remained most comfortable was his mother, who was always loving and protective, if at times overbearing. His father, a humble man who worked long hours in the composing room of the New York *Daily News*, was never a forceful presence in the home, and the only influential male in Stanley's youth would be an NYU student named Bernard Hewitt, who during the 1930s began to date, and would eventually marry, Stanley's sister Florence. Assuming the role of an older brother, Hewitt often interceded in Stanley's behalf for more independence from his mother; and when Stanley turned eighteen, Hewitt convinced Mrs. Fleishman that her son should be sent to a college far from home, to a campus on which he would be free to progress as best he could without her persistent attention and concern; and Stanley, endorsing the suggestion, announced that he wanted to attend the University of Georgia.

He was aware of Georgia because it was the state in which his hero and fellow polio victim, Franklin D. Roosevelt, went to relax and swim in the miracle waters of Warm Springs. While Fleishman had no idea how far the health spa in Warm Springs was from the campus in Athens, he assumed that it would be close enough for him to enjoy frequent visits with the President; and with this image vividly in mind Stanley Fleishman hobbled up the steps of a railroad car in Pennsylvania Station in 1939 and began the long southward journey to the sound of steel wheels clacking in the night.

On the following day, he met a group of gregarious soldiers on the train who taught him how to shoot craps; and after he expressed a willingness to try his luck at their game, they proceeded to relieve him of seventy-two dollars, which was all the cash that he had in his pocket. Fortunately, on arriving at the railroad station in Athens, a university-bound vehicle was waiting to carry him to the campus; but once there he discovered that he had greatly overestimated his ability to function as an independent student. Unlike the buildings he had known in the North, the grand academic halls in Georgia did not have handrails, and it took him hours to maneuver up and down the steps. There were also no handrails affixed to the shower room in his dormitory, and he was so disoriented during his first three weeks at school that, despite the help extended to him by a few amiable but awkward students, it took him three weeks to unpack his luggage, and longer to learn how to balance himself on the slippery tiles of the bathroom.

But within the first year he began to gain confidence and a sense of liberation in being away from his mother's dominating support; and while he was only an adequate student, he passed all of his courses. In the dormitory at night, he enjoyed the rap sessions with the other freshmen, being particularly impressed by the many differing attitudes between Southerners and Northerners with regard to politics, government, and life in general. During the latter part of his first year at Georgia, he considered himself ready to make his first pilgrimage by train halfway across the state to Warm Springs, thinking that the great Liberal Democrat would graciously open the gates on learning of the arrival of a crippled student who admired him. But on reaching the entrance of the estate, which reminded him of pictures he had seen in books of southern plantations, he was confronted by tall black custodians who were gently-spoken but steadfast in informing him that "outpatients" were not accepted at the spa. When Fleishman inquired as to the whereabouts of the President, to whom he wished to make a personal appeal, he was told that Mr. Roosevelt was in Washington. Summoning the verbal skill that would later distinguish him as a lawyer, Fleishman prevailed upon the gatekeepers to permit him at least to enter the grounds, explaining that he had traveled for hours in the hope of visiting the President's renowned Little White House. Finally they agreed to give him a cursory tour and lunch—after which they put him on the next train headed back to the Georgia campus.

Much more hospitable was Stanley Fleishman's visit to an off-campus whorehouse, a place in Athens called "Effie's" that was patronized by townsmen and a few college boys. Here for the first time Fleishman experienced intercourse, an act of such wondrous satisfaction that he decided as he left the brothel that he should definitely return, which he did. During his sophomore year he became sufficiently self-assured to approach co-eds and ask them for dates; but while they seemed to enjoy accompanying him to the movies and to the local meal halls, the evenings invariably ended with the young ladies' relative virtue in no way affected.

As he was about to enter his junior year, Fleishman began to see his future in the field of law, envisioning himself as a wise counselor and artful debator whose professional fulfillment

would not be restricted by the braces and crutches that would
always be his burden. Receiving financial aid to attend Columbia University during the summer of 1941, he decided to forgo
the trip South and to reside full-time in his native New York,
while maintaining his independence from his family by living
in a campus apartment on Morningside Heights.

But after graduation from Columbia Law School in 1944, and
two years' employment as a legal associate working on probate
cases and labor disputes—and after losing his balance and often
falling during the winter on New York's icy streets as taxis and
buses swerved past his prone body—Fleishman concluded that
his destiny would be better served in a balmy, palm-lined city
of tropical climate. Leaving for Los Angeles in 1946, and passing the California bar examination a year later, he would never
regret his move to the West Coast—even though, while riding
in an automobile driven by a colleague in 1948, his body was
battered and bruised in an auto accident that hospitalized him
for nine months.

Practicing law from bed in his own behalf, he sued the driver
and collected $10,000 in damages. Fleishman also befriended
the hospital dietitian, a woman he would marry in 1949. When
the hospital refused to grant her an extra week's salary that she
insisted was long owed her, Fleishman sued the hospital—and
collected the money with interest.

Fleishman first gained professional recognition in Los Angeles during the early 1950s, the period of the Hollywood purge
of reputed Communists working in the film industry. While
Fleishman's clients did not include any of the famous names on
the Hollywood blacklist, he nonetheless was noticed and admired by other lawyers for his vigorous efforts in a number of
obscure cases involving alleged subversives. One defendant was
a screenwriter and teacher who had been arrested as a party
sympathizer and was held without bail indefinitely in a Los Angeles jail despite Fleishman's outraged protests to the judge. On
the following day, Fleishman read in the newspapers that Justice
William O. Douglas had arrived in San Francisco to attend a
conference of federal jurists of the Ninth Circuit, the western
judicial region over which Douglas presided; and although
Fleishman did not have an appointment to see Justice Douglas,
nor was he sure that it was entirely proper to privately approach
a justice of the Supreme Court, Fleishman quickly left his office
for the airport, flew to San Francisco, took a taxi to the locale
of the meeting, and waited for hours in the corridor until the

message he had sent into Douglas' conference room had been replied to—resulting in Douglas' recommendation of bail and a hearing that would free Fleishman's client from prison.

During the later 1950s, as the pornographers gradually replaced the Communists as the caitiffs of society, Fleishman sometimes worked without a fee for the opportunity to defend obscenity cases on First Amendment grounds, a legal position that in those days was as untenable to most judges as it was confusing to most pornographers, only a few of whom had ever heard of the First Amendment, and fewer still shared young Fleishman's lofty illusions about their constitutional rights. While the pornographers feared and resented imprisonment, they were, like most gamblers, quietly resigned to bad luck; and since their principal passions in life had little to do with literary freedom or even sex, and much to do with making money, their pragmatic solution to avoiding jail was in offering payoffs to the police or trying to dodge the law by constantly changing their business addresses.

But Fleishman was instrumental in altering the pornographers' thinking—not by lecturing them on the law, although he did much of that, but by proving with his achievements in court that the obscenity laws were flexible, were capable of being bent, shaped, extended to allow greater freedoms. Like the English writer Kenneth Tynan, Fleishman saw pornography as beneficial to much of mankind—it "assuages the solitude," Tynan wrote, and offers the "illusion of release" to people who are "sexually condemned to solitary confinement" or are unable for varied reasons to bring sexual variety into their lives. Since Fleishman had been on compatible terms with pornography since his college days, enjoyed looking at pictures of well-formed bodies engaged in freedoms that he could appreciate, he was a sort of surrogate-defendant in every obscenity case he argued; and there was no case too small for him to handle if it involved sex and censorship.

In Los Angeles he successfully defended a proprietor of a topless tavern; a mail-order merchant who was selling coasters showing a nude picture of Marilyn Monroe; and also the owner of a Beverly Hills store that displayed nude statuary in its window, including a replica of Michelangelo's David. Among Fleishman's major triumphs was the Supreme Court case of *Smith* v. *California* in which he argued that his client—a bookstore owner named Eleazer Smith who had been arrested for having on his shelf an obscene book called *Sweeter Than Life*—

could not be held responsible unless the police could prove that Smith was aware of the obscene nature of the book. In another Supreme Court ruling—*A Quantity of Copies of Books* v. *Kansas*—Fleishman gained from the justices rigid restrictions on the search and seizure tactics that could be employed by vice agents while raiding warehouses or bookshops. Fleishman also traveled to several states—Michigan, Iowa, Texas, Arizona, Hawaii—in defending Sanford Aday's right to publish *Sex Life of a Cop*; and once after flying through a snowstorm into Chicago, and being assisted down the slippery steps of the airplane by male traveling companions, Fleishman walked into court to argue in behalf of a cigar store merchant who had been caught selling a magazine called *Exotic Adventures*. Insisting that the description and discussion of sex should be entitled to the same legal protection as the description and discussion of religion and politics, Fleishman told the jury: "At the root of all suppression is the fear of unorthodoxy, whether in religion or politics or morals—a fear that has no place in our country"; and he added: "Only people who are afraid of sex think *Exotic Adventures* dangerous. Those with a healthy attitude toward sex may find it dull or entertaining, depending on their taste. They properly dismiss as preposterous, however, the idea that the magazine can corrupt an average person."

After deliberating for six hours, the jury voted for acquittal.

Although Stanley Fleishman had previously won all the cases involving his client William Hamling, this latest trip to Washington in mid-April 1974, in defense of Hamling's illustrated brochure, was a source of deep concern, for he now would be facing a conservative Supreme Court majority that—if it voted as it had a year ago in the *Miller* ruling—would inevitably put his client behind bars. While Fleishman was reasonably confident that his legal position in court today would be supported by Justices Douglas and Brennan, Stewart and Marshall—the four who had sided with Miller—he knew he would have trouble with the other five, whose aversion to pornography was not only evident in their past voting records but was further emphasized in newspaper articles written by such Washington correspondents as Nina Totenberg, who obviously had close sources within the Supreme Court building. Describing how the justices reacted while watching porno films in their screening room, Miss Totenberg wrote that Justice Powell seemed highly embarrassed, that Justice Blackmun became almost "catatonic," and that Justice White became restless and referred to such films as "filth." Although the junior member of the Court, Justice William H. Rehnquist, had once been characterized in the New York *Times* as being a surreptitious "girl watcher" in court, he was known to be as antipathetic to pornography as Chief Justice Burger, who usually boycotted the screenings.

Also absent most of the time, but for reasons different from Burger's, was Justice Douglas—who, interpreting the First Amendment as disallowing sexual censorship no matter what was being shown on the screen, could not justify spending part of his busy workday sitting in a dark room watching what was purportedly the latest X-rated scandal. Justice Brennan, an aging Catholic who had once opposed pornography, had in recent years seemingly become so accustomed to it that it no longer bothered him—and thus he usually voted with Douglas to allow it on First Amendment grounds. The only justice who, according to Nina Totenberg, seemed amused while watching the films was Justice Thurgood Marshall, who had been overheard by clerks to be laughing in the screening room, and occasionally expressing words of encouragement to the actors. Justice Potter Stewart, the fourth member of the Court who generally opposed sexual censorship, wrote ten years ago in his *Jacobellis* opinion that obscenity was indeed difficult to define, but "I know it when I see it"—a comment that later gave rise to what members of the press would privately call Stewart's Casablanca standard: i.e., if what Justice Stewart saw in sex films was not worse than what he had seen during his wartime navy days while visiting the salacious seaport of Casablanca, then it was not obscene.

Sitting at the counselors' table, knowing that within moments he would be addressing the Supreme Court bench, Fleishman felt mounting anxiety and also a touch of irritation—the latter being partly attributable to his having to sit during the last hour and listen to attorney Louis Nizer's argument in the *Carnal Knowledge* case. In pleading for his client's vindication, Nizer was needlessly hurting Hamling by emphasizing rather excessively the artistic merits of the Mike Nichols film, separating it from the X-rated fare normally shown along Forty-second Street—whereas Fleishman knew that such Hollywood directors as Nichols would never enjoy full professional freedom if the directors of films like *Deep Throat* did not.

But Fleishman tried to repress his resentment and concentrate on what he would say in defense of Hamling. The main point of his argument today would be that Hamling had been unfairly trapped in a period of legal transition, that he had been sentenced in 1972 to a lengthy prison term and an enormous fine by a San Diego judge who had instructed the jury to apply "national" standards instead of "community" standards in deciding whether or not Hamling's illustrated brochure was socially acceptable. At the trial in California Fleishman would have preferred that Hamling be judged by community standards as well as national standards because then Fleishman could have introduced as relevant evidence a city-wide survey showing that the San Diego community was more sexually permissive than the nation as a whole, and he also could have presented to the jury a number of reputable San Diego citizens who would have articulately testified in Hamling's behalf. But after Fleishman's efforts in this direction had been overruled as irrelevant, and the government had gained a conviction under national standards, the Supreme Court interpreted the law in its *Miller* decision to read that community standards, instead of national, should prevail in all obscenity cases—prompting Fleishman to demand that Hamling be given a retrial in San Diego, one to be conducted under the test of the community. The Court of Appeals for the Ninth Circuit in California, however, rejected his argument, and affirmed Hamling's prison term and fine. And so now on this spring day in Washington in 1974, Fleishman's only hope, however remote, was that at least five of the nine justices would veto the rulings of the lower courts, believing it unjust to imprison a man for four years and fine him $87,000 for having mailed out glossy brochures that praised the Illustrated Report, criticized President Nixon's rejection of the commission's conclusions, and also featured several color photographs showing nude people masturbating, fellating, and participating in group sex.

The photographs, of course, and how each justice responded to them while examining Hamling's brochure in their private chambers prior to today's hearing, would largely determine Hamling's future—and, Fleishman knew, *that* was why obscenity rulings were so often unpredictable: They were decided so subjectively, emotionally, and in the end, so personally. There is an old saying among First Amendment counselors that "obscenity" is whatever gives a judge an erection. Fleishman believed the same was true of many prosecutors, censors, members of juries: A man might enjoy a stag movie one night at the American Legion hall, and the next day as a juror he might vote to convict the filmmaker. Ultraliberal citizens who favor reha-

bilitation for convicted murderers, and oppose harsh sentences
for drug smugglers, and affix their signatures to countless radical petitions, will often condone, and even applaud, the police
raids on "dirty" bookstores and the incarceration of their owners. "While moralists of the Left are opposed to censorship in
principle," wrote Alain Robbe-Grillet, "they also have principles—i.e., moral values inherited from the past, and they soon
find themselves opposed to the pornographers and on the side
of the censors." Or, as Gershon Legman commented on the
American ethic: "Murder is a crime. Describing murder is not.
Sex is not a crime. Describing it is."

Of course part of the problem, as Fleishman knew, and as
Tynan wrote, is that pornography is "orgasmic in intent"—one
of its fundamental purposes is to give men erections and allow
them to masturbate; and therefore it is difficult to defend pornography without defending masturbation, and *that*, quoth
Shakespeare, is the rub, for masturbation remains in the minds
of many people an unmanly act, a delinquent pleasure, an admission of failure in wooing a woman who might be a superior
substitute for the paper princess who reigns for ten minutes on
a bedroom pillow. Masturbation is deplored as wasted seed by
the Church, as sexual selfishness by many married couples; and
books that induce masturbation are rarely regarded as literature,
even though the critic Lionel Trilling once acknowledged that he
saw no reason "why literature should not have as one of its intentions the arousing of thoughts of lust." But lustful literature, and
its orgasmic culmination, has never been tolerated as a proper act
of free expression by the judicial interpreters of the First Amendment, in part because the Supreme Court has been primarily composed, since the eighteenth century, of elderly men whose
ascension was marked by conformity to the law and the social
norm, and who have maintained in their personal lives, at least
on the surface, an almost mythical standard of morality. Except
for Justice Douglas, none has ever been divorced; and except for
one justice who had a fatal heart attack decades ago while allegedly in the bed of an unmarried woman, no member of the Court
has even been rumored to have kept a mistress.

If the element of aphrodisia inherent in pornography has ever
influenced the controlled habits or private proprieties of a justice, none has ever acknowledged this in a posthumously published diary or memoir; and during obscenity hearings in the
Supreme Court building, the justices' demeanor is entirely tem-
pered and dispassionate, and all of their references to sex are

cloaked in circumlocution and the arcane language of law, *even* when the material they are judging reeks of ribaldry and seduction, of rakish barons and sullied scullery maids, of lissome ladies and muscled men swinging sweatily in circuses of debauchery—or, as in the case of Hamling's brochure, which the government had produced in evidence and Fleishman was now about to defend, unabashedly exhibits couples copulating, masturbating, and sodomizing.

In a stentorian voice, Chief Justice Warren Burger announced to the Court: "We'll hear arguments next in 73505—Hamling against the United States." Nodding from his high-backed black chair down toward the attorney, Burger added: "Mr. Fleishman, I think you may proceed whenever you are ready."

Fleishman pushed himself up from behind the counselors' table, and, in a rolling motion, pivoted his five-foot body between two crutches and moved by the strength of his shoulders toward the podium. At first his body seemed almost gnomish, a small figure in a dark tailored suit, advancing slowly, noisily, heavily in front of the bench. But when he stopped at the podium and turned toward the justices, after pounding his rubber-tipped crutches into a firm position on the floor, he seemed suddenly to transcend any sense of frailty. His shoulders were massive. His head was held high and was topped by thick curly black hair. With a sharp jaw, a prominent nose, and deep penetrating eyes, his was a sculptor's face, chiseled and strong, and as he stood alone in the front of the room his presence suggested an unfinished masterwork, a heroic head and torso supported by scaffolding. When he began to speak, his voice was resonant and reverberated through the large chamber, reaching the farthest row. Unlike many attorneys who appear before the High Tribunal, Fleishman seemed unintimidated, exuding a manner that would have bordered on cockiness were it not for his attitude of respect and formality. He was defense counselor who was not on the defensive.

"Mr. Chief Justice, may it please the Court . . ." he began. "Mr. Hamling has been given a prison term of four years . . . including [a fine of] $87,000 for mailing a brochure that hurt no one. The brochure advertises a book, a book of plain serious political value. The book is an illustrated version of a government report which basically concluded that the law of obscenity in a free community such as ours requires that willing adults be permitted to make their own choice with regard to whether or not they will or will not expose themselves to sexually explicit material. . . ."

Chief Justice Burger leaned forward and asked, "Was the original report illustrated, Mr. Fleishman?"

"No, sir, it was not," Fleishman replied, but he quickly added that at Hamling's trial in San Diego two former members of the presidential commission had testified that Hamling's illustrated report was "more valuable" than the original report because its pictures clarified for the reader the specific sort of sexual material that had concerned the Congress and had led to the creation of the President's fact-finding commission.

"Was there any reason," asked Justice Rehnquist, "why the jury wouldn't be free to disbelieve these witnesses just as they would any other witness?"

"I believe not, your honor . . ." Fleishman said. "A commissioner who spent two years on the commission report simply has an opinion that is better than that of a lay jury."

"But," Rehnquist insisted, "juries *do* disbelieve experts for a number of reasons, don't they? And there is no rule of law that says they *have* to believe."

"Yes, sir," Fleishman hastily agreed, not wanting to debate further this oblique point; he was allowed only a half hour to speak, and part of this time would be used by his co-counselor, Sam Rosenwein, in defending the three Hamling staff members who had collaborated on the illustrated book and brochure. Also, even before the hearing had begun today, Fleishman had all but written off Rehnquist's vote, knowing that the latter was as opposed to pornography as Burger and Blackmun. Fleishman had decided instead to direct most of his argument toward Justices White and Powell, one of whom he hoped would vote with the four liberal members of the Court. Although White and Powell were hardly liberal interpreters of the First Amendment, they had in the past seemed less self-righteous and predictable than Rehnquist, Blackmun, and Burger; and they might even find merit in Fleishman's argument that his client had been caught in a "period of transition," a constitutional "no-man's-land"—Hamling had been victimized in San Diego by a courtroom verdict based on legal logic that in 1973 had been declared illogical by the very members of the Supreme Court that Fleishman now faced.

As Fleishman continued his speech to the justices, he went on (referring to the 1973 *Miller* ruling): "This Court has said there are no national standards—they are unascertainable, they are unprovable, they are unrealistic, they are abstract. And this

Court has said that a jury trying to answer the question of obscenity within the framework of national standards was engaged in an exercise in futility. Therefore," Fleishman continued, his voice rising, "the petitioners [Hamling et al.] were convicted of offending standards that, simply on the Court's own terms, do not exist."

Fleishman reasoned further that, since community standards are now sovereign in obscenity cases, his client deserved better than he had received in San Diego, where the judge had thwarted every attempt by the defense to introduce evidence relating to the sexual standards of the community. "We, for example, had called a witness who had made a survey in the San Diego area with regard to the identical brochure in question," Fleishman recalled, "and on a scientific basis, she asked 718 people their opinion with regard to the brochure. Overwhelmingly, as the record shows, they were of the view essentially that the brochure as it stood should be allowed to be circulated to the American people generally. That evidence was excluded, however, solely on the grounds that the only test that was applicable was the national standards, and not the local standards. So that if again we are to follow the suggestion of the government that local standards are to be used, then plainly there has to be a reversal in this case. . . ."

William Hamling, sitting in the crowded room surrounded by people who did not recognize him as the offstage protagonist in this case, occasionally nodded his head in agreement with the points his attorney was making. Next to him sat his wife, Frances, looking at the distant faces of the justices and searching for some indication of how they might be reacting to Fleishman's words. She sensed nothing. On the other side of her daughter, Deborah, who seemed tense, sat Fleishman's nineteen-year-old daughter, Judy, who seemed calm. Judy Fleishman had accompanied her father to court before, and she was confident that this case, like the others, would be favorably concluded.

Meanwhile the bailiffs of the Supreme Court walked up and down the aisles as Stanley Fleishman spoke, watching the spectators and making sure that nobody was using a tape recorder or a camera, or was even taking notes; whispering was forbidden, as was sitting with legs crossed or arms resting over the back of the pews. Suddenly, one of the bailiffs stopped in the aisle next to where the Hamlings were seated and glared at Judy Fleishman, shaking his finger. Judy had been caught chewing gum. As ca-

sually as she could, she removed it from her mouth, wrapped it
into a Kleenex, and deposited it in the pocket of her dress.

When she directed her attention once more to the podium,
she saw that her father was temporarily relinquishing his place
to his co-counselor, Sam Rosenwein, a balding gray-haired man
in his late sixties, who explained to the justices: "The issue I
am devoting myself to is the issue of scienter—the question of
guilty knowledge, and what is the mental element requisite for
a constitutionally permissible prosecution. . . ." Rosenwein
paused, then continued, "In answer to our motion for a bill of
particulars, the [prosecution] stated it was *not* claiming that these
defendants knew in fact that the material was obscene—all that
it was claiming was that they knew the *contents* of the brochure,
and *that* was sufficient to satisfy the scienter requirement."

"Do you suggest, Mr. Rosenwein," asked Chief Justice
Burger, "in order to make out a case, the handler of the material
must acknowledge that it's obscene before he exposes it or dis-
tributes it?"

"My contention," Rosenwein replied, "is simply this: that
one has to prove beyond a reasonable doubt that he *knew* the
contents; and, with that knowledge, intentionally disseminated
the material with a specific intent to appeal to a prurient interest.
That, I think, is a burden that is upon prosecution in an obscenity prosecution. . . ."

Listening nearby, at the government's table, sat Hamling's
accuser—a bearded, youthful Yale man from the Solicitor General's office named Allan Tuttle. Having trimmed his dark beard
earlier on this day to a judicial length, and having rehearsed
many times in private the argument that he would momentarily
deliver, Tuttle felt both personally and professionally prepared;
and adhering to a tradition followed by all federal government
lawyers when appearing before the justices of the Supreme
Court, Tuttle was formally attired, wearing a black cutaway coat,
gray striped trousers, a black vest, a white shirt, and a silver silk
tie. Though he was not personally offended by sexually explicit
pictures, and untimidly perused the pages of *Penthouse* when in
his favorite Washington barbershop, Tuttle believed that Hamling's brochure was excessively graphic and legally obscene. If
Hamling had only included a few excerpts from the text of the
Presidential Report, the brochure might have presumed to at
least a modicum of serious purpose; and while Stanley Fleishman's rebuttal to Tuttle's forthcoming remarks would be the last
words heard in today's oral argument, Tuttle could not imagine

what Fleishman could say in defense of such pictures as the brochure's nude Godiva mouthing the penis of her horse.

When Chief Justice Burger finally nodded toward Allan Tuttle after Rosenwein had sat down, Tuttle lost no time in challenging the worthiness of the brochure. "Mr. Chief Justice, may it please the Court . . ." Tuttle began. "I invite the Court to consider the material which is here for review. The brochure consists of a single page: On one side is a photograph of the cover of the Illustrated Report, together with a coupon indicating where copies can be obtained; the other side consists entirely of a collage of photographs showing a variety of sexual scenes, including group-sex scenes, heterosexual and homosexual intercourse, sodomy, bestiality, and masturbation. This is hard-core pornography by *any* definition, and judged by the standards of *any* community.

"Petitioners nonetheless say that their conviction should be reversed," Tuttle went on. "They argue that *Miller* teaches us that the federal obscenity statutes were unconstitutionally vague, at least until *Miller* was decided . . . [but] as I read *Miller*, the Court found that the *Roth* definition, or some aspects of the *Roth* definition—for instance, the 'utterly without redeeming social value' test—was constitutionally unnecessary, and difficult to prove, if not impossible to prove; and the Court formulated a different formulation. But I don't take the Court to be saying, when it decided that *Miller* would be the standard for judging obscenity in the future, that all the prior convictions, using the *Roth* definition, were unconstitutional, or unconstitutionally obtained, or that the formulation under which they were obtained made the convictions void. . . ."

"Then those cases went on to say," interjected Justice Potter Stewart, "that in order not to be deficient constitutionally, the statutes had to be *very* specific."

"Yes, Mr. Justice, I was going to say that . . . the requirement in *Miller* that the obscenity statutes be limited to depictions of sexual conduct specifically described in applicable state law . . . [and] it says if and when a serious doubt is raised as to the vagueness of the federal statutes, we are prepared to construe them as limited to the examples of hard-core sexual conduct. And in point of fact . . ."

"That can't very well be done *after* a conviction, can it?" Justice Stewart said.

Tuttle and Stewart debated further; and then Tuttle spoke without interruption for several minutes, until Justice Stewart began once more to ask questions, most of which dealt with the problem of how various and sundry communities could fairly interpret and enforce the federal postal law that had ensnared Hamling. "*Miller* was dealing with a state law," Stewart reminded Tuttle, "which had no wider scope than statewide. But here [in *Hamling*] we are dealing with a federal law [the Comstock Act]," and Stewart added that now this ancient federal postal law had countless local interpretations across the land. It would be as if, Stewart suggested, "somebody in the Solicitor General's office stood up and told us that the Internal Revenue Code was to have a different meaning" in numerous different parts of the nation.

But, Tuttle replied, "the reason why the Court returned to temporary community standards in a state case [*Miller* v. *California*] was because it found that the juries' efforts to articulate and grasp a national standard had not been wholly successful. If that's true, it's equally true with respect to a jury attempting to judge a federal obscenity prosecution. . . ."

"Does the First Amendment have nothing to do with the national standards?" asked Justice Douglas.

"Of course," Tuttle said, "the Court, construing the First Amendment, developed a requirement of a national standard. All I'm saying [with regard to Comstock's federal postal restrictions] . . . was that Congress, I don't think, had in mind either a local or a national standard—they had in mind obscene material as a jury would find it—and that again is the lesson of *Miller*."

"I suppose it's true," Chief Justice Burger added in elaboration, "that running an unlicensed still in Kentucky, or some of the other states, might get a different reaction from jurors than it would in yet other states, where it is not so much a way of life. Yet, the statute would be the same statute, would it not?"

"Yes," Tuttle answered, "there are a number of crimes, in fact I would say in most instances, where the crime is . . ."

"Well," said Justice Thurgood Marshall, "could you say that in the State of New York a still is not a still?" Tuttle was confused by the question. "It's either a still or it's *not* a still!" Marshall cried out impatiently, surprising Tuttle. "It's the same still in New York that it is in Kentucky!"

"I quite agree, Mr. Justice Marshall," Tuttle said, "and that is why I said in those instances . . ."

"But in this," Marshall continued, "you could have *Carnal Knowledge*, a still in Kentucky, and not in New York . . ."

"*Carnal Knowledge* maybe exceeds the limits of candor of Albany, Georgia," Tuttle said, "and *Carnal Knowledge* may in fact be found to appeal to the prurient interest of the average person in Albany, Georgia, but it still lies with this Court . . ."

"Mr. Tuttle," Marshall interrupted, more softly, "my only quarrel is: I thought you were inferring that *Miller* changed the [Comstock] statute's determination."

"I don't think *Miller* was simply, if you will, a determination."

"Let me ask you—what did *Miller* do to this statute?"

"*Miller*, the statute speaks only of obscene material . . ."

"Right," said Marshall.

"The Court had since *Roth* undertaken to give content to what that means," Tuttle continued, "and in each of these cases the Court's formulation has been a slightly different formulation. *Miller* gave a formulation, which has been recited today, and *Miller* said that with respect to the community-standards element, reference should be had to the contemporary community standards of the forum community."

"Would you be able to advise a client whether to plead guilty?" Justice Douglas asked, adding: ". . . is [the statute] sufficiently clear, or is it so obscure that it is open to guesswork?"

"I think," Tuttle replied, "that it is quite evident, Mr. Justice, that the concept of obscenity does not lend itself to the precise kinds of measurement that many other elements of criminal statutes do. . . ."

"Under this federal statute," Douglas theorized, ". . . the act of mailing from New York could be innocent, but the act of receiving and selling from California could be a crime—is that right?"

"It's conceivable," said Tuttle. "We would be speculating to know, but it is conceivable [that] the judgment of criminality would turn on the place in which the matter is disseminated and the crime is committed."

"Mr. Tuttle," Chief Justice Burger added, as if wanting to help clarify, if not justify, the fickled character of obscenity laws, "the Court over the period of the last fifteen years has had at least three different definitions—there's nothing new about altering these definitions, is there? . . . Coming back from *Roth* to *Jacobellis* to the other cases down the line, it's been a revolution . . ."

"It's been a continuing effort," Tuttle agreed, "to attempt to formulate manageable standards . . ."

"Mr. Tuttle," asked Justice Byron White, "you suggested that before *Miller* there was a third requirement that material be 'utterly without redeeming social value'—what cases do you rely on for that?"

"I would rely on *Memoirs* v. *Massachusetts*."

"How many votes did that test have there?"

"That test had three votes."

"Well, under what case did it ever have five?"

". . . Excuse me," Tuttle corrected himself, "*Memoirs* is the case."

Justice White frowned slightly, seeming displeased with Tuttle's answer. While it was true that five justices during the mid-1960s had allowed the legalization of *Fanny Hill* in the *Memoirs* case, it was also true that only three justices could agree on the precise language to be used in that splintered opinion—and even now, eight years later, Justice White (who had opposed the book) seemed rankled by the outcome; and in a clear, hard voice he reminded Tuttle that *Memoirs* "did not have five votes."

"The reason why I think there were five votes," Tuttle persisted in explaining, as White's lips tightened, "is that you had *two* members of the Court who would have found the publication constitutionally protected under *any* circumstances, and you had *three* members of the Court who would have found it constitutionally protected unless it was shown to be 'utterly without redeeming social value.' . . ."

"But the fact remains," White said, looking down at Tuttle, "at *no* time did five members of the Court subscribe to that test." As Tuttle remained silent, Stanley Fleishman watched with interest the emergence of Justice White's unrelenting nature. Earlier, Fleishman had thought that he had a fair chance of converting White to Hamling's side, but now Fleishman saw his only hope in Justice Lewis Powell, the lean, quiescent Virginian who sat on the extreme left, stroking with his thin fingers his pallid, pointed chin. Meanwhile the loquacious Allan Tuttle, having wisely terminated his debate with White by conceding the accuracy of White's remembrance of *Memoirs*, continued with his prepared speech, ignoring momentarily Justice William Brennan's efforts to interrupt him.

"Please pause, Mr. Tuttle," Justice Brennan said finally. Tuttle turned toward the scowling, round-faced septuagenarian, the author of the controvertible and now moribund *Memoirs* opinion, and Tuttle heard Brennan ask: "Does all of this discussion suggest that maybe even *Miller* isn't the last word in this very troubled area?"

"*Miller* gave us . . ."

"That's *not* my question," Brennan cut in; "my question is whether you think *Miller* is necessarily the last word in this area?"

"*Miller* of course is not the last word," Tuttle said, "because we are here today, and we are here today with some problems. But our problems relate to the application of *Miller*. We are not here to question the standards of obscenity articulated in *Miller*, but we are merely attempting to determine whether a pre-*Miller* conviction can be sustained under that definition.'' Tuttle waited for a reaction; and when there was none, he continued: ''Now, we don't believe that the criticism of local standards which is contained in *Miller* v. *California* necessarily implies that all federal obscenity prosecutions antedating *Miller* have to be voided. And we don't think the Courts had any such idea in mind. In the first place there have been, since *Miller*, a large number of cases which have been remanded to Courts of Appeal for reconsideration in the light of *Miller*. And these are federal cases where the jury was charged to use the national standard, as was the jury here [in the San Diego trial involving Hamling]. And we believe that if the use of a national standard had made the statute unconstitutionally vague, prior to *Miller*, we would have had reversals, and not remands. . . .''

Seeing the small light flashing on the podium, signaling that his time was nearly up, Tuttle raised his voice as he concluded: ''. . . and if there is any question that the defendant was incorrectly tried under a national standard, we would say it was harmless error because [Hamling's] material is obscene under *any* standard, and there is no community whose limits of candor are not exceeded by the petitioner's publication.'' He paused, then said, ''Thank you,'' and turned toward his seat.

Chief Justice Burger nodded, then turned to his right and said: ''Mr. Fleishman.''

Fleishman was clearly riled by Tuttle's closing remarks, and as soon as he had settled himself at the podium he began to aggressively refute the contentions of the government prosecutor.

''Chief Justice,'' Fleishman began, ''. . . the brochure simply is *not* obscene! It is not obscene under national standards. It is not obscene under local standards. . . . The prosecution says it is obscene under *any* standards. I would remind the Court that a film, *Deep Throat*, which was thought to be obscene by any standards is being found *not* obscene continuously throughout the country by local juries.''

As to the government's indictment against Hamling, Fleishman continued, it is capriciously conceived, vaguely defined, and legally defective. The indictment is characterized by such Comstockian words as ''lewd,'' ''lascivious,'' ''indecent,'' ''filthy,'' and ''vile,'' and yet it fails to substantiate the charge that Hamling had personally violated, either willfully or inadvertently, a crime against the public morality. "Look at the indictment—is the specificity there?" he demanded. "No," he answered, "it is *not*. . . . What *was* the legal definition of obscenity at the time the indictment came down? Justice White suggests that 'utterly without redeeming social value' was not part of it. For the present purposes, I don't care whether it was or was not part of the definition. I don't care whether it was a local standard or a national standard. I don't care whether you measure prurient interest by national or local standards or *no* standards. I *do* say that where you have a statute which is so up in the air as this one is, absolutely the irreducible minimum is that we are entitled to have in our *indictment* what the charge is, and not have these vague words 'lewd,' 'lascivious,' and the like, and say that *everybody* knows what that is, of course we have *always* known what that is.

"Now," he continued, "we do have other points, and I would like to emphasize, if I may, some of the vices that came from the infirmity of the indictment. For example, we were charged, in statutory language only, in response to a bill of particulars, that the material was offensive because it appealed to the prurient interest of the average person. And yet [the San Diego jury] . . . was told that they could convict if it appealed to a prurient interest of the average person *or* a clearly defined sexually deviant group. When we complained to the Court of Appeals, the Court of Appeals said we were right, that it should have been solely measured by the average person, but it was harmless error. . . .

"Pandering, also," Fleishman went on, "there isn't a word of pandering in the indictment, nothing in the bill of particulars—and *yet* the jury was instructed that they could convict on a pandering doctrine without the slightest evidence of any pandering. There isn't a case that I know of which holds that an advertisement can pander itself. . . ."

"What was the situation in the *Ginzburg* case, Mr. Fleishman?" asked Chief Justice Burger. "Was there anything?"

"No," said Fleishman, "in *Ginzburg*, your honor, as I read *Ginzburg*, the Court held that the books involved were rendered obscene because the brochure advertising them in effect said that they were obscene and therefore that could be taken into account. But *Ginzburg* did not at *all* suggest that the advertisement could pander itself. It's logically inconsistent, because in this case if the brochure was mailed, either it's obscene or it's not obscene. It doesn't in any way lend itself to a pandering instruction. . . ."

"Mr. Fleishman, does the record show how the mailing list of fifty-five/fifty-eight thousand people was compiled?" It was the soft Tidewater-Richmond inflection of Justice Lewis Powell, speaking for the first time today; and as Fleishman shifted on his crutches so that he could directly face his interrogator seated to his extreme left, this jurist who might represent the "swing vote" in this case, the lawyer responded in a conciliatory manner: "It does not, your honor. What we do have is, for sure, that twelve people were offended. That is all we know. That fifty-five/fifty-eight thousand [brochures] were mailed, and that twelve people were offended. . . ."

"Does the record show whether any of the fifty-five/fifty-eight thousand people had requested the brochure?"

"The record is silent on that point, your honor."

"Does the record show," Powell went on, "whether it was received by any minors?"

"The record *does* show that it was *not* received by any minors at all," Fleishman replied, pleased with the opportunity to impart this fact to the justices of the Supreme Court; and he also took the opportunity to add that, after Hamling's office had learned of the twelve complaints to the Post Office, all twelve names were immediately removed from the distributor's mailing list, guaranteeing that the complainants would be spared the receipt of more sexually oriented mail in the future.

"I suppose," Justice Powell continued softly, "there was no way to tell the number of children in the fifty-five thousand homes into which this brochure was mailed?"

"No," Fleishman admitted, "but I would say this, since we are supposing, your honor: I know that the list was purportedly a list of persons who had previously indicated their desire to receive sexually explicit material. Those are the only mailing lists that are *worth* anything, because one tries to mail to those persons who are interested. . . . If you want to sell cat food, you want to mail material to people who have cats."

Perceiving what might have been the mildest of smiles on Justice Powell's sober countenance, Fleishman continued: "So the truth of the matter is, the brochure was mailed, as fully as one could, to those adults who had indicated that they did want it. Now that's not in the record, and I don't want to mislead the Court, but I think that is the true answer as to who were in fact the recipients of the ad. We have, as I say, twelve people who are offended. But," he concluded, "there are twelve people who are offended by receiving many political brochures, too, your honor."

Justice Powell, who seemed satisfied with Fleishman's answer, had no further questions. Since the allotted time of his rebuttal had expired, Fleishman thanked the Court and heard Chief Justice Burger announce: "The case is submitted." As the marshal banged the gavel, the nine justices stood, turned, and quickly disappeared through the red velvet draperies. The spectators began to leave their pews and move slowly through the crowded aisles toward the rear exits; but Hamling edged his way forward toward the counselors' table to shake hands with Fleishman, to congratulate him on his handling of the case, and to express optimism about the outcome. Fleishman smiled, but warned him against overconfidence. The vote, to be announced in ten weeks, would be close, Fleishman predicted; it would probably be a five-to-four decision, with the private musing and vicissitudes of Justice Powell perhaps determining the conclusion of the entire case.

On June 24, 1974, Stanley Fleishman received from Washington the disturbing news: In a five-to-four vote, Hamling had lost. Hamling had been supported by the Court's liberal foursome—Douglas and Marshall, Brennan and Stewart—but Justice Powell had remained allied with the other Nixon appointees, and Justice White, in forming the majority. The prevailing opinion, written by Justice Rehnquist, overruled every objection that Fleishman had raised in Hamling's behalf. Rehnquist declared that the government's indictment had been "sufficiently definite" in clarifying the charges against Hamling; that such words as "lewd," "lascivious," "indecent," etc., in the Comstock postal statute were not "too vague" to justify Hamling's conviction; and that it had *not* been "constitutionally improper" of the California judge to employ national standards, and to disallow local evidence, at Hamling's trial in San Diego. While Hamling might have sincerely believed that his brochure was not legally obscene, Rehnquist said in effect that that was no defense; and Rehnquist supported his position by citing the 1896 case of *Rosen* v. *United States*, in which a New York publisher named Lew Rosen, after claiming that he did not know that the ladies photographed in his periodical were obscenely posed, was told by the Supreme Court that his knowledge of obscenity was irrelevant: His conviction was affirmed because he was aware of the content of the material he had mailed.

While the film *Carnal Knowledge* was vindicated by the Court in a companion opinion that was also authored by Rehnquist—

"there are occasional scenes of nudity," Rehnquist wrote, "but nudity alone is not enough to make material legally obscene"—the Hamling brochure was, in Rehnquist's words, "a form of hard-core pornography well within the types of permissibly proscribed depictions described in *Miller*." And so Hamling's conviction was final; a stay in prison was inevitable; the $87,000 fine was payable.

In newspapers throughout the land, Hamling received little sympathy on the editorial pages, and only minimal coverage in the news columns—except for the CDL's *National Decency Reporter*, where there was a front-page photograph of Justice Rehnquist with an adulating article about his ruling, under a headline that read: "All Systems 'Go' for Obscenity Prosecutions."

At Fleishman's request, several lawyers, writers, publishers, and editors joined Hamling's family in writing mercy-pleading letters to the San Diego judge who now controlled Hamling's immediate fate; but the only concession that Fleishman could achieve after the payment of the fine was a reduction of the prison term to less than a year in Terminal Island on the understanding that Hamling would sever all business connections with erotic publishing, and thereafter cease to write, to edit, or to distribute any material even mildly related to sex. Hamling also understood that, at the risk of violating his five-year probationary period, he would be wise to refrain from writing magazine articles or books about the vagaries of sex laws, or lamentations about his own predicament and punishment—meaning that his written views about his case would be restricted to personal letters he mailed to his friends or attorney. In one letter to Fleishman, he wrote, as if he could yet barely believe it, "I am a criminal. . . . It has been determined. One vote in nine has determined the brochure for the book illegal and my sentence thus affirmed. Irrelevant thought, traumatic in its perplexity: Justice Black was sitting at the time the brochure was mailed. . . .The one vote would have been different. I would not be a criminal. . . . But Justice Black is not now sitting [having been replaced by Justice Powell], therefore I am a criminal, consigned to the limbo of convict life and brand. How does one adjust to this? A question of personal taste and legal ambiguity that swings the scales of justice 5 to 4 either way . . . as capricious as the changing wind at sunset."

24

IN HIS MORE visionary moments, sitting on his round bed in his private airplane, a sleek black DC-9 jet that regularly transported him and several playmates between his mansion in Chicago and his mansion in Los Angeles, Hugh Hefner saw himself as the embodiment of the masculine dream, the creator of a corporate utopia, the focal point of a big-budget home movie that continuously enlarged upon its narcissistic theme month after month in his mind—a film of unfolding romance and drama in which he was simultaneously the producer, the director, the writer, the casting agent, the set designer, and the matinee idol and lover of each desirable new starlet who appeared on cue to enhance, but never upstage, his preferred position on the edge of satiation.

Ever since his adolescent days as an usher at the Rockne Theater in Chicago, Hefner had been enchanted with movies, had accepted uncritically their most improbable plots, had languished in their emotions and reveled in their adventures; and as he stood watching in the darkened theater, he often wished that the lights would never turn on, that the story on the screen would continue indefinitely and delay forever his return to the mundane, tidy home of his German accountant father and his prim Swedish mother. It was his mother who had first perceived his escapist tendencies and had learned from an examining psychologist that her son was a kind of genius with afflictions of immaturity, an appraisal that had worried her but would never embarrass Hugh Hefner. On the contrary, he coveted his youthful illusions, intensifying them to a passion; and now in the mid-1970s, relaxing in his plane or luxuriating in his mansions, he could look back on the many happy years in which he had escaped the boredom that other people rationalized as "maturity,'' and had expanded his fantasies into a multimillion-dollar empire.

The initial source of his fortune had been, of course, *Playboy* magazine, which he began in 1953 with $600 that he borrowed against his wedding furniture; and the success of his magazine marked the end of his marriage and the beginning of a continuous courtship with nude photographs and the models who had posed for them. The women in *Playboy* were Hefner's women, and after their photo sessions he complimented them, bought them expensive gifts, and took many of them to bed. Even after they had stopped modeling for *Playboy*, and had settled down with other men to raise families of their own, Hefner still considered them *his* women, and in the bound volumes of his magazine he would always possess them.

In 1960 he had opened in Chicago his first Playboy Club, introducing into his life numerous Bunnies from around the nation, some of whom came to live in the dormitories of his forty-eight-room mansion near the lake on Chicago's exclusive Gold Coast. When he first saw the mansion it reminded him of some of the great houses he had seen in mystery movies, the sort that had hidden tunnels and secret doors; and after he had bought the property and discovered that such features were lacking, he had his own private passageways built, together with walls and bookcases that moved by the press of a button. He also added within the mansion's grand interior a movie studio and a popcorn machine, a bowling alley and steam room, and, though he did not swim, he installed in the basement a full-sized swimming pool. The pool was partly encased in glass, and it often presented in Hefner's underwater bar a view of Bunnies swimming in the nude.

Since Hefner's large kitchen staff and many dark-suited butlers worked in shifts around the clock, it was possible for him and his house guests to order breakfast or dinner at any time of the day or night; and since Hefner preferred that all the windows of the house be heavily shaded, draped, and soundproofed, he was able to dwell in baronial seclusion for many months without ever becoming aware of the weather outside, the activity in the street, the season of the year, or the time of day. Like the fated Jay Gatsby, the hero of Hefner's favorite novelist, Hefner often gave large parties for hundreds of people; and, like Gatsby, he occasionally failed to appear, choosing to remain instead in his private suite beyond the oaken steps to work on the layout of a forthcoming *Playboy*, or to enjoy the company of a smaller group of intimates, or to watch on the movie screen opposite his bed one of the several hundred films that he stored in his cinema library.

His suite, which he designed so that he would rarely have to leave it, offered every imaginable comfort and convenience: He had visual and sound equipment that allowed him to communicate from his bed to his executives in the Playboy building blocks away; and by pressing buttons, he could spin his bed 360 degrees in either direction, could make it shake, vibrate, or suddenly stop in front of a fireplace, or a brown couch, or television sets, or a low flat curved headboard that served as a desk and dining table and contained a stereo, telephones, and a refrigerator in which was stocked champagne and—his favorite drink—Pepsi-Cola, of which he consumed more than a dozen bottles daily. Also in his mirrored room was a television camera focused on his bed, permitting him to film and preserve the imagery of his joyful moments with a lady lover—or, as was sometimes the case, with three or four lovers at the same time. One night a newly arrived resident of the mansion opened the door to Hefner's suite and discovered him lying naked in the center of the bed surrounded by a half-dozen nude *Playboy* models and Bunnies, each of whom was gently massaging him with oil, while he watched attentively, seeming to be getting as much pleasure from what he was seeing as from what he was feeling: It was as if the pictures of his magazine had suddenly come to life and were anointing him in an erotic ritual.

After buying his jet for nearly $6 million, Hefner had its cabin redesigned, reproducing as much as possible the familiar comforts of his mansion. Reducing the plane's seating capacity from 110 passengers to barely 35, he installed plush chairs that could be converted into beds; he added tables for business conferences and his favorite games of Monopoly and backgammon; he included two 16 mm movie projectors, nine television monitors, three sky-phones with extensions, an elaborate eight-track stereo system, and also reserved enough floor space in the front of the cabin for dancing. Playboy stewardesses, wearing tight-fitting black uniforms trimmed with white bunny emblems, matching the exterior colors of the plane, were prepared to serve eight-course dinners with enough silver, crystal, and china for thirty-six people. In the rear of the plane, in Hefner's suite, was a round bed, a step-down shower, and a desk with a Dictaphone, tape recorder, and a light-box on which he could examine color transparencies for future issues of the magazine.

Although the plane's extra fuel tanks enabled Hefner to take occasional trips overseas, his frequent flights from Chicago mostly took him back and forth to Los Angeles, where his company in the late 1960s had begun investing heavily in television and film production, and where in 1968 Hefner became enchanted with Barbara Klein, an eighteen-year-old UCLA co-ed whom he had recently met. He had been introduced to her on the set of the "Playboy After Dark" television variety show, where he was the host and she had been hired as an extra model by a Hefner associate who had spotted her one night in a Beverly Hills discotheque and knew immediately that her looks would appeal to Hefner. Barbara Klein was the quintessential girl-next-door, a green-eyed brunet with a perfect complexion, a cute little upturned nose, and a graceful, budding body unselfconsciously enhanced by clothes that were casual but well tailored. Before enrolling as a premed student at UCLA, Barbara Klein had been a high school cheerleader and a Miss Teenage America contestant from her hometown of Sacramento; and after arriving in Los Angeles, she occasionally worked after class as a television model, doing commercials for Certs and posing as a mermaid for Groom & Clean.

When Hefner first saw her, he was amazed at how much she resembled his estranged wife, Mildred—not the contemporary Mildred but the virginal bright-eyed brunet with bangs and bobby socks whom he had fallen in love with during the summer of 1944 after graduation from Steinmetz High School. Mildred Williams had been the original girl-next-door, the cynosure of his purest dreams and desires, and, also, the source of his greatest pain when she admitted—after they had become engaged, and she was teaching school in a small Illinois town—that she was having an affair with a man on the faculty. Although this had shattered Hefner, they proceeded with their scheduled wedding in June 1949, a decision that within a few years, and after the birth of two children, they both recognized as a mistake. Following their divorce, Mildred would marry an attorney who had helped with her settlement; while Hefner's personal involvements would thereafter remain in the realm of romantic courtships with *Playboy* inamoratas.

But after he had gone out on a number of occasions with Barbara Klein, Hefner suddenly seemed interested in a more committed relationship. He was now in his early forties, and, though she was not much older than his daughter Christie (who was living in Chicago with her mother and stepfather), Barbara was different from the dozens of other young women he had known since his divorce: She was more intellectually curious, more vivacious and socially poised; as the product of a prominent Jewish family in Sacramento, and the daughter of a physician, she was less awed than most of Hefner's girl friends by his wealth or position. When they went out on dates, she insisted that he not pick her up at her apartment in his chauffeured limousine, preferring to drive her own car and meet him at the restaurant or party they were attending. She also avoided ever being alone with him in a room, having no intention of losing her virginity to a man of his reputation and advanced years. Early in their acquaintanceship, she explained, "You're a nice person, but I've never dated anyone over twenty-four"; to which he replied: "That's okay, neither have I."

During his first few months of seeing her whenever he was in Los Angeles, Hefner remained reasonably proper and patient; and when she finally agreed to fly with him and his friends for overnight visits to Las Vegas, and to go skiing in Aspen, where his brother Keith had a large house, arrangements were made for Barbara Klein to have a private bedroom. Their traveling together, however, was soon publicized in the Hollywood press, which offended her parents in Sacramento and revived against Hefner familiar allegations that he dated nymphets because he feared older, more challenging women. To such assumptions Hefner answered that older women were not necessarily more challenging than younger ones, and in any case he was not seeking challenges in his love life. "I'm not looking for a female Hugh Hefner," he told one reporter, adding: "A romantic relationship for me is an escape from the challenges and problems I face in my work. It's a psychological and emotional island I slip away to."

As Barbara Klein spent more time in his company, and came to know his many friends in publishing and show business, she became increasingly comfortable in his world and responsive to Hefner personally. He was quick-witted but never derisive; he seemed unaffected by his millions, and possessed a sense of boyish adventure that made her forget the difference in their ages. By 1969, during a visit to his mansion in Chicago, Barbara Klein was not only ready but eager to consummate their relationship in the big round bed; and she also agreed while in Chicago to pose for the cover of *Playboy*, the first of many pictorial appearances that would bring her national attention under the name "Barbi Benton." Hefner was enthralled with Barbi

Benton, dazzled by her wholesome appeal, and, as she reacted with girlish delight to beautiful things and places that Hefner had taken for granted, she motivated within him a drive to explore still further the limitless possibilities of his life. During a weekend in Acapulco, despite his inability to swim, Hefner followed her and his friends in taking a turn on a flying water-kite pulled by a motorboat, and for many perilous moments the irreplaceable head of Playboy Enterprises was seen hanging by his arms high over Acapulco Bay.

Because of Barbi Benton, Hefner spent more time than ever before in Los Angeles; and in 1970 he purchased for $1.5 million a Gothic-Tudor chateau on a lush estate near Sunset Boulevard in which Barbi Benton would be the chatelaine. Together they discussed how they would redecorate the thirty-room, ivy-covered manor that would become Playboy Mansion West, and for many months architects and workmen reshaped the surrounding five and a half acres into gently rolling hills and lawns, built a lake and waterfall behind the main house, and also created a stone grotto that sheltered a series of warm Jacuzzi baths in which guests could bathe in the nude. Music was piped into the steaming grotto, through the surrounding forest of redwoods and pines, across the sprawling green lawns on which dozens of Hefner's newly acquired animals were allowed to roam—llamas and squirrel monkeys, raccoons and rabbits, and even peacocks. On the ponds were ducks and geese; in the aviary were condors, macaws, and flamingos. On other parts of the property there was a greenhouse filled with rare flowers and plants; guest cottages furnished with antiques; a game house in which was a pool table, pinball and Pong machines, and small private bedrooms with mirrored ceilings. There was also built within a wide clearing of trees a step-down tennis court that was overlooked by an outdoor dining area where lunch or dinner could be served, and where black-tied butlers would provide on trays, to each arriving racket-carrying couple, *two* unopened cans of tennis balls.

Visible from almost every part of the estate, despite the high hedges and trees, was the mansion, a castlelike structure with towering chimneys and turrets that was modeled after a fifteenth-century English manor. In front of the mansion's main entrance was a white marble fountain with cherubs and lions' heads spouting water; and after passing through an arched stone portal and a heavy oak door, visitors entered a grand hallway with marble floors and a high-beamed ceiling from which was sus-

pended an enormous golden chandelier with candles nearly the
size of baseball bats. To the right was a baronial dining room
with a long polished wood table surrounded by twelve blue-
velvet-covered chairs; to the left was a large living room with a
concert piano, leather sofas, and many chairs that would be
occupied by guests on those evenings when Hefner would convert the room into a movie studio. Rising from the entrance hall
was a wooden twin-balustrade Gothic staircase that led to several private suites, including the master bedroom that would be
occupied by Barbi Benton and, when he was in town, by Hugh
Hefner.

The Los Angeles mansion, like the one in Chicago, would
feature round-the-clock kitchen service, a Hefnerian lack of interest in whether it was day or night, and large parties hastily
arranged by Hefner's social secretaries whenever it suited his
pleasure. Since most of the renowned movie moguls had in
recent years become too old to host the gaudy, tinseled gatherings that had once been the hallmark of Hollywood, Hefner's
presence in Los Angeles was particularly welcomed, and as
soon as his mansion was ready in 1971 for his first private party,
the electrically operated iron gates at the bottom of the hill were
opened to a procession of Rolls-Royces and Bentleys, Mercedes-
Benzes, Jaguars and customized Jeeps that transported up the
winding ivy-walled road dozens of top producers and directors,
film stars and models, all of whom were greeted in the marble
hallway by a pipe-smoking silk-robed Hugh Hefner holding an
open bottle of Pepsi, and by his ultrabright princess in a high-
collared low-cut blouse and tailored spangled blue denims.

As tokens of his affection, Hefner gave Barbi Benton a Mas-
erati automobile, exquisite jewelry, beautiful clothes, and a red
cotton-candy machine; and he commissioned a sculptor to do a
bust of her that emphasized her sprightly sensuality and her firm
pointed breasts. When Hefner was away from Los Angeles he
telephoned her every day from his airplane, or from his limousine, or from his big Chicago bed, telling her that he loved her
and missed her—which was true enough; but what he did not
admit during their separations was that he was often sharing his
Chicago bed with one of the new Bunnies or models who were
residing temporarily at the mansion while training as waitresses
at the Playboy Club or undergoing a series of test shots in the
Playboy building's photo studios.

Although Hefner was approaching forty-five, and had been
involved with hundreds of photogenic women since starting his

magazine, he enjoyed female companionship now more than ever; and perhaps more significant, considering all that Hefner had seen and done in recent years, was the fact that each occasion with a new woman was for him a novel experience: It was as if he was always watching for the first time a woman undress, rediscovering with delight the beauty of the female body, breathlessly expectant as panties were removed and smooth buttocks were exposed—and he never tired of the consummate act. He was a sex junkie with an insatiable habit.

He was also convinced that his hyperactive sex life was the regenerative source of his creative drive and business success, his confidence and uniqueness as a man; it was what separated him from the melancholy Fitzgeraldian characters that he otherwise identified with, those stylish romantics who feared growing older and who finally faded at forty into obscurity and despair. For the aging Hefner, the opposite had so far been true: He was happier in his forties than he had been in his thirties, and he had no doubt that in his fifties he would be even more fulfilled, that his many business enterprises would continue to thrive, and that he would possess in the center of his private paradise, as he did now, a young woman whom he loved—while he simultaneously had access to skeins of migratory beauties who would bring variety and spice to his most personal moments.

During such moments in Chicago, hundreds of miles away from Barbi Benton, in the early summer of 1971, Hugh Hefner became particularly appreciative of a green-eyed zaftig blonde from Texas named Karen Christy. Endowed with large, firm, magnificent breasts and curly platinum-blond hair that flowed over her shoulders and halfway down her back, Karen Christy had been discovered in Dallas during a "Bunny hunt" conducted by one of Hefner's associates, a Playboy Club executive named John Dante, who often traveled from city to city interviewing those women who, in reply to local newspaper ads, had expressed interest in working for one of the fifteen Playboy Clubs located around the nation. In Dallas, Karen and two hundred other applicants had assembled at the Statler-Hilton Hotel to pose in bikinis and meet with John Dante and other *Playboy* representatives. Notified weeks later that she was hired, she received an airplane ticket to Chicago and was invited to stay at the mansion while being trained to work at the Playboy Club in Miami.

Karen reacted to her acceptance with as much trepidation as joy, having never before been east of Texas and having spent most of her youth in the rural surroundings of Abilene, in a family that was unaccustomed to receiving good news. When Karen was three, her mother died from a complicated kidney disorder. Her father remarried, but this unhappy relationship ended in divorce when Karen was nine; and four years later, Karen's father was fatally shot in a hunting accident. During those years Karen and a younger sister were alternately reared in the well-intending but barely solvent households of various aunts, uncles, or grandparents; and although Karen received federal aid as an orphan, and saved whatever money she could from her after-school jobs and her full-time secretarial position in a business office following her graduation from Cooper High in Abilene, insufficient funds forced her to drop out of North Texas State University after her freshman year.

At nineteen, however, she saw the *Playboy* ad in the local press, and later, concluding that employment as a cotton-tailed waitress had to be more interesting and remunerative than working as a secretary in an office, she packed her suitcase in May 1971 and, landing at the Chicago airport, taxied to the ornate black wrought-iron front gate of Hefner's limestone and brick domain on North State Parkway. After the security guards in the vestibule had verified her identity, Karen Christy was escorted by a butler through a marble hall up an oaken staircase to the fourth floor, where she was directed to a door leading into the Bunny dormitory.

Behind the door she heard the sound of showers and laughter, electric hair dryers and radio music; and as she walked through the hall she saw several nude young women rushing in and out of rooms, presumably getting ready to go to work at the Playboy Club. Amazed and mildly discomfited by their extreme informality, Karen became even more self-conscious when, on entering her assigned suite, she noticed standing in front of a mirror a nude brunet brushing her hair, and a short-haired blonde seated at the dresser polishing her fingernails. While both women were friendly as Karen introduced herself, and also patiently answered her many questions about the job she would begin on the following day, Karen sensed as they talked to her that they were critically appraising her, surveying the outline of her body under her clothing; and after she had removed her blouse but not her brassiere, one of the women lightly commented: "We don't wear those around here." Karen smiled but did not take off her brassiere as she continued to unpack; and it was not until after they had left for work, and the dormitory was quiet and empty, that she removed all of her clothes and entered the shower room.

Later, feeling refreshed and dressed in new clothes she had bought in Dallas, Karen ventured out of the dormitory and down the grand staircase, soon finding herself in a sixty-foot-long living room that had teakwood floors and a more than twenty-foot-high ceiling inlaid with flowered frescoes. At one end of the massive room was a carved marble fireplace large enough for her to stand in; at the other end, perched on pedestals, were silver polished medieval suits of armor; and in between was a mixture of antique and modern furniture, a concert piano, and a stereo console softly resounding with jazz. Around a coffee table, near the distant fireplace, sat a group of young women and older men who were engaged in conversation. Hefner was not among them, but Karen did recognize the man she had met in Dallas, John Dante; and when Dante saw her, he immediately got up and came forward to greet her. Dante was a ruggedly stylish man in his early forties with a small, neatly trimmed mustache and friendly ruddy face, and he wore an open silk shirt with a gold medallion around his neck and sharply creased, tapered trousers. Although he was soft-spoken and unassuming, the butlers in the room, responsive to his status in the Hefner hierarchy, remained attentive as Dante shook hands with Karen; and when Dante asked her if she wanted something to eat or drink, two butlers were quickly at her side ready to fulfill her request.

She was introduced to the people around the coffee table, and sat among them for several moments in awkward silence as they chatted and relaxed in the surrounding splendor; then the group was joined by an attractive woman of about thirty with lean delicate features, large expressive eyes, and a manner that, while sophisticated, seemed warm and natural. Her name was Bobbie Arnstein, and, as Karen later learned, Miss Arnstein was Hefner's social secretary and confidante; among other duties she helped to entertain Hefner's house guests and visiting celebrities, scheduled the *Playboy* business meetings held in Hefner's suite, and did most of Hefner's personal shopping, including the Christmas and birthday gifts that he sent to his parents and children. Years ago, briefly and casually, Bobbie Arnstein had been romantically involved with Hugh Hefner; but since then their relationship had ripened into a deep and special friendship—

and, like Hefner, she now preferred lovers who were years younger than herself. Bobbie Arnstein's presence at the table, and her subtle way of including Karen Christy in the conversation without necessitating a response from the obviously shy Texas beauty, allowed Karen to feel more at ease among the many strangers. But Karen nonetheless welcomed the graceful exit that Dante provided when he offered to give her a tour of the mansion.

For the next half hour, Karen followed Dante through corridors and secret passageways, past antique furnishings and pinball machines, and down a curved staircase into the underwater bar that could also be reached by sliding down a brass fireman's pole from the floor above. Dante, who had moved into the mansion at Hefner's suggestion years ago and knew something of its history, told Karen that it had first been erected before the turn of the century by a Chicago industrialist who later entertained in the house such guests as Theodore Roosevelt and Admiral Peary. Until Hefner had purchased it, for less than a half million dollars in 1960, it had been empty and gathering dust for years; and since acquiring it Hefner had spent at least a half million on modernization and such features as the bowling alley, the swimming pool, and his private apartment that was replete with electronic gadgetry and custom-made furniture of his own design. When Karen asked if she could see Hefner's quarters, Dante at first hesitated, explaining that Hefner had arrived in Chicago earlier in the day from Los Angeles and might be sleeping; but a few minutes later, after Dante had gone off by himself to check, he returned to say that Hefner was awake and would be glad to meet her.

With Dante at her side, Karen walked across the oak-paneled living room in which they had been sitting earlier, climbed two steps, and passed through a door that led into a room that was abundantly appointed with electronic equipment, including eight separate television monitors, one for each channel in Chicago, thus permitting Hefner to have a variety of programs taped simultaneously and replayed at his convenience. Opening a second door, Dante guided Karen onto the thick white carpeting of a paneled room that was dominated by the round bed in the center of which, eating a hamburger and sipping a Pepsi, while reading page proofs, sat Hugh Hefner.

With raised eyebrows and an exaggerated smile, Hefner bounced out of bed to welcome her; and for the next ten minutes, in addition to bantering with Dante for Karen's amusement, he conversed with her in a serious but convivial manner, asked her questions about her background and her future aspirations, and took her through the apartment, showing her his luxuriously furnished library with walls lined with books, his bathing area with a Roman tub large enough for a dozen people, and the many buttons and knobs that activated his rotating bed, which was eight and a half feet in diameter and had been built at a cost of $15,000. Near the bed, and pointed toward it, was an Ampex television camera that was designed to produce both instantaneous and delayed transmissions, on the wall screen above, of Hefner's amorous activities, which he found endlessly stimulating; but in his guided tour with Karen Christy he tactfully avoided any mention of this apparatus.

Before Karen had left, Hefner explained that he would be playing pool later in the evening with the actor Hugh O'Brian and a few other house guests, and he added that he would be very pleased if Karen would join them. She replied that she would. Later, relaxing alone in her room, she was surprised at how comfortable she had felt in Hefner's presence, and how convincingly contented he had seemed within himself. Having watched him one night a year ago on the Johnny Carson television show in her college dormitory, she had sensed him to be somewhat artificial and forced in his manner; but in person he was more free-spirited, unassuming, and physically more attractive. She also found endearing the signs of adolescent sloppiness she had observed in his private quarters—the floors littered with scraps of paper and old magazines, bits of clothing carelessly tossed across chairs, the suitcase from his California trip opened but not yet unpacked. Despite the valets and many housekeepers dedicated to maintaining order and tidiness around the clock, Hugh Hefner conveyed the impression of having to be looked after more carefully, catered to more personally.

In the poolroom hours later with Hefner's guests, and still later standing around the pinball machines that Hefner skillfully nudged and patted with the palms of his hands, Karen Christy was constantly aware of Hefner's attention. He smiled at her as he chalked his cue tip, winked following each good shot, and, after delivering a joke or witty comment to the crowd, he would invariably look in her direction to study her reaction. While his lack of subtlety might have cost him points with a more worldly woman, Karen was flattered by it, preferring by far his open approach to the indirect tactics of a less forthright man. He seemed to be acknowledging not only to her but to the room at large—and particularly to the other attractive women gathered there—that he was overwhelmingly drawn to her; and while she chose not to dwell on where this all might lead, she was for the moment enjoying it immensely.

After a midnight supper, which had been carried on silver trays by butlers into the game room—and had been served on the glass tops of the pinball machines that Hefner and some of his guests continued to play while eating—the group drifted down to the underwater bar for drinks, swimming, and conversation. Hefner stayed close to Karen; and gradually the other people, sensing that he wanted privacy, left the two of them alone. It had been after one o'clock when they arrived, and three hours later they were still there, sitting together and talking softly at a small table under the hazy blue-green light glowing through the pool. He seemed avidly interested in learning more about her past, her schooling, her friends, how she had endured the hardships and the many deaths in her family. Although his questions were endless, he did not appear to be merely probing in the professional manner of a magazine editor—he seemed sincerely interested in knowing her intimately, eager to hear from her what nobody had ever taken the time to hear, and he listened for long periods without interrupting, allowing her to develop her thoughts in an unhurried way. She also listened while he discussed his own past, his disappointing marriage, his hopes for his children, and his current love affair in Los Angeles with Barbi Benton. Karen was especially appreciative of his candor regarding Barbi, a subject that a less honest man might have conveniently ignored on a first evening with someone new. As it happened, Karen was well aware of Barbi Benton, having seen her with Hefner on the Johnny Carson show, where their eventual marriage was mentioned as a possibility, although Karen remembered doubting at the time that Hefner would ever destroy his renowned bachelorhood for Barbi Benton or anyone else. And now, a year later, with Hefner in person, seeing how he enjoyed his life in his mansion filled with toys, Karen was even more convinced that he was a poor candidate for marriage— which was not meant as a criticism on her part; on the contrary, she relished the idea of being close to a rich and busy older man who had somehow retained a youthful vigor for fun and frolic. And as the hours passed in the underwater atmosphere of this timeless place, Karen was aware only of her pleasure and comfort in his company; and when he suggested that they return to his apartment to watch a movie, she stood and took his hand. Later, when he asked her to spend the night with him, she accepted without hesitation.

The marvelous mood of their first evening extended through the following day and into the next night; and much to Karen's delight and surprise, they remained compatible lovers and congenial companions throughout the entire week—interrupted only by his business meetings and her hours of training at the Playboy Club. But before she had been fitted for her Bunny uniform, Hefner asked if she would mind quitting her job so they would have more time together at night; he assured her she would not have to worry about the loss of salary, suggesting she could earn much more as a magazine model adorning the pages of *Playboy*. When she agreed to pose, Hefner instructed his photo editor to arrange for her test shots; and after days of shooting, Karen Christy became the *Playboy* centerfold for the December issue of 1971, for which she received $5,000.

Her sudden emergence as Hefner's lover in Chicago caused some astonishment and envy among the Bunnies in the dormitory; but as they realized that Hefner was serious about her, they resigned themselves to her privileged presence, and in time they came to like her. Though she now had access to a limousine and had charge accounts at his expense in Chicago stores, she remained essentially the same country girl she had been on the day of her arrival from Texas. She often walked around the mansion in bare feet, shorts, and a T-shirt. If influenced at all by her new surroundings, it was only evident in her abandonment of her brassiere, and in her developing skill at the games that Hefner and his close friends spent so much time playing—backgammon, Monopoly, and the pinball machines. She spent her days as she had done since her girlhood, watching soap operas on television, including "Another World," her favorite show, which she had begun watching at fourteen while living on her grandmother's farm; and if occasionally she missed it due to spending the afternoon in bed with Hefner, she knew that she could see it later at her convenience because the house engineer had been instructed by Hefner to tape its every installment.

When Hefner left for Los Angeles, as he did every other week, Karen expressed no resentment about his continuing interest in Barbi Benton; although as the months passed, and as Karen was becoming more emotionally involved with Hefner, she felt an increased loneliness and she privately wondered what, if anything, Barbi knew about her. But the telephone calls she received each day from Hefner when he was in California, and the gifts he gave her, reassured her. During their first month together, he had given her a diamond watch inscribed "with love"; and his Christmas gift to her in 1971 was a full-length white mink coat. In March 1972, on her twenty-first birthday, he gave her a five-karat diamond cocktail ring from Tiffany's. He also gave her an emerald ring, a silver fox jacket, a Matisse painting, a Persian cat, a beautiful metallic reproduction of the *Playboy* cover on which she was featured; and for her Christmas gift in 1972, she received a white Mark IV Lincoln.

With the money she was earning from her modeling and public appearances for *Playboy*, she bought for his Monopoly board such specially designed items as hand-carved hotels shaped like the Playboy Plaza Hotel in Miami, and tiny individual statues of the six people who were most often seen seated around the board; in addition to Hefner, whose two-and-a-half-inch-high sculptured likeness wore a colorful bathrobe and smoked a pipe, the other figurines represented Karen, Bobbie Arnstein, and John Dante, and two old Hefner friends and habitués of the mansion, Gene Siskel, the Chicago *Tribune* movie critic, and Shel Silverstein, the cartoonist and children's writer. She also commissioned a Chicago artist to do a three-dimensional portrait of Hugh Hefner, a large oil painting that showed him seated in a chair wearing a silk robe and smoking a pipe, while above his head was a cloud of white smoke in which was a small nude picture of Karen Christy. When she presented him with the gift, she amused him by pointing out that the section showing her was detachable, and that whenever he became tired of looking at it he could easily replace it with an inset of someone else.

But throughout 1972 into 1973, during their every-other-week reunions in Chicago, Hugh Hefner tired of neither her picture nor her presence, and he also began asking her to join him on airplane trips. He took her to Orlando, Florida, to see Disney World; to a resort hotel in the Caribbean, where he was being honored at a convention of magazine distributors; and to New York City, where there was a backgammon tournament. While in New York, after Karen had expressed a wish to do some shopping, Hefner reached into his pocket and handed her his wallet, then left to attend a meeting. In the wallet was $3,000. But as Karen wandered through stores along Fifth Avenue, she found herself checking the prices and resisting the impulse to buy; as outlandishly generous as Hefner was capable of being, Karen also knew that he was quietly conscious of how money was spent—and, not wanting to take advantage of him, nor to waste money herself on things she did not really need, she later returned the wallet with only $200 missing.

Karen Christy's sensitivity to certain conflicts in Hefner's nature, to his varying moods and unexpressed wishes, contributed greatly to the harmony of their relationship. One day when they were playing Monopoly in the Chicago mansion, a butler announced that Hefner's plane was ready to leave for Los Angeles; and Karen, though barefoot, quickly followed him out the door and accompanied him in the limousine to the airport. As Hefner boarded the plane with his business associates and friends, one of them playfully suggested that Karen come along for the ride—which, with Hefner's sudden approval, she did. During the flight west, she and the others resumed their game of Monopoly and enjoyed a festive lunch, while the pilots, following Hefner's instructions, radioed ahead for a separate limousine that would take Karen to a Beverly Hills shoe store, and then back to the Los Angeles airport, where an airline ticket would be waiting for her return trip to Chicago.

After this flight, Karen sometimes traveled from Chicago on commercial planes to join Hefner at the Los Angeles airport, and then fly back with him on the Playboy jet so that they could gain extra hours of pleasure together. Time—not money—was of primary importance to Hefner if love and pleasure were involved. He had often said following his fortieth birthday—when his personal fortune exceeded $100 million dollars—that money was no longer a factor in his life, but time was; and that he would spare no expense in gaining time to fulfill his romantic desires. Once, when Karen was visiting her relatives in Texas, Hefner dispatched a Lear jet at the cost of more than $10,000 to pick her up in Dallas and bring her to the Los Angeles airport so that she could be with him on the Playboy DC-9 jet headed back to Chicago.

On another occasion, when he returned to Chicago without her, he was surprised to see that the trees outside the Chicago mansion were festooned with yellow ribbons, a decoration inspired by a song currently popular around the nation—''Tie a Yellow Ribbon''—a recording of which Karen had bought for him weeks before; the song described a returning lover for whom the sign of continued affection was a yellow ribbon tied to an oak tree, and Hefner had immediately responded to the song, and asked that it be played repeatedly on the mansion's big stereo. But since the song was on a 45 rpm recording that was not made for continuous play, Hefner asked one of the butlers to stand next to the stereo and, as soon as the record was finished, lift the needle and put it back to the beginning. The butler spent an entire evening replaying the song.

As *Playboy* magazine in 1973 approached its twentieth anniversary in publishing, with its monthly circulation at 6 million, Hugh Hefner continued to divide his time evenly and happily between his two mansions and his two women. At forty-six, he seemingly had enough time, money, power, and imagination to control every aspect of his life except his final fate; and as a one-time movie usher who had wishfully dreamed in a darkened theater of escaping the tedious world of reality, he had finally achieved his long-sought ambition: Hugh Hefner was now living a movie. Sheltering himself in elaborate sets, controlling the lights and the music, he was the leading man in a Captain's Paradise that continued uninterruptedly through the unnoticed hours of succeeding weeks and months.

In the larger world outside, as inflation and higher taxes victimized American families, it seemed grossly unfair to many people that a man like Hugh Hefner should have it so good, that his businesses should continue to expand and flourish—as his publicity department proclaimed—while he concentrated on chasing women and playing Monopoly. Although there were numerous men who were far wealthier than Hefner, the public was either unaware or unenvious of them since they rarely appeared on television and never called attention to the fact that they were enjoying themselves. Typical among them were the Rockefeller brothers, who seemed burdened with responsibility; J. Paul Getty, a feeble old man who appeared to be lonesome in his every public photograph; and Howard Hughes, a paranoiac recluse hiding in hotel rooms while dependent on sober Mormon male nurses. The photographs of harem-keeping Arab potentates sometimes published in *Paris Match* and American news-magazines showed men who were invariably obese or scowling, complaining of personal ailments and fearful of armed fanatics. The power brokers in American politics, when they kept mistresses on the payroll, seemed to be sooner or later exposed in the press and sometimes further vilified in confessional autobiographies by the ladies themselves.

But Hefner's constant and well-publicized philandering with

his female employees and centerfold starlets was heralded in *Playboy* as an "alternate lifestyle," and with each passing year he seemed to be undermining more defiantly the Judeo-Christian tradition that associated excessive pleasure with punishment. Though his aging body was allegedly subjected to the exhaustive daily demands of frisky females, he never looked better in his life. Though he ate much junk food, he never gained weight; and his consumption of caseloads of Pepsi apparently failed to erode his teeth. While he confronted many problems as the head of a major corporation that had several subsidiaries, with thousands of employees around the nation and overseas, he rarely hinted that he was under pressure, nor was he known to have ever visited a psychiatrist.

The successful launching of a raunchy, gynecologically specific sex magazine called *Hustler*, whose founder, Larry Flynt, believed that *Playboy* would soon become obsolete—and the fact that *Penthouse* now had a rising monthly circulation of 4 million—did not alarm Hugh Hefner; and after his editors had reacted to such competition by publishing pinups in *Playboy* that seemed too brazen by Hefner's standards, he reminded his staff that he did not want the girl-next-door to look like a trollop.

Even when there appeared to be legitimate causes for concern in the casual way his corporation was functioning, Hefner's natural optimism and enormous ego prevented him from taking quick corrective measures. He saw positive signs in each unfavorable report: To the news that Playboy's movie division had lost millions in producing such films as *The Naked Ape* and Roman Polanski's version of *Macbeth*, Hefner emphasized that his company had gained valuable experience from these ventures and he also pointed out that *Macbeth* had been named Best Film of the Year by the National Film Review Board; and in responding to evidence that his key clubs around the nation—and his resort hotels in Miami Beach and Jamaica, in Lake Geneva, Wisconsin, and Great Gorge, New Jersey—were with few exceptions unprofitable, Hefner said that he was not discouraged, that better days were ahead. Meanwhile he continued to support with unimpressive results a book division, a music publishing and record company, movie theaters in Chicago and New York, a limousine service, a model agency, and a firm that manufactured gadgets and gewgaws bearing Bunny emblems. His Playboy Towers Hotel in Chicago was loosely managed and losing money; and *Playboy* magazine's somewhat kinky sister publication, *Oui*, which was introduced in 1972 to more directly

compete with *Penthouse*, was apparently more successful in luring readers away from *Playboy*, which during the year following
Oui's appearance went from a peak monthly circulation of
7 million down to 6. And while *Playboy* magazine remained the
most lucrative men's magazine in the world, and additional
millions were being earned overseas by Playboy's three gambling casinos in England, the Playboy corporate stock had
dropped a dozen points in as many months on the New York
Stock Exchange—circumstances that Hefner attributed not to
the condition of his company, but to the national recession, inflation, and poor leadership in Washington. When an inter-
viewer asked him if, in view of what seemed to be happening
to his corporate investments, he might soon return to the Playboy building as a day-to-day executive, he insisted that his office
days were over. "I have something more important to do," he
replied. "It's called living."

Elaborating on his position that he was more efficient in a
mansion than he would be in an office, Hefner explained in an
interview that was published in *Playboy*: "Man is the only animal capable of controlling his environment, and what I've created is a private world that permits me to live my life without a
lot of the wasted time and motion that consume a large part of
most people's lives. The man who has a job in the city and a
house in the suburbs is losing two or three hours a day simply
moving himself physically from where he lives to where he works
and back again. Then he has to take the time and energy to go
out for lunch in some crowded restaurant, where he's more than
likely dealt with in a rushed and impersonal fashion. He's living
his life according to a preconceived notion—certainly not his
own—of what a daily routine ought to be. . . . The details of
most people's daily regimen," Hefner went on, "are dictated
by the clock. They eat breakfast, lunch and dinner at a time
generally prescribed by social custom. They work during the
day and sleep at night. But in the mansion it is, quite literally,
the time of day that you want it to be. . . . One of the greatest
sources of frustration in contemporary society is that people feel
so powerless, not only in relation to what happens in the world
around them but in influencing what happens in their own lives.
Well, I don't feel that frustration, because I've taken control of
my life."

But there was part of his life over which he suddenly lost
control during the summer and fall of 1973, and, because it
involved his two favorite women, he displayed to his household

staff an uncharacteristic lack of composure and even signs of panic. What provoked this was a story in *Time* magazine in July entitled "Adventures in the Skin Trade"; and in addition to stressing the heightened rivalry between *Playboy* and *Penthouse*, as well as speculating on how the Supreme Court's *Miller* ruling might inhibit men's magazines, *Time* printed a photograph showing Hefner in Los Angeles being embraced by Barbi Benton, and a second picture of him sitting in the Chicago mansion with his arm around Karen Christy. "Long a two-of-everything consumer," *Time* wrote, "Hefner has lately extended the principle to his romantic life. Former Playmate Barbi Benton, his longtime escort, lives in the California mansion; blonde Karen Christy, an ex-Bunny in the Chicago Playboy Club, is ensconced in his Chicago quarters. Somehow the arrangement continues to work."

The magazine provided Barbi Benton with the first indication that Hefner was more than casually involved with another woman; and that he had knowingly allowed himself to be photographed with Karen Christy for a newsmagazine was inexcusable to Barbi. Without telephoning or notifying Hefner in any way, Barbi packed a suitcase and left the mansion. When Hefner learned of her departure, he immediately summoned his pilots to fly him to California—greatly upsetting Karen Christy, who had been led to believe in recent months that Hefner was more in love with her than with Barbi, a view that he had not only expressed but had further demonstrated by spending more time of late in Chicago than in Los Angeles.

Reassuring Karen as he kissed her good-bye that she was paramount in his life, but nonetheless insisting that he felt obliged to appease Barbi—and that he had to do it in person—he left for Los Angeles. Karen seemed to understand his leaving; Barbi had been in Hefner's life before she had, and Hefner had convinced Karen that Barbi deserved his direct explanation. What Hefner did not admit to Karen was that he wanted Barbi to return, that he needed them both, that he was attracted to each for different reasons. He admired Barbi Benton for her vitality and blithe spirit; and the fact that he could not completely control this financially independent Californian, who was also striving to establish her identity as a country-and-western singer, made her more challenging to him, and constantly desirable. Like his mother, his former wife, and his daughter completing college, Barbi Benton was a woman of wholesome appeal and uncommon character; but in other areas that were important to

Hefner—and particularly within the walls of his bedroom—Barbi
was no match for Karen Christy. Though shy in a crowd, Karen
was uninhibited in private; and during his vast and varied exotic
past, he had never known anyone who could surpass her skill
and ardor in bed. The sight of her removing her clothes thrilled
him; and after he had covered her body with oil—which she
seemed to enjoy as much as he—the smooth, soothing, glistening lovemaking on the satin sheets aroused him to peaks of
passionate pleasure. Unlike Barbi, who was often tired in the
evening after rehearsing in studios, and who disliked it when oil
got into her hair on those nights when she had auditions on the
following morning, Karen was not ambitious about a career and
she had many free hours during the day for the washing and
drying of her hair. Hefner was also pleased that Karen shared
his enthusiasm for backgammon and the other games, and was
always willing and available to travel with him, or to take planes
to meet him whenever he called. When he was in the mood to
be with just one other person, that person was usually Karen
Christy; but when he was serving as a host at a large party—and
especially at one of the fund-raisers for social causes that he
frequently sponsored—he preferred to have Barbi Benton at his
side. She had more social poise than Karen, was a better con-
versationalist, was capable of making a speech. Although her
television appearances as a singer and comedienne had so far
made her seem trivial and superficial, she was in person intelligent and astute; and she was the only woman he had met in
recent years who he thought could make him an acceptable wife.

While he had no intention of offering marriage to Barbi as a
possible inducement for her return, he also could not imagine
being happy in his West Coast mansion if she was not in residence; and as soon as he landed in Los Angeles, and located
her by telephone at a hotel in Hawaii—where he was relieved to
learn that she was staying with a lady friend—he pleaded for
forgiveness and urged that she not allow the one article in *Time*
to destroy their years of love and understanding. Though she
remained cool on the phone, and insisted that she would stay
another week in Hawaii, she did agree to speak with him in
person after her return to Los Angeles. But when he next saw
her, she was still upset and remote; and while she conceded that
she still loved him and hoped that their relationship could be
revived, she announced that she had gotten an apartment of her
own in Beverly Hills, a place to which she could go when she

wanted to get away from the house guests, the Bunnies, and the ongoing backgammon games at the mansion.

After Barbi Benton had joined Hugh Hefner in bed, she promised that she would not date other men, and Hefner promised that he would be faithful in his fashion; and from then on he sent flowers proclaiming his love each and every day to her apartment. During this time he was speaking on the telephone daily to Karen Christy, who seemed eager for his return; but when he moved back into the Chicago mansion, he could sense that she, too, was somehow different, more reserved, less free with him, even though she told him nothing had changed between them.

The routine of the mansion slowly returned to normal: The pinball machines and table games were played through the night; the Bunnies shuttled back and forth between the dormitory and the club; the *Playboy* editors regularly arrived for meetings in Hefner's suite—but a sense of restiveness permeated the big house. Extra teams of security guards, hired to stand watch around the property ever since the kidnapping of Patricia Hearst, lent an air of emergency by their very presence behind the gates; and in addition there were signs of anxiety in the manner of Hefner's secretary, Bobbie Arnstein, once a gentle influence in the house but now involved in a troubled love affair with a handsome and erratic young drug dealer who quietly and unpredictably visited her lower-floor apartment in the rear of the mansion.

Hefner's most trusted male friend, John Dante, announced one day during this time that he had to get away. For years he had lived in the mansion as Hefner's emissary to the clubs, but the job was now very undemanding and often boring, and recently Dante had referred to himself bitterly as an aging "game player." Though he remained devoted to Hugh Hefner—and would be forever grateful for Hefner's loan in 1968 of nearly $40,000 that allowed Dante to pay off the Chicago bookies to whom he was in debt for gambling on pro football games— Dante seemed desperate for a vacation from Hefner's paradise; and with Hefner's reluctant blessing, Dante climbed into a Jeep, together with the 1973 Bunny of the Year, and headed for Taos, New Mexico.

And then one evening, after emerging for a business meeting, Hefner discovered that Karen Christy was missing from the mansion. She had been seen earlier in the afternoon by some of the house guests and guards, but a quick inspection of every

room of the house, including the secret passageways and hide-
aways, failed to reveal a trace of her. By midnight Hefner was
visibly shaken and exasperated; and responding to a suggestion
that she might be visiting the apartment of a Bunny friend named
Nanci Heitner, with whom Karen Christy often spent time while
Hefner was out of town, Hefner quickly put on a coat over his
pajamas, jumped into his chauffeur-driven Mercedes, and, accompanied by guards, drove through a light snow into the Lincoln Park section of Chicago.

When the driver stopped in front of the old four-story red
brick building where Nanci Heitner lived, Hefner and the guards
hastened toward a dark doorway that had no overhead light, and,
as they lit matches, they squinted at the mailbox in an attempt
to locate the Heitner name and apartment number. There was a
row of six buttons along the box, but the plastic nameplates were
either missing or illegible; and so the impatient Hefner began
to press all six buttons repeatedly. When the door was finally
buzzed open, he stood at the staircase and called up in a loud
voice: "Hello, I'm Hugh Hefner—is Karen Christy up there?"

The two guards carrying walkie-talkies, and Hefner carrying
an open Pepsi, waited momentarily for a sign of response. When
none came, Hefner proceeded to climb the steps and to knock
on each door, repeating: "I'm Hugh Hefner, and I'm looking
for Karen Christy." Soon, on the second floor, he heard noises
coming from the other side of a door, saw a streaming through
the cracks and the peephole.

"What do you want?" a woman cried from behind the
peephole.

"I'm Hugh Hefner, and . . ."

"Are you *really* Hugh Hefner?" she asked, still not unlock-
ing the door. Then Hefner heard a man's voice in the background asking the woman what the commotion was about, and
she replied: "Some nut outside says he's Hugh Hefner."

Nobody on the second floor or the third would open doors,
but Hefner continued up another flight of steps; and after he
knocked on apartment 4-A, he heard a dog barking and a voice
announcing: "Karen's not here." The door opened, and Nanci
Heitner, a blondish young woman wearing a black robe, and
holding back her Tibetan watchdog, let Hefner and the guards
in. "She's not here—you can see for yourself." As Hefner apologized for the late-hour interruption, the guards searched
through Nanci Heitner's rooms, in her closets, under her bed.
Hefner looked haggard and desolate, his hair was blown wild,

his Pepsi bottle was empty. After the guards had completed their search, Nanci Heitner walked with him to the door, feeling sorry for him.

Hefner's car had barely pulled away from the curb when, moments later, the telephone rang. It was the sobbing voice of Karen Christy saying that she was in a phone booth and wanted to come over, adding that she *had* to get away from the faithless Hugh Hefner. After Karen had arrived, wearing a heavy coat and boots, her hair wet from the snow and her mascara smeared with tears, she explained that earlier in the day, as she awoke from a nap, she had overheard Hefner in the next room talking on the telephone to Barbi in Los Angeles, reaffirming his love and even making arrangements to join her for a weekend in Aspen. The night before, Karen told Nanci, Hefner had declared that it was all over with Barbi, claiming that during his recent visit to California he realized that Barbi no longer enthralled him. Obviously, Karen concluded, Hefner was deceiving her; and Nanci Heitner, concurring, suggested that she pack her things at the mansion and leave it forever.

Nanci Heitner was beginning to grow weary of hearing Karen constantly talking about Hefner, complaining about his selfish nature and how painful it was being involved with him. Frustrated in her desire to possess him exclusively, and lonely in the mansion when he was out of town, Karen had lately gotten into the habit of calling Nanci at all hours of the night, interrupting Nanci's sleep after she had come home tired from work, or interrupting Nanci when she was in bed with a man. While Nanci always listened patiently, her lovers invariably became restless, piqued, or continued to make love while Nanci held the phone to her ear—which Nanci minded less than acknowledging to Karen that she was too busy to listen, for she had become concerned of late about Karen's mental stability and health, being aware that Karen had lost fifteen pounds and was indulging heavily in sleeping pills. Nanci was also very fond of Karen and identified with her. Like Karen, Nanci Heitner had been reared in a family of much hardship and death; and, like Karen, she had come to work for *Playboy* hoping that it would somehow introduce her to influential people and social opportunities that had previously been lacking in her impoverished past. Although nothing very special had yet happened to Nanci, she had reveled in the Cinderella situation of her friend; and, in a small way, Nanci had benefited from it. At the club, where the managers knew that she was close to the woman who was closest to Hefner in Chicago, Nanci was deferentially treated as a person who, through Karen, could get messages to Hefner much faster than if they were sent through official channels. Indeed, Nanci frequently spoke directly to Hefner himself since he recently had begun calling her from Los Angeles on those occasions when an anguished Karen had hung up on him; he would call Nanci and ask her to deliver messages to Karen, asking her to call him back with Karen's reaction. Since he never told Nanci to call him collect, the discord between Hugh Hefner and Karen Christy was greatly escalating Nanci Heitner's telephone bill.

Still, Nanci was slow in complaining because she was flattered by her trusted role as their intermediary, and she also knew that Karen was often too confused to act rationally in her own behalf. Had Karen fallen in love with a married man with children, she would have better understood the ground rules; but the dilemma was in becoming ensnared in a whirlwind romance with an adolescent tycoon who wanted to monopolize the love of two women—and every time he chose to be with one, it was doubly destructive to the ego of the other, because he was clearly signifying his choice rather than fulfilling an obligation to a wife and family. Nanci knew that it was particularly depressing for Karen during holidays: While Hefner usually spent Christmas with Karen in Chicago, he was with Barbi for the big New Year's Eve party at Playboy Mansion West. And Nanci was quite sure that if Hugh Hefner was not with Barbi Benton he would be with another young woman—he would always want what he did not have, he enjoyed the chase, and he would always be simultaneously drawn to two different types of women: the healthy, perky "good" girl personified by Barbi, and the big-breasted, sexy "bad" girl that Karen represented. Nanci knew that the situation with Hefner was impossible for Karen; he would never marry her, which had lately become her hope, nor could he offer her even a semblance of the personal commitment that her insecurity required. And now, following this latest visit by Hefner and his guards to her apartment, Nanci Heitner had all but exhausted her patience with Karen's ongoing soap opera. She felt compassion but emphasized to Karen that there was no future for a woman in Hefner's bed; and Karen, though tearful at times, nodded in agreement and promised that she would end the affair at once.

The two young women spoke for hours, leaving the apartment

at 2 A.M. for a final drink in the more cheerful ambience of the nearby Four Torches bar. But as they returned to the apartment building two hours later, they saw Hefner's car cruising along the street; and when Hefner spotted them, he jumped out of the car and ran toward Karen with outstretched arms. Karen, stopping next to Nanci, cursed under her breath; but as he approached her with tears in his eyes, and his arms reaching out to her, Karen suddenly moved forward to embrace him, and she too began to cry. As the two of them held one another tightly and exchanged tender words, Nanci turned; and as Hefner led Karen toward the open door of the limousine, Nanci Heitner climbed up the steps leading to her apartment.

Hefner assured Karen on the following day that the phone call she had overheard regarding the Aspen weekend was not to Barbi Benton, but rather to his daughter, Christie Hefner. This somewhat assuaged Karen's hurt feelings, although in truth she was almost less enamored of Hefner's Phi Beta Kappa daughter than she was of Barbi Benton. Karen had met Christie Hefner several times when Christie was visiting from college with her friends, and she recently had been upset when she overheard one of the boy friend's disparaging remark about Hefner's "concubinage." Karen also had heard that Hefner's daughter and Barbi Benton got along well in Los Angeles, and had gone on a shopping spree together in Beverly Hills, and this made Karen, at this sensitive time, even more insecure. But Hugh Hefner had given no indication, at least to Karen, that he could be influenced by his daughter's judgment of his women; and she was encouraged when he suggested that they take a short vacation in Acapulco. It had been a long, cold winter for Karen in Chicago and she looked forward to a few days of lying in the sun.

They were accompanied by a couple of Hefner's friends whom Karen liked, and the visit to Acapulco was for her a reprieve from all the turmoil of the past months; Hefner was giving her his most valuable gift—his time—and during the effulgent days and nights that followed she luxuriated in his presence and wished that it could continue indefinitely. But the warm outdoors and tranquil evenings were of limited appeal to Hefner; and after one week, citing office problems that demanded his immediate attention, the restless publisher prepared for his premature departure while convincing Karen to remain with his friends through the weekend.

On the way to the airport, sitting close to him in the back of

the car, Karen wondered aloud when they would next be together. After he had offered a vague reply, she pressed him to
be specific, wanting to know approximately how long his business would take, and when she might count on seeing him again.
But he remained stubbornly noncommittal and distant—it was
as if he were already in the air, miles away, out of range. And
as she walked with him arm in arm through the crowded terminal, and out toward the glaring runway where the Playboy
plane was waiting, she felt her anxiety rising; and before kissing
him good-bye, she tried one more time to elicit from him a direct
answer to her urgent question—at which point, suddenly and
furiously, he took the hard leather attaché case that he was carrying and hurled it high in the air toward his plane. As the case
bounced heavily on the ground and skidded forward several feet,
Hefner bolted toward it like a greyhound chasing a mechanical
rabbit; and when he reached it, he jumped on top of it with both
feet, stomping up and down many times. While his pilots observed with astonishment, and groups of suntanned straw-hatted
tourists also stopped to look, the petrified Karen Christy ran
toward him; but before she reached him, he had miraculously
calmed down, his tempestuous outburst having exhausted itself
within a few seconds. As he stepped down from his case, he
seemed neither embarrassed nor even fully aware of what he
had done. And after he had retrieved his somewhat battered
valise, and had kissed Karen good-bye, he proceeded without
delay up the metal staircase into the cabin of his plane.

Later that night he telephoned her at the hotel, said he was
sorry if he had frightened her, told her that everything was fine,
and promised that he would notify her as soon as he had resolved
the problems he was confronting. In a telephone conversation
days later, after Karen had expressed a wish to visit her relatives
in Texas, he encouraged her to go, and even offered to fly the
Playboy plane from Los Angeles to Dallas at the completion of
her visit and accompany her back to Chicago. This was a grand
gesture on his part—the trip from Los Angeles to Chicago via
Dallas was hardly the direct route that he preferred to travel,
and he also said that he would be happy to meet her uncle, aunt,
and her other relatives who would be with her at the Dallas
airport.

True to his word, the black DC-9 with the white bunny emblem painted on its tail landed at the new Dallas/Fort Worth
Airport; and as the unusual plane came slowly to a halt in front

of the observation deck of the white terminal, several hundred people—travelers, ticket agents, baggage porters, bathroom attendants, ruddy men wearing ten-gallon hats, women holding children, long-haired young people carrying guitars—all suddenly turned and gazed through the gigantic window that overlooked the field.

The plane was the only big jet ever to be painted black, which was exactly why Hefner had chosen that color; and as the plane's steps were lowered and the cabin door swung open, Hefner stood momentarily alone on the top step, his hair and silk shirt moving in the breeze, his intense dark eyes focused on the mass of silent faces staring down at him from behind the massive pane of glass. He had not been in the state of Texas in nearly thirty years. When he had first visited Texas, in the summer of 1944, he arrived on a troop train headed for Camp Hood—a skinny, eighteen-year-old recent high school graduate who had been voted by his class the third most likely to succeed. Now, at forty-seven, he had returned to lay claim to one of Texas' most curvesome blondes, to greet her relatives, and, with no intentions toward marriage, to carry her away to Chicago—an act that in an earlier time would have surely aroused the rancor of her kinfolks and provoked the sound of shotguns.

Walking toward the terminal, with his guards a few paces behind, Hefner spotted Karen waving at him from the top of the ramp, smiling from under her straw hat. Wearing clogs, a slim skirt, and a T-shirt that left little to the imagination, Karen edged through the crowd to greet him, and to introduce him to the relatives with whom she had stayed at a cabin on Eagle Mountain Lake. There were her aunt and uncle, her three cousins, her two gangly teenaged stepbrothers wearing jeans, her twenty-year-old sister, Bonnie, who was carrying a crying one-year-old baby, and Bonnie's husband, an Air Force sergeant on leave from his base in Tokyo.

Removing his pipe, Hefner shook hands with them, smiled, and engaged them in conversation; and when a photographer came over, Hefner agreed to pose with the group. Meanwhile his friends from the plane—men wearing gold medallions and open-necked shirts, jet Bunnies in shiny black skintight uniforms, and a plume-hatted centerfold model carrying a poodle—had stepped onto the runway, seeming restless, and were looking up at the crowd; and Hefner, concluding his chat with Karen's relatives, took her arm and headed back toward the plane.

The crowd, not moving, continued to watch as the engines started; and they were still watching when the black airplane had become a distant object in the sky.

Having established a stronger sense of herself, and what she wanted, during her time away from Chicago, Karen was slow in readjusting to the routine of the mansion. The absence of John Dante had deprived her of the one male friend that she could confide in when Hefner was away; and when Hefner was there, his many business meetings and the personal problems of his secretary, Bobbie Arnstein, so preoccupied him that an uncharacteristic air of foreboding and even gloom pervaded the Chicago household. Days before Karen had returned, Bobbie Arnstein was arrested outside the mansion on charges of having earlier conspired with her boy friend, among other young men, to transport a half pound of cocaine from Florida to Chicago. On the day of her arrest she was discovered to be carrying in her purse a variety of pills, including a small quantity of cocaine. Freed on $4,500 bail, her name and photograph were thrust onto front pages around the country, and, by implication, Hefner and the mansion staff and his entourage were under suspicion of indulging, and perhaps even trafficking, in drugs. Although Hefner steadfastly supported Bobbie Arnstein throughout the litigation and paid the bills of her attorneys, the abundant publicity was clearly disturbing him, particularly when he believed that there was probably less drug consumption in his mansions than in the average dormitory on an American campus.

The drug probe was not Hefner's only distraction at this time: There was a charge of discrimination brought against *Playboy* by a black employee who had been passed over for promotion in the company's personnel department; there was an intensified IRS investigation originally initiated by the Nixon White House after Hefner was placed on the ''enemies list''; and there were continuing reports of Playboy's declining stock prices and the conspicuous losses in its hotel operations and other subsidiary ventures. Suddenly, after years of astounding profits, abysmal bliss, and apparent control over his environment, Hefner's foundation seemed shaken; and while Karen Christy would have willingly remained at his side if she felt she had a real place in his world, she was convinced at this time that it was foolish of her to remain. She was only a part of his folly, a prop for his image. Though she knew it was silly, she felt old at twenty-three, a shrew who eavesdropped on his phone calls, a bed partner whom he easily replaced when they were apart. She had been told by one of the jet Bunnies that, on the day before his plane landed in Dallas, Hefner had spent the night in his Los Angeles bed (while Barbi Benton was out of town on a singing assignment) with the centerfold model who had ridden with the poodle on the plane; and though Karen was not so naïve as to ever expect Hefner's sexual fidelity to extend much longer than a week, she was no longer willing to abide by his expectations that she remain uninvolved with other men. There was a young man in Dallas whom she knew and had even dated secretly. She was sure there were other men in the world outside whom she would enjoy meeting. And so with much encouragement from her Bunny friend Nanci Heitner, Karen Christy decided at last that she would pack her bags and, without a word to Hefner, permanently leave the mansion.

The problem of getting her things past the security guards was not inconsiderable, but she eventually devised a plan that enabled her to send her possessions to Dallas without alerting anyone in the house who might report it to Hefner. Explaining to the maids and butlers that she was sending her unwanted clothes to her poor relatives in Texas, she packed in cardboard boxes, little by little, her furs, her jewels, and her vast wardrobe of dresses and negligees that Hefner had given her. After mailing more than thirty boxes during a two-week period to her aunt in Dallas, Karen Christy managed to get her white Lincoln into the hands of a former Bunny whom she knew she could trust; and, on a day when Hefner was in Los Angeles, she used a chauffeured limousine to go shopping at one of her favorite boutiques on Rush Street.

While the chauffeur and a security guard sat waiting in the car, Karen entered the shop and, with the help of a saleslady she knew, was able to exit through a rear door to a parallel street, where she hailed a taxicab that took her to the place where her car and two girl friends were waiting. One of them, Nanci Heitner, was there to help with the long drive to Dallas—a trip that they would accomplish in sixteen hours, using Dexedrine to stay awake. Along the way, many miles from Chicago, Karen paused to use a roadside phone to say good-bye to Bobbie Arnstein and to explain that she simply could not stay at the mansion any longer.

After Bobbie Arnstein had relayed the message to Hefner in Los Angeles, he became agitated and fretful, and for the next week he telephoned Karen repeatedly and tried to convince her to return. But while she wanted to maintain their friendship, and agreed to visit him from time to time in Los Angeles, she told him she would never go back to Chicago. She had just gotten a small apartment in Dallas, had been hired as a model by a local agency, and was dating a young executive with a computer firm, whom she had met previously in Dallas. While she continued to drive her white Lincoln, she had no use for her furs and expensive jewelry. Around her neck she was soon wearing a gold chain given her by her new boy friend; and suspended from it was a fourteen-karat price tag on which was printed: ''Sold.''

In a federal courtroom in November 1974, having been found guilty of conspiracy in bringing a half pound of cocaine into Chicago, Hefner's secretary Bobbie Arnstein was sentenced to fifteen years in prison—five years longer than the harshest sentence received by her male co-conspirators who had negotiated and carried out the transaction. Although federal agents knew from personal surveillance and the wiretaps placed on her boy friend, Ron Scharf, that she was aware and approving of his activities, and was a drug user herself—and had accompanied him to Miami where the deal was made—her lawyer insisted that she had mainly gone ''along for the ride,'' being enamored of young Scharf, who was seven years her junior, and wanting to prove her compatibility in the hip and daring drug culture that he personified to her.

The fact that her long sentence was ''provisional,'' and could be greatly reduced and maybe suspended if she would become a government informer against other drug users or distributors of her acquaintance—which was the method the federal agents had used in inducing a narcotics convict to implicate Bobbie Arnstein, Ron Scharf, and another young man—convinced Arnstein's attorneys that the lawmen were less interested in punishing her than in using her to get the man for whom they suspected she might be obtaining the drugs, namely her boss, Hugh Hefner.

For years in Chicago, law-enforcement authorities and church groups had been offended by Hefner's hedonism and expanding wealth, but they had so far been unable to imprison him as a criminal. In 1963, after a pictorial display of Jayne Mansfield in *Playboy* was declared to be obscene, a vice squad with a warrant forced its way into the mansion, accused Hefner of publishing filth, and literally dragged him out of bed to be booked at the station house. But he was released on bail, and in the subsequent trial he won his freedom after a hung-jury verdict.

However, the drug case against Bobbie Arnstein, his most intimate employee, seemed to present a more promising opportunity to finally check Hefner and his influence, which now, eleven years after the obscenity arrest, had spread to the extent that his magazine was openly displayed on newsstands all over the nation, even in the drugstores of very conservative communities. With part of his fortune, Hugh Hefner had established a foundation that lobbied for the decriminalization of marijuana and opposed all forms of authoritarian repression; and because he was a party-giver whose invitees regularly included rock stars, jazz musicians, and young political radicals, it was reasonable for the federal and state investigators to assume that, even though Hefner himself might not indulge, his generosity as a host would prompt him to cater to the habits of his guests. In the forefront of the investigation against Hefner was the United States attorney for the Northern District of Illinois, James R. Thompson, who years before in Chicago had prosecuted the case against Lenny Bruce and who, following the wide press attention he received during the Arnstein-Hefner inquiry, would become the next governor of Illinois.

One month after Bobbie Arnstein had been sentenced, James Thompson summoned her and her attorney to his office and informed them that he had learned from reliable sources that there was a "contract" out on her life, and he warned her that during the time she was free on bail she should trust "neither friend nor foe." The Arnstein attorney interpreted this as an attempt to further frighten an already intimidated defendant into suspecting her employer, and perhaps terrify her to a point where she would testify against him. If this was the government's intention, it did not succeed; but although Bobbie Arnstein had no doubt of Hefner's continued loyalty and affection, she began to feel somewhat uneasy in the mansion and even wary when the butlers brought to her room her usual drink and midnight snack.

Adding further to her sense of isolation and discomfort in this place that had so long been her home was the guilt she felt each day as she saw the newspapers and read of the government's widening probe into the private lives of Hefner's friends and associates, his house staff, the Bunnies, and many of the celebrities whom he had entertained not only in Chicago but in Los Angeles. The investigators also pulled from their files the case of a Bunny named Adrienne Pollack, whose death in 1973 was suspected to be the result of an overdose of Quaaludes. Though Hefner claimed to have never met Adrienne Pollack, and though at the time of her death she was living with a boy friend who was an admitted user of narcotics, the headlines linked Hefner with her demise, and a separate grand jury was established to reinvestigate the Pollack case.

Among the dozens of people who were questioned about Hefner was a former *Playboy* editor named Frank Brady, who had recently written an unauthorized biography of the publisher; but instead of concentrating on the extent of Hefner's possible involvement with the procurement or use of drugs, Brady was mainly asked about Hefner's sexual affairs and the type of activity that transpired in his bedroom. The same line of questioning was followed with others who were queried—the investigators seemed eager to present the Arnstein conspiracy case in an atmosphere of sex and drugs, degeneracy and death. While Hefner could not protect himself against deprecations upon his character, he was determined to thwart any possible attempt by investigators to infiltrate his property and "plant" in obscure places sample of drugs that they would later uncover as evidence against him. After ordering his security force to search every nook, cranny, and medicine cabinet in his two mansions, he called for stricter vigilance at the gates and a closer scrutiny of all delivery boys, maintenance crews, and other outsiders who passed through the service entrance. His engineers periodically checked the phones against wiretapping and electronically "swept" the rooms and halls for any evidence of "bugs."

In this time of heightened suspicion Bobbie Arnstein became increasingly morose, and on two occasions, while her appeal was pending, she took an overdose of sleeping pills and required medical treatment. Although Hefner invited her to work in the sunnier surroundings of the California office, where he was now spending most of his time since Karen Christy's departure, his attorneys urged that she not live in the Los Angeles mansion, warning that she might still be dependent on drugs. When a close woman friend in Chicago, a former *Playboy* employee named Shirley Hillman, discussed moving with her family to Los Angeles to share a home with Bobbie, the shift to the Coast seemed tempting; but Bobbie resisted because she knew that in California she would be reliant on an automobile. She had been afraid of driving ever since an accident in 1963 when, on a road in Kentucky with her fiancé, an associate editor named Tom

Lownes—a brother to the *Playboy* executive Victor Lownes—she had hit a bump in the road, veered onto the dirt shoulder into a tree, and overturned Lownes' Volkswagen. Thrown out of the vehicle, she broke an arm and suffered other injuries; but Lownes, trapped in the car, died instantly. For many months thereafter Bobbie Arnstein was haunted by moods of depression, and could not be left alone day or night as she relived the accident and blamed herself again and again for her fiancé's death.

Still, after Hefner's suggestion during the winter of 1974 that she join him in California, she promised she would fly out soon after the New Year's holiday. During the second week in January, on a Saturday night, she had dinner at the North Side apartment of Shirley and Richard Hillman, and appeared to be optimistic about her future and also hopeful about the outcome of her case. She said that it was unlikely that she would be sent to prison.

At 1:30 A.M. a male friend drove her back to the mansion, where, after checking her messages—there were none—she obtained a fifth of liquor from the night houseman and carried it to her bedroom. After a few drinks, she packed a cosmetics case and left the mansion for a walk. Blocks south, on North Rush Street, she pushed through the revolving door of the aging Hotel Maryland, where, in the basement nightclub during the 1950s, Lenny Bruce had entertained audiences that often included Hugh Hefner. Signing the hotel register under the name "Roberta Hillman," Bobbie Arnstein took the elevator to the seventeenth floor and, after entering her room, hung a "Do Not Disturb" sign on the knob and double-locked and bolted the door. Through the window of her room she could see the thirty-seven-story skyscraper topped by a large-lettered sign beaming in the night: PLAYBOY. Shortly before 3 A.M., she made three telephone calls—one to the man who had driven her home (there was no answer); one to the mansion to check if there were any late messages (there were none); and one to the Hillman apartment. Richard Hillman answered, and, though Shirley was asleep, he said he would awaken her; but Bobbie told him not to, adding, "Just tell her I called." In Bobbie Arnstein's cosmetics case were bottles containing barbiturates, sleeping pills, and tranquilizers. After consuming enough of each in a quantity that would kill her, she composed her final statement on hotel stationery and put it in an envelope on which she wrote: "boring letter of explanation within. . . ."

The next afternoon, when a chambermaid was unable to enter

the room, the manager ordered the lock broken. Bobbie Arnstein, still dressed, was found dead, lying on the edge of the bed. Her letter began: "It was I alone who acted and who conceived of this act. Because of recent developments, it behooves me to specify that it was definitely not the result of *any* determination or action on the part of my employers—who have been most generous and patient during my recent difficulties. . . .

"Despite the (perjured) testimony of the government's 'star' witness," her note continued, "I was never a part of any conspiracy to transport or distribute the alleged drugs connected with the case. . . . I don't suppose it matters that I say it, but Hugh M. Hefner is—though few will ever really realize it—a staunchly upright, rigorously moral man—and I know him well and he has never been involved in the criminal activity which is being attributed to him now." In conclusion, she added: "If—as has been said before about someone else, my veneer (or psychological make-up) couldn't permit any defenses against my sense of reality, then it has comforted me to know that this last decision—being of my own choosing . . . was the only one I've felt able to exercise over which *I've* had complete control. . . ."

The announcement of Bobbie Arnstein's suicide brought a despondent and angry Hefner flying into Chicago; and at a crowded press conference near the fireplace in the main room of the mansion, he attacked the prosecutors and mourned his friend. Unshaven, his eyes red, reading from the prepared statement, he began: "For the last several weeks, I have been the subject of a series of sensational speculations and allegations regarding supposed illicit drug activities at the Playboy Mansions in Chicago and Los Angeles—attempting to associate me with the recent cocaine conspiracy conviction of Playboy secretary Bobbie Arnstein and the death of Chicago Bunny Adrienne Pollack from a drug overdose sixteen months ago. Although I had no personal connection of any kind with either case, I reluctantly agreed to make no initial public statement on the subject because our legal counsel was convinced that anything I said would only be used to further publicize what—in our view—is not a legitimate narcotics investigation at all, but a politically motivated, anti-Playboy witch-hunt.

"The suicide of Bobbie Arnstein makes any further silence impossible," he continued. "Whatever mistakes she may have made in her personal life, she deserved better than this. She deserved—among other things—the same impartial consideration accorded any other citizen similarly accused. But because of her association with Playboy and with me, she became the central focus in a cocaine conspiracy case in which it appears she was only peripherally involved. There is ample reason to believe that if she had provided the prosecutors with evidence to support any serious drug charge against me, she would never have been indicted. Faced finally with a conditional sentence of fifteen years, the pressures of a lengthy appeal and increasing harassment from government prosecutors and their agents, an already emotionally troubled woman was pushed beyond endurance—and she killed herself. . . .

"It is difficult," he said, "to describe the inquisitional atmosphere of the Bobbie Arnstein trial and related Playboy probe. In the infamous witchcraft trials of the Middle Ages, the inquisitors tortured the victims until they not only confessed to being witches, but accused their own families and friends of sorcery as well. In similar fashion, narcotics agents frequently use our severe drug laws in an arbitrary and capricious manner to elicit the desired testimony for a trial." After referring to Bobbie Arnstein as "one of the best, brightest, most worthwhile women I have ever known," Hefner was forced to pause. His hands gripped the lectern, tears fell, and, except for the sound of the cameras, there was silence in the room. Finally, he went on to say: "For the record, I have never used cocaine, or any other hard drug or narcotics—and I am willing to swear to that fact under oath, and penalty of perjury, if that will put an end to the groundless suspicions and speculations. . . . The zeal with which certain government agents are pursuing this case says more about the prosecutors, I think, than it does about the accused. It appears that the 'enemies list' mentality of Watergate is still with us; and the repressive legacy of puritanism that we challenged in our first year of publication remains as formidable an opponent to a truly free and democratic society as ever."

While many newspaper columnists and editorialists agreed with Hefner's criticism of the investigation, other newspapers were less sympathetic, and a writer for the Chicago *Tribune* accused Hefner of trying "to cop a plea through publicity." In a statement from the United States attorney's office, James R. Thompson emphasized that "no one, including Hugh Hefner, is above the law"; and in response to the charge that Hefner was being targeted because he was the publisher of *Playboy*, Thompson commented: "I'm not sure that what Hefner stands for these days is all that relevant—or that any prosecution of him would mean much.''

Still, the scrutiny of Hefner and his associates continued after the funeral; and although the Justice Department eleven months later would announce that it was dropping the drug case due to insufficient evidence, the media kept the spotlight on Hefner and focused on his problems with his company. In front-page stories it reported that *Playboy* magazine had lost advertising revenue because of the publicity linking Hefner to drugs; and the negative publicity, together with the belief that Hefner's corporation was too loosely managed, caused the First National Bank of Chicago to deprive Hefner of two lines of credit totaling $6.5 million. During this period, two men who were influential on Wall Street resigned as members of Hefner's Board of Directors; and Playboy's corporate stock, which in 1971 was selling to investors for as much as $23.50 a share, had at one point in 1975 dropped to as low as $2.25 a share. Although Playboy's gambling casinos in England, patronized prominently by oil-rich Arabs, were earning $7 million a year; and although *Playboy* magazine, despite its monthly circulation drop to below 6 million, was still the world's most profitable men's periodical, the media continued to stress the circulation gains of Hefner's rival publishers. Robert Guccione's *Penthouse*, offering readers "pinups without the hangups,'' was edging to 4.5 million in monthly sales; and Larry Flynt's *Hustler*, begun in June 1974, was already approaching a circulation of 2 million—and it had astounded the men's market in August 1975 by publishing a series of color photographs showing Jacqueline Kennedy Onassis sunbathing in the nude on the island of Skorpios, pictures taken by an Italian photographer using a telescopic lens and crouched in a fishing boat.

Flynt also had in his possession, and was planning to publish in *Hustler*, a photograph of a nude Hugh Hefner having sex with a young woman, a picture that Flynt had somehow acquired after it was taken from Hefner's personal files in Chicago. When Hefner first learned of Flynt's intentions—being told by *Playboy* executive Nat Lehrman, who had been tipped off by Al Goldstein of *Screw*—Hefner urged Lehrman to contact Flynt and ask that the photograph be returned, explaining that it was stolen property and that its unauthorized publication would be very unfair to the woman involved. While Flynt was noncommittal after Lehrman had first discussed it, Lehrman came away with the impression that Flynt could be reasoned with. An eighth-

grade dropout, a dirt-poor Kentucky sharecropper's son who
had grown rich by shocking the magazine world with clinical
closeups of life in the haystack, Flynt might be flattered by an
invitation to dine and be entertained at Hefner's Los Angeles
mansion; and when Lehrman suggested this to Hefner, an invitation was proffered, and Larry Flynt accepted. Throughout
the visit, Hefner was charming and solicitous; he introduced
his fellow publisher to attractive guests, and personally took
Flynt on a tour of the mansion and the surrounding grounds.
Although Larry Flynt had arrived with certain misgivings about
Hefner, doubting that Hefner would fully support any cause
except his own, Flynt was nonetheless impressed with what Hefner had achieved with his life and had bought with his money;
and before leaving the mansion, as a gesture of friendship, Larry
Flynt reached into his jacket pocket and turned over to Hefner
the desired photograph, assuring him that no duplicate had been
made.

It was not only Nat Lehrman who successfully served Hefner's interests during this uncertain period—Victor Lownes, the
Playboy casino viceroy in London, was also summoned to alleviate certain difficulties, especially the financial problems of
Playboy's resort hotels and clubs. During the past four years,
the hotels alone had lost in excess of $10 million; and, with
Playboy's clubs also unprofitable—along with the movie and
record division—the corporate profits had dropped in 1975 to
$1.1 million as compared with $11.3 million two years earlier.
Victor Lownes, a privately wealthy Chicago divorcé who in
recent years had been living in an English country manor and
traveling to his office in a chauffeured Rolls-Royce, was a self-
assured, pragmatic man of forty-seven who had never sought
approval or popularity from his fellow executives at Playboy;
and the fact that Lownes would agree to leave even temporarily
the good life in London to become Hefner's hatchetman in Chicago was less an act of altruism than a response to his own self-
interest as Playboy's second largest stockholder. Lownes was
tired of seeing the earnings of the casinos, and the profits of
Playboy magazine, siphoned off by a number of slipshod subsidiaries; and immediately after arriving in Chicago, he began
to carve the corporate fat, to cut excessive spending, and to fire
unessential employees, caring little that in the home office he
was commonly referred to as "Jaws."
Aware that the Chicago mansion, which Hefner had all but

abandoned, had a house staff of fifty, Lownes cut the number
to twelve; and after trimming the service staffs in the Chicago
hotel and the local Playboy Club, he discontinued a magazine
called *V.I.P.* that was circulated to Playboy Club key holders
around the nation, thus saving the company $800,000 a year in
publishing costs. Striving to attract convention business, Lownes
removed Playboy's name from the hotels in Chicago and Great
Gorge, New Jersey; and, with Hefner's approval, plans were
soon made to dispose of the resort hotel in Jamaica and to eliminate the unprofitable clubs in Baltimore and New Orleans, San
Francisco, Montreal, and Atlanta. The company's recording
business was phased out, and Playboy film production was held
in abeyance. While Lownes had no authority over the operation
of *Playboy* magazine, which had achieved editorial distinction
under Arthur Kretchmer, the successor to the late A. C. Spec-
torsky, Lownes' mere presence in the editorial offices was
enough to stir some editors' snappish complaints to Hefner—
who, while always a sympathetic listener and sometimes even
himself critical of Lownes' peremptory nature, secretly endorsed what Lownes was doing, so long as it did not greatly
inconvenience Hefner's own lifestyle.

Having already taken a 25 percent pay cut, reducing his annual $300,000-plus salary to $230,000, and having relinquished $1,200,000 by refusing three semi-annual dividend
checks that were credited instead to Playboy's other sharehold-
ers, Hefner believed he had sacrificed sufficiently in the name
of solvency; and when Hefner learned through the newspapers
of Lownes' announcement that the Chicago mansion was probably for sale, along with Hefner's airplane, the astonished publisher no longer was so impressed with Lownes' cost-cutting
talents.

After chiding Lownes in private, Hefner publicly denied the
report; and while the Chicago mansion remained in his custody,
complete with cool cases of Pepsi awaiting his unscheduled arrival, Hefner stubbornly clung to his favorite toy, the Playboy
jet, which sat idly in the California sun because, if it were to
fly, its operational cost to the company would be at least $16,000
a day. However, when the company received an offer of $5 mil-
lion for the five-year-old plane, Hefner's practical German genes
dominated his Fitzgeraldian romanticism, and he felt compelled
to agree to its sale, especially since the new owner would be
painting the black plane a different color, would not be exploiting the fact that it had belonged to Playboy, and also would be

operating it far from American borders. The purchaser of the Big Bunny was the Venezuelan government.

Still, when the DC-9's ownership officially changed hands—after Hefner had reacquired from the plane his stereo equipment, his flying robes and pajamas, and the Tasmanian opossum fur coverlet that had fit over his round bed—it was a mournful day at the Los Angeles mansion, not only for Hugh Hefner but for his friends who had grown accustomed to the many free joy rides in sumptuous surroundings; and they would have perhaps been even more depressed had they witnessed the fate of the Playboy plane after its final flight from Los Angeles.

It was flown to Wilmington, Ohio, where in time special workmen completely gutted the interior, destroyed the colorful banquettes, Hefner's step-down shower, and his special round bed. Along the aisles where Hefner had installed his gaming tables and dance floor, the workmen now bolted tidy rows of nearly one hundred standard passenger seats. The plane was repainted white, and instead of the familiar Playboy rabbit on the exterior there was now the seven-starred flag of Venezuela.

When it finally arrived in 1976 in the Venezuelan capital, the DC-9 looked like any other domestic commuter plane; and the sober, serious-looking bureaucrats and businessmen who soon boarded it each day, and flew it back and forth between Caracas and Maracaibo, had no idea that the bland cabin in which they sat elbow to elbow had recently been a pleasure craft of popping corks and laughter, of sybarites in silk shirts and buxom backgammon players without bras.

Although Hefner remained in psychic contact with his departed airplane by often watching home movies that showed him climbing aboard the black jet and hosting revelries in the sky, no amount of fantasizing or reminiscing could comfort him in March 1976 when, in order to attend the gala opening of the renovated Playboy Club in New York, Hefner and his retinue were obliged to stand in line holding tickets at the Los Angeles Airport and to board a commercial carrier whose scheduled departure would in no way be influenced by the sleeping habits or moods of the *Playboy* publisher. The trip thus required some mental adjusting not only by Hefner but also by his long-pampered traveling companions; and while he had purchased every seat in the first-class cabin to ensure ample room for his ten friends (three seats, however, had been presold to jockeys traveling from Santa Anita to Aqueduct), Hugh Hefner announced with a forced smile to his group before they settled in their seats and had opened the backgammon boards: "Somehow I feel I owe you people an apology."

But the New York visit, if not the ride itself, was a source of satisfaction to Hefner. For the first time in years, Playboy received a favorable press. The remodeled club on Fifty-ninth Street off Fifth Avenue was complimented on its appearance, its superior cuisine and entertainment, and dozens of photographers wandered through the crowded bar and dance floor taking pictures of everyone from Howard Cosell to Lenny Bruce's mother. While Hefner in his new white suit and Barbi Benton in her long black gown served as the host and hostess, much more attention and curiosity seemed to be directed toward the stunning young brunet who stood at Hefner's side, smiling with alert dark eyes that matched his own—she was his twenty-three-year-old daughter, Christie, and, in a sense, this night in New York was her coming-out party.

Brought into the organization as a junior executive in 1975, a year after she had graduated *summa cum laude* from Brandeis University with an A.B. in English literature, Christie Hefner had already demonstrated to many skeptical *Playboy* editors in Chicago an astute mind and mature disposition, an ability and desire to learn without ever expecting or wanting special treatment as the boss's daughter. Although special treatment was unavoidable within the Playboy building—particularly after her father had publicly stated that she might one day take over the organization—Christie's tact and sensitivity made the best of a situation that could have easily caused resentment; and by the time of the New York opening, she had already earned the goodwill and respect of nearly all of her father's associates.

Beginning with the interviews she gave in New York, and the subsequent ones in other cities around the nation, Christie Hefner diverted the press from its predominantly critical coverage of *Playboy* to the personal story of herself and her sudden rise to the position that *Cosmopolitan* called "Hare Apparent." Described by writer Judy Klemesrud as having the "wholesome, well-scrubbed face of a Big Ten cheerleader grown up to become a Breck girl," Christie was clearly the type that would appeal to her father; and, by her own admission, they shared a mutual attraction that was far more romantic than familial.

During most of her girlhood her father had been a virtual stranger, a kind of reclusive uncle living in mysterious and opulent notoriety that she found both alluring and confusing. He had moved out of the family apartment when Christie was two, and, following her mother's remarriage in 1960, the eight-year-old Christie and her younger brother of five took the surname of their stepfather and she resided quietly, if not happily, in the North Shore community of Wilmette. After Christie had entered high school she was occasionally allowed to visit her father at the mansion, there to sit in wonderment at his extraordinary toys and women; but it was not until her college years that she and her father were able to communicate in a personal way, and to recognize and appreciate the traits and qualities that they had in common. Like him, she had a quick mind and high I.Q., a strong ego and a drive to succeed, and a commitment to individualism and sexual freedom.

During her freshman year at Brandeis, she began living in an apartment with a male student she had met on the campus; and while her mother was initially not pleased when Christie brought the young man home during a holiday and shared with him the same bed, her father wholeheartedly approved of the relationship after he had met Christie's friend, and he preferred to believe that his daughter's happy private life had contributed to her success as a student and her eventual election in June 1973 to Phi Beta Kappa.

For this occasion, Christie insisted that her surname on the honored scroll be printed as "Hefner," a decision that pleased her father immensely; and after she had graduated in 1974 from Brandeis and had spent a year in Boston as a freelance writer—while her boy friend went on to law school in Georgetown University—she accepted her father's offer to return to Chicago and work in the Playboy building as his special assistant. During her first year on the job, she periodically visited the company's paper mill and printing plant, its casinos and clubs, attended business meetings and familiarized herself with the corporate structure and the individuals who headed the various departments. She also attended office parties and conventions, and, like her father, she did not adhere to the adage that discouraged sexual activity among office acquaintances. One of the men with whom Christie became temporarily involved, with her father's full knowledge and limited enthusiasm, was a senior officer in the company with wide corporate responsibilities. In truth, Hefner had more confidence in his daughter's capacity to handle the situation than he did the older man's; and when the affair finally ended amicably, and with no resultant signs of corporate disarray or bruised egos, Hugh Hefner was relieved. On her part, Christie Hefner did not hesitate to tell her father what she thought of his young women friends; and while she was never harsh in her opinions, being aware of her own lack of objectivity in this area, she believed that none of his lovers was really as important in his life as he liked to think—and *none*, in her view, came close to possessing the intelligence and substance of the lady who had once been his wife.

Christie's reunion with her father in no way detracted from her close ties to her mother, Mildred, whom she continued to telephone almost daily and to visit nearly each week, not out of a sense of obligation but one of affection; and though she knew that it was highly unlikely, even after her mother's divorce in 1971 from her second husband, that her parents would re-marry—one reason being that her mother was now deeply in-volved in a three-year romance and sharing her home with a charming hairdresser twelve years her junior—Christie did suc-ceed in strengthening the bonds of friendship between her es-tranged parents. At Christie's suggestion and instigation, a number of Hefner family reunions were held during the mid-1970s, bringing under one roof her parents with their young lovers; her divorced uncle Keith from Aspen, usually accom-panied by one of his après-ski starlets; her collegian brother, David, an aspiring photographer who retained the surname of his former stepfather; her own male companion, invariably an older man; and her white-haired conservative grandparents, Grace and Glenn Hefner, who seemed to enjoy the reunions while privately believing in the superior wisdom of their ways. The elder Hefners made no secret of the fact that their lifetime experience with sex had been strictly limited to one another; and after more than fifty years of marriage, they said they had no regrets. Although Glenn Hefner had become a millionaire through investing in his son's stock, and had for years helped to audit the corporation's books, he claimed that he had never once in his life looked at a nude photograph in *Playboy*. The only magazines he enjoyed, he insisted, were *Fortune* and *Business Week*.

Except for a few quiet references to nepotism expressed by middle-level executives, there was throughout the Playboy building a celebratory response to the announcement that Chris-tie Hefner was being promoted to the rank of vice-president in her third year with the company, earning at the age of twenty-six a salary approaching $50,000; and even those employees who believed that she was being elevated too quickly had to admit that, more than any other individual, she had improved the public image of *Playboy* since the bleak days of the drug probe, the stock decline, and the death of Bobbie Arnstein.

But coinciding with her success as a media attraction were a number of unrelated events that also contributed to the company's restored stature with the advertising agencies, the bankers, and the investors. The magazine, for example, in continuing to buy and publish outstanding work by prestigious writers—John Cheever, Irwin Shaw, Alex Haley, David Halberstam, Saul Bellow—was finally receiving in literary circles the recognition that had long been its due; and of special significance were news-making *Playboy* interviews with such individuals as the deposed union boss Jimmy Hoffa (his final interview prior to his disappearance) and the future President of the United States Jimmy Carter, who made world headlines for the magazine as well as himself in admitting: "I've looked on a lot of women with lust. I've committed adultery in my heart many times. This is something God recognizes I will do and God forgives me for it."

Hefner's decision in 1976 to install as his chief operating officer a top newspaper executive named Derick J. Daniels, hired away from the thirty-two-paper Knight-Ridder chain, would also prove to be a wise move; for Derick Daniels, possessing the special clarity of mind that an outsider can often bring to solving the problems of a somewhat muddled management, discovered ways to cut costs beyond what Victor Lownes had already done without greatly disturbing staff morale or undermining the gains the company was already making. The most conspicuous gains were in *Playboy* magazine's advertising revenue, which, although the monthly circulation had now settled at the 5 million mark, would soon approach a record $50 million a year, double that of its closest competitor, *Penthouse*. The company's other magazine, *Oui*, also began to show profits, while the hotel-club losses gradually lessened. Although nearly one hundred employees were either fired or retired during Daniels' first two years in charge, as certain departments and subsidiaries were consolidated or eliminated, Daniels did not espouse a policy of conservatism or defensiveness. Recognizing that a vital organization must at times take risks in the interest of high profits, Playboy Enterprises, Inc., under Daniels' direction, announced plans for the building and opening in late 1980 of a multimillion-dollar hotel casino in Atlantic City, where gambling had recently been legalized by the New Jersey legislature. Partly because the first casino established by Resorts International proved to be a bonanza, and reinforced by Playboy's gambling success in England, the Playboy company stock rose to $16 a share.

Among the decisions for which Daniels claimed full credit was the elevation of Christie Hefner to vice-president; and, while serving as her regent, he put her in charge of the Playboy Foundation (which contributed several thousand dollars annually to civil libertarian causes and medical-sexual research) and the publicity-promotion department of Playboy Enterprises, Inc., which involved her in such duties as speechmaking before advertising groups, appearing on television talk shows, and traveling around the nation giving interviews to the press.

The question she was most often and curtly asked by women journalists, in view of her claim to being an ardent feminist, was how she could justify working for a male chauvinist organization that had made its fortune through demeaning the female body. Christie Hefner denied that the depiction of women as sexual beings was in any way demeaning, and she declared that sexuality was just as much a part of a woman's self as her intelligence and her independence. When interviewers cited *Playboy* photographs showing a nude woman with a finger on her clitoris, and asked if *that* was not exploitative of women, Christie responded: "I do not think that masturbation is a bad thing," and she pointed out that "for the first time women are shown involved with their bodies, which is what the women's movement is all about."

Emphasizing that *Playboy* does not display women with chains, whips, and other kinky accoutrements—which, curiously, she discovered in such women's high-fashion magazines as *Vogue*—Christie Hefner recalled: "As the women's movement took hold, there was a feeling for a while that if you were a feminist you wore jeans and combat boots. So all of a sudden, nudity and eroticism were exploitative, and there was in the movement a little bit of anti-sexual, anti-male bias that came down very hard on *Playboy*, because *Playboy* is obviously very pro-heterosexuality and very pro the sexual relationship between men and women." But, she went on, she saw no inherent incompatibility between *Playboy* and feminism; to her, feminism represented having vast opportunities and options in life, and to tell women that they should not appear in the nude—as certain puritanical feminists were now urging, and as male censors and priests have been urging for ages—was, she insisted, contrary to the goals of independence and self-determination sought by a majority of women liberationists. While she conceded in an interview in the New York *Times* that *Playboy* offered a limited perspective on womanhood, she stressed that it was a man's magazine, and its mission was not concerned with the varied complexities of being a woman any more than the women's magazines in America dealt with the complexities of being a man. Most women's magazines, in fact, "don't even deal with the complexities of being a woman," she said, adding that she was a lot more eager to change the way women were being presented in *Family Circle* magazine than in *Playboy*.

In December 1978 *Playboy* magazine celebrated its twenty-fifth anniversary in publishing; and during the next several weeks—in Chicago, in Los Angeles, and in New York—there were a series of parties and dinners, disco dances and banquets and other extravaganzas costing the company more than $1 million, all of which were organized under the supervision of Christie, who clearly was now the most important woman in Hugh Hefner's life. Barbi Benton was still a friend, but, at twenty-eight, she felt she was stagnating in his Jacuzzi-land and decided to live full-time in her Beverly Hills apartment and to date other men. Karen Christy, who after returning to Texas had visited Hefner in Los Angeles in 1976 and 1977, had recently written him a note telling him that she had just married, in Dallas, the Baltimore Colts linebacker Ed Simonini. Hefner's former wife, Mildred, having happily cohabitated for years with the young Swiss-born hairdresser named Pierre Rohrbach, also decided to get married; while Hugh Hefner, at fifty-two, courted his newest chatelaine, Sondra Theodore, *Playboy*'s twenty-two-year-old Miss July who was a blond blend of Barbi Benton and Karen Christy and other girls-next-door who inexorably aged and changed in real life but never in Hefner's mind.

In the 410-page anniversary edition that contained photographs of every playmate in the magazine's history, Hugh Hefner in the publisher's page editorial recalled: "When I conceived this magazine a quarter of a century ago, I had no notion that it would become one of the most important, imitated, influential and yet controversial publishing ventures of our time. The early Fifties was an era of conformity and repression—of Eisenhower and Senator Joe McCarthy—the result of two decades of Depression and war. But it was also a period of reawakening in

America—with a re-emphasis on the importance of the individual, on his rights and opportunities in a free society—a period of increasing affluence and leisure time. I wanted to publish a magazine that both influenced and reflected the socio-sexual changes taking place in America but that was—first and foremost—fun. *Playboy* was intended as a response to the repressive antisexual, anti-play-and-pleasure aspects of our puritan heritage. Big dreams for a young man only recently graduated from college, who quit his $60-a-week job as a promotion copy writer for *Esquire* when refused a request for a five-dollar raise. . . ."

On January 11, 1979, at the anniversary finale before hundreds of guests gathered at the Tavern-on-the-Green restaurant in New York's Central Park, one of the speakers, a representative of *Esquire*, stood up and presented Hugh Hefner with a blown-up replica of a five-dollar bill in recognition of the raise that had been so adamantly denied him decades ago.

25

We have to cultivate women's chastity as the highest national possession, for it is the only safe guarantee that we really are going to be the fathers of our children, that we work and labor for our own flesh and blood. Without this guarantee there is no possibility of a secure family life, this indispensable basis for the welfare of the nation.

This, and not masculine selfishness, is the reason why the law and morals make stricter demands on the woman than on the man with regard to premarital chastity and to marital fidelity. Freedom on her part involves much more serious consequences than freedom on the part of the man.

—MAX GRUBER, German sex hygienist, 1920s

Among the many issues involved in the liberation of women, the two major fronts in my own personal liberation have been sexuality and economics. Ultimately, they are not separable— not as long as the female genitals have economic value instead of sexual value for women. Saving sex for my lover/husband was my gift to him in exchange for economic security—called "meaningful relationship" or "marriage." My future depended upon finding the right partner whom I would possess forever with my gift of sex and love.

With that romanticized image of sex, in a society that doesn't have economic equality between the sexes, I was forced to bargain with my cunt for any hope of financial security. Marriage under those circumstances is a form of prostitution.

—BETTY DODSON, American artist-feminist, 1970s

GIVEN THE TRANSFORMATION of Betty Dodson from a dependent housewife into a liberated individual, it was not surprising that her days and nights as a visitor to Sandstone would be compatible with her evolution as a self-proclaimed Phallic Woman. Although the definition of "phallus," as Ms. Dodson discovered long ago in her dictionary, referred equally to the clitoris as well as to the penis, this fact had little chance of popular acceptance in a world where, in her view, the "denial of the woman's phallus has for centuries been the essence of male dominance and female subjugation." Partly in compensation, and partly because it appealed to her emerging erotic nature, Betty Dodson in recent years had dedicated herself, as a painter and writer, to exposing female sexual imagery to a society that preferred to conceal it.

Even before she visited Sandstone, where she would meet feminists as phallic as herself, Betty Dodson had conducted seminars for women in her New York apartment, consciousness-raising sessions in which the participants were encouraged to scrutinize their own and each other's genitals without shame or diffidence. Using mirrors for self-examination, and then taking turns spreading their legs for observation by others, the women were amazed at how varied were their genitals' shapes, designs, textures, patterns: Some were heart-shaped, others resembled shells, wattles, or orchids; and when the pubic hair and foreskin above the vagina was pulled back, fully revealing the clitoris, many women saw clearly for the first time the feminine center of arousal, and they were surprised to discover that clitorises could vary in size and shape from recessed pearls to protruding bullets.

The women learned, too, that the position of the clitoris with regard to the vaginal opening differed from one woman to the next, as did the coloring of the outer and inner lips, ranging from dark brown to light pink. At Ms. Dodson's suggestion, the women not only observed but also touched, smelled, and tasted their own genitals, and sometimes those of their friends, in an attempt to overcome their childhood inhibitions and Bible-based traditions that marked this physical area as evil, unclean, the site of the curse.

On the walls of Betty Dodson's apartment were hung several of her artful drawings of female genitalia, and occasionally she projected on a screen for her groups' edification and admiration color slides showing nude women untimidly revealing themselves and exhibiting an attitude that Betty Dodson called "cunt positive." Most of the women who attended her sessions were, like herself, middle-class heterosexual or bisexual women in their thirties or forties who were divorced or still married, and, while supportive of the feminist movement, they did not share the asexual or antimale inclinations of some of their activist sisters. As an artist whose drawings and paintings had been called pornographic, Dodson had been criticized by a few feminists for contributing to the degradation of women; but, never apologetic about her work, she commented: "If a woman has had nothing but sex-negative experiences, then looking at pictures about sex will understandably make her feel degraded."

Attractive and energetic, with gamine-styled dark hair and a short athletic body that was often nude when she greeted guests at her door, Betty Dodson was born in 1929 in the Kansas Bible Belt region of Wichita and had been reared with idealistic notions about marriage and fidelity. As a teenager she masturbated to images of her anticipated wedding night, and she visualized herself as an elegantly groomed woman wearing an exquisite lace peignoir and walking across a bedroom with poise and confidence toward a faceless obscure male figure reclining on her marital bed; and as she dropped her long gown to the floor, exposing her naked loveliness, she achieved her desired orgasm.

Such solitary pleasure, while she privately acknowledged its wickedness, was beyond her will to resist during her adolescent years, even though she suspected that her habitual masturbation was deforming her vaginal lips. She arrived at this conclusion one day when, behind the closed door of her bedroom, while borrowing her mother's large ivory hand mirror, she sat with her legs spread near the window light and examined her genitals. With feelings of horror and fear, she noticed that the inner lips were extended, and the sight of these small folds of jagged tissue hanging out convinced her that she was the victim of self-abuse. Immediately she took a vow of lifelong autoerotic abstinence, which lasted for little more than a week; but she nonetheless did modify her masturbatory technique: Having observed that the vaginal lips on her left side were shorter than on the right side, she restricted her stroking thereafter to the left, hoping that in time her vaginal lips would even up. And although the condition remained unchanged, she persisted in this manner of masturbation throughout her young womanhood in Kansas, where she worked as a newspaper artist, and she continued to touch only her left side after she had moved to New York in 1950, where she would study at the Art Students League, at the National Academy, and at Columbia University.

Following her marriage, in which she would remain monogamous during its five-year duration, she neglected her career as an artist while trying to please her husband as a full-time homemaker; but her connubial relations with a premature ejaculating spouse were rarely fulfilling, and thus masturbation continued to be her primary source of pleasure. However, after her divorce in 1965, Betty Dodson was finally able to enjoy complete satisfaction with male lovers; and in a book that she published in 1974, entitled *Liberating Masturbation: a Meditation on Self-love*, she recalled one episode that was central to her sexual emancipation:

When I got divorced and re-entered the world of Romance, candle-lit dinners and the handsome dark stranger, I was very excited and turned on to all the adventure that was now just around the corner . . . [and] nearly paralyzed with self-consciousness about how I looked, and how I was going to handle sex.

One of my first lovers was a devoted appreciator of female genitals. We got into oral sex (I was determined to try everything) and once after I had a really great orgasm he said, "You have a beautiful cunt. Let me look for a moment." Oh groan . . . oh no, I felt a sinking feeling and I told him I would really rather he didn't. . . . He wanted to know what was the matter. Evidently I had turned a bit green, and I said I had those funny inner lips that hung down like a chicken, unfortunately a result of childhood masturbation. Convinced my genitals were certainly not pretty, I didn't particularly want anyone looking at them. "Wow," he said, "a lot of women are made like that. It's perfectly normal, actually, it's one of my favorite styles of genitals." Off he goes to a closet, coming back with a stack of magazines of crotch shots. Forty-second Street porno shop Beaver Books. (Beaver is a slang expression for women's genitals and split beaver is the term applied to a woman holding her genitals open.) I was shocked—but interested. I thought how it must be very degrading for those poor women to pose in underwear, garter belts, black net stockings and to have to expose themselves like that, but nonetheless, I began looking at the pictures. Indeed, there was a cunt just like mine, and another and another. By the time we had gone through several magazines together I had an idea of what women's genitals looked like. What a relief! In that one session I found out I wasn't deformed, funny looking or ugly . . . I was normal, and as my lover said, actually beautiful.

Encouraged by her new sexual confidence, her art became increasingly sensual, and in 1968—the year when nudity was much in vogue in the avant-garde theater, films, and the counterculture—she was featured in a one-woman show at the Wickersham Gallery on Madison Avenue, an event that attracted during its two-week run more than 8,000 visitors who viewed with rapt attention and blushing appreciation her lusty depictions of several heroic nude figures touching or kissing one another and, in some instances, making love. This show appealed to those who thought themselves *engagé* in uptown Manhattan, the art patrons and brownstone liberals and parents of flower children, and she was praised by critics for her classic draftsmanship, her creative authority and flair. She was further gratified by the many sales to her unabashed admirers and by the fact that a few samples of her work were scheduled to be reproduced in art anthologies.

And if she was not so successful during a subsequent two-week exhibition at the Wickersham, a show that drew only 3,000 visitors, she was far from dismayed, for this second presentation was closer to her heart and emotions, was artistically more relevant and uncompromising, dwelling as it did on sexuality in isolation and acts of deviation. Among the thirty pictures that she prepared for the Wickersham were drawings and paintings of naked figures engaged in autoeroticism, of men participating in mutual fellatio, of a solitary black male fondling his enlarged penis, of white women with erect clitorises tenderly touching one another's genitals, of women bedded with men in body but not in spirit. There were expressions on some of the female faces that suggested dispassion, anguish, even rage, and Dodson was clearly saying, as dramatically as any contemporary novelist or playwright, that there was in the contraceptive society still a continuing war between the sexes and much alienation in the bedrooms of America. Not only was she convinced that this was true but it was confirmed for her frequently in the comments she overheard among the crowds gathered around her pictures, or in what she had been told by people, most of them women, who spoke to her quietly in a corner of the gallery. Although some women confessed to being rarely if ever orgasmic in their marital relationship, they also admitted that they were too embarrassed to masturbate, or feared that if they tried using a vibrator they might become "hooked." Some of the men, in studying the pictures of the masturbating women, admitted that they had no idea that women ever masturbated, while a few men were prompted to make hostile remarks, particularly after they saw Dodson's six-foot drawing of a blond woman lying on her back with her eyes closed and masturbating with a vibrator. "If that was my woman," said one man, "she wouldn't have to use that thing."

Rather than being deterred by the negative reaction to her show, Dodson and her feminist followers became more convinced than ever that the acceptance of masturbation, and the guiltless practice of it, was essential to the sexual liberation of women. "If I had any doubts about it before I started, the two weeks I spent in the gallery made it very clear that repression relates directly to masturbation," Dodson wrote in her book. "It follows then that masturbation can be important in reversing the process and achieving liberation. Seeking sexual satisfaction is a basic drive, and masturbation, of course, is our first natural sexual activity. It's the way we discover our eroticism, the way we learn to respond sexually, the way we learn to love ourselves and build self-esteem. . . . When a woman masturbates, she learns to like her own genitals, to enjoy sex and orgasm, and furthermore, to become proficient and independent about it. Our society is made uncomfortable by sexually proficient and independent women."

Betty Dodson asserted that it was very significant that a woman gives up her surname when she marries, adding: "It is really her identity she is giving up"; and the sex-negative conditioning in which most middle-class women were reared, and which they often reinforced in their daughters, tended to perpetuate the double standard and to deny to a majority of married women the "reclamation of the female body as a source of strength, pride and pleasure." Betty Dodson also insisted that the social pressure on women to conform to male-defined standards of respectability—lest these women encounter the social ostracism that befalls the "prostitute or tramp," the very females that are patronized by many male moral hypocrites—resulted too often in women becoming "crippled" sexually: "Our pelvises are severely locked. Our shoulders are frozen forward. Our genitals are made repulsive to us and a source of constant discomfort. Our bodies lack muscle tone and often are armored with fat. The insidious thing about this system is that we end up accepting the self-serving male definitions of 'normal' female sexuality. We vehemently or sullenly put down masturbation and overt displays of healthy female sexuality. At this point we embellish our own pedestals and become the keepers

of Social Morality . . . sexless mothers and house-slaves.''
Conversely, Dodson declared, in a magazine interview in the
Evergreen Review: ''If we women all got together and became
one unified 'yes' for sex, it would show us [that] men are just
as uptight about sex as we are, only they don't have to confront
that. Since women act out all of their sex fears and reservations,
men get to act and feel very sex-positive. Unconsciously they
depend upon our saying 'no' or being hesitant, fearful, or passive.'' And when men failed to satisfy women in bed, Dodson
wrote in her book, they rationalized their failures by assuming
that the women were frigid, even when these women were capable of satisfying themselves through masturbation. ''If a
woman can stimulate herself to orgasm, she is orgasmic and
sexually healthy,'' Dodson declared. '' 'Frigid' is a man's word
for a woman who cannot have an orgasm in the missionary position
in five minutes with only the kind of stimulation that is good for
him. We must no longer cling to the notion that we 'should' have
orgasm from intercourse alone. And we must not be intimidated
by chauvinists in white coats who still refer to 'coital inadequacy'
in women when their own laboratory and statistical evidence clearly
contradicts this male concept of female response. The truth is very
few women ever consistently reach orgasm in intercourse without
additional stimulation. To be liberated a woman must be free to
choose and state her preference in sexual activity without prejudice
or judgment when it is her turn.''

At the sexual gatherings in Betty Dodson's apartment, to which
male friends and husbands were often invited, and where the
activities might include anything from yoga to group sex, the
women were generally uninhibited and fully capable, in Dodson's words, of ''running the fuck.'' Dodson's women had developed through attendance at her seminars the confidence and
ability to take the sexual initiative, to tell their male lovers how
they wished to be touched, how much pressure they enjoyed,
what positions they preferred, going so far as straddling a man's
face and controlling the movements, and discovering in the process that men often welcomed the opportunity of switching the
traditional roles and becoming the passive partner. And the
''cunt positive'' attitude that many of Dodson's female friends
assumed enhanced not only their sexual lives but also their entire
sense of self-worth. One woman, who, like Dodson years ago,
believed that her genitals were deformed and ugly, was persuaded by Dodson's color slides of female genitalia that she was

as attractive as most other women; and the next day in her office, reassured and confident, she demanded a raise—and got it.

But although Betty Dodson was aware and proud of the progress made by the women in her group, she was not so naïve to think that they were representative of American women in the 1970s, a large percentage of whom still opposed the women's Equal Rights Amendment and doubted that they could, or even wanted to, survive personally or economically outside the conventional system of marriage. Women were not as sexually spontaneous as men, Dodson conceded, but she again attributed this to the historical conditioning of the double standard; and until this tradition was altered, until more women could enjoy one-night stands and "open-ended" marriages—in which the man and woman both maintained casual sex outside the marital unit—too many women would remain largely dependent on a husband or a single lover, instead of on themselves, for sexual, economic, and emotional fulfillment. "It takes a lot of courage to be who you are in any life situation . . ." Betty Dodson said, and "when you get into varietal sex, you have to confront your orgastic potential on a social basis just as a man does," which was another way of saying that varietal sex for women would be less restricted to the "meaningful relationship" and more to fun and recreation, experimenting and experiencing. "To love only one person is anti-social," Dodson said, reflecting a view expressed more than one hundred years ago by Oneida's John Humphrey Noyes; and she added: "It's a beautiful concept, social sex for life-affirmative pleasure instead of sex based on economics and power, buying and selling, and manipulating with your genitals."

The problem remained, however, that there were very few safe places in America where an adventuresome woman could go to learn through experience what men had been living for centuries. There were numerous swing clubs, of course, but these tended to be surreptitious gatherings in overcrowded suburban houses with the shades pulled down, and they were frequently raided by the police following complaints by prying neighbors. Indeed, probably the only place in the nation where recreational sex could be indulged in by women in a pleasant and open environment was Sandstone Retreat; and when Betty Dodson first arrived there during an extended visit to California, she was pleased to discover that it was exactly as it had been described to her by friends on the West Coast. The grounds were beautiful, the hilltop setting was ideally remote, and her host and hostess, John and Barbara Williamson, clearly had a marriage that epitomized equality between the sexes; it was a union of two committed people to whom adultery was not a taboo and lying was never a necessity.

Among Sandstone's hundreds of club members there were a few familiar faces and bodies that Betty Dodson recognized from her parties in New York, and there was also among the membership her close friend and sister feminist, the anthropologist Sally Binford. Dodson made new friends, too, during her days and nights at Sandstone, one of the most interesting of them being a gray-haired English gentleman whom she had first noticed one night in the downstairs "ballroom." At the time, she had been lying nude on a mat with two equally nude men, lightly engaged in a massaging threesome and pleasantly preoccupied; and yet she could not avoid being aware of the riveting attention she was receiving from a man who sat alone across the room, an owlish-looking bespectacled man who seemed unembarrassed by the fact that she was watching *him* watching her. Finally she waved to him, gesturing for him to join them; and, unhesitatingly, he got up and did so. When he arrived and sat at her side, she extended her hand in greeting and then took his hand and placed it between her legs, realizing as she did so that his hand was lacking fingers. This was Betty Dodson's introduction to the gentleman who was then the most successful writer and observer of sex in America, Dr. Alex Comfort.

As unlikely as it might have seemed to an occasional visitor, the "ballroom" at Sandstone Retreat, in addition to presenting the mazurka of sexual cotillions, was also a place where love could be kindled and cultivated—which had been the happy experience of one of Sandstone's most sophisticated and perspicacious women, Dr. Sally Binford. After three divorces, assorted affairs, some varietal after-hours cavorting near the campuses where she taught anthropology, and much recreational romping on the unhallowed grounds of Sandstone itself, Sally Binford became acquainted in the ballroom one day with a handsome and sensitive character-actor named Jeremy Slate, who had appeared in several Hollywood films and had discovered Sandstone in 1970 while dating a Los Angeles journalist who had written an article about the Williamsons.

A six-foot blondish man in his forties with blue eyes, a graceful athletic body, and an equally graceful sense of humor, Jeremy Slate had begun his acting career in 1958 on the New York stage with a substantial supporting role in the Broadway version of Thomas Wolfe's *Look Homeward, Angel*. His performance in that Pulitzer prize-winning play was instrumental in getting him to Hollywood, where during the next decade he appeared in dozens of films and television shows: He costarred in the CBS TV series "Malibu Run," playing a scuba diver; portrayed a rocket captain in "Men in Space"; made guest appearances in such shows as "The Defenders" and "Naked City." Slate was an outlaw in the film *True Grit*, starring John Wayne; a Canadian airman in *Devil's Brigade*, featuring William Holden and Cliff Robertson; and played character roles in a number of other action films, Westerns, and comedies starring such performers as Bob Hope and Elvis Presley. In 1968, after being divorced from his second wife, actress Tammy Grimes, he injured himself in a motorcycle accident while acting in a film about the Hell's Angels; and for the next eight months, with a broken leg encased in a forty-pound cast, he lived in virtual isolation in his Laurel Canyon apartment, brooding and meditating, smoking pot and masturbating—a supporting actor unsupported for the first time in years by roles, directors, and controllable scenarios.

It was during this time that he spent long hours reading books, including the works of Wilhelm Reich; and after he was again mobile, he decided to concentrate less on the business of playing parts and more on trying to piece together his own disjointed life. Moving into a new apartment at Venice Beach in a community of artists and hippies, he stopped scanning the Hollywood trade papers each day, avoided the actors' bar he had once frequented, and became interested in the peace movement, the counterculture, and alternate life-styles. Among the young women he was then dating was the journalist who had told him about the Williamsons and Sandstone; and with a minimum of convincing, he agreed to accompany her there, thinking that it would be fun to mingle with people in the nude. But after he had driven up the curved roads to the mountaintop, and had toured the estate with its uninhibited house, and had caught erotic glimpses of the bodies in the dim downstairs light, he felt almost vertiginous and intensely self-conscious—and impotent with his girl friend when they tried to make love.

Still, he was not discouraged from returning, for he did enjoy being nude in the outdoors; and as he gradually became better acquainted with other people, and more comfortable with himself, he reveled in the rarity of being sexually approached by Sandstone women, among them Dr. Sally Binford. Though he was attracted to her when he first saw her, and was delighted by their later lovemaking in the ballroom, the recreational sex was mainly an excuse for them to be together and to explore within their embrace the deeper intimacy that they both sensed was there. They were two people in their mid-forties who, until now, had preferred much younger lovers, using sex as an escape from the intellectual challenges and uncertainties of their lives. But after years of disenchantment with the values of their contemporaries, and seeing at times their entire generation as symbolized by materialism and racism, police dogs and napalm, they were overjoyed to discover in one another a fellow dropout from the fifties. Although Sally Binford had been more politically active than Slate in the Los Angeles antiwar movement, he soon joined her at rallies and demonstrations; and after Daniel Ellsberg's fellow conspirator, Anthony Russo, had been arrested during the Pentagon Papers controversy, Jeremy and Sally went together to visit Russo at the federal prison on Terminal Island, which was an hour's drive from Sandstone, where Russo had been given a farewell bacchanal just prior to his incarceration.

It was after the Russo party, in fact, that Jeremy and Sally began living together in Venice; and since she had stopped teaching at UCLA, and he was not working as an actor, they were free to move around the country as they wished, and in 1972 they settled for months in the San Francisco Bay Area, existing financially on their savings and on Jeremy's acting residuals and his song royalties from two country-western hits that he had written—one for Tex Ritter entitled "Just Beyond the Moon," and another that was written with Glen Campbell and appeared on the subside of Campbell's popular "Galveston" record; it was called: "How Come Every Time I Itch, I Wind Up Scratching You?"

Later in 1972, Jeremy and Sally moved temporarily to Vermont, where during the next nine months Sally taught courses in anthropology and women's studies at the progressive, freethinking Goddard College, and Jeremy conducted a male consciousness-raising seminar in which he disseminated Sandstone's equal-rights sex doctrine, getting a positive reaction from many men who shared his view that the elimination of the double standard would be liberating for men as well as women. On weekends, Jeremy and Sally occasionally visited couples in New England or New York who had been to Sandstone, and who enjoyed sharing their beds with socially compatible house guests; and it was only a matter of time, Jeremy thought, before ersatz versions of Sandstone's ballroom would go public—an event that would indeed begin to happen years later with the opening of Plato's Retreat in Manhattan and similar clothes-optional recreational centers for couples in other cities.

In the fall of 1973, after Sally Binford had purchased an elaborate motor home, she and Jeremy headed back to California via Canada, stopping for a few days near the Glacier National Park in Montana to visit the recently arrived John and Barbara Williamson, who had just optioned about two hundred acres of land in a community called White Fish, hoping to create another Sandstone in a more spacious setting than their fifteen acres atop Topanga Canyon that had suddenly seemed very confining. In recent months, along the adjacent hills of the canyon within sight of Sandstone, a number of new homes were being built, intruding upon what had once been an uninterrupted view of trees and mountainsides extending down to the misty edge of the Pacific. And after years of being at the center of an often intense group marriage—and simultaneously trying to operate a couples club in which new members constantly had to be guided and reassured through their traumatic introductions to open sexuality—the Williamsons felt emotionally exhausted and claustrophobic, in need of a reprieve from other people's intimacies. While waiting for a successor to buy and carry on the work in Topanga Canyon, the Williamsons had brought with them to Montana a select few from Sandstone; and though many people in Los Angeles had expressed an interest in taking over the canyon property, it was not until 1974 that a marriage counselor and Gestalt therapist named Paul Paige had acquired enough capital and bank loans to buy Sandstone and to reopen the couples club, which in the interim months had been inactive.

Paul Paige, who at thirty-four was eight years younger than John Williamson, and had graduated with a master's degree in social work from UCLA, was a six-foot, trimly muscular former United States Marine with blue eyes and neatly trimmed dark hair; and while he was soft-spoken and exuded the poised manner of a professional counselor, he nonetheless gave the impression that there was simmering within him much restless energy and conflict that he was trying with some difficulty to control. He smoked excessively, and the articulate flow of his speech was sometimes marred by a slight stutter. Except for his interest in sex, and his belief that much of world history had been influenced by the demons dwelling in human erotic nature, Paul Paige had little in common with John Williamson, whose slum-

berous style he atypified and whose portly, potbellied body he
saw as consistent with the sloppy manner in which Williamson
had kept the business records at Sandstone. Paige was a man
striving for order, discipline, and good management; and he
saw no reason why these traits could not blend in with whatever
utopian principles Sandstone presumed to represent.

Having been a frequent visitor and dues-paying member of
Sandstone since early 1972, Paige had a sense of its failing long
before he bought the place. The building and landscaping were
not receiving the fastidious maintenance that was required; the
approach roads had become cracked and bumpy, and John Williamson appeared to have lost his enthusiasm as the resident
guru. Instead of mixing with the crowds in the main house before dinner, Williamson often took his meals in the motor home
that he parked on Sandstone's highest peak, or he sat alone in
the living room reading a book near the fireplace; or, if he
deigned to converse with anyone in the living room, it was usually with one of the few people he looked upon as a peer, such
as the columnist Max Lerner, or Dr. Comfort, or Dr. Ralph D.
Yaney, a Beverly Hills psychoanalyst and psychiatrist who had
long been a habitué of Sandstone.

Although Sandstone had received much publicity in newspapers and magazines in 1972, the Sandstone management had
lacked the imagination and energy to take advantage of this by
recruiting large numbers of new members; and it was no secret
among the Sandstone regulars that Williamson had lost considerable money in the past year—which Paige attributed not only
to Williamson's listless leadership but also to the fact that he had
kept the annual membership dues down to $240 per couple, a
figure that Paige quickly doubled after he had purchased the
property and had begun to make improvements. Among other
things, Paige ordered that the main house be repainted and re-
decorated, that the sun deck be enlarged, and a Jacuzzi be installed on the front lawn. The surrounding grounds were
restored, the roads were repaired, and the guest houses were
remodeled. He advertised Sandstone in the press and made himself available for television interviews (which the camera-shy
Williamson had avoided); and joined by his piquant, raven-haired
lady friend, Theresa Breedlove, who lived with him at Sandstone, Paul Paige warmly greeted the arriving guests and members in the living room and was a decisive factor in Sandstone's
successful revitalization.

Influenced by the Esalen Institute at Big Sur, which Paige had often visited in the past, he added to Sandstone's staff several specialists who, for a fee, offered the members and guests everything from sessions in Rolfing and the Esalen massage to bioenergetics and hatha-yoga. For the price of $250 that included room and board, nonmember couples were invited to spend an entire weekend at Sandstone, using the facilities and attending Gestalt therapy clinics under Paige's supervision; and among the participants one weekend was the actor and television personality Orson Bean, accompanied by his wife, Carolyn, both of whom soon became friendly with Paul Paige and actively involved at Sandstone. Bean, who had once undergone treatment in Reichian therapy—and had described it in his book *Me and the Orgone*—now wrote about Sandstone in his column in the Los Angeles *Free Press*, and he favorably referred to Sandstone on the Johnny Carson show. Sandstone was also featured in a *Playboy* article by Dan Greenburg; by Herbert Gold in *Oui*; by Robert Blair Kaiser in *Penthouse*. And in his second bestselling book, *More Joy*, Alex Comfort devoted a chapter to Sandstone, in which he wrote: "California abounds in 'encounter' and 'sensitivity' centers—people who go there do or don't find themselves . . . [and] a high proportion have the air of going through a lot of psycho-make-work and verbal behaviors when the real object of the exercise is to get laid. At Sandstone, one could quite frankly go to get laid—but having got that out of the way, participants were surprised to find that 'sensitivity,' 'encounter' and a good deal of genuine self-education quite often followed; they both enjoyed themselves and did reassess their goals and self-image. As a result," Comfort continued, "disciples of Sandstone (some of whom may only have been there once) are widely scattered in sex counseling—including that sponsored by the churches. For its size, and the fact that the original experiment, started by John and Barbara Williamson, ran only four years, it has a potential influence through contacts which will only become evident with time—it was many 'straight' people's first and only encounter with genuinely open sexuality in a structured setting. The fact that it recreated an intense experience of infantile innocence in hungup adults makes many who went there nostalgic or overenthusiastic about it, but allowing for this its capacity to facilitate the sort of 'growth' at which individual psychology aims was pretty remarkable."

At Paul Paige's request, Dr. Comfort became an unofficial adviser to Sandstone, and his name was listed among its staff in the brochure that was periodically mailed out; and on special occasions, such as the open-house weekend in early June 1974, Dr. Comfort delivered a speech before an audience that had paid $25 each to listen. More than two hundred people had driven up the foggy roads to attend, joining in the crowded house such veteran members as Sally Binford and Jeremy Slate, who had weeks before parked their motor home on an upper hill and were now residing at Sandstone. It was so cloudy and chilly during the day of Comfort's presentation that most of the audience kept its clothes on, an uncommon sight at Sandstone.

In addition to the speech by Alex Comfort, the audience heard briefly from Al Goldstein, the publisher of *Screw*, and Nat Lehrman, the associate publisher of *Playboy*; and they also were addressed at length by the second featured speaker of the day, a writer from New York named Gay Talese, who was researching a book about sex in America for Doubleday & Company.

A lean, dark-eyed man of forty-three whose brown hair was beginning to turn gray, Talese was not entirely a stranger to the people in the room. He had visited Sandstone often in the past, including its ballroom, and his book-in-progress had already received inordinate amounts of publicity in many newspapers and magazines. Most of what had been written about Talese in the press, however, had been jocularly presented, strongly suggesting that his reportorial technique as a "participating observer" in the world of erotica—his patronage of massage parlors, his dark afternoons in X-rated cinemas, his intimate familiarity with swing clubs and orgiasts across the land—was an ingenious ploy on his part to indulge his carnality and to be unfaithful to his wife, while justifying it in the name of sexual "research."

While Talese had never openly refuted this notion, assuming that any attempt to deny it might mark him as a man on the defensive, which he often felt he was—or might label him a First Amendment hypocrite who condoned pornography but was antipathetic to the media's right to fair comment when it focused on him—he was nonetheless keenly aware that his allegedly ideal assignment was frequently less pleasurable than other people generally believed. And what bothered him even more was that after three years of research and many months of pondering behind his typewriter, he had been unable to write a single word. He did not even know how to begin the book. Nor how to organize the material. Nor if what he hoped to say about sex had not already been said in dozens of other recently published works written by marriage therapists, social historians, and talk-show celebrities.

Indeed, Talese himself had lately become a frequent talk-show guest, being invited because of the publicity he had received after a newsman had discovered him working as a manager of a New York massage parlor, a prurient Plimpton wallowing in oily delight—an image that Talese always sought to counter, too earnestly at times, by emphasizing on television the seriousness of his literary intentions. His speech at Sandstone was similarly directed—he wanted to present himself to his audience, simply and unpretentiously, as a committed researcher and writer who, apart from his personal life and vices, was currently working on one of the most important stories of his lifetime: It was a story that would intimately describe many of the people and events that in recent decades had influenced the redefinition of morality in America.

After he had been introduced to the crowd by a young Sandstone staff member named Martin Zitter, one of the few people in the room who was completely nude, Talese walked to the podium with a prepared text and began his speech. "This nation," he said, "is being gradually overtaken by a silent revolution of the senses, a departure from conventionality. And even within the middle class, which is where I'm concentrating my research, there is now an ever-increasing tolerance for sexual expression in films and books, and a more accepting attitude among couples in the bedroom with regard to what had once been considered 'kinky'—having mirrors around the room, colored lights and candles, vibrators at bedside, Frederick's of Hollywood lingerie, X-rated movie cassettes, oral sex and other acts that many state laws still condemn as 'sodomy.' The success of *The Joy of Sex*, which would have been labeled 'smut' a few years ago, is another example of how middle-class society has become less squeamish about depictions of erotica," Talese continued, nodding toward Dr. Comfort, who sat nearby. "That book has sold 700,000 copies in hard cover to date—it's a mass-market book that you see in store windows on Main Street, and on the coffee tables of Middle America, even though it displays explicit drawings of nude couples making love in every conceivable manner.

"At polite dinner parties," Talese went on, "you now hear people discussing the intimate aspects of their private lives in ways that in the mid-sixties would have been socially unacceptable. Homosexual bars are no longer the constant targets of police raids since homosexual activists have organized. And most middle-class parents of college students are resigned to the fact that premarital sex is hardly uncommon in off-campus apartments or even in dormitories. While I can't prove it, I think that middle-class American husbands now, more than ever before in American history, can live with the knowledge that their wives were not virgins when they married—and that their wives have had, or *are* having, an extramarital affair. I'm not saying that husbands are not bothered by this," Talese emphasized, looking up from his text. "I'm only suggesting that the contemporary husband, unlike his father and grandfather before him, is not so shocked or shattered by such news, is more likely to accept women as sexual beings, and only in extreme cases will he retaliate with violence against his unfaithful wife or male rival. . . ."

Unlike most of his audience, who were ten or twenty years younger than himself, Talese could recall personally the rigid moral atmosphere of the 1930s and 1940s, particularly as it existed in such small, homogenous towns as the one in which he had been born and reared, a Victorian community in southern New Jersey where even now, in the 1970s, the sale of liquor was forbidden. He remembered hearing, as an adolescent at Sunday Mass, which he served as an altar boy, the parish priest's strident predictions of heavenly punishment against any parishioner who read a book that was listed on the Index or who patronized theaters that featured films banned by the Legion of Decency. In his parochial school, the nuns had advised him and his classmates that they should sleep each night on their backs with their arms crossed on their chests, hands on opposite shoulders—a presumably holy posture that, not incidentally, made masturbation impossible. Talese had been a sophomore in college before he masturbated, being aroused by the imagery of a co-ed he was then dating rather than by a photograph in a men's magazine, which he would have been too embarrassed to purchase.

And yet suddenly in the late 1950s and early '60s, or so it seemed to him, the men's magazines had come up from under the counter, erotic novels were no longer outlawed, nudity appeared in Hollywood films—and these changes were not only evident in the larger cities through which he traveled as a newspaper reporter and freelance writer, but also in conservative places like his hometown, which he regularly visited; and in 1971, while he was contemplating possible subjects for his next book, he decided that what most intrigued him was America's new openness about sex, its expanding erotic consumerism, and the quiet rebellion that he sensed within the middle class against the censors and clerics that had been an inhibiting force since the founding of the Puritan republic.

After reading several books on sex laws and censorship, watching many obscenity trials in courtrooms, and interviewing the editors of *Screw* and similar publications, Talese began his personal odyssey in the sex world by venturing into massage parlors and becoming a regular customer. He had first noticed a massage parlor in his neighborhood one night while returning home from P. J. Clarke's tavern with his wife. Flickering from a third-story window on Lexington Avenue, near Bloomingdale's, was a red neon sign that read *Live Nude Models*, and he was amazed that such an establishment could operate so openly.

The next day at noon, alone, he returned to the building, climbed three flights of steps, and passed through a curtained portal into what looked like the living room of an old neglected house. The oriental rug was frayed and faded; the sofas, tables, and floor lamps had probably come from junk shops; and the silent middle-aged men who sat waiting, like patients in a dentist's office, seemed unable to concentrate on the newspapers and magazines they held before them.

Approaching the manager at the desk, a long-haired young man wearing blue denims and peace beads, Talese was told that the price was eighteen dollars for a half-hour session, and that he could select as his masseuse any of the half-dozen women whose photographs appeared in the picture album that lay open in front of him. Talese chose a pleasant-looking young blonde named June, who was posed in a bikini on a tropical beach; and after he had waited for twenty minutes, dividing his time between glancing at *Newsweek* and watching the quiet arrivals and departures of the men, most of whom were his own age or older and wore suits and ties—and were, he supposed, largely businessmen on furtive lunch-hour visits—the manager waved toward him. As Talese got up he saw, standing in the hallway, a freckled-faced blond woman who bore only a slight resemblance to the June in the photograph—and was perhaps not even the same person—but who was nonetheless quite attractive. She was sloe-eyed and willowy, wore a pink wraparound skirt, a yellow T-shirt, and sandals. As she escorted him down the hall and led him into Room No. 5, carrying a single starched sheet that she had taken from the linen closet, she spoke with a southern accent.

She was from Alabama, she said—the state in which Talese had attended college; and while she briefly listened in the massage room while he reminisced about the South, she soon became impatient. This was a business appointment, she reminded him, the clock was ticking, and she suggested that he take off his clothes and lie on the table over which she had just flipped the sheet. After he had done so, she began to undress, and, turning, revealed a well-conditioned body that he found exciting.

"Oil or powder?" she asked, approaching the table. He looked uncertainly around the room.

"Are there showers in here?" he asked, after a pause.

"No," she said.

"Then I'll take powder."

She reached for a can of Johnson's baby powder, and soon he felt her fingers gently stroking his shoulders and chest, and then she moved down toward his stomach and thighs. He watched as she leaned over his body, her arms and breasts moving, her hands chalk-white from the talc. He could smell her perfume, feel his palms perspire, see his penis rising. He closed his eyes and heard the sighs of other men in the adjoining rooms, and he also heard the street noise from Lexington Avenue, the honking of cars, the grinding of buses pulling away from the curb, and he thought of Bloomingdale's and Alexander's across the street, and the crowds of customers and saleswomen who at this moment were leaning over counters, buying and selling . . .

"Do you want anything special?" she asked.

He opened his eyes. He saw her looking at his penis.

"Can we have sex?" he asked. She shook her head.

"I don't do that," she said. "I don't French either. I only give locals."

"Locals?"

"Hand jobs," she explained.

"Okay," he said, "I'll have a local."

"That will be extra."

"How *much* extra?"

"Fifteen dollars."

Too much, he thought. But in his aroused condition he was in no mood for bargaining, and so he nodded and watched with curiosity and anticipation as she sprinkled his groin with puffs of powder and adroitly proceeded to stroke his orgasm—expertly sensing, not a second too soon, the moment to whish a Kleenex from the nearby box.

While some people might have found the experience degrading or demeaning, Talese enjoyed the strangeness and impersonal nature of such contact; and after his first visit he returned often, taking sessions not only with June but with several other masseuses, and through them he learned that similar places existed throughout New York City.

During the remainder of that year and in 1972, he visited dozens of parlors on such a regular basis that he became socially acquainted not only with the masseuses but also with the young managers and owners. A few of them, having majored in English or studied journalism in college, were familiar with Talese's work and they thought it ''groovy'' that he was both a customer and an aficionado of their service; and they accepted his invitations to dine with him in restaurants, submitted to his interviews, and allowed the use of their names in his possible forthcoming book—and two of them finally permitted him to work in their parlors as a nonsalaried manager.

Talese's first job was at the Secret Life Studio, a third-floor walkup at 132 East Twenty-sixth Street, on the corner of Lexington Avenue; and for many weeks during the spring and summer of 1972 he worked behind the desk from noon to six, being responsible for collecting the money and checking the linen supply, conversing with the waiting customers and watching the clock after the masseuse had escorted a man into a private room. When the customer left, if there was a lull in the business activity, Talese would question the masseuse about the session, asking her what the man had talked about, what he had revealed of his personal and business life, his frustrations, aspirations, and fantasies. Talese soon convinced the masseuses to keep journals for him—documents that would describe daily each customer, recount what had been said and done behind closed doors, and reveal what the masseuse herself had been thinking as she catered to her customer's desires. It was Talese's intention, though he had yet to organize the scenes and story line, to write about a relationship between two real-life characters in a massage parlor—a middle-aged conservative businessman and a hippie coed who services his erotic needs, capitalizes on his inhibitions, and eventually befriends him and helps to extricate much of the shame and guilt that he usually brought with him into the massage parlor. From meeting and chatting with hundreds of male customers, and later reading about them in the journals, the author knew he had little difficulty in identifying with them—he *was* them in many ways, and as he read the masseuses' writings he recognized observations that could have accurately described himself.

Like a majority of the men, Talese was emotionally committed to a long-term marriage that he wanted to continue. While he had had affairs, he had never wanted to leave his wife for these other women, although he continued to admire them and maintain close friendships with many of them. Prostitutes had never appealed to him, especially since the contemporary streetwalker was invariably a poorly educated young woman from the ghetto with a drug problem who was rarely even attractive. But he had responded very much to the college-educated masseuse—a different type of "prostitute," one that a "John" could relate to in ways not merely sexual.

Many male habitués of massage parlors, like Talese, did not like solitary masturbation; in the parlance of the younger generation, it was a "downer." And yet to be masturbated by an appealing masseuse, to be in the physical presence of a woman with whom there was some communication and understanding, if not love, was gratifying and fun. As the months went by, Talese began to see the masseuse as a kind of unlicensed therapist. Just as thousands of people each day paid psychiatrists money to be heard, so these massage men paid money to be touched.

And if the majority of massage customers were anything like Talese—and his conversations with the men and his reading of the journals convinced him that they were—their sexual activities with masseuses did not diminish their passions for their wives at home; in fact, most men told him that they desired their wives even more on nights that followed an afternoon session in a parlor—the masseuses apparently activated the sex drives of the older men, made them feel better about themselves, more contented at home, more eager to please their wives in bed and out of it.

But as Talese listened to the men and talked with the young masseuses during his months behind the desk at the Secret Life Studio, and during his subsequent job as manager of the Middle Earth parlor on East Fifty-first Street, he gradually became aware that the telephone had never once rung with a call from a woman asking if there were young masseurs available for the pleasure of females. It was not that women were unaware of massage parlors: There were ads in the backs of taxicabs, on the wall posters of buildings, and in newspapers such as the New York *Post* and *The Village Voice* announcing sensual satisfaction for men *and* women. And Talese was sure that throughout New York there must be numerous women—aging widows, spinsters, liberated middle-aged female executives—who might welcome a midday massage with erotic delicacies, including oral sex or intercourse, in a balmy and bountiful East Side ambience that would offer some of the pampering features of an Elizabeth Arden salon or a ladies' luxurious health club. But the parlor owners and masseuses that Talese spoke with assured him that there was no such market. One highly advertised establishment had been started within a good East Side hotel, but, failing to lure female customers to its young masseurs, it was soon forced out of business. Women, it was concluded, were unwilling to pay for such personal servicing. Women would pay men to shampoo their hair, to design their clothing, to soothe their psyches, to flatten their stomachs in exercise classes—but they would not pay men money for manual masturbation, cunnilingus, or credit-card coitus.

Even the role of the gigolo was largely misunderstood, Talese was told by men who were well qualified to comment; while there were wealthy women who did support gigolos, these young men mainly functioned as escorts and sons rather than as lovers. Most gigolos were homosexual, it was explained, and the matrons who mothered them were often privately referred to, even by their subsidized suitors, as "fag hags." It seemed that the penis per se, except to male homosexuals, was not a very salable commodity in the sexual marketplace of America. Few women could be aroused by the sight of an erect penis *unless* they were warmly disposed to the man who was attached to it. Quite apart from the potential danger involved in picking up stray men in public places, the average heterosexual woman did not enjoy intercourse without a feeling of familiarity or personal interest in her partner. If it was merely an orgasm that she sought, she would prefer masturbating in her bedroom with a penis-shaped vibrator to engaging the genuine article of a male stranger. "It is just as natural for a woman to reject the sexual apparatus of a male stranger as it is for the human body to try to reject any other foreign object, be it a microscopic virus or an incompatible organ transplant," a marriage therapist once told Talese. "The key word is foreign; if a man is a stranger to a woman, his penis is foreign to her, and she is not likely to want it inside of her, because then her person would be invaded. But if it is not alien to her, if it is a part of somebody she knows, trusts, desires a relationship with, then she can take it into her, embrace it and feel in harmony with it.''

It was therefore logical, the therapist continued, that women did not respond to photographs of nude men in magazines in the way that men reacted to pinups—an opinion that many women themselves later confirmed in interviews with Talese; it was a rare woman who said she masturbated to pictures of unknown nude men, no matter how handsome or endowed was the male model. While the newsstands were stacked with endless "skin" magazines for men, there was only one slick periodical, *Playgirl*, that exposed males for an allegedly female audience; another publication, *Viva*, had earlier tried to interest women in such pictures but had abandoned its effort, and later failed entirely as a publication.

In 1973 Talese visited major cities in Europe to see if Continental women, unaffected by the vestiges of American Puritanism, might be more responsive to mercenary sex in massage parlors (sometimes called "sauna clubs"), and more interested in depictions of male nudity in magazines; but he discovered the European women seemed no different from their New York sisters. In London, in Paris, and even in the very permissive city of Copenhagen, Talese found no women who patronized massage parlors, very few women who enjoyed live sex shows or hard-core films, and he infrequently saw photos of nude men in women's magazines. During his wanderings at night in European streets, Talese saw what he had seen in New York: solitary men walking in and out of parlors, men negotiating with prostitutes in doorways, men staring silently at performing women in topless or bottomless bars. Men admitted to being endlessly fascinated with the naked female form; they appreciated women in a detached, impersonal way that women, even those women who were flattered by such attention, rarely understood. Men were natural voyeurs, women were exhibitors. Women sold sexual pleasure; men bought it. In social situations at cocktail parties, or in quest of an office affair or romance, the initiators were nearly always men and the inhibitors were nearly always women. A recently divorced husband of a famous European actress told Talese: "Men and women are natural enemies. Women begin as teenaged girls, often unconsciously, to arouse men—they wear tight sweaters, they paint their lips, they scent themselves with perfume, they swing their hips—and when they have made men hungry for them, they become suddenly coy and proper.'' Men want what women have to give, he conceded,

but women withhold it until certain conditions are met or promises are made. Women can give a powerless man a temporary
sense of strength, or at least the reassurance that he is not entirely impotent; and for a man, he elaborated, there is no substitute for the warm, welcoming place between a woman's legs,
the birthplace to which men continuously try to return. But there
is nearly always a price for readmission, he added, and sometimes the price is high. The church and the law try to "socialize
the penis," he said, to restrict its use to worthy occasions such
as monogamous marriage. "Marriage is a form of arms control
over the penis," but it is unable to entirely contain the excess
male sexual energy, and it is much of this energy that is spent
in the pornographic industry and the red-light districts of cities—
the areas that the vice squads, the celibate priests, and some
man-hating females want to eliminate. "These 'clean-up' campaigns," he concluded, "are really a battle against male biology, and they have been going on, in one form or another, since
the Middle Ages."

After returning from Europe, Talese continued his survey of
America by traveling into the interior, interviewing ordinary
men and women as well as civic leaders and local celebrities;
he spoke with admittedly monogamous couples and acknowledged swingers, with prosecutors and defense attorneys, theo-
logians and marriage counselors. He spent weeks in West
Virginia and Kentucky, Indiana, Ohio, and then down into the
Bible Belt, where he attended church sermons and town meetings, eavesdropped in cocktail bars, visited precinct houses as
well as the tenderloin areas. During the day he strolled through
the business districts, noting the close proximity of Woolworth's
and J.C. Penney to the local massage parlor and X-rated theater.
At night he lingered in the lobbies of the Holiday Inns, the
Ramadas, and other motels watching as the gray-suited men
with attaché cases purchased at the newsstand a copy of *Playboy*
or *Penthouse* before heading up to their rooms.

He also observed young couples with children and station
wagons driving into shopping centers; solid Rotarians and Ki-
wanians wearing flamboyant satin shirts, hurling bowling balls
down narrow glistening lanes; freckled country women in curl-
ers checking Gothic novels out of high school libraries; suntanned suburbanites playing mixed doubles on tennis courts;
members of the Pepsi Generation singing in the church choir on
Sundays. In such places, and after lengthy conversations with
such people, Talese sensed that normal American family life

and traditions were enduring on the surface but in private were being pondered and reappraised. Constantly throughout his travels he reminded himself that, despite the social and scientific changes relevant to the Sexual Revolution—the Pill, abortion reform, and the legal restraints against censorship—there were millions of Americans whose favorite book remained the Bible, whose marriages were unadulterous, whose daughters in college were still virgins. The *Reader's Digest* was unquestionably thriving in America; and though the national divorce rate was higher than ever, so was the rate of remarriage.

Still, Talese was more impressed by the vast changes that had altered the consciousness of the American middle class since his graduation from college; and while there were many people in the 1970s who were hopefully predicting a return to the more conservative 1950s, Talese doubted that such was possible. It would necessitate the outlawing of abortion and contraceptives, the imprisonment of adulterers, the censuring not only of *Playboy* but also of *Vogue* and the Maidenform advertisers in the New York *Times* Sunday magazine. Although the Supreme Court's *Miller* ruling in 1973 appeared at the time to be an ominous pronouncement, and would victimize such men as William Hamling, the attorneys, whom Talese subsequently spoke with and accompanied to obscenity trials, predicted that *Miller* would not sustain the trend that had at first alarmed civil libertarians. Most contemporary juries were more liberal than the nation's aging judges, it was said; and even in the conservative city of Wichita, the New York publisher of *Screw* triumphed over the federal prosecutors in an obscenity trial. On the national newsstands, a year after the *Miller* ruling, *Hustler* magazine appeared in print to extend the limits of explicitness—and its staff remained editorially unintimidated by the fact that its publisher would be permanently crippled from bullets fired outside a Georgia courthouse by an unidentified assailant. And in various parts of the country, surprisingly attractive actresses agreed to perform in hard-core sex films—one of which, in the secluded hills of Pennsylvania, Talese watched as it was being made.

The film was shot in the manor of a large estate that had been rented for the occasion, and Talese spent a week with the cast and technical crew. Several members of the group, including the director, had previously collaborated on *Deep Throat* and *The Devil in Miss Jones*; and although the film being made in Pennsylvania—entitled *Memories Within Miss Aggie*—would prove to be less lucrative than *Deep Throat* and *Miss Jones*, it resembled its more successful forerunners in its contrived plot, its group-sex scenes, its views of ejaculating penises, and the aggressive sexual behavior of its actresses on screen. Talese suspected that it was these scenes of women blithely inviting men into bed, and appearing to be uninhibited about impersonal sex, that catered to the wish-fulfillment fantasies of the majority of middle-aged male customers who frequented most X-rated cinemas in large cities and small towns. The porno starlets in the films, unlike women in real life, made their bodies quickly available, rejected no man's advances, required a minimum of foreplay, seemed multi-orgasmic, and sought no romantic promises. Such X-rated heroines as Georgina Spelvin, Marilyn Chambers, and Linda Lovelace used men for their pleasure, even beckoning a second or third actor after the first had exhausted himself; and while critics of pornography often accused sex films of exploiting women and glorifying violence, such views did not conform to what Talese was watching in person, or what he had seen in the numerous films that he had sat through in Times Square and in shabby theaters elsewhere around the nation.

If it was violence that an audience wanted, then it was more readily available in the R-rated and even the PG-rated films—war movies, the Godfather epics, the psycho-spiritual horror thrillers that were shown in endless imitation of *The Exorcist*. Sex films were passive by comparison; and if there was a legitimate grievance against them it was that the box office's admission fee of five dollars per customer was too high a cost to pay for the inferior quality of the films, the sophomoric scenarios, the unconvincing acting even in the bedroom scenes in which the actors were constantly losing their erections and futilely trying to simulate intercourse. During his cinematic excursions Talese did see examples of "kiddie porn," films exhibiting the sexuality of minors; but such films were few indeed, having a very limited audience; and although he saw several S&M films, these tended to show as many women as men in sexually dominant roles—such as high-heeled goddesses flailing men with whips, squeezing their genitals, and not infrequently squatting over the body of a prone man and urinating in his face. Whatever else might be said of such scenes, Talese guessed that many men found the close-up view of squatting women sexually educational, for Talese had long theorized that most men of his generation had no idea that a woman urinated from a different opening than the one she used for making love.

After he had left the movie troupe in Pennsylvania, where the shooting schedule had been extended for an extra day because of the failure of an actor to ejaculate on cue, Talese traveled to Chicago, where in time he met and befriended a massage parlor proprietor on South Wabash Avenue named Harold Rubin. A somewhat short, robust man in his mid-thirties with a jutting haw, blue eyes and long wet-combed blond hair, Rubin's manner, when Talese first met him, was dominated by unbridled contempt for Mayor Daley, for the Chicago police, and for the city's fire and building inspectors who he claimed were harassing him and trying to close him down. From his desk he removed and showed Talese an eviction notice sent by the landlord—citing, among other alleged misdeeds, the fact that Rubin had displayed in his front window a sign reading: "Dick Nixon Before He Dicks Us." Rubin said that he had recently been fined $1,200 by a judge for selling reputedly obscene books, and had been accused, falsely, of dumping a cubic yard of horse manure on the steps of the City Hall of Berwyn, the Chicago suburb in which he lived. Rubin's pretty brunet wife, a masseuse who had lately become disturbed by his continuing controversies with the law, had just abandoned him and gone off to Florida, leaving behind their three-year-old son to pedal his tricycle and scatter his toys in the reception room and the hallway of Rubin's massage parlor.

Business had greatly declined since the acceleration of the raids, Rubin conceded; and having little else to do during the afternoons, Rubin spoke at length to Talese about his vague hopes for the future, his recollections of a misspent youth, and his history of trouble in Chicago. Despite his protestations and feuds with the authorities, however, Rubin seemed to enjoy his image as a rebel and rake in a largely conformist city; and after Chicago headline writers had begun calling him "Weird Harold," he adopted the moniker as the official name of his parlor. But when he was away from the neon lights and pornographic posters of his business, he seemed to be as socially conservative as his most righteous critics; he lived quietly in the community of Berwyn, visited his widowed grandmother twice each week, and kept the apartment that he shared with his son in a fashion that was obsessively tidy if highly ornamental. He was a collector of objects d'art, antique gadgetry, and fragile trinkets which he kept in glass cases or brass boxes that he regularly dusted and polished. On the walls were turn-of-the-century posters, and in his living room were chairs and sofas that were older than his grandmother. He played music on an Edison phonograph built in 1910, and took pride in his wooden icebox, his Packard juke-box, and his equally old Pulver chewing-gum machine. On the bookshelves of his orderly bedroom were old leather-bound vol-umes; and in his closet were neatly stacked piles of 1950s nudist magazines, most of which featured the photographs of the woman who had been central to his fantasies during most of his life—Diane Webber.

The masseuse that he married resembled more than slightly the California model of his dreams, and during their first year together in 1969, Rubin would escort her into the Cook County forest preserves, where, in hidden places in the woods, he would take pictures of her in the nude, posing her in the exact way that he had seen Diane Webber in the magazines he had so carefully kept in his closet. Harold Rubin's rhapsodic recollections of his imaginary meetings with Diane Webber in his boyhood bed-room soon prompted Talese to fly to Southern California and seek his own rendezvous; and after discovering her home ad-dress and private telephone number with the help of photogra-phers with whom she had once worked, and after writing her and leaving several messages on her answering machine, none of which she replied to—and then enlisting the cooperation of her husband, a documentary film editor in Hollywood—an in-terview was finally granted in her Malibu home on a gray, cool afternoon made more chilly by the reception he received.

Diane Webber did not smile as she opened the door. A bare-foot woman in her forties whose diminutive, somewhat plump figure was concealed in faded blue jeans and an oversized man's shirt, and whose long brunet hair and dark-rimmed glasses sug-gested the current fashion of many feminists, her first words to Talese were more in the form of a lecture than a gesture of greeting. She had *not* been impressed by his persistence in track-ing her down, she said, and she stressed as well that the inter-view she was about to give would hopefully be brief. She was now a private citizen, she reminded him, turning to lead him toward a modern sofa in a tidy living room overlooking the beach; and while she admitted to having enjoyed nude modeling at the time, she was now totally devoted to her full-time career as a dance instructor of female classes in the nearby community of Van Nuys. She taught the demanding art of belly dancing at Everywoman's Village, she said, and occasionally she also per-formed this dance, accompanied by her top students and a band playing Middle Eastern music, in public places in and around Los Angeles.

As she spoke, Talese listened without interruption, and in time she seemed to relax and to resent his presence less. Though he found her attractive, and would as the interview progressed become even more aware of her intelligence and articulateness, he believed that if Harold Rubin had been in the room he would have been disappointed. As erotic and free-spirited as she appeared to be in the old photographs, she projected none of this in person, and Talese guessed that this was probably just as true when she had posed years ago. After she had removed her clothes and had sprawled nude on the California sand dunes during her youth, most likely nothing was further from her mind than erotica or pornography, although Talese would not have bet that such thoughts were far from the minds of the male photographers who were working with her. They were males taking male pictures, and they no doubt knew, if she did not, that the pictures they eventually selected for publication would soon excite the male magazine audience, would flourish in the world of male sexual fantasy, and would in many feverish male minds subject her to wild scenes of ravishment and a lifetime of captivity behind the closed doors of bedroom closets.

But as *she* interpreted her modeling career to Talese during their interview, her posing in the nude was an expression of photographic ''art''—and Talese resisted the impulse to suggest that ''art'' to her might be ''pornography'' to her male admirers. His prudence at this juncture was possibly rewarded, for she later agreed to a second interview, and still later a third; and through her he came to know her husband, to whom she had been married for twenty years, and also her nineteen-year-old son, John Webber, a handsome onetime hippie who had recently become gainfully employed in a nudist colony in the hills southeast of Malibu, a colony called Elysium Fields, which was owned by a former photographer who had specialized in taking Diane Webber photographs, the gray-bearded Ed Lange.

John Webber lived at the colony, performing many menial chores and working long hours; but periodically he wandered off and returned to his parents' home in Malibu. Late one afternoon, after a dance class, Diane Webber walked into her living room and discovered her son lying nude on the living room floor, his legs spread wide, masturbating to photographs of actress Ursula Andress in *Playboy* magazine. Diane Webber was not pleased.

It was while Talese was on this trip to California that he first ventured into Sandstone Retreat. A writer in New York named

Patrick McGrady, Jr., had earlier in the year told him about Sandstone and the experiment in open sexuality that was being conducted by John and Barbara Williamson in their private estate in Topanga Canyon, and after Talese had seen a Sandstone advertisement in the Los Angeles *Free Press* he telephoned the listed number and was invited by the club manager to drive up the hill for an afternoon's visit.

Motoring up the zigzagging roads, and twice getting lost, Talese finally located the stone pillars of the main entrance and pulled into the parking lot, never expecting that his brief visit to this permissive paradise would extend from that day through the night, and through most of the next two months. Talese was mesmerized by the place, its tranquillity and freedom, its minimum of rules and regulations, its ballroom and aggressive women. Nothing in his earlier research had quite prepared him for Sandstone—not the massage parlors, not the swing bars, not the live shows, nor what he had read or been told by the sexual gazetteers of his acquaintance. Sandstone, during the early 1970s, was undoubtedly the most liberated fifteen acres of land in America's not-always-democratic Republic: It was the only place he knew where there was no double standard, no place for mercenary sex, no need for security guards or the police, no reason for fantasies as substitute stimulants. It was here, during his first night, that Talese became involved in a group experience, a recreational scene in the ballroom in the exalted company of Dr. Comfort and a famous Hollywood ventriloquist who, though his head was buried between the thighs of a schoolmistress, nevertheless continued a humorous dialogue between himself and his absent wooden-headed alter ego.

It was at Sandstone that Talese gradually became comfortable as a nudist; and though he was not bisexual, he learned at Sandstone to relax in the close naked presence of men, and to develop in this uninhibiting environment a bond of friendship with some men that would lead to greeting them with an embrace as natural as a handshake. But there was much about Sandstone that Talese found not altogether pleasant, especially during the quiet afternoons when the property was occupied only by ten full-time residents—John Williamson's "family," who, with a few notable exceptions, seemed cool to his presence, skeptical of his intentions, and openly wondered at times why Talese had not brought his wife. After Talese had been living at Sandstone for less than a month, he sensed that John Williamson himself was becoming more remote and unfriendly; it was as if Williamson, after inviting Talese to occupy a guest house and remain for an undetermined length of time, had privately acknowledged that he had made a mistake—but rather than admitting that mistake by suddenly evicting him, Williamson seemed resigned to Talese's increasing discomfort.

Talese thought at the time that it was possible he was over-reacting to Williamson's nonverbal nature, about which Talese had been forewarned in New York by the writer McGrady; and Talese also speculated on the possibility that he was being subjected to one of the special stress tests that Williamson was known to employ occasionally on outsiders who had chosen to live even briefly among his naked followers and fellow deviants from the deceptive ways of the world below. But Talese remained at Sandstone, dreading the day and eagerly anticipating the nighttime arrival of the club members and their merriment; and that he withstood as long as he did the daily vibrations of Williamson's silence, and a sense of isolation from most of the family, was attributable in part to the fact that Talese was not unfamiliar with the condition of being an outsider. Indeed it was a role for which his background had most naturally prepared him: an Italo-American parishioner in an Irish-American church, a minority Catholic in a predominantly Protestant hometown, a Northerner attending a southern college, a conservative young man of the fifties who invariably wore a suit and tie, a driven man who chose as his calling one of the few professions that was open to mental masqueraders: he became a journalist, and thus gained a license to circumvent his inherent shyness, to indulge his rampant curiosity, and to explore the lives of individuals he considered more interesting than himself.

As a journalist, not unexpectedly, he had been attracted to people who had strayed from the straight and narrow, the unnoticed wanderers in the city of New York, the itinerant bridge workers on high steel, the eccentric Bartlebys on the New York *Times* copydesk, the children of the Mafia, the smugglers of illegal literature, the dropout co-eds in massage parlors, and now Williamson's pioneers in impropriety. But even to such an individual as Talese, who prided himself on his capacity to long endure incompatible company if he thought he would ultimately be rewarded with a good story, there nevertheless were limits; and just as he was ready to acknowledge to himself that his limit had been reached, the door to the guest house opened one afternoon, and, unannounced and nude, there appeared the demurely smiling countenance of John Williamson's wife. Softly placing her hands on his shoulders as he remained seated behind his typewriter at his desk, she began to massage his back and to stroke his neck; and with a minimum of words and no resistance on his part, she guided him into the bedroom and proceeded to make love.

It was the first time that he had been so directly sought out by a sexually aggressive woman, and there was no doubt in Talese's mind or body that he was receptive to the experience. After she had finished, and *only* after she had finished, Barbara Williamson began to talk freely, confiding in him for the first time since he had arrived at Sandstone. While not apologizing for her husband's sullenness, she sought to explain that a number of business reversals concerning the sale of the property had constantly frustrated her husband's desire to resettle in Montana. But, she added, John Williamson was, like most dreamers, a man given to exaggerated despondence, and she recalled that back in 1970—after his adoring Oralia Leal had run away with David Schwind and gotten married in Elyria, Ohio—he had brooded in his bedroom and had barely spoken to anyone at Sandstone for nearly two months.

As Talese listened with interest, and prompted her with questions, Barbara Williamson began to tell him the story of how Sandstone had begun, recalling her affair with John Bullaro, and her husband's later relationship with Bullaro's wife, describing as well the dramatic weekend at Big Bear Lake in which the two couples had shared a cabin and each other's spouses. Although John and Judith Bullaro a year later had quit Sandstone and had ceased living with one another, they had subsequently become partners in an open marriage, Barbara said, adding that the couple was still friendly with the Williamsons and that, if Talese wished, she would arrange for him to meet them.

A week later, this was done; and during the next two years, as Talese flew back and forth between New York and California, he often visited the Bullaros in Woodland Hills, where he gradually gained their confidence and permission to write about them, and to make use of the diary and other notes that John Bullaro had kept during those traumatic days when Judith had been lured away by Williamson and the group that would form Sandstone's charter membership.

During this time, Talese's own marriage, which had been in existence since 1959, and which now included two young daughters, was responding adversely to the flagrance of his research, its attendant publicity, and his recent agreement to be interviewed at length by a reporter from *New York* magazine about the challenges and difficulties Talese was confronting in his new project. The reporter was a friend, someone he had known for years, a journalist he thought would write more about the method of his work than his intimate involvement with the subject; and so Talese felt confident that there was little in his life he would need to hide.

One evening, with the reporter at his side, Talese returned home to find his house quiet and an envelope awaiting him on the dining room table. Opening it, he read that his wife had left the house and she did not say when she would return. Her right of privacy, which she valued like few other possessions, was being violated, she declared, by his unwitting willingness to discuss with the press what was none of its business; and she warned further that his candor on the subject of sex, while it might titillate some magazine readers, would only bring ridicule upon himself.

Distressed by her departure, but eager to conceal the contents of the letter from the *New York* reporter who stood silently next to him, waiting to accompany him to a restaurant to conclude the interviews that had been going on for days, Talese put the note in his pocket. Repressing his emotions, Talese spent the next few hours in the restaurant conversing with the reporter, hoping that the tension and anxiety he felt was going unnoticed.

It had been a Friday when he received the note, and on the following Monday she was back without explanation. She did not volunteer where she had been, nor did he feel he had the right to ask. Their marriage continued through the fall of 1973 and winter of 1974 with an uncertain aura of reconciliation. That the marriage survived at all was due not only to their love but more to the fact that through the years they each had developed an insight into the labyrinth of one another's ways, a special and not-always-spoken language, a respect for one another's work, a history of shared experiences good and bad, and a recognition that they genuinely liked one another. There are times in marriage when it is more important to ''like'' than to ''love''—and thus the marriage continued and deepened through a second decade, and during the summer of 1974 Talese returned, as he did each year with his wife and children, to the Victorian beach house he owned in his hometown of Ocean City, New Jersey.

The negative reaction to his publicized ''research'' had, as his wife predicted, preceded his arrival and had become the subject of an unflattering editorial in the weekly newspaper where he had begun his journalistic career as a high school sportswriter. This editorial, more than all the gossip and articles in the big-city dailies and national magazines, most offended his parents, who still resided in the town, and who for a half century had exemplified the moral propriety that had characterized at least the surface of this small seaside city. While Talese was at first irritated and made self-conscious by the effect his book-in-progress was having on his family, he gradually ceased to care about what people thought of him personally. He had now found a way to begin the book, his first chapter was completed, and during midday breaks from his work he would walk through the town, visit the local newsstand and casually thumb through the racks of men's magazines, and continue to explore the changing sexual mores that surrounded him—both in his hometown and in the larger resort of nearby Atlantic City, and in the extended area of provincial farms and villages.

Twenty miles from where Talese had been raised, concealed deep in the woodlands along the Great Egg Harbor River, there was a nudist park that he had been aware of since his boyhood, but, as a young man, had never dared to enter. It was called Sunshine Park, and had been founded in the mid-1930s by a stocky, volatile, controversial minister named Ilsley Boone, who was recognized by a small group of shameless adherents of nudism as the father of the movement in America. A onetime pastor of the Ponds Reformed Church in Oakland, New Jersey, Reverend Boone discovered nudism in 1931 during his travels through Germany, where, until closed down by Hitler, there had been a number of private parks used by naturists who believed that the removal of clothing in the outdoors was liberating and healthy for both the body and spirit. Although Reverend Boone's first attempt at founding a naturist settlement in Schooley's Mountain in central north Jersey was terminated by an eviction notice from the landlord, he did succeed in acquiring eighty acres of forest land in south Jersey from a German-American family living in the community of Mays Landing; and in 1935, driven by a messianic fervor and assisted by his followers, Boone built within the shading of tall oak trees and cedar and clusters of pine, a riverside retreat he called Sunshine Park. He erected a large white frame house, in which he lived with his wife and children, and also smaller houses and cabins, an auditorium, and a school. He published a nudist newsletter and a picture magazine called *Sunshine & Health*, which, though regularly banned by the local postmaster in Mays Landing, was just as regularly defended in countersuits by Boone himself, who asserted in an editorial: "Until the 'moral' leaders of America accept reality in the body and allow the hoi polloi to become perfectly familiar with the body's complete physical appearance, a more or less feverish interest in the 'forbidden' parts of the body will continue."

A "feverish interest" in the body's "forbidden" parts—no phrase was more appropriate to Talese's boyhood in Ocean City; and while he always lacked the nerve to inquire if *Sunshine & Health* magazine was available for sale under the counter at the corner cigar store, where the most indiscreet publication on display was the *Police Gazette*, he listened with unabated interest whenever his school chums discussed the daring possibility of sneaking into the park at night and climbing the trees and hiding until daylight brought its promised view of naked female splendor. And whenever he was taken to baseball games in Philadelphia, and was driven along the riverside road that led past Sunshine Park's stone gate and its bold white billboard sign, he looked into the blurring trees futilely searching for a forbidden sight. He had also heard that there were boat owners in his town who, particularly on weekends, sailed or motored their vessels along the Great Egg Harbor River and anchored opposite the shoreline of Sunshine Park in order to catch the wondrous view of the wicked bathers sprawled along the wooden pier and tiny beach.

One summer weekend, returning to Ocean City after a few days' visit to Sandstone, Talese drove alone through the tree-lined road leading to Sunshine Park. Noting that the park's familiar white sign had been unchanged since his boyhood, he turned into the entrance and followed a long, winding dirt road that led past thick trees and bushes, and finally ended at a log-cabin gatehouse where an elderly nude man sat in the sun behind a rustic wooden desk. The man welcomed Talese, handed him a registration card to be filled in, and accepted a fee. In reply to Talese's question, the old man said that he was not Ilsley Boone, who died in 1968, but added that he had helped Boone build the park, which, except for the motor homes, still looked essentially as it did when it was opened forty years ago. After the man had waved him through the inner gate, Talese drove along a sandy roadway toward the river, where he could now see dozens of people of all ages, shapes, and coloring, strolling or lying nude in the sun, and swimming in the river. There were parents holding babies, old folks with tan, sagging skin, young women with—or lacking—beautiful bodies, men who were muscular, flabby, frail, and teenagers of both sexes who lay next to one another on beach towels or stood talking in a casual manner.

After parking his car and removing his clothing, Talese walked slowly toward the water, feeling unselfconscious and pleasant. It was a sweltering July afternoon, but the shaded ground was cool under his feet, and the cedar-colored water, when he entered it, was warm and soothing. He waded in the water toward a wooden ladder leading up to the pier; and when he climbed up and mingled with a crowd of other nudists, none of whom he had ever seen before, he noticed that a few of them were facing and waving toward a number of sailing vessels and motorboats that were anchored beyond the long extended line of rope that separated the park property from the common sea.

Painted on the stern of most of the boats beneath the declaration of their names was the lettering of their locale: "Ocean City, N.J."; and seated on the decks were people wearing Bermuda shorts and sailing caps, bathing suits, straw hats, and dark glasses; and in their hands they held cans of beer, Thermos bottles, transistor radios, and handkerchiefs that they waved at the nudists. There were also some catcalls coming from the boats, whistles and cheers; and after watching for a few moments, Talese stepped forward on the deck, separating himself from the other quiet nudists, and he faced the boats, recognizing a few of the sailing ships and, he thought, some of their passengers. He also noticed for the first time that many of the passengers held silvery telescopes and dark binoculars, and they sat rigidly on their decks and swayed in the water and squinted in the sun. They were unabashed voyeurs looking at him; and Talese looked back.

AUTHOR'S NOTE

DURING THE NINE years it took me to complete *Thy Neighbor's Wife*, I interviewed hundreds of people, some of them more than fifty times each; but what made the research particularly difficult and time-consuming was establishing such trusting relationships with the interviewees that they would allow the use of their names in connection with the intimate stories they told me about themselves.

After finishing my last book in 1971—a five-year project during which I gained the confidence of the Bonanno organized crime family and was able to describe the changing social traditions of certain men, women and children within the Mafia—I hoped to follow with a larger work that would reflect the social and sexual trends of the entire nation: a book that would both deal with the history of sex laws and censorship, as well as describe some of the people and events that in recent decades influenced or reflected the redefinition of morality in America.

I wanted to combine in one book such individuals as Hugh Hefner and Samuel Roth, Alex Comfort and Sally Binford, and also more ordinary people such as Judith and John Bullaro, who, though they drifted into an unusual situation, were not really unlike many couples that I came to know during my research travels around the country. In obtaining the use of the Bullaros' and Williamsons' names, and the names of others in this book, I was fortunate in persuading them that their stories would be recounted accurately and in the same nonjudgmental tone that had characterized my previous work. In the interest of credibility and verification, I was joined during several interviews by my research associate from Los Angeles, Ms. Cynthia Sears, who tape recorded my conversations with the Bullaros, the Williamsons, Diane Webber and several other people. Ms. Sears carefully transcribed these dialogues, which gave me an additional record so that I could play back and hear again what was said about the events and emotions involved, and thus verify the accuracy of my material.

In addition to my own interview notes and the transcripts, several people provided me with writings of their own: diaries, journals, and unpublished personal reminiscences that recounted their sexual thoughts and activities. These private papers further authenticated the sexual scenes and attitudes, feelings and fantasies, that appear in the book.

G.T.
January 18, 1980

INDEX